PENGUIN ⓟ CLASSICS

DEMONS

FYODOR MIKHAYLOVICH DOSTOYEVSKY was born in Moscow in 1821, the second of a physician's seven children. When he left his private boarding school in Moscow he studied from 1838 to 1843 at the Academy of Military Engineers in St Petersburg, graduating with officer's rank. His first novel to be published, *Poor Folk* (1846), was a great success. In 1849 he was arrested and sentenced to death for participating in the 'Petrashevsky circle'; he was reprieved at the last moment but sentenced to penal servitude, and until 1854 he lived in a convict prison at Omsk, Siberia. Out of this experience he wrote *The House of the Dead* (1860). In 1860 he began the review *Vremya* (*Time*) with his brother; in 1862 and 1863 he went abroad, where he strengthened his anti-European outlook, met Apollinaria Suslova, who was the model for many of his heroines, and gave way to his passion for gambling. In the following years he fell deeply in debt, but in 1867 he married Anna Grigoryevna Snitkina (his second wife), who helped to rescue him from his financial morass. They lived abroad for four years, then in 1873 he was invited to edit *Grazhdanin* (*Citizen*), to which he contributed his *A Writer's Diary*. From 1876 the latter was issued separately and had a large circulation. In 1880 he delivered his famous address at the unveiling of Pushkin's memorial in Moscow; he died six months later in 1881. Most of his important works were written after 1864: *Notes from Underground* (1864), *Crime and Punishment* (1865–6), *The Gambler* (1866), *The Idiot* (1868), *Demons* (1871–2) and *The Brothers Karamazov* (1880).

ROBERT A. MAGUIRE (1930–2005) held the position of Boris Bakhmeteff Professor Emeritus of Russian Studies at Columbia University. He taught at Yale, Princeton and Harvard, and was a Visiting Fellow at St Antony's College, Oxford. His two main areas of specialization, on which he wrote widely, were the Soviet period and the early nineteenth century. Among his books are *Red Virgin Soil: Soviet Literature in the 1920s* (1968; 3rd edition, 2000), *Gogol from the Twentieth Century* (1974) and *Exploring Gogol* (1994). His translations include Andrei Bely's Symbolist novel *Petersburg* (with John Malmstad, 1978) and Nikolay Gogol's *Dead Souls* (Penguin, 2004), as well as the works of several contemporary Polish poets, notably Tadeusz Różewicz and the Nobel laureate Wisława Szymborska.

ROBERT L. BELKNAP studied Russian and other literatures at Princeton University, the University of Paris, Columbia University and Leningrad State University. He has taught most of his life at Columbia University, where he has also been a Dean of Columbia College, Director of the Russian (now Harriman) Institute and Chair of the Slavic Department. He is now Director of the University Seminars. He has written two books on Dostoyevsky's *Brothers Karamazov* and worked for many years on Russian prose fiction and literary theory.

RONALD MEYER teaches Russian literary translation at Columbia University. He is the editor of Anna Akhmatova's *My Half-Century: Selected Prose* (1992); co-translator, with David Lowe, of *The Complete Letters of Fyodor Dostoevsky*, volume 1 (1988); and co-editor of *Russian Literature of the 1920s: An Anthology* (1987). His other translations include works by Babel, Chekhov, Gogol, Lipkin, Nagibin and Palei. He is currently translating a volume of Dostoyevsky's short fiction, *The Gambler and Other Stories*, for Penguin Classics.

FYODOR DOSTOYEVSKY

Demons

A Novel in Three Parts

Translated by ROBERT A. MAGUIRE
Edited by RONALD MEYER
Introduction by ROBERT L. BELKNAP

PENGUIN BOOKS

PENGUIN CLASSICS

Published by the Penguin Group
Penguin Books Ltd, 80 Strand, London WC2R ORL, England
Penguin Group (USA) Inc., 375 Hudson Street, New York, New York 10014, USA
Penguin Group (Canada), 90 Eglinton Avenue East, Suite 700, Toronto, Ontario, Canada M4P 2Y3
(a division of Pearson Penguin Canada Inc.)
Penguin Ireland, 25 St Stephen's Green, Dublin 2, Ireland (a division of Penguin Books Ltd)
Penguin Group (Australia), 250 Camberwell Road, Camberwell, Victoria 3124, Australia
(a division of Pearson Australia Group Pty Ltd)
Penguin Books India Pvt Ltd, 11 Community Centre, Panchsheel Park, New Delhi – 110 017, India
Penguin Group (NZ), 67 Apollo Drive, Rosedale, North Shore 0632, New Zealand
(a division of Pearson New Zealand Ltd)
Penguin Books (South Africa) (Pty) Ltd, 24 Sturdee Avenue, Rosebank, Johannesburg 2196, South Africa

Penguin Books Ltd, Registered Offices: 80 Strand, London WC2R ORL, England

www.penguin.com

First published 1871–2
This translation first published 2008

1

Translation copyright © The estate of Robert A. Maguire, 2008
Editorial material copyright © Ronald Meyer, 2008
Introduction copyright © Robert L. Belknap, 2008
All rights reserved

The moral right of the translator and editors has been asserted.

Set in 10.25/12.25 pt PostScript Adobe Sabon
Typeset by Rowland Phototypesetting Ltd, Bury St Edmunds, Suffolk
Printed in England by Clays Ltd, St Ives plc

ISBN: 978-0-141-44141-2

www.greenpenguin.co.uk

Contents

Chronology

1821 (30 October)* Born Fyodor Mikhaylovich Dostoyevsky, in Moscow, the son of Mikhail Andreyevich, head physician at Mariinsky Hospital for the Poor, and Marya Fyodorovna, daughter of a merchant family.

1823 Pushkin begins *Eugene Onegin*.

1825 Decembrist uprising.

1831–6 Attends boarding schools in Moscow together with his brother Mikhail (b. 1820).

1836 Publication of the 'First Philosophical Letter' by Pyotr Chaadayev.

1837 Pushkin is killed in a duel.

Their mother dies and the brothers are sent to a preparatory school in St Petersburg.

1838 Enters the St Petersburg Academy of Military Engineers as an army cadet (Mikhail is not admitted to the Academy).

1839 Father dies, apparently murdered by serfs on his estate.

1840 Lermontov's *A Hero of Our Time*.

1841 Obtains a commission. Tries his hand at historical drama without success.

1842 Gogol's *Dead Souls*.

Promoted to second lieutenant.

1843 Graduates from the Academy. Attached to St Petersburg Army Engineering Corps. Translates Balzac's *Eugénie Grandet*.

1844 Resigns his commission. Translates George Sand's *La dernière Aldini*. Works on *Poor Folk*, his first novel.

---

* Dates are old style (see p. 791).

1845 Establishes a friendship with Russia's most prominent
and influential literary critic, the liberal Vissarion Belinsky,
who praises *Poor Folk* and acclaims its author as Gogol's
successor.

1846 *Poor Folk* and *The Double* published. While *Poor Folk*
is widely praised, *The Double* is much less successful.
'Mr Prokharchin' also published. Utopian socialist M. V.
Butashevich-Petrashevsky becomes an acquaintance.

1847 Nervous ailments and the onset of epilepsy. 'A Novel in
Nine Letters' and 'The Landlady' are published.

1848 Several short stories published, including 'White Nights',
'A Weak Heart', 'A Christmas Party and a Wedding' and 'An
Honest Thief'.

1849 *Netochka Nezvanova* published. Arrested along with
other members of the Petrashevsky Circle, and convicted of
political offences against the Russian state. Sentenced to
death, and taken out to Semyonovsky Square to be shot
by firing squad, but reprieved moments before execution.
Instead, sentenced to an indefinite period of exile in Siberia,
to begin with eight years of penal servitude, later reduced to
four years by Tsar Nicholas I.

1850 Prison and hard labour in Omsk, western Siberia.

1853 Outbreak of Crimean War.
    Beginning of periodic epileptic seizures.

1854 Released from prison, but immediately sent to do compul-
sory military service as a private in the infantry battalion at
Semipalatinsk, south-western Siberia.

1855 Alexander II succeeds Nicholas I as Tsar: some relaxation
of state censorship.
    Promoted to non-commissioned officer.

1856 Promoted to lieutenant. Still forbidden to leave Siberia.

1857 Marries the widowed Marya Dmitriyevna Isayeva. Publication of 'The Little Hero', written in prison during the
summer of 1849.

1858 Works on *The Village of Stepanchikovo and its Inhabitants* and *Uncle's Dream*.

1859 Allowed to return to live in European Russia; in
December, the Dostoyevskys return to St Petersburg. First

chapters of *The Village of Stepanchikovo and its Inhabitants* (the serialized novella is released between 1859 and 1861) and *Uncle's Dream* published.

Mikhail starts a new literary journal, *Vremya* (*Time*). Dostoyevsky is not officially an editor, because of his convict status. First two chapters of *The House of the Dead* published.

1861 (19 February) Emancipation of serfs. Turgenev's *Fathers and Sons*.

Vremya begins publication. *The Insulted and the Injured* published in *Vremya*. First part of *The House of the Dead* published.

1862 Second part of *The House of the Dead* and *A Nasty Tale* published in *Vremya*. Makes first trip abroad, to Europe, including England, France and Switzerland. Meets Alexander Herzen in London.

1863 *Winter Notes on Summer Impressions* published in *Vremya*. After Marya Dmitriyevna is taken seriously ill, travels abroad again. Begins liaison with Apollinaria Suslova. Nikolay Chernyshevsky's *What Is to Be Done?* is published.

1864 First part of Tolstoy's *War and Peace*.

In March with Mikhail founds the journal *Epokha* (*Epoch*) as successor to *Vremya*, now banned by the Russian authorities. *Notes from Underground* published in *Epokha*. In April death of Marya Dmitriyevna. In July death of Mikhail. The International Workingmen's Association (the First International) founded in London.

1865 *Epokha* ceases publication because of lack of funds. Suslova rejects his proposal of marriage. Gambles in Wiesbaden. Works on *Crime and Punishment*.

1866 Dmitry Karakozov attempts to assassinate Tsar Alexander II.

Crime and Punishment and *The Gambler* published. The latter written in 26 days with the help of his future wife, the stenographer Anna Grigoryevna Snitkina (b. 1846).

1867 Marries, and hounded by creditors, the couple leaves for Western Europe and settles in Dresden.

1868 Birth of daughter, Sofia, who dies only three months old. *The Idiot* published in serial form.

1869 Birth of daughter, Lyubov.

The Nechayev Affair – Ivan Ivanov is murdered by fellow members of a clandestine revolutionary cell led by Sergey Nechayev.

1870 V. I. Lenin is born in the town of Simbirsk, on the banks of the Volga. Defeat of France in Franco-Prussian War.

The Eternal Husband published.

1871 Moves back to St Petersburg with his wife and family. Birth of son, Fyodor.

1871–2 Serial publication of *Demons*.

1873 Becomes contributing editor of conservative weekly journal *Grazhdanin (Citizen)*, where his *A Writer's Diary* is published as a regular column. 'Bobok' published.

1875 *The Adolescent* published. Birth of son, Aleksey.

1876 'The Meek One' published in *A Writer's Diary*.

1877 'The Dream of a Ridiculous Man' published in *Grazhdanin*.

1878 Death of Aleksey. Works on *The Brothers Karamazov*.

1879 Iosif Vissarionovich Dzhugashvili (later known as Stalin) born in Gori, Georgia.

First part of *The Brothers Karamazov* published.

1880 *The Brothers Karamazov* published (in complete form). Anna starts a book service, where her husband's works may be ordered by mail. Speech in Moscow at the unveiling of a monument to Pushkin is greeted with wild enthusiasm.

1881 Assassination of Tsar Alexander II (1 March).

Dostoyevsky dies in St Petersburg (28 January). Buried in the cemetery of the Alexander Nevsky Monastery. The funeral procession from the author's apartment numbers over 30,000.

Introduction

*New readers are advised that this Introduction makes
details of the plot explicit.*

I.

Fyodor Mikhaylovich Dostoyevsky was born 30 October
1821,* and brought up in a Moscow hospital for the poor. His
father, Mikhail Andreyevich Dostoyevsky, was a chief physician and resided in the hospital; although the son of a modest
priest, his ancestry as a member of the hereditary nobility
entitled him to own villages and their inhabitants. Mikhail's
career, first in military medicine, and after his marriage, in the
civil service, gave him the resources to buy two villages after
1831. Fyodor's mother, Marya Fyodorovna Nechayeva, was a
deeply religious woman who came from the merchantry, a
separate, defined estate in Russian society, where ninety per
cent of the population were peasants, most of them the property
of the state or the nobles until 1862. Dostoyevsky lovingly
described a moment when a farm serf comforted him as a small
boy with a panic attack,[1] but he never showed any desire to
live in the countryside or even a small city.

In 1837, Dostoyevsky's mother died; his father retired and
moved to the country; and Fyodor and his older brother Mikhail travelled to study at the Military Engineering Academy in
the St Petersburg palace where the Emperor Paul had lived until
his murder in 1801. Dostoyevsky's father died two years later,
apparently murdered by his own serfs after a drunken episode
with a serf's wife, but several scholars doubt that his death was
violent. In a corrupt bureaucracy, disreputable facts are hard
to confirm or disprove almost two centuries later; literarily,

* Dates are old style (see p. 791).

what Dostoyevsky thought happened matters more than what actually did happen. He never mentioned this story, and gambled away his small inheritance.

The brothers studied calculus, physics, fortifications, etc., but also French, German and religion. Dostoyevsky boasted of reading Goethe and E. T. A. Hoffmann in German, Shakespeare and others in English, but probably relied on French or Russian versions for most of his reading of foreign writers. From the days when his family would read translations of Sir Walter Scott aloud together to the engineering-school days when the brothers read Victor Hugo and George Sand, or when the romantic wanderer Ivan Nikolayevich Shidlovsky excited them over Friedrich Schiller, to his first literary work, which was a translation of Honoré de Balzac, and all his life thereafter, Dostoyevsky was drenched in Western European, as well as Russian and occasionally Asian or American, literature. The spookiest and most 'Dostoyevskian' passages in his writings often come not from the fastnesses of his alien soul, but from Dickens or from sensationalist Western writers like Anne Radcliffe, 'Monk' Lewis, Eugène Sue, whom the Russians loved, or Edgar Allan Poe, whom Dostoyevsky's own journal introduced more generally into Russia.

After serving a year in the army in return for his education, Dostoyevsky resigned in 1844. His shrewd understanding of literary careers led him to translate *Eugénie Grandet*, which had been adapted to the theatre – Balzac had visited St Petersburg for this and been lionized – and had other novels translated. Dostoyevsky's first novel, *Poor Folk*, still erupted in 1846 with an éclat that startled Petersburg. He met the radicals of the Forties, including Vissarion Belinsky, Nikolay Nekrasov and Alexander Herzen, and fell under the spell of the liberal, Europeanized gentleman and writer Ivan Turgenev, who drew some of his thought from the Hegelian idealism of Timofey Granovsky, Professor of History in Moscow. A few years later Dostoyevsky joined the utopian socialist group that gathered in the dwelling of M. V. Butashevich-Petrashevsky. There they would discuss phalansteries, the perfectly organized communes that Charles Fourier and others worked to design and establish all over Europe and America, little utopias where human beings would have the chance to realize their full potentialities. Dostoyevsky knew the Russian radical youth of the 1840s from the inside, and suffered for this involvement when with the Petrashevsky leaders he was arrested in 1849, sentenced to death, put through a mock execution and walked to prison camps in Siberia. Dostoyevsky's execution might have been real had the authorities learned of his role in a Petrashevsky subgroup that owned a press that could print manifestos. Luckily, in Tsar Nikolay I's Russia, the police had never seen a printing press and did not recognize it in a conspirator's chemistry laboratory. As it was, Dostoyevsky served four years of hard labour in the Omsk camp, among the thieves, murderers, Polish political exiles, and others he described in *The House of the Dead* (1860). Even there, he kept a notebook of peasant jokes and criminal slang for use in later writing. After his release in 1854, he served five years of exile as a private obliged to stay in Semipalatinsk, south-western Siberia, where the Russian Empire used to marshal its armies for the ongoing conquest of Central Asia. Siberia taught Dostoyevsky much that would be fictionalized in *Demons*, including criminal speech, the criminal mind and the ways of officialdom. He also experienced personally the complexities of passion his stories and novels of the 1840s had already explored; he wooed a close friend's wife, Marya Dmitriyevna Isayeva, and married her after she became a widow burdened with a troubled family and the hectic hysteria of advanced tuberculosis.

In 1859, the regime of the new tsar, Alexander II, allowed the Dostoyevskys to leave Siberia for Tver, a hundred miles north of Moscow; this provincial capital on the upper Volga River, and its geography, architecture and society, provided much of the setting for *Demons*. Within a year, Dostoyevsky was allowed to return to St Petersburg, where he re-entered the literary world and with his brother Mikhail started his own highly successful journal, *Time*, which was reincarnated after a brush with the censorship in 1863 as *Epoch*. In the early 1860s, Dostoyevsky's journals tried at some level to find a middle course between the conflicting political and intellectual positions he had encountered in the past. His doctrine of *Poch-vennichestvo*, or Grassroots, rested on the idea that Peter the Great's Westernization of Russia in the first quarter of the eighteenth century had been desirable and necessary, but that many movements, ideas and attitudes, including the Fourierist and other communes the Russians imported from Europe, ignored the social inventions the Russian serfs had been perfecting for centuries, such as the village commune, land redistribution and the leadership of rural elders; Grassroots held that Russia's own roots offered richer solutions to political and human problems than imported fads could.

But the old 1840s split between the religious, patriotic, Slavophile establishment and the progressive, humane, revolutionary Westernizers was giving way to the exacerbated conflict between the alienated positivist radicals of the 1860s who adopted the name Turgenev had given them, Nihilists, and those who thanked Russian Nationalism, Orthodoxy and Autocracy for the bloodless liberation of the serfs, introduction of trial by jury, reduction of the draft from twenty-five to five years, partial decentralization of local government, and other reforms of 1862. The 'men of the sixties' – Dmitry Pisarev, Nikolay Dobrolyubov, Nikolay Chernyshevsky, Mikhail Saltykov-Shchedrin, and many others – argued more and more savagely that Internationalism, Positivism, Atheism, Democracy, Materialism, Scientism, Feminism, Westernization, established through violence if necessary, were indispensable for the achievement of social justice. The middle ground disappeared. A writer who sought it, such as Turgenev, became virtually an émigré, and Dostoyevsky was drawn more and more to the right as he wrote *Notes from Underground* and *Crime and Punishment*, his two most political novels of the 1860s, but even more powerfully in his journalism.

In the year 1864, the death of his first wife on 15 April, and of his brother Mikhail on 10 July, disrupted Dostoyevsky's emotional and professional life. He inherited two rather dysfunctional families and a collection of debts sufficient to crush *Epoch* a year later. He travelled to Europe, gambled compulsively, had an ill-advised affair with Apollinaria Suslova, a fiercely intelligent and aggressively independent woman, and returned to Russia in 1866 with much of *Crime and Punishment* written, but an overhanging obligation to write another novel in six weeks. He hired a stenographer, Anna Grigoryevna Snitkina, from the only agency in St Petersburg and dictated *The Gambler*, before completing *Crime and Punishment*. A few months later, he married her, one of the smartest moves he ever made. She adored him, bore him four children, cured him of gambling and set his business affairs in order. They spent the next four years in Dresden, Geneva, and other Swiss, German and Italian cities, beyond the reach of his families and creditors. These were years of political tension in all these countries, culminating in France's defeat in the Franco-Prussian War (1870–71) and the frightening Paris Commune of 1871, several of whose leaders fled when it collapsed to Swiss cantons, including Uri, that had no extradition treaties. But Europe meant more to Dostoyevsky than revolutionary unrest. It was the repository of traditional high culture. He completely ignored the emerging Impressionists and Symbolists, but he would gaze obsessively at Holbein's *Deposition of Christ* in Basel or Raphael's *Sistine Madonna* in Dresden. Religious art transcended his Russian Orthodox hostility to the Catholic Church, and to Protestantism, which he saw as a doomed reaction to a doomed heresy. America was even worse, the soulless wasteland Dickens and Mrs Trollope had sometimes described, where commercial exploitation might be benign, but often crushed the blacks and all the vulnerable. He hungered for Russia all these years, but they were among his most creative. In eleven monthly instalments of the *Russian Herald*, he published *The Idiot* in 1868 and by then was already at work on *Demons*.

II

Russian radicalism had changed after 1865. On 4 April 1866, Dmitry Karakozov fired a shot at Tsar Alexander II. The assassination attempt failed, but it ended the period of the great reforms and the diffused social unrest that went with them. The liberation of the serfs in 1861 had been accompanied by hundreds of local uprisings, secretly printed manifestos, urban and village conflagrations, and by '*glasnost*', or uncensored, and often splendidly vicious, journalism. The greatest radical journal, Nekrasov's *Contemporary*, was closed, bureaucratic controls were tightened, and the pros and cons of terrorism became a central consideration for the 'Populists', who succeeded the Nihilists of the 1860s. The most shocking of these populists, Sergey Nechayev, claimed a large network of five-man cells linked to foreign leaders, and was famous for his 'Catechism of a Revolutionary', a document of twenty-six short paragraphs that describes and also exemplifies an obsession with human domination that still inspires those who send others to their death for a cause. A few paragraphs can give a sense of the theory and the personality that would propound it:

1. The revolutionist is a dedicated man. He has no interests of his own, no affairs, no ties, no possessions, not even a name. Everything in him is swallowed up in a single exclusive interest, a single idea, a single passion – revolution.

3. The revolutionist scorns all ideology and rejects worldly science, relegating it to future generations. He knows only one science – the science of destruction. For that and that alone he studies mechanics, physics, chemistry and, if you please, medicine. For that he studies living science day and night – people, character, positions, and all the conditions of the current social structure in all possible classes. For the goal is one – the swiftest and surest destruction of this vile structure.

10. Every comrade must have under his thumb several second- and third-level revolutionaries, that is, not quite consecrated. He must regard them as part of the common revolutionary capital which has been put at his disposition. He must expend his part of the capital economically, trying to extract the maximum use from it. He regards himself as capital dedicated to be expended for the triumph of the revolutionary work, but not as capital which he has at his sole disposal without the agreement of the whole comradeship of the fully consecrated.

14. With the goal of merciless destruction, the revolutionist can and often must live within society, pretending to be not at all what he is. The revolutionary must appear everywhere, in all the upper and middle classes, in the merchant's shop, the church, the lordly home, the bureaucratic world, the military, in literature, in the secret police, and even in the imperial palace.[2]

This catechism was published in 1871, during the trial of a group of young men who had murdered the student Ivanov in a garden grotto under Nechayev's tutelage. From Europe, Dostoyevsky had already been following Nechayev and other Populists. Dostoyevsky's letters and notebooks make it plain that Nechayev is a major source for Pyotr Stepanovich Verkhovensky, that Ivanov is a source for Shatov, Turgenev for Karmazinov, and Granovsky for Stepan Trofimovich Verkhovensky, but Dostoyevsky's character types are almost always composites. There has been a long dispute about whether Mikhail Bakunin, the great Russian anarchist whom Dostoyevsky may even have met in Geneva, actually wrote the Catechism, or whether Dostoyevsky's fellow Petrashevskian, Nikolay Alexandrovich Speshnev, or the intellectual Populist, Pyotr Nikitich Tkachev, played a major part in generating it. In any case, they all entered into the making of Pyotr, and, less directly, of Stavrogin.

In the genesis of *Demons*, Dostoyevsky twisted many strands together. As he completed *The Idiot*, he worked on the plans of two works that he never wrote: 'Atheism' and 'The Legend of a Great Sinner'. Both reflect Dostoyevsky's deep religious concerns and his love of melodramatic exaggeration, and both contributed elements to *Demons* and later to *The Adolescent* (also known as *A Raw Youth*) (1875), and *The Brothers Karamazov* (1879–80). The roots of the novel go much further back. Five pages from the end of *Crime and Punishment*, Raskolnikov has the last of his extraordinary dreams:

In his sickness he dreamed that all the world was doomed to be the victim of some sort of fearsome pestilence, unseen and undescribed before, and coming into Europe from the depths of

Asia. Everyone would have to die except a chosen few. Certain trichinae had appeared, microscopic beings that infested human bodies. But these beings were spirits endowed with mind and will. Humans who had ingested them immediately became possessed and mad. But never, never, had humans considered themselves so shrewd and unshakeable in their truth as the infected did. Never had they considered their pronouncements so unshakeable, or their scholarly deductions, or their moral convictions and beliefs. Whole settlements, whole cities and peoples were infected and went mad ... Fires began, and hunger. All things and people were destroyed. The plague spread and moved farther and farther. Only a handful of people could be saved in all the world; these were the elect and clean, destined to begin a new race of humans and a new life, to renew and clean the earth, but no one saw these people anywhere; no one heard their words and voices.[3]

Crime and Punishment treats radicalism as a disease, while *Demons* treats it as madness or possession by evil spirits, but the conscious trichinae in this dream show Dostoyevsky well on the way towards *Demons* before he had finished *Crime and Punishment*.

III

Demons belongs to a cluster of 1870s works that experimented with mixtures of apparently incompatible sub-genres of the novel. While *Demons* was gestating, Leo Tolstoy's *Anna Karenina* (1875–8) was developing a different kind of mixture: the tragic novel of Karenin, Vronsky and Anna, with their grand but broken families and final horror; the satiric novel of her aimless brother Oblonsky, Dolly and their overwhelmed family; and the comic novel of her sister, Kitty, Levin and their burgeoning family at the end. The sibling linkage unites these plots, and characters exchange many visits between family groupings, but Tolstoy keeps presenting the events within one family for a number of chapters and then shifts to one of the other two. It is an elegant structure and derives much of its power from the clarity with which readers can differentiate the three sub-genres. *Demons* also mixes three sub-genres of novel, but these are divided along a different axis: the Society Tale, primarily in Part I; the Anti-Nihilist Novel in Part II; and the Psychological Novel in Part III.

The Russian Society Tale thrived in the 1830s, emerging from the French novels about royal courts, from before Mme de Lafayette's *Princess of Cleves* (1678) to Stendhal's *Charterhouse of Parma* (1839). They also reflected English novels of manners that followed the tradition set by Scott's *St Ronan's Well*. Both Stendhal and Scott looked back to such Romantic favourites as *Hamlet*, with its picture of a staid, reprehensible, small-time court laid waste by the irruption of an unmanageable gang of young Europeanized elite, whose charismatic leader is sane except when the wind blows north-north-west. Dostoyevsky loved Shakespeare, but *Henry IV*, with its vision of a successful usurper beleaguered by new rebellions, also entered *Demons* indirectly through Alexander Pushkin, whose usurper, Boris Godunov, is ruined by the False Dmitry, who is actually Grishka Otrepev, a runaway novice from a monastery.[4] Society Tales explore the interplay between power and manners, emotion and manipulation in a world whose hierarchical social structure is as important as any character. The governing tone of these works is ironic. The implied author and the reader know far more than many of the characters do. In *Demons* three central and rather typical characters in the 'Society Tale' are Varvara Petrovna Stavrogina, Stepan Trofimovich Verkhovensky and their confidant, Anton Lavrentyevich G—v, the chronicler for the novel. In Part I, the central concerns are underlined by the frequent refusal of the characters even to discuss them: Stavrogin's sanity, his marital status and his possible impregnation of Darya Pavlovna, who is to be married off, all typical concerns for a Society Tale, which traditionally aspires to advance virtue by laying vice bare.

The Anti-Nihilist Novel is a darker genre, making vice ugly and sometimes fearsome. Its tone is that of a pamphlet, or a comedy of bad manners. It has its origin not so much in fiction as in the nasty diatribes and exposés of the 1860s. The Anti-

Nihilist Novel attracted many reactionary hacks, but also some of the finest literary minds of the nineteenth century – Nikolay Leskov, Aleksey Feofilaktovich Pisemsky and Ivan Goncharov. Charles Moser, who wrote the best book on the Anti-Nihilist Novel, considers *Demons* the culmination of the genre. Kirillov, Shigalyov and Pyotr Stepanovich Verkhovensky give monologues in Part II that enunciate and embody different implications of Nechayevism: Kirillov links it to self-destruction; Shigalyov to enslavement; Pyotr Stepanovich to madness; but all three to domination by the will. Dostoyevsky boasted that his imagination was prophetic and could use limited data to deduce truths not yet evident; later readers have said that the clarity of his understanding of Nechayev and the many extremists of his time gave him uncanny prescience.

Kirillov and Shigalyov exist almost entirely in the Anti-Nihilist Novel, but Pyotr Stepanovich moves, as Nechayev had said a revolutionist should, between this world and that of the Society Tale. Some characters are split almost evenly between the two. Karmazinov wears 'a short, quilted jerkin, a sort of jacket, with little mother-of-pearl buttons, but it was much too short and was therefore anything but becoming to his plump little belly and firmly rounded thighs. But tastes do vary' (Part II, Chapter 6, §5). This description, with the kindly narrator's refusal to judge, is typical of the Society Tale. Karmazinov's opinions in the same passage, however, belong in an Anti-Nihilist Novel: 'Russia is now pre-eminently the one place in the whole world where anything you want can happen without the slightest resistance. I understand only too well why Russians with means have all made tracks abroad . . . If the ship is about to sink, the rats are the first to desert it.' So many characters in *Demons* belong like Karmazinov to both the Society and the Anti-Nihilist plot that Dostoyevsky needed special devices to guide the reader as to when to react ironically and when angrily.

Even more confusing, in the third part of *Demons*, a third kind of novel comes into its own, although it too has been present at some level from the start. Dostoyevsky himself had invented it, though it had been invented and reinvented many times before: the Psychological Novel. In this part of *Demons*,

Dostoyevsky addresses a question he had raised at certain
points in *Notes from Underground*. Chernyshevsky, the most
publicized radical of the 1860s, had characterized his hero
Lopukhov, in *What Is to Be Done?* (1863), as the kind of man
who had thrown a self-satisfied and well-dressed officer into a
muddy ditch for expecting the shabbily dressed Lopukhov to
give way for him on a pavement. Dostoyevsky understood the
political, economic and even moral meaning of this action, but
asked a question Chernyshevsky had no time for: 'What sort of
human psyche would behave this way?' The Underground Man
in *Notes from Underground* was his devastating answer, a man
so worried about his insignificance that he prepared epically
for a pavement collision with a man who ignored him, and
sought reassurance that he existed in the attention that he could
get only by insulting people, including his readers. Chernyshevsky had disinvented the existing Psychological Novel, and Dostoyevsky reinvented it to ridicule him. A decade later, Nechayev
was the most visible radical, and in Dostoyevsky's eyes, the
creator of a persuasive fiction about a huge conspiracy. Dostoyevsky again wondered about the kind of psyche that would
need this anti-social violence. The answer this time took the
form of a huge novel, with two instantiations of Nechayev –
Stavrogin and Pyotr Stepanovich. Psychologically, Dostoyevsky
made them self-dramatizing human beings, power-hungry,
atheistic, manipulative, but above all, eager to display their
power, their unbelief and even their manipulative skill. In a
famous letter of 15 January 1880, Dostoyevsky would charac-
terize the unbelieving as 'such *lightweights* that they have no
scholarly preparation for knowing what it is that they are
denying . . . infected with the general sick contemporary feature
of all the Russian intelligentsia, this frivolous relation to the
object, the extraordinary self-esteem, which would not occur to
the mightiest minds in Europe, and the phenomenal ignorance
about the matter they are judging'.[5] He already believed this in
the 1870s. His initial characterization of Pyotr Stepanovich
Verkhovensky emphasizes something that the horror of
Nechayev's actions and enunciated doctrines had obscured: he
was on what a later generation would call an ego trip. Stavrogin

lives centrally in the Society Tale plot and secondarily in the Anti-Nihilist plot, while Pyotr Stepanovich lives primarily in the Anti-Nihilist plot and secondarily in the Society Tale.

The Psychological Novel links Pyotr Stepanovich's outrageousness and Stavrogin's mental and marital states not to Society, but to the ways they dominate Shatov's and Kirillov's wildly different modes of thought; Lizaveta Nikolayevna's, Darya Pavlovna's and Marya Ignatyevna's wildly different kinds of desire; Varvara Petrovna's and Stepan Trofimovich's social existence; and each other's dreams of an anti-utopia, which somehow become contagious enough to infect the youth of the town and many of their servile elders. The Psychological Novel turns into an exploration of domination and helplessness, with Varvara Petrovna exploiting aristocratic power, Governor von Lembke and those around him bureaucratic power, and the holy fool Semyon Yakovlevich, no longer a parenthetical figure, the power of religious fanaticism, pure of birth or rank or intellect.

Stavrogin, with his hypnotic, inexplicable power, stands at the centre of this exploration, but here, under the tightened censorship of the 1870s, the magisterial editor of the *Russian Herald*, Mikhail Katkov, as he did with *Anna Karenina*, rejected the key chapter of the novel. He refused to publish the war-as-suicide ending of *Anna Karenina*, and he refused to publish the chapter in which Stavrogin confesses to the rape of a child who then commits suicide. This monstrous passage is the culmination of the Psychological Novel Dostoyevsky had in mind, because it absorbs all three kinds of novel into a study of unbridled power. Stavrogin's social, ideological and sexual power becomes nothing but power in the encounter with the child. This edition appends the suppressed chapter at the end. Other good editors have tried to insert it, but Dostoyevsky did not do so when he republished *Demons*, probably because he had partly compensated for its absence when he wrote the chapters that came after it. Stavrogin's child rape explains the motivation for Pyotr Stepanovich's drive to dominance: unbridled power is not the means to utopia or sex; it is the source of a sick gratification that comes from trampling on helplessness. As with Svidrigailov and Luzhin in *Crime and Punishment*, Smerdyakov and Rakitin in *The Brothers Karamazov*, or Rogozhin and a group of radicals in *The Idiot*, Dostoyevsky pairs his sensually enormous, self-destructively murderous villains with lightweight political villains. Unlike the other lightweight villains, Pyotr Stepanovich becomes a murderer too, consciously using his frivolity, as Stavrogin uses his mysterious magnetism, to reduce others to helplessness.

IV

Until the First World War, the literary world considered Dostoyevsky a mysterious force, able to strike our emotions, but lacking the form and control to create proper literature. André Gide in the West and Leonid Grossman in Russia[6] were among the first to explore Dostoyevsky as a consummate literary craftsman who achieved his effects by adopting and adapting the techniques of literary classics, popular literature and journalism. When Henry James described the Russian novels as 'loose and baggy monsters',[7] one of the disorderly elements he had in mind would certainly have been the old, old matter of narrative technique. Plato had distinguished epic from drama as demanding a narrator, and the inventors of the modern novel in the seventeenth and eighteenth centuries experimented very self-consciously with narrators they learned about from epics, romances, histories, biographies, collections of letters and earlier prose fiction. They learned directly and indirectly from the *Arabian Nights* about narrators who told about narrators who told about narrators who told a story, and what it means to readers if some of these narrators were liars and others were stupid or biased. In *Don Quixote* (1605–15), Cervantes made fun of the whole process of narration, with lost and interrupted manuscripts and characters in the novel who have already read part of it. A century and a half later, the funniest element in one of the funniest novels ever, Laurence Sterne's *Tristram Shandy* (1760–67), is the mockery of the storytelling itself. Still the first sophisticated analysis of narrative technique came near the beginning of the twentieth century in James's prefaces. He knew, as Plato did, that we can only encounter the world of a novel or an epic through some sort of narration, and he believed that this encounter will collapse if the narration abandons its consistency. Narrators may be sane or insane, intelligent or stupid, honest or dishonest, biased or neutral, and James tried most of these variants in different stories, but a narrator whose literary identity keeps changing will lose the capacity to transmit a believable world. For all his international sophistication, James was treating a local, Western novelistic custom as a basic psychological truth. Russian novelists from Gogol on rejected this particular consistency, not out of laziness or ignorance, but because it deprived them of other shaping devices that they considered more important.

Two of the key elements in narrators' identities are their ability to know what the characters are thinking and the ability to make moral, social and psychological judgements about people. Some narrators are omniscient and can see into everybody's mind, while others, including most first-person narrators, usually present one character's thoughts and dreams at first hand, but learn about all others from their looks, actions or words. Both kinds of narrator may or may not be given the power to judge whether a character or action is good or evil, sensible or foolish, noble or vile, etc. Writers as different as Ernest Hemingway and Andrey Platonov sometimes evoke terror by withholding this judging capacity from their narrators. Dostoyevsky's narrator in *Demons* shifts among these identities many times. In the first important article about narration in this novel, Vladimir Tunimanov[8] considered the dozens of places where the first-person chronicler slips into omniscience. The two easiest explanations for such slippage are Dostoyevsky's carelessness or his ignorance. The notebooks and letters exclude ignorance, but no theoretical basis exists for excluding carelessness. As the Hellenistic critics knew, even Homer nods. Critical humility, and scientific optimism, however, teach us that anomalies often lead us to unpredictable insights, and serious readers accept their challenge and take the easy way out only when ingenuity is exhausted. If *Demons* sacrificed narratorial consistency for a rhetorical or an aesthetic goal that

Dostoyevsky considered more important, then James's rules for narration become simply one of the options in the community of novelistic traditions.

In fact, Slobodanka Vladiv has accepted the challenge of this slippage and written a persuasive book on the function of this chronicler in a structure that generates and communicates the political and religious positions Dostoyevsky takes. Yury Karyakin takes almost the opposite stand, seeing the chronicler as a powerful artistic counterweight to Dostoyevsky's premeditated tendentiousness. To no small degree, he thinks the chronicler makes the novel, originally conceived as a pamphlet, into a 'poem'.[9]

If *Demons* is hard to read because it belongs to three different literary genres, shifting in importance, but not elegantly segmented like those in *Anna Karenina*, Dostoyevsky uses narrative technique to guide our reactions to these different sets of concerns and kinds of discourse. Anton Lavrentyevich often calls himself a chronicler, and at the beginning of the novel is almost always that. He lives in the town, is fond of Stepan and Lizaveta, is proud to be the confidant of the two most distinguished ladies and the most distinguished intellectual in the town, and has all the sensibilities of small-town society. The tension between his admiration for Stepan and Stepan's laughable career as a radical generates much of the irony which is the governing reader reaction to most of Part I. In the Society Tale, Dostoyevsky withholds Anton Lavrentyevich's capacity to judge and makes him participate on the edges of the action in such a way as to see much of it for himself and to hear much of the rest in the confidences of his close friend Stepan. He is given very little judgement about Stepan and others, and very little information that he does not see or hear.

In the polemical Anti-Nihilist Novel, the narration is much more judgemental and often ignores the question of how the narrated is known. Neither of these changes is a part of the chronicler's biography, as some critics have tried to make it. The narrator of the Anti-Nihilist *Demons* would size up Stepan as severely as the reader does. He looks at von Lembke, the new governor, as not very bright, not well connected socially, and – worst of all – German. Von Lembke's wife aspires to popularity among the Radical youth and becomes subject to the will of Karmazinov and Pyotr.

> But let me continue with Yuliya Mikhaylovna. The poor lady (I'm very sorry for her) could have achieved everything she found so attractive and alluring (renown and all the rest) without any of the drastic and eccentric moves she set her mind to ... But whether from an excess of poetry in her soul, or whether from the long, sad failures of her early youth, she suddenly felt, as soon as her fortunes had changed, that she had somehow been specially called, almost anointed, as one 'over whom this tongue of fire had blazed', and it was precisely this tongue that caused all the trouble: after all, it was not a chignon, which can fit any woman's head. (Part II, Chapter 6, §1)

The comic element here is nasty, and the anti-nihilist manifesto takes hold. The great issues of the Society Tale were Stavrogin's sanity, his marital state and Stepan Trofimovich's reaction to a forced marriage. None of these issues is pursued in Part II, but as Stepan's intellectual and biological offspring, Stavrogin and Pyotr Stepanovich, move in from the geographical and narrative fringes, the narrator develops strong opinions. In Part III, where the Psychological Novel dominates, the narrator often almost disappears. To make us explore what is going on in the minds of these people and what can motivate Pyotr Stepanovich and Stavrogin to behave the way they do, Dostoyevsky needs to guide us past irony and anger into his understanding of the insane drives actuating all the radicals. His narrative voice here exchanges its validating participation for a transparency that makes the readers themselves participate. In Part III, we are often there, unaware of Plato's and James's mediacy. The shifting narrative technique tracks and guides us through the shifting genres that shape our experience of the novel.

V

From its title to its final sentence, this novel deals with insanity. Immediately after the title, readers encounter the two epigraphs, from Pushkin and the Gospel according to St Luke. The early Christians, like the pagans before them, treated dreams as external visitations, and insanity as possession by unclean spirits. Both epigraphs identify the demons of the title as earlier words for and understandings of madness. In Dostoyevsky's own time, the intellectual high ground belonged to the neurologists who believed that no insanity could exist without a visible lesion on the brain, something twenty-first-century neurology has yet to prove. It is often said that there are two kinds of novel, those that tell the reader what is happening, and those that show the reader what is happening. In the nineteenth century, Dostoyevsky and other Russians were inventing a third kind of novel, one that also made the reader experience what is happening. *Demons* not only tells us about scandals and catastrophes, and shows them to us; it uses its whole structure to carry us through irony, then anger, then into the experience of being manipulated towards madness.

The second epigraph connects madness with both self-destruction and a return to sanity, and Stavrogin, who has been scientifically diagnosed as delirious after biting the governor's ear, is called completely sane at the time of his suicide, with the same scientific authority. Stepan Trofimovich, his foolish mentor, seeks salvation, while all the conspirators are destroyed, except Pyotr Stepanovich who, like Nechayev, flees to Europe, where so many of these mad ideas originated. Kirillov, Lizaveta Nikolayevna and Stavrogin may be the most appealing of the major figures in the novel, and they all destroy themselves. Mikhail Bakhtin maintained that we should not begin a sentence, 'Dostoyevsky said . . .' and end it with a quotation from any of his characters, including the narrator, since the meaning of a Dostoyevskian text resides in the dialogue among the ideas, and the authorial spokesman was an anachronism for him. One exception might be the hero of the last short story Dostoyevsky wrote, 'The Dream of a Ridiculous

Man' (1877), who outdoes those wonderful Tolstoy heroes who pursue the meaning of life. The Ridiculous Man believes that life is more important than the meaning of life. Kirillov and Shigalyov have complementary theories opposed to this doctrine, one a theory that outweighs his own life, and the other a theory worth a hundred million other lives.

Both the subject matter and the genre of the typical Society Tale belonged to the years of Dostoyevsky's childhood. The Anti-Nihilist Novel belongs to the angry years when he was writing *Demons*, and the Psychological Novel perhaps belongs best to the twentieth century, when a few Stavrogins empowered thousands of Pyotr Stepanovichs to drive herds of 'capital', to use Nechayev's term, to slaughter about a hundred million people, the very number Shigalyov and Pyotr hit upon. In the twenty-first century, journalists and other writers have been fascinated by the motives, the backgrounds and the psyches of those who killed themselves on suicide missions, just as they were with the kamikazes in the twentieth century, but they have devoted surprisingly little study to the trainers and motivators who recruit them and send them on their missions. Pyotr Stepanovich and Stavrogin offer rich bodies of understanding for such figures. Like Nechayev, Stavrogin uses ideological virtuosity and Pyotr Stepanovich conspiratorial authority to empower their will to send others to destruction for the sake of purposeless power, to shock and awe. It is a scary book.

Robert L. Belknap

NOTES

1. 'Muzhik Marey' (February 1876), in *A Writer's Diary*, p. 351 (for bibliographical details, see Further Reading).
2. My translation from Feliks Moiseevich Lur'e, *Nechaev, sozdatel' razrusheniya* (*Nechayev. The Builder of Destruction*) (Moscow: Molodaya Gvardiya, 2001), pp. 104–9.
3. My translation from F. M. Dostoevskii, *Polnoe sobranie sochinenii v tridsati tomakh, Tom VI, Prestuplenie i nakazanie* (*Crime and Punishment*) (Leningrad: Akademiia nauk, 1973), p. 419.

4. In *Boris Godunov* (1825).
5. My translation. See Fyodor Dostoyevsky, *Complete Letters*, tr. and ed. David Lowe, vol. 5, p. 178.
6. André Gide, *Dostoevski* (Paris, 1923) and Leonid Grossman, 'Dostoevskii i Evropa', *Russkaya Mysl'* (November–December 1915).
7. Henry James, *Letters*, ed. Leon Edel (London and Cambridge, Massachusetts: Belknap Press, 1984), vol. 4, p. 619.
8. See Further Reading.
9. For Vladiv, see Further Reading. Yurii Fyodorovich Karyakin, *Dostoevskii i kanun XXI veka* (*Dostoyevsky and the Eve of the Twenty-first Century*) (Moscow: Sovetskii pisatel', 1989), p. 244.

Further Reading

Paul Avrich, *Bakunin and Nechaev* (London: Freedom Press, 1974)

—, *Russian Anarchists* (Princeton, New Jersey: Princeton University Press, 1967)

Mikhail Bakhtin, *Problems of Dostoevsky's Poetics*, tr. and ed. Caryl Emerson (Minneapolis: University of Minnesota Press, 1984)

Richard Palmer Blackmur, 'In the Birdcage', *Eleven Essays in the European Novel* (New York: Harcourt Brace, 1964)

Jessie Coulson, *Dostoevsky: A Self Portrait* (London: Oxford University Press, 1962)

Anna Dostoevskaya, *Reminiscences*, tr. and ed. Beatrice Stillman (New York: Liveright, 1975)

Fyodor Dostoevsky, *Complete Letters*, tr. and ed. David Lowe and Ronald Meyer (Ann Arbor, Michigan: Ardis, 1988–91), 5 vols.

—, *Dostoevsky as Reformer: The Petrashevsky Case*, tr. and ed. Liza Knapp (Ann Arbor, Michigan: Ardis, 1987)

—, *Notebooks for The Possessed*, tr. Victor Terras, ed. and introduction by Edward Wasiolek (Chicago: University of Chicago Press, 1968)

—, *A Writer's Diary*, tr. and ed. Kenneth Lantz (Evanston, Illinois: Northwestern University Press, 1993)

Joseph Frank, *Dostoevsky: The Miraculous Years, 1865–1871* (Princeton, New Jersey: Princeton University Press, 1995)

William Leatherbarrow (ed.), *The Cambridge Companion to Dostoevsky* (Cambridge: Cambridge University Press, 2002)

—, *Devil's Vaudeville: The Demonic in Dostoevsky's Major*

Fiction (Evanston, Illinois: Northwestern University Press, 2005)

—, *Dostoevsky's 'The Devils': A Critical Companion* (Evanston, Illinois: Northwestern University Press, 1999)

Deborah Martinsen, *Surprised by Shame* (Columbus: Ohio State University Press, 2003)

Konstantin Mochul'skii, *Dostoevsky: His Life and Work*, tr. Michael Minihan (Princeton, New Jersey: Princeton University Press, 1971)

Charles A. Moser, *Anti-Nihilism in the Russian Novel of the 1860's* (The Hague: Mouton, 1964)

Vladimir Tunimanov, 'Rasskazchik v *Besakh* Dostoevskogo', in *Issledovaniia po poetike i stilistike* (Leningrad, 1972), pp. 87–162. Partial tr. in Robert L. Jackson, (ed.), *Dostoevsky: New Perspectives* (Englewood Cliffs, New Jersey: Prentice Hall, 1984), pp. 145–75

Slobodanka D. Vladiv, *Narrative Principles in Dostoevsky's 'Besy'* (Bern: Peter Lang, 1979)

A Note on the Text

In October 1870, after a number of false starts, Dostoyevsky sent off half of the first part of his new novel *Demons* to the *Russian Herald*, the journal which had serialized his previous novel *The Idiot*, apologizing for the late submission and at the same time asking for another advance, a frequent refrain in his correspondence. Dostoyevsky's situation was dire. The author and his new wife had been living abroad since 1867, homesick and virtually penniless, their financial situation made worse by Dostoyevsky's disastrous forays at the gaming tables. He had promised the *Russian Herald* that his new novel would be ready to begin publication in the January 1870 issue. Instead, he had been working on the novella *The Eternal Husband*, originally conceived as a relatively short piece for another journal. The novella, however, grew in length and ambition and was not submitted to *Dawn* until December 1869. Casting around for a suitable subject for the *Russian Herald*, Dostoyevsky hit upon the idea of writing a novel that would treat 'contemporary issues'. As he explained in a letter to the critic Nikolay Strakhov: 'I have great hopes for the work that I'm writing for the *Russian Herald*, not from the artistic but from the tendentious point of view; I want to express several ideas – even if my artistry should suffer as a result ... Even if it turns out to be nothing more than a lampoon – I'll have my say' (24 March/5 April 1870). The Nechayev Affair (see Introduction, Section II) provided the impetus for Dostoyevsky's political lampoon, which traces the excesses of the radicals of the 1860s–70s to their forefathers, the liberals of the 1840s – in the novel neatly illustrated by

Stepan Trofimovich Verkhovensky, the representative of the 1840s, and his son Pyotr, the radical revolutionary.

However, during the course of his work on the novel that would become *Demons*, another figure usurped the position of central hero, namely, Nikolay Vsevolodovich Stavrogin, whom Dostoyevsky describes in a letter as a 'gloomy figure', a 'villain' and a 'tragic' character, whom he had 'wanted to depict for a long time now' (8/20 October 1870). As we know from Dostoyevsky's notebooks and letters for the period 1869–70, the character of Stavrogin had its genesis in the plans for a work that was to be called 'The Life of a Great Sinner', a multi-volume epic that was to rival Tolstoy's *War and Peace* in scope. But Dostoyevsky had put aside this project, thinking that he would be able to write his political lampoon quickly, fulfil his obligation to the *Russian Herald* and return to write what he regarded as his life's work. Instead, Stavrogin took centre stage in the ever-shifting early plans for *Demons*, as is seen in this entry from Dostoyevsky's notebooks: 'NB. Everything turns on Stavrogin's character. Stavrogin is *everything*' (16 August 1870). As was often the case, Dostoyevsky had severely underestimated the time required to write the novel, which had now grown more complex with the introduction of the Stavrogin plot line. *Demons* was serialized in fits and starts in the *Russian Herald* from January 1871 to December 1872, the lags not always the result of the author's lateness with submitting the text. A separate book edition was published in 1873.

The novel *Demons* was introduced to the English reader in 1913 by the indefatigable Constance Garnett, the woman who single-handedly created the 'Russian craze' through her translations of the collected works of Dostoyevsky, Chekhov, Gogol, Tolstoy and Turgenev. Garnett dubbed the novel *The Possessed*, a title which held sway for decades, even influencing translations into other languages, for example, the stage adaptation *Les Possédés* (1959) by Albert Camus. But fashions in translation, as in so much else, change with the times, as evidenced by Garnett's own take on the problems of translating Dostoyevsky, whom she finds to be 'so obscure and so careless a writer that one can scarcely help clarifying him – sometimes it needs some penetration to see what he is trying to say' ('Russian Literature in English', *Listener*, January 1947). She was not alone then in her opinion of Dostoyevsky's carelessness, but today's reader now embraces those same instances that Garnett erased or smoothed over and wishes to grapple with the obscurities, rather than have them clarified or interpreted. In other words, rather than attempting to adapt Dostoyevsky's prose to the norms of 'good' English prose, whatever that may be, the modern translator seeks to reproduce as faithfully as possible Dostoyevsky's text in all its complexity, sometimes at the expense of the 'good, smooth' English so favoured by reviewers. This faithfulness to Dostoyevsky's text must begin with the title. *The Possessed* was an inspired choice on the part of Garnett, but the fact of the matter remains that it is not the title that Dostoyevsky gave his novel. The title in Russian is *Besy*, literally *Demons*, which is reinforced by the repetition of the word *bes* in the two epigraphs. Furthermore, Garnett's title redirects the action: Dostoyevsky's title, like the epigraphs, speaks of the demons by which one is possessed, not of those who are possessed. As he writes in his letter to his frequent correspondent, the poet Apollon Maikov:

> True, the facts also indicate that the sickness that had held civilized Russians in its grip was much stronger than we had realized and that the matter did not end with the Belinskys, Krayevskys and so forth. But then took place that to which the Evangelist Luke bears witness: there were demons sitting in a man, and their name was Legion; and they asked Him: order us to enter into the swine, and he allowed them to do so. The demons entered the swine and the whole herd threw itself from the steep bank into the sea and they all drowned . . . That's exactly what happened with us. The demons went out of Russian man and entered the herd of swine, that is, the Nechayevs . . . and their ilk. They have drowned or will certainly do so, and the man who has been healed, out of whom the demons have come, sits at the feet of

Jesus. And that's just how it should be ... He who loses his people and his national character loses both the faith of his fathers and God. Well, if you want to know – that's precisely what my novel is about. It's called *Demons*, and it's a description of how these demons entered the herd of swine.

(9/21 October 1870)

This translation of *Demons* is based on the authoritative text as found in the 'Academy' edition of Dostoyevsky's *Complete Collected Works in Thirty Volumes* (*Polnoe sobranie sochinenii*), volumes 10–12 (Leningrad: Nauka, 1974–5). Volume 10 prints the complete text of the novel; volume 11 has the suppressed chapter 'At Tikhon's' (see Appendix) as well as manuscript materials, notes and variants; and volume 12 contains extensive commentary and notes, as well as sketches and plans.

A NOTE FROM THE EDITOR

Robert A. Maguire died on 8 July 2005, after a lengthy bout with cancer. He had completed, literally just a few weeks earlier, the first round of revisions on his translation of *Demons*. While engaged in his painstaking read-through of the translation, he reminded me, and others, on more than one occasion of my promise to him to prepare the translation for publication should he be unable to do so. (His long-time Columbia University colleague Robert Belknap had been pressed into service to write the Introduction.) I inherited some 950 pages of typescript covered in a scrawl of red ink. In addition to straightforward corrections and revisions to the translation, there were questions to be answered, proposed alternate readings of words and phrases, cross-references to other instances of Dostoyevsky's use of a certain word or phrase, as well as reminders on what should be explained in the Notes about the translation. All of this I have incorporated to the best of my ability; in addition, I compiled the Notes. Bob and I had been discussing the *Demons* translation from the beginning, and his work on his translation of Gogol's *Dead Souls* before that, so I had a good idea of how to proceed, and would like to think that he might approve of the translation in its present state.

I would like to take this opportunity to thank Peter Carson and Lindeth Vasey, both editors at Penguin Classics, and E. Thomas Maguire, Bob's brother, for the generous assistance and support that made the completion of this book possible.

Ronald Meyer

Demons

A Novel in Three Parts

Strike me dead – can't see the way,
It's lost we are, what can we do?
(Could be) a demon's leading us through fields
In circles, and we've gone astray.

. . .

What's driving them? And such a band!
What is their doleful song about?
Laying a house-sprite in the ground?
Giving in marriage a witch's hand?
       – Alexander Pushkin, 'Demons' (1830)[1]

Now a large herd of swine was feeding there on the hillside; and they begged him to let them enter these. So he gave them leave. Then the demons came out of the man and entered the swine, and the herd rushed down the steep bank into the lake and were drowned. When the herdsmen saw what had happened, they fled, and told it in the city and in the country. Then people went out to see what had happened, and they came to Jesus, and found the man from whom the demons had gone, sitting at the feet of Jesus, clothed and in his right mind; and they were afraid. And those who had seen it told them how he who had been possessed with demons was healed.

       – Luke 8:32–6 [RSV]

Contents

PART I

CHAPTER I

Instead of an Introduction: A Few Details from the Biography of the Much-Esteemed Stepan Trofimovich Verkhovensky

I.

As I embark on a description of the very strange events that recently occurred in our town, which until then had not been notable for anything, I am compelled, owing to my lack of experience, to begin in a rather roundabout way, namely, with a few biographical details concerning the talented and much-esteemed Stepan Trofimovich Verkhovensky. Let these details serve merely as an introduction to my proposed chronicle, whereas the story itself that I intend to tell is yet to come.

I'll say it straight out: Stepan Trofimovich was constantly playing a certain special role among us, one that might be called civic, and he passionately loved this role, so much so that I even think he could not have gone on living without it. It's not that I'm putting him on the same level with a stage actor, by no means: God forbid, the more so as I myself have great respect for him. It could all have been a question of habit, or rather, of a constant and high-minded tendency, from childhood on, to indulge in pleasant daydreams about the fine figure he would cut as a citizen of our town. For example, he was inordinately fond of his position as a man who was 'persecuted' and, so to speak, 'exiled'.[1] Both these little words have a kind of classical lustre to them, which had proved enduringly seductive to him, and, with the passage of so many years, had gradually raised him in his own opinion of himself and finally placed him on a pedestal that was very lofty and gratifying to his self-esteem. In a certain English satirical novel of the last century, one Gulliver, on returning from the land of the Lilliputians, where the people stood no more than about four inches tall, had become so accustomed to regarding himself as a giant among them that, while walking through the streets of London, he could not keep from shouting to passers-by and carriages to get out of his way and take care that he didn't crush them, imagining that he was still a giant and they were small.[2] For this they jeered at him and abused him, and crude coachmen gave the giant a taste of their whips. But was that just? What is habit not capable of? Habit had brought Stepan Trofimovich to almost the same position too, but in a more innocent and inoffensive way, if one can put it like that, because he was a splendid human being.

I'm even of the opinion that towards the end he had been forgotten everywhere and by everyone; but one certainly can't really say that he was not altogether unknown before that. There's no gainsaying that for some time he too was a member of the distinguished pleiad[3] of some of the celebrated figures of our generation just past – albeit for only the very briefest of moments – and that his name was uttered by many of the impetuous people of that time in practically the same breath with the names of Chaadayev, Belinsky, Granovsky and Herzen,[4] who was only then beginning his career abroad. But Stepan Trofimovich's activity ended almost the very moment it began, because of a 'whirlwind of concurrent circumstances',[5] so to speak. And what do you know? It later turned out that there was not only no 'whirlwind' but not even any 'circumstances', at least in his case. Only recently, just a few days ago, I learned, to my utter astonishment, yet from a completely reliable source, that Stepan Trofimovich had been living among us, in our province, not only not in exile, as we had been accustomed to think, but had never even been under surveillance. Such is the power of one's own imagination! He himself sincerely believed, as long as he lived, that in certain circles he was constantly feared, that every step he took was invariably known and noted, and that each of our three successive governors over the past twenty years, on arriving to take charge of the province, had already brought with him some particular and disturbing notion of Stepan Trofimovich, which had been communicated from on high as the first order of business during the transition of power. If anyone had then adduced irrefutable

proof by way of assuring Stepan Trofimovich, the soul of
honour, that he had absolutely nothing to fear, he would certainly have taken offence. And yet he was actually a most
intelligent and gifted man, even a man, one might say, of learning, although, come to think of it, in learning . . . well, in a
word, he didn't accomplish so much in the area of learning,
and, it would seem, nothing at all. But after all, this happens
pretty often with people of learning in this Rus[6] of ours.

He returned from abroad and performed brilliantly in the
capacity of university lecturer at the very end of the 1840s. But
he managed to deliver no more than a few lectures, about the
Arabs, it would seem. He also managed to defend a brilliant
dissertation on the budding civic and Hanseatic significance of
the small German town of Hanau,[7] in the period between 1413
and 1428, as well as on the specific and undetermined reasons
why this significance had never come to anything. This dissertation was a deft and painful jab at the Slavophiles[8] of the time
and immediately won him numerous and bitter enemies among
them. Later – although it was after he had lost his university
position – he managed to publish (by way of revenge, so to
speak, and to show who it was they had lost) in a progressive
monthly journal, which offered translations from Dickens and
championed George Sand,[9] the beginning of a very probing
piece of research – apparently on the reasons for the unusually
moral sense of nobility of certain knights in a particular age,[10]
or something of the sort. At least, some lofty and unusually
noble idea was advanced. People later said that the continuation
of the study was quickly forbidden, and that even the progressive journal suffered for having published the first half. That was
entirely possible, because what didn't happen in those days?
But in this case, it is more likely that nothing happened, and
that the author himself was too lazy to finish his study. And he
curtailed his lectures on the Arabs because someone (evidently
from among his reactionary enemies) had somehow intercepted
a letter to someone with an account of certain 'circumstances',
as a result of which someone had demanded certain explanations from him. I don't know whether that's true, but people
went on to assert that in Petersburg, at the very same time,

some vast, bizarre anti-government association, consisting of about thirteen members and practically shaking the foundations of the state, had been discovered. It was said that they were supposedly intending to translate none other than Fourier[11] himself. As though by design, at the very same time in Moscow a long poem[12] by Stepan Trofimovich was also seized, which he had written some six years earlier, in Berlin, in the first flush of youth, and which had passed from hand to hand, in copies, among two admirers and one student. This poem is now lying on my writing table; I received it no more than a year ago from Stepan Trofimovich himself in a very recent copy in his own hand, inscribed by him and in a magnificent red morocco-leather binding. Incidentally, it is not lacking in poetic merit or even a certain talent; it is a strange creation, but in those days (more accurately, that is, in the thirties) people often wrote like that. As for relating the plot, I find that difficult, because to tell the truth, I don't understand a thing in it. It's some sort of allegory, in lyrical dramatic form, reminiscent of the second part of *Faust*.[13] The first scene opens with a chorus of women, then a chorus of men, then a chorus of spirits of some kind, and at the very end, a chorus of souls, which have never yet been alive, but would very much like to come to life. All these choruses sing about something very vague, mostly about someone's curse, but with a shade of high-minded humour. But the scene suddenly changes and then there begins some sort of 'Festival of Life', in which even insects sing, a tortoise appears with some sacramental words in Latin, and even, if I remember rightly, a certain mineral – that is, an entirely inanimate object – bursts into song about something. And in general, all sing incessantly, and if they do speak, then it is to rail at one another in some vague way, but again, with a shade of some higher meaning. Finally, the scene changes again, and before us appears a wild place, a civilized young man wanders among crags, plucking and sucking herbs of some sort, and when a fairy asks him why he is sucking these herbs, he replies that since he feels an overabundance of life within himself, he seeks oblivion and finds it in the juices of these herbs, but that what he desires most of all is to lose his mind as quickly as possible (a desire that is perhaps superfluous). Then an indescribably handsome youth suddenly rides in on a black steed, followed by a huge number of all the peoples of the world. The youth represents death, and all the peoples are longing for it. And finally, in the very last scene, the Tower of Babel suddenly appears, and some athletes are busy bringing it to completion, with a song of fresh hope, and when they reach the very top, the lord of – let's say it's Olympus[14] – runs off in comical fashion, and mankind, which has grasped the situation, occupies his place, and immediately begins a new life with a new and deeper understanding of things. Well then, this is the poem that was deemed dangerous at that time. Last year I proposed to Stepan Trofimovich that he should publish it, because in our day and age it is completely innocuous, but he rejected this proposal with obvious displeasure. He was not pleased by my opinion that it was completely innocuous, and I even attribute to that a certain coldness towards me on his part, which lasted two whole months. And then look what happened! Suddenly, and at virtually the same time I proposed that it be published here, our poem was published *there*, that is, abroad, in one of the revolutionary anthologies, and totally without the knowledge of Stepan Trofimovich. At first he was terrified; he rushed off to see the governor and wrote a most high-minded letter of self-justification to Petersburg and read it to me twice, but didn't send it, not knowing whom to address it to. In a word, he was agitated for an entire month; but I am convinced that in the secret recesses of his heart he was extraordinarily flattered. He virtually slept with the copy of the anthology that had been delivered to him, and during the day he hid it under the mattress, and didn't even allow his maid to make the bed, and although every day he expected a telegram to arrive from somewhere, he turned a haughty face to the world. No telegram ever arrived. It was then that he made peace with me once again, which is ample testimony to the extraordinary kindness of his gentle and forgiving heart.

2.

I'm not asserting, mind you, that there was absolutely no reason for him to suffer. I've merely become fully convinced now that he could have continued with his Arabs as much as he wanted, as long as he provided the necessary explanations. But he was filled with arrogance at that time, and managed to convince himself, once and for all, and far too hastily, that his career had been permanently shattered by the 'whirlwind of circumstances'. But if the whole truth be told, the real reason for his change of career was the extremely delicate proposal that had earlier been made to him and was now renewed by Varvara Petrovna Stavrogina, the wife of a lieutenant general and a very wealthy woman, that he should take on himself the education and the entire intellectual development of her only son, in the capacity of a superior pedagogue and friend, not to mention a generous remuneration. This proposal had been made to him for the first time while they were still in Berlin, precisely when he was widowed for the first time. His first wife had been a flighty girl from our province, whom he married in the first flush of his still reckless youth, and with this person, even though she was fetching, he apparently experienced a great deal of sorrow, lacking as he did the means to support her, and for other, somewhat delicate reasons besides. She died in Paris, after being separated from him for the final three years, and left him with a five-year-old son, 'the fruit of my first, joyous and as yet unclouded love', words that had once burst from the grieving Stepan Trofimovich in my presence. The fledgling was promptly sent back to Russia, and there he remained, his upbringing entrusted to some distant aunts somewhere in the backwoods. Stepan Trofimovich declined Varvara Petrovna's proposal at that time and quickly married again, before even a year had elapsed, to a tactiturn German girl from Berlin, and, most importantly, without any particular need for it. But in addition, there proved to be other reasons as to why he declined the position of tutor. He was intrigued by the fame of a certain prominent professor that resounded far and wide at that time, and in turn he flew to accept a university lectureship for which he had been preparing himself, in order to try his own eagle wings. And now, his wings singed, he naturally remembered the proposal that earlier had made him hesitate as well. The sudden death of his second wife, who had lived with him for less than a year, finally settled things once and for all. I'll say it straight out: everything was resolved by Varvara Petrovna's ardent concern and her priceless, or, so to speak, classical friendship for him, provided it's possible to speak of friendship in this way. He threw himself into the arms of this friendship, and the matter was settled for twenty years and more. I have used the expression 'threw himself into the arms', but God forbid that the thought of anything frivolous and uncalled-for should cross anyone's mind. These 'arms' have to be understood strictly in the very highest moral sense. The most refined and most delicate tie bound these two most remarkable beings forever.

The position of tutor was also accepted because the property that was left after the death of Stepan Trofimovich's first wife – a very small one – happened to be located directly next to Skvoreshniki, the magnificent estate of the Stavrogin family not far from our provincial town. Besides, it would always be possible, in the quiet of one's study and no longer distracted by the burden of university duties, to devote oneself to the cause of scholarship and to enrich the nation's literature with highly original studies. No such studies appeared; but on the other hand, it did prove possible to spend the entire remainder of one's life, more than twenty years, as 'a reproach incarnate', so to speak, to one's fatherland, as the people's poet puts it:

> Reproach incarnate, grand,
> . . .
> You stood before your native land,
> A liberal and idealist.[15]

But the person about whom this people's poet was speaking perhaps did have the right to strike that pose his whole life long, if he so desired, boring though it is. As for our Stepan Trofimovich, if truth be told, he was just an imitator when compared with persons of that kind, and what's more, he would grow tired of standing erect, and would very often just lie about. But even while lying about, 'reproach incarnate' would be maintained lying down in a recumbent position as well – one has to give credit where credit is due, the more so since that was quite sufficient for our province. You should have seen him in our club whenever he sat down to play cards. His whole manner said: 'Cards! I am sitting down with you to play whist! Is that really in keeping with who I am? Who will answer for that, then? Who has destroyed my activity and turned it into a mere card game? Eh, perish Russia!' – and he would grandly trump with hearts.

And if truth be told, he dearly loved a good game of cards, and as a result – and especially in recent times – he had frequent and unpleasant squabbles with Varvara Petrovna, the more so because he constantly lost. But more about that later. I will merely note that this was a man who was even conscientious (sometimes, that is), and therefore he often brooded. In the entire course of his twenty-year friendship with Varvara Petrovna he would regularly, some three or four times a year, sink into what in our circles was called 'civic grief',[16] that is, simply into depression, though the much-respected Varvara Petrovna preferred the former term. Subsequently, besides civic grief, he began sinking into champagne as well; but the alert Varvara Petrovna protected him from all trivial propensities his whole life long. What he really needed was a nursemaid, because he sometimes became very strange: in the midst of his loftiest transports of sorrow, he would suddenly take to laughing like the simplest peasant. Moments would come when he even began to talk about himself in a humorous vein. But Varvara Petrovna feared nothing more than a humorous vein. She was a classic kind of woman, a female Maecenas,[17] who acted strictly out of the highest considerations. Of fundamental importance was the influence of this exalted lady on her poor friend for twenty years. About her we shall have to speak separately, which I propose to do.

3.

There are strange friendships: two friends almost want to devour each other, and they spend their entire lives living that way, but meanwhile they cannot part. There is not even a way they can part: the one who takes to acting up and breaks the tie will be the first to fall sick and perhaps die, if that should happen. I know for a fact that on several occasions, Stepan Trofimovich, sometimes even after the most intimate effusions to Varvara Petrovna in private, would suddenly jump up from the sofa as soon as she left and begin beating his fists against the wall.

All this happened quite literally, even to the point where he once broke some plaster off the wall. People may ask: How could I have learned such a tiny detail? And what if I had witnessed it myself? What if Stepan Trofimovich himself had more than once sobbed on my shoulder, depicting all the ins and outs for me in the brightest colours? (And there wasn't a thing he didn't tell me on these occasions!) But here is what would almost always happen after these sobbing sessions: by the next morning he was prepared to crucify himself for his ingratitude; he would hastily summon me to see him or would come running to me himself, solely to inform me that Varvara Petrovna was an 'angel of honour and delicacy, and he was just the opposite'. He would not only come running to me but on more than one occasion would describe all this to the lady herself in the most eloquent letters and would confess to her, over his full signature, that as recently as, for instance, the day before he had been telling a third party that she was keeping him out of vanity, that she was envious of his learning and his talents; that she hated him but was simply afraid to show her hatred openly, fearing that he would leave her and thereby damage her literary reputation; that in consequence of all this he despised himself and resolved to die a violent death, and was only awaiting the final word from her that would decide everything, and so on and so forth, all in this manner. After that, you can imagine the hysterical pitch that the nervous outbursts of this most innocent of all fifty-year-old boys sometimes reached! I myself once read one such letter of his, after some quarrel between them that had started over a trivial matter but had turned venomous as it developed. I was horrified, and pleaded with him not to send the letter.

'That's impossible . . . it's more honourable . . . my duty . . . I shall die if I don't confess everything to her, everything!' he replied, almost in a fever, and he went ahead and sent the letter.

Here is precisely where the difference between them lay: Varvara Petrovna would never have sent such a letter. True enough, he was mad about writing; he would write to her even while living in the same house with her, and when in a state of hysteria, even two letters a day. I know for certain that she always read through these letters with the greatest of care, even when it came to two letters a day, and, after reading them, would put them away, numbered and sorted, in a special little box; besides which she laid them up in her heart. Then, after making her friend wait an entire day without an answer, she would meet him as if nothing at all were different, as if absolutely nothing out of the ordinary had occurred the day before. Little by little she trained him so well that he himself no longer dared even to mention what had happened the day before, but only kept glancing into her eyes now and again. But she forgot nothing, whereas he sometimes forgot much too quickly, and encouraged by her composure, would, that very same day, not infrequently laugh and behave like a schoolboy over the champagne if friends came to visit. The venomous looks she must have cast in his direction at such moments, while he noticed nothing at all! A week later, perhaps, or a month later, or even six months later, at some special moment, chancing to recall some phrase from one of these letters, and then in fact the entire letter, with all the accompanying circumstances, he would suddenly burn with shame and feel such torment that he would fall ill with one of his attacks of cholerine.[18] These peculiar attacks of his, which resembled cholerine, were in some cases the natural result of shocks to his nervous system, and represented a certain feature, curious in its way, of his physical makeup.

In fact, Varvara Petrovna probably did very often hate him,

but there was one thing he did not perceive in her until the very end: that he had at last become a son in her eyes, her creation, even, one might say, her invention; that he had become flesh of her flesh,[19] and that she was keeping and supporting him not only out of 'envy of his talents', by no means. And how insulted she must have been by such suppositions! Lodged deep within her was an unbearable love for him, amid the constant hatred, jealousy and contempt. She protected him from every little speck of dust, fussed over him for twenty-two years, and would have spent sleepless nights worrying about him, if there were the slightest question of his reputation as a poet, a scholar and a public figure. She had invented him and was the first to have complete faith in her own invention. He was something like a dream of hers . . . But in return she really did require a great deal from him, sometimes even slavery. And she was unbelievably unforgiving. Apropos of this I will tell two little stories.

4.

On one occasion, when early rumours of the emancipation of the peasants had just begun to circulate,[20] when all of Russia was exulting and preparing to undergo a complete rebirth, Varvara Petrovna was visited by a certain baron who was passing through from Petersburg, a man with the highest connections and very close to the reform. Varvara Petrovna set an extremely high value on visits of this kind, because her connections in high society, after the death of her husband, had grown weaker and weaker, and finally had ceased altogether. The baron stayed for an hour with her and had tea. No one else was present, but Varvara Petrovna did invite Stepan Trofimovich and put him on display. The baron had even heard something of him previously, or pretended that he had heard of him, but paid little attention to him at tea. Naturally, Stepan Trofimovich was incapable of committing a social misstep, and his manners were most elegant. Although he was not well born by origin, I believe, it so happened that he had been brought up, from his earliest childhood, in a certain distinguished household in Moscow, and therefore, with propriety; he spoke French like a Parisian. Consequently, the baron, from the very outset, was to understand the kind of people with whom Varvara Petrovna surrounded herself, albeit even in provincial solitude. However, that was not how things worked out. When the baron gave positive confirmation of the reliability of the first rumours about the great reform that were just then beginning to spread, Stepan Trofimovich suddenly could not restrain himself and cried 'Hurrah!' and even made a gesture with his hand that signified his delight. His exclamation was not loud, and was even genteel; his delight was perhaps even premeditated, and his gesture purposely practised in front of the mirror half an hour before tea. But something must not have quite come off, since the baron permitted himself a faint smile, although he promptly put in an extraordinarily polite phrase about the appropriate swell of emotion in all Russian hearts in view of the great event. Then he quickly took his leave, and as he was departing, did not forget to extend two fingers to Stepan Trofimovich. When Varvara Petrovna returned to the drawing room, she remained silent at first for a good three minutes, as if searching for something on the table; but suddenly she turned to Stepan Trofimovich and, pale, with flashing eyes, slowly hissed:

'I shall never forgive you for that!'

The next day she met her friend as if nothing at all were wrong. She never mentioned what had happened. But thirteen years later, at a certain tragic moment, she did remember it, and reproached him for it, and grew just as pale as she had thirteen years previously, when she had taken him to task the first time. Only twice in her entire life did she say to him 'I shall never forgive you for that!' The incident with the baron was actually the second incident; but the first incident was also highly characteristic and seemed to bear so significantly on the fate of Stepan Trofimovich that I venture to mention it as well.

This was in 1855, in the spring, in May, just after news had been received in Skvoreshniki of the demise of Lieutenant General Stavrogin, a frivolous old man, who died from a stomach disorder on his way to the Crimea,[21] where he was hastening to join the army on active duty. Varvara Petrovna was left a widow and put on deep mourning. True enough, she couldn't grieve very much, since for the past four years she had lived apart from him, on account of their incompatibility of character, and had provided him with an allowance. (The total wealth of the lieutenant general himself amounted to a hundred and fifty souls[22] and his salary, in addition to his high position and his connections; while all the money and Skvoreshniki belonged to Varvara Petrovna, the only daughter of a very rich liquor franchisee.[23]) Nonetheless, she was shaken by the sudden news and retreated into complete solitude. Naturally, Stepan Trofimovich was constantly by her side.

May was in full flower; the evenings were astonishing. The cherry trees were in bloom. The two friends got together every evening in the garden, and sat in the gazebo until nightfall, pouring out their feelings and thoughts to one another. These moments were poetic. Varvara Petrovna, under the influence of the change in her life, talked more than usual. She clung to the heart of her friend, as it were, and several evenings passed in this manner. A strange thought suddenly flashed through Stepan Trofimovich's mind: 'Isn't the inconsolable widow counting on him, and isn't she waiting for him to propose to her at the end of the year of mourning?' A cynical thought; but the loftiness of a man's constitution sometimes even fosters a tendency to cynical thoughts, if only by virtue of the many-sidedness of his spiritual development. He began to look deeper, and found something of the sort. He fell to thinking: 'Her fortune is immense, true enough, but . . .' In fact, Varvara Petrovna did not altogether resemble a beauty: she was a tall, yellow, bony woman, with an excessively long face reminiscent of a horse. Stepan Trofimovich grew increasingly hesitant, tormented himself with doubts, and twice even burst into tears of indecisiveness (he cried rather often). But in the evenings, that is, in the gazebo, his face involuntarily somehow began to express something capricious and mocking, something coquettish and at the same time haughty. This somehow happens accidentally and involuntarily, and in fact the more noble the person, the more noticeable it is. Lord knows how to judge matters in this case, but more likely than not, absolutely nothing was stirring in Varvara Petrovna's heart that could fully justify Stepan Trofimovich's suspicions. And what's more, she would certainly not change the name of Stavrogin for his name, however renowned it may be. Perhaps it was nothing more than just a feminine game on her part, the manifestation of an unconscious feminine need, which is so natural in some extremely feminine women. However, I won't swear to it; the depths of the female heart are unfathomable to this very day! But let me continue.

It must be supposed that she soon figured out for herself the strange expression on her friend's face; she was quick and observant, while he was sometimes very innocent. But their evenings passed as before, and their conversations were just as poetic and interesting. And then on one occasion, as night was coming on, after a very lively and poetic conversation, they parted in a friendly manner, warmly pressing each other's hands on the steps of the lodge in which Stepan Trofimovich lived. Each summer he moved out of the huge manor-house of Skvoreshniki into this small lodge, which stood almost in the garden. He had just stepped into his quarters, and, in a state of restless preoccupation, picked up a cigar, and without yet having lighted it, stood weary and motionless before the open window, gazing at the small white clouds, fluffy as down, that scudded around the clear bright moon, when suddenly a faint rustle gave him a start and made him turn around. Standing before him once again was Varvara Petrovna, whom he had left a mere four minutes earlier. Her yellow face looked almost blue, her lips were pressed tightly together and quivered at the corners. For a full ten seconds she stared silently into his eyes, with a hard, implacable look, and suddenly said in a rapid whisper:

'I shall never forgive you for that!'

A good ten years later, when Stepan Trofimovich told me this melancholy story in a whisper, after first closing the door, he swore to me that he had been so petrified that he neither heard nor saw Varvara Petrovna disappear. Since she never once hinted subsequently at what had happened, and since everything went on as if nothing had occurred, he was inclined to think, for the rest of his life, that this had all been a hallucination that had come on before an illness, the more so because that very same night he really did fall ill and it lasted for two whole weeks, which, incidentally, also put an end to the meetings in the gazebo.

But despite his theory that this was a hallucination, every day, for the rest of his life, he seemed to be expecting a continuation and, so to speak, a denouement of this incident. He simply could not believe that it had ended in such a way! And if it had, then he must have sometimes looked strangely at his friend.

5.

She herself had even created a costume for him, in which he walked around for the rest of his life. The costume was elegant and what one would expect: a black frock-coat with long skirts, buttoned almost to the top, but which looked stylish on him; a soft hat (straw in the summer) with a wide brim; a white cambric tie, with a large knot and dangling ends; a walking stick with a silver handle; all topped off with his hair down to his shoulders. His hair was dark brown, and only recently had begun to go a bit grey. He was clean-shaven. People said that in his youth he had been extremely handsome. But in my opinion, even in his old age he was unusually striking. Besides, how can one talk of old age at fifty-three? But because of a certain coquettish sense of his position as a civic figure, he not only didn't try to look younger, but even seemed to flaunt the solidity of his years, and in his costume – tall, lean, with shoulder-length hair, he looked something like a patriarch, or rather, like the lithograph portrait of the poet Kukolnik[24] made in the 1830s for some edition of his works, especially when he was sitting in the garden in the summer, on a bench, under a blossoming lilac bush, both hands resting on his walking stick, a book open beside him and poetically contemplating the setting sun. Regarding books, I will note that towards the end he somehow began to give up reading. However, this was at the very end. The profusion of newspapers and journals to which Varvara Petrovna subscribed were his constant reading. He also took a constant interest in the achievements of Russian literature, although without the slightest loss of a sense of his own worth. At one point he became keen on studying the higher politics of our present-day domestic and foreign affairs, but soon, with a wave of his hand, he dropped the project. It also sometimes happened that he would take Tocqueville into the garden with him, and carry a Paul de Kock[25] hidden in his pocket. However, all that's just a trivial detail.

I will note one thing parenthetically about the portrait of Kukolnik: this engraving had first come into Varvara Petrovna's hands when she was still a pupil in the boarding school for young girls of noble origin in Moscow. She instantly fell in love with the portrait, as is the wont of all young girls in boarding schools, who fall in love with anything that comes along, including of course their teachers, especially those of penmanship and drawing. But what's curious in this case is not the habits of young girls, but the fact that even at the age of fifty, Varvara Petrovna preserved this engraving among her most cherished treasures, and that's perhaps the only reason why she created a costume for Stepan Trofimovich that was somewhat similar to the costume depicted in the portrait. But that of course is also a trivial detail.

In the first few years, or, more accurately, during the first half of his stay at Varvara Petrovna's, Stepan Trofimovich was mulling over some large work, and each day he was seriously intending to write it. But in the second half, he must have forgotten even what he had known virtually by heart. More and more often he would say to us: 'I seem to be ready to get down to work, my materials are all collected, and then I just can't do anything! Nothing gets accomplished!' – and his head dropped in dejection. The purpose of this was no doubt to increase his stature in our eyes, as a martyr to learning; but he himself had something else in mind. 'They've forgotten me, I'm of no use to anyone!' burst from his lips more than once. He was particularly prone to such extreme depression at the very end of the 50s. At last Varvara Petrovna understood that it was a serious matter. And besides, she could not endure the thought that her friend was forgotten and of no use. To take his mind off things, and at the same time to restore his fame, she then took him to Moscow, where she had several elegant acquaint-

ances in literature and scholarship; but Moscow proved unsatisfactory.[26]

That was a special time: something new was afoot, something
very unlike the tranquillity of the past, and something very
strange too, but which could be felt everywhere, even in Skvoreshniki. Various rumours began to reach us. The facts were
generally known, more or less, but it was obvious that apart
from the facts there were certain ideas accompanying them,
and, most importantly, a great number of them. But this is what
was truly confusing: it proved utterly impossible to adapt to
these ideas and find out exactly what they meant. Varvara
Petrovna, owing to her female nature, was bound and determined to get to the bottom of whatever secrets they contained.
She undertook to read for herself the newspapers and journals,
forbidden foreign publications and even the manifestos that
were beginning to appear at that time (she got her hands on all
these things); but they did nothing but make her head spin. She
set about writing letters: she received few replies, and the longer
she persisted, the more incomprehensible the ideas became.
Stepan Trofimovich was solemnly invited to explain 'all these
ideas' to her once and for all; but she remained completely
dissatisfied with his explanations. Stepan Trofimovich's view
of the direction in which things were generally moving was
highly condescending; to his mind, it all came down to the fact
that he himself had been forgotten and was of no use to anyone.
At last mention was made of him too: at first in foreign publications, as an exiled martyr, and immediately thereafter in
Petersburg, as a former star in a famous constellation; he was
even compared with Radishchev[27] for some reason. Then someone stated in print that he was already dead, and promised an
obituary of him. In an instant, Stepan Trofimovich came back
to life and assumed the air of a person of consequence. His
condescending attitude towards his contemporaries immediately vanished for good and all, and a dream began to glow in
his heart: of joining the new movement and demonstrating
his powers. Varvara Petrovna at once regained her faith in
everything, and began bustling about furiously. It was decided
to go to Petersburg without a moment's delay, to find out how

matters there actually stood, to look into everything personally, and, if possible, to plunge into all this new activity whole-heartedly and unreservedly. She announced, by the way, that she was prepared to establish her own magazine and devote her entire life to it from then on. Seeing that things had gone so far, Stepan Trofimovich became still more condescending, and on the journey he began to treat Varvara Petrovna almost patroniz-ingly, something she immediately laid up in her heart. However, she had yet another important reason for making the trip, namely, the renewal of her high connections. It was necessary, as far as possible, to remind society of her existence, or at least to make the attempt. But the ostensible reason for the journey was a meeting with her only son, who just then was completing a course of studies at a Petersburg lyceum.[28]

6.

They went off to Petersburg and lived there for almost the entire winter season. By Lent, however, everything had burst like a rainbow-coloured bubble. Their dreams melted away, and the fog of confusion not only didn't clear up, but became even more repellent. In the first place, the high connections virtually failed to materialize, except in the most microscopic form and only after humiliating efforts. An offended Varvara Petrovna tried to throw herself headlong into the 'new ideas', and began giving soirées[29] at her place. She invited literary people, and they were immediately brought to her in great numbers. Then they began to come on their own, without invitations: one would bring another. Never before had she seen men of letters like these. They were impossibly vain, but very openly so, as if that was their duty. Some (though by no means all) would even turn up drunk, but they seemed to see this as evidence of some beautiful, special truth that had been discovered only the day before. All of them were strangely proud of something. On all their faces it was written that they had just discovered some extremely important secret. They would abuse each other, and reckon it to their honour. It was rather difficult to determine just what they had written; but critics, novelists, playwrights, satirists and specialists in exposés were in attendance. Stepan Trofimovich even penetrated their very highest circle, from which the movement was directed. He had an impossibly long way to climb before he reached the people in charge, but he received a hearty welcome, although none of them, of course, knew anything about him and had heard nothing except that he 'represented an idea'. He manoeuvred so skilfully around them that on two occasions he managed to persuade them to put in an appearance at Varvara Petrovna's salon as well, despite all their Olympian detachment. These men were very serious and very polite; they comported themselves well; the others were evidently afraid of them; but it was obvious that they had no time for anyone else. Two or three former literary luminaries who happened to be in Petersburg just then and with whom Varvara Petrovna had long maintained the most refined relations, also turned up. But to her surprise, these genuine and certainly incontestable luminaries never uttered a peep, and some of them tried to ingratiate themselves with all this new rabble and shamelessly sucked up to them. At first Stepan Trofimovich fared well. People took him up and began presenting him at public literary gatherings. When he walked out on stage for the first time to take his turn at one of the public literary readings, there was a burst of frenzied clapping, which didn't subside for a good five minutes. Nine years later he recalled this with tears, but more because of his artistic nature than out of gratitude. 'I swear to you, and I'm prepared to wager,' he himself said to me (but only to me, and in secret), 'that not a single member of this entire audience knew a thing about me – absolutely nothing!' An extraordinary admission: it followed that he had a keen intelligence if he was able, then and there, on that stage, to understand his position so clearly, despite all his excitement; and it further followed that he did not have a keen intelligence if even nine years later he couldn't recall this episode without feeling offended. He was compelled to sign his name to two or three collective protests (against what, he himself had no idea); he signed. Varvara Petrovna was also compelled to sign in protest against some 'outrageous act',[30] and she signed. However, the majority of these new people, although they did pay visits to Varvara Petrovna, regarded themselves as somehow obliged to regard her with contempt and unconcealed mockery. Stepan Trofimovich later hinted to me, in moments of bitterness, that her envy of him dated from precisely that time. Of course, she understood that she shouldn't associate with these people, yet she continued to receive them eagerly, with all the impatience of a hysterical woman, and, most importantly, kept waiting for something to happen. She had little to say at her soirées, although she could have said a lot; instead, she mostly listened carefully. The talk was of the abolition of censorship and of spelling reforms, of the substitution of the Latin alphabet for the Russian, of the exile of someone the day before, of some scandal in the Arcade, of the advantages of splitting up Russia by nationalities, which would be united in a voluntary federation, of the abolition of the army and the navy, of the restoration of Poland as far as the Dnieper River, of the peasant reform and of leaflets, of the abolition of inheritance, the family, children, and priests, of the rights of women, of Krayevsky's house,[31] for which no one could ever forgive Mr Krayevsky, and so on and so forth. It was obvious that this clutch of dubious new people contained many scoundrels, but there was no doubt that it also contained many honest, even very attractive persons, despite certain subtle but nonetheless surprising shades of difference. The honest ones were much harder to understand than the dishonest and rude ones; but it couldn't be ascertained who was at whose beck and call. When Varvara Petrovna announced her idea of establishing a magazine, even more people surged to her soirées, but accusations that she was a capitalist and an exploiter of labour were immediately hurled in her face. The unceremoniousness of these accusations was equalled only by their unexpectedness. The superannuated General Ivan Ivanovich Drozdov, a former friend and colleague of the late General Stavrogin, a most honourable man (but in his own way), and known to all of us here, a man who was extremely obstinate and short-tempered, who ate an awful lot and was awfully afraid of atheism, began to quarrel at one of Varvara Petrovna's soirées with a certain celebrated young man. The latter promptly retorted: 'You must be a general if you talk like that', meaning, in other words, that he could come up with no greater term of abuse than 'general'. Ivan Ivanovich rose to the bait at once: 'Yes, sir, I am a general, and a lieutenant general, and I have served my Sovereign, and you, sir, are an impudent boy and an atheist!' A dreadful scene ensued. The next day the incident was reported in the press, and people began collecting signatures for a petition against the 'outrageous conduct' of Varvara Petrovna, who had refused to banish the general instantly from her house. A cartoon appeared in an illustrated magazine,[32] where Varvara Petrovna, the general and Stepan Trofimovich were caricatured all together as three reactionary friends; the cartoon was also accompanied by some verses, written by the people's poet exclusively for this occasion. I will note, for my part, that many persons with the rank of general really do have the absurd habit of saying 'I have served my Sovereign', that is, as if they had a different Sovereign from the rest of us ordinary subjects of the Tsar, as if he were theirs alone, someone special.

Naturally, it was impossible to remain in Petersburg any longer, the more so since the ultimate fiasco befell Stepan Tro- fimovich. He couldn't restrain himself, and began proclaiming the rights of art, whereupon people began to laugh even more loudly at him. At his final reading he conceived the notion of impressing them with his eloquence in civic matters, imagining that he could touch their hearts and relying on their respect for his 'banishment'. He expressed unconditional agreement with the uselessness and absurdity of the word 'fatherland'; he agreed with the idea that religion was harmful;[33] but he loudly and firmly asserted that boots were inferior to Pushkin,[34] and even much more so. He was mercilessly hissed, so much so that then and there, he burst into tears in public, without leaving the stage. Varvara Petrovna took him home more dead than alive. '*On m'a traité comme un vieux bonnet de coton!*'[35] he kept babbling senselessly. She looked after him all night long, gave him laurel water[36] and kept repeating until daybreak to him: 'You are still useful; you will still make your mark; you will be valued . . . in some other place.'

The very next day, early in the morning, five men of letters appeared at Varvara Petrovna's. Three of them were complete strangers, whom she had never even laid eyes on. With stern expressions they announced to her that they had looked into the matter of her magazine and had come to a decision on this matter. Varvara Petrovna most certainly had never entrusted anyone with looking into her magazine and deciding anything about it. The decision was as follows: that after establishing the magazine, she should immediately turn it over to them along with the funds to run it on the basis of a free cooperative association; and as for her, she should leave for Skvoreshniki, not forgetting to take with her Stepan Trofimovich, 'who had grown old'. Out of considerations of delicacy, they agreed to acknowledge her right of ownership and to send her, annually, one-sixth of the net profit. Most touching of all was the fact that of these five men, certainly four had no monetary goals in mind, but were acting only in the name of the 'common cause'.

'We departed in a daze,' as Stepan Trofimovich recounted it, 'I couldn't make head or tails of it, and I remember that I kept babbling, to the pounding of the wheels:

> Vek and Vek and Lev Kambek,
> Lev Kambek and Vek and Vek . . .[37]

and the Devil only knows what else, all the way to Moscow. Only in Moscow did I come to my senses, as if we would really find something different there. Oh, my friends!' he would sometimes exclaim to us in an inspired tone, 'you cannot imagine what sadness and anger take hold of your entire soul when a great idea that you have long held in sacred esteem is picked up by clods and dragged out into the street for idiots like themselves, and you suddenly come across it in a flea market, unrecognizable, covered with dirt, absurdly presented all askew, without proportion, without harmony, a plaything for stupid children! No! Things were not that way in our time, and that is not what we strove for. No, no, not for that at all! I can't recognize anything . . . Our time will come once again, and once again we shall steer everything that's shaky, everything as it is now, on to a firm course. Otherwise, what will happen?'

7.

Immediately after their return from Petersburg, Varvara Petrovna sent her friend abroad, 'for a rest'. Besides, it was necessary to part with him for a while, she felt. Stepan Trofimovich set out with enthusiasm. 'There I shall come back to life!' he exclaimed. 'There I shall at long last take up my scholarly work!' But in the very first letters he wrote from Berlin, he sounded the same old refrain. 'My heart is shattered,' he wrote Varvara Petrovna, 'I cannot forget anything! Here, in Berlin, everything reminds me of my youth, my past, my first joys and first sorrows. Where is she? Where are both of them now? Where are you two angels, of whom I was never worthy? Where is my son, my beloved son? Where ultimately am I, I myself, the former I, with a will of steel, solid as a rock, when some *Andrejeff* (in the French spelling),[38] a Russian Orthodox buffoon with a beard, *peut briser mon existence en deux*',[39] and so on and so forth. As for Stepan Trofimovich's son, he had seen him only twice in his life, the first time when he had been born, and the second time recently in Petersburg, where the young man was preparing to enter the university. As has already been mentioned, the boy had spent his entire life being raised by his aunts in O— Province (at Varvara Petrovna's expense), which was 700 versts[40] from Skvoreshniki. As for *Andrejeff*, that is, Andreyev in Russian, he was nothing more nor less than our local merchant, a shopkeeper, a highly eccentric man, a self-taught archaeologist, a passionate collector of Russian antiquities, who sometimes engaged in verbal fencing with Stepan Trofimovich on points of knowledge, and especially on political trends. This estimable merchant, with his grey beard and his large silver-rimmed spectacles, had not finished paying Stepan Trofimovich the 400 roubles he owed for several desyatinas of forest he had bought for timber on the latter's small estate (next to Skvoreshniki). Although Varvara Petrovna had lavishly provided her friend with expenses as she sent him off to Berlin, Stepan Trofimovich was especially counting on these 400 roubles before he left, probably to cover his secret expenses, and he nearly burst into tears when *Andrejeff* asked him to wait a month, although he was certainly within his rights to request such a delay, inasmuch as he had made the first payments almost six months in advance, because Stepan Trofimovich had particularly needed the money at that time. Varvara Petrovna had read his first letter avidly, and, after underlining in pencil his exclamation, 'Where are both of you?', she numbered it and consigned it to her little box. Of course, he was reminiscing about his two deceased wives. In the second letter that came from Berlin, the song had undergone some variation: 'I'm working twelve hours a day.' ('He could have said eleven,' grumbled Varvara Petrovna.) 'I'm poking about in libraries, checking things, copying, running hither and yon; I've visited some professors. I have renewed my acquaintance with the excellent Dundasov family. Nadezhda Nikolayevna is still such a charming woman! She sends you greetings. Her young husband and all three nephews are in Berlin. In the evening I converse with the young people until dawn, and we have almost Athenian evenings,[41] but only with respect to refinement and elegance; everything is genteel: a great deal of music, Spanish motifs, dreams of the renewal of all mankind, the idea of eternal beauty, the Sistine Madonna,[42] light alternating with darkness, but even the sun has spots! Oh, my friend, my noble, faithful friend! In my heart I am with you, and am yours, only with you, always, *en tout pays*, and even *dans le pays de Makar et de ses veaux*,[43] of which we used to talk, all a-tremble, in Petersburg before our departure. I am smiling as I remember it. Once I had crossed the border, I felt safe – a strange and new feeling, for the first time after so many long years', and so on and so forth.

'Oh, it's all sheer nonsense!' Varvara Petrovna decided, as she put this letter away too. 'If they're holding Athenian evenings until dawn, then he's certainly not sitting over his books twelve hours a day. Was he drunk when he wrote it, I wonder? This Dundasova woman dares send me greetings? But then, let him have his bit of fun.'

The phrase '*dans le pays de Makar et de ses veaux*' meant 'where Makar doesn't drive his calves', in other words, 'the back of beyond'. Stepan Trofimovich would sometimes deliberately translate Russian proverbs and folk sayings into French in the most stupid manner, although he was undoubtedly able to understand and translate them better; but he would do this because he thought it was particularly chic, and found it witty.

But his bit of fun was short-lived. He didn't last more than four months, and dashed back to Skvoreshniki. His final letters consisted of nothing but outpourings of the most heartfelt love for his absent friend and were literally wet with the tears of separation. There are natures that are extremely attached to a house, like lapdogs. The reunion of the two friends was ecstatic. In two days, everything began to move along in its old way, and even more boringly than before. 'My friend,' Stepan Trofimovich said to me after two weeks, but strictly in secret, 'I have discovered something new that is dreadful for me: *je suis* simply a sponger, *et rien de plus! Mais rien de plus!*'[44]

8.

After this followed a period of calm that stretched on for virtually these entire nine years. The hysterical outbursts and sobbings on my shoulder, which continued at regular intervals, had no effect on our state of well-being. I am surprised that Stepan Trofimovich didn't get fat during this time. His nose simply grew rather red, and he became more benign, that was all. Gradually a circle of friends formed around him, albeit never large. Although Varvara Petrovna had little to do with this circle, we nonetheless recognized her as our patroness. After the lesson of Petersburg, she settled for good in our town. In winter she lived in her house in town, and in summer on her estate just out of town. She had never had as much importance and influence in the society of our town as in the past seven years, that is, right up to the time when our present governor was appointed. Our former governor, the mild and unforgettable Ivan Osipovich, was a close relative of hers and had once been beholden to her. His wife trembled at the very thought of not pleasing Varvara Petrovna, and the homage rendered her by the society of the province became so marked that it verged on outright sin. Consequently, Stepan Trofimovich was living very well indeed. He was a member of the local club, lost at cards in lordly manner and won well-deserved esteem, although many regarded him merely as a 'learned man'. Subsequently, when Varvara Petrovna allowed him to live in a house of his own, we began to enjoy even greater freedom. We would gather at his place about twice a week; we were a merry band, especially when he didn't stint on the champagne. The wine was procured from the shop of that same Andreyev. The bill was paid twice a year by Varvara Petrovna, and the day on which it was paid was almost always the day of one of Stepan Trofimovich's attacks of cholerine.

By far the senior member of the circle was Liputin, a provincial clerk, a man who was no longer young, a great liberal and reputed in town to be an atheist. He was married for the second time to a quite young and quite pretty woman, who came with a dowry and with three adolescent daughters besides. He threw the fear of God into the entire family, and kept them under lock and key, was extraordinarily stingy and had saved enough of his salary to acquire a small house and some capital. He was a restless man, and not of very high rank; he commanded little respect in the town, and was not received in the highest circle of society. In addition, he was an out-and-out gossipmonger, and had been punished for that more than once, and painfully punished, once by a certain officer, and another time by a respectable paterfamilias, a landowner. But we liked his sharp wit, his inquisitive nature, his particular brand of jolly malice. Varvara Petrovna didn't like him, but he always managed somehow to ingratiate himself with her.

She didn't like Shatov either, who had become a member of the circle only in the past year. Shatov had formerly been a student, and had been expelled from the university after an incident involving some students. But as a child he had been a pupil of Stepan Trofimovich, though he had been born a serf, the son of Varvara Petrovna's deceased valet, Pavel Fyodorovich, and she had taken him under her wing. She didn't like him because of his pride and ingratitude, and simply couldn't forgive him for having failed to come to her immediately after being expelled from the university. Quite the contrary: he didn't even reply to the letter she had expressly sent him on that occasion, preferring instead to enslave himself to some cultivated merchant as a teacher of his children. He accompanied this merchant's family abroad, more in the capacity of a babysitter than a tutor; but he very much wanted to go abroad just then. The children also had a governess, a lively young Russian lady, who had also come into the household just before they departed, and had been hired mainly because she came cheap. In a couple of months the merchant dismissed her for 'freethinking'.[45] Shatov tagged along behind her, and hastily married her in Geneva. They lived together for about three weeks, and then went their separate ways, being free and not bound by anything – and also, of course, because they had no money. Then he spent a long time wandering through Europe, living God knows how; people said that he cleaned boots on the streets and was a stevedore in some port. Finally, about a year ago, he returned to us, to his native nest, and settled down with an old aunt, whom he proceeded to bury within a month. He had a sister, Dasha, who had also been brought up by Varvara Petrovna and lived in her house as her favourite and as an equal in all respects; but he maintained an extremely infrequent and distant relationship with her. In our circle he was unfailingly gloomy and untalkative; but occasionally, when the conversation touched on his convictions, he would become morbidly irritated and completely lose control of his tongue. 'Shatov has first to be tied up, and only then can you discuss anything with him,' Stepan Trofimovich sometimes said jokingly; but he liked him. While abroad Shatov radically revised certain of his former socialist convictions and jumped to the opposite extreme. He was one of those idealistic Russian beings who are suddenly struck by some powerful idea and immediately, then and there, seem to be crushed by it, even sometimes permanently. They are never equipped to deal with it, and instead come to believe in it passionately, and so their entire life from then on passes in its final throes, as it were, under the stone that has fallen upon them and already crushed them half to death.

In appearance, Shatov was all of a piece with his convictions. He was clumsy, fair-haired, dishevelled, short in stature, with broad shoulders, thick lips, very bushy beetling whitish

eyebrows, a brow knitted into a frown and hostile eyes stubbornly fixed on the ground and seemingly ashamed of something. One tuft of hair simply resisted smoothing down, and was
always sticking up. He was about twenty-seven or twenty-eight
years old. 'I'm no longer surprised that his wife ran away
from him,' opined Varvara Petrovna on one occasion, after
scrutinizing him carefully. He made an effort to dress neatly,
despite his extreme poverty. Once again he didn't turn to
Varvara Petrovna for help, but struggled along with whatever
God sent; he also did some odd jobs for the local merchants.
Once he worked in a shop, and later he was just on the point
of going off on a freighter as a clerk's assistant, but fell ill just
before he was to set sail. It's difficult to imagine the poverty
that he was capable of enduring, without even giving it the
slightest thought. After his illness Varvara Petrovna sent him a
hundred roubles secretly and anonymously. However, he found
out the secret, and after giving it some thought he accepted the
money and went to thank Varvara Petrovna. She received him
warmly, but on this occasion, too, he shamefully disappointed
her expectations: he remained sitting for only five minutes,
saying nothing, staring vacantly at the floor with a stupid smile,
and then suddenly, without waiting for her to finish the most
interesting part of the conversation, stood up, made a clumsy
kind of sideways bow, felt crushed with shame, and in the
process brushed against her expensive and fancy little work-
table,[46] sent it crashing to the floor, smashed to pieces, and
walked out, nearly dead from humiliation. Liputin later took
him to task severely for not refusing (and with contempt) those
hundred roubles at the outset, coming from his despotic former
patroness, and for not only accepting them, but even crawling
to thank her for them. Shatov lived in isolation, on the outskirts
of town, and didn't like anyone to come and visit him, even
one of us. He always appeared at Stepan Trofimovich's soirées
and took newspapers and books from him to read.

   Another young man also used to appear at these soirées, one
Virginsky, a local civil servant, who bore a certain resemblance
to Shatov, even though to all appearances he was his complete
opposite in every respect. But he was also a paterfamilias. He

was a pathetic and extremely quiet young man, already almost thirty years old, with considerable education, but more self-taught than anything else. He was poor, married, employed in a government office, and the sole support of his aunt and his wife's sister. His spouse and in fact all the ladies of the family held the very latest views, but all in a rather crude form, instances of 'an idea that has ended up in the street', as Stepan Trofimovich once put it in another context. They took everything out of books, and at even the first whisper from our progressive corners in the capital, were prepared to throw absolutely everything out of the window, provided they were advised to throw it out. Madame Virginskaya worked as a professional midwife in our town; as a young girl she had lived for a long time in Petersburg. Virginsky himself was a man of a rare purity of heart, and I have rarely met a soul that burned more brightly and honestly. 'I shall never, ever forsake these radiant hopes,' he would tell me with shining eyes. About his radiant hopes he would always speak quietly, sweetly, in almost a whisper, as if in secret. He was rather tall, but extremely thin and narrow in the shoulders, with extraordinarily fine, lanky hair of a reddish shade. All the condescending gibes that Stepan Trofimovich aimed at certain of his opinions he accepted meekly, but sometimes he came up with very serious objections and often painted him into a corner. Stepan Trofimovich treated him affectionately, and in general behaved like a father to us all.

'None of you has sat long enough to hatch anything,' he would remark jocularly to Virginsky, 'they're all like you; although in you, Virginsky, I really haven't noticed that nar-row-ness that I've encountered in Petersburg *chez les séminaristes*,[47] but still and all, you've not sat long enough to hatch anything. Shatov would very much like to hatch something, but even he hasn't sat long enough.'

'And what about me?' Liputin would ask.

'Oh, you're just the golden mean[48] who will get along anywhere . . . in your own way.'

Liputin would take offence.

The story was told about Virginsky, and, unfortunately, very accurately, that his wife, after spending less than a year with him in lawful wedlock, suddenly announced to him that he had been 'retired' and that she preferred Lebyadkin. This Lebyadkin, who was just passing through, later turned out to be a highly suspicious character and wasn't even a retired staff captain at all, as he styled himself. The only thing he could do was twirl his moustache, drink and babble the most embarrassing nonsense that one could possibly imagine. This person, in a grossly indelicate manner, proceeded to move in with them, glad to partake of another man's bread, ate and slept there, and finally began to treat the master of the house condescendingly. People asserted that Virginsky, when his wife announced his retirement, said to her: 'My dear friend, until now I have merely loved you, but now I respect you'; but it is hardly likely that such an ancient Roman sentiment[49] was uttered; on the contrary, people said, he burst into sobs. But then, some two weeks after he'd been retired, all of them, the whole 'family', set off for a picnic with friends in a grove of trees outside town. Virginsky was in a kind of frenetically cheerful mood, and joined in the dancing; but suddenly, and without any preliminary quarrel, he seized by the hair with both hands the gigantic Lebyadkin, who had just broken into a solo cancan, pulled his head down and began dragging him with squeals, shrieks and tears. The giant was so terrified that he didn't even try to defend himself and scarcely uttered a sound all the time he was being dragged. But as soon as it was over, he became outraged with all the passion of which a man of noble birth is capable. Virginsky spent the whole night on his knees begging his wife's forgiveness; but he did not obtain forgiveness, because when all was said and done he did not agree to go and apologize to Lebyadkin. In addition, he was chided for the feebleness of his convictions and for his stupidity, the latter because he went down on his knees while explaining himself to a woman. The staff captain soon disappeared and reappeared in our town only very recently, with his sister and with fresh objectives; but more about him later. It was no wonder that the poor paterfamilias would unburden his soul to us and had need of our company. About his home life, however, he never uttered a word in our presence. Only once, on returning from Stepan Trofimovich's with me, did he begin to speak indirectly about his situation, but then, grabbing me by the arm, he exclaimed heatedly:

'It's nothing; it's only an individual case; it won't have the slightest effect on the "common cause", not the slightest!'

Occasional visitors used to show up in our circle too: a little Jew named Lyamshin came, as did a Captain Kartuzov. An inquisitive little old man was with us for a time, but he died. Liputin brought an exiled Polish priest named Sloncewski, and for a time we received him on principle, but then we stopped receiving him.

9.

At one time word was going around town that our circle was a hotbed of freethinking, depravity and godlessness; and these rumours kept growing. And yet all we were engaging in was the most innocent, nice, completely Russian, cheerful, liberal idle talk. 'Higher liberalism' and a 'higher liberal', that is, a liberal without any programme in mind, are possible only in Russia. Stepan Trofimovich, like any truly witty man, needed an audience, and in addition, he needed the recognition that he was fulfilling the higher duty of propagating ideas. And finally, it was also necessary to have someone to drink champagne with, and to exchange, over the wine, cheerful thoughts of a certain kind about Russia and 'the Russian spirit', about God in general and the 'Russian God' in particular, and to repeat, for the hundredth time, the scandalous Russian stories that were known to all and repeated by all. We were not averse to rehashing the gossip of the town either, which sometimes led us to hand down severe and highly moral verdicts. We also fell into generalizations on the human condition, and indulged in uncompromising discussions of the future destiny of Europe and humanity. We didactically predicted that France, after Caesarism,[50] would immediately sink to the level of a second-rate state, and were utterly certain that this could happen awfully quickly and easily. We had long ago predicted that in a united Italy[51] the Pope would function as nothing more than the head of the Church, and were fully convinced that this thousand-year-old question, in our age of humanism, industry and railways, was nothing more than a trivial matter. But then, 'lofty Russian liberalism' couldn't treat such questions in any other way. Stepan Trofimovich would sometimes go on about art, and very well, but in rather an abstract way. He would sometimes reminisce about the friends of his youth – always about people who had distinguished themselves in our progress through history – reminisce emotionally and reverentially, but also with a dash of what seemed like envy. And if things got really boring, then the little Jew Lyamshin (a minor clerk in the post office), a master of the piano, would sit down to play, and between numbers would provide musical imitations of a pig, a thunderstorm, childbirth and the baby's first cry, and so on and so forth; in fact, that was the only reason he was invited. If we had had a great deal to drink – and that did happen, though not often – we would get carried away, and on one occasion we even sang the *Marseillaise*,[52] with Lyamshin accompanying, except I don't know whether it came out very well. We greeted the great day of February nineteenth with enormous enthusiasm, and long before it arrived we began to drain our glasses in its honour. That all happened a very long time ago, before Shatov or Virginsky were on the scene, and while Stepan Trofimovich was still living under the same roof as Varvara Petrovna. For some time before the great day, Stepan Trofimovich had taken to muttering to himself the well-known, albeit rather forced-sounding verses that must have been written by some liberal landowner of old:

> The muzhiks are coming with axes in hand,
> Something most dreadful will happen.[53]

Or something of the sort, I think, though I don't remember it word for word. Once Varvara Petrovna overheard it, and shouted at him: 'Rubbish! Rubbish!' – and walked out in a rage. Liputin, who happened to be present on this occasion, observed sarcastically to Stepan Trofimovich:

'It would be a pity if their former serfs do celebrate by doing something really unpleasant to their lords and masters.'

And he drew his forefinger across his throat.

'*Cher ami*,'[54] Stepan Trofimovich noted with equanimity, 'believe me, *this*' – and he made the same gesture across his throat – 'will bring no benefit at all to our landowners, or to any of the rest of us. Without heads on our shoulders there is no way we can organize anything, despite the fact that it is our heads that are the greatest impediment to our understanding of things.'

I will note that many people among us expected that something unusual would happen on the day of the proclamation, along the lines predicted by Liputin, all of them, I may say, so-called experts on the common people and the government. Stepan Trofimovich apparently shared these ideas as well, to the point that almost on the eve of the great day he even began to beg Varvara Petrovna to allow him to go abroad; in brief, he began to worry. But the great day came and went, a certain period of time came and went, and the condescending smile again appeared on Stepan Trofimovich's lips. He treated us to a few noteworthy thoughts on the character of the Russian in general, and the Russian muzhik in particular.

'We, as people in a hurry, have acted too hastily with our muzhiks', was the way he concluded his series of noteworthy thoughts, 'we have made them fashionable, and an entire branch of literature, for several years on end, has been making a fuss over them as if they were a newly discovered treasure.[55] We have placed laurel wreathes on louse-ridden heads. The only thing the Russian village has given us, over the past thousand years, has been the Komarinsky.[56] A wonderful Russian poet, who was also not lacking in wit, when he saw the great Rachel for the first time on the stage, exclaimed rapturously: "I wouldn't trade Rachel for a muzhik!"[57] I am prepared to go further: I would exchange all the muzhiks of Russia for just one Rachel. It's high time we took a more sober look at things and stopped mixing our lumpy native tar with *bouquet de l'impératrice*.'[58]

Liputin promptly agreed, but noted that it was nonetheless essential at that time to go against one's conscience and praise the muzhiks for the sake of the movement; that even high-society ladies broke out in tears while reading *Anton Goremyka*,[59] and some of them even wrote from Paris to the stewards of their estates to treat the peasants as humanely as possible from now on.

As luck would have it, it happened that immediately after rumours about the Anton Petrov affair[60] began to circulate, a certain misunderstanding occurred in our own province, and no more than fifteen versts from Skvoreshniki, so that in the heat of the moment a detachment of troops was dispatched. This time Stepan Trofimovich became so agitated that he even frightened us. In the club he cried out that more troops were needed, that they should be summoned from the adjoining district by telegraph; he ran to the governor and assured him that he had nothing to do with it; he asked that he not be dragged into the whole business in any way, out of force of habit; and he proposed that a written account of his statement be sent immediately to the proper authorities in Petersburg. It was a good thing that all this soon passed and amounted to nothing; but at the time I must say I was surprised at Stepan Trofimovich.

Some three years later, as we know, people began talking about nationality, and 'public opinion' came into being. Stepan Trofimovich had a good laugh at this.

'My friends', so went the lesson, 'our nationality, if in fact it has "come into being", as we are now being assured in the newspapers, is still sitting in school, in some German *Peterschule*,[61] reading a German book and repeating its eternal German lesson, while the German teacher makes it go down on its knees whenever necessary. I have only the highest praise for the German teacher; but it's most likely that nothing has happened, and that nothing of the sort has come into being, and that everything has been following the same old course, that is, under God's protection. In my opinion, that would be quite sufficient for Russia, *pour notre sainte Russie*.[62] Besides, all these pan-Slavisms[63] and nationalities are too old a thing to be new. Nationality, if you like, has certainly never appeared in this country except in the form of an amusing pastime in a gentleman's club, and a Moscow one at that. Needless to say,

I am not speaking of the time of Prince Igor.[64] And, finally, it all comes from idleness. Everything in this country comes from idleness, both the good and the bad. Everything comes from the nice, cultivated, whimsical idleness of our gentlemen! I've been harping on this for thirty thousand years. We cannot live by our own labour. And the fact that people have now started making such a fuss about some sort of public opinion that has "come into being" – has it really fallen from the sky all of a sudden, just like that? Don't they really understand that to acquire an opinion the very first thing needed is labour, one's own labour, one's own initiative in matters, one's own practical experience! Nothing will ever be gained for nothing. If we labour, we shall have our own opinion as well. But since we never shall labour, then opinion will also be expressed for us only by those who until now have done the work instead of us, in other words, that same old Europe, those same old Germans – our teachers for the last two hundred years. Besides, Russia is too great a misunderstanding for us to sort out by ourselves, without the Germans and without labour. It's twenty years now that I've been sounding the alarm and summoning people to labour! I've given my life to making this appeal, and, madman that I am, I've put all my faith in it! Now I no longer have faith, but I am still ringing the bell and will go on ringing it to the end, until I die. I shall keep pulling on the rope until the bell summons people to my own funeral service!'

Alas! We simply went along with him. We applauded our teacher, and very warmly indeed! And what do you think, gentlemen, don't we hear even now, sometimes rather often, the same sort of 'nice', 'intelligent', 'liberal' old Russian nonsense?

Our teacher believed in God. 'I don't understand why everyone here makes me out to be an atheist,' he would sometimes say, 'I do believe in God, *mais distinguons*,[65] in God as a being that is conscious of himself only in me. I certainly can't believe the way my Nastasya (his servant) believes, or some nobleman, who believes "just in case", or like our dear Shatov – however, no, Shatov doesn't count, Shatov believes *of necessity*, like a Moscow Slavophile. And with regard to Christianity, for all my sincere respect for it, I am not a Christian. Rather, I am an ancient pagan, like the great Goethe,[66] or like an ancient Greek. And it's quite enough that Christianity has never understood women, a point that George Sand has so splendidly developed in one of her novels of genius.[67] And as for the bowing, the fasting and all the rest, I don't understand what that has to do with me. However tireless our local informers, I do not wish to be a Jesuit. In 1847, Belinsky, while abroad, sent his famous letter to Gogol in which he passionately reproached him for believing in "some god".[68] *Entre nous soit dit*,[69] I can't imagine anything more comic than the moment when Gogol (the Gogol of that particular time!) read this expression and – the whole letter! But leaving aside the amusing aspect, and being, as I am, in agreement with the essence of the matter, then I'll point to them and say: those were men! They really knew how to love their people, they also knew how to suffer for them, they knew too how to sacrifice everything for them and at the same time they knew how, when necessary, to maintain a distance from them, knew how to avoid pandering to them when it came to certain ideas. Belinsky, after all, could not possibly have sought salvation in Lenten oil,[70] or in radishes with peas!'

But at this point Shatov stepped in.

'These men of yours never did love the people, didn't suffer for them and sacrificed nothing for them, no matter how they themselves may have imagined they did to make themselves feel good!' he growled sullenly, staring at the floor and shifting impatiently in his chair.

'Are you saying that they didn't love the people?' Stepan Trofimovich began to shriek. 'Oh, how they loved Russia!'

'Neither Russia nor the people!' Shatov also began to shriek, his eyes flashing. 'It's impossible to love what you don't know, and they had no understanding of the Russian people! All of them, including you, turned a blind eye to the Russian people, and especially Belinsky: it's obvious from that very letter to Gogol. Belinsky, precisely like the inquisitive man in Krylov's fable, didn't notice the elephant in the museum of curiosities, but focused all his attention on the French social insects, and simply never went any further than that.[71] And yet he was perhaps even more intelligent than all of you! It's not enough that you overlooked the people – you treated them with sickening contempt, for the sole reason that you couldn't imagine "the people" to be anything other than the French people, and only Parisians at that, and you were ashamed that the Russian people weren't like that. That's the unvarnished truth! And anyone who has no people has no God either! You can be quite sure that all who cease to understand their own people and lose their ties with them, immediately and to the same extent, also lose the faith of their fathers, and either become atheists or indifferent. I'm telling the truth! This is a fact that will be corroborated. That's why all of you and all of us now are either vile atheists or indifferent, depraved rubbish, and nothing more! And you too, Stepan Trofimovich, I'm not making the slightest exception for you, I was even saying it on your account, you should know that!'

Usually, after delivering himself of such a monologue (as was often the case with him), Shatov would grab his cap and rush to the door, fully convinced that everything was now over and that he had completely and permanently severed his friendly relations with Stepan Trofimovich. But the latter always managed to stop him in time.

'Shouldn't we make peace, Shatov, after all these nice little words?' he would say, good-naturedly extending a hand to him from his armchair.

The awkward but bashful Shatov didn't like displays of affection. Outwardly he was a coarse man, but inside, he was very sensitive. Although he often lost a sense of proportion, he himself was the first to suffer from it. After growling something under his breath in response to Stepan Trofimovich's appeal, and stomping in place like a bear, he would suddenly and unexpectedly give a smirk, put down his cap and sit down in the same chair as before with his eyes fixed on the floor. Naturally, wine was brought in, and Stepan Trofimovich would propose some appropriate toast, for example, to the memory of one of the activists of the past.

CHAPTER 2

Prince Harry. Matchmaking

I.

There existed one other person on this earth to whom Varvara Petrovna was no less attached than to Stepan Trofimovich – her only son, Nikolay Vsevolodovich Stavrogin. He was the one whose upbringing had been entrusted to Stepan Trofimovich. The boy was about eight years old at that time. The frivolous General Stavrogin, his father, was then already living apart from his mother, so that the boy grew up in her sole care. In all fairness to Stepan Trofimovich, he knew how to create a bond with his young charge. The whole secret lay in the fact that he himself was just a boy. I had not come on the scene as yet, and he constantly needed a true friend. He didn't hesitate to make this small being his friend, just as soon as he had grown up a little. Somehow things worked out very naturally in such a way that there was not the slightest distance between them. More than once he woke up his ten- or eleven-year-old friend at night, for the sole purpose of tearfully pouring out his wounded feelings to him or revealing some family secret, without noticing that this was simply improper. They threw themselves into each other's arms and wept. The boy knew that his mother loved him very much, but he didn't really love her very much at all. She had little to say to him, and rarely interfered with him in any way, but he was always somehow morbidly aware that she was keeping a close watch on him. However, the mother entrusted his whole education and moral development entirely to Stepan Trofimovich. At that time she still had complete faith in him. One is inclined to think that the pedagogue unsettled his pupil's nerves somewhat. When he was taken, at age sixteen, to the lyceum, he looked frail and wan, strangely quiet and pensive. (Subsequently he was noted for his extraordinary physical strength.) One must also suppose that when the two friends threw themselves into each other's arms at night, they were not just weeping over some domestic drama. Stepan Trofimovich knew how to reach into his young friend's heart and pluck the deepest chords and evoke in him the first, still vague sense of that eternal, sacred anguish which some elected souls, once having tasted and known it, would never again exchange for some cheap gratification. (There are also lovers of such anguish who prize it more than its most radical gratification, if such indeed were even possible.) But in any event, it was good that pupil and preceptor,[1] albeit rather late, were separated and went in different directions.

In the first two years the young man would come home on vacation from the lyceum. During the trip that Varvara Petrovna and Stepan Trofimovich took to Petersburg, he would sometimes be present at the literary soirées that were held at his mother's, listening and observing. He said little and, as before, was quiet and shy. Towards Stepan Trofimovich he behaved tenderly and attentively, as before, but now in a somewhat more reserved way: he obviously kept away from discussions of lofty topics and reminiscences of the past with him. After completing his course of studies, he bowed to his mother's wishes and entered military service and was soon posted to one of the most distinguished regiments of the horse guards.[2] He did not come to show himself in uniform to his mother, and his letters from Petersburg grew infrequent. Varvara Petrovna sent him money unstintingly, despite the fact that after the reform the income from her estates fell so sharply that at first she did not take in even half of what she previously had. However, a long habit of economizing had enabled her to accumulate a not inconsiderable sum. She was very much interested in the success of her son in the highest circles of Petersburg society. Where she had not succeeded, the young officer, rich and with prospects, did succeed. He renewed acquaintanceships of which she could no longer even dream, and was everywhere received with great delight. But very soon rather strange rumours began to reach Varvara Petrovna; the young man had suddenly taken up a life of almost mad dissipation. It wasn't that he was gambling or drinking a lot; what people were talking about was only a certain wildness and unruliness, people trampled by horses, the brutal treatment of a certain lady of good society with whom he had had a liaison and had then insulted publicly. There was something even too openly sordid about this affair. In addition, it was said that he had become a bully of sorts, attaching himself to people and then insulting them for the pleasure of it. Varvara Petrovna was upset and miserable. Stepan Trofimovich tried to reassure her that these were only the first stormy outbursts of a richly endowed nature, and that the sea would grow calm and that all this was like the youthful years of Prince Harry, who roistered with Falstaff, Poins and Mistress Quickly, as described by Shakespeare.[3] On this occasion Varvara Petrovna didn't shout 'Rubbish, rubbish!' as she had recently so often taken to shouting at Stepan Trofimovich, but on the contrary, listened carefully, ordered him to explain the details, picked up Shakespeare herself and read the immortal chronicle through with the closest attention. But the chronicle didn't set her mind at ease, and besides, she didn't find that much similarity. She feverishly awaited replies to several of her letters. The replies were not slow in coming; soon the fateful news arrived that Prince Harry had fought two duels almost at the same time, was entirely to blame for both, had killed one of his opponents outright and crippled the other, and as a result of these exploits had been put on trial. The upshot was a reduction to the ranks, with deprivation of his rights as a nobleman, and banishment to service in one of the army's infantry regiments,[4] and even that was only by special favour.

In 1863[5] he managed somehow to distinguish himself; they gave him a decoration and he was promoted to non-commissioned officer, and then, rather quickly somehow, to officer. During this entire time Varvara Petrovna sent perhaps as many as a hundred letters to the capital with requests and entreaties. She was willing to demean herself somewhat in such extraordinary circumstances. After his promotion, the young man suddenly resigned his commission, did not return to Skvoreshniki and stopped writing to his mother altogether. Eventually it was learned, through third parties, that he was again in Petersburg, but that there was no longer any sign of him in his old haunts; he seemed to have hidden himself away somewhere. After inquiries, it was learned that he was living in strange company, that he had hooked up with the dregs of the Petersburg population, some down-at-heel government clerks, retired military officers who were genteel beggars, and drunkards, that he was visiting their filthy families, spending his days and nights in dark slums and in God only knows what back alleys, that he'd sunk very low, was all rags and tatters, and that he therefore found it all to his liking. He didn't ask his mother for any money; he had his own small estate, the former country property of General Stavrogin, which after all did yield some income, and which, as rumour had it, he had rented out to a certain Saxon German. Finally, his mother prevailed on him to come and see her, and Prince Harry appeared in our town. It was then that I had a good look at him for the first time; until then I had never seen him.

He was a very handsome young man, of twenty-five or so, and, I must confess, he made an impression on me. I had been expecting to meet some filthy ragamuffin, haggard from debauchery and reeking of vodka. On the contrary, he was the most elegant gentleman of any I had ever happened to meet, extremely well dressed, and comported himself in a way that only a man accustomed to the finest and most elegant things could comport himself. I was not the only one to be surprised: the entire town was surprised as well, knowing, as they of course already did, the entire life-story of Mr Stavrogin, and even in detail of a kind that one couldn't imagine where it had come from, and most surprising of all, half of which turned out to be true. All our ladies were besotted with the new visitor. They divided sharply into two camps: one adored him, while the other hated him with a vengeance; but both were besotted nonetheless. Some were especially intrigued by the possibility that a fateful secret lay hidden in his soul; others positively liked the fact that he was a murderer. It also turned out that he had been very decently educated, and even knew a thing or two. Not much knowledge was required, of course, to surprise us; but he was able to express opinions about timely, highly interesting topics, and, what was most valued, with remarkable good sense. I will mention as an oddity that everyone in our town, from almost the first day, found him a man of extremely good sense. He wasn't very much inclined to talk; he was elegant but not ostentatiously so, surprisingly modest and at the same time bold and self-assured, like no one else among us. Our dandies regarded him with envy and receded into the background in his presence. I was also struck by his face: his hair was somehow almost too black, his bright eyes were somehow too calm and clear, his complexion was somehow too delicate and white, the colour of his cheeks was somehow too bright and clear, his teeth were like pearls, his lips like coral – you might say that he was a picture of beauty, but at the same time there was also something repellent about him. They said that his face resembled a mask; but they talked a great deal, by the way, about his extraordinary physical strength. He was almost tall. Varvara Petrovna looked at him with pride, but with constant worry. He lived with us for six months – listlessly, quietly, rather sullenly; he appeared in society and observed all our provincial etiquette with unflagging attention. He was related to the governor on his father's side, and was received in his house as a close relative. But several months passed, and suddenly the beast showed its claws.

By the way, let me mention parenthetically that our dear, mild Ivan Osipovich, our former governor, was a bit of an old woman, but of a good family and with connections, which explains the fact that he had held on to his position here for so many years while constantly brushing aside any official duties. With his hospitality and his graciousness towards guests, he should have been a marshal of the nobility[6] in the good old days, and not a governor in such a troublesome time as ours. People in town were constantly saying that it was not he who ran the province, but Varvara Petrovna. Of course this was said caustically, but still and all, it was an outright lie. And indeed, no little wit was expended on this particular topic. On the contrary, in recent years Varvara Petrovna had made a point of consciously distancing herself from any higher vocation, despite the extraordinary respect in which she was held by all of society, and voluntarily confined herself within strict limits that she herself had set. Instead of a higher vocation she suddenly began to look after the management of her estate, and within two or three years she had raised its profitability to almost its previous level. Instead of her former poetic enthusiasms (her trip to Petersburg, her intention of establishing a magazine, and so on), she began to watch her money and save it. She even kept Stepan Trofimovich at a distance, allowing him to rent lodgings in another house (something that he had long been badgering her to do under various pretexts). Little by little Stepan Trofimovich began referring to her as a prosaic woman, or more jokingly, as 'my prosaic good friend'. Naturally, he allowed himself such jokes only in an extremely respectful way and spent a long time in choosing the right occasion.

All of us who were close to her understood – and Stepan Trofimovich more acutely than any of us – that her son had now appeared to her as something like a new hope and even a new dream. The passion she felt for her son had begun at the time of his success in Petersburg society, and grew particularly intense from the moment she received the news of his demotion to the rank of a common soldier. Yet at the same time she was obviously afraid of him, and seemed to act like a slave in his presence. One could see that she was afraid of something vague, something mysterious, which she herself could not have articulated, and very often she would imperceptibly and closely study Nicolas, pondering and trying to figure out something . . . and then – the beast suddenly showed its claws.

2.

Suddenly our prince, for no apparent reason, perpetrated two or three gross outrages against various people, the important thing being, in other words, that these outrages were utterly without precedent, utterly unimaginable, utterly unlike anything usually done, utterly rotten and childish, and the Devil knows why, utterly without provocation. One of the most

respected senior members of our club, Pavel Pavlovich
Gaganov, a man well along in years and even honoured for his
service, had adopted the innocent habit of accompanying his
every word with a vehement 'No, indeed, they won't lead me
by the nose!' Well, there was nothing wrong with that. But on
one occasion in the club, when during a heated discussion he
uttered this phrase to a handful of club members that had
clustered round him (and all of them people of some importance), Nikolay Vsevolodovich, who was standing by himself to
one side and to whom no one was paying any attention, suddenly walked up to Pavel Pavlovich, seized him unexpectedly
but firmly by the nose with two fingers, and managed to drag
him two or three steps across the room. He couldn't possibly
have felt any animus towards Mr Gaganov. It might be thought
of as just a schoolboy prank, of the most unforgivable kind, to
be sure. And yet, as people subsequently described it, at the
very moment of the operation, he was almost in a reverie, 'as if
he had lost his mind'; but that was recalled and reflected on
only long afterwards. In the heat of things everyone at first
remembered only the next moment, when he must have realized
what had actually happened, and not only showed no embarrassment, but on the contrary, gave a malicious and happy
smile, 'without the slightest regret'. A truly dreadful din arose;
people clustered round him. Nikolay Vsevolodovich kept turning and looking around, not replying to anyone and peering at
the shouting people with curiosity. Finally, he suddenly seemed
to become lost in thought once more – that, at least, is the way
it was reported – gave a frown, marched resolutely up to the
affronted Pavel Pavlovich and in evident annoyance, quickly
muttered:

'Of course, I beg your pardon . . . I really don't know why I
suddenly felt the urge . . . it was stupid . . .'

His casual apology amounted to a new affront. The exclamations grew even louder. Nikolay Vsevolodovich shrugged his
shoulders and walked out.

All this was very stupid, to say nothing of its ugliness –
an ugliness that was calculated and deliberate, as it appeared
at first sight, and therefore constituted a deliberate and

unbelievably insolent affront to our entire society. So it was understood by everyone. They began by immediately and unanimously expelling Mr Stavrogin from membership in the club; then they decided, in the name of the entire club, to turn to the governor with an immediate request (not waiting until the matter was formally taken up by the court) that this dangerous brawler, this Petersburg bully, be restrained 'by the administrative powers entrusted to him, thereby protecting the peace of the entire decent circle of people in our town from harmful infringements'. To this they appended, with malicious innocence, the statement that 'perhaps some law can be found that applies even to Mr Stavrogin'. These words were a personal jab at the governor because of Varvara Petrovna. They were embroidered with relish. As it happened, the governor wasn't in town at the time; he had made a short trip to stand godfather to the child of an attractive recent widow, who had been left in an interesting condition after the death of her husband; but they knew that he would soon return. In anticipation, they arranged a real ovation for the respected and affronted Pavel Pavlovich: they embraced him and kissed him; the entire town called upon him. They even planned a subscription dinner in his honour, and only after an urgent request on his part did they abandon this idea – perhaps realizing at last that a man had after all been dragged around by the nose, and that therefore there was nothing much to celebrate.

And, for that matter, how did this actually happen? How could this happen? Particularly remarkable is the circumstance that none of us, in the entire town, attributed this savage act to insanity. This meant that people were inclined to expect acts precisely of this nature from Nikolay Vsevolodovich even when he was in his right mind. As for me, I don't know to this day how to explain it, even despite an incident that followed shortly thereafter, which seemed to explain everything and evidently appeased everyone. I will also add that four years later Nikolay Vsevolodovich, in reply to my cautious question about what had occurred in the club, said with a frown: 'Yes, I was not entirely in good health at the time.' But there's no need to get ahead of myself.

What I found curious was the general outburst of hatred with which everyone in town then fell upon the 'brawler and bully from the capital'. They were intent on seeing insolent determination and a calculated intention to offend our whole society at once. This man genuinely did not please anyone; on the contrary, he set everyone against him – and how could that possibly be? Until the recent incident he had not had a single quarrel with anyone, and had never offended anyone, but instead was as courteous as a stylish gentleman in a fashion plate, if only the latter had been capable of speech. I suppose that he was hated for his pride. Even our ladies, who had begun by adoring him, were now railing against him more loudly than the men.

Varvara Petrovna was dreadfully shaken. Later she admitted to Stepan Trofimovich that she had had some inkling of this for a long time, every day for these six months, and even in 'precisely this form' – an admission that was remarkable coming from a mother. 'It has begun!' she thought with a shudder. The morning after the fateful evening in the club she initiated, cautiously but decisively, a discussion with her son, all the while simply trembling, poor woman, despite her decisiveness. She hadn't slept all night and even went early in the morning to consult with Stepan Trofimovich and burst into tears at his lodgings, which had never before happened to her in anyone's presence. She was hopeful that Nicolas would at least say something to her, deign, for instance, to explain himself. Nicolas, who was always so courteous and respectful towards his mother, listened to her for a time, frowning but very serious. Suddenly he got up, without having uttered a word in reply, kissed her hand and walked out. And that very same day, in the evening, as though by design, another scandal came along, although it was far milder and more ordinary than the first one, but nonetheless it raised the volume of protests in the town considerably, because of the prevailing mood.

What happened was that our friend Liputin turned up. He appeared at Nikolay Vsevolodovich's immediately after the young man's talk with his mother, and entreated him to do him the honour of coming to his house that very evening to celebrate the occasion of his wife's birthday. Varvara Petrovna had long been watching and shuddering at Nikolay Vsevolodovich's tendency to seek out low company, but didn't dare say anything about it to him. In addition, he had already struck up several other acquaintanceships on this third-rate level of our society and even lower still – but such was his inclination. He hadn't yet been a guest in Liputin's house, although he had met him several times. He guessed that Liputin was inviting him now because of the scandal at the club the previous day, and that Liputin, as the local liberal, was thrilled by the scandal, and sincerely thought that this was precisely the way to act towards the senior members of the club and that this was a very good thing. Nikolay Vsevolodovich gave a hearty laugh and promised to come.

A great many guests had gathered. The company was not much to look at, but was lively. Liputin, a touchy and envious man, invited guests only twice a year, but he didn't stint on these occasions. The most honoured guest, Stepan Trofimovich, didn't come because of illness. Tea was served, and there was a generous spread of *zakuski* and vodka. Three tables had been set up for cards, and the young people, while waiting for supper, were dancing to the accompaniment of the piano. Nikolay Vsevolodovich offered his arm to Madame Liputina, an extremely pretty little woman who was dreadfully timid with him, took two turns around the room with her, sat down beside her, chatted and made her laugh. Finally, noticing how pretty she was when she laughed, he suddenly put his arm around her waist, in front of all the guests, and kissed her on the lips, some three times in a row, with genuine gusto. The terrified young woman fainted. Nikolay Vsevolodovich picked up his cap, went up to the dumbstruck husband amid the general commotion, seemed confused himself as he looked at him, quickly muttered 'Don't be angry' and walked out. Liputin ran after him into the front hall, gave him his fur coat with his own hands and accompanied him down the stairway, bowing. But the very next day there followed, with perfect timing, a rather amusing sequel to this essentially innocent story (comparatively speaking), a sequel which even conferred a certain esteem on Liputin from that time forward, and which he learned to use to his full advantage.

At about ten in the morning, Liputin's servant Agafya, an easy-going, spunky and rosy-cheeked peasant woman of about thirty, appeared at the house of Mrs Stavrogina. She had been sent by him with a message for Nikolay Vsevolodovich and insisted on seeing 'the master himself, and none other'. He had a bad headache, but he came out. Varvara Petrovna managed to be present when the message was delivered.

'Sergey Vasilyich' (that is, Liputin), Agafya began rattling away spunkily, 'first off, he told me to give you his best greetings and ask about your health, how you was pleased to rest after yesterday, and how you're pleased to feel now, after yesterday.'

Nikolay Vsevolodovich grinned.

'Send my greetings and thanks, and tell your master for me, Agafya, that he's the most intelligent man in the entire town.'

'And he told me to answer you, sir, in return,' Agafya added even more spunkily, 'that he knows about that anyway, and wishes you the same.'

'Really! But how could he know what I would say to you?'

'I don't rightly know in what manner he came to find out, sir, but when I stepped out and had walked all the way down the lane, I heard him running after me, and without his cap on. "Agafya," he says, "just in case he tells you: 'Say to your master that he's more intelligent than anyone in town', then don't you forget to answer him right back: 'We know about that very well, yes indeed, and we wish you the same, sir.'"'

3.

At last the talk with the governor took place as well. Our dear, mild Ivan Osipovich had just returned and had just had time to hear the heated complaint from the club. There was no doubt that something had to be done, but he was in a state of confusion. Our hospitable old man also seemed to be a little afraid of his young relative. However, he finally resolved to prevail on him to apologize to the club and to the man he'd insulted, but in satisfactory form, and, if required, in writing as well; and then gently persuade him to leave us, travelling, for example, to Italy for self-improvement, and in general anywhere abroad. In the reception room, where on this occasion he emerged to greet Nikolay Vsevolodovich (who on other occasions, in keeping with his rights as a relative, had been entitled to wander unrestricted through the entire house), Alyosha Telyatnikov, a well-bred clerk, and at the same time a member of the governor's household, was sitting at a table in the corner unsealing envelopes, and in the next room, by the window closest to the door of the reception room, a visitor had installed himself, a stout, healthy-looking colonel, a friend and former colleague of Ivan Osipovich, who was reading the *Voice*,[7] without of course paying the slightest attention to what was going on in the reception room; he was even sitting with his back turned. Ivan Osipovich began speaking circuitously, almost in a whisper, but kept getting somewhat muddled. Nicolas looked very unobliging, not at all as a relative should; he was pale, sat with his eyes fastened on the floor and listened with knitted brows, as if trying to overcome an acute pain.

'You have a good heart, Nicolas, and a noble one,' the old man interjected, among other things, 'you are a highly educated person, you have moved in the highest circles, and here, too, you have been a model of good behaviour to this point, and have thereby reassured the heart of your loving mother, who is so dear to all of us ... And now everything has once again appeared in such a puzzling light, so dangerous to everyone! I am speaking to you as a friend of your family, as an old man and your relative, who loves you sincerely, and at whom you cannot take offence ... Tell me, what impels you to commit such unbridled acts, which are beyond the bounds of all accepted conventions and rules? What can be the meaning of such escapades, which seem to have been perpetrated in a state of delirium?'

Nicolas kept listening with annoyance and impatience. Suddenly there was a gleam of something cunning and mocking in his eyes.

'I'll tell you, if you like, what it is that impels me,' he said sullenly, and, looking around, bent down to Ivan Osipovich's ear. The well-bred Alyosha Telyatnikov retreated another three steps towards the window, and the colonel gave a cough behind the *Voice*. Poor Ivan Osipovich hastened to incline a trusting ear; he was extremely curious. And then something happened suddenly that was absolutely unbelievable, yet at the same time, all too clear in a certain sense. The little old man suddenly felt that Nicolas, instead of confiding some interesting secret to him in a whisper, had suddenly seized the upper part of his ear in his teeth, and clamped down on it rather firmly. He began to tremble, and gave a gasp.

'Nicolas, what kind of joke is this?' he moaned mechanically, in a voice no longer his own.

Alyosha and the colonel had not yet had time to make sense of anything, and in any event they couldn't see what was happening and until it was all over the two seemed to be exchanging whispers; but meanwhile, the old man's despairing face alarmed them. They looked at each other wide-eyed, not knowing whether to rush over and help him, as had been agreed, or to continue to wait. Nicolas perhaps noticed this and bit down on the ear even harder.

'Nicolas! Nicolas!' the victim moaned again. 'Come now, that's enough joking.'

A minute more and of course the poor fellow would have died of fright; but the monster took pity and released the ear. The old man's mortal fear had lasted a full minute, after which he had some kind of fit. But half an hour later Nicolas was arrested and taken, for the time being, to the guardhouse, where he was locked in a special cell, with a special guard at the door. The decision was harsh, but our gentle superior was so angry that he made bold to take the responsibility on himself even if it meant facing Varvara Petrovna. To everyone's astonishment, this lady, who arrived at the Governor's house posthaste and in a state of irritation to demand an immediate explanation, was refused admittance at the front steps, upon which she simply returned home, without getting out of her carriage, utterly incredulous.

And at long last everything became clear! At two o'clock in

the morning, the prisoner, who until then had been surprisingly calm and had even fallen asleep, suddenly raised a rumpus, set up a frenzied pounding on the door with his fists, tore the iron grating out of the small window in the door with superhuman strength, smashed the glass and cut up his hands. When the officer on duty ran in with a detachment of men and the keys and ordered the cell opened, so that they could rush the raging young man and tie him up, he proved to be in the throes of an acute attack of brain fever;[8] he was taken home to his mother. Everything suddenly became clear. All three of our doctors ventured the opinion that even for the previous three days the patient could already have been in the grip of delirium, and though he might have seemed to possess full awareness and cunning, the same could not be said about his common sense and self-control, which, of course, was confirmed by the facts as well. Thus it turned out that Liputin had guessed the truth sooner than anyone else. Ivan Osipovich, a man of delicate and sensitive feelings, was highly embarrassed; but curiously enough, that meant that even he had regarded Nikolay Vsevolodovich as capable of any insane act while fully rational. The people at the club felt ashamed and puzzled as to why they had missed the obvious and overlooked the only possible explanation for all these wonders. Naturally, there were some sceptics as well, but they didn't hold out for long.

Nicolas spent more than two months in bed. A famous doctor was called in from Moscow for a consultation; the entire town visited Varvara Petrovna. She forgave them. When, in the spring, Nicolas had already made a full recovery, and, without the slightest objection, had agreed to his mother's proposal of a trip to Italy, then she also begged him to pay farewell visits to all of us, and at the same time, as far as possible and wherever necessary, to make his apologies. Nicolas very willingly agreed. It became known at the club that he had gone to Pavel Pavlovich Gaganov's house for a highly delicate talk, with which the latter was fully satisfied. As he made his rounds of visits, Nicolas was very serious and even somewhat morose. All seemed to receive him with complete sympathy, but all for some reason felt embarrassed and were glad that he was leaving for Italy. Ivan

Osipovich's eyes even brimmed with tears, but for some reason he made no move to embrace him even at their final leave-taking. To be sure, some of us remained firmly convinced that this good-for-nothing had simply been making fun of us, and that his illness had nothing to do with it. He went round to see Liputin as well.

'Tell me,' he asked him, 'how could you have guessed ahead of time what I would say about your intelligence, and supply Agafya with the answer?'

'Why, this is how,' said Liputin with a laugh. 'I do regard you as an intelligent person, you know, and so I was able to predict what your answer would be.'

'Still and all, it's a remarkable coincidence. But please allow me: you actually regarded me as an intelligent person when you decided to send Agafya, and not as a madman?'

'As a highly intelligent and highly sensible man, and I only gave the impression that I believed you were not in your right mind . . . And anyway, you yourself immediately guessed what I was thinking at the time, and through Agafya you issued me a licence for my wit.'

'Well, there you're somewhat mistaken. In fact . . . I was unwell . . .' Nikolay Vsevolodovich muttered with a frown. 'Really, now!' he exclaimed. 'Do you actually think that I'm capable of attacking people when I have my wits about me? Why, what would be the point of that?'

Liputin hunched his shoulders, and didn't know how to answer. Nicolas paled slightly, or perhaps it only seemed so to Liputin.

'In any event, you have a very amusing way of thinking,' Nicolas continued, 'and as for Agafya, I understand of course that you sent her to be rude to me.'

'I couldn't challenge you to a duel, sir, now could I?'

'Ah, yes, that's right! I've actually heard that you don't like duelling.'

'Well, why translate from the French?' Liputin hunched his shoulders again.

'You cling to national customs?'

Liputin hunched his shoulders even more.

'Well, well, look what I see here!' exclaimed Nicolas, suddenly noticing a volume by Considérant[9] lying in a highly conspicuous place on a table. 'Does this mean you're a Fourierist? Why, you may very well be! But isn't that the same sort of translation from the French?' he said with a laugh, drumming his fingers on the book.

'No, it's not a translation from the French!' Liputin said rather angrily and jumped up, 'This is a translation from the universal language of humanity, and not just from the French! From the language of mankind's universal social republic and harmony, that's what it is! And not just from the French!'

'Ugh! The Devil with it, why, no such language as that exists!' Nicolas continued laughing.

Sometimes even a trifle arrests your attention for a long time and excludes everything else. Everything important that is to be said about Mr Stavrogin lies in the future; but now I shall mention, as a curiosity, that of all the impressions that struck him during the entire time he spent in our town, the one that left the sharpest imprint on his memory was the unattractive and almost loutish little figure of the petty provincial clerk, a coarse and jealous family despot, a miser and usurer, who would put leftovers from dinner and candle-ends behind lock and key, yet who at the same time was a fierce partisan of heaven knows what future 'social harmony', who spent his nights revelling ecstatically in fantastic visions of a future phalanstery, and in whose imminent implementation, in Russia and in our province, he believed as he did in his own existence. And all this was in the place where he himself had saved up for a 'nice little house', where he had married for the second time and taken a spot of cash in exchange for his wife, and where for a hundred versts around there was perhaps not a single person, beginning with himself, who bore even the remotest resemblance to a future member of 'mankind's universal social republic and harmony'.

'Lord knows where such people come from!' Nicolas wondered, when he would sometimes recall the improbable Fourierist.

4.

Our prince travelled for three years and then some, and as a result was almost forgotten in our town. But through Stepan Trofimovich it became known to us that he had travelled the length and breadth of Europe, had even been to Egypt and had made a short trip to Jerusalem; then he hooked on somewhere to some scientific expedition to Iceland and actually spent some time in Iceland. It was also reported that he had spent a winter attending lectures at a certain German university. He wrote to his mother infrequently – once every six months and even less often; but Varvara Petrovna was neither angry nor offended. The relations with her son that had been established once and for all she accepted without complaint and submissively, but, quite naturally, every day during these three years she constantly worried about, longed for and dreamed about her Nicolas. She shared neither her dreams nor her complaints with anyone. She even seemed to have distanced herself somewhat from Stepan Trofimovich. She was making some plans in secret, and seemed to have become more miserly than before, and began to save even more and to be angry at Stepan Trofimovich for his losses at cards.

Finally, in April of the present year, she received a letter from Paris, from Praskovya Ivanovna Drozdova, the widow of a general and her childhood friend. In her letter Praskovya Ivanovna – whom Varvara Petrovna had not laid eyes on or corresponded with for some eight years now – informed her that Nikolay Vsevolodovich had become an intimate of her family and had formed a close friendship with Liza (her only daughter), and that he intended to accompany them to Switzerland that summer, to Vernex-Montreux, despite the fact that he had been received like a son in the family of Count K. (a highly influential personage in Petersburg), who was presently staying in Paris, and that he was almost living at the Count's house. The letter was brief, and revealed its purpose clearly, although except for the above-mentioned facts, it drew no conclusions. Varvara Petrovna spent little time thinking about it; in an instant she came to a decision and made preparations, took her ward Dasha with her (Shatov's sister), and in the middle of April set off for Paris and then for Switzerland. She returned in July alone, having left Dasha with the Drozdovs; and the Drozdovs themselves, according to the news she had brought, promised to arrive in our town at the end of August.

The Drozdovs were also landowners of our province, but the service career of General Ivan Ivanovich (a former friend of Varvara Petrovna and a fellow officer of her husband) had always prevented them from ever visiting their magnificent estate. But after the general's death, which had occurred the previous year, the inconsolable Praskovya Ivanovna had gone abroad with her daughter, among other things to take the grape cure, which she proposed to do in Vernex-Montreux[10] in the second half of the summer. Then, after returning to her native country, she intended to settle in our province for good. She had a large house in town, which had stood empty for many years, with its windows boarded up. They were wealthy people. Praskovya Ivanovna, who was Mrs Tushina in her first marriage, was, like her school friend Varvara Petrovna, also the daughter of a liquor franchisee of the old days, and had also received a large dowry when she got married. Tushin, a retired cavalry staff captain, was himself a man of means and of some ability. On his deathbed he bequeathed a large sum of money to his seven-year-old (and only) daughter Liza. Now that Lizaveta Nikolayevna had already reached the age of twenty-two or so, her personal fortune could safely be estimated at 200,000 roubles, not to mention the property that in time would pass to her after the death of her mother, who had no children from her second marriage. Varvara Petrovna seemed to be highly pleased with her trip. In her opinion, she had come to a satisfactory understanding with Praskovya Ivanovna and immediately after she arrived home, she told Stepan Trofimovich everything; she was even very expansive with him, something that had not been the case with her for a very long time.

'Hurrah!' exclaimed Stepan Trofimovich, and he snapped his fingers.

He was absolutely thrilled, the more so since he had spent

the whole time that his friend was away in utter dejection. On going abroad, she had not even bade him a proper farewell, and had told nothing of her plans to 'this old woman', perhaps fearing that he would blab something. She was angry at him then because of a significant loss at cards that had suddenly come to light. But while in Switzerland, she began to feel in her heart that her abandoned friend should be rewarded when she returned, the more so since she had been treating him harshly for quite some time now. Her rapid and mysterious departure had startled Stepan Trofimovich and filled his timid heart with anguish, and, as luck would have it, other troubling things happened at the same time. He was tormented by a certain very considerable monetary obligation of long standing, which could never be satisfied without the help of Varvara Petrovna. Furthermore, in May of this year an end finally came to the governorship of our kind, gentle Ivan Osipovich. He was replaced, and even unpleasantly so, and, while Varvara Petrovna was still away, the arrival of our new superior, Andrey Antonovich von Lembke, occurred, and with it began a perceptible change of attitude towards Varvara Petrovna on the part of practically our entire provincial society, and consequently, towards Stepan Trofimovich as well. At least, he had already managed to gather a few unpleasant, albeit valuable observations, and he seemed very apprehensive without Varvara Petrovna. He was alarmed by the suspicion that people had already informed the new governor that he was a dangerous man. He learned definitely that certain of our local ladies intended to curtail their visits to Varvara Petrovna. About the new governor's wife (who was expected here only in early fall) people were repeating that although rumour had it that she was a proud woman, nonetheless she was a real aristocrat, and not 'someone like our poor unfortunate Varvara Petrovna'. From somewhere or other everyone knew for a fact, and in detail, that the new governor's wife and Varvara Petrovna had already met socially at one time and had parted enemies, so much so that the mere mention of Mrs von Lembke would supposedly produce a painful impression on Varvara Petrovna. Varvara Petrovna's buoyant and triumphant air, her contemptuous indifference when she heard of the opinions of our ladies and of the agitated state of our society, raised the flagging spirits of the timid Stepan Trofimovich and instantly restored him to cheerfulness. With his special brand of gleeful yet obsequious humour, he set about describing the arrival of the new governor for her.

'You are undoubtedly aware, *excellente amie*,' he said coquettishly, in a foppish drawl, 'what is meant by a Russian administrator, speaking generally, and what is meant by a new, that is, a newly-baked, newly-installed Russian administrator ... *Ces interminables mots russes!* ... But you could hardly have gained practical knowledge of the meaning of administrative ecstasy[11] and precisely what sort of thing that is.'

'Administrative ecstasy? I don't know what that is.'

'In other words ... *Vous savez, chez nous* ... *En un mot*, you appoint a nobody, some utter nonentity to sell utterly worthless railway tickets, and this nonentity will immediately regard himself as entitled to look down on you like Jupiter when you go to buy a ticket, *pour vous montrer son pouvoir*. "All right, then," he says, "let me show you the power I have over you ..." And for them this reaches the point of administrative ecstasy ... *En un mot*, I actually read that some sacristan in one of our churches abroad – *mais c'est très curieux* – drove, that is, literally drove, a distinguished English family out of the church, *les dames charmantes*, just before the Lenten service was scheduled to begin – *vous savez ces chants et le livre de Job* ... – solely on the grounds that "it is contrary to good order for foreigners to lounge about in Russian churches, and they should come at a designated time ...", and he sent them into fainting fits. This sacristan was having an attack of administrative ecstasy, *et il a montré son pouvoir* ...'[12]

'Cut it short if you can, Stepan Trofimovich.'

'Mr von Lembke has set out on a tour of the province. *En un mot*, this Andrey Antonovich, although he is a Russian German of the Orthodox persuasion, and even – I'll grant him this – a remarkably handsome man, somewhere in his forties ...'

'Whatever gave you the idea that he's a handsome man? He has sheep's eyes.'

'To an extreme degree. But I yield, after all – so be it – to the opinion of our ladies . . .'

'Let's change the subject, Stepan Trofimovich, I beg you! By the way, you're wearing a red tie. Has it been for long?'

'I . . . only today . . .'

'And are you taking your exercise? Are you going out for a six-verst walk every day, as the doctor prescribed?'

'. . . Not . . . not always.'

'I just knew it! I had a feeling about that when I was still in Switzerland!' she exclaimed in irritation. 'Now you will walk not six, but ten versts every day! You've let yourself go dreadfully, dreadfully, dread-ful-ly! You haven't exactly grown old, but you have grown decrepit . . . I was shocked when I saw you a little while ago, despite your red tie . . . *quelle idée rouge!*[13] Continue with von Lembke, if in fact there is anything to tell, and do bring it to an end eventually, I beg you; I am tired.'

'Well, then, *en un mot*, I simply wanted to say, you see, that he's one of those administrators who begin their career at the age of forty, and who until the age of forty have been vegetating in obscurity, and then suddenly make something of themselves by unexpectedly acquiring a wife or by some other, no less desperate means . . . That is, he has now left . . . that is, I mean to say that people lost no time in whispering into both his ears that I am a corrupter of youth and a breeding-ground of atheism in this province. He immediately began making inquiries.'

'Why – is that true?'

'I have even taken measures. When people "re-por-ted" that you "were running the province", *vous savez*, he permitted himself to say that "such things will not be permitted in the future".'

'Did he really say that?'

'That "such things will not be permitted in the future", and *avec cette morgue*[14] . . . His wife, Yuliya Mikhaylovna, we will see here at the end of August, direct from Petersburg.'

'From abroad. We met there.'

'*Vraiment?*'[15]

'In Paris and in Switzerland. She is related to the Drozdovs.'

'Related? What a remarkable coincidence! She is said to be ambitious, and . . . supposedly has important connections?'

'Rubbish! Piddling little connections! Until she was forty-five she was an old maid still, without a kopeck to her name, and now she's hooked up with von Lembke, and of course her whole purpose now is to make something out of him. They're both intriguers.'

'And they say she's two years older than he is?'

'Five. Her mother used to wear out her skirts on my doorstep in Moscow; she would beg to be invited to my fancy-dress balls as a favour, when Vsevolod Nikolayevich was still alive. And this one, her daughter, would sit all night long in the corner not dancing, with a turquoise fly on her forehead, so that by the time it got to be after two in the morning, I would send over her first partner, just out of pity. She was already twenty-five at that point, and they would take her out in a short skirt like a little girl. It became indecent to have them in my house.'

'I seem to see that fly.'

'I'm telling you, I arrived there and I immediately stumbled on an intrigue. Well, you've just read Drozdova's letter, what could be clearer? And what is it I find? This fool Drozdova – she was always nothing but a fool – suddenly looks at me questioningly, as if to ask: why have I come? You can imagine how surprised I was! I look and there's this Lembke woman scheming away and this cousin of hers, the nephew of old man Drozdov – everything is clear! Of course, I fixed everything in an instant and Praskovya is again on my side, but the intrigue, the intrigue!'

'Which you, however, got the better of. Oh, you Bismarck!'[16]

'Without being Bismarck, I am capable nonetheless of discerning falsehood and stupidity when I come across them. Lembke is falsehood, and Praskovya is stupidity. I've rarely met a more limp woman, and besides, her legs are swollen, and besides, she is kind. What can be more stupid than a stupid, kind person?'

'An evil fool, *ma bonne amie*,[17] an evil fool is even more stupid,' Stepan Trofimovich parried nobly.

'Perhaps you're right. Do you happen to remember Liza?'

'*Charmante enfant!*'[18]

'Well, now she's no longer an *enfant*, but a woman, and a woman of character. Honourable and impassioned, and what I love in her is that she doesn't defer to her mother, the credulous fool. Something very unpleasant very nearly occurred because of that cousin.'

'Well, in fact, he's actually not related to Lizaveta Nikolayevna at all . . . Does he have designs on her, or what?'

'You see, he's a young officer, very taciturn, even shy. I always want to be fair. It seems to me that he himself is opposed to this whole intrigue and doesn't want anything for himself, and that it's only the Lembke woman who's been scheming. He had great respect for Nicolas. You understand, the entire matter depends on Liza, but when I left her, she felt very kindly disposed toward Nicolas, and he himself promised me that he would come to see us in November without fail. And so, it's only the Lembke woman who is doing the intriguing, and Praskovya's just blind. Suddenly she says to me that all my suspicions are fantasies; I tell her to her face that she's a fool. I'm prepared to affirm it at the Last Judgement.[19] And if it hadn't been for Nicolas's begging me to drop the matter for the time being, I wouldn't have left that place without exposing that false woman. She tried to use Nicolas to ingratiate herself with Count K., she wanted to separate a son from his mother. But Liza is on our side, and I've come to an understanding with Praskovya. Do you know that Karmazinov is a relative of hers?'

'What? A relative of Madame von Lembke?'

'Why, yes. A distant one.'

'Karmazinov, the novelist?'

'Why, yes, the writer. What are you surprised at? Of course, he regards himself as a great writer. The puffed-up creature! She will come here with him, but now she's making a big fuss over him there. She's intent on starting up something here, some sort of literary gatherings. He's coming for a month; he wants to try to sell the last piece of property he owns here. I very nearly ran across him in Switzerland and I certainly didn't want to. However, I do hope he will deign to recognize me here. In the old days he used to write me letters, and he would visit me at home. I would like you to dress a little better, Stepan Trofimovich; you're becoming so untidy with every passing day ... Oh, how you torment me! What are you reading now?'

'I ... I ...'

'I understand. The same as before: friends, drinking bouts, the club and cards, and a reputation as an atheist. I don't like that sort of reputation, Stepan Trofimovich. I would rather you weren't called an atheist, especially now. I didn't like it before either, because it's all really just empty chatter, you know. This is something that has to be said once and for all.'

'*Mais, ma chère* ...'[20]

'Listen, Stepan Trofimovich, in all learned matters I am of course an ignoramus compared with you, but as I was on my way back here I was thinking about you a great deal. I've come to a certain conclusion.'

'And what was that?'

'That you and I aren't smarter than everybody else in the world, and that there are people who are smarter than we are.'

'That's witty and to the point. There are those who are smarter, therefore, there are those who are more right than we are, and we can make mistakes, isn't that so? *Mais, ma bonne amie*, let's suppose I'm mistaken, I do nonetheless have my human, perpetual, supreme right of freedom of conscience, don't I? I do have the right not to be a hypocrite and a bigot, if I don't want to, and for that, naturally, I will be hated to the end of time by various gentlemen. *Et puis, comme on trouve toujours plus de moines que de raison*,[21] and inasmuch as I am in complete agreement with this ...'

'What? What did you say?'

'I said: *on trouve toujours plus de moines que de raison*, and inasmuch as I am in complete ...'

'That can't be yours: you must have taken it from somewhere.'

'It was Pascal who said it.'

'"Well, that's what I thought ... it wasn't you! Why don't you ever say anything like that, so succinctly and to the point, instead of always dragging things out at such length? This is much better than the "administrative ecstasy" you've just been talking about . . .'

'*Ma foi, chère*[22] . . . why? In the first place, probably because I am not Pascal, after all, *et puis* . . . in the second place, we Russians don't know how to say anything in our own language . . . At least, we haven't said anything so far . . .'

'Hmm! That perhaps is not true. At least you should write such sayings down and memorize them, for conversational purposes, you know . . . Oh, Stepan Trofimovich, I've come here to have a serious, a very serious talk with you!'

'*Chère, chère amie!*'

'Now, when all these Lembkes, all these Karmazinovs . . . Oh, my heavens! How you've let yourself go! Oh, how you torment me! . . . I would very much like these people to feel respect for you, because they aren't worth one of your fingers, your little finger, but how do you behave? What will they see? What will I have to show them? Instead of bearing witness honourably, continuing to set an example, you surround yourself with all sorts of scum, you've acquired some unbelievable habits, you've become decrepit, you can't get along without wine or cards, all you read is Paul de Kock and you write nothing, whereas all of them are writing away; all your time is frittered away in chatter. Is it possible, is it permissible to be friends with scum like your inseparable Liputin?'

'Why do you say he's "mine" and "inseparable"?' Stepan Trofimovich protested meekly.

'Where is he now?' Varvara Petrovna continued sternly and sharply.

'He . . . he has boundless respect for you, and he's gone to S—k, to receive his inheritance after his mother's death.'

'The only thing he does is receive money, it seems. What about Shatov? The same?'

'*Irascible, mais bon.*'[23]

'I can't bear your Shatov; he's malicious, and he thinks a great deal of himself!'

'How is Darya Pavlovna's health?'

'Do you mean Dasha? What possesses you to ask about her?' Varvara Petrovna looked at him curiously. 'She's well, I left her with the Drozdovs . . . In Switzerland I heard something about your son, something bad, not good.'

'*Oh, c'est une histoire bien bête! Je vous attendais, ma bonne amie, pour vous raconter* . . .'[24]

'Enough, Stepan Trofimovich, leave me in peace, I'm exhausted. We will have time to talk to our hearts' content, especially about bad things. You're beginning to splutter when you laugh, and that's a sure sign of senility! And how strangely you've begun to laugh now . . . Heavens, you've accumulated so many bad habits! Karmazinov won't come to visit you! And even as it is, people here are glad of anything . . . You've revealed yourself completely now. Enough then, enough, I'm tired! Really, you might have mercy on a person!'

Stepan Trofimovich did have some 'mercy on a person', but withdrew in confusion.

5.

Bad habits had in fact developed in our friend in no small number, especially of late. He had let himself go visibly and rapidly, and it was true that he had become untidy. He was drinking more, had become more given to tears and more nervous; he had also become very sensitive to the finer things. His face had taken on the strange facility of changing with unusual rapidity, from the most solemn expression, for instance, to the most ridiculous and even stupid one. He couldn't bear being alone, and was constantly craving instant amusement from people. He absolutely had to be told some gossip, something interesting that was going on in town, and it had to be something new every day besides. If no one came to visit for a long time, he would wander through his rooms in misery, go up to the window, bite his lips pensively, heave a deep sigh and end by virtually snivelling. He was always apprehensive about something, always afraid that something unexpected and unavoidable would happen; he became fearful; he began to take his dreams very seriously.

He had spent this entire day and evening in an extremely melancholy state; he sent for me, was very agitated, spoke at length and told me everything at length, but all in a rather disconnected way. Varvara Petrovna had long been aware that he concealed nothing from me. It finally struck me that he was troubled by something in particular, something that he very likely couldn't put into words himself. Before then, whenever we would get together in private and he would begin complaining to me, the usual thing was that after a time a bottle was almost always brought in and the atmosphere would become much more comfortable. On this occasion there was no wine, and he was obviously suppressing his repeated desire to send for it.

'But why is she always so angry!' he complained incessantly, like a child. '*Tous les hommes de génie et de progrès en Russie étaient, sont et seront toujours des* gamblers *et des* drunkards *qui boivent en zapoi* . . . but I'm not yet such a gambler or such a drunkard, by no means. She reproaches me for not writing anything. What a strange idea! . . . Then too: why am I just lying around? You, she says, ought to stand as "an example and a reproach". *Mais, entre nous soit dit,*[25] if a man is destined to stand as a "reproach", then what in the world is he to do besides lie around – doesn't she understand that?'

And at last I clearly understood what was mainly responsible for the anguish that lay in his heart and tormented him so relentlessly on this occasion. Many times that evening he went up to the mirror and stood before it for a long time. Finally, he turned away from the mirror towards me and said with a strange sense of despair:

'*Mon cher, je suis un*[26] man who's let himself go!'

Yes, in fact, until that time, until that very day, he had remained unshakeably certain of one thing only, despite all the 'new views' and all the 'changing ideas' of Varvara Petrovna, namely, that he was still an object of fascination to her female heart, that is to say, not only as an exile or a famous scholar, but also as a handsome man. For twenty years this flattering and reassuring conviction had been fixed deeply in his mind, and of all his convictions, it would have been perhaps hardest of all for him to part with this one. Did he have a premonition that evening of the colossal test that was being prepared for him in the very near future?

6.

Now I will embark on a description of that rather amusing incident with which my chronicle actually begins.

At the very end of August the Drozdovs finally did return. Their appearance occurred shortly before the arrival of their kinswoman, who had long been awaited by the whole town – the wife of our new governor, and in general created a remarkable impression on society. But about all these curious events I shall speak later; for the present, I shall merely confine myself to the fact that Praskovya Ivanovna brought Varvara Petrovna, who had long been impatiently awaiting her, a certain, very troubling puzzle: Nicolas had parted company with them back in July, and after meeting Count K. on the Rhine, set off for Petersburg with him and his family. (NB: The Count has three unmarried daughters.)

'I got nothing out of Lizaveta, owing to her pride and her stubbornness,' Praskovya Ivanovna concluded, 'but I could see with my own eyes that something had happened between her and Nikolay Vsevolodovich. I don't know the reasons for it, but I think you, my dear friend Varvara Petrovna, will have to ask your Darya Pavlovna for the reasons. If you want my opinion, Liza was highly offended. I'm as happy as happy can be that at last I've brought you your favourite and I'm turning her over to you: that's a load off my shoulders.'

These venomous words were uttered with remarkable irritation. It was evident that the 'limp woman' had prepared them ahead of time and had anticipated their effect with pleasure. But Varvara Petrovna was not a woman who could be taken aback by sentimental effects and puzzles. She sternly demanded the most precise and satisfactory explanations. Praskovya Ivanovna instantly softened her tone, and even ended by bursting into tears and launching into the friendliest effusions. This irritating but sentimental lady, like Stepan Trofimovich himself, had a constant need for sincere friendship, and her principal complaint against her daughter, Lizaveta Nikolayevna, was precisely that 'her daughter was not a friend to her'.

But from all her explanations and effusions only one thing

could be gathered for certain: that some falling-out indeed had occurred between Liza and Nicolas, but as for the kind of falling-out, Praskovya Ivanovna obviously could form no definite idea. Not only did she finally and fully take back the blame she had laid at Darya Pavlovna's door, but asked in particular that no importance should be attached to what she had just said, because she had spoken 'in irritation'. In a word, everything proved in the end to be very unclear, even suspicious. As she related it, the falling-out began because of Liza's 'stubborn and sarcastic nature'; 'and the proud Nikolay Vsevolodovich, although he was deeply in love, could not bear the sarcastic remarks and began to be sarcastic himself'.

'Shortly thereafter we became acquainted with a certain young man, the nephew, I think, of your "professor", anyway his last name is the same . . .'

'His son, not his nephew,' Varvara Petrovna corrected her. Even before this, Praskovya Ivanovna could never remember Stepan Trofimovich's last name, and always called him 'the professor'.

'Well, be that as it may, his son, so much the better, it's really all the same to me. An ordinary young man, very lively and easygoing, but there's nothing special about him. Well, then Liza proceeded to act badly; she deliberately became friendly with the young man with an eye to making Nikolay Vsevolodovich jealous. I don't really condemn her that very much: it's a young girl's way, it's the usual thing, it's even sweet. Except that Nikolay Vsevolodovich, instead of getting jealous, did the opposite; he himself made friends with the young man, as if he didn't see a thing, or as if he didn't care a bit. That made Liza simply explode. The young man departed in haste (he was very much in a hurry to get somewhere), and Liza started picking on Nikolay Vsevolodovich at every opportunity. She noticed that he sometimes talked with Dasha, so she started flying into such rages that my own life became sheer misery, my dear. The doctors have forbidden me to get irritated, and I grew so sick of that lake of theirs that everyone praises: all it did was make my teeth ache and give me terrible rheumatism. They even write in the papers that Lake Geneva makes the

teeth ache:[27] that's one of its properties. And then Nikolay
Vsevolodovich suddenly received a letter from the Countess
and picked up and left us, he packed his things in one day. But
they said goodbye on friendly terms, and what's more, Liza
became very cheerful and silly and laughed a lot as she was
seeing him off. Except it was all just an act. He left, and she
got very broody and what's more, stopped mentioning him
altogether, and wouldn't let me either. And what's more, I
would advise you, my dear Varvara Petrovna, not to start up
with Liza on this topic now, you'll only spoil things. But if you
keep quiet, she herself will be the first to start talking to you;
then you'll learn more. In my opinion, they'll get together again,
provided Nikolay Vsevolodovich isn't too long in arriving, as
he promised.'

'I'll write to him immediately. If everything was as you say,
then it's nothing more than a tiff – all nonsense! And I know
Darya too well – it's nonsense.'

'I'm very sorry about Dashenka – I did her wrong. Their
conversations were entirely ordinary, and what's more, they
talked aloud. But all that upset me terribly at the time, my dear.
What's more, Liza, I could see, became friends with her again
and just as close as before . . .'

That very same day Varvara Petrovna wrote to Nicolas and
begged him to come at least a month earlier than he had
planned. Still and all, there was something that remained
unclear and mysterious to her about the whole business. She
pondered it all evening long and all night long. Praskovya's
opinion seemed too innocent and sentimental to her. 'Praskovya
has been too sentimental her entire life, ever since she was in
boarding school,' she thought, 'Nicolas is not the kind of person
to run away because of some silly young girl's sarcastic remarks.
There's something else going on here, if it really was just a tiff.
That officer, however, is here, they brought him back with
them, and he's settled into the house like a relative. And as for
Darya, Praskovya was much too quick to apologize: I imagine
she's keeping something to herself that she doesn't want to tell
me . . .'

By morning Varvara Petrovna had developed a plan to clear

up at least one misunderstanding once and for all – a plan that was remarkable for its very unexpectedness. What lay in her heart when she conceived it is hard to say, and I won't undertake an explanation ahead of time of all the contradictory factors that entered into it. As a chronicler, I am confining myself solely to presenting incidents in the exact form in which they occurred, and I am not at fault if they seem improbable. However, I'm obliged to attest once more to the fact that by morning she harboured no suspicions about Dasha, and, in truth, there had never even been a trace of any – she had too much confidence in her. What's more, she could not allow herself to think that her Nicolas might have been keen on her Darya. That morning, as Darya Pavlovna was pouring tea at the tea table, Varvara Petrovna took a long and searching look at her and, perhaps for the twentieth time since the previous day, said to herself confidently:

'It's all rubbish!'

The only thing she noticed was that Darya looked tired and was somewhat quieter than before, and more apathetic. After tea, according to a custom that had been established for all time, both sat down to their needlework. Varvara Petrovna instructed her to provide a full account of her impressions abroad, primarily of the weather, the people, the towns, the customs, their art, their industries – everything she had managed to observe. There was not a single question about the Drozdovs or about life with the Drozdovs. Dasha, who was sitting beside her at the work-table and helping her with the embroidery, had already been talking for half an hour in an even, monotonous, but rather weak voice.

'Darya,' Varvara Petrovna suddenly interrupted her, 'don't you have something special you would like to tell me?'

'No, nothing,' Darya said after a moment's thought, and glanced at Varvara Petrovna with her bright eyes.

'In your soul, in your heart, on your conscience?'

'Nothing,' Dasha repeated softly, but with a certain sullen firmness.

'I just knew it! You should know, Darya, that I never doubted you. Now sit there and listen. Move to this chair, sit opposite me, I want to see all of you. That's it. Listen – do you want to get married?'

Dasha's reply was a long, questioning look, which did not, however, betray much surprise.

'Stop, be quiet. In the first place, there is a disparity in your ages, a very big one; but after all, you yourself know better than anyone what nonsense that is. You are a sensible girl, and there should be no mistakes in your life. Besides, he's still a handsome man . . . In a word, Stepan Trofimovich, for whom you've always had respect. Well?'

Dasha looked even more questioningly, and this time not only with surprise, but even with a perceptible blush.

'Stop, be quiet; don't be hasty! Although you'll have money, according to the provisions of my will, what will become of you when I die, even if you have money! You'll be deceived and your money will be taken away, and that will be the end of you. And if you marry him you'll be the wife of a well-known man. Now look at it from another angle: if I should die right now – although I've made provisions for him – what will become of him? It's you that I'm relying on. Stop, I haven't finished: he's flighty, he dithers, he's cruel, he's an egotist, he has base habits, but you should appreciate him, first of all, if only because there are those who are far worse. Listen, I don't want to get rid of you by marrying you off to some scoundrel, you don't think that, do you? The main thing is that because I'm asking you, you will appreciate him' – she broke off suddenly in irritation – 'do you hear me? Why are you refusing to speak?'

Dasha maintained her silence and continued to listen.

'Stop, wait one minute more. He's an old woman, but after all, that's even better for you. And a pitiful old woman at that. He wouldn't ordinarily deserve the love of a woman. But he does deserve to be loved for his helplessness, and you will love him for his helplessness. Are you sure you understand me? Do you understand?'

Dasha nodded her head in affirmation.

'I just knew it, I expected no less of you. He will love you, because he should, he should; he should adore you!' Varvara Petrovna shrilled in a peculiarly irritated way. 'And besides, he will fall in love with you even without being obliged to, I know him well. Besides, I myself will be here. Don't worry, I will always be here. He'll start complaining about you, he'll begin to say slanderous things about you, he'll whisper about you with the first person he meets, he'll whine, he'll constantly whine; he'll write letters to you from one room to the next, two letters a day; but he won't be able to survive without you all the same, and that's really the main thing. Make him obey; if you don't know how to, you're a fool. He'll want to hang himself, he'll threaten to do it, but don't believe him – it's nothing but nonsense! Don't believe him, but still, be on your guard, you never know whether he actually will hang himself. It happens with people like him; they hang themselves not because they're strong, but because they're weak, and that's why you should never push him to the limit – that's the first rule of marriage. Remember, too, that he's a poet. Listen, Darya: there's no greater happiness than to sacrifice yourself. And besides that, you'll give me great pleasure, and that's the main thing. Don't think that I've been babbling on because I'm stupid. I understand what I'm saying. I'm an egotist, you be an egotist too. I'm not forcing you, you know: it's all up to you, whatever you say is the way it will be. Well, why are you just sitting there, say something!'

'It's really all the same to me, Varvara Petrovna, if I really must get married,' Dasha said firmly.

'Must? What are you hinting at?' Varvara Petrovna looked sternly and intently at her.

Dasha said nothing, and kept picking at the embroidery frame with her needle.

'You may be intelligent, but what you're saying is absurd. Even though it's certainly true that I've resolved to marry you off, it's not out of necessity, but simply because it occurred to me, and only to Stepan Trofimovich. If Stepan Trofimovich weren't in the picture, I wouldn't for a moment think of marrying you off now, even though you're already twenty years old . . . Well, then?'

'I'll do whatever you like, Varvara Petrovna.'

'So, you agree! Stop, be quiet, where are you rushing off to,

I haven't finished. According to the terms of my will, I'm leaving you fifteen thousand roubles. I shall hand that over to you immediately after the wedding. Out of that you will give eight thousand to him, that is, not to him, but to me. He's running a debt of eight thousand; I'll be the one to pay it, but he should know that it's with your money. Seven thousand will remain in your hands, but you shouldn't under any circumstances ever give him even one rouble. You should never pay his debts. Once you begin paying, you'll never see the end of it. However, I shall always be here. Each of you will receive an allowance of twelve hundred roubles a year from me, and five hundred for extras, besides lodging and board, which will also be at my expense, just like he has now. You will only have to arrange for your own servants. I will give the money for the whole year directly to you, and all at once. But do be kind to him: also give him something sometimes, and allow his friends to come and visit, once a week, but if they come more often, then get rid of them. But I myself shall be here. And if I should die, your allowances will continue until *his* death, you hear, only until *his* death, because this is his allowance, not yours. And I shall leave you an additional eight thousand in my will, besides the present seven thousand, which will remain untouched if you're not stupid. And there will be nothing more coming from me, you should know that. Well, do you agree, then? Will you finally say something?'

'I've already said it, Varvara Petrovna.'

'Remember that it's entirely up to you; whatever you want, that's the way it will be.'

'But allow me, Varvara Petrovna, has Stepan Trofimovich already said anything to you?'

'No, he hasn't said anything, and he doesn't know, but . . . he'll soon start talking!'

She jumped up in a flash and threw on her black shawl. Dasha once again coloured slightly, and followed her with an inquisitive look. Varvara Petrovna suddenly turned round and looked at her, her face burning with anger, and said:

'You're a fool!' – she pounced on her like a hawk. 'An ungrateful fool! What's in your head? Do you really think I would compromise you in the slightest, even *this* much! Why, he himself will come crawling on his knees to beg, he ought to die of happiness – that's how this will be arranged! You know perfectly well that I would never allow any harm to come to you! Or do you think that he'll take you in exchange for these eight thousand roubles, and that I'm running off to sell you now? Fool, fool, you're all ungrateful fools! Give me my umbrella!'

And she dashed off on foot off over the wet brick pavements and wooden planks to see Stepan Trofimovich.

7.

It was true that she would never allow any harm to come to Darya; on the contrary, even now she continued to regard herself as her benefactor. Indignation of a most noble and irreproachable kind began to burn in her breast when, as she put on her shawl, she caught the puzzled and mistrustful eyes of her ward fixed upon her. She had genuinely loved her from earliest childhood. Praskovya Ivanovna was justified in calling Darya Pavlovna her favourite. Varvara Petrovna had long since decided, once and for all, that 'Darya's character was not like her brother's' (that is, like the character of her brother Ivan Shatov), that she was quiet and meek and capable of great self-sacrifice, that she was remarkable for her loyalty, uncommon modesty, rare common sense and, most importantly, gratitude. Until now, Dasha had seemed to live up to all her expectations. 'There will be no mistakes in this life,' Varvara Petrovna said when the girl was just twelve years old, and since it was in her nature to attach herself stubbornly and passionately to any dream that captivated her, to any new scheme of hers, to every idea of hers that presented itself to her in a bright light, she promptly resolved to bring Dasha up as her own daughter. She immediately set aside a sum of money for her, and invited a governess into the house, a Miss Criggs who lived with them until the ward had reached the age of sixteen, and was then suddenly dismissed for some reason. Teachers came from the high school, among them a real Frenchman, who proceeded to teach Dasha French. This one was also dismissed suddenly, virtually thrown out of the house. One impoverished lady, not a native of the town, but a widow from a noble family, taught her the piano. But her principal pedagogue was still Stepan Trofimovich. In point of fact, he was the first to discover Dasha: he had begun to teach the quiet child even before Varvara Petrovna had given her any thought. I'll repeat once again: it is surprising how attached children were to him! Lizaveta Nikolayevna Tushina studied with him from the age of eight to eleven (naturally, Stepan Trofimovich taught her without recompense and wouldn't have dreamed of taking anything from the Drozdovs). But he himself fell in love with the delightful child, and would recite long poems to her about the creation of the world and the earth, and about the history of mankind. His lectures about primitive peoples and primitive man were more entertaining than the Arabian Nights. Liza, who was fascinated by these stories, would do very amusing imitations of Stepan Trofimovich at home. He found out about this, and once caught her by surprise. An embarrassed Liza threw herself into his arms and burst out crying. So did Stepan Trofimovich, from sheer delight. But Liza soon went away, and there remained only Dasha. When teachers began to come to Dasha, Stepan Trofimovich dropped his lessons with her and little by little stopped paying any attention to her at all. This went on for a long time. Once, when she was already seventeen years old, he was suddenly struck by how pretty she was. This happened at Varvara Petrovna's table. He began talking with the young girl, was very pleased with her answers and ended by offering to give her a serious and extensive course on the history of Russian literature. Varvara Petrovna praised and thanked him for his wonderful idea, and Dasha was in ecstasy. Stepan Trofimovich began to prepare specially for the lectures, and finally they began. They started out with the most ancient period. The first lecture went off delightfully; Varvara Petrovna was present. When Stepan Trofimovich finished, and, as he was leaving, announced to his pupil that the next time he would undertake an analysis of 'The Song of Igor's Campaign', Varvara Petrovna suddenly stood up and announced that there would be no more lectures. Stepan Trofimovich winced but kept quiet. Dasha flushed, but the venture ended then and there nonetheless. This happened exactly three years before Varvara Petrovna's latest unexpected fantasy.

Poor Stepan Trofimovich was sitting by himself with no premonition of anything. Sad and pensive, he had been glancing out of the window for quite some time to see whether any of his acquaintances was coming. But no one wanted to come near the house. It was drizzling outside and turning cold; the stove should have been lighted; he gave a sigh. Suddenly a dreadful sight appeared before his eyes: Varvara Petrovna, coming to see him in weather like this and at such an inopportune time! And on foot! He was so startled that he forgot to change into his costume and received her as he was, in his usual pink cotton-wadded dressing jacket.

'*Ma bonne amie!*' he exclaimed feebly as he went to meet her.

'You're alone, I'm glad: I can't bear your friends! Your house is always full of smoke; Lord, what kind of air is this! You haven't even finished drinking your tea, and it's after twelve o'clock. Your idea of bliss is disorder! Your idea of enjoyment is litter! What are those scraps of torn paper on the floor? Nastasya, Nastasya! What does your Nastasya do? My good woman, open the windows, the vents, the doors, everything wide open. And we'll go into the sitting room. I've come to you on business. Now, do give everything a good sweeping for once in your life, my good woman!'

'He makes such a mess, he does!' Nastasya whined in a tiny irritated and complaining voice.

'Well, you sweep then, sweep fifteen times a day! Your sitting-room is filthy.' (After they had gone into the sitting room.) 'Shut the door as tight as you can, she'll try to eavesdrop. You've really got to change the wallpaper. Come now – I did send you a decorator with samples, why didn't you select anything? Sit down and listen. Sit down, will you please, I beg you. Where are you going? Where are you going? Where *are* you going!'

'I'll be . . . right back,' Stepan Trofimovich shouted from the next room, 'here I am again!'

'Ah, you've changed clothes!' she said derisively as she looked him over. (He had thrown a frock-coat over his dressing jacket.) 'Yes, that will be far more suitable for what we have to say. Do sit down, will you please, I beg you.'

She explained everything to him at once, abruptly and cogently. She also hinted at the eight thousand, which he urgently needed. She told him about the dowry in detail. Stepan Trofimovich sat wide-eyed and trembling. He heard everything, but could make no clear sense of it. He wanted to say something, but his voice kept breaking. All he knew was that everything would be as she said it would, that it was useless to raise objections and not agree, and that he was irrevocably a married man.

'*Mais, ma bonne amie*, for the third time and at my age . . . and to such a child!' he finally brought out. '*Mais c'est une enfant!*'[28]

'A child who is twenty years old, thank God! Don't keep rolling your eyes, please, I beg you, you're not in some theatre. You're very intelligent and learned, but you understand nothing of life, a nursemaid should be looking after you constantly. If I should die, what will become of you? But she will be a good nursemaid for you; she's a modest, steadfast, sensible girl. Besides, I'll be here, I'm not going to die right away. She's a stay-at-home girl, she's an angel of meekness. This happy thought came to me while I was still in Italy. Do you understand if I tell you myself that she's an angel of meekness!' she suddenly shouted in a frenzy. 'Your house is filthy, she'll introduce cleanliness, order, everything will shine like a mirror . . . Ugh, do you really imagine that I'm obliged to keep bowing before you with such a treasure, enumerating all the advantages, arranging a match! Why, you ought to go down on your knees . . . Oh, you empty, empty, weak-spirited man!'

'But . . . I'm already an old man!'

'What do your fifty-three years matter! Fifty is not the end of life, but only the first half. You're a handsome man, and you know it yourself. You also know how much she respects you. If I should die, what will become of her? But married to you she'll feel reassured and I'll feel reassured. You have stature,

a name, a loving heart; you are receiving an allowance, which
I regard as my obligation. Perhaps you will save her, save her!
In any event, you will do her an honour. You will prepare her
for life, you will develop her heart, guide her thoughts. So many
people nowadays are lost because their thoughts are badly
guided! By then your book will be finished, and at the same
time you will remind people of your existence.'

'Actually, I am . . .' he mumbled, already flattered by the deft
flattery, 'actually, I'm planning to get down to work now on
my "Tales from Spanish History".'[29]

'Well, then, you see, a perfect coincidence.'

'But . . . what about her? Have you spoken to her?'

'Don't worry about her, and there's no need for you to be
curious. Of course, you must ask her yourself, implore her to
do you the honour, do you understand? But don't worry,
I myself will be here. Besides, you love her.'

Stepan Trofimovich's head began to spin; the walls started
going round and round. There was one dreadful idea here that
he could not contend with.

'*Excellente amie!*' his voice suddenly began to quiver. 'I . . .
I could never have imagined that you would venture to marry
me off . . . to another . . . woman!'

'You're not a young girl, Stepan Trofimovich; only young
girls are married off, but you yourself are getting married,'
Varvara Petrovna hissed venomously.

'*Oui, j'ai pris un mot pour un autre. Mais . . . c'est égal,*'[30]
he stared at her with a lost look.

'I see that *c'est égal,*' she said scornfully through clenched
teeth. 'Lord! Why, he's fainted! Nastasya, Nastasya! Water!'

But there was no need for water. He came to. Varvara
Petrovna picked up her umbrella.

'I see there's no point in talking to you now . . .'

'*Oui, oui, je suis incapable.*'[31]

'But by tomorrow you'll have rested and thought it over.
Stay at home, and if anything happens, let me know, even if it's
late at night. Don't write me any letters, I won't read them.
Tomorrow, at the very same time, I'll come again, alone, for
your final answer, and I hope it will be satisfactory. Try to see

that no one else is here, and that there's no clutter, because it's just beyond belief. Nastasya, Nastasya!'

Naturally, the following day he gave his consent; and he couldn't have failed to give his consent. For there was one special circumstance here . . .

8.

What we used to call Stepan Trofimovich's estate (about fifty souls according to the old method of reckoning, and adjacent to Skvoreshniki) was not his at all, but had belonged to his first wife, and consequently, was now his son's. Stepan Trofimovich merely held it in trust, and therefore, now that the fledgling had sprouted wings, acted as manager of the estate according to a formal power of attorney from him. The arrangement was profitable for the young man: he received up to a thousand roubles a year from his father ostensibly as income from the estate, although under the new order of things it didn't yield even five hundred (and perhaps even less). Heaven knows how such an arrangement had been arrived at. However, the whole one thousand was provided by Varvara Petrovna, while Stepan Trofimovich didn't contribute a single rouble to it. On the contrary, the entire income from the small parcel of land remained in his pocket, and in addition, he had utterly ruined the land by letting it to some entrepreneur, and, without Varvara Petrovna's knowledge, selling its woods, that is, its principal asset, for timber. He had been selling off the small patch of forest in bits and pieces for quite some time. In its entirety it was worth at least eight thousand, but he had taken only five for it. But he would sometimes lose too much at cards at the club, and was afraid to ask Varvara Petrovna for it. She gnashed her teeth when she finally found out everything. And now his young son suddenly informed him that he himself was coming to sell his holdings for whatever they would yield, and entrusted his father with arranging for the sale without delay. Naturally, Stepan Trofimovich, given his honourable and generous nature, felt ashamed of the way he had treated *ce cher enfant* (whom he had last seen nine whole years ago, when he was a student, in Petersburg). Originally the entire estate might have been worth about thirteen or fourteen thousand, but now it was hardly likely that anyone would give even five for it. Undoubtedly Stepan Trofimovich had every right, by the terms of the formal trust, to sell the woods and, taking into account the incredible annual income of a thousand roubles that for so many years had been sent abroad punctually, could have defended himself at the final settlement. But Stepan Trofimovich was an honourable man with higher impulses. A wonderful and beautiful idea flashed through his mind: when Petrusha arrived, he would generously place upon the table the maximum price, that is, as much as fifteen thousand, without the slightest reference to the amounts that had been sent abroad, and would clasp *ce cher fils*[32] firmly, ever so firmly to his breast, whereupon all accounts would be closed once and for all. He had begun, indirectly and cautiously, to unfold this picture before Varvara Petrovna. He hinted that this would even give a special, noble cast to their bond of friendship – to their 'idea'. This would present the 'fathers' and in general the people of the previous generation in a highly generous and magnanimous light compared with the new, frivolous and socialist youth. He said a great deal else, but Varvara Petrovna kept silent. At last she announced to him dryly that she was willing to buy their land and would give the maximum price for it, that is six or seven thousand (it could actually be bought for four). About the remaining eight thousand, which had vanished along with the woods, she didn't say a word.

This happened a month before the matchmaking episode. Stepan Trofimovich was stunned, and began to reflect. Previously there might have been some hope that his young son would perhaps not come at all – that is, some hope if looked at from the perspective of an outsider. But Stepan Trofimovich, as his father, would have rejected the very idea of such a hope with indignation. Whatever the truth of the matter, the strangest rumours about Petrusha had hitherto been reaching us. First, after completing his course of study at the university some six years ago, he had been knocking about Petersburg doing nothing. Suddenly we received the news that he had taken part in composing some anonymous manifesto and had been implicated in the whole business. Then, that he had suddenly turned up abroad, in Switzerland, in Geneva – a fugitive, for all we knew.

'It's astonishing to me,' Stepan Trofimovich used to declaim to us at that time, in great embarrassment, 'Petrusha *c'est une si pauvre tête!* He is kind, honourable, very sensitive, and I was so delighted then, in Petersburg, when I compared him with today's young people, but *c'est un pauvre sire tout de même* . . .*[33]* And, you know, it's all the result of that same immaturity, that same sentimentalism! They are captivated not by realism, but by the sentimental, idealistic side of socialism, so to speak, its religious tinge, its poetry . . . secondhand, naturally. And what about me, me, how do you think I feel! I have so many enemies here, and even more *there*, they'll ascribe it to his father's influence . . . Heavens! Petrusha a social force! What times we live in!'

However, Petrusha very soon sent his exact address from Switzerland so that the usual sum of money could be sent to him; therefore, he was certainly not really an émigré. And now, having lived abroad for some four years, he suddenly appeared in his native land again and announced his impending arrival: consequently, he stood accused of nothing. What was more, it even appeared that someone had taken an interest in him and was protecting him. Now he wrote from the south of Russia, where he was on some private but important mission and was busy with something. That was all well and good, but still, where were the remaining seven or eight thousand roubles to be found, so that a decent maximum price could be put on the property? And what if there should be an outcry, and instead of a grand picture matters should come to a lawsuit? Something told Stepan Trofimovich that the sensitive Petrusha would not forego his own interests. 'Why is it, as I've observed,' Stepan Trofimovich whispered to me on one occasion just then, 'why is it that these desperate socialists and communists are at the same time so unbelievably stingy, so interested in acquiring things, so devoted to private property, and even to the point that the more a man is a socialist, the deeper he's into it, the stronger his property instinct ... Why is that? Could this be the result of sentimentalism too?' I don't know if there's any truth to this observation of Stepan Trofimovich's; all I know is that Petrusha had certain information about the sale of the woods and the rest of it, and that Stepan Trofimovich knew that he had this information. I also had occasion to read Petrusha's letters to his father. For him to write was extremely rare – once a year, and even less often. Only recently, by way of notifying us of his forthcoming arrival, he sent two letters, one virtually following on the other. All his letters were rather brief and dry, and consisted of nothing but instructions, and inasmuch as father and son had been on terms of familiar address ever since Petersburg, as was the fashion, this meant that Petrusha's letters had the unmistakably old-fashioned look of the orders that landowners in both capitals once used to send their house-serfs whom they had put in charge of administering their properties. And now these eight thousand roubles, which would decide the matter, suddenly fluttered down from Varvara Petrovna's offer, and at the same time she let it be clearly understood that no more could possibly come fluttering down from anywhere else. Naturally, Stepan Trofimovich agreed.

Immediately after she had left, he sent for me, and refused to admit anyone else the entire day. Of course, he cried a little, talked a great deal and, well, fell into frequent and glaring self-contradictions, made a pun quite by chance and was happy with it, then suffered a slight attack of cholerine – in a word, everything went as it should. After that he brought out a picture of his little German wife, who had died twenty years ago, and began calling out to her plaintively: 'Will you forgive me?' In general he was somehow disoriented. In our sorrow we got a little drunk. However, he soon fell into a peaceful sleep. The next morning he knotted his tie expertly, dressed himself carefully, and often went up to the mirror to have a look. He sprayed his handkerchief with scent, but only so slightly, and, as soon as he caught sight of Varvara Petrovna through the window, he hastily picked up another handkerchief, and hid the scented one under a pillow.

'That's excellent!' Varvara Petrovna said approvingly, after she had heard him agree. 'In the first place, an honourable decisiveness, and in the second place, you have harkened to the voice of reason, to which you so often harken in your personal affairs. There is no need to hurry, by the way,' she added, inspecting the knot of his white tie, 'say nothing for the time being and I shall say nothing. It will soon be your birthday; I will be with you, along with her. Give us an evening tea and, please, no wine or *zakuski*; I, however, shall arrange everything. Invite your friends – however, we shall choose them together. The day before you'll have a talk with her, if it's necessary; but at your evening party we shall not exactly announce anything or make any formal agreement, but merely hint or let it be known, without any ceremony. And then in two weeks or so the wedding, without any more fuss than necessary . . . Both of you could even go away for a while, directly from the church, to Moscow, for instance. I'll also go with you, perhaps . . . But the main thing is to say nothing until then.'

Stepan Trofimovich was surprised. He tried to stammer that he couldn't do that sort of thing, that he really had to talk things over with the bride-to-be, but Varvara Petrovna fell upon him in irritation:

'But what for? In the first place, nothing has happened yet, and perhaps nothing will . . .'

'What do you mean nothing will!' muttered the bridegroom, utterly stunned.

'Just that. I'll give it some further thought . . . But everything will be as I have said, and don't you worry, I'll prepare her myself. There's no need at all for you to do anything. Everything necessary will be said and done, and there's no need for you to go there. What for? What part would you play? And don't go on your own, and don't write letters. Not a word out of you, I beg you. I won't say anything either.'

She certainly didn't want to explain herself, and left visibly discomposed. Stepan Trofimovich's excessive willingness apparently took her aback. Alas, he had absolutely no conception of his situation, and the matter had not yet presented itself to him from certain other points of view. On the contrary, there was now something new in his manner, something triumphant and frivolous. He swaggered.

'How do you like that!' he exclaimed, standing before me with his arms outstretched. 'Did you hear? She wants to bring things to such a point that ultimately I won't want to go through with it. You know, I can also lose my patience and . . . not feel like it! "Just sit, and there's no need for you to go there." But when it comes down to it, why must I absolutely get married? Just because some silly fantasy has popped into her head? But I'm a serious person, and capable of not wishing to subordinate myself to the empty fantasies of an eccentric woman! I have obligations to my son and . . . and to myself! I'm making a sacrifice – does she understand that? Perhaps I agreed because I've grown tired of life and it's all the same to me. But she can irritate me, and then it will no longer be all the same to me: I will take offence and refuse. *Et enfin, le ridicule* . . . What will they say at the club? What will . . . Liputin say? "Maybe nothing will really come of it at all" – what sort of thing is that! That really tops it all! That's . . . what is that, anyway? *Je suis un forçat, un Badinguet, un*[34] man who's been pressed to the wall!'

And yet at the same time a kind of capricious self-indulgence, a kind of frivolous playfulness showed through all these plaintive exclamations. That evening we once again had a bit to drink.

CHAPTER 3

Another Man's Sins

I.

A week or so passed, and then things began to move somewhat.

I will note in passing that during this unhappy week I suffered a great deal of anguish, remaining as I did virtually inseparable from my poor engaged friend in my capacity as his closest confidant. What lay heaviest on him was shame, even though we saw no one during that week and remained by ourselves; but he was even ashamed in my presence, and to the point where the more he opened himself up to me, the more irritated he became with me because of it. His anxious nature led him to suspect that everything was already known to everyone, to the entire town, and he was afraid to show himself not only at the club, but even in his own circle. He even went out for a walk, for the obligatory constitutional, only well after dusk, when it had already grown quite dark.

A week passed, and he still didn't yet know whether he was a bridegroom-to-be or not, and he simply couldn't find out for sure, no matter how he tried. He hadn't yet had a meeting with his bride-to-be, and didn't even know whether she was his bride-to-be; he didn't even know whether to take any of this remotely seriously or not! For some reason, Varvara Petrovna had absolutely no desire to allow him to come to see her. In reply to one of his first letters (and he wrote a great many to her), she bluntly asked him to spare her all dealings with him for the time being, because she was busy, and since she herself had much of importance to communicate to him, she was deliberately waiting for a freer moment to do so than now, and would certainly let him know *in due time* when he could come to see her. As for his letters, she promised to return them unopened, because they were 'nothing but self-indulgence'. I myself read this note; he made a point of showing it to me.

Yet all this rudeness and vagueness were nothing compared to his main anxiety. It tormented him acutely and relentlessly; he lost weight over it and grew despondent. It was something that he was more ashamed of than anything else and about which he didn't wish to speak even with me; on the contrary, when the occasion arose he would lie and be evasive in my presence, like a little boy; and yet he himself would send for me every day, he couldn't live without me for two hours, he needed me like water or air.

Such behaviour wounded my pride somewhat. It goes without saying that I had long since guessed this great secret on my own, and saw through everything. It was my deepest conviction at the time that the revelation of this secret, this enormous anxiety of Stepan Trofimovich's, would not have done him honour, and therefore, being still a young man, I was somewhat indignant at the coarseness of his feelings and the ugliness of certain of his suspicions. In a temper – and, I admit, out of boredom from being his confidant – I perhaps put too much of the blame on him. In my cruelty, I tried to get him to confess everything to me, although, to be sure, I did allow that it was very likely difficult to confess to some things. He also understood me thoroughly, that is, he clearly saw that I understood him thoroughly and was even angry at him, and he himself was angry at me because I was angry at him and understood him thoroughly. Perhaps my irritation was petty and stupid; but mutual isolation sometimes proves extremely harmful to true friendship. From a certain angle he had an accurate understanding of some aspects of his situation and could even assess it quite subtly on those points where he didn't feel obliged to hold back.

'Oh, that's not the way she was then!' he would sometimes blurt about Varvara Petrovna. 'That's not the way she used to be, when she and I would talk. Do you know that at that time she still knew how to talk? Can you believe that at that time she had ideas, her own ideas? Now everything has changed! She says that all that is nothing but ancient chatter! She has contempt for what once was ... Now she is some sort of steward or housekeeper, an embittered person, and is angry all the time ...'

'Why, what does she have to be angry about, since you've done what she demanded?' I objected.

He merely looked at me.

'*Cher ami*, if I had simply refused to agree, she would have grown dreadfully angry, dread-ful-ly! But in any event less so than now, when I have agreed.'

He was pleased with this nice turn of phrase, and we finished off a bottle that evening. But that was only momentary: the next day he was in an even more dreadful and morose mood than ever before.

But more than anything else I was annoyed with him because he had not bestirred himself, as duty required, to go to visit the Drozdovs, who had just arrived, to renew their acquaintance-ship, which, word had it, they themselves desired, inasmuch as they had already been asking about him; and this was a daily source of misery for him. About Lizaveta Nikolayevna he spoke with a kind of ecstasy that I found incomprehensible. Undoubtedly he remembered her as the child he had once loved so much; but besides that, he imagined, for some unknown reason, that at her side he would immediately find relief for all his present torments and would even resolve his most pressing doubts. In Lizaveta Nikolayevna he expected to meet some kind of extraordinary being. And yet he did not go to see her, although he intended to do so every day. The main thing was that I myself at that time was desperate to be presented and introduced to her, and could rely solely on Stepan Trofimovich for that. My frequent encounters with her made an extraordin-ary impression on me at that time – in the street, of course, when she would come out on horseback, in riding habit and on splendid mount, accompanied by her so-called relative, a handsome officer, the nephew of the late General Drozdov. I was blinded for just a moment, and I very quickly realized that my dream was utterly impossible, but, though only for a moment, it really did exist, and therefore you can imagine how

indignant I sometimes was at my poor friend in those days for
his stubborn reclusiveness.

From the very beginning, everyone in our circle was officially
notified that Stepan Trofimovich would not be receiving guests
for some time, and was asking to be left in complete peace. He
insisted that people be notified one by one, although I strongly
advised against it. And I was the one who made the rounds, as
he requested, and divulged to everyone that Varvara Petrovna
had entrusted our 'old man' (as all of us called Stepan Trofimovich among ourselves) with an urgent task, that of putting in
order some correspondence that had extended over several
years; that he had shut himself up, and that I was helping him,
and so on and so forth. Liputin was the only one I did not get
around to visiting, and I kept putting it off – more accurately,
I was afraid to visit him. I knew in advance that he would not
believe a word I said, would certainly imagine that there was
some secret here, which people wanted to hide from him and
no one else, and that as soon as I had left his place, he would
immediately go all over town trying to find out what it was and
start gossiping. While I was picturing all this, it so happened
that I unexpectedly ran across him in the street. It turned out
that he had already learned about everything from the people
in our circle who had just been informed by me. But strangely
enough, he not only showed no curiosity and didn't inquire
about Stepan Trofimovich, but, on the contrary, was quick to
interrupt me when I tried to make my excuses for not visiting
him earlier, and promptly switched to another topic. True
enough, he had a fund of things to regale me with; he was in
an extraordinarily excited state of mind and was delighted that
he had found an audience in me. He began talking about the
town news, about the arrival of the governor's wife 'with fresh
material for conversation', about the opposition that had
already built at the club, about the fact that everyone was
shouting about new ideas and how this had infected everyone,
and so on and so forth. He went on talking for a quarter of an
hour, and so entertainingly that I couldn't tear myself away.
Although I couldn't bear him, I admit that he had the gift of
compelling people to listen to him, especially when he was very

angry at something. This man, in my opinion, was a genuine born-spy. At any moment he knew all the very latest news and all the ins and outs of our town, primarily where abominations were concerned, and one had to marvel at the extent to which he took to heart things that sometimes didn't concern him at all. It always seemed to me that his main character trait was envy. When I told Stepan Trofimovich that same evening about my encounter that morning with Liputin and about our conversation, he became extremely agitated, to my surprise, and asked me a strange question: 'Does Liputin know or not?' I began trying to show him that there was no chance of his finding out so soon, and besides, there was no one to tell him; but Stepan Trofimovich stuck by what he had asked.

'Well, you may believe it or not,' he finally concluded unexpectedly, 'but I am convinced that not only is everything known to him about *our* situation in all its details, but that he knows a great deal more than that, something that neither you nor I know yet, and perhaps will never find out, or will find out when it is already too late, when there is no longer any turning back!'

I said nothing, but his words hinted at a great deal. Thereafter we didn't utter a word about Liputin for five whole days; it was clear to me that Stepan Trofimovich was very sorry that he had revealed such suspicions in my presence and had let the cat out of the bag.

2.

One morning – it was the seventh or eighth day after Stepan Trofimovich had agreed to become engaged – at about eleven o'clock, while I was hurrying, as usual, to meet my mournful friend, I had an adventure along the way.

I came across Karmazinov, 'the great writer', as Liputin had dubbed him. I had been reading Karmazinov since I was a child. His novels and short stories were well known to everyone of the previous generation and even of our own; I for one used to revel in them; they had been the delight of my adolescence and young manhood. Then I grew rather cool towards his work; the novels with a message, which he had been writing of late, no longer held my interest as much as the earlier ones had, his first works, which contained so much spontaneous poetry; and his most recent works weren't at all to my liking.

Generally speaking, if I may take the liberty of expressing my own opinion on such a delicate matter, all our talented gentlemen of the middling sort, who are usually regarded as nothing short of geniuses during their lifetime, not only disappear from people's memory when they die, rather suddenly somehow and virtually without a trace, but it also happens that even during their lifetime, as soon as a new generation comes of age and takes the place of the one in which they have been active, they are mysteriously forgotten and neglected by all. In our country this somehow happens all of a sudden, like changing the scenery in a theatre. Oh, it's not at all the same thing as with the Pushkins, Gogols, Molières and Voltaires,[1] with all those figures who had come to utter their new word! It's also true that these talented gentlemen of the middling sort here in Russia usually write themselves out in the most pitiable way in the declining period of their distinguished years, without even noticing it in the least. Not infrequently it turns out that a writer whom people have long credited with an extraordinary depth of ideas and whom they have expected to exert an extraordinary and major influence on the direction of society, displays in the end such a watered-down and minuscule version of his basic little idea that no one is even sorry that he's succeeded in writing himself out. But the grey-haired little old men don't notice this and become angry. Their vanity, just towards the end of their careers, sometimes reaches proportions that are truly astonishing. Heaven knows who it is they begin to take themselves for – for gods, at the very least. About Karmazinov it was said that he cherished his connections with powerful people and higher society almost more than his own soul. It was said that he would meet you, treat you kindly, flatter you and charm you with his open-heartedness, especially if he needed you somehow, and, quite naturally, if you'd been recommended to him ahead of time. But let the first prince come along, the first countess, the first person he fears, and he would consider it his most sacred duty to forget all about you in the most insulting and offhanded manner, as if you were a splinter of wood, a fly, right then and there, before you even had time to leave his presence. He regards this in all seriousness as the most refined and elegant form. Despite his complete self-possession and his thorough knowledge of good manners, he is so vain, they say, so hysterically vain, that he is utterly unable to conceal his authorial annoyance even in those circles of society where people take little interest in literature. But if by chance someone should unexpectedly display utter indifference towards him, then he would become morbidly offended and would try to take his revenge.

About a year ago I read an article of his in a magazine, which was written with frightful pretensions to extremely naive poetry and to psychology at the same time. He was describing a shipwreck somewhere on the coast of England, which he himself had witnessed, and he watched as drowning people were saved and dead bodies pulled out.[2] This entire article, which was rather long and wordy, was written with the sole purpose of displaying himself. You could read between the lines: 'Take an interest in me, look at the way I was at those moments. Why do you need the sea, the storm, the rocks, the shattered splinters of the ship? After all, I have described all this to you adequately with my mighty pen. Why are you looking at this drowned woman with the dead child in her dead arms? Look at me instead, and see how I endured this spectacle and turned away from it. You see, I stood with my back to it; you see, I am horrified and have not the strength to look back; I am shutting my eyes tight – that's so interesting, is it not?' When I told Stepan Trofimovich what I had thought of Karmazinov's article, he agreed with me.

When recent rumours of Karmazinov's arrival began to circulate among us, I desperately wanted to see him, of course, and if possible, make his acquaintance. I knew I could do this through Stepan Trofimovich; they had been close friends at one time. And now, suddenly I met him at a street crossing. I recognized him at once; people had already pointed him out to me some three days ago, when he was driving by in a carriage with the governor's wife.

96

DEMONS

He was a very short, prim little old man, although no more
than about fifty-five, with a rather ruddy little face, thick little
grey curls that peeped from under a stovepipe hat[3] and twined
round his clean, rosy little ears. His clean little face was not
altogether handsome, with its thin, long, slyly-set lips, its rather
fleshy nose and its sharp, intelligent little eyes. He was dressed
rather shabbily, with a kind of cloak thrown over his shoulders,
of a style that would, for instance, be worn this season somewhere in Switzerland or Northern Italy. But at least all the small
details of his costume – cuff-links, collars, buttons, tortoiseshell
lorgnette[4] on a slender black ribbon, signet ring – were exactly
as they were worn by people of impeccably good taste. I'm
certain that in the summer he undoubtedly went around in
coloured prunella[5] shoes with mother-of-pearl buttons on the
side. When we bumped into each other, he had paused at a
turning in the street and was looking around attentively. Noticing that I was looking at him with curiosity, he asked me in a
mellifluous though penetrating thin voice:

'Be so good as to tell me the shortest way to Bykova Street.'

'To Bykova Street? Why, that's right here, very close by,' I
exclaimed in great excitement. 'You go straight along this street
and then take the second turn to the left.'

'Very much obliged to you.'

A curse on this moment: I think I was intimidated, and threw
him an obsequious look! He noticed all this in a flash, and of
course understood everything immediately, that is, he understood that I already knew who he was, that I had read and
revered him since I was a child, that I was now feeling intimidated and was looking at him obsequiously. He gave a smile,
nodded his head again and walked straight on in the direction
I had indicated. I don't know why I turned back and followed
him; I don't know why I ran alongside him for ten steps. He
suddenly stopped again.

'And could you please tell me where the nearest cab-stand
is?' he shouted at me again.

A nasty shout; a nasty voice!

'A cab-stand? The cab-stand is very close by . . . they stop at
the cathedral, that's where they always stop', and then I nearly

turned and ran to get him a cab. I suspect that's precisely what he expected from me. Of course, I immediately collected my wits and stopped, but he had definitely detected my movement, and was still watching me with the same nasty smile. Then something happened that I shall never forget.

He suddenly dropped a tiny bag that he had been holding in his left hand. Actually, it wasn't a bag, but a box of some kind, or, more accurately, a small portfolio of some kind, or, rather, a small reticule,[6] like an old-fashioned lady's reticule. Actually, I don't know what it was, but I do know that I seem to have rushed to pick it up.

I am utterly convinced that I didn't pick it up, but my initial movement was unmistakable; I could not conceal it, and I blushed like an idiot. The crafty fellow promptly extracted everything from the situation that he possibly could.

'Don't trouble yourself, I'll get it myself,' he said charmingly, that is, when he finally realized that I wouldn't pick up his reticule for him, he picked it up, as if anticipating me, nodded his head again, and set out on his way, leaving me looking like an idiot. It was the same as if I had picked it up myself. For a good five minutes I thought I had been completely and permanently disgraced; but as I walked up to Stepan Trofimovich's house, I suddenly burst out laughing. The encounter seemed so funny to me that I immediately decided to amuse Stepan Trofimovich with an account of it, and even act out the whole scene for him.

3.

But on this occasion, to my surprise, I found him drastically changed. To be sure, he swooped down on me with a certain avidity the moment I came in, and began listening to me, but with such a distracted expression on his face that at first he obviously didn't understand what I was saying. But as soon as I spoke the name Karmazinov, he completely lost his self-control.

'Don't speak of him! Don't utter his name!' he shouted in almost a frenzy. 'Look, look at this! Read it! Read it!'

He pulled out a drawer and threw on to the table three small scraps of paper that had been hastily written on with pencil, all from Varvara Petrovna. The first note was from two days ago, the second from the day before, and the last one had arrived today, just an hour ago. Their contents were utterly trivial, all about Karmazinov, and revealed Varvara Petrovna's anxiety, born of egotism and ambition, that Karmazinov would forget to pay her a visit. Here is the first of them, from two days previously (there was also probably one three days ago, and perhaps four days ago as well).

If he does finally favour you today, then I beg you, not a word about me. Not the slightest hint. Don't speak of me and don't mention me.

V.S.

Yesterday's:

If he finally ventures to pay you a visit this morning, the most honourable thing, I think, is not to receive him at all. That's my opinion, I don't know what your opinion is.

V.S.

Today's note, the last one:

I am convinced that there's a whole cartload of rubbish and clouds of tobacco smoke in your house. I will send you Marya and Fomushka; they'll tidy it up in half an hour. And don't you get in their way – sit in the kitchen while they're tidying up. I'm sending a Bukhara carpet[7] and two Chinese vases – I have long been intending to make you a present of them – and in addition, my Teniers[8] (temporarily). The vases you can place on a window sill, and you will hang the Teniers above and to the right of the portrait of Goethe, it can be seen better there and it's always light in the morning. If he does finally appear, receive him with exquisite politeness, but try to talk about trivial matters, about something learned, and make it look as if you'd said goodbye to each other only yesterday. About me – not a word. Perhaps I'll look in this evening.

V.S.

P.S. If he doesn't come today, then he won't come at all.

I read these notes and was astonished that he was upset by such trifles. I glanced at him questioningly and suddenly noticed that while I had been reading, he had managed to change the white tie he always wore for a red one. His hat and cane lay on the table. He was pale, and his hands were even trembling.

'I don't want to hear about her anxieties,' he exclaimed in a fury, in response to my questioning glance. '*Je m'en fiche!* She has the nerve to get upset about Karmazinov, and doesn't even answer my letters! Look, here's an unopened letter of mine that she returned to me yesterday, right there on the table, under that book, under *L'Homme qui rit.*[9] What do I care that she's grieving over Ni-ko-len-ka! *Je m'en fiche et je proclame ma liberté. Au diable le Karmazinoff! Au diable la Lembke!* I've hidden the vases in the front hall and the Teniers in the closet, and I've demanded that she receive me this very moment. Do you hear: I've demanded it! I've had Nastasya take her a scrap of paper just like hers, in pencil, not sealed, and I'm waiting. I want Darya Pavlovna herself to tell me with her own lips and before heaven, or at least before you. *Vous me seconderez, n'est-ce pas, comme ami et témoin.*[10] I don't want to blush, and I don't want to lie, I don't want any secrets, I will not allow any secrets in this matter! Let them confess everything to me, openly, sincerely, honourably, and then . . . then perhaps I will astonish an entire generation with my magnanimity! Am I a scoundrel or not, my dear sir?' he concluded suddenly, looking at me threateningly, as if I were the one who had regarded him as a scoundrel.

I suggested he drink some water; I had never seen him in such a state. All the time that he was talking he was running from one corner of the room to another, but he suddenly stopped in front of me and struck an unusual pose.

'Do you really think,' he began again with morbid haughtiness, looking me over from head to foot, 'can you really suppose that I, Stepan Verkhovensky, am unable to find sufficient moral strength within myself to take up my box – my beggar's box! – and hoisting it on to my weak shoulders, walk through the gate and disappear from here forever, when that is required by honour and the great principle of independence? It would not be the first time that Stepan Verkhovensky responded to despotism with magnanimity, albeit the despotism of a crazy woman, that is to say, the most tiresome and cruel kind of despotism that can possibly exist in this world, despite the fact that you seem to have permitted yourself just now to make fun of my words, my dear sir! Oh, you don't believe that I can find enough magnanimity within myself to be able to end my life as a tutor for a merchant family, or die of hunger next to a fence! Answer me, answer me at once: do you believe me or not?'

But I deliberately remained silent. I even gave the impression that I would not venture to offend him with a negative answer, but that I could not answer in the affirmative. In all this irritation of his there was something that certainly offended me, but not personally, oh no! But . . . I will explain later.

He even turned pale.

'Perhaps you are bored with me, G—v,' (that's my surname),[11] 'and you would like . . . not to come to visit me at all?' he muttered in that blandly calm tone that usually precedes some unusual outburst. I jumped up in alarm. At that very moment in came Nastasya and silently handed Stepan Trofimovich a piece of paper on which something had been written in pencil. He glanced at it and tossed it over to me. Written on the paper were just two words, in Varvara Petrovna's hand: 'Stay home.'

Stepan Trofimovich silently snatched up his hat and stick and quickly left the room; I walked after him automatically. Suddenly voices and the sound of someone's quick steps were heard in the hallway. He stopped as if struck by lightning.

'It's Liputin, and I'm done for!' he whispered, seizing me by the arm.

At that very moment Liputin walked into the room.

4.

Why he should be done for because of Liputin I didn't know, and I didn't attach any value to what he had said; I attributed everything to nerves. Still and all, his alarm was unusual, and I made up my mind to observe everything closely.

If nothing else, Liputin's look, as he came in, announced that on this occasion he had a special right to come in, despite all the prohibitions. He brought with him an unknown gentleman, someone new in town in all likelihood. In response to the blank stare of the dumbfounded Stepan Trofimovich, he promptly and loudly exclaimed:

'I'm bringing a visitor, and a special one at that! I make bold to intrude on your solitude. Mr Kirillov, a most remarkable civil engineer. And most importantly, he knows your son, the much-esteemed Pyotr Stepanovich – very intimately, I must say; and he has a message from him, sir. And he has just arrived.'

'You've added the part about the message,' the visitor observed sharply, 'there never was any message, but true enough, I do know Verkhovensky. I left him in Kh— Province, about ten days before we got here.'

Stepan Trofimovich offered his hand mechanically and motioned them to sit down. He looked at me, he looked at Liputin, and suddenly, as if recovering his senses, hastened to sit down himself, while continuing to hold his hat and walking stick in his hand and not noticing that he was doing so.

'Oh, I see you're on your way out! But I was told that you were quite indisposed on account of your studies.'

'Yes, I'm not well, and I just now wanted to take a walk, I . . .' Stepan Trofimovich paused, quickly threw his hat and walking stick on the sofa, and – blushed.

Meanwhile I was giving the visitor a quick once-over. He was still a young man, about twenty-seven, decently dressed, slender and good-looking, with dark hair and a pale, somewhat ashen face, and black, lustreless eyes. He seemed rather pensive and distracted, spoke haltingly and somehow ungrammatically, somehow transposing his words and getting all mixed up if he had to create a longer sentence. Liputin was fully aware of

Stepan Trofimovich's extraordinary apprehension, and was obviously pleased. He seated himself on a wicker chair that he had dragged almost into the middle of the room so that he could be at an equal distance from the host and the guest, who had stationed themselves on two facing sofas. His sharp, curious eyes darted all over the room.

'I . . . haven't seen Petrusha for a long time now . . . Did you two meet abroad?' Stepan Trofimovich managed to mumble to the guest.

'Both here and abroad.'

'Aleksey Nilych himself has just returned from abroad, sir, after an absence of four years,' Liputin chimed in. 'He went there to perfect himself in his speciality, and has come back to us with good reason to hope that he will obtain a position on the construction of our railway bridge, and he's now awaiting an answer. He is acquainted, sir, with the Drozdovs and with Lizaveta Nikolayevna through Pyotr Stepanovich.'

The engineer sat as if his feathers had been ruffled, listened attentively and seemed uncomfortable and impatient. It struck me that he was angry at something.

'He is also acquainted with Nikolay Vsevolodovich, sir.'

'You know Nikolay Vsevolodovich as well?' inquired Stepan Trofimovich.

'I know that one as well.'

'I . . . it's been an extraordinarily long time now since I've seen Petrusha and . . . I have so little right to call myself his father . . . *c'est le mot*;[12] I . . . How was he when you left him?'

'Well, I just left him, that's all . . . he will be coming himself,' Mr Kirillov again hastened to get off the topic. He was definitely angry.

'He will be coming! At last I . . . you see, it's been too long now since I've seen Petrusha!' Stepan Trofimovich was stuck on this phrase. 'I'm waiting for my poor boy now, whom . . . oh, whom I feel so guilty about! That is to say, I, strictly speaking, want to say that when I left him in Petersburg then, I . . . in a word, I regarded him as a nonentity, *quelque chose dans ce genre*. He was a nervous boy, you know, very sensitive, and . . . fearful. When he went to bed, he would bow to the ground as he said his prayers and make the sign of the cross on his pillow, so that he wouldn't die in the night . . . *je m'en souviens. Enfin*, he had no feeling for the finer things at all, that is, for anything higher, anything fundamental, the tiniest germ of any future idea . . . *c'était comme un petit idiot.*[13] But I seem to be muddled, forgive me, I . . . you caught me . . .'

'Are you serious that he made the sign of the cross on his pillow?' the engineer suddenly inquired with obvious curiosity.

'Yes, he did . . .'

'Well, I was just asking; do go on.'

Stepan Trofimovich looked questioningly at Liputin.

'I'm very grateful for your visit, but I admit that just now I'm . . . not in any condition . . . However, do tell me where you're staying.'

'In Bogoyavlenskaya Street, in Filippov's house.'

'Ah, that's the same place that Shatov lives,' I couldn't help but remark.

'That's right, in the very same house,' Liputin exclaimed, 'except that Shatov is staying upstairs, in the attic, while Mr Kirillov has taken lodgings downstairs, with Captain Lebyadkin. Mr Kirillov knows both Shatov and Shatov's wife. He used to be on very close terms with her abroad.'

'*Comment!* Do you really know something, then, about the unhappy marriage *de ce pauvre ami*[14] and this woman?' exclaimed Stepan Trofimovich, suddenly carried away with emotion. 'You are the first person I've met who knows her personally; and if only . . .'

'What nonsense!' snapped Kirillov, flushing all over. 'How you add to things, Liputin! I never saw Shatov's wife; only once, from a distance, and not close up at all . . . Shatov I do know. Why is it you add on various things?'

He turned abruptly on the sofa, snatched up his hat, and set it aside again and, settling down as before, fixed his burning black eyes on Stepan Trofimovich in a kind of challenge. I simply couldn't understand such strange irritability.

'Pardon me,' Stepan Trofimovich observed importantly, 'I understand that this matter can be extremely delicate . . .'

'There's absolutely no extremely delicate matter here, and

it's even shameful, and I wasn't shouting "nonsense" at you but at Liputin, why he adds things. Excuse me if you took it as referring to you. I do know Shatov, but I don't know his wife at all . . . I don't know her at all!'

'I understand, I understand, and if I was pressing the matter, then it was merely because I very much love our poor friend, *notre irascible ami*, and have always taken an interest . . . In my view, this man has made too abrupt a change in his former ideas, which were perhaps too youthful, but nonetheless correct. And now he's shouting various things about *notre sainte Russie*, to such an extent that I've long been attributing this sudden change in his organism – I can't call it anything else – to some powerful shock in his home life, namely, his unhappy marriage. I, who have studied my poor Russia as closely as I know my own two fingers, and who have given my entire life to the Russian people, I can assure you that he does not know the Russian people,[15] and in addition . . .'

'I don't have the slightest knowledge of the Russian people either and . . . I have absolutely no time to study them!' the engineer again snapped, and again turned abruptly on the sofa. Stepan Trofimovich stopped dead in mid-sentence.

'Mr Kirillov is studying them, he is studying them,' Liputin picked up. 'Mr Kirillov has already begun his study and is writing a most interesting article on the reasons for the increase in incidents of suicide in Russia,[16] and in general on the factors that promote or retard the spread of suicide in society. He has come up with astonishing results.'

The engineer was frightfully agitated.

'You have absolutely no right,' he began muttering angrily, 'I'm not writing any article. I'm not going to do anything stupid. I asked you in confidence, quite by chance. There's no article here at all, I'm not publishing anything, and you have no right . . .'

Liputin was visibly enjoying himself.

'Begging your pardon, perhaps I was mistaken in calling your literary work an article. Mr Kirillov is only collecting observations, and not at all touching on the essence of the problem, or, so to speak, its moral side, and even rejects the principle of morality altogether, and is holding to the latest principle of general destruction in the name of ultimately good purposes. Mr Kirillov has already demanded more than a hundred million heads for the establishment of common sense in Europe, many more than were demanded at the last peace congress.[17] In this sense Aleksey Nilych has gone further than anyone.'

The engineer was listening with a scornful and pale smile. No one said a word for a good half-minute.

'All that's stupid, Liputin,' Mr Kirillov finally stated with a certain dignity. 'If by chance I have mentioned some points to you, and you caught them up, then it's as you like. But you have no right, because I never say anything to anyone. I scorn to speak ... If I do have convictions, then for me it is clear ... but you've done stupidly. I don't argue about those points where everything is completely settled. I can't bear to argue. I never want to argue ...'

'And perhaps you do well not to,' Stepan Trofimovich couldn't refrain from putting in.

'I beg your pardon, but I'm not angry at anyone here,' the guest continued in an excited patter, 'I have seen few people for four years ... I have conversed little for four years, and have tried not to meet people, for my own purposes, which are no one's business, for four years. Liputin found this out and is laughing. I understand and don't care. I'm not touchy, I'm just annoyed at his liberties. And if I don't expound my ideas with you,' he concluded unexpectedly, and swept a firm look over all of us, 'then it's certainly not because I'm afraid that you will inform on me to the government. That's not it; please don't think any such nonsense in this regard.'

None of us had a thing to say in reply to these words, but merely exchanged glances. Even Liputin forgot to giggle.

'Gentlemen, I am very sorry,' said Stepan Trofimovich, resolutely rising from the sofa, 'but I feel unwell and upset. Excuse me.'

'Ah, this is so we should leave,' Mr Kirillov gave a start, seizing his cap, 'it's good you said something, because I'm forgetful.'

He rose, and walked up to Stepan Trofimovich with an outstretched hand and an ingenuous look.

'It's too bad you're unwell and I came.'

'I wish you every success here in our town,' replied Stepan Trofimovich, pressing his hand genially and unhurriedly. 'I understand that if you, as you put it, have lived abroad for so long, avoiding people for your own purposes, and – have forgotten Russia, then of course you are bound to be surprised when you look on us homegrown Russians, just as we are when we look on you. *Mais cela passera.*[18] There's only one thing that causes me difficulty: you want to build our bridge, and at the same time you announce that you stand for the principle of universal destruction. They won't let you build our bridge!'

'What? What did you say? Oh, damnation!' Kirillov exclaimed in astonishment and suddenly burst out into the merriest and brightest laughter imaginable. For an instant his face took on an absolutely childlike expression which struck me as very well suited to him. Liputin was rubbing his hands in ecstasy at Stepan Trofimovich's felicitous expression. But I kept marvelling to myself: why was Stepan Trofimovich so afraid of Liputin, and why did he exclaim 'I'm done for' when he heard him coming?

5.

We were all standing in the doorway. It was the moment when hosts and guests hasten to exchange their final and most cordial words, and then happily part.

'Mr Kirillov is so sullen today,' Liputin suddenly interjected just as he was going out of the room, and was, so to speak, on the wing, 'because he had a dust-up earlier today with Captain Lebyadkin over his sister. Captain Lebyadkin beats his beautiful young sister, the crazy one, every day with a whip, a real Cossack whip, mornings and evenings. So Aleksey Nilych has even rented the small building in the yard to avoid being a party to it. Well then, goodbye.'

'A sister? Who's sick? With a whip?' Stepan Trofimovich positively cried out, as if he himself were suddenly being lashed with a whip. 'What sister? What Lebyadkin?'

His earlier fear came back in an instant.

'Lebyadkin? Ah, the retired captain; formerly he referred to himself only as a staff captain . . .'

'Oh, what do I care about his rank! What sister? My Lord . . . did you say Lebyadkin? But didn't there used to be a Lebyadkin living here . . .'

'The very same, *our* Lebyadkin, you remember, at Virginsky's?'

'But wasn't he caught with counterfeit banknotes?'

'Well, here he is, back with us, almost three weeks now, and under the most peculiar circumstances.'

'But he's a scoundrel!'

'As if there couldn't be any scoundrels among us?' Liputin suddenly grinned, as if he were groping Stepan Trofimovich with his furtive little eyes.

'Oh, my Lord! That wasn't at all what I . . . although, actually, I'm entirely in agreement with you about the scoundrel, particularly with you. But what more is there, what more? What did you mean by that? . . . You definitely did mean something by that, didn't you!'

'Oh well, it's all just such trivial stuff, you know . . . That is to say, the captain, to all appearances, left here at that time not because of the counterfeit notes, but for the sole purpose of finding this younger sister of his, and she had supposedly hidden from him in some unknown place. Well, now he's brought her back, and that's the whole story. Why do you seem so frightened, Stepan Trofimovich? Besides, I'm only telling you what I gather from his own drunken babbling; but when he's sober he himself keeps his mouth shut about it. He's an irritable man, and, how should I put it, a military aesthete, only with very bad taste. And this sister of his is not only insane, but crippled as well. She was supposedly seduced by someone, lost her virtue, and for that our Mr Lebyadkin has supposedly been receiving compensation from the seducer every year for many years now, in recompense for the insult to his honour, or so at least his babbling would have us believe. But in my opinion, it's nothing but a lot of drunken talk. He's just boasting. And that sort of thing costs a good deal less. But as for his having large sums of money, that's absolutely true; a week and a half ago he was walking around barefoot, and now, I've seen it for myself, he's got hundreds. His sister has some kind of seizures every day; she screams, and he "puts her back in working order" with his whip. You have to instil respect in a woman, he says. What I can't understand is how Shatov gets on with them, living as he does right above. Aleksey Nilych stayed with them just three days; they already knew each other from Petersburg, and now he's rented the small house in the yard to get away from all the turmoil.'

'Is all that true?' Stepan Trofimovich turned to the engineer.

'You're blathering an awful lot, Liputin,' he grumbled angrily.

'Mysteries, secrets! Where did so many mysteries and secrets suddenly appear from!' exclaimed Stepan Trofimovich, unable to restrain himself.

The engineer frowned, flushed, shrugged his shoulders and started out of the room.

'Aleksey Nilych even tore the whip out of his hands, you know, broke it and threw it out of the window, and they had a big argument,' Liputin added.

'What are you blathering for, Liputin, it's stupid. What for?' Aleksey Nilych spun round in a flash.

'Why be modest and try to conceal the noblest impulses of one's soul, that is, of your soul, I mean, I'm not speaking of my own.'

'How stupid it is . . . and completely unnecessary . . . Lebyadkin is stupid and utterly empty – and useless for any action . . . and utterly harmful. Why are you babbling stuff like that? I'm leaving.'

'Oh, what a pity!' exclaimed Liputin with a bright smile. 'Otherwise I would have told you another nice little story, Stepan Trofimovich, one that would have made you laugh, yes, sir. I even came here with the intention of passing it on to you, although you've probably actually heard it yourself. Well, another time, then, Aleksey Nilych is in such a hurry . . . Goodbye, sirs. It's an interesting little story, concerning Varvara Petrovna. She made me laugh the other day; she sent for me just for that purpose; it just killed me. Goodbye, sirs.'

But at this point Stepan Trofimovich simply pounced on him: he seized him by the shoulders, spun him abruptly around back into the room and sat him down on a chair. Liputin was absolutely terrified.

'But what's this all about?' he began, looking warily at Stepan Trofimovich from his chair. 'She suddenly summoned me and asked me "confidentially" what my own opinion of the matter was: was Nikolay Vsevolodovich insane or in his right mind? Don't you think that's astonishing?'

'You're out of your mind!' muttered Stepan Trofimovich and he suddenly seemed to lose control of himself: 'Liputin, you know very well that the only reason you came here was to pass on something vile of this sort and . . . something even worse!'

In a flash I recalled his conjecture that Liputin not only knew something more about our business than we ourselves did, but even something else that we ourselves would never learn.

'For pity's sake, Stepan Trofimovich!' Liputin kept muttering as though he were frightened to death, 'for pity's sake . . .'

'Keep quiet and begin! I beg you, Mr Kirillov, to come back as well and stay, I beg you in all earnestness! Please sit down. And you, Liputin, begin directly, simply . . . and without reservations of any kind!'

'If I'd only known that this would shock you so, I wouldn't have started it at all, no, sir . . . And I really did think that everything was already known to you from Varvara Petrovna herself!'

'You didn't think any such thing! Begin, begin immediately, I tell you!'

'Except do me the favour of taking a seat yourself, otherwise how can I possibly go on sitting here if you're standing in front of me in such an agitated state. Everything will come out all incoherent, yes, sir.'

Stepan Trofimovich restrained himself and lowered himself imposingly into the armchair. The engineer gloomily fixed his eyes on the floor. Liputin looked at them in a frenzy of delight.

'Well then, how am I to begin . . . you've confused me so . . .'

6.

'The day before yesterday she suddenly sends her man-servant to me. "She asks you," he says, "to be present at twelve o'clock." Can you imagine? I dropped everything, and yesterday on the dot of noon I ring. They show me straight into the drawing room. I wait a minute or two – out she comes, asks me to sit down and sits down herself, right opposite. I'm sitting there and refusing to believe my eyes; you yourself know how she's always treated me! She begins straight off, in her usual way, without any beating about the bush. "You remember," she says, "that four years ago Nikolay Vsevolodovich, being in an ill condition, committed several strange acts, which left the whole town baffled until everything was explained. One of these acts concerned you personally. Nikolay Vsevolodovich then came to see you after he had recovered, and at my request. It is also known to me that he had several conversations with you even before that. Tell me frankly and straightforwardly, how you..." (here she hesitated a bit) "how you found Nikolay Vsevolodovich on that occasion... How you regarded him in general ... what opinion you were able to form of him and ... now hold?"

'Here she breaks off altogether, even letting a whole minute pass, and suddenly flushes. I get really scared. Then she begins again, not in a way that would move you, that wouldn't be her style, but in a very imposing sort of tone.

'"I desire," she says, "that you understand me well and unequivocally. I've sent for you now because I consider you a discerning and sharp-witted man, capable of making accurate observations." (Such compliments!) "You," she says, "will also of course understand that a mother is speaking to you ... Nikolay Vsevolodovich has experienced certain misfortunes and many ups and downs in his life. All that," she says, "could have affected his state of mind. Naturally," she says, "I am not speaking of mental illness, that could never be!" (Firmly and proudly uttered.) "But there might have been something strange, something peculiar, a certain turn of thought, a tendency to look at things in a special way." (These are all her exact words, and I was surprised, Stepan Trofimovich, by the preciseness with which Varvara Petrovna is capable of explaining things. A lady of high intelligence!) "At least," she says, "I myself have noticed in him a certain chronic restlessness and a tendency towards special inclinations. But I am a mother, while you are a third party, so you are capable, given your intelligence, of forming a more independent opinion. I beseech you, finally" (that's exactly what was said: "I beseech") "to tell me the whole truth, without any distortions, and if at the same time you will give me your word never to forget in the future that I have been speaking to you in confidence, then you can expect my complete and constant readiness to show my gratitude at every opportunity henceforth." Well, then, sir, what do you think of that!'

'You ... you have given me such a shock ...' Stepan Trofimovich babbled, 'that I don't believe you ...'

'But observe, observe,' Liputin went right on, as if he hadn't even heard Stepan Trofimovich, 'how great her agitation and anxiety must have been if she turned to a man like me with such a question from such a lofty height, and furthermore condescended to the extent of asking me to keep it a secret. What's going on here? Perhaps she's received some unexpected news about Nikolay Vsevolodovich?'

'I don't know ... there's no news ... I haven't seen her for several days, but ... I will observe to you,' babbled Stepan Trofimovich, who was visibly having trouble wrestling with his thoughts, 'I will observe to you, Liputin, that if that was conveyed to you in confidence, and you now, in everyone's presence ...'

'In complete confidence! But may God strike me dead if I ... And if here ... well, then, what of it? Are we strangers, even if we include Aleksey Nilych?'

'I do not share such a view. Undoubtedly the three of us here will keep it a secret, but you, the fourth, I fear and I don't believe anything you say!'

'But why do you say that, sir? Why, I have a greater interest than anyone, seeing that eternal gratitude has been promised me! And I really did want in this connection to point out an extraordinarily strange incident, more psychological, so to speak, than simply strange. Last evening, under the influence of my conversation with Varvara Petrovna (you can imagine the impression it made on me), I turned to Aleksey Nilych with an indirect question. "You," I say, "knew Nikolay Vsevolodovich before, both abroad and in Petersburg. How," I say, "did you find him as far as his mind and capacities are concerned?" He proceeds to answer very laconically, as is his manner, that "he's a man of subtle intelligence and sound judgement", to use his own words. "And didn't you observe over the years," I say, "a certain, I say, deviation in his ideas, or a peculiar turn of thought, or a certain," I say, "so to speak insanity, as it were?" In a word, I repeated the question that Varvara Petrovna herself asked. Just imagine: Aleksey Nilych suddenly begins thinking and wrinkles his brow, just like he's doing now. "Yes," he says, "at times something has seemed strange to me." Note, moreover, that if something could seem strange to Aleksey Nilych, of all people, then what might really be going on in point of fact, eh?'

'Is that true?' Stepan Trofimovich turned to Aleksey Nilych.

'I don't wish to talk about it,' replied Aleksey Nilych, suddenly raising his head, his eyes flashing. 'I want to dispute your right, Liputin. You have absolutely no right to say anything about me in this case. I haven't spoken my entire opinion by any means. Although I was acquainted with Nikolay Stavrogin in Petersburg, that was a long time ago, and now, although I've met him again, I know Nikolay Stavrogin very little. I ask you to keep me out of all this and ... and all that sounds like gossip.'

Liputin spread his arms in a gesture of offended innocence.

'Me, a gossip! Why not a spy too? It's all very well for you, Aleksey Nilych, to criticize, when you've kept yourself out of everything. Why, you wouldn't believe, Stepan Trofimovich – well, just take Captain Lebyadkin, he seems, why, as stupid as ... that is, I'm simply ashamed to say how stupid. There's a Russian comparison that indicates the degree of stupidity, and even he, don't you know, considers himself offended by Nikolay Vsevolodovich, even though he does worship his wit. "I'm amazed," he says, "by this man: a wise serpent" (his own words). And I say to him (still under the very same influence as yesterday, and after my conversation with Aleksey Nilych): "So then, Captain," I say, "what's your opinion in this matter, is your wise serpent crazy or not?" Believe me, it was as if I'd suddenly lashed him with a whip from behind, without his permission. He simply jumped to his feet: "Yes," he says, "yes," he says, "only that," he says, "can have no influence on . . .", but he didn't say what it could have no influence on. And then he turned sad and fell to thinking, and thought so hard that he sobered up in a flash. We were sitting in Filippov's tavern. And only half an hour later did he suddenly bang his fist on the table. "Yes," he says, "maybe he really is crazy, except that it can have no influence on . . .", and again, he didn't say what it could have no influence on. Naturally, I'm only giving you a summary of the conversation, but the idea of it is perfectly clear: no matter who you ask, the same thought comes to all of them, even though it hadn't occurred to them before then. "Yes," they say, "he's crazy; very intelligent, but maybe he's crazy too."'

Stepan Trofimovich was sitting there pensive and engrossed in thought.

'And how does Lebyadkin know?'

'But it would be better to make inquiries about that of Aleksey Nilych, who has just called me a spy. I'm a spy, yet I don't know – but Aleksey Nilych knows all there is to know and keeps quiet about it.'

'I don't know anything, or very little,' replied the engineer, in the same irritated tone. 'You got Lebyadkin drunk so as to try and find out. You brought me here too so that you could find out and so that I'd talk. Therefore, you're a spy!'

'I haven't got him drunk yet, and what's more, he isn't worth spending that much money on, despite all his secrets – that's what they're worth to me – but I don't know about you. On the contrary, he's the one who's throwing money around, though twelve days ago he came to try and get fifteen kopecks out of me, and he was the one plying me with champagne, and it wasn't me doing the plying. But you've given me an idea, and if need be, then I'll certainly get him drunk, precisely to try and find out – and maybe I will find out, yes, all your little secrets,' Liputin snapped maliciously.

Stepan Trofimovich watched in perplexity as the two men argued. Both were giving themselves away, and most importantly, weren't standing on ceremony. It occurred to me that Liputin had brought this Aleksey Nilych fellow to us precisely for the purpose of using him as a third person to draw us into a conversation he wanted to have with us, a favourite manoeuvre of his.

'Aleksey Nilych knows Nikolay Vsevolodovich only too well,' he continued in irritation, 'except he's trying to conceal it, yes, indeed. And as for what you asked about Captain Lebyadkin, he made his acquaintance some five or six years ago in Petersburg, before any of us, in that little-known – if I can put it that way – period of Nikolay Vsevolodovich's life, when he as yet had no intention of adding to our happiness by coming here. Our prince, we must conclude, surrounded himself with a rather strange choice of acquaintances at that time in Petersburg. That was when, or so it appears, he got to know Aleksey Nilych as well.'

'Watch yourself, Liputin, I'm warning you that Nikolay Vsevolodovich is planning to be here soon, and that he knows how to stand up for himself.'

'Why, what are you picking on me for? I'm the first to shout for all to hear that he's a man with a highly subtle and refined mind, and yesterday I reassured Varvara Petrovna fully in this respect. "But I can't vouch for his character," I tell her. Lebyadkin also said the very same thing: "I've suffered from his character," he says. Ah, Stepan Trofimovich, it's all very well for you to shout about gossip and spying, but observe that it's after you've squeezed everything out of me, and with such an excess of curiosity besides. But take Varvara Petrovna, she just went straight to the point yesterday: "You," she says, "had a personal interest in the matter, and that is why I am turning to you." Well, it would be surprising if she didn't, sir! Why wonder about motives here, when I swallowed a personal insult from His Excellency in front of our local society! I would seem to have good reason to be interested, and not just for the sake of gossip. Today he shakes your hand, but the next day, out of the blue, he rewards your hospitality by slapping you on both cheeks in front of a whole gathering of honest people, just because he feels like it. It comes from having it too good, sir! For these people the main thing is the female sex: butterflies and strutting little cocks of the walk! Landowners with delicate little wings, like the ones on ancient cupids, lady-killing Pechorins![19] It's all very well for you, Stepan Trofimovich, as a confirmed bachelor, to talk this way and to call me a gossip because of His Excellency. But if you were to get married, since you're still such a fine figure of a man even now, to someone who's both pretty and young, then you'd most probably lock and bolt the door against our prince and set up barricades in your own house! Well, never mind. Take this Mademoiselle Lebyadkina, the one who's being beaten with whips, if only she weren't crazy and bowlegged, then I swear, I'd think she's the one who's the victim of our young general's passions, and that it was from him that Captain Lebyadkin suffered "in his family dignity", to use his own expression. Except maybe that's contrary to his refined taste, but to people like him that doesn't matter. Any little berry is worth the picking, so long as it's there when he's in a particular mood. Here you are talking about gossip, but there's no need for me to shout about it when the whole town is chattering away, and I'm just listening and nodding in agreement. There's no law against nodding in agreement, sir.'

'The town is shouting? What's the town shouting about, then?'

'That is to say, it's Captain Lebyadkin who's shouting in a drunken state for all the town to hear, well, then, isn't that the same as if the entire marketplace were shouting? How am I to blame? I'm only interested in it as among friends, sir, because I do, after all, consider myself as being among friends here' – he scanned us with an innocent look. 'There's an incident that occurred here, just consider it: it turns out that His Excellency supposedly sent from Switzerland with a most honourable young lady and modest orphan, so to speak, whom I have the honour to know, three hundred roubles to be handed over to

Captain Lebyadkin. And a little while later Lebyadkin received the most precise information, I won't say from whom, but also from a most honourable person, and consequently a most reliable one, that it wasn't three hundred but a thousand that was sent! Consequently, Lebyadkin shouts, the girl stole seven hundred roubles from him, and he wants to get it back if not quite by calling the police, then at least by threatening to do so, and he's chattering away for the whole town to hear.'

'That's vile, vile of you!' The engineer suddenly jumped up from his seat.

'But after all, you yourself are that most honourable person who confirmed for Lebyadkin, in the name of Nikolay Vsevolodovich, that it wasn't three hundred but a thousand roubles that had been sent. Look, the Captain himself told me this in a drunken state.'

'That's . . . that's an unfortunate misunderstanding. Someone made a mistake and it turned out that . . . It's nonsense, and you are vile!'

'Why, I really do want to believe that it's nonsense, and I'm listening to all this with regret, because, say what you like, a most honourable young lady is implicated, in the first place, in a matter of seven hundred roubles, and in the second, in obvious intimacies with Nikolay Vsevolodovich. After all, what does it cost His Excellency to disgrace a girl of impeccable honour, or to bring shame upon someone else's wife, as was recently the case with me? Some person brimming with generosity will turn up, and His Excellency will proceed to force him to cover up another man's sins with his own good name. That's precisely what I had to tolerate, sir; I'm speaking about myself, sir.'

'Watch yourself, Liputin!' Stepan Trofimovich rose from his armchair and turned pale.

'Don't you believe it, don't you believe it! Someone made a mistake, and Lebyadkin was drunk,' exclaimed the engineer in indescribable agitation. 'Everything will be explained, and I can't stand it any longer . . . I regard it as low behaviour . . . and enough! Enough!'

He ran out of the room.

'Why, what's wrong with you? Why, I'm going with you,

after all!' Liputin shouted in alarm, jumped up and ran after Aleksey Nilych.

7.

Stepan Trofimovich remained standing for a moment in hesitation, looked at me somehow without seeing me, picked up his hat and stick, and quietly walked out of the room. I followed him again, as before. As we were going out of the gate, he noticed that I was accompanying him, and said:

'Ah, yes, you can serve as a witness . . . *de l'accident. Vous m'accompagnerez, n'est-ce pas?*'[20]

'Stepan Trofimovich, are you really going there again? Just think what might come of it.'

With a pitiable and lost smile – a smile of shame and utter despair, and of a certain strange exultation at the same time – he whispered to me, pausing for a moment:

'I simply cannot get married to "another man's sins"!'

These were precisely the words I was waiting for. At last this phrase, cherished in his heart and hidden from me all along, had been spoken after a whole week of evasions and dodges. I completely lost my temper.

'And that such a dirty, such a . . . low thought could even occur to you, Stepan Trofimovich, to your luminous mind, to your kind heart and . . . even before Liputin showed up!'

He looked at me, made no reply and began to walk on in the same direction. I didn't want to lag behind him. I wanted to bear witness in front of Varvara Petrovna. I would have forgiven him if his womanly faint-heartedness had led him simply to believe Liputin, but now it had become clear that he himself had invented everything long before Liputin, and Liputin had only confirmed his suspicions and had poured oil on the fire. He hadn't hesitated to suspect the girl from the very first day, without as yet having any grounds for it, even Liputin's. He had explained Varvara Petrovna's despotic actions to himself as merely the result of her desperate desire to gloss over the aristocratic peccadilloes of her priceless Nicolas with marriage to someone respectable! It made me yearn for him to be punished for that.

'*O! Dieu qui est si grand et si bon!*[21] Oh, who will console me!' he exclaimed, having walked another hundred steps or so, and suddenly stopped.

'Let's go home right now, and I'll explain everything to you!' I shouted, forcibly turning him in the direction of the house.

'That's him! Stepan Trofimovich, is that you? You?' A fresh, playful young voice rang out next to us, like a kind of music.

We could see nothing, but suddenly a girl on horseback appeared beside us. It was Lizaveta Nikolayevna, with her constant escort. She reined in her horse.

'Come here, do come here right away!' she called, loudly and merrily. 'I haven't seen him for twelve years but I recognized him . . . You really don't recognize me?'

Stepan Trofimovich grasped the hand she had extended to him, and gave it a reverential kiss. He looked at her as if in prayer, and could not utter a word.

'He recognized me and he's glad! Mavriky Nikolayevich, he's ecstatic at seeing me! Why haven't you come to visit these two whole weeks? My aunt's been trying to convince me that you've been sick and couldn't be disturbed; but I knew she was lying, you see. I kept stamping my feet and scolding you, but I really wanted, I really did want you to call on us first, and that's why I didn't send for you. Good heavens, he hasn't changed at all.' She was examining him as she leaned down from the saddle. 'It's funny how much he hasn't changed! Oh, no, there are some tiny wrinkles, many tiny wrinkles around the eyes and on the cheeks, and there's some grey hair, but the eyes are the same! And have I changed? Have I? But why don't you say something?'

At that moment I recalled the story of how she had been almost ill when she was taken off to Petersburg at the age of eleven; during her illness she supposedly kept crying and asking for Stepan Trofimovich.

'You . . . I . . .' he was now babbling, his voice breaking with joy. 'I had just shouted: "Who will console me?" – and then your voice rang out. I consider this a miracle *et je commence à croire.*'

'*En Dieu? En Dieu, qui est là-haut et qui est si grand et si bon?* You see, I remember all your lectures by heart. Mavriky

Nikolayevich, what faith he taught me then *en Dieu, qui est si grand et si bon*! And do you remember your stories of how Columbus was on his way to discovering America, and how everyone began to shout: "Land, land!" My nurse Alyona Frolovna says that after that I was delirious all night and shouted in my sleep: "Land, land!" And do you remember how you told me the story of Prince Hamlet? And do you remember how you described the way the poor emigrants were transported from Europe to America? It wasn't true, any of it, I found out later how they were transported; but how well he lied to me then, Mavriky Nikolayevich, it was almost better than the truth! Why are you looking at Mavriky Nikolayevich like that? He's the best and most faithful man on the face of the earth, and you absolutely must come to love him the same way you love me! *Il fait tout ce que je veux.*[22] But, dear, dear Stepan Trofimovich, does it mean you're unhappy again, if you're shouting in the street for someone to console you? You're unhappy, isn't that so? Isn't that so?'

'Now I'm happy . . .'

'Is my aunt being mean to you?' she went on without listening. 'The same wicked, unjust aunt who's so priceless to us! And do you remember how you used to throw yourself into my arms in the garden, and I tried to soothe you and cried – why, don't be afraid of Mavriky Nikolayevich: he knows everything about you, he's known for a long time, you can cry on his shoulder all you want, and he'll stand there as long as you want! . . . Remove your hat, take it off for just a minute, raise your head, stand on your tiptoes, I'll give you a kiss on the forehead right now, just the way I kissed you the last time, when we were saying goodbye. Look, that young lady is admiring us from the window . . . Well, come closer, closer. Good heavens, how grey he's become!'

And, leaning forward in the saddle, she kissed him on the forehead.

'Well then, now let's go to your house! I know where you live. I'll be there right away, this very minute. I'll make the first visit to you, you stubborn man, and then I'll drag you back to my place for the entire day. Get a move on, prepare to meet me.'

And she galloped off with her escort. We went back. Stepan Trofimovich sat down on the sofa and began to cry.

'*Dieu! Dieu!*' he exclaimed. '*Enfin une minute de bonheur!*'[23]

No more than ten minutes later she appeared as promised, accompanied by her Mavriky Nikolayevich.

'*Vous et le bonheur, vous arrivez en même temps!*'[24] He rose to greet her.

'Here's a bouquet for you: I've just been to Madame Chevalier's, she'll have bouquets all winter for name-days.[25] Here's Mavriky Nikolayevich for you too, please get to know each other. I did want to bring a cake instead of a bouquet, but Mavriky Nikolayevich assures me that it's not in the Russian spirit.'

This Mavriky Nikolayevich was a captain of artillery, of about thirty-three, a tall gentleman, handsome and faultlessly correct in appearance, with an imposing and, at first glance, even stern face, despite a surprising sensitivity and kindness, of which everyone became aware from virtually the first moment of making his acquaintance. However, he didn't have much to say, was very cool and composed, and didn't put himself out to make friends. Later many people here said that he was none too bright; but that was not entirely justified.

I will not try to describe Lizaveta Nikolayevna's beauty. The whole town was already singing the praises of her beauty, although certain of our ladies and young girls indignantly disagreed with those who were doing the singing. There were some among them, too, who had already conceived a hatred of Lizaveta Nikolayevna, first of all for her pride: the Drozdovs had hardly begun to pay any visits, which offended people, although the obvious reason for the delay was actually the poor state of Praskovya Ivanovna's health. In the second place, they hated her for being a relative of the governor's wife; in the third place, for going horseback riding every day. Before this there had never yet been any horsewomen in our town; naturally, the appearance of Lizaveta Nikolayevna on horseback and not paying visits was bound to offend society. True enough, everyone already knew that she went riding on her doctor's orders; even so, they talked sarcastically about her sickly condition.

She really was sick. The one feature that stood out at first glance was her sickly, nervous, constant restlessness. Alas! The poor girl was suffering a great deal, and everything became clear later on. Now, as I remember the past, I would no longer say that she was as much of a beauty as she then seemed to me. Perhaps she was not even good-looking at all. Tall, slender, but supple and strong, she was rather striking by virtue of the irregularity of the lines of her face. Her eyes were set somewhat like a Kalmyk's,[26] at a slant; she was pale, with prominent cheekbones, and her face was dark complexioned and thin; but there was something triumphant and attractive about that face! A certain power showed forth in the burning glance of her dark eyes; she looked as if she had come as a conquerer and to conquer. She seemed proud, and sometimes even cheeky; I don't know whether she succeeded in being kind; but I do know that she desperately wanted to be, and took great pains to compel herself to be somewhat kind. There were, of course, many splendid impulses in her nature, and she undertook many very admirable things; but everything in her seemed constantly to be seeking its level without finding it, everything was in a state of chaos, agitation, restlessness. Perhaps her demands on herself had been too severe, and she never could find in herself the strength to satisfy these demands.

She sat down on the sofa and looked around the room.

'Why do I become so melancholy at moments like these – can you work that out, my learned friend? My entire life I have thought that I would be heaven knows how happy when I saw you and recalled everything, and now here I am apparently not happy at all, despite the fact that I love you ... Oh, Lord, my portrait is hanging on his wall! Give it here, I remember it, I remember!'

The superb miniature watercolour portrait of a twelve-year-old Liza had been sent to Stepan Trofimovich from Petersburg by the Drozdovs some nine years previously. Since then it had always hung on his wall.

'Was I really such a pretty child? Is that really my face?'

She stood up, and with the portrait in her hands, looked at herself in the mirror.

'Take it immediately!' she exclaimed, handing back the portrait. 'Don't hang it now, but later; I don't want to look at it.' She sat down again on the sofa. 'One life has passed, a second has begun, then the second one has passed, and a third has begun – and so on, until it's all over. It clips all the ends off, as if with scissors. You see what old things I'm telling you, yet there's so much truth in them!'

She looked at me with a smile; she had already glanced at me several times, but Stepan Trofimovich in his agitation had simply forgotten that he had promised to introduce me.

'And why is my portrait hanging there under those daggers? And why do you have so many daggers and sabres?'

In fact, hanging on his wall, I don't know for what purpose, were two crossed Turkish daggers and above them a genuine Circassian[27] sabre. As she was asking, she looked at me so directly that I was on the point of answering her question, but I stopped short. Stepan Trofimovich finally caught on and introduced me.

'I know, I know,' she said, 'I'm very glad. Mother has also heard a great deal about you. Let me introduce you to Mavriky Nikolayevich as well. He's a splendid fellow. I've already formed an amusing notion of you; aren't you Stepan Trofimovich's confidant?'

I flushed.

'Oh, please excuse me, I went and used the wrong word; I didn't mean "amusing" at all, it just . . .' (She turned red and grew flustered.) 'However, why feel ashamed of being a splendid person? Well, time for us to go, Mavriky Nikolayevich! Stepan Trofimovich, I want you to be at our house in half an hour. Heavens, how much we'll talk! Now I'm the one who's your confidante, and regarding everything, *regarding everything*, do you understand?'

Stepan Trofimovich took fright immediately.

'Oh, Mavriky Nikolayevich knows everything; don't be embarrassed in front of him!'

'What is it that he knows?'

'Why, what do you mean!' she exclaimed in astonishment. 'Look, it's perfectly true that they're hiding things! I didn't want to believe it. They're also hiding Dasha. My aunt wouldn't let me in to see Dasha this morning, she says she has a headache.'

'But . . . but how did you find out?'

'Oh, my heavens, the same way as everyone else! It doesn't take much!'

'Do you really mean everyone?'

'Why, of course! Mother, to be sure, first found out about it through Alyona Frolovna, my nurse. Your Nastasya had run to tell her. Are you the one who told Nastasya? She says that you told her yourself.'

'I . . . I said once . . .' Stepan Trofimovich babbled, all flushed, 'but . . . I merely hinted . . . *j'étais si nerveux et malade et puis . . .*'[28]

She burst out laughing.

'So your confidant wasn't close to hand, as it happened, but Nastasya turned up – well, that's all I need to hear! And that one has a whole town full of gossips! Well, enough of that, now, it really makes no difference: let them know, it's even better that way. Come to see us as soon as you can, we dine early. Oh, I forgot.' She sat down again. 'Listen, what is Shatov all about?'

'Shatov? He's Darya Pavlovna's brother . . .'

'I know he's her brother, you don't have to tell me that, really!' she interrupted him impatiently. 'I want to know what he's all about, what kind of person he is.'

'*C'est un pense-creux d'ici. C'est le meilleur et le plus irascible homme du monde . . .*'[29]

'I myself have heard that he's rather strange. But that's not what I'm asking about. I've heard that he knows three languages, including English, and can do literary work. If that's the case, I have a lot of work for him: I need an assistant, and the sooner the better. Does he take on work or not? He's been recommended to me . . .'

'Oh, certainly, *et vous fairez un bienfait . . .*'[30]

'I'm not doing it as a *bienfait*; I need an assistant for myself.'

'I know Shatov rather well,' I said, 'and if you entrust me with a message to him, I'll go to him this very minute.'

'Tell him to come to me tomorrow at noon. Wonderful! Thank you. Mavriky Nikolayevich, are you ready?'

They drove off. Naturally, I started to Shatov's immediately.

'*Mon ami!*' Stepan Trofimovich caught up with me on the porch. 'Be here without fail at ten or eleven o'clock, when I return. Oh, I feel extremely, extremely guilty about you and . . . about everyone, about everyone.'

8.

I didn't find Shatov at home. I dropped by two hours later – he still wasn't there. Finally, when it was already past seven, I set off, either to catch him or leave him a note; once again, I didn't find him in. His apartment was locked, and he lived alone, with no servant. It crossed my mind that I should go downstairs and knock on Captain Lebyadkin's door, to ask about Shatov; but everything there was locked too, and there was no sound or glimmer of light from inside, as if the place were empty. The stories I'd heard that morning piqued my curiosity, as I walked past Lebyadkin's door. Finally, though, I decided to drop by very early the next morning. In all honesty, I didn't put much trust in a note; Shatov might ignore it, he was so stubborn and shy. Cursing my bad luck, I was already on my way through the gate when I suddenly bumped into Mr Kirillov; he was coming into the house and saw me first. Since he was the one who started asking questions, I proceeded to give him the general picture of everything, and to tell him that I had a note.

'Let's go,' he said, 'I'll arrange everything.'

I remembered that Liputin had told us that he had rented the wooden house in the yard that very morning. It was too big for him, and some deaf old woman, who saw to his needs, lived there too. The landlord lived in his other house, a new one in another street, where he kept a tavern, and this old woman, who seemed to be a relative of his, stayed behind to look after the whole of the old house. The rooms of the house in the yard were rather clean, but the wallpaper was dirty. In the room we entered, the furniture had been collected from here and there, was all of different sizes and styles, and utterly worthless: two card tables, an alderwood chest of drawers, a large plank table from some peasant hut or kitchen, chairs and a sofa with latticed backs and hard leather cushions. One corner held an ancient icon,[31] in front of which the old woman had lit a lamp before we came in, and on the walls hung two large dark oil portraits: one of the late Emperor Nikolay Pavlovich,[32] which had been executed, to judge by the face, in the 1820s, the other depicting some bishop.

On entering the room, Mr Kirillov lit a candle and took an envelope, sealing wax and a crystal seal out of his valise, which was standing in a corner and hadn't yet been unpacked.

'Seal your note and address the envelope.'

I was about to object that this wasn't necessary, but he insisted. I addressed the envelope and picked up my cap.

'But I was thinking you'd have tea,' he said. 'I bought tea. Want some?'

I didn't refuse. The old woman soon brought in the tea, that is, an enormous teapot with hot water, a small teapot with a generous brew, two large, crudely decorated earthenware cups, a kalach and a whole soup-plate of lump sugar.

'I like tea,' he said, 'at night.[33] A lot of it. I walk and I drink it till dawn. Abroad it's inconvenient to drink tea at night.'

'You go to bed at dawn?'

'Always; for a long time now. I don't eat much; it's always tea. Liputin's crafty, but impatient.'

I was surprised that he wanted to talk, and I resolved to take advantage of the moment.

'There were some unpleasant misunderstandings this morning,' I observed.

He gave an enormous frown.

'That's stupid; that's a lot of trivial stuff. It's all trivial stuff because Lebyadkin was drunk. I didn't say anything to Liputin, but just explained the trivial stuff, because he'd got things all wrong. Liputin's got a big imagination, he was making mountains instead of nonsense. Yesterday I believed Liputin.'

'And today it's me you believe?' I began laughing.

'Well, you already know about everything that happened this morning, after all. Liputin's either weak, or impatient, or harmful, or . . . he's envious.'

This last word took me aback.

'But you've created so many categories he's bound to fit one of them.'

'Or all of them together.'

'Yes, that's true, too. Liputin is chaos! Is it true what he was babbling about this morning, that you want to write something?'

'Why do you say he was babbling?' he frowned again, his eyes fixed on the floor.

I apologized and began to assure him that I wasn't prying. He flushed.

'He was speaking the truth; I am writing. Except it doesn't make any difference.'

We fell silent for a moment; suddenly he smiled the same childlike smile as this morning.

'That business with the heads – he invented it himself, took it out of a book, and at first told me himself, and he doesn't understand it very well, but I'm only looking for the reason why people don't dare kill themselves; that's all. And it makes no difference.'

'What do you mean they don't dare? Are there really so few suicides?'

'Very few.'

'Do you really find that to be so?'

He made no reply, stood up, and began walking back and forth, lost in thought.

'What is it that in your opinion deters people from suicide?' I asked.

He looked at me distractedly, as if suddenly remembering what we'd been talking about.

'I . . . I still don't know much . . . two prejudices deter them, two things; only two; one is very small, the other is very big. But even the small one is also very big.'

'Well, what's the small one, then?'

'Pain.'

'Pain? Is it really so important . . . in this case?'

'It's the very first thing. There are two kinds of people: those who kill themselves either from some great sorrow, or from anger, or the crazy ones – it amounts to the same thing . . . they do it suddenly. They don't think about pain very much, but do it suddenly. But those who do it for good reason – they think a lot.'

'Why, are there people who do it for good reason?'

'A great many. If there were no prejudice, there'd be more of them; a great many; everyone.'

'Do you really mean everyone?'

He remained silent.

'But are there really no ways of dying without pain?'

'Imagine,' he stopped in front of me, 'imagine a stone as large as a big house; it's hanging, and you're under it; if it falls on you, on your head, will you feel pain?'

'A stone as big as a house? It would be frightening, of course.'

'I'm not talking about fear; would it be painful?'

'A stone as big as a mountain, a million poods? It wouldn't be painful at all, that goes without saying.'

'But stand there in reality, and while it's hanging, you'll be very much afraid that it will be painful. Every learned scholar, every first-rate doctor, everyone, everyone will be very much afraid. Everyone will know that it's not painful, and everyone will be very much afraid that it would be painful.'

'Well then, the second reason, the big one?'

'The next world.'

'You mean punishment?'

'That doesn't matter. The next world; just the next world.'

'And you think there aren't atheists who absolutely don't believe in the next world?'

Again he remained silent.

'Perhaps you're judging by yourself?'

'Everyone can't help but judge by himself,' he said, flushing. 'Full freedom will come only when it makes no difference whether to live or not to live. That's the goal for everyone.'

'The goal? Why, then no one, perhaps, will even want to live?'

'No one,' he stated flatly.

'Man is afraid of death because he loves life, that's how I understand it,' I observed, 'and nature has ordained it so.'

'That's vile, and that's the basis of the whole deception!' His eyes began to flash. 'Life is pain, life is fear and man is unhappy. Now all is pain and fear. Now man loves life because he loves pain and fear. And that's how he's been made. Now life is given in exchange for pain and fear, and that's the basis of the whole deception. Now man is still not what he should be. There will be a new man, happy and proud. Whoever doesn't care whether he lives or doesn't live, he will be the new man. Whoever conquers pain and fear, he himself will be God. And that other God will no longer be.'

'So, that other God does exist, in your opinion?'

'He doesn't exist, but he does exist. In the stone there's no pain, but in the fear of the stone there is pain. God is the pain of the fear of death. Whoever conquers pain and fear will himself become God. Then a new life, then a new man, everything new . . . Then history will be divided into two parts: from the gorilla to the annihilation of God, and from the annihilation of God to . . .'

'To the gorilla?'

'. . . to the change of the earth and of man, physically. Man will be God and will change physically. And the world will change, and deeds will change, and thoughts, and all feelings. What do you think, will man change physically then?'

'If it doesn't matter whether one lives or doesn't live, then everyone will kill himself, and that's perhaps what the change will consist of.'

'It doesn't matter. Deception will be killed. Everyone who wants the main freedom must dare to kill himself. Whoever dares to kill himself has learned the secret of deception. There's no freedom beyond that; that's all there is, and there's nothing beyond it. Whoever dares to kill himself is God. Now everyone can do it so that there will be no God, and there will be nothing. But no one has yet done it, not even once.'

'There have been millions of suicides.'

'But never for that reason, always with fear and not for that purpose. Not to kill fear. Whoever kills himself only for the purpose of killing fear will immediately become God.'

'He won't have time, perhaps,' I observed.

'It doesn't matter,' he replied softly, with a calm pride, almost with disdain. 'I'm sorry that you seem to be laughing,' he added a few seconds later.

'I find it strange that you were so irritable this morning, and now you're so calm, even though you're speaking with some passion.'

'This morning? This morning was laughable,' he replied with a smile. 'I don't like to abuse people, and I never laugh,' he added sadly.

'Yes, you can't be very happy spending your nights drinking tea.'

I got up and took my cap.

'You think not?' He smiled in some surprise. 'Why is that? No, I . . . I don't know,' he suddenly became confused. 'I don't know how it is with other people, but I feel that I can't be like everyone else. Everyone thinks and then immediately thinks about something else. I can't think about something else, my whole life I've thought about one thing. I've been tormented by God my whole life,' he suddenly concluded, with a surprising expansiveness.

'But tell me, if you will, why do you speak such incorrect Russian? Have you actually forgotten it during your five years abroad?'

'Do I really speak incorrectly? I don't know. No, it's not because I was abroad. I've spoken this way all my life . . . it doesn't matter to me.'

'Another more delicate question: I fully believe that you're not inclined to meet with people and that you don't speak to people very much. Why have you been so chatty with me just now?'

'With you? You were sitting so nicely there this morning and you . . . but it doesn't matter . . . you are very much like my brother, extraordinarily so,' he stated, flushing. 'He's been dead for seven years; he was older – much, very much.'

'He must have had a great deal of influence on your way of thinking.'

'N-no, he didn't talk much; he didn't say anything. I'll deliver your note.'

He accompanied me as far as the gate with a lantern, so that he could lock up after me. 'Of course, he's deranged,' I decided to myself. At the gate a new encounter occurred.

9.

No sooner had I set my foot across the high sill of the gate than suddenly someone's powerful hand seized my chest.

'Who's this?' roared a voice, 'Friend or foe? Confess!'

'He's one of us, one of us!' squealed the high little voice of Liputin nearby. 'It's Mr G—v, a young man with a classical education and connections with the highest society.'

'I like him if he's connected with society, and with a good class-ic ... that means he's highly ed-u-ca-ted ... Retired Captain Ignat Lebyadkin, at the service of the world and his friends ... provided they're true, true, the scoundrels!'

Captain Lebyadkin, who was over six feet tall, portly, fleshy, curly-haired, ruddy and extremely drunk, was barely able to remain on his feet in front of me and was having difficulty articulating his words. I had seen him before, however, at a distance.

'Ah, and this one too!' he roared again, noticing Kirillov, who had not yet walked away with his lantern. He made to raise his fist, but immediately lowered it.

'I forgive you for your learnedness! Ignat Lebyadkin – highly ed-u-ca-ted ...

> A cannon ball of love aflame
> Burst in Ignat's tender soul.
> And, armless, now in bitter pain
> He wept once more for Sevastopol.[34]

Even though I was never in Sevastopol and I'm not even one-armed, still – just listen to the rhymes!' He thrust his drunken mug up close to me.

'The gentleman has no time, no time, he's on his way home,' Liputin said cajolingly, 'the gentleman will tell Lizaveta Nikolayevna tomorrow.'

'Lizaveta!' he began howling again, 'Stop, don't move! A variant:

> The star of all the girls who ride
> Their steeds, aristocratic child,
> You deign on me while still astride
> To lean down and bestow a smile.

"To a Star-Horsewoman". Now that's a hymn if ever I heard one! It's a hymn, if you're not a complete ass! The drones wouldn't understand it! Wait!' He caught hold of my overcoat, even though I was trying to push through the gate with all my strength. 'Tell her I'm a knight of honour, and Dashka ... Dashka I can ... with two fingers ... she's a serf-girl and doesn't dare ...'

At this point he fell, because I forcibly wrenched myself out of his hands and started running down the street. Liputin followed in my tracks.

'Aleksey Nilych will pick him up. Do you know what I just found out from him?' he was jabbering breathlessly. 'Did you hear those verses? Well, he's had those same verses, "To a Star-Horsewoman", printed, and is sending them tomorrow to Lizaveta Nikolayevna over his own signature. What a fellow!'

'I'll bet you were the one who put him up to it.'

'You lose!' Liputin began laughing away. 'He's in love, he's as smitten as a cat, and do you know that it all began with hatred. At first he conceived such a hatred for Lizaveta Nikolayevna on account of her horseback riding that he almost cursed her out loud on the street; and what's more, he did curse her! Just two days ago he swore at her when she was riding by. Luckily, she didn't hear him, and suddenly today he's writing poetry! Do you know that he wants to risk proposing to her? Seriously, seriously!'

'I'm surprised at you, Liputin, wherever something vile is going on you seem to be right on the spot, directing and managing everything!' I muttered in a fury.

'Come now, you're going too far, Mr G—v; maybe your

tender little heart's skipped a beat or two, in fear of a rival, eh?'

'Wha-a-at?' I shouted, coming to a stop.

'Well then, as a punishment I'm not going to say another word to you! And how you'd love to hear more, right? Just one thing: this idiot isn't an ordinary captain, but a landowner of our province, and a rather important one at that, because just a few days ago Nikolay Vsevolodovich sold him his entire estate, along with his two hundred serfs, and that's God's truth, I'm not lying! I've just found out – and from a most reliable source. Well, now go ahead and poke around for the rest yourself, I'll say no more. Goodbye!'

10.

Stepan Trofimovich was waiting for me in hysterical impatience. It had already been almost an hour since he had returned. I found him in what seemed to be a drunken state. For the first five minutes, at least, I thought he was drunk. Alas, his visit to the Drozdovs had unhinged him completely.

'*Mon ami*, I've completely lost the thread of things ... Lise ... I love and respect that angel as before, exactly as before; but it seems to me that they were both waiting for me solely to worm something out of me, that is, simply to drag it out of me, and then just send me on my merry way ... That's how it was.'

'Shame on you!' I couldn't keep from exclaiming.

'My friend, I'm now completely alone. *Enfin, c'est ridicule*. Just imagine, everything's simply teeming with mysteries there, too. They just swooped down on me about those noses and ears, and about some other Petersburg mysteries. It's only here, you know, that both of them learned for the first time about the incidents involving Nicolas four years ago here. "You were here, you saw that he was out of his mind, didn't you?" And where this idea came from, I don't understand. Why is Praskovya so keen on Nicolas's being out of his mind? This woman is really keen on it, really keen! *Ce* Maurice, or what do they call him, Mavriky Nikolayevich, *brave homme tout de même*,[35] can it really be in his interest, and after she herself was the first to write from Paris to *cette pauvre amie . . . Enfin*, this Praskovya, as *cette chère amie* calls her, she's a type: she's Gogol's immortal Korobochka,[36] except she's a malicious Korobochka, a hot-tempered Korobochka and in an infinitely magnified form.'

'Well then, that would make her a trunk. Is she really a magnified version?'

'All right, then, a smaller version, it doesn't matter, only don't interrupt me, because all this is whirling around in my head. They're completely at daggers drawn there, except Lise; she's just the same, with her "Auntie, Auntie", but Lise is crafty, and there's still something going on there. Mysteries. But they did have a falling out with the old woman. *Cette pauvre* Auntie, it's true, tyrannizes everyone . . . and then there's the governor's wife too, and disrespect on the part of society, and disrespect on the part of Karmazinov; and then suddenly this idea about madness, *ce Lipoutine, ce que je ne comprends pas* and – and they say she's wet her head with vinegar,[37] and then there's you and I as well, with our complaints and our letters . . . Oh, how I have tormented her, and at such a time! *Je suis un ingrat!*[38] Just imagine, I come back and I find a letter from her; read it, read it! Oh, how despicable it was of me!'

He handed me the letter he had just received from Varvara Petrovna. She seemed to have had second thoughts about her 'Stay home' of that morning. The note was polite, yet decisive and brief. She was asking Stepan Trofimovich to come and see her the day after tomorrow, on Sunday, at exactly twelve o'clock, and advised him to bring along one of his friends (my name was in parentheses). On her part, she promised to summon Shatov, as Darya Pavlovna's brother. 'You can receive a final answer from her, will that be enough for you? Is this the formality you were so eager to obtain?'

'Note the irritable phrase about formality at the end. Poor woman, poor woman, my lifelong friend! I admit that I felt crushed by this *sudden* decision about my fate . . . I admit that I continued to nurture some hope, and now *tout est dit*, and I do know that it's all over: *c'est terrible*.[39] Oh, would that this

Sunday should never come, and that everything should be as of old: you would have come to see me, and I would have been here . . .'

'You've been unhinged by all those vile things, all that gossip from Liputin this morning.'

'My friend, you've just put your friendly finger on another painful spot. In general, these friendly fingers are pitiless, and sometimes clumsy, *pardon*, but would you believe it, I have almost forgotten about all that, about the nasty things, I mean – that is, I haven't actually forgotten, but through my stupidity, all the time I was at Lise's, I tried to be happy and tried to convince myself that I was happy. But now . . . oh, now I'm thinking about that generous, humane woman, who is so patient when it comes to my crude shortcomings – that is to say, perhaps not entirely patient, but after all, just look at me, with my empty, horrible character! You know, I'm a capricious child, with all the egotism of a child, but without a child's innocence. For twenty years she's looked after me, like a nurse-maid, *cette pauvre* Auntie, as Lise so charmingly calls her . . . And suddenly, after twenty years, the child has taken it into his head to get married – find me a wife, find me a wife, in letter after letter, while she wets her head with vinegar, and finally I've got what I wanted, on Sunday I'll be a married man, no joking about it . . . And why was I myself so insistent, why did I write those letters? Yes, I forgot: Lise worships Darya Pavlovna, at least she says so. She says of her "*C'est un ange*, but not very forthcoming." They both advised me to marry her, even Praskovya . . . actually, Praskovya didn't advise it. Oh, the venom that's locked up in that Korobochka! What's more, Lise didn't actually advise it either: "What do you want to get married for? Your scholarly pleasures should be enough for you." She laughed heartily. I forgave her for laughing, because she has something gnawing at her heart, too. However, she says, "You can't get along without a woman. The infirmities of your old age are approaching, and she'll tuck you in all snug, or something of the sort . . ." *Ma foi*, all the time I've been sitting here with you I have actually been thinking about myself, that Providence is sending her to me in the declining years of my turbulent life, and that she will tuck me in snugly, or something of the sort . . . *enfin*, she'll be needed to keep house. What a mess the place is, just look how everything is lying around, I ordered it to be tidied up this morning, and there's a book on the floor. *La pauvre amie* was always angry at the mess in my house . . . Oh, now her voice will no longer be heard! *Vingt ans!* And . . . and they've received anonymous letters, it seems – imagine, Nicolas has supposedly sold his property to Lebyadkin. *C'est un monstre;*[40] *et enfin*, who is Lebyadkin anyway? Lise listens and listens – oh, how she listens! I forgave her for laughing, I saw the expression on her face as she was listening, and *ce* Maurice . . . I wouldn't want to be playing the part he is now, *brave homme tout de même*, but rather shy; however, let's forget about him . . .'

He fell silent. He was tired and befuddled, and sat with his head down, staring at the floor with tired eyes. I took advantage of this interlude to tell him about my visit to Filippov's house, while expressing my opinion curtly and dryly, that Lebyadkin's sister (whom I'd never seen) could in fact have once been one of Nicolas's victims during the enigmatic period of his life, as Liputin put it, and that it was entirely possible that Lebyadkin for some reason was receiving money from Nicolas, but that was all. But as far as the gossip about Darya Pavlovna went, it was all nonsense, all attempts by that scoundrel Liputin to stretch things; at least that was what Aleksey Nilych had heatedly maintained, and there was no reason not to believe him. Stepan Trofimovich listened to my assurances until I had finished, his distracted manner suggesting that they had nothing to do with him. I also mentioned in passing my conversation with Kirillov, and added that he might very well be insane.

'He's not insane, but he's one of those people whose minds aren't very far-ranging,' he mumbled listlessly and reluctantly, or so it seemed. '*Ces gens-là supposent la nature et la société humaine autres que Dieu ne les a faites et qu'elles ne sont réellement.* People play up to them, but at least Stepan Verkhovensky does not. I used to see them in Petersburg then, *avec cette chère amie,*' (Oh, how I used to offend her then!) 'and not only did their abuse not frighten me, their praise didn't either. I will

not be afraid now either, *mais parlons d'autre chose*[41] . . . I seem
to have done a lot of dreadful things; just imagine, yesterday I
sent Darya Pavlovna a letter and . . . how I curse myself for
that!'

'Well, what did you write?'

'Oh, my friend, believe me that it was all done with the
utmost nobility of spirit. I informed her that I had written to
Nicolas, some five days previously, and also in a noble spirit.'

'Now I understand!' I exclaimed heatedly. 'And what right
did you have to put their names together like that?'

'But, *mon cher*, don't crush me completely, don't shout at
me; I'm utterly squashed as it is, like . . . like a cockroach, and
when all is said and done, I still think it was all very noble. Just
suppose that something had actually happened there . . . *en
Suisse*[42] . . . or was beginning to happen. I felt an obligation to
question their hearts beforehand, in order . . . *enfin*, in order
not to constrain their hearts and not become an obstacle in
their path . . . My motives were strictly noble.'

'Oh heavens, what a stupid thing you've done!' unwittingly
burst from me.

'Stupid, stupid!' he repeated, even eagerly. 'You have never
said anything more intelligent, *c'était bête, mais que faire, tout
est dit*.[43] I will get married all the same, albeit for "another
man's sins", and so what was the point of writing even? Isn't
that so?'

'You're back at the same old thing!'

'Oh, don't try to frighten me with your shouting now, the
old Stepan Trofimovich no longer stands before you. He is dead
and buried; *enfin, tout est dit*. And what are you shouting for
anyway? Only because you yourself are not getting married and
will not have to wear a certain ornament on your head. Does
this grate on you again? My poor friend, you don't know
women, whereas I've done nothing else but study them. "If you
want to conquer the entire world, conquer yourself" – that's
the only thing that another man like yourself, a romantic,
Shatov, my fiancée's brother, has succeeded in saying well. I
gladly borrow his maxim. Well. Here I am, ready to conquer
myself by getting married, while wondering what I shall gain

instead of the whole world. Oh my friend, marriage is the moral death of any proud soul, of any independence. Married life will corrupt me, will take away my energy and my courage in the service of the institution; children will come along, though perhaps not mine, that is, of course not mine; a wise man is not afraid to look the truth in the face ... This morning Liputin proposed that I save myself from Nicolas by erecting barricades; he's stupid, that Liputin. A woman will deceive the all-seeing eye itself. *Le bon Dieu*,[44] in creating woman, of course knew what he was subjecting himself to, but I am convinced that she herself interfered in it and forced him to create her in such a form and ... with such attributes; otherwise, who on earth would wish to take such troubles on himself for nothing? Nastasya, I know, will probably be very angry with me for such freethinking, but ... *Enfin, tout est dit.*'

He would not have been running true to form if he had dispensed with the sort of cheap, freethinking witticism that had been so much in vogue in his time, but at least on this occasion he consoled himself with the semblance of a witticism, though not for long.

'Oh, why could this day after tomorrow, this Sunday, not come to pass at all!' he suddenly exclaimed, but now in utter despair. 'Why could there not be at least this one week without a Sunday, *si le miracle existe*? Now, what would it cost Providence to strike from the calendar just one Sunday, if only to prove his power to an atheist, *et que tout soit dit*![45] Oh, how I have loved her! Twenty years, all these twenty years, and she never understood me!'

'But who is it you're talking about; I don't understand you!' I asked in surprise.

'*Vingt ans!* And she hasn't understood me once, oh, that's cruel! And does she really think that I'm getting married out of fear, out of need? Oh, shame! Auntie, Auntie, I'm doing it for you! ... Oh, let her find out, this Auntie, that she is the only woman whom I have adored for twenty years! She must find out about this; otherwise it won't come to pass, otherwise they'll have to use force to drag me under *ce qu'on appelle le*[46] wedding crown!'

This was the first time I had heard this confession, and so vigorously uttered. I won't hide the fact that I had a horrible urge to burst out laughing. I was wrong.

'He is the only one, the only one who remains to me now, my only hope!' He suddenly clasped his hands, as if unexpectedly struck by a new thought. 'Now he alone and only he, my poor boy, will save me, and – oh, why doesn't he come! Oh my son, oh my Petrusha . . . and even though I am unworthy of the name of father – tiger would be better – but . . . *laissez-moi, mon ami*, I am going to lie down for a while, to collect my thoughts. I am so tired, so very tired, and I think it's time for you to go to bed too, *voyez-vous*,[47] it's twelve o'clock . . .'

CHAPTER 4

The Crippled Woman

I.

Shatov didn't baulk and, in response to my note, he appeared at Lizaveta Nikolayevna's at noon. We went in almost at the same time; I had also come to pay my first call. All of them, that is, Liza, her mother and Mavriky Nikolayevich, were sitting in the large drawing room having an argument. Mother was demanding that Liza play some waltz for her on the piano, and when she began to play the waltz that had been demanded, her mother started insisting that it was not the right one. Mavriky Nikolayevich, in his innocence, stood up for Liza and began insisting that the waltz was the right one; the old woman burst out crying in anger. She was ill and even walking was difficult. Her legs were swollen, and for several days now she had done nothing but act up and nag everyone, despite the fact that she was always a little afraid of Liza. She brightened up when we came in. Liza blushed in pleasure, and after saying *merci* to me, of course, for bringing Shatov, she went up to him and studied him with curiosity.

Shatov paused awkwardly in the doorway. After thanking him for coming, she led him up to her mother.

'This is Mr Shatov, whom I was telling you about, and here is Mr G—v, a great friend of mine and Stepan Trofimovich's. Mavriky Nikolayevich also made their acquaintance yesterday.'

'And which one is the professor?'

'There's no professor here at all, maman.'

'No, there is, you said yourself that there would be a professor; this must be the one.' She pointed at Shatov disapprovingly.

'I certainly never told you that there would be a professor.

Mr G—v is in the civil service, and Mr Shatov is a former student.'

'Student, professor – they're both from a university. All you want to do is argue. But there was a Swiss with a moustache and a beard.'

'Maman always calls Stepan Trofimovich's son a professor,' said Liza, leading Shatov away to the sofa at the other end of the drawing room.

'When her legs are swollen, she's always like this; she's sick, you understand,' she whispered to Shatov, while continuing to study him with the same extraordinary curiosity, especially his unruly lock of hair.

'Are you a military man?' The old woman turned to me, after both of us had been so pitilessly abandoned by Liza.

'No, ma'am, I'm in the civil service . . .'

'Mr G—v is a great friend of Stepan Trofimovich's,' Liza immediately responded.

'Do you serve under Mr Verkhovensky? He's also a professor, isn't he?'

'Oh, maman, you must dream of professors all night long,' Liza cried in annoyance.

'There are far too many of them when I'm awake. And you're always saying something to contradict your mother. Were you here when Nikolay Vsevolodovich came to visit four years ago?'

I replied that I was.

'And was there some Englishman with you?'

'No, there wasn't.'

Liza began to laugh.

'Ah, you see, there was no Englishman at all, so it's just a lot of talk. Both Varvara Petrovna and Stepan Trofimovich tell lies. What's more, everyone tells lies.'

'It was yesterday Auntie and Stepan Trofimovich discovered what they thought was some resemblance between Nikolay Vsevolodovich and Prince Harry, in Shakespeare's *Henry the Fourth*, and maman's reply to that is there was no Englishman here,' Liza explained to us.

'If there was no Harry, then there was no Englishman. It was just Nikolay Vsevolodovich being mischievous.'

'I assure you that maman is saying this on purpose,' Liza found it necessary to explain to Shatov. 'She knows very well about Shakespeare. I myself read her the first act of *Othello*;[1] but she's suffering a great deal just now. Maman, listen, the clock's striking twelve; it's time to take your medicine.'

'The doctor is here.' The maid appeared in the doorway.

The old woman half rose and began to call the dog. 'Zemirka, Zemirka, you'll come with me at least.'

The disgusting old lapdog Zemirka didn't obey and crawled under the couch where Liza was sitting.

'You don't want me? Then I don't want you. Farewell, dear sir, I don't know your name and patronymic,' she turned to me.

'Anton Lavrentyevich . . .'

'Well, it doesn't matter, with me it goes in one ear and out the other. Don't see me out, Mavriky Nikolayevich, Zemirka was the only one I was calling. I can still walk by myself, praise God, and tomorrow I'll go for a stroll.'

She walked out of the drawing room in anger.

'Anton Lavrentyevich, you talk with Mavriky Nikolayevich in the meantime. I assure you that you'll both profit if you get to know one another better,' said Liza, and she bestowed a friendly smile on Mavriky Nikolayevich, who began to glow all over as she looked at him. And, with no choice in the matter, I was left to talk with him.

2.

Liza's business with Shatov, to my surprise, did indeed turn out to be purely literary. I don't know why, but I kept thinking that she had invited him for some other reason. We, that is, Mavriky Nikolayevich and I, on seeing that they weren't hiding from us and were speaking very loudly, began to listen. Then they invited us to join the conference as well. It all boiled down to this: Lizaveta Nikolayevna had long been planning to publish a certain book, which, as she saw it, would be useful; but owing to her complete lack of experience, she needed a collaborator. The serious manner in which she undertook to explain her plan to Shatov even astonished me. 'She must be one of the new people,'[2] I thought. 'She wasn't in Switzerland for nothing.' Shatov was listening attentively, his eyes fixed on the floor and without showing the slightest surprise that a scatter-brained young society lady should be taking up matters that were seemingly so unsuited to her.

The literary undertaking[3] was of the following nature. In Russia a great many newspapers and other periodicals are published in the capitals and the provinces, and every day a great many events are reported in them. When the year was over, the newspapers were stacked in cupboards everywhere, or turned into litter, torn up, and used for wrappers and hats. Many published facts make an impression and remain in the public's memory, but then are forgotten as the years pass. Many people would subsequently like to consult them, but what a dreadful task it was to plough through this sea of pages, often having no idea of the day, or the place, or even the year in which the event occurred. Meanwhile, if all these facts for an entire year were to be compiled in a single book, following a certain plan and a certain theme, with headings, references and categories according to months and days, then such a compilation, all in one place, would serve as an outline of the characteristics of Russian life for an entire year, even though an extremely small percentage of the facts would be published in comparison with everything that had happened.

'Instead of a great many pages, the result would be several thick books, that's all,' Shatov observed.

But Lizaveta Nikolayevna hotly defended her scheme, despite her difficulty and her inadequacy in expressing herself. There ought to be only one book, not even very thick, she insisted. But even supposing it were thick, it would be clear, because the main thing was the plan and the way the facts were presented. Of course, not everything could be collected and reprinted. Official decrees, government acts, local ordinances, laws – all were very important facts, to be sure, but facts of this kind could be omitted altogether from her proposed publication. One could omit a great deal and limit oneself just to a selection of the events which more or less reflected the personal moral life of the people, the personality of the Russian people at a given moment. Of course, everything could go in: curious incidents, fires, donations, all kinds of good and bad things, all kinds of statements and speeches, perhaps even reports of floods, perhaps even certain government decrees as well, but only things that depicted the times should be selected from all this. Everything included would reflect a certain point of view, a direction, an intention, an idea that illuminates the facts as a whole, the sum total. And finally, the book should be interesting even as light reading, not to speak of the fact that it should be essential as a reference tool! This would be, so to speak, a picture of the spiritual, moral inner life of Russians over the course of an entire year. 'Everyone should buy it, the book should become a household item everywhere,' Liza affirmed. 'I understand that it's all a matter of the way it's planned, and that's why I'm turning to you,' she concluded. She was flushed with excitement, and even though her explanations were unclear and incomplete, Shatov began to understand.

'So, the result would be something with a tendency, a selection of facts according to a certain tendency,' he murmured, still without raising his head.

'Not at all. It won't be necessary to select things according to a tendency, and no tendency is needed. Just impartiality – that's the tendency.'

'Well, a tendency isn't such a bad thing,' Shatov began to stir. 'Besides, it can't be avoided, the moment any principle of selection becomes evident. The very selection of facts will indicate how they are to be understood. Your idea isn't bad.'

'So, you're saying that such a book is possible?' said Liza happily.

'We'll have to wait and see, and give it some thought. It's an enormous undertaking. You won't be able to come up with everything all at once. Experience is necessary. Why, even when it comes time to publish the book, we will probably not yet have figured out how to publish it. Only after many trials; but I'm beginning to get the idea. The idea is useful.'

Finally, he raised his eyes, and they began to shine with pleasure, so great was his interest.

'Did you think this up all by yourself?' he asked Liza affectionately and somewhat bashfully.

'Why, to think it up was no trouble, the basic plan was the trouble,' Liza smiled. 'I don't understand very much, I'm not very intelligent and I pursue only things that are clear to me . . .'

'You pursue them?'

'That's probably not the right word?' Liza inquired quickly.

'Perhaps it is the right word; I don't object to it.'

'It occurred to me while I was still abroad that I, too, could be useful in some way. I have my own money, and it's just lying around, so why shouldn't I do some work for the common cause? Besides, the idea somehow suddenly came all by itself; I didn't spend any time thinking it up, and I was very happy about it; but now I've come to see that it can't be done without a collaborator, because I don't know how to do anything on my own. The collaborator would of course become co-publisher of the book. We would go halves: yours would be the planning and the work, and mine would be the original idea and the means of financing the publication. Do you think the book would pay for itself?'

'If we can dig up the right kind of plan, then the book will sell.'

'I'm advising you ahead of time that I'm not doing this to make a profit, but I would very much like the book to find an audience, and I will be proud of any profits it does make.'

'Well, what's my role in all this?'

'Why, you're the one I'm inviting to collaborate with me . . . to go halves. You'll come up with the plan.'

'What makes you think that I'm capable of coming up with a plan?'

'People have been telling me about you, and I've heard here . . . I know that you're very intelligent and . . . that you're busy with useful work and . . . that you think a lot. Pyotr Stepanovich Verkhovensky spoke about you to me in Switzerland,' she added hastily. 'He's a very intelligent person, isn't that so?'

Shatov cast a momentary, barely fleeting glance at her, but then promptly lowered his eyes.

'Nikolay Vsevolodovich has also told me a great deal about you . . .'

Shatov suddenly flushed.

'However, here are the newspapers.' Liza hastily reached over to the chair and picked up a bundle of newspapers that had already been prepared and tied up. 'Here I've tried to mark the facts to be selected and sort them out, and I've numbered them . . . you'll see.'

Shatov took the bundle.

'Take them home, look them over. Where do you live?'

'On Bogoyavlenskaya Street, in Filippov's house.'

'I know it. They say that some captain apparently lives there too, next door to you, a Captain Lebyadkin?' Liza said in the same hurried manner.

Shatov simply sat for a full minute without replying, staring at the floor, with the bundle in his outstretched hand, just as he had picked it up.

'For this sort of thing you should choose someone else. I won't be the right person for you at all,' he said, lowering his voice to virtually a whisper, in a way that was somehow frighteningly strange.

Liza flared up.

'What sort of thing are you talking about? Mavriky Nikolayevich!' she cried. 'Bring me that letter that came this morning, if you please!'

I followed Mavriky Nikolayevich over to the table.

'Take a look at this,' she suddenly turned to me, unfolding the letter in great agitation. 'Have you ever seen anything like it? Read it aloud, please. I need Mr Shatov to hear it as well.'

With no little astonishment I read the following missive aloud:

To the Perfection of the Tushina Girl.

Gracious Young Lady, Yelizaveta Nikolayevna!

Yelizaveta Tushina,
Oh, what a beautiful queen!
When side saddle with her cousin forth she rides
And breezes disport with her tresses besides,

And when in church she bows low with her mother
And blushes suffuse the face of many another,
Then I desire the joys of lawfully married pleasure,
And so I dispatch a tear to her mother and her, my treasure.
    Composed by an Unlearned Man During an Argument.

Gracious Young Lady!

I pity myself more than all others that I was not deprived of
an arm at Sevastopol for glory's sake, not having been there at
all, but instead having served out the entire campaign issuing
paltry provisions and regarding that as beneath me. You are a
goddess of antiquity, and I a nothing, but I have caught an
intimation of infinity. Look on these as verses and nothing more,
for verses are, after all, mere rubbish, and a justification of that
which in prose would be regarded as impertinence. Can the sun
be angry at the infusorian,[4] if said being composes something for
it out of a drop of water, where there are a great many like him,
if you look through a microscope? Even the high-society club in
Petersburg dedicated to the humane treatment of large animals,
rightly feeling compassion for the dog and the horse, despises
the short-lived infusorian, making no mention of it whatsoever,
because it has not grown big enough. I haven't grown big enough
either. The idea of marriage might appear incredibly funny. But
I shall soon have two hundred former souls, courtesy of a mis-
anthrope whom you despise. There is much that I can tell, and
can volunteer the documents – enough for a trip to Siberia. Don't
despise my proposal. The letter from the infusorian is of course
in verse.

    Captain Lebyadkin, your friend most lowly,
        with the leisure to move most slowly.

'This was written by a man in a drunken state, and a scoundrel!' I cried out in indignation. 'I know him!'

'I received this letter yesterday,' Liza said, flushing and
hastening to explain to us: 'I immediately understood that this
was from some idiot, and I haven't yet shown it to maman,
because I don't want to upset her even more. But if he continues
with this, then I don't know what to do. Mavriky Nikolayevich

wants to go to his place and forbid him to write. Since I was looking on you as a collaborator' – she turned to Shatov – 'and since you live there, I wanted to ask you so that I might judge what else I can expect from him.'

'A drunken man and a scoundrel!' Shatov grumbled with apparent reluctance.

'Well then, is he always so stupid?'

'Oh, no, he's definitely not stupid when he's not drunk.'

'I used to know a general who wrote verses exactly like those,' I noted with a laugh.

'It's evident even from this letter that he's in his right mind,' the taciturn Mavriky Nikolayevich interjected unexpectedly.

'He's living with a sister, they say?' Liza asked.

'Yes, with his sister.'

'They say he tyrannizes her, is that true?'

Shatov glanced at Liza again, knitted his brows and, after growling 'What business is it of mine!', moved towards the door.

'Oh, wait,' Liza exclaimed in alarm, 'wherever are you going? We still have a great deal to talk over . . .'

'What's there to talk about? I'll let you know tomorrow . . .'

'Why, about the most important thing, the printing press! Please believe me, I'm not joking, I do want to do this in all seriousness!' Liza insisted with mounting alarm. 'If we decide to publish, where then will we have it printed? Really, that's the most important question, because we won't go to Moscow for that, and the local printing press is impossible for a publication of this kind. I long ago made up my mind to set up my own printing press, perhaps in your name, and maman, I know, will permit it only if it's in your name.'

'How can you conceivably know that I could be a printer?' Shatov asked sullenly.

'Why, while we were still in Switzerland, you were expressly the one that Pyotr Stepanovich identified as able to set up a printing shop and familiar with its workings. He even wanted to give me a note for you, but I forgot.'

Shatov's face, as I now recall it, underwent a change. He remained standing for a couple of seconds longer, and suddenly walked out of the room.

Liza grew very angry.

'Does he always walk off like that?' she turned to me.

I was about to shrug my shoulders when Shatov suddenly came back in, went directly up to the table and put down the bundle of newspapers he had taken with him.

'I will not be a collaborator, I have no time . . .'

'But why, but why? You're very angry, it would seem?' Liza was asking in a distressed and pleading tone.

The sound of her voice seemed to startle him; for a few moments he scrutinized her, as if wishing to penetrate to her very soul.

'It doesn't matter,' he muttered softly, 'I don't want to . . .'

And then he was gone for good. Liza was utterly stunned, even somewhat excessively so, or so it seemed to me.

'A surprisingly strange man!' Mavriky Nikolayevich loudly observed.

3.

Of course he was 'strange', but there was a great deal about all this that was unclear. Something was lying under the surface here. I certainly didn't take this publication seriously. Then there was that stupid letter, which contained all too clearly a hint that some denunciation would be made with 'documents', and about which they all maintained a silence, talking instead about something entirely different. Finally, there was this business of the printing press and Shatov's sudden departure specifically because the conversation had turned to the printing press. This all suggested to me that something had already happened here before I'd turned up, of which I knew nothing; that, consequently, I was superfluous, and that none of this was any of my business. And it was time to go – I'd been there long enough for a first visit. I went up to Lizaveta Nikolayevna to take my leave.

She simply seemed to have forgotten that I was in the room, and remained standing in the same place at the table, immersed in thought, her head bowed and her eyes singled out a certain spot in the carpet.

'Oh, you too, goodbye,' she babbled in her habitually affectionate tone. 'Give my regards to Stepan Trofimovich, and persuade him to come and see me as soon as possible. Mavriky Nikolayevich, Anton Lavrentyevich is leaving. Forgive maman for not being able to come out and say goodbye to you . . .'

I went out, and had even walked down the stairs when a servant suddenly caught up with me on the porch.

'The mistress begs you to come back . . .'

'The mistress or Lizaveta Nikolayevna?'

'The young lady, sir.'

I found Liza no longer in the large drawing room where we had been sitting, but in an adjoining reception room. The door to the drawing room, where Mavriky Nikolayevich now remained alone, was tightly shut.

Liza smiled at me, but was pale. She was standing in the middle of the room, in obvious hesitation and obviously struggling with herself, but suddenly she took me by the hand and led me to the window, quietly and quickly.

'I want to see *her* without fail,' she whispered, looking at me with burning, powerful, impatient eyes that did not brook the slightest contradiction, 'I must see *her* with my own eyes, and I am asking for your help.'

She was in a state of utter frenzy and despair.

'Whom do you wish to see, Lizaveta Nikolayevna?' I asked in alarm.

'This Lebyadkin woman, the crippled one . . . Is it true that she's crippled?'

I was astounded.

'I have never seen her, but I've heard that she's crippled, I heard it just yesterday,' I hastened to babble with alacrity and also in a whisper.

'I must see her without fail. Could you arrange it for me today?'

I felt dreadfully sorry for her.

'That's impossible, and besides, I would have absolutely no idea of how to go about it,' I began, begging off. 'I'll go and see Shatov . . .'

'If you don't arrange it by tomorrow, then I'll go to her

myself, alone, because Mavriky Nikolayevich has refused. I am relying solely on you, and I have no one else. What I said to Shatov was stupid . . . I'm sure you're a completely honest man, and perhaps devoted to me, but please do arrange it.'

I felt a passionate desire to help her in every way.

'Here's what I'll do,' I said, after a moment's thought, 'I myself will go, and most likely, *most likely* I'll see her today! I'll arrange it so that I *will* see her, I give you my word of honour. Except, please allow me to confide in Shatov.'

'Tell him that I desire that too and that I cannot wait any longer, but that I was not deceiving him just now. He left perhaps because he is very honest and didn't like it that I seemed to be deceiving him. I wasn't deceiving him; I really do want to try to publish something and set up a printing press . . .'

'He's an honest man, an honest man . . .'

'However, if it isn't arranged by tomorrow, then I'll go myself, whatever may happen and even though everyone finds out about it.'

'I can't be here tomorrow any earlier than three o'clock,' I noted, collecting my wits somewhat.

'Three o'clock, then. So I was right in supposing yesterday, at Stepan Trofimovich's, that you are somewhat devoted to me?' She smiled, hastily pressing my hand by way of goodbye, and hurrying back to the abandoned Mavriky Nikolayevich.

I went out, feeling the weight of my promise, and not understanding what had happened. I had seen a woman in genuine despair, who was not afraid of compromising herself by confiding in a man she virtually did not know. Her womanly smile at a time that was so difficult for her, and her hint that she had already taken note of my feelings the day before, was like a stab in the heart; but I felt sorry for her, I felt sorry – that was all! Her secrets suddenly became something sacred to me, and even if anyone should begin to reveal them to me now, I think I would stop up my ears and not want to listen to any more. All I had was a presentiment of something . . . And yet I had absolutely no idea how I could arrange anything of this sort. Moreover, I still didn't know even now what exactly it was I had to arrange: a meeting, but what kind of meeting? What's more, how would I bring them together? I rested all my hopes on Shatov, although I should certainly have known in advance that he would not be any help at all. But I rushed off to see him all the same.

4.

Only that evening, when it was already past seven, did I find him at home. To my surprise, he had company – Aleksey Nilych, and another gentleman with whom I was half-acquainted, a certain Shigalyov, the brother of Virginsky's wife.

This Shigalyov must have been staying in our town for some two months by then. I don't know where he came from; all I'd heard about him was that he had published some article in a progressive Petersburg magazine. Virginsky had happened to introduce me to him on the street. Never in my life have I seen such gloom, moroseness and sullenness on a person's face. He looked as if he were anticipating the destruction of the world, not at some time in the future, according to prophecies that might not even come to pass, but as a fixed and definite thing, the day after tomorrow, let's say, precisely at 10.25 in the morning. However, on that occasion we hardly uttered a word to each other and merely shook hands with the air of two conspirators. What struck me most of all were his unnaturally large ears, long, wide, broad and sticking out in a rather peculiar way. His movements were clumsy and slow. If Liputin had in fact ever dreamed that a phalanstery could be established in our province, then this man certainly knew the day and the hour it would happen. He had produced a sinister impression on me; meeting him now at Shatov's, I was surprised, the more so since Shatov in general didn't like having company.

While still going up the stairs I could hear them talking very loudly, all three at once, and apparently quarrelling; but no sooner had I made my appearance than all three fell silent. They had been standing up while they quarrelled, and now they all suddenly sat down, so that I too had to sit. A stupid silence remained unbroken for three full minutes. Shigalyov, while recognizing me, pretended he didn't know me, and probably not out of hostility, but for no particular reason. Aleksey Nilych and I exchanged slight bows, but in silence, and without shaking hands for some reason. Shigalyov began finally to look at me sternly and with a frown, in the naive assurance that I would suddenly get up and leave. Finally, Shatov stood up from his chair, and everyone else also jumped up suddenly. They went out without saying goodbye; except that Shigalyov, still standing in the doorway, said to Shatov, who was showing him out:

'Remember that you're obliged to give an account.'

'To hell with your accounts, and I'm not obliged to any devil,' said Shatov as he showed him out, and then locked the door with the latch.

'Pipsqueaks!' he said, glancing at me and giving a kind of crooked grin.

His face had an angry look, and I found it strange that he had actually begun to speak. Until now it had usually happened that whenever I stopped by to see him (which was, however, very rarely), he would seat himself in the corner with a frown and make angry replies, and only after a long time would he fully come to life and begin speaking with pleasure. Then, when saying goodbye, he would again unfailingly frown each time, and let you out as if he were getting rid of his personal enemy.

'Yesterday I was drinking tea with that Aleksey Nilych,' I noted. 'He seems to be demented on the subject of atheism.'

'Russian atheism has never gone any further than a joke,' Shatov growled, inserting a new candle in place of the burnt-out end.

'No, this one, it seemed to me, isn't a joker; he simply doesn't seem to know how to talk, let alone try to make jokes.'

'Paper men. It's all the result of a lackeyism of thought,'[5] Shatov calmly observed, sitting down on a chair in the corner and resting the palms of both hands on his knees.

'There's also hatred here,' he stated, after a minute of silence, 'they'd be the first to be dreadfully unhappy if Russia should somehow rebuild itself, even the way they want it, and should somehow become boundlessly rich and happy. Then there would be no one for them to hate, no one to spit on, nothing to make fun of! What we have here is nothing but a boundless

animal hatred for Russia which has eaten into their organism
... And in this case there are no tears unseen by the world
behind the laughter that the world can see![6] Nothing more false
has ever yet been said in Russia than this business of invisible
tears!' he shouted almost in a rage.

'What on earth are you talking about!' I began to laugh.

'And you're a "moderate liberal",' Shatov grinned in turn.
'You know,' he rejoined suddenly, 'maybe I was talking a lot
of rot about "lackeyism of thought". You'd probably come
right back with: "You're the one who was born of a lackey, but
I'm not a lackey."'

'I wouldn't have said any such thing ... what's wrong with
you!'

'Why, don't apologize, I'm not afraid of you. At the time I
was merely born of a lackey, but now I've become a lackey
myself, the same as you. Our Russian liberal is first of all a
lackey, and is merely looking for someone's boots to clean.'

'What boots? What sort of allegory is this?'

'What sort of allegory is this! You're laughing, I see ...
Stepan Trofimovich was right when he said that I'm lying under
a stone, crushed but not squashed, and that I'm just writhing;
he made an apt comparison.'

'Stepan Trofimovich insists that you've gone crazy over the
Germans,' I laughed, 'and we have, after all, swiped something
from them and stuck it in our pockets.'

'We've taken a twenty-kopeck piece, and given back a hundred roubles of our own.'

For a minute we said nothing.

'He got that from lying around too long in America.'

'Who? What did he get from lying around?'

'I'm speaking of Kirillov. We spent four months there lying
on the floor of a hut.'

'Did you really go to America?' I asked in surprise. 'You
never said anything about it.'

'What is there to tell? The year before last three of us set out
for the United States of America on an emigrant ship with our
last remaining kopecks, "in order to try out for ourselves the
life of the American worker and in that way to learn from our

personal experience the condition of a human being in the most difficult of social conditions".[7] That was our purpose in making the trip.'

'Good Lord!' I laughed. 'Why, you would have done better to go to one of our provinces when the harvest was in full swing, in order to have "personal experience" of it, instead of dashing off to America!'

'There we hired ourselves out as labourers to an exploiter. There were six of us Russians working for him – students, landowners straight from their estates, even officers, and all with the same grand purpose. And so we worked, got soaked with sweat, suffered and wore ourselves out, until finally Kirillov and I left: we fell sick, we couldn't endure it. The exploiter, our boss, cheated us when he paid us off. Instead of the thirty dollars that had been agreed on, he paid me eight, and Kirillov fifteen. He also beat us more than once. And so then we were without work, and we lay around on a floor in some horrible little town for four straight months. He was thinking about one thing, and I was thinking about something else.'

'Did the boss really beat you; did this happen in America, of all places? How you must have cursed him!'

'Not at all. On the contrary, Kirillov and I immediately decided that "we Russians, next to the Americans, are little children and that you have to be born in America or at least spend many years living with Americans in order to rise to their level". Why, you know, when we were asked to pay a dollar for something worth just a kopeck, then we paid it, not only with pleasure, but with enthusiasm. We were full of praise for everything: spiritualism, lynch law, six-shooters, tramps. Once we were travelling, and a man reached into my pocket, took out my hairbrush[8] and began using it; all Kirillov and I did was exchange glances and decide that this was a good thing and that we liked it very much . . .'

'Strange that such things not only pop into our heads, but are actually carried out,' I observed.

'Paper men,' Shatov repeated.

'Still and all, to sail across an ocean on an emigrant ship, to an unknown land, even with the purpose of "learning from personal experience", etc., really and truly there's a certain high-minded determination about it . . . Well, how did you get away from there?'

'I wrote to a man in Europe and he sent me a hundred roubles.'

As he was speaking, Shatov kept staring at the floor, as was his habit, even when he was excited. But now he suddenly raised his head.

'Do you want to know the name of the man?'

'Who was he, then?'

'Nikolay Stavrogin.'

He suddenly stood up, turned to his lindenwood[9] writing table and began to rummage for something on it. A vague but reliable rumour was circulating among us that his wife had had an affair with Nikolay Stavrogin for some time in Paris, about two years earlier, that is, when Shatov was in America – to be sure, long after she had left him in Geneva. 'If that's the case, then whatever possessed him to come out with the name now and make so much of it?' I thought.

'I still haven't paid him back.' He suddenly turned to me again, and staring hard at me, sat down in his former place in the corner and asked curtly, now in an entirely different tone of voice:

'You came here for some reason, of course; what is it you want?'

I proceeded to relate everything, in strict chronological order, and added that although I had now had ample time to think better of it after the first flush of that morning, I was even more confused. I understood that there was something very important to Lizaveta Nikolayevna involved here, I had a strong desire to help her; the trouble was that I not only had no idea how to keep the promise I had given her, but that I now didn't even understand exactly what it was that I had promised her. Then I assured him once again, and in all seriousness, that she didn't want to deceive him and had no thought of doing so, that this was the result of some misunderstanding, and that she was very distressed by his unusual departure earlier in the day.

He heard me out very attentively.

'Perhaps I really did something stupid this morning, as I usually do ... Well, if she herself didn't understand why I left as I did, then ... so much the better for her.'

He rose, went up to the door, opened it part way and began listening for anything on the stairs.

'Do you wish to see this person for yourself?'

'I'd like to very much, but how can it be done?' I jumped up eagerly.

'Let's just go there, while she's alone. When he comes, he'll give her a dreadful beating if he finds out we've been there. I often go on the quiet. I thrashed him not long ago when he started beating her again.'

'What do you mean?'

'Just this: I dragged him away from her by his hair. He was about to give me a good thrashing, but in return I frightened him, and that was the end of it. I'm afraid he'll come back drunk and remember – and then will really let her have what for.'

We immediately went downstairs.

5.

The door to the Lebyadkins was shut and not locked, and we went in without any trouble. The whole premises consisted of two disgusting little rooms, with soot-begrimed walls, on which dirty paper was literally hanging in shreds. For several years an eating house had been maintained here, until the landlord, Mr Filippov, had moved it to his new house. The remaining rooms, located under the eating house, were now locked up, except the two that had fallen to Lebyadkin. The furniture consisted of simple benches and deal tables, except for an old easy chair that was missing an arm. Standing in the corner of the second room was a bed with a cotton spread, belonging to Mademoiselle Lebyadkina, whereas the Captain himself, when the time came for him to sleep, always collapsed on the floor, often in whatever he had been wearing. There were crumbs, litter and puddles everywhere: a large, thick rag, still wet, lay in the middle of the floor in the first room, and there too, in the very same pool of water, was an old worn-out shoe. It was obvious that no one looked after anything here: the stoves were not lit, meals were not prepared; they didn't even have a samovar, as Shatov recounted in detail. The Captain, along with his sister, had arrived utterly impoverished, and at first, as Liputin said, he actually went from house to house begging; but having unexpectedly come into some money, he promptly took to drink and completely lost his mind from wine, and was no longer capable of maintaining the house.

Mademoiselle Lebyadkina, whom I had so been wanting to see, was sitting meekly and silently in a corner of the second room on a bench, at the deal kitchen table. She didn't call out to us when we were opening the door, and didn't even stir from her place. Shatov had said that their door didn't lock, and that on one occasion it had stood wide open to the entryway all night long. By the dim light of a spindly candle in an iron candlestick, I could make out a woman of perhaps thirty, sickly and gaunt, wearing an old, dark cotton dress, her long neck uncovered and her scanty dark hair twisted at the nape of her neck into a knot as thick as the fist of a two-year-old child. She glanced at us rather happily. There on the table before her, besides the candlestick, were a small peasant-style looking glass, an old pack of cards, a tattered songbook of some kind and a white German roll, out of which one or two bites had already been taken. It was noticeable that Mademoiselle Lebyadkina used powder and rouge, and smeared something on her lips. She also darkened her eyebrows, which were long, thin and black anyway. On her narrow, high forehead, despite the powder, three long wrinkles were rather sharply etched. I already knew that she was a cripple, but on this occasion she didn't get up or walk while we were present. At some time in her early youth this emaciated face might even have been attractive; but her soft, gentle grey eyes were still remarkable even now; something dreamy and sincere shone in her gentle, almost joyful gaze. This gentle, calm joyfulness, which found expression in her smile as well, surprised me after everything I had heard about the Cossack whip and all the other enormities of her brother. It was strange that instead of the oppressive and even apprehensive revulsion that is usually felt in the presence of all such beings who have been punished by God, I almost took pleasure in looking at her from the very first moment, and only pity, certainly not revulsion, overcame me later on.

'That's how she sits, literally for days on end, all by herself, without stirring, and she tells her fortune or looks at herself in the glass,' Shatov pointed her out to me from the doorway. 'He gives her absolutely nothing to eat, you see. The old woman from the other house sometimes brings her something out of charity; how can she be left alone with just a candle!'

To my surprise, Shatov was speaking loudly, as if she were not in the room at all.

'Hello, Shatushka!' Mademoiselle Lebyadkina called out in greeting.

'I've brought you some company, Marya Timofeyevna,' said Shatov.

'Well, the company is quite welcome. I don't know whom you've brought, somehow I don't remember seeing him before.' She looked at me intently from behind the candle and immediately turned to Shatov again (and then didn't bother with me at all, during the entire conversation, as if I weren't standing there beside her).

'Have you got bored with walking around in your garret all alone?' she laughed, in the process exposing two rows of magnificent teeth.

'Got bored, and I felt like paying you a visit.'

Shatov moved a small bench up to the table, sat down and had me sit beside him.

'I'm always glad for some conversation, except I find you funny, Shatushka, you look just like a monk. When did you last comb your hair? Let me comb it for you,' she said, extracting a comb from her pocket, 'I'll bet you haven't touched it since the last time I combed it.'

'But I don't have a comb,' Shatov laughed.

'Really? Then I'll make you a present of mine; not this one, but another one, only remind me.'

She began combing his hair in a very serious manner, even

made a parting on one side, leaned back a little, looked to see whether it was right and put the comb back into her pocket.

'You know what, Shatushka,' she shook her head, 'you may be a sensible man, but you're bored. I find it strange to watch all of you. I don't understand how people can be bored. Sorrow isn't boredom. I'm happy.'

'And are you happy with your brother?'

'Are you talking about Lebyadkin? He's my lackey. And it makes absolutely no difference to me whether he's here or not. I shout at him: "Lebyadkin, bring me some water, Lebyadkin, hand me my shoes", and he runs to fetch them. Sometimes I feel like such a sinner – it's so funny to look at him.'

'And that's precisely how it is,' Shatov turned to me again, loudly and without ceremony, 'she treats him just like a lackey. I myself have heard how she shouts at him: "Lebyadkin, bring me some water", and then bursts out laughing. The only difference is that he doesn't run to fetch her water, but beats her for it. But she's not in the least afraid of him. She has some kind of nervous attacks, almost daily, and they knock out her memory, so that after them she forgets everything that's just happened, and is always confused about the time. You think she remembers our coming in? Perhaps she does remember, but it's more likely that she's refashioned everything in her own way, and now takes us for some other people, although she does remember that I'm Shatushka. It doesn't matter that I'm speaking loudly; she immediately stops listening to those who aren't speaking to her and immediately plunges into daydreams about herself; yes, literally plunges. She's an extraordinary dreamer; for eight hours on end, for an entire day she remains sitting where she is. See that roll lying there, since morning she's perhaps taken one bite from it, and she'll finish it tomorrow. Look, now she's begun to tell her fortune with the cards . . .'

'That's just what I'm doing, Shatushka, telling my fortune, but somehow it keeps coming out all wrong,' Marya Timofeyevna, on catching the last word, suddenly chimed in, and without looking, reached out with her left hand for the roll (having probably heard something about it as well). At last she grasped the roll, but after holding it for a while in her left hand and distracted by the conversation that had started up again, she laid it back down on the table, without noticing, and without having bitten off a single piece. 'The same thing keeps coming out: a road, an evil man, someone's perfidiousness, a deathbed, a letter from somewhere or other, unexpected news – it's all a bunch of lies, I think. Shatushka, how do you see it? If people tell lies, then why shouldn't cards tell lies?' She suddenly mixed up the cards. 'I said this very thing to Mother Praskovya once, an honourable woman she is, she'd always be coming by my cell for me to read some cards, in secret from the Mother Superior. And she wasn't the only one who came by. They'd "ooh" and "aah", and shake their heads, and hash and rehash everything, and I'd just be laughing away: "How do you figure on getting a letter, Mother Praskovya, if it hasn't come all these twelve years?" Her husband took her daughter away somewhere to Turkey, and there hasn't been hide nor hair of her for twelve years. Except there I am sitting the very next evening having tea with the Mother Superior (a princess by birth), there's some visiting lady sitting there too, a great dreamer, and some nice little monk visiting from Athos,[10] a pretty funny man, in my opinion. And what do you think, Shatushka, none other than this nice little monk had brought Mother Praskovya a letter from her daughter in Turkey that very morning – that's the jack of diamonds for you – totally unexpected news! And so there we are drinking tea, and the nice little monk from Athos goes and says to the Mother Superior: "Most of all, Reverend Mother Superior, the Lord has blessed your cloister with the fact that you are preserving such a valuable," he says, "treasure in its depths." "What treasure is that?" asks the Mother Superior. "Why, blessed Mother Lizaveta." And this Blessed Lizaveta is enclosed in our cloister wall, in a cage a sazhen long and two arshins high, and she's been sitting there behind an iron grating for seventeen years, winter and summer in just a hempen shift, and she keeps picking away at her shift, at her sackcloth, either with a piece of straw, or whatever twig is at hand, and she doesn't say a word, and she doesn't scratch herself, and she hasn't washed these seventeen years. In wintertime, a sheepskin coat is pushed

through to her, and every day a crust of bread and a mug of
water. The pilgrims look, ooh and ah, sigh, and put down some
money. "Some treasure they've found," the Mother Superior
answers. (She was angry: she had an awful dislike of Lizaveta.)
"Lizaveta's sitting there just out of spite, just to be stubborn,
she's just pretending." I didn't like that: in those days I was
thinking about shutting myself up too. "And in my opinion," I
say, "God and nature are all one." All of them answer me in
one voice: "Is that so!" The Mother Superior burst out laughing, began whispering to the lady about something, called me
over, was really nice to me, and the lady gave me a little pink
ribbon. If you want, I'll show it to you. Well, the little monk
started preaching at me then and there, and he talked so nice
and humble and I guess with such intelligence, I just sit and
listen. "Do you understand?" he asks. "No," I say, "I don't
understand a thing, and just leave me," I say, "in peace."
And so since then they've left me alone, in complete peace,
Shatushka. And at that time one of our little old ladies, who
was living with us as a penance for prophesying the future,
whispered to me as she was coming out of the church: "The
Virgin, what is she, do you imagine?" "The Great Mother, the
hope of the human race." "That's so," she says, "the Virgin is
Sacred Mother Earth, and in that lies great joy for mankind.
And every earthly sorrow and every earthly joy is a joy for us;
and when you have watered the earth beneath you with your
own tears to the depth of half an arshin, then you will at once
take delight in everything. And sorrow will no longer, no longer
be yours," she says, "such," she says, "is the prophecy." These
words sank into my soul at the time. Since then when I'm at
prayer, bowing to the earth, I've begun kissing the earth each
time, I actually kiss it and I weep. And I'm going to tell you
something, Shatushka: there's nothing bad in these tears; and
even though no misfortune may come your way at all, your
tears will still start to flow from pure joy. The tears flow all on
their own, that's the truth. I used to go off to the shore of the
lake. On one side is our monastery, and on the other, our
Pointed Mountain, that's what they call it, Pointed Mountain.
I would climb the mountain, turn my face to the east, fall to

the ground, weep and weep, and be unable to remember how long I'd been weeping and that's when I didn't remember anything and that's when I didn't know anything. Then I would get up and turn back, and the sun is going down – oh, so big, so gorgeous, so wonderful – do you like to look at the sun, Shatushka? It's nice, but sad. I would turn back towards the east again, and there's a shadow, a big shadow flying from our mountain over the lake, far over, like an arrow, narrow, long, oh, so long and a whole verst beyond, right up to the island in the lake, and it would cut that rocky island right in two, the whole of it; and as it's cutting it in two, the sun goes down altogether, and all the light suddenly goes out. And that's when I begin to feel very sad, that's when my memory suddenly comes back, I'm afraid of the dark, Shatushka. And what I weep for most is my little baby . . .'

'Was there really a baby?' Shatov nudged me with his elbow, all the time listening intently.

'Of course there was: little, all pink, with tiny little nails, and the only thing that makes me really sad is that I can't remember if it was a boy or a girl. Sometimes I remember it as a boy, sometimes as a girl. And when I gave birth to it, I wrapped it right up in cambric and lace, tied pink ribbons around it, scattered flowers over it, got it all ready, said a prayer over it, carried it away, even though it hadn't been christened, and carried it through the forest. I'm afraid of the forest, and I feel scared, and what I weep for most is that I gave birth to it and I don't know who my husband was.'

'Perhaps you really did have one?' Shatov asked cautiously.

'You're a funny man, Shatushka, with the way you think. I did have one, maybe I really did, but what difference does it make if I had one if it doesn't make a difference whether I didn't have one? There's an easy riddle for you, so go and figure it out!' She smiled.

'Where was it you took the baby, then?'

'I took it to the pond,' she sighed.

Again Shatov nudged me with his elbow.

'And what if you didn't have a baby at all, and all this is just your imagination?'

'It's a hard question you're asking me, Shatushka,' she replied thoughtfully and without showing the slightest surprise at such a question. 'About that I won't tell you anything, maybe I really didn't; in my opinion, it's just your curiosity; but still, I won't stop weeping over him, it wasn't just a dream, was it?' And large tears began to glisten in her eyes. 'Shatushka, Shatushka, is it true that your wife ran away from you?' She suddenly put both her hands on his shoulders and looked pityingly at him. 'Now, don't get angry, I feel sick about it myself. You know, Shatushka, here's the dream I had: he comes to me again, he beckons to me, he calls out to me: "My little puss," he says, "my puss, come to me!" It was the "little puss" that delighted me more than anything: he loves me, I thought.'

'Maybe he really will come,' Shatov muttered under his breath.

'No, Shatushka, it's just a dream . . . he won't really come. You know how the song goes:

> I don't need a tall new house,
> It's in this little cell I'll stay,
> Here I'll live and save my soul,
> And pray to God for you.[11]

Oh, Shatushka, Shatushka, my dear friend, why don't you ever ask me about anything?'

'Why, you won't tell me, that's why I don't ask.'

'I won't tell, I won't tell, for the life of me I won't tell,' she picked up on it quickly. 'You may burn me, I won't tell. And no matter how much I suffer, I won't tell anything; people won't find out!'

'Well there, you see, to each his own, then,' Shatov said even more quietly, hanging his head lower and lower.

'But if you should ask, maybe I'd tell, maybe I'd tell,' she repeated ecstatically. 'Why won't you ask? Ask me, ask me nicely, Shatushka, maybe I really will tell you; beg me, Shatushka, so that I'll go ahead and agree . . . Shatushka, Shatushka!'

But Shatushka said nothing; general silence prevailed for

about a minute. Tears were gently trickling down her powdered cheeks; she sat there, forgetting the two hands that she had placed on Shatov's shoulders and no longer looking at him.

'Oh, I can't be bothered with you, and besides, it's a sin,' Shatov said, suddenly getting up from the bench. 'You, stand up!' He angrily pulled the bench out from under me, and, lifting it, put it back in its former place.

'He'll be coming, and he shouldn't find out what's been going on; besides, it's time we were going.'

'Ah, you're still talking about my lackey!' Marya Timofeyevna suddenly began laughing. 'You're afraid of him! Well, farewell, dear guests, but listen for just a minute to what I have to say. That Nilych fellow came here this morning with Filippov, the landlord, the one with the big red beard, just as my brother came flying at me. The landlord suddenly grabs him and starts dragging him around the room, and my brother is shouting: "I'm not at fault, someone else is to blame and I'm suffering for it!" And would you believe it, we just stood there and started roaring with laughter . . .'

'Oh, Timofeyevna, why, I was the one, not the red beard; why, I was the one who pulled him away from you by his hair this morning, and the landlord came the day before yesterday and quarrelled with you; you've simply mixed things up.'

'Wait, maybe I really did mix things up, maybe it really was you. Oh, well, why quarrel about trivial things? Does it really matter to him who pulled him away?' She began to laugh.

'Let's go,' Shatov suddenly yanked me by the arm. 'The gate's squeaking; he'll catch us and beat her up.'

We didn't get all the way up the stairs before a drunken shout and a shower of oaths were heard at the gate. Shatov let me into his place, and locked the door.

'You'll have to sit for just a minute if you don't want a scene. Just listen, he's squealing like a pig, he must have stumbled over the threshold again; he falls flat on his face every time.'

However, we didn't escape without a scene.

6.

Shatov was standing by his locked door and straining to hear what was happening on the stairway. Suddenly he jumped back.

'He's coming here, I just knew it!' he whispered savagely. 'Now we probably won't get rid of him till midnight.'

Then came several powerful blows of a fist at the door.

'Shatov, Shatov, open up!' the captain began howling. 'Shatov, friend!

> I have come to you with a greeting
> To tell you the dawn has broken,
> The sun, bright and burning, is beating
> On woodlands, and birds have spoken.
> To tell you I've woken, the Devil take you,
> Come fully awake 'neath the boughs . . .

Just like 'neath birch-rods, ha, ha!

> Each little bird is thirsting.
> To tell you I'm going to drink,
> To drink . . . but I don't know what I'll drink.[12]

Oh, the Devil take your stupid curiosity! Shatov, do you understand how good it is to be alive!'

'Don't answer,' Shatov whispered to me again.

'Open up, I tell you! Do you understand there's something higher than fighting . . . among people. There are moments when a person is hon-our-able. Shatov, I'm good; I forgive you . . . Shatov, the Devil with manifestos, eh?'

Silence.

'Do you understand, you ass, that I'm in love. I've bought a set of tails, look, the tail-coat of love, for fifteen silver roubles. A captain's love requires worldly proprieties . . . Open up!' He suddenly began roaring savagely and pounding his fists on the door in another frenzy.

'Go to the Devil!' Shatov suddenly roared as well.

'Sla-a-ave! Serf, and your sister's a slave and a serf . . . a thief!'

'And you sold your sister.'

'You lie! I'm putting up with slander when with a single explanation I can . . . do you understand what kind of woman she is?'

'Who?' Shatov suddenly went up to the door, curious.

'Well, can you understand?'

'I can understand; I will, just tell me who.'

'I dare to say it! I always dare to say everything in public!'

'Well, you hardly dare,' Shatov taunted him and signalled for me to listen.

'I don't dare?'

'In my opinion, you don't dare.'

'I don't dare?'

'Well, you tell me if you're not afraid of the master's whip . . . You're just a coward, captain or no captain!'

'I . . . I . . . she . . . she is . . .' the captain began to babble in a trembling, agitated voice.

'Well?' Shatov put his ear to the door.

A silence fell, lasting at least thirty seconds.

'Scoun-drel!' finally came from behind the door, and the captain beat a hasty retreat downstairs, puffing like a samovar, and noisily stumbling on each step.

'No, he's crafty, and he won't let anything slip even when he's drunk.' Shatov moved away from the door.

'What's that all about?' I asked.

Shatov dismissed me with a wave of his hand, opened the door and again began listening on the stairs to what was happening. He listened for a long time, and even quietly walked down a few steps. Finally he came back.

'Can't hear a thing, he's not fighting with her; he must have collapsed and fallen asleep straight away. Time for you to go.'

'Listen, Shatov, what am I supposed to conclude from all this now?'

'Oh, conclude what you like!' he replied in a tired and disgusted voice and sat down at his writing table.

I left. An improbable idea was growing stronger and stronger in my imagination. I thought with anguish of the day to come.

7.

This 'day to come', that is, the very Sunday on which the fate of Stepan Trofimovich was to be irrevocably decided, was one of the most remarkable days in my chronicle. It was a day of surprises, a day of unravellings of the old and ravellings of the new, of sudden elucidations and confusion confounded. In the morning, as the reader already knows, I was obliged to accompany my friend to Varvara Petrovna's, at her own bidding, and by three o'clock in the afternoon I was supposed to be at Lizaveta Nikolayevna's, in order to tell her – I myself didn't know what – and to help her – I myself didn't know how. And meanwhile everything was settled in a way no one could have imagined. In a word, it was a day of extraordinary coincidences.

It began when Stepan Trofimovich and I appeared at Varvara Petrovna's at precisely twelve o'clock, the time appointed by her, and didn't find her at home. She hadn't yet returned from mass. My poor friend was so arranged, or, better said, so deranged that he was immediately crushed by this circumstance. In a state of virtual collapse he sank into an armchair in the drawing room. I offered him a glass of water; but despite his pallor and even a tremor in his hands, he proudly declined it. By the way, his outfit on this occasion was remarkable for its extraordinary good taste: an embroidered cambric shirt that almost looked destined for a fancy-dress ball, a white tie, a new hat in his hands, gloves the colour of fresh straw, and even the faintest hint of scent. We had no sooner sat down when in came Shatov, escorted by the butler, and obviously by official invitation. Stepan Trofimovich half-rose to extend his hand, but Shatov, after a close look at both of us, turned away into a corner, sat down there and didn't even nod his head. Stepan Trofimovich bestowed another frightened glance on me.

And so we sat for several minutes more in complete silence. Stepan Trofimovich suddenly tried to whisper something to me very rapidly, but I couldn't hear it; and then he himself was too agitated to finish it and let it go. The butler came in again to adjust something on the table, but more likely to have a look at us. Shatov suddenly turned to him and in a loud voice said:

'Aleksey Yegorych, do you know whether Darya Pavlovna went with her?'

'It pleased Varvara Petrovna to go to the cathedral by herself, and it pleased Darya Pavlovna to remain in her room upstairs, and she does not feel so very well, sir,' Aleksey Yegorych reported sententiously and decorously.

My poor friend again exchanged a fleeting and frightened glance with me, so that I at last began to turn away from him. There came the sudden rumble of a carriage at the front entrance, and a kind of distant stirring in the house announced to us that the lady had returned. We all jumped up from our armchairs, but then came another surprise: the sound of many footsteps could be heard, which meant that the lady hadn't returned alone, and that was really rather strange, inasmuch as she herself had set the time for us. Finally, there was the sound of someone coming in rapidly, as if running, and that was strange, because Varvara Petrovna would not have been coming in like that. And suddenly she virtually flew into the room, breathing heavily and extraordinarily agitated. Trailing slightly behind her, and much more quietly, came Lizaveta Nikolayevna, and arm in arm with her – Marya Timofeyevna Lebyadkina! If I had seen it in a dream, even then I wouldn't have believed it.

By way of explaining this utterly surprising turn of events, it's necessary to go back an hour and give a detailed account of the extraordinary adventure that befell Varvara Petrovna in the cathedral.

In the first place, virtually the entire town – that is, of course, the upper stratum of our society – had assembled for mass. They knew that the governor's wife would favour them by attending for the first time since she had arrived here. I will note that rumours had already begun to circulate that she was a freethinker and an adherent of 'the new principles'. It was also known to all the ladies that she would be dressed magnificently and in extremely good taste; and for that reason, the outfits of our ladies were remarkable for their elegance and splendour. Alone among them Varvara Petrovna was modestly dressed entirely in her usual black; this is the way she had routinely dressed for the past four years. After arriving at the cathedral, she established herself in her usual place, in the first row on the left, and a lackey in livery placed in front of her a velvet cushion for her to kneel on: in a word, everything was as usual. But people also noted that on this occasion she was somehow praying with unusual fervour throughout the service; they also insisted later, when they recalled everything, that she even had tears in her eyes. At last the mass came to an end, and our archpriest, Father Pavel, stepped forth to deliver the solemn homily. People in our town loved his homilies and valued them highly; they even tried to persuade him to publish them, but he never could make up his mind to do so. On this occasion, the homily somehow turned out to be especially lengthy.

And while the homily was still under way, a lady drove up to the cathedral in a light hired droshky of a bygone era, that is, of the kind where ladies could sit only sideways, holding on to the driver's belt and swaying from the jolting of the carriage, like a blade of grass in the wind. Such cabbies still drive about in our town to this day. Stopping at a corner of the cathedral – for many carriages and even mounted police were standing at the gates – the lady jumped out of the droshky and gave the cabby four silver kopecks.

'What's the matter, cabby, isn't it enough?' she cried out, seeing him make a face. 'It's all I have,' she added mournfully.

'Oh, well, God be with you, I let you get in and didn't say nothin' 'bout the cost,' the cabbie waved dismissively, and looked at her as if thinking: 'Why, 'twould be a sin to offend you', following which he thrust his leather purse inside his coat, got his horse moving and rolled off, sent on his way by the gibes of the coachmen who were standing nearby. Gibes and even astonishment accompanied the lady as well, all the time she was picking her way towards the cathedral gates between the carriages and the servants waiting the imminent emergence of their masters. And in fact everyone did find something unusual and unexpected in the sudden appearance of such an individual from Lord knows where, on the street amid the common people. She was painfully thin, walked with a limp, was heavily powdered and rouged; her long neck completely bare, without kerchief or cloak; clad only in an old dark-coloured dress, despite the cold and windy, albeit clear September day; her head completely uncovered, her hair twisted into a small knot at the nape, with only an artificial rose thrust into it on the right, of the kind used to decorate cherubim on Palm Sunday. I had noticed just such a Palm Sunday cherubim the day before in the corner, beneath the icons, wearing a crown of paper roses, when I was sitting at Marya Timofeyevna's. To top everything off, the lady, although she was walking with modestly lowered eyes, was at the same time smiling happily and slyly. If she had slowed her pace even slightly, she might not have been allowed into the cathedral. But she managed to slip through, and after entering, pushed forward inconspicuously.

Although the homily was half over, and the entire dense crowd that filled the church was listening to it with full and hushed attention, several eyes nonetheless glanced sideways in curiosity and bewilderment at the woman who had come in. She dropped on to the dais of the church, lowered her powdered face to it, lay there for a long time and was evidently weeping; but after raising her head once again, and getting up off her knees, she very quickly recovered and began to enjoy herself. Happily, and obviously with extreme pleasure, she began to run her eyes over the faces and the walls of the cathedral. She peered at the other ladies with particular curiosity, even standing on tiptoe for that purpose, and even laughed a couple of times, with a strange sort of giggle as she did so. But the homily came to an end, and the cross was carried out. The governor's wife was the first to begin walking towards the cross, but, before she had taken two steps, she paused, evidently wishing to make way for Varvara Petrovna, who on her part was moving forward unswervingly, seemingly without noticing anything in front of her. This unusual display of courtesy by the governor's wife undoubtedly concealed an obvious and clever rebuff of a sort; so it was understood by all, and so Varvara Petrovna must have understood it as well; but, without noticing anyone, as before, and with the most imperturbable expression of dignity, she applied her lips to the cross and immediately made for the exit. The lackey in livery cleared the way before her, even though everyone was already stepping aside. But just at the exit, on the porch, a densely packed throng of people blocked her way for an instant. Varvara Petrovna paused, and suddenly a strange, unusual being, a woman with a paper rose in her hair, squeezed between the people and fell on her knees before her. Varvara Petrovna, who was not easily taken aback by anything, especially in public, looked at her imposingly and sternly.

I will hasten to note here, as briefly as possible, that Varvara Petrovna, although in recent years she had become excessively thrifty, as people put it, and even rather tight, didn't at times begrudge money for strictly charitable purposes. She was a member of a charitable society in the capital. In the recent year of famine[13] she had sent to Petersburg, to the main committee for the relief of sufferers, five hundred roubles, and this was talked about in our town. Finally, and most recently, just before the appointment of the new governor, she had been on the point of founding a women's committee for aid to the very poorest of new mothers in the town and province. Among us she was heartily reproached for being ambitious; but the well-known impetuosity of Varvara Petrovna's character, combined with her fixity of purpose, almost always triumphed over obstacles. The charitable society had almost been established, and the original idea kept growing and developing in the enthusiastic mind of its founder; she was already dreaming of founding the same kind of committee in Moscow, and of the gradual spread of its activities throughout all the provinces. And then, with the sudden change of governor, everything came to a halt; and the new governor's wife, it was said, had already contrived to register in society some sarcastic and, most importantly, apt and sensible objections about the supposed impracticability of the basic idea of such a committee, which, naturally, and with embellishments, had already been passed on to Varvara Petrovna. Only God knows the depths of human hearts, but I imagine that it was with a certain pleasure that

Varvara Petrovna now paused at the very doors of the
cathedral, knowing that the governor's wife must pass by at
any moment now, followed by everyone else, and 'then let her
see for herself how little I care what she may think, and what
other sarcastic remarks she might make concerning the vanity
of my charitable works. So much for all of you!'

'What's wrong, my dear? What are you asking for?' Varvara
Petrovna peered attentively at the supplicant kneeling before
her, who was staring at her with a dreadfully apprehensive,
shamefaced but almost reverential look and suddenly laughed
with the same strange giggle.

'What does she want? Who is she?' Varvara Petrovna swept
a commanding and inquiring look across the assembled company. All remained silent.

'Are you unhappy? Are you in need of assistance?'

'I'm in need of . . . I have come . . .' babbled the 'unfortunate
one' in a voice breaking with emotion. 'I've come only to kiss
your hand', and she giggled again. With an utterly childlike
look, which children assume when they are trying to wheedle
something out of someone, she reached forward to grasp Varvara Petrovna's hand, but suddenly pulled back her hands as if
frightened.

'Is that all you've come for?' Varvara Petrovna gave a com-
passionate smile, but promptly extracted her mother-of-pearl
purse from her pocket, and from it a ten-rouble note which she
handed to the unknown woman. She took it. Varvara Petrovna
was very interested, and evidently didn't regard the stranger as
some common beggar.

'Look, she's given her ten roubles,' someone in the crowd said.

'Do please give me your hand,' babbled the 'unfortunate'
one, firmly grasping with the fingers of her left hand the corner
of the ten-rouble note she had just received, which was fluttering
in the wind. For some reason Varvara Petrovna frowned
slightly, and held out her hand with a serious, almost severe
expression; the other woman kissed it reverentially. Her grateful eyes even gleamed with a kind of rapture. And it was just
then that the governor's wife came up, and a whole crowd of
our ladies and senior officials surged behind her. The governor's

wife had no choice but to pause for a moment in the crush; many other people stopped.

'You're trembling, are you cold?' Varvara Petrovna suddenly observed, and flinging off her cloak, which was caught by a servant, she removed her black (and far from inexpensive) shawl from her shoulders, and with her own hands wrapped it around the bare neck of the petitioner who was still on her knees before her.

'Do get up, get up off your knees, I beg you!' The young woman stood up.

'Where do you live? Doesn't anyone really know where she lives?' Varvara Petrovna again looked around impatiently. But the former cluster of people had disappeared; all that could be seen were the familiar faces of society people who were scanning the scene, some in stern surprise, others with sly curiosity and, at the same time, naively eager for a juicy little scandal, while still others were even beginning to chuckle.

'I believe she's a Lebyadkin, ma'am,' a kind man finally ventured in response to Varvara Petrovna's query. He was our estimable merchant Andreyev, respected by many, with spectacles and a grey beard, wearing Russian clothing and a stovepipe hat, which he was now holding in his hands. 'They live in the Filippovs' house, in Bogoyavlenskaya Street.'

'Lebyadkin? The Filippovs' house? I've heard something . . . I thank you, Nikon Semyonych, but who is this Lebyadkin?'

'A captain is what he styles himself; a man, it should be said, who's not very careful. And this one, in all likelihood, is his sister. Chances are she's just now escaped from supervision,' Nikon Semyonych stated, lowering his voice and looking significantly at Varvara Petrovna.

'I understand; thank you, Nikon Semyonych. My dear, are you Miss Lebyadkina?'

'No, I'm not Lebyadkina.'

'Then is your brother perhaps Lebyadkin?'

'My brother is Lebyadkin.'

'Here's what I'm going to do. I'm going to take you with me now, my dear, and from my house you'll be taken back to your family. Do you want to come with me?'

'Oh, yes, I do!' Miss Lebyadkina clapped her hands together.

'Auntie, Auntie? Take me with you to your house as well!' The voice of Lizaveta Nikolayevna was suddenly heard. I should note that Lizaveta Nikolayevna had come to mass together with the governor's wife, while Praskovya Ivanovna, on doctor's orders, had gone for a ride in her carriage, and taken Mavriky Nikolayevich with her for diversion. Liza suddenly abandoned the governor's wife and came running up to Varvara Petrovna.

'My dear, you know I'm always glad to see you, but what will your mother say?' Varvara Petrovna began loftily, but suddenly grew flustered on noticing that Liza looked uncommonly agitated.

'Auntie, Auntie, I really have to go with you now,' Liza pleaded, kissing Varvara Petrovna.

'*Mais qu'avez-vous donc*,[14] Lise!' asked the governor's wife with marked surprise.

'Oh, forgive me, darling, *chère cousine*, I'm going to my aunt's.' Liza turned to her *chère cousine*, who was unpleasantly surprised, and kissed her twice as she flew past.

'And tell maman also that she should come and fetch me at my aunt's; maman really, really did want to drop by; she's been talking about it lately, I forgot to let you know,' Liza chattered away, 'I beg your pardon, don't be angry, Julie . . . *chère cousine* . . . Auntie, I'm ready!'

'If you don't take me, Auntie, then I'll run behind your carriage and scream,' she whispered in a hurried and desperate voice directly into Varvara Petrovna's ear; it was a good thing that no one heard her. Varvara Petrovna even took a step back and fixed a penetrating look on the mad girl. This look settled everything: she had definitely decided to take Liza with her!

'There must be an end to this!' escaped from her. 'Very well, I'll take you with pleasure, Liza,' and she immediately added in a loud voice, 'of course, if Yuliya Mikhaylovna will agree to let you go,' she said, turning directly to the governor's wife with a candid look and unmistakable dignity.

'Oh, of course, I wouldn't want to deprive her of this pleasure, the more so since I myself . . .' Yuliya Mikhaylovna began babbling with surprising amiability. 'I myself . . . I know very well what a fantastically wilful little head sits on our pretty little shoulders . . .' (Yuliya Mikhaylovna gave a charming smile.)

'I am extremely grateful to you,' Varvara Petrovna rendered her thanks with a courteous and dignified bow.

'And I am even more pleased,' Yuliya Mikhaylovna went on babbling, now almost in ecstasy, even flushing all over in the pleasure of her excitement, 'that, besides the gratification of being with you, Liza is being carried away by such a splendid, I can say such a lofty feeling . . . compassion' – she glanced at the 'unfortunate' woman . . . – 'and on the very porch of the church . . .'

'Such a view does you honour,' Varvara Petrovna bestowed her approval grandly. Yuliya Mikhaylovna extended her hand impulsively, and Varvara Petrovna was more than ready to touch it with her fingers. The general impression was excellent; the faces of some of those present beamed with pleasure, a few sweet and ingratiating smiles appeared.

In a word, it suddenly became clear to the entire town that it was not Yuliya Mikhaylovna who had been ignoring Varvara Petrovna until then and not paying her a visit, but, on the contrary, Varvara Petrovna herself who 'was keeping Yuliya Mikhaylovna within bounds, while the latter would have run to pay her a visit, on foot perhaps, if only she were certain that Varvara Petrovna would not have chased her away'. Varvara Petrovna's authority soared.

'Do sit down, my dear,' Varvara Petrovna directed Mademoiselle Lebyadkina to a carriage that had drawn up. The 'unfortunate woman' ran joyfully to the door, where a footman caught her up.

'What! You're crippled!' cried Varvara Petrovna, as if thoroughly alarmed, and turned pale. (Everyone noticed it at the time, but didn't understand it.)

The carriage rolled off. Varvara Petrovna's house was located very close to the cathedral. Liza told me later that Lebyadkina was laughing hysterically for the full three minutes of the journey, while Varvara Petrovna was sitting 'as if in some mesmeric dream', Liza's own expression.

CHAPTER 5

The Wise Serpent

I.

Varvara Petrovna rang the bell and flung herself into an armchair by the window.

'Sit here, my dear.' She directed Marya Timofeyevna to a seat in the middle of the room, at a large round table. 'Stepan Trofimovich, what is all this about? Here, here, look at this woman, what is all this about?'

'I . . . I . . .' Stepan Trofimovich began babbling.

But a footman appeared.

'A cup of coffee, immediately, made specially, and as soon as possible! The carriage is not to be unharnessed.'

'*Mais, chère et excellente amie, dans quelle inquiétude . . .*'[1] Stepan Trofimovich exclaimed in a fading voice.

'Oh! In French, in French! You can see right away it's high society!' Marya Timofeyevna clapped her hands, ecstatic at the prospect of hearing a conversation in French. Varvara Petrovna stared at her almost in fear.

We all remained silent and waited for a denouement of some kind. Shatov didn't raise his head, while Stepan Trofimovich was in a state of confusion, as if he were to blame for everything: perspiration broke out on his temples. I glanced at Liza (she was sitting in a corner, almost next to Shatov). Her sharp eyes kept darting from Varvara Petrovna to the crippled woman and back; a crooked but unattractive smile appeared on her lips. Varvara Petrovna saw this smile. And meanwhile, Marya Timofeyevna was utterly transported: she was examining, with pleasure and without the slightest embarrassment, Varvara Petrovna's beautiful drawing room – the furnishings, the carpets, the pictures on the walls, the old-fashioned decorated ceiling, the large bronze crucifix in the corner, the china lamp, the albums, the knick-knacks on the table.

'So, you're here too, Shatushka!' she suddenly exclaimed. 'Imagine: I've been looking at you for a long time now, but I'm thinking: no, it's not him! How could he have got here!' and she began laughing merrily.

'Do you know this woman?' Varvara Petrovna immediately turned towards him.

'Yes, I do,' Shatov mumbled, shifting in his chair, but remaining seated.

'What is it that you know? Tell me quickly, please!'

'Why, that . . .' he gave an unnecessary grin and stammered, '. . . you can see for yourself.'

'What can I see? Come now, say something!'

'She lives in the same house where I . . . with her brother . . . a certain officer.'

'And?'

Shatov stammered again.

'It's not worth saying . . .' he mooed and lapsed into a determined silence. He even blushed at his determination.

'Of course, one couldn't expect anything more from you!' Varvara Petrovna snapped indignantly. It was now clear to her that everyone knew something, yet everyone was afraid of something and was dodging her questions, wanting to hide something from her.

The footman came in and brought her a small silver tray with the cup of coffee she had specially ordered, but in response to a wave of her hand, promptly went over to Marya Timofeyevna.

'You got very chilled this morning, my dear; drink up quickly and warm yourself.'

'*Merci*,' Marya Timofeyevna took the cup and suddenly burst out laughing because she had said *merci* to the footman. But, on meeting Varvara Petrovna's menacing look, she quailed and set the cup on the table.

'Auntie, you aren't angry with me, are you?' she babbled in a rather mindlessly playful tone.

'Wha-a-at?' Varvara Petrovna jerked upright in her armchair.

'What sort of aunt am I to you? What do you mean by that?'

Marya Timofeyevna, not anticipating such an angry reaction, began trembling all over in tiny convulsive shudders, as if she were having a seizure, and recoiled in her chair.

'I . . . I thought that was how I should,' she babbled, looking wide-eyed at Varvara Petrovna, 'that's what Liza called you.'

'Which Liza do you mean?'

'Why, that young lady there,' Marya Timofeyevna pointed at her.

'So she's already become Liza to you?'

'That's what you yourself called her this morning,' Marya Timofeyevna replied, somewhat emboldened. 'And I had a dream about a beautiful girl just like her,' she smiled, as if unintentionally.

Varvara Petrovna pondered the matter, and calmed down somewhat; she even allowed herself a faint smile at Marya Timofeyevna's last utterance. Catching her smile, the latter got up from her chair and limped timidly towards her.

'Take it, I forgot to give it back, don't be angry at my bad manners,' she said, suddenly removing from her shoulders the black shawl that had been draped over her that morning by Varvara Petrovna.

'Put it on again at once, and keep it with you. Go and sit down, drink your coffee, and, please, don't be afraid of me, my dear, calm yourself. I am beginning to understand you.'

'*Chère amie* . . .' Stepan Trofimovich was about to allow himself to speak again.

'Oh, Stepan Trofimovich, nothing makes any sense here even without you; you at least spare me . . . Please, ring that bell there beside you, for the maids' room.'

A silence ensued. Her eyes glided suspiciously and irritably across all our faces. Agasha, her favourite maid, appeared.

'Bring me the checked shawl, the one I bought in Geneva. What is Darya Pavlovna doing?'

'She's not quite well, ma'am.'

'Go and ask her to come here. Tell her that I'm asking her as a special favour, even though she doesn't feel well.'

At that instant there again came the unusual noise of footsteps and voices from the adjoining rooms, as before, and suddenly a panting and 'distraught' Praskovya Ivanovna appeared in the doorway. Mavriky Nikolayevich was supporting her by the arm.

'Oh, Lord, I could hardly drag myself here. Liza, you mad creature, what are you doing to your mother!' she squealed, putting all her accumulated irritation into this squeal, as all weak but highly irritable people are wont to do.

'My dear lady, Varvara Petrovna, I've come to fetch my daughter!'

Varvara Petrovna glowered at her, half rose in greeting and, scarcely concealing her vexation, said:

'Good day, Praskovya Ivanovna, please be seated. I knew you would come.'

2.

Such a reception could not have occasioned any surprise in Praskovya Ivanovna. From the time they were children, Varvara Petrovna had always treated her old school friend despotically and, under the guise of friendship, almost with contempt. But in the present case, the situation was truly special. Over the past few days things had almost reached the point of a complete rupture between the two houses, as I have already mentioned in passing. The reasons for the incipient rupture were still a mystery to Varvara Petrovna, and therefore all the more annoying; but the main thing was that Praskovya Ivanovna had managed to assume a kind of haughty attitude towards her, which was out of character. Naturally, Varvara Petrovna was hurt, and meanwhile certain strange rumours were already beginning to reach her and proved exceedingly irritating to her, precisely because they were so vague. Varvara Petrovna had a direct and proudly open character, with a tendency towards sudden attacks, if one is permitted to put it that way. Least of all could she tolerate secret, surreptitious accusations, and she always preferred open warfare. Be that as it may, it was now five days since the two ladies had seen each other. The last visit had come from Varvara Petrovna, who had driven away 'from that Madame Drozdova' offended and flustered. I can say without risk of error on this occasion that Praskovya Ivanovna came in naively convinced that Varvara Petrovna for some reason ought to be afraid of her; just the expression on her face made that obvious. But it was obvious, too, that Varvara Petrovna would be possessed by the demon of overweening pride precisely whenever she had the slightest grounds for suspecting that she was supposed to feel humiliated. And Praskovya Ivanovna, like many weak people who have long allowed themselves to be offended without protesting, was known to attack with extraordinary vigour the moment events turned in her favour. To be sure, she was not feeling well just now, and her illness had made her even more irritable. I will add, finally, that the mere presence of all of us in the drawing room wouldn't particularly have helped restrain either of these childhood friends if a quarrel should flare up between them; we were regarded as members of the family and virtual underlings. I realized this with some alarm at the time. Stepan Trofimovich, who had not sat down from the moment Praskovya Ivanovna arrived, sank on to his chair in exhaustion when he heard Praskovya Ivanovna squeal, and began desperately trying to catch my eye. Shatov turned abruptly in his chair, and even mumbled something to himself. It seemed to me that he wanted to get up and leave. Liza looked as if she were about to get up, but immediately sank back on to her chair, without even having paid the necessary attention to her mother's squeal, not out of a 'stubbornness of character', but apparently because she remained in thrall to some other powerful emotion. Now she was looking off somewhere into the air, almost absentmindedly, and had even stopped paying any attention to Marya Timofeyevna.

3.

'Ugh, here!' Praskovya Ivanovna indicated the chair at the table, and sank heavily on to it with the help of Mavriky Nikolayevich. 'I wouldn't sit down in your house, dear lady, if it weren't for my legs!' she added in a voice breaking with emotion.

Varvara Petrovna raised her head a little, and with a tormented look on her face pressed the fingers of her right hand

to her right temple, which was evidently causing her sharp pain
(*tic douloureux*).[2]

'Why do you say that, Praskovya Ivanovna, why shouldn't
you sit down in my house? I enjoyed the sincere friendship of
your late husband all his life, and you and I used to play dolls
when we were little girls at boarding school.'

Praskovya Ivanovna began waving her hands.

'Well, I just knew it! You always start in about boarding
school whenever you're of a mind to find fault with me – that's
a trick of yours. But in my opinion, it's just a lot of fine talk. I
simply can't endure this boarding school of yours.'

'You seem to have come here in a very bad mood. How are
your legs? Here, they're bringing you some coffee; please, drink
it and don't be angry.'

'My dear lady, Varvara Petrovna, you're treating me like a
little girl. I don't want any coffee, so there!'

And she testily waved away the servant who was bringing
her coffee. (Incidentally, the others refused coffee as well, except
Mavriky Nikolayevich and me. Stepan Trofimovich started to
pick up his cup, but set it back down on the table. Marya
Timofeyevna, although she really wanted another cup, and had
even held out her hand, thought better of it and primly declined
it, obviously pleased with herself for doing so.)

Varvara Petrovna gave a crooked smile.

'You know what, my dear friend Praskovya Ivanovna, you've
probably imagined something again, and that's why you've
come here. You've lived your entire life imagining things. You
flew into a rage about our boarding school; but don't you
remember how you came in and assured the entire class that
the hussar Shablykin had proposed to you, and how Madame
Lefebure immediately caught you in the lie? But you weren't
really lying, you were simply imagining it for the fun of it.
Come on, speak up. What are you here for now? What else
have you imagined, what are you dissatisfied with?'

'Well, in boarding school you fell in love with the priest who
taught catechism – so much for you, since you still harbour
such resentment to this day – ha, ha, ha!'

She burst into petulant laughter and had a coughing fit.

'A-ah, you haven't forgotten about the priest,' Varara Petrovna glanced at her with hatred.

Her face turned green. Praskovya Ivanovna suddenly assumed a dignified air.

'My dear woman, I'm in no laughing mood now. Why have you involved my daughter in your scandal, for the entire town to see? That's what I've come about!'

'In my scandal?' Varvara Petrovna suddenly and menacingly drew herself up.

'Maman, I'm also begging you to control yourself,' Lizaveta Nikolayevna said suddenly.

'What did you say?' Her mother was on the point of squealing again, but suddenly retreated before her daughter's flashing eyes.

'How could you talk about a scandal, maman?' Liza flared up. 'I came here on my own, with Yuliya Mikhaylovna's permission, because I wanted to learn the story of this unfortunate woman, so that I could be of use to her.'

' "The story of this unfortunate woman"!' Praskovya Ivanovna drawled with spiteful laughter. 'Is it your business to interfere in such "stories"? Oh, my dear woman! We've had enough of your despotism!' She turned to Varvara Petrovna in a fury. 'They say, whether it's true or not, that you've got the whole town marching in close-order drill, but I guess your time has finally come!'

Varvara Petrovna was sitting straight as an arrow that's ready to leap from the bow. For a good ten seconds she looked, stern and unmoving, at Praskovya Ivanovna.

'Well, Praskovya, you should thank God that everyone here is one of us,' she finally uttered with ominous composure. 'You've said a lot that didn't need saying.'

'But my dear woman, I am not as afraid as some others of what people will think. You're the one who calls it pride and yet trembles over what people will think. And the fact that everyone here is one of us is certainly better for you than if outsiders were listening.'

'Have you grown wiser this week, is that it?'

'I haven't grown any wiser this week, but the truth has evidently come out this week.'

'What truth has come out this week? Listen here, Praskovya Ivanovna, don't irritate me. Explain yourself this very minute, I urge you; what truth is it that's come out?'

'Why, there it is, the whole truth's sitting right there!' Praskovya Ivanovna suddenly pointed at Marya Timofeyevna with that desperate decisiveness that is no longer concerned with consequences, but seeks only to shock. Marya Timofeyevna, who had been watching her all this time with cheerful curiosity, laughed merrily at the sight of the angry visitor's finger pointed at her and began to shift gleefully in her chair.

'Lord Jesus Christ, has everyone gone stark raving mad then!' Varvara Petrovna exclaimed, and turning pale, threw herself against the back of her chair.

She turned so pale that it even caused some commotion. Stepan Trofimovich was the first to rush to her; I also went nearer; even Liza stood up, although she remained by her chair; but Praskovya Ivanovna was the one who was most frightened: she let out a scream, stood up as best she could and began almost to wail in a mournful voice:

'Dear friend, Varvara Petrovna, please forgive my malicious foolishness! Someone give her some water!'

'Don't whimper, please, Praskovya Ivanovna, I ask you. And step aside, gentlemen, do me the favour. I don't need any water!' Varvara Petrovna stated firmly, albeit not very loudly, through pale lips.

'My dear!' continued Praskovya Ivanovna, calming down a bit. 'My friend, Varvara Petrovna, even though I'm guilty of speaking carelessly, I've been most irritated by these anonymous letters that some horrible people have been bombarding me with. Well, they should be sending them to you, since you're the one they're writing about, but I have a daughter, my dear!'

Varvara Petrovna was looking at her speechless and wide-eyed, listening in astonishment. At that moment a side door in the corner of the room opened, and Darya Pavlovna appeared. She paused and looked around; she was struck by the commotion in the room. She probably didn't make out Marya Timofeyevna right away, since no one had forewarned her. Stepan Trofimovich was the first to notice her, made a quick movement, flushed and loudly announced, for some reason, 'Darya Pavlovna!' so that all eyes turned on the newcomer at the same time.

'Oh, so this is your Darya Pavlovna!' exclaimed Marya Timofeyevna. 'Well, Shatushka, your sister doesn't look like you! How can my man possibly call a treasure like this by such a serf-girl's name as Dasha!'

Meanwhile Darya Pavlovna had already gone up to Varvara Petrovna, but startled by Marya Timofeyevna's exclamation, she quickly turned around and remained standing in front of her chair, bestowing a long, unwavering look on God's fool.[3]

'Sit down, Dasha,' Varvara Petrovna said, with terrifying composure. 'Closer – that's it; you can see this woman even when you're sitting down. Do you know her?'

'I've never seen her,' Dasha replied softly, and, after a moment of silence, immediately added: 'This must be the invalid sister of a certain Mr Lebyadkin.'

'And I'm only seeing you, dear heart, for the first time now, even though I've long been curious to make your acquaintance, because in your every gesture I see good upbringing,' Marya Timofeyevna cried eagerly. 'And as for my lackey saying bad things about you, is it really possible that you took money that belonged to him, someone as well brought up and nice as you? Because you are nice, nice, nice, I say that to you from my heart!' she concluded ecstatically, waving her small hand in front of her.

'Do you understand anything?' asked Varvara Petrovna with proud dignity.

'I understand everything, ma'am.'

'Have you heard about the money?'

'That must be the same money that I took it on myself to hand over to this Mr Lebyadkin, her brother, at the request of Nikolay Vsevolodovich, when we were still in Switzerland.'

A silence followed.

'Nikolay Vsevolodovich himself asked you to deliver it?'

'He very much wanted to send this money, three hundred roubles in all, to Mr Lebyadkin. But since he didn't know his address, and knew that he would be coming to our town, he entrusted me with handing it over, in case Mr Lebyadkin did come.'

'What money was it that . . . got lost? What was this woman talking about just now?'

'That I really don't know, ma'am. I've also heard the rumours that Mr Lebyadkin was spreading about me publicly, that I didn't deliver all the money to him; but I don't understand that. There were three hundred roubles, and three hundred roubles were what I sent him.'

Darya Pavlovna had now calmed down almost completely. And I will note in general that it was difficult to rattle this girl or throw her off the track for long, whatever she may really have been feeling. She produced all her answers now without haste, promptly replying to each question precisely, quietly, evenly, without any trace of her initial sudden agitation, and without the slightest embarrassment, which might have betrayed an awareness of some kind of guilt on her part. Varvara Petrovna's eyes didn't leave her the whole time she was speaking. Varvara Petrovna thought for a moment.

'If,' she finally uttered firmly, and evidently for the benefit of the onlookers, although she kept looking just at Dasha, 'if Nikolay Vsevolodovich didn't turn even to me with his errand, but asked you, then of course he had his reasons for doing so. I don't believe that I have the right to wonder about them, if they are kept secret from me. But the very fact of your participation in this matter reassures me completely about everything, you should know that, Darya, first and foremost. But don't you see, my friend, that you, with a clear conscience, might have committed some indiscretion through lack of knowledge of the world; and you did commit it by entering into dealings with some scoundrel. The rumours that were spread by this wretch are confirmation of your error. But I will find out about him, and since I am your protectress, I will do what I can to stand up for you. And now it's necessary to put an end to all this.'

'The best thing is when he comes to see you,' Marya Timofeyevna suddenly took up the conversation, thrusting forward in her chair, 'to pack him off to the servants' quarters. Let him play his trumps with them there on top of a trunk, while we sit here and drink coffee. A cup of coffee could be sent to him, but I have only profound contempt for him.'

And she shook her head expressively.

'We must put an end to this,' Varvara Petrovna repeated, after carefully hearing Marya Timofeyevna out. 'Please ring, Stepan Trofimovich.'

Stepan Trofimovich rang and suddenly stepped forward in great agitation.

'If . . . if I . . .' he began babbling excitedly, flushing, breaking off and stammering, 'if I had also heard highly disgusting news, or, better said, slander, then . . . in complete indignation . . . *enfin, c'est un homme perdu et quelque chose comme un forçat évadé . . .*'[4]

He stopped short without finishing. Varvara Petrovna, squinting, looked him over from head to toe. The ceremonious Aleksey Yegorovich came in.

'The carriage,' Varvara Petrovna ordered, 'and you, Aleksey Yegorovich, prepare to take Miss Lebyadkina home, and she will give you directions herself.'

'Mr Lebyadkin himself has been waiting downstairs for some time, ma'am, and begs to be announced, ma'am.'

'That's impossible, Varvara Petrovna,' Mavriky Nikolaye-vich, who had observed an unruffled silence all this time, sud-denly announced anxiously. 'If you will permit me to say it, this is not the kind of person who can be admitted into society . . . this is . . . this is . . . an impossible person, Varvara Petrovna.'

'Wait,' said Varvara Petrovna, turning to Aleksey Yegoro-vich, and he disappeared.

'*C'est un homme malhonnête et je crois même que c'est un forçat évadé ou quelque chose dans ce genre,*'[5] Stepan Trofimo-vich again muttered, again flushed and again broke off.

'Liza, it's time to be going,' Praskovya Ivanovna announced disdainfully, and got up from her chair. She now seemed to regret that in her fright she had called herself a fool just a few moments ago. While Darya Pavlovna was speaking, she was listening with superciliously pursed lips. But I was struck above all by the expression on Lizaveta Nikolayevna's face ever since

Darya Pavlovna had come in: her eyes were flashing with hatred and contempt, which were utterly unconcealed.

'Wait a moment, Praskovya Ivanovna, I beg you,' Varvara Petrovna stopped her, still with the same extreme composure. 'Please be seated. I intend to have my say about everything, and your legs are hurting you. That's it, I thank you. I recently lost my temper and said several things to you in haste. Please forgive me. I acted stupidly, and I am the first to feel contrite, because I like there to be fairness in everything. Of course, when you also lost your temper you mentioned some anonymous letters. Any anonymous slander is worthy of contempt because it hasn't been signed. If you see it otherwise, I don't envy you. In any event, if I were in your place I wouldn't have made a point of dragging out such rubbish; I wouldn't have dirtied my hands. But you did dirty yours. But since you yourself have already brought it up, I'll tell you that six days or so ago I also received an anonymous letter from some clown. In it some scoundrel assures me that Nikolay Vsevolodovich has lost his mind and that I must fear some crippled woman, who "is fated to play an extraordinary role in my life". The expression has stuck in my mind. After thinking it over, and knowing that Nikolay Vsevolodovich has an extraordinary number of enemies, I immediately sent for a certain person who lives here, one of the most secret, vindictive and contemptible of all his enemies, and from my conversations with him, I immediately became convinced that I knew the source of this contemptible letter. If you, my poor Praskovya Ivanovna, have also been bothered by the same sort of contemptible letters *on account of me*, and were, as you put it, "bombarded", then of course I am the first to regret that I was the innocent cause of it. That's all I wanted to say to you by way of explanation. I am sorry to see that you are very tired and out of sorts now. Moreover, I have definitely made up my mind to *admit* this suspicious person at once, whom Mavriky Nikolayevich described, not quite aptly, as being impossible to *receive*. There is no need for Liza, in particular, to be here. Come here, Liza, my friend, and let me kiss you again.'

Liza walked across the room and paused silently in front of

Varvara Petrovna. The latter kissed her, took her by the hands, moved her back a little, looked at her with feeling, then made the sign of the cross over her and kissed her again.

'Well, goodbye, Liza,' (tears could almost be heard in Varvara Petrovna's voice) 'believe me when I say that I shall never stop loving you, whatever fate may have in store for you ... May God be with you. I have always blessed his holy right hand ...'

She wanted to add something more, but restrained herself and fell silent. Liza was about to go back to her seat, still saying nothing and seemingly wrapped in thought, but suddenly stopped in front of her mother.

'I'm not going yet, maman, I'll stay with Auntie a little while longer,' she said in a soft voice, but an iron determination came through these quiet words.

'Good Lord! What's going on!' Praskovya Ivanovna wailed, clasping her hands helplessly. But Liza didn't answer, and didn't even seem to have heard; she sat down in the same corner as before, and began looking off into space again.

Something triumphant and proud shone in Varvara Petrovna's face.

'Mavriky Nikolayevich, I have a great favour to ask of you. Do me the kindness of going downstairs and taking a look at that man down there, and if there is any possibility of *admitting* him, then bring him here.'

Mavriky Nikolayevich bowed and went out. A minute later he brought in Mr Lebyadkin.

4.

I have already had something to say about this gentleman's appearance: a tall, curly-haired, thick-set fellow of about forty, with a somewhat puffy, flabby purple face; cheeks that quivered with each movement of his head; small, blood-shot, sometimes rather cunning eyes; a moustache, side whiskers; and a fleshy Adam's apple that was just beginning to protrude and was rather unpleasant to look at. But what was most striking about him was that this time he appeared in a tail-coat and clean linen. 'There are people on whom clean linen looks positively

indecent, sir,' as Liputin once objected when Stepan Trofimovich jokingly reproached him about his untidiness. The captain
was also wearing black gloves, holding the right one in his
hand, while the left one, which was tightly stretched and left
unbuttoned, half-covered his fleshy left paw, in which he was
holding a brand-new, shiny round hat that had probably been
pressed into service for the first time. It turned out, therefore,
that yesterday's 'tail-coat of love', which he had been shouting
to Shatov about, actually did exist. All of this, that is, the
tail-coat and the linen, had been procured (as I later learned)
on the advice of Liputin, for some mysterious purposes. There
was absolutely no doubt that he had arrived just now (in a
hired carriage) at someone else's instigation and with someone
else's help. He wouldn't have been able to figure all this out for
himself, let alone dress himself, get ready and make up his
mind, all within three-quarters of an hour, even supposing that
the scene on the cathedral porch had become known to him
immediately. He wasn't drunk, but was in the heavy, ponder-
ous, foggy state of a man who had suddenly awakened after
many days of hard drinking. It seemed all you would have to
do was shake him a couple of times by the shoulder and he
would promptly be drunk again.

He was about to come flying into the drawing room, when
he suddenly tripped on the carpet in the doorway. Marya Timofeyevna nearly died laughing. He looked at her fiercely and
suddenly took several quick steps towards Varvara Petrovna.

'I have come, madam . . .' he began to blare as if through a
trumpet.

'Be so good, my dear sir,' Varvara Petrovna said, drawing
herself up, 'as to take a seat over there, on that chair. I will be
able to hear you from there as well, and it will be easier for me
to see you from here.'

The captain stopped short, staring vacantly ahead; still, he
turned and sat in the place indicated, right by the door. A great
lack of self-assurance, together with insolence and a certain
chronic irritability were betrayed in the expression on his face.
He was dreadfully scared, that was evident, but his self-esteem
was suffering as well, and it was easy enough to guess that

irritated self-esteem might even lead him, despite his cowardice, to venture on some insolent act, given the opportunity. He was obviously afraid of every movement of his clumsy body. It's well known that the main source of suffering for all gentlemen of this kind, when by some miraculous happenstance they appear in society, is their own hands and their awareness, at every moment, of their inability to find an appropriate place to put them. The captain sat like a statue on his chair, with his hat and gloves in his hands, and without shifting his blank stare from the stern face of Varvara Petrovna. Perhaps he really would have liked to have a good look round, but as yet he hadn't summoned up the courage to do so. Marya Timofey-evna, probably again finding his appearance terribly funny, broke into laughter once more, but he didn't stir. Varvara Petrovna kept him in this position for an unmercifully long time, a whole minute, subjecting him to a relentless scrutiny.

'First of all, permit me to learn your name, from your own lips,' she pronounced the words in a measured and distinct manner.

'Captain Lebyadkin,' the captain blared. 'I have come, madam . . .' he started to stir again.

'Just a moment!' Varvara Petrovna stopped him again. 'This pitiful person, in whom I have taken such an interest, is this really your sister?'

'My sister, madam, who slipped away from supervision, being in such a condition . . .'

He suddenly hesitated and turned red.

'Don't take that the wrong way, madam,' he said, dreadfully flustered, 'her own brother won't start blackening her . . . in such a condition – I mean, not in such a condition . . . in the sense of tarnishing her reputation . . . recently . . .'

He broke off abruptly.

'My dear sir!' Varvara Petrovna raised her head.

'I mean in *this* condition,' he suddenly concluded, tapping the middle of his forehead with his finger. A silence followed.

'And has she been suffering from this for a long time?' asked Varvara Petrovna with a slight drawl.

'Madam, I have come to thank you for the generosity you

showed her on the cathedral porch, in a Russian, in a brotherly way . . .'

'In a brotherly way?'

'That is, not brotherly, but only in the sense that I am my sister's brother, madam, and believe me, madam,' he hurried on, turning red again, 'that I am not so uneducated as I might at first appear to be in your drawing room. My sister and I are nothing, madam, compared with the magnificence we see here. Having enemies who are slandering us, besides. But as far as reputation goes, Lebyadkin is proud, madam, and . . . and . . . I have come to thank you . . . Here is the money, madam!'

Here he retrieved a wallet from his pocket, pulled a wad of cash out of it and began thumbing through it with trembling fingers in a frenzy of impatience. It was evident that he was eager to explain something as quickly as possible, and in fact that it was quite necessary to do so; but probably aware himself that fussing with the money was making him look even more foolish, he lost his last remaining shred of self-possession. The money simply didn't want to be counted, he was all fingers, and, to make his shame complete, one green banknote,[6] which had slipped out of the wallet, zig-zagged on to the carpet.

'Twenty roubles, madam,' he jumped up suddenly with the wad in his hands, his face sweaty from his agony. Noticing the banknote that had floated to the floor, he began bending to retrieve it, but for some reason was overcome with shame and waved his hand dismissively.

'For your servants, madam, for your footman, when he picks it up – let him remember Lebyadkina!'

'I simply cannot permit this,' Varvara Petrovna said hurriedly, and with some apprehensiveness.

'In that case . . .'

He bent down, picked up the note, turned red and suddenly going up to Varvara Petrovna, held out the money that he had counted.

'What is this?' she asked, thoroughly frightened at last and even recoiling in her armchair. Mavriky Nikolayevich, Stepan Trofimovich and I each took a step forward.

'Calm yourselves, calm yourselves; I'm not a madman, I

swear, I'm not a madman!' the captain kept assuring one and all excitedly.

'Yes, my dear sir, you've lost your mind.'

'Madam, it's not at all what you think! Of course, I'm an insignificant link . . . Oh, madam, yours is a house rich in many mansions, but poor are they in the case of Marya the Unknown, my sister, who was born Lebyadkina, but whom we shall call Marya the Unknown for the time being, for the time being, madam, only *for the time being*, inasmuch as God himself will not countenance it forever! Madam, you gave her ten roubles, and she took them, but only because they were from *you*, madam! Listen, madam! She would not take them from anyone else in the world, this Unknown Marya, otherwise her grandfather, a staff officer killed in the Caucasus in full view of Yermolov[7] himself, would turn over in his grave, but from you, madam, from you she would take anything. But she would take it with one hand, and with the other she would hold out to you a full twenty roubles, by way of a contribution to one of the charitable committees in the capital, of which you are a member, madam . . . inasmuch as you yourself, madam, have published a notice in the *Moscow Gazette*[8] that you are in charge of a local subscription book for a charitable society in our town, where anyone can register his name . . .'

The captain broke off suddenly. He was breathing heavily, like someone who had just brought off a difficult feat. All this business of a charitable committee had most likely been prepared in advance, perhaps also with Liputin as editor. He began to sweat even more heavily; drops of sweat literally stood out on his temples. Varvara Petrovna fixed a penetrating look on him.

'That book,' she intoned sternly, 'is always located downstairs with the porter of my house; there you can enter your contribution, if you wish. And therefore I ask you to put away your money now and stop waving it in the air. That's it. I also ask you to go back to where you were sitting before. That's it. I very much regret, my dear sir, that I was mistaken about your sister and gave to her as if she were poor when she is so rich. The only thing I don't understand is why she can only take something from me, but under no circumstances from others. You've made such a point of it that I wish to have an absolutely clear explanation.'

'Madam, that is a secret that can be buried only in the grave!' replied the captain.

'But why?' asked Varvara Petrovna, though now in a somewhat less firm tone.

'Madam, madam! . . .'

He fell into a gloomy silence, staring at the floor and with his right hand clapped to his heart. Varvara Petrovna waited, not taking her eyes off him.

'Madam!' he suddenly bellowed. 'Will you permit me to ask you one question, only one, but openly, frankly, in the Russian manner, from the heart?'

'Please do.'

'Have you ever suffered in your life, madam?'

'You merely want to say that you have suffered or are suffering at someone's hands?'

'Madam, madam!' He jumped up again, probably without even noticing, and struck himself on the chest. 'Here, in this heart, so much has accumulated, so much that God himself will be astonished when it is revealed on Judgement Day!'

'Hmm, that's a strong way of putting it.'

'Madam, perhaps I am speaking in too irritable a way . . .'

'Don't worry, I myself will know when it's necessary to stop you.'

'May I propose another question to you, madam?'

'Propose one more question.'

'Can one die solely from the generosity of one's soul?'

'I don't know; I've never asked myself such a question.'

'You don't know! You've never asked yourself such a question!' he shouted with pathos-laden irony. 'But if that's so, if that's so:

Be still, my hopeless heart!'[9]

And he thumped his breast in a fury.

He again began to walk around the room. One mark of

such people is an utter powerlessness to keep their desires to themselves. On the contrary, they have an irresistible impulse to let them out, even in all their messiness, just as soon as they arise. Once he finds himself in a strange milieu, such a gentleman usually begins timidly, but if you give him an inch, he immediately makes the leap to insolent behaviour. The captain was worked up now, pacing, waving his arms, not listening to questions, talking about himself rapidly, very rapidly, so that he sometimes tripped over his own tongue, and without finishing what he was saying, would jump to another sentence. True enough, he was not what you would call completely sober. And also Lizaveta Nikolayevna was sitting there, at whom he did not glance even once, but whose presence seemed to be putting his head into a terrific spin. However, that's nothing more than a supposition. Therefore, there must have been some reason why Varvara Petrovna, overcoming her revulsion, had made up her mind to hear such a man out. Praskovya Ivanovna was simply quaking with fear, while not quite understanding what was going on, to be sure. Stepan Trofimovich was also trembling, but, on the contrary, because he was always inclined to understand too much. Mavriky Nikolayevich was standing in the pose of protector of one and all. Liza was very pale, and was staring wide-eyed at the wild captain. Shatov was sitting in his previous pose. But what was strangest of all was that Marya Timofeyevna had not only stopped laughing, but had become terribly sad. She was leaning on the table with her right arm, and with a long, sad gaze was watching her brother as he declaimed. The only one who seemed calm to me was Darya Pavlovna.

'These are all just stupid allegories,' Varvara Petrovna finally grew angry enough to say. 'You haven't answered my question: "Why?" I'm waiting, I insist on an answer.'

'I didn't answer your "why"? You expect an answer to "why"?' The captain tossed the question back with a wink. 'This tiny little word "why" has been spread throughout the entire universe from the very first day of creation, madam, and all of nature at every moment cries out to its creator: "Why?" And for seven thousand years now it has received no answer.

Is it really up to Captain Lebyadkin alone to provide an answer, and is that fair, madam?'

'That's all nonsense, and not to the point!' Varvara Petrovna was growing exasperated and losing patience. 'That's an allegory. Besides, your way of speaking is too overblown, my dear sir, and I regard it as impertinence!'

'Madam,' the captain was not listening. 'Perhaps I would like to have been called Ernest, but meanwhile I am compelled to bear the vulgar name of Ignat – why is that, do you think? I would like to have been called Prince de Montbars,[10] but meanwhile I'm just Lebyadkin, from the word *lebyed*, "swan". I am a poet, madam, a poet in my soul, and I could have been receiving a thousand roubles from a publisher, but meanwhile I'm forced to live in a washtub – why, why? Madam! In my opinion, Russia is a freak of nature, nothing more!'

'You can say absolutely nothing more definite than that?'

'I can recite a piece called "The Cockroach" to you, madam!'

'Wha-a-at?'

'Madam, I'm not yet crazy! I will be crazy, I probably will be, but I'm not crazy yet! Madam, a friend of mine – a most hon-our-able person – has written a Krylov fable entitled "The Cockroach". May I recite it?'

'You want to recite some fable by Krylov?'

'No, it's not a fable by Krylov that I want to recite, but my fable, my very own, composed by me! Do believe me, madam, without any offence to you, that I am not really so uneducated and depraved that I don't understand that Russia possesses a great writer of fables in Krylov, to whom a monument has been erected[11] by the Ministry of Education in the Summer Garden, for the diversion of people still at the age of childhood. And so, madam, you are asking "Why?" The answer lies at the bottom of this fable, written in letters of fire!'

'Recite your fable.'

> 'In this world a roach did dwell,[12]
> From birth a cockroach, proud and wise,
> One day into a glass he fell
> All chockablock with cannibal flies.'

'Lord, what is this!' exclaimed Varvara Petrovna.

'It means that in the summer,' the captain hastened to explain, waving his arms wildly, with the irritated impatience of an author whose recitation has been interrupted, 'when flies get into a glass in the summer, then fly-cannibalism occurs, any fool can understand that; don't interrupt, don't interrupt, you'll see, you'll see.' (He kept waving his arms.)

> 'The cockroach took his rightful place,
> The flies, they buzzed and clamoured,
> "Our glass is full, there's no more space"
> To Jupiter they yammered.
>
> Before the shouts and screams abated
> Up came Nikifor, old and grizzled,
> A worthy soul, much venerated . . .

This part's not yet finished, but it doesn't matter, I'll tell it in plain words!' the captain jabbered. 'Nikifor picks up the glass, and despite the shouting, he pours the entire comedy out into a bucket, flies and cockroach both, which should have been done long ago. But take note, take note, madam, the cockroach doesn't grumble! Here's the answer to your question "Why?"' he cried triumphantly. 'The cock-a-roach does not grumble! As for Nikifor, he represents nature,' he added in a quick patter, and, pleased with himself, began walking around the room.

Varvara Petrovna grew dreadfully angry.

'And what about the money, if I may ask you, supposedly received from Nikolay Vsevolodovich and supposedly not given to you in full – money that you dared accuse a certain member of my household of taking?'

'Slander!' roared Lebyadkin, raising his right hand in a tragic manner.

'No, it's not slander.'

'Madam, there are circumstances that compel one to endure familial disgrace rather than proclaim the truth loudly. Lebyadkin will not let the cat out of the bag, madam!'

He was like a blind man; he was overcome with inspiration;

he sensed his importance; he had probably dreamed about something of the sort. Now he felt the urge to deliver insults, play dirty tricks somehow, show his power.

'Ring, please, Stepan Trofimovich,' Varvara Petrovna asked.

'Lebyadkin is cunning, madam!' He winked, with a nasty smile. 'Cunning, but he has his limitations too, there is a threshold to his passions as well! And this threshold is the old bottle of the fighting hussar, as celebrated by Denis Davydov.[13] And it's when he's standing on this threshold, madam, that he may happen to send a letter in verse, a truly mag-ni-fi-cent one, but one that he would then like to take back with the tears of his entire life, for the sense of beauty is destroyed. But the bird has flown, there's no catching it by the tail! It's on this very threshold, madam, that Lebyadkin might even have let something slip about a noble girl, in the form of the noble indignation of a soul roused to anger by insults, a fact that his slanderers have taken advantage of. But Lebyadkin is cunning, madam! And all for naught does the sinister wolf sit over him, constantly filling his glass and awaiting the end: Lebyadkin will not blab, and at the bottom of the bottle, instead of what is expected, there always turns out to be – Lebyadkin's cunning! But enough, oh, enough! Madam, your magnificent mansions could have belonged to the most noble of persons, but the cockroach doesn't grumble! Note, please, just note, in conclusion, that he doesn't grumble, and recognize a great spirit!'

At that moment a bell sounded from the porter's room downstairs, and almost immediately Aleksey Yegorych appeared, in a somewhat delayed response to Stepan Trofimovich's ring. The ceremonious old servant was in an unusually excited state.

'Nikolay Vsevolodovich has been pleased to arrive this moment and is on his way here, ma'am,' he said in response to Varvara Petrovna's inquiring look.

I particularly recall her at that instant: at first she turned pale, but suddenly her eyes began to flash. She straightened up in her armchair with an air of uncommon resolution. Everyone in fact was astounded. The completely unexpected arrival of Nikolay Vsevolodovich, who had been expected here no earlier than a month from now, was strange not only because of its unexpectedness, but precisely because of its fateful coincidence with the present moment. Even the captain stood still as a post in the middle of the room, his mouth agape, looking at the door with a dreadfully stupid expression.

And then, from the adjoining hall, a long and large room, came the sound of rapidly approaching steps, small and very quick steps; it was as if someone were running, and into the drawing room suddenly flew – not Nikolay Vsevolodovich at all, but a young man who was an unknown to everyone.

5.

I will permit myself to pause and give a quick sketch, in a few broad strokes, of this person who had appeared so suddenly.

He was a young man of twenty-seven or thereabouts, some-what taller than average, with rather long, thin fair hair and a patchy, barely discernible moustache and beard. His clothes were clean and even stylish, but not foppish. At first glance he looked rather round-shouldered and clumsy, but even so, he wasn't at all round-shouldered, and even had an easygoing manner about him. He seemed to be an odd sort, yet everyone in our circle subsequently found his manners very decent, and his conversation always to the point.

No one would say that he was ugly, yet no one liked his face. His head was elongated towards the back and somehow flattened on the sides, making his face look sharp. His forehead was high and narrow, but his features were small: sharp eyes, a tiny, sharp little nose, and long, thin lips. His face suggested sickliness, but that was deceptive. He had a sort of deep wrinkle on each cheek and around his cheekbones, which gave him the appearance of a man recovering from a severe illness. Yet he was completely healthy and strong, and had never even been sick.

He walked and moved like a man in a great hurry, but he was never in a hurry. It seemed nothing could fluster him; in any circumstances and in any social situation at all, he would remain exactly the same. He was very complacent, but hadn't the slightest inkling of it himself.

He spoke quickly, hurriedly, but at the same time in a self-assured manner, and was never at a loss for words. Despite his hurried air, his thoughts were unruffled, precise and final – and that stood out in particular. He articulated his words in a surprisingly clear manner; his words fell from his lips like large, perfectly formed grains, always well chosen and always ready to be of service. At first you would find this very much to your liking, but then it would become repellent, precisely because of this excessively clear articulation, and this string of ever-ready words. You somehow began to imagine that his tongue must be of some special shape, unusually long and thin somehow, terribly red and extraordinarily sharp, its tip in constant and spontaneous movement.

So, it was this young man who had just now flown into the drawing room, and to this day it seems to me that he had started talking while he was still in the adjoining room, and came in already talking. In a flash there he was standing in front of Varvara Petrovna.

'. . . Just imagine, Varvara Petrovna' – his words fell like beads – 'I come in and I'm thinking I'll find that he's been waiting for me a good quarter of an hour; he arrived in town an hour and a half ago; we met at Kirillov's; he set off half an hour ago to come directly here, and told me to come here too in a quarter of an hour . . .'

'Who do you mean? Who told you to come here?' Varvara Petrovna questioned him.

'Why, Nikolay Vsevolodovich! Is this really the first you've heard of it? But his luggage must have arrived quite a while ago; how is it you weren't told? So then, I'm the first to announce it. One could, of course, send someone out to find him; however, he himself will probably turn up any minute now, and, I should think, precisely at the time that is eminently suited to certain of his expectations and, insofar at least as I'm capable of judging, to certain of his calculations.' Here his eyes swept around the room, and came to rest on the captain in particular. 'Ah, Liza-veta Nikolayevna, how glad I am to meet you right at the outset, I'm very glad to shake your hand,' he quickly flew to her, to take the hand that a happily smiling Liza had extended

to him, 'and, as far as I can see, our much-respected Praskovya
Ivanovna has also not forgotten, I believe, her "professor" and
is not even angry with him any more, although she always was
angry in Switzerland. But let me ask, how are your legs now
that you're here, Praskovya Ivanovna, and was your medical
consultation in Switzerland correct in sentencing you to living
in the climate of your native land? . . . What's that? Wet compresses? That must be very helpful. But how I regret, Varvara
Petrovna,' he quickly turned to her again, 'that I wasn't in time
to find you abroad on that occasion, and to present my respects
to you personally, and besides, I had so much to report to you
. . . I sent word to my old man here, but, as is his wont, he
seems to . . .'

'Petrusha!' Stepan Trofimovich exclaimed, momentarily
snapping out of his state of stupefaction. He clasped his hands
and rushed to his son. 'Pierre, *mon enfant*,[14] why, I didn't
recognize you!' He clasped him in an embrace, and tears began
to trickle down his cheeks.

'Come now, Papa, don't be naughty, don't be naughty, no
grand gestures, enough, enough, please, I beg you,' Petrusha
mumbled hurriedly, as he attempted to free himself from the
embrace.

'I've always felt guilty for the way I've treated you, always!'

'Enough of that, now; we'll talk about it later. I just knew
you'd start acting naughty. Now, do be a little more temperate,
please, I beg you.'

'But after all, I haven't seen you for ten years!'

'All the less reason for such effusions.'

'*Mon enfant!*'

'Come now, I believe you love me, I believe it, take your arms
away. You're embarrassing the others, you see . . . Ah, here's
Nikolay Vsevolodovich at last, now please stop acting naughty,
I beg you in all seriousness.'

In fact, Nikolay Vsevolodovich was already in the room. He
had come in very quietly and paused for a moment in the
doorway, casting a quiet glance over the assembled company.

As had been the case four years ago, when I had seen him for
the first time, so now on this occasion, too, I was struck when

I first saw him. I hadn't forgotten him in the least; but I think there are faces which, each time they appear, always seem to have something new to offer, something that has previously gone undetected by you, even though you've seen them at least a hundred times before. To all appearances, he was exactly the same as he had been four years ago: just as elegant, just as imposing – he came in just as imposingly as he had done then; he even looked almost as young. His slight smile was just as officially amiable and just as complacent; he had the same stern, pensive and apparently distracted look to him. In a word, it seemed as if we had parted only the day before. But one thing did strike me: previously, although he was considered handsome, his face really did 'look like a mask', as some of the evil-tongued ladies of our circle put it. But now – but now, I don't know why, he seemed to me, at the very first glance, to be definitely, unquestionably handsome, so much so that no one could possibly have said that his face looked like a mask. Perhaps it was because he had become ever so slightly paler than before, and seemed to have lost a little weight? Or perhaps he now had the gleam of some new idea in his eyes?

'Nikolay Vsevolodovich!' Varvara Petrovna exclaimed, sitting bolt upright but not getting out of her chair and stopping him with an authoritative gesture. 'Stay there for just a minute!'

But in order to explain the dreadful question that suddenly followed this gesture and this exclamation – a question whose implications I could not have imagined even Varvara Petrovna capable of – I will ask the reader to remember the kind of character Varvara Petrovna had possessed her whole life long, and her exceptional impulsiveness at other extraordinary moments. I will also ask the reader to consider that, despite her exceptional firmness of character and the large grain of common sense and practical, even, so to speak, managerial shrewdness that she possessed, still and all her life was not yet completely free of the kind of moments to which she suddenly abandoned herself entirely, wholly and, if I may so express myself, utterly without restraint. Finally, I ask you to take into consideration that the present moment might actually have been for her one of those in which the entire essence of her life

– everything that had been experienced, the entire present, and perhaps the future – was concentrated and focused. I will again mention in passing the anonymous letter she had received, and which she had earlier let slip about to Praskovya Ivanovna, in such a state of irritation, while saying nothing, I think, about what else was contained in the letter; and that perhaps was where the answer lay to the riddle of how she could possibly ask the dreadful question that she now suddenly put to her son.

'Nikolay Vsevolodovich,' she repeated, accentuating each word in a firm voice that had the menacing ring of a challenge, 'I ask you to tell me immediately, without moving from your place: is it true that this unfortunate, crippled woman – there she is, sitting over there, look at her! – is it true that she is . . . your lawful wife?'

I remember this moment all too well. Without even batting an eyelid he stared at his mother; not the slightest change registered on his face. Finally, he gave a kind of slow, condescending smile, and without saying a word, quietly walked up to his mother, took her hand, raised it respectfully to his lips and kissed it. And so powerful was the irresistible influence he always had on his mother that even now she didn't dare pull her hand away. She merely kept looking at him, all of her being one big question, and her entire manner said that in another instant she wouldn't be able to endure the uncertainty.

But he continued to remain silent. After kissing her hand, he glanced over the whole room once more, and, without hurrying, as before, headed directly for Marya Timofeyevna. It's very difficult to describe the way people look at certain moments. I seem to have remembered, for example, that Marya Timofeyevna, paralysed with fear, rose to greet him and clasped her hands in front of her, as if beseeching him; and at the same time I can remember the ecstasy in her eyes as well, a kind of mad ecstasy, which almost distorted her features – the kind of ecstasy that is difficult for people to endure. Perhaps both were present, both fear and ecstasy, but I remember that I quickly moved towards her (I was standing almost next to her); it seemed to me that she was about to faint.

'You shouldn't be here,' Nikolay Vsevolodovich said to her

in an affectionate, melodious voice, and an uncharacteristic tenderness glowed in his eyes. He was standing before her in an extremely deferential pose, and his every movement showed an utterly sincere respect for her. The poor girl impulsively began babbling to him in a breathless half-whisper:

'And may I . . . now . . . get on my knees before you?'

'No, that's absolutely impossible,' he bestowed a magnificent smile on her that made her grin in sudden joy. In the same melodic voice, and in a tenderly coaxing manner, as if she were a child, he added weightily:

'Keep in mind that you are a girl, and that even though I am your very devoted friend, I am still an outsider to you, not a husband, not a father, not a fiancé. Here, give me your hand, and let's go: I'll escort you to the carriage, and, if you will permit me, I'll take you to your house.'

She heard him out and bowed her head, as though deep in thought.

'Let's go,' she said, sighing and giving him her hand.

But at this point a small accident befell her. She must have turned carelessly somehow and stepped on her short, ailing leg – in a word, she fell sideways on to the chair and if it hadn't been for this chair, she would have landed on the floor. In a flash he caught her and held her, took her firmly by the arm and led her to the door carefully and solicitously. She was obviously distressed at having fallen; she became flustered, flushed and dreadfully ashamed. Quietly looking at the floor, and limping heavily, she hobbled along behind him, almost hanging from his arm. And so they went out. Liza, I saw, suddenly jumped up from her chair, for some reason, while they were walking out, and followed them with an unwavering stare until they reached the door. Then she sat down again in silence, but her face went into a kind of spasm, as if she had touched a viper.

While this scene between Nikolay Vsevolodovich and Marya Timofeyevna was being played out, everyone observed an astonished silence; you could have heard a fly; but as soon as they had gone out, everyone suddenly began talking.

6.

There was little actual talking, however, and more exclaiming. I don't quite remember the order in which everything occurred, because there was such confusion. Stepan Trofimovich exclaimed something in French and clasped his hands together, but Varvara Petrovna paid him no mind. Even Mavriky Nikolayevich presently muttered something abruptly and quickly. But Pyotr Stepanovich was more worked up than anyone else: he was desperately trying to convince Varvara Petrovna of something, with broad gestures, but for a long time I couldn't understand what he was saying. He also kept turning to Praskovya Ivanovna and Lizaveta Nikolayevna, and in a fit of temper even shouted something in passing at his father – in a word, he was spinning round the room like a top. Varvara Petrovna, all flushed, jumped up from her seat and shouted at Praskovya Ivanovna: 'Did you hear, did you hear what he just said to her here?' But Praskovya Ivanovna simply couldn't come up with an answer, and only muttered something, waving her hand dismissively. The poor woman had her own troubles: she kept constantly turning her head towards Liza and looking at her in unaccountable fear, no longer daring even to think of getting to her feet and leaving until her daughter had got up. At the same time the captain most likely wanted to slip away, I could see that. He had been in a state of utter and unmistakable panic from the very moment Nikolay Vsevolodovich turned up; but Pyotr Stepanovich seized him by the arm and wouldn't let him leave.

'It's essential, quite essential,' he kept dropping his verbal beads for Varvara Petrovna, still continuing his efforts to convince her. He was standing before her, and she was once again sitting in her armchair, and, I remember, listening to him eagerly; he had finally succeeded in getting her attention.

'It's essential. You can see for yourself, Varvara Petrovna, that this is just a misunderstanding, and there's a great deal that looks peculiar, while actually the matter is clear as glass and simple as grass. I understand only too well that I have not been empowered by anyone to tell you this, and perhaps I look ridiculous in trying to push myself forward. But in the first place, Nikolay Vsevolodovich himself doesn't attach any importance to this matter, and finally, there are, after all, cases where it is difficult for a man to make up his mind to explain himself personally, and it is absolutely necessary that a third party, who finds it easier to say certain delicate things, should take it upon himself. Believe me, Varvara Petrovna, when I say that Nikolay Vsevolodovich is in no way to blame for failing to reply straightaway and with some thorough explanation to the question you asked just now, even though the entire matter is utterly trivial. I have known him since Petersburg. Besides, the whole story only does honour to Nikolay Vsevolodovich, if it's absolutely necessary to use this vague word "honour".'

'Do you mean to say that you were witness to some incident that gave rise to this ... misunderstanding?' asked Varvara Petrovna.

'A witness and a participant,' Pyotr Stepanovich hastily confirmed.

'If you will give me your word that this will not offend Nikolay Vsevolodovich's delicacy with respect to certain of his feelings towards me, from whom he does not conceal an-y-thing ... and if, in addition, you are sure that by doing so you will even give him pleasure ...'

'Of course, it will give him pleasure, that's why I regard it as a special pleasure for myself. I'm sure he would have asked me himself.'

A rather strange thing it was, and quite contrary to customary form, this insistent desire on the part of a gentleman who had dropped so suddenly from the sky to tell other people's stories. But he had hooked Varvara Petrovna by touching on an extremely sensitive spot. As yet I didn't have full knowledge of the character of this man, let alone his intentions.

'I am listening,' Varvara Petrovna announced guardedly and cautiously, somewhat embarrassed by her own condescending manner.

'It's a short account, even, if you wish, not really a story at all,' he said, dropping another bead. 'Still and all, a novelist might be able to concoct a novel from it if he had nothing else to do. It's a rather interesting little thing, Praskovya Ivanovna, and I'm sure that Lizaveta Nikolayevna would be curious to hear it, because it has many if not wonderful, then passing strange things to offer. About five years ago, in Petersburg, Nikolay Vsevolodovich got to know this gentleman, the very gentleman who's standing there with his mouth open and who seemed to be hoping to slip out just now. Pardon me, Varvara Petrovna. However, I advise you not to cut and run, Mr Retired Clerk of the Commissariat Department (you see, I remember you very well). And the funny business you've been up to here, for which you will have to give an accounting, and don't you forget it, is well known to Nikolay Vsevolodovich and me. Once again, I beg your pardon, Varvara Petrovna. At that time Nikolay Vsevolodovich used to call this gentleman his Falstaff;[15] this must be,' he suddenly explained, 'some character in an old burlesque, whom everyone laughs at and who allows everyone to laugh at him provided they pay him money. At the time Nikolay Vsevolodovich was leading a life in Petersburg that was, so to speak, a mockery – I can't find any other word to define it, because he's not the kind of man who becomes easily discouraged, and he himself scorned the whole idea of undertaking any work at that time. I am speaking only of that particular period, Varvara Petrovna. This Lebyadkin had a sister – the very person who was just sitting here. Neither brother nor sister had a corner to call their own, and would make the rounds staying at other people's lodgings. He would hang around under the arches of the Gostiny Dvor,[16] always wearing his old uniform, and would stop the more respectable-looking passers-by, and whatever he would take in, he would drink up. But his sister lived like the birds of heaven. She would work as a charwoman in various corners in exchange for the bare necessities. It was a truly dreadful Sodom;[17] I shall omit giving you a picture of this life in the corners, a life to which, out of mere eccentricity, Nikolay Vsevolodovich was also devoted at that time. I'm speaking only of that period, Varvara Petrovna; and as far as "eccentricity" is concerned, that's his own expression. He doesn't hide very much from me. Mademoiselle Lebyadkina, who at one time had occasion to meet Nikolay Vsevolodovich far too often, was struck by his appearance. He was, so to speak, a diamond set against the filthy background of her life. I don't describe emotions very well, and I'll therefore let them pass, but some rotten little people immediately took to making fun of her, and she became very depressed. People generally used to laugh at her there, but before then she hadn't given it the slightest notice. Even then her head was no longer in good working order, but it was still not as bad as it is now. There is reason to suppose that in her childhood she almost received an education, through some benefactress. Nikolay Vsevolodovich never paid the slightest attention to her, and mostly played preference with greasy old cards for quarter-kopeck stakes with various clerks. But on one occasion, when she was being insulted, he (without inquiring as to the reason) grabbed a clerk by the scruff of the neck and threw him out of a second-storey window. There was no question of chivalrous indignation on behalf of injured innocence here; the whole business was carried out with everyone laughing away, and Nikolay Vsevolodovich himself laughing more than anyone else. And when everything ended happily, they all made peace and started drinking punch. But the injured innocent didn't forget about it. Naturally, the end result was the final derangement of her mental capacities. I repeat, I am not very good at describing feelings, but in this case the main thing was her fantasy. And Nikolay Vsevolodovich aggravated the fantasy, deliberately it would seem. Instead of laughing at her, he suddenly began to treat Mademoiselle Lebyadkina with unexpected respect. Kirillov, who was present there (an extraordinarily original and extraordinarily curt man; perhaps you'll see him some day, he's here now), well then, this Kirillov who had the habit of never opening his mouth, suddenly got all hot and bothered, and observed to Nikolay Vsevolodovich, I remember, that he was treating this young lady like a marquise and that this would finish her off for good. Let me add that Nikolay Vsevolodovich had some respect for this Kirillov. And what do you think? He replied as follows: "You are supposing, Mr Kirillov, that I'm laughing at her: disabuse yourself of that; I actually respect her, because she is better than all of us." And, you know, he said it in such a serious tone. Meanwhile, during these two or three months he essentially hadn't said a single word to her beyond "hello" and "goodbye". I was there at the time, and I remember clearly that she finally reached the point of regarding him as something like her fiancé, who didn't dare "elope with her" only because he had many enemies and family obstacles, or something of the sort. There was a lot of laughter about that! It ended when Nikolay Vsevolodovich had to leave for home at that particular time, and, as he was departing, he made arrangements for her support and, I think, for a substantial annual allowance, of at least three hundred roubles, if not more. In short, let's suppose this was all just a game on his part, the fancy of a prematurely weary man; let's even go as far as to grant, as Kirillov said, that this was a new experiment on the part of a jaded man whose purpose was to find out how far he could take a crazy crippled woman. "You," he said, "have purposely picked out the most hopeless of creatures, a cripple, who's constantly shamed and beaten, while fully aware, besides, that this creature is dying of a comic love for you, and suddenly you deliberately set out to fool her, simply to see what will come of it!" But when all is said and done, how can a man be particularly blamed for the fantasies of a crazy woman, to whom – mark it well – he has hardly uttered two words the entire time! There are things, Varvara Petrovna, of which it is not only impossible to speak intelligently, but of which it is not intelligent even to begin to speak. Well, let's grant that it's eccentricity, but it's really impossible to say more than that. Meanwhile, they've now created a whole story out of it ... To some extent I am familiar with what's going on here, Varvara Petrovna.'

The speaker suddenly broke off and was about to turn to Lebyadkin, but Varvara Petrovna stopped him. She was in an elevated state of exultation.

'Have you finished?' she asked.

'Not yet. For the sake of completeness, I would need to question this gentleman here about something, if you will permit it ... You will soon see what's at issue, Varvara Petrovna.'

'Enough, later; leave it for now, I ask you. Oh, what a good thing it was that I let you speak!'

'And note, Varvara Petrovna,' Pyotr Stepanovich said with renewed energy, 'could Nikolay Vsevolodovich himself really have explained all of this to you earlier, in answer to your question, which was perhaps too categorical?'

'Oh yes, much too much!'

'And wasn't I right in saying that in certain cases it's much easier for a third party to explain something than for the interested party himself?'

'Yes, yes ... But you were mistaken about one thing, and I see to my regret that you continue to be mistaken.'

'Really? What's that?'

'You see ... However, if you would sit down, Pyotr Stepanovich.'

'Oh, as you wish; I'm very tired myself, I thank you.'

In an instant he had pulled up an armchair and positioned it so that it stood between Varvara Petrovna on the one side and Praskovya Ivanovna at the table on the other, and was facing Mr Lebyadkin, from whom he didn't take his eyes for a moment.

'You are mistaken in calling this "eccentricity" ...'

'Oh, if that's all ...'

'No, no, no, wait,' Varvara Petrovna stopped him, obviously preparing to say a great deal and in a state of ecstasy. As soon as he noticed this, Pyotr Stepanovich was all attention.

'No, this was something higher than eccentricity, and, I assure you, even something sacred! A man who is proud and who has been humiliated at an early age, who has reached the stage of "mockery", as you so aptly put it – in a word, Prince Harry, to use the magnificent comparison that Stepan Trofimovich once made, and which would be perfectly accurate if he didn't resemble Hamlet[18] even more, at least as I see it.'

'*Et vous avez raison*,'[19] Stepan Trofimovich replied weightily and with feeling.

'I thank you, Stepan Trofimovich, you I thank especially and in particular for your unwavering faith in Nicolas, in the loftiness of his soul and his vocation. You even strengthened this faith in me, whenever I lost heart.'

'*Chère, chère* ...' Stepan Trofimovich made to take a step

forward, but he paused, deciding that it was dangerous to interrupt.

'And if Nicolas' (Varvara Petrovna was now almost singing) 'had had someone quiet by his side, great in his humility, a Horatio (another fine expression of yours, Stepan Trofimovich), then perhaps he would long ago have been saved from the "sudden demon of irony", which has tormented him all his life. (Again, the "demon of irony" is a marvellous expression of yours, Stepan Trofimovich.) But Nicolas never had either a Horatio or an Ophelia.[20] He had only his mother, but what can a mother possibly do by herself in such circumstances? You know, Pyotr Stepanovich, it's becoming perfectly understandable to me how a being like Nicolas could turn up even in such filthy holes as you were describing. I can now so clearly picture this "mockery" of life (a wonderfully apt expression of yours!), this insatiable thirst for contrast, this dark background of the picture against which he appears like a diamond, to use your comparison once again, Pyotr Stepanovich. And there he comes across a creature mistreated by all, a half-crazy cripple, yet someone who at the same time perhaps has the noblest of feelings!'

'Hmm, yes, let's suppose so.'

'And after all that you can't understand that he is not laughing at her, like everyone else! Oh, you people! You can't understand that he is defending her from those who mistreat her, that he's surrounding her with respect, "like a marquise" (this Kirillov must have an exceptionally deep understanding of people, although he had absolutely no understanding of Nicolas!). If you like, it was precisely this contrast that caused all the trouble. If the unfortunate woman had been in different circumstances, then perhaps she wouldn't have come up with such a hysterical fantasy. A woman, only a woman can understand that, Pyotr Stepanovich, and what a pity it is that you're ... that is, not that you're not a woman, but at least for this one occasion, so that you could understand!'

'That is to say, in the sense that the worse things are, the better – I understand, I understand, Varvara Petrovna. It's like religion: the worse a man's life is, or the more cowed or poorer an entire people is, then the more stubbornly they dream of a reward in paradise, and if a hundred thousand priests keep harping on it, fanning the flames of their dream and seeking to profit by it, then . . . I understand you, Varvara Petrovna, rest assured.'

'Well, that's not entirely what I meant, but tell me, was it really the case that Nicolas, in order to extinguish the fantasy in this unfortunate organism' (for what reason Varvara Petrovna used the word 'organism' in this context, I couldn't understand) 'had to laugh at her himself and treat her the same way the other clerks did? Are you really rejecting the lofty compassion, the noble tremor that shook his entire organism when Nicolas suddenly and sternly answered Kirillov: "I'm not laughing at her." A lofty, sacred answer!'

'*Sublime*,' muttered Stepan Trofimovich.

'And note that he is nowhere near as rich as you think; I'm the one who's rich, not he, and at that time he was taking almost nothing at all from me.'

'I understand, I understand all that, Varvara Petrovna,' said Pyotr Stepanovich, now fidgeting rather impatiently.

'Oh, that's my character! I recognize myself in Nicolas. I recognize this youthfulness, this possibility of stormy, violent impulses . . . And if you and I ever become close, Pyotr Stepanovich, which on my part I sincerely desire, the more so since I am already so indebted to you, then perhaps that is when you will understand . . .'

'Oh, believe me, on my part I do desire it,' Pyotr Stepanovich muttered abruptly.

'That is when you will understand the impulse that compels one, out of a blind sense of nobility, to take up a man who is even unworthy of one in every respect, who is profoundly lacking in any understanding of you, who is prepared to torment you at the first opportunity, and suddenly to incarnate such a man, despite everything, into some ideal, into one's own dream, fastening all one's hopes on him, bowing before him, loving him your entire life, without having the slightest idea what for, perhaps precisely because he is unworthy of it . . . Oh, how I've suffered my entire life, Pyotr Stepanovich!'

Stepan Trofimovich, a sickly expression on his face, began trying to catch my eye, but I avoided him in time.

'. . . And not long ago, not long ago – oh, how guilty I feel towards Nicolas! . . . You won't believe how they've tormented me from all quarters, everyone, everyone, enemies, and dreadful little people, and friends – friends perhaps more than enemies. When the first of those contemptible anonymous letters was sent to me, Pyotr Stepanovich, you won't believe it, but in the end I didn't have enough contempt in me to respond to all this malice . . . Never, never will I forgive myself for my faint-heartedness!'

'I've already heard some general talk about the anonymous letters here,' Pyotr Stepanovich suddenly came to life, 'and I'll find out for you who sent them, rest assured.'

'But you wouldn't believe the intrigues that have begun here! They've even tormented our poor Praskovya Ivanovna – and what reason is there to pick on her? Perhaps I've been very unjust to you today, my dear Praskovya Ivanovna,' she added, in an impassioned rush of magnanimity, but not without a certain triumphant irony.

'Oh, come now, dear lady,' Praskovya Ivanovna murmured reluctantly, 'in my opinion, an end should be put to all this; too much has been said . . .' and she stole another timid glance at Liza, who, however, was looking at Pyotr Stepanovich.

'And as for this poor, this unfortunate creature, this mad woman who has lost everything and has kept only her heart, I myself intend to adopt her,' Varvara Petrovna suddenly exclaimed. 'This is a sacred duty that I intend to fulfil. From this very day on, I am taking her under my protection!'

'And that will even be very good indeed, in a certain sense,' said Pyotr Stepanovich, now fully alert. 'Pardon me, I did not finish what I had to say a moment ago. It's precisely about patronage. Can you imagine that when Nikolay Vsevolodovich departed just then (I am beginning precisely from the place where I left off, Varvara Petrovna), that gentleman, that very gentleman standing there, Mr Lebyadkin, instantly imagined that he had the right to do what he wanted with the allowance that had been provided for his sister, without anything left over;

and so he did. I don't have exact knowledge of how it was set up by Nikolay Vsevolodovich, but within a year, while he was still abroad, he learned of what was happening and was compelled to make other arrangements. Again I don't know the details, he'll tell you himself; I know only that the interesting individual in question was placed somewhere in a remote convent, all very comfortably, but under friendly supervision – do you understand? What do you think Mr Lebyadkin made up his mind to do? First, he bent all his efforts to snoop out where his annuity, that is, his sister, was being hidden from him, and he achieved his goal not long ago; he removed her from the convent, after laying some claim to her, and brought her straight here. Now he doesn't feed her; he beats her, he tyrannizes her and, when he finally receives by some means a considerable sum of money from Nikolay Vsevolodovich, he proceeds to get drunk, and instead of gratitude he ends by issuing an impertinent challenge to Nikolay Vsevolodovich, making senseless demands, and threatening, in the event that the pension is not paid directly to him in advance, to take him to court. And so, he takes Nikolay Vsevolodovich's voluntary gift as something that's owed him. Can you imagine that? Mr Lebyadkin, is *everything* that I've just been saying here true?'

The captain, who until now had been standing silently with his eyes lowered, took two quick steps forward and flushed deeply.

'Pyotr Stepanovich, you've acted cruelly towards me,' he said abruptly.

'How is that being cruel, and why do you say that? But excuse me, we can talk about cruelty or kindness later, but now all I'm asking you is to answer my first question: is *everything* that I've been saying true or not? If you find that it's not true, then you can immediately make a declaration to that effect.'

'I . . . you yourself know, Pyotr Stepanovich . . .' the captain mumbled, broke off and fell silent. It should be noted that Pyotr Stepanovich was sitting in an armchair, with his legs crossed, while the captain stood in front of him in an extremely respectful pose.

Mr Lebyadkin's hesitations were apparently not at all to

Pyotr Stepanovich's liking; his face twisted in an angry spasm.

'Do you mean there's really nothing you want to say?' He looked shrewdly at the captain. 'If there is, please do say. Everyone's waiting.'

'You yourself know, Pyotr Stepanovich, that there's nothing I can say.'

'No, I don't know that; it's the first time I've even heard it. Why is it that you can't say anything?'

The captain remained silent, his eyes looking at the floor.

'Allow me to leave, Pyotr Stepanovich,' he said firmly.

'But not before you give some answer to my first question: is *everything* that I've been saying true?'

'Indeed, it's true,' Lebyadkin said in a dull voice, raising his eyes to his tormentor. Beads of sweat broke out on his temples.

'*Everything* is true?'

'Indeed, everything is true.'

'Do you find that you have anything to add, to comment on? If you feel that we're being unjust, then say so; protest, announce your dissatisfaction for all to hear.'

'No, nothing.'

'Did you recently make threats against Nikolay Vsevolodovich?'

'That . . . that was more the drink that anything else, Pyotr Stepanovich.' (He suddenly raised his head.) 'Pyotr Stepanovich! If family honour and the heart's unmerited disgrace cry out among people, then is a man really to blame?' he roared, suddenly forgetting himself as he had before.

'And are you sober now, Mr Lebyadkin?' Pyotr Stepanovich fixed a penetrating look on him.

'I . . . am sober.'

'What is the meaning of family honour and the heart's unmerited disgrace?'

'I wasn't saying that about anyone, I didn't have anyone in mind. I was talking about myself . . .' the captain collapsed again.

'You seem to have been highly offended by what I said about you and your behaviour. You are easily irritated, Mr Lebyadkin. But just wait, I haven't even begun to say anything yet

about your behaviour in its present form. I'll begin to speak
about your behaviour in its present form. I'll begin to speak,
that's very likely to happen, but I haven't yet begun to do so –
not in its *present* form.'

Lebyadkin shuddered and stared wildly at Pyotr Stepanovich.

'Pyotr Stepanovich, I'm only now beginning to wake up!'

'Hmm. And am I the one who woke you?'

'Yes, you're the one who woke me, Pyotr Stepanovich, and
I've been asleep for four years with a storm cloud hanging over
me. May I withdraw now, Pyotr Stepanovich?'

'Now you may, provided that Varvara Petrovna does not
find it necessary to . . .'

But she waved her hand in dismissal.

The captain bowed, took two steps towards the door, suddenly stopped, placed his hand on his heart, was about to say
something, didn't say it and quickly ran out. But just as he was
going through the doorway he bumped into Nikolay Vsevolodovich, who stepped aside. The captain seemed to shrink
before him somehow and remained rooted to the spot, without
tearing his eyes from him, like a rabbit facing a boa constrictor.
After waiting a moment, Nikolay Vsevolodovich pushed him
gently aside and walked into the drawing room.

7.

He was cheerful and calm. Perhaps something very good had
just happened to him, which we didn't yet know about; but he
even seemed to be particularly gratified by something.

'Do you forgive me, Nicolas?' Varvara Petrovna couldn't
restrain herself, and quickly stood up to greet him.

But Nicolas positively burst out laughing.

'Just as I thought!' he exclaimed in a good-natured and joking
way. 'I see that everything is already known to you. And as
soon as I'd left here, I got to thinking in the carriage: "I should
at least have told you the story, because who after all goes off
like that!" But as soon as I remembered that Pyotr Stepanovich
was still with you, then all my worries disappeared.'

As he was speaking, he gave a cursory glance around.

'Pyotr Stepanovich told us a certain old Petersburg story from the life of a certain odd fellow,' Varvara Petrovna picked up the thread enthusiastically, 'a certain individual who was eccentric and crazy, but always with lofty feelings, and always chivalrous and noble . . .'

'Chivalrous? Did it really come to that?' Nicolas was laughing. 'However, this time I'm very grateful to Pyotr Stepanovich for being hasty.' (Here he exchanged a fleeting glance with him.) 'You should know, maman, that Pyotr Stepanovich is a universal peacemaker; that's his role, his sickness, his hobby horse, and I especially recommend him to you on this point. I think I can guess the sort of line he's been handing you here. He can't help handing out a line whenever he has something to tell; he has a whole record office in his head. Note that in his capacity as a realist he cannot tell a lie, and that truth is dearer to him than success . . . except of course for those special cases where success is dearer than the truth.' (As he was saying this, he kept looking round.) 'And so, you can clearly see, maman, that it's not up to you to ask my forgiveness, and if there's any craziness going on anywhere here, then of course it comes from me, and in the final analysis that means I'm the one who's deranged – after all, I have to keep up the reputation I have in these parts . . .'

At this point he embraced his mother tenderly.

'In any event, this matter is now done with and talked about, and we can therefore let it drop,' he added, and a certain dry, resolute tone could be heard in his voice. Varvara Petrovna understood this tone, but her exaltation did not pass – quite the contrary.

'I wasn't expecting you for at least a month, Nicolas!'

'Naturally, I'll explain everything to you, maman, but now . . .'

And he went over to Praskovya Ivanovna.

But she barely turned her head in his direction, despite the fact that she had been stunned half an hour ago when he first appeared. Now she had new things to worry about: from the moment the captain had walked out and bumped into Nikolay Vsevolodovich in the doorway, Liza had suddenly begun to laugh – at first quietly and fitfully, but her laughter kept growing and growing, louder and more audible. She had turned crimson. The contrast with her recent gloomy look was extraordinary. While Nikolay Vsevolodovich was talking with Varvara Petrovna, she beckoned Mavriky Nikolayevich over to her once or twice, as if wishing to whisper something to him; but no sooner had he bent over her than she burst into peals of laughter. One might conclude that it was precisely Mavriky Nikolayevich who was the butt of her laughter. However, she was making an obvious effort to control herself and kept pressing her handkerchief to her lips. Nikolay Vsevolodovich turned to greet her with the most innocent and ingenuous look.

'Please excuse me,' she responded in a rapid patter, 'you, you of course have met Mavriky Nikolayevich . . . Lord, how inexcusably tall you are, Mavriky Nikolayevich!'

And again, laughter. Mavriky Nikolayevich was tall, but by no means inexcusably so.

'Have you . . . been here long?' she murmured, again trying to control herself, and even looking flustered, but with flashing eyes.

'A couple of hours or so,' Nicolas replied, looking at her intently. I will note that he was unusually reserved and polite, but, politeness aside, he had an utterly indifferent, even listless look to him.

'And where will you be staying?'

'Here.'

Varvara Petrovna was also watching Liza, but she was suddenly struck by a thought.

'Where have you been until now, Nicolas, all these two hours and then some?' She went up to him. 'The train arrives at ten o'clock.'

'I first took Pyotr Stepanovich to Kirillov's. I met Pyotr Stepanovich at Matveyevo,' (three stations away) 'we travelled here in the same railway carriage.'

'I had been waiting in Matveyevo since dawn,' Pyotr Stepanovich chimed in, 'our rear carriages were derailed during the night; my legs were almost broken.'

'Your legs broken!' Liza exclaimed. 'Maman, maman, and

you and I wanted to go to Matveyevo last week, so our legs would have been broken too!'

'Good Lord!' Praskovya Ivanovna crossed herself.

'Maman, maman, dearest ma, don't you be frightened if I should really break both legs; that could certainly happen to me, since as you tell me that I gallop on my horse every day at the risk of breaking my head. Mavriky Nikolayevich, will you be my guide when I'm crippled?' She began to laugh again. 'If that happens, I won't let anyone but you be my guide, you can safely count on that. Well, let's suppose I break only one leg ... Now, be nice, tell me you'll consider that good luck.'

'What kind of good luck is that, just one leg?' Mavriky Nikolayevich frowned solemnly.

'But you'll be my guide, only you, no one else!'

'Then it's you who'll be my guide, Lizaveta Nikolayevna,' Mavriky Nikolayevich grumbled even more solemnly.

'Good heavens, he actually wanted to make a joke!' Liza exclaimed almost in horror. 'Mavriky Nikolayevich, don't you ever dare strike out on that path! But what an egotist you are! I am convinced, to your credit, that you're now slandering yourself. On the contrary: then you'll be trying to reassure me, from morning till night, that I've become more interesting without a leg! There's one thing that can't be fixed: you're so much taller than I am, and without a leg I'll become really tiny; how are you going to lead me by the arm? We won't be much of a couple!'

And she burst into unhealthy peals of laughter. Her jokes and innuendoes fell flat but evidently she cared nothing about making a good impression.

'Hysterics!' Pyotr Stepanovich whispered to me. 'A glass of water as quickly as possible.'

He had put his finger on it; a moment later and everyone was bustling about, water was brought. Liza was hugging her mother, kissing her warmly, crying on her shoulder, and then, suddenly rearing back and peering into her face, proceeded to start laughing. Finally, even her mother began whimpering. Varvara Petrovna quickly led them both off to her own quarters, through the same door from which Darya Pavlovna had earlier emerged into the drawing room. But they didn't remain there for long; four minutes or so, no more . . .

I'm now trying to recall each detail of the last moments of that memorable morning. I remember that when we had been left alone, without the ladies (except for Darya Pavlovna, who hadn't budged from her seat), Nikolay Vsevolodovich went round and exchanged greetings with each of us except Shatov, who continued sitting in his corner, his head bowed even lower than before. Stepan Trofimovich was on the point of making some extremely witty remark to Nikolay Vsevolodovich, but the young man quickly moved off towards Darya Pavlovna. But on the way, Pyotr Stepanovich grabbed him almost by force and dragged him over to the window, where he proceeded to tell him something in a rapid whisper, evidently very important, to judge by the expression on his face and the gestures that accompanied the whispering. But Nikolay Vsevolodovich was listening very lackadaisically and distractedly, wearing his official smile, and, in the end, even impatiently, as if eager to leave. He walked away from the window at the moment the ladies returned: Varvara Petrovna had Liza sit in the same chair, trying to reassure her by saying that they should delay their departure at least ten minutes to rest, and that at the moment fresh air would hardly be beneficial for weak nerves. She was very attentive to Liza and took a seat next to her. Pyotr Stepanovich, who was free now, immediately trotted over to them and initiated a rapid and cheerful conversation. Upon which Nikolay Vsevolodovich finally went up to Darya Pavlovna at his unhurried pace; Dasha actually began to sway in her seat as he approached, and quickly leaped up in evident confusion and with her face all crimson.

'I take it that you can now be congratulated . . . or not yet?' he said with a peculiar sort of furrow on his face.

Dasha made some reply, but it was hard to hear.

'Forgive my indelicacy,' he raised his voice, 'but you see, I was expressly informed. Did you know that?'

'Yes, I know that you were expressly informed.'

'I hope, however, that I haven't disturbed anything with my congratulations,' he laughed, 'and if Stepan Trofimovich . . .'

'What's the occasion for congratulations, then?' Pyotr Stepanovich suddenly trotted up. 'What are you to be congratulated
for, Darya Pavlovna? Oh, I see! Is it really for that? Your
blushing tells me that I've guessed right. In fact, what does one
congratulate our pretty and well-behaved young girls for, and
what kind of congratulations make them blush the most? Well
then, please accept mine as well, if I have guessed right, and
pay your bet: you remember that in Switzerland you bet me that
you would never get married. Oh, yes, speaking of Switzerland,
what am I thinking of? Just imagine, it's half the reason I've
come here, and I almost forgot. Tell me,' he quickly turned
to Stepan Trofimovich, 'when is it you're actually going to
Switzerland?'

'I . . . to Switzerland?' Stepan Trofimovich was astonished
and flustered.

'What? Are you really not going? Why, you're getting
married too . . . didn't you write to me?'

'Pierre!' Stepan Trofimovich exclaimed.

'What do you mean "Pierre"? Don't you see, that if it pleases
you, I've come flying here to say that I have nothing at all
against it, since you absolutely wanted my opinion as soon as
possible. But if' (another bead dropped) 'you need to be
"saved", as you wrote and pleaded at the very same time in the
very same letter, then I'm again at your service. Is it true that
he's getting married, Varvara Petrovna?' He turned to her
quickly. 'I hope I'm not being indiscreet; he himself writes that
the whole town knows and that everyone is congratulating him,
so to avoid it he only goes out at night. I have the letter in my
pocket. But would you believe it, Varvara Petrovna, I don't
understand anything in it! Just tell me one thing, Stepan Trofimovich, are you to be congratulated or "saved"? You wouldn't
believe it, but one line sounds as happy as can be, and the next
is written in the depths of despair. In the first place, he asks my
forgiveness; well, let's suppose that's just his way . . . Still and
all, it's impossible not to say it: just imagine, the man has seen
me twice in my life, and quite by accident at that, and suddenly
now, as he enters upon his third marriage, he imagines that he
is violating some parental obligations he has towards me, and

at a distance of a thousand versts he begs me not to get angry and to give my permission! Please, don't be offended, Stepan Trofimovich, it's a sign of the times; I have a broad outlook on things and I don't judge, and that, let's suppose, does you honour, etc., etc., but once again the main thing is that it's precisely the main thing that I don't understand. There's something here about some "sins in Switzerland". I'm getting married, it says, on account of sins, or because of another man's sins, or however it's stated there – in short, "sins". "The girl," he says, "is a pearl and a diamond", and naturally enough, "he's unworthy" – that's his expression. But because of some sins or circumstances there, he is "forced to make a trip to the altar and go to Switzerland", and I'm supposed to "drop everything and come flying to save" him? Do you understand anything of all this? And yet ... and yet, I see from the expression on your faces,' (letter in hand, he was turning to scrutinize each face with an innocent smile) 'that I seem to have committed a blunder, as is usual with me ... through this stupid outspokenness of mine or, as Nikolay Vsevolodovich says, haste. I really did think we were all good friends here, that is, all your good friends, Stepan Trofimovich, all your good friends, whereas I am essentially an outsider, and I can see ... I can see that everyone knows something, and I'm precisely the one who doesn't know.'

He continued to look around him.

'Stepan Trofimovich actually wrote to you that he's getting married for "another man's sins that were committed in Switzerland", and that you should come flying to "save" him, these were his exact words?' Varvara Petrovna suddenly came up to him; all yellow, her face distorted, her lips quivering.

'That is to say, don't you see, if there's something I didn't understand here,' said Pyotr Stepanovich, as if alarmed and speaking even more rapidly than before, 'he's the one to blame, of course, for writing it. Here's the letter. You know, Varvara Petrovna, the letters are endless and relentless, and in the past two or three months there's simply been one letter after another, and sometimes, I confess, I couldn't bring myself to finish reading them. Please forgive me, Stepan Trofimovich, for my stupid confession; but you will agree, after all, that although I was the one you were addressing them to, you were really writing more for posterity, so you really shouldn't mind a bit. Come now, don't be offended. You and I are good friends, after all! But this particular letter, Varvara Petrovna, this letter I did read through to the end. These so-called "sins" – these "another man's sins"– these are probably some of our own peccadilloes and as innocent as can be, I'll bet; but because of them we've suddenly taken it into our heads to kick up a dreadful scandal with a noble tinge to it – and it was precisely for the sake of the noble tinge that we kicked it up. There's something not quite sound, you see, in our accounts department – that should be acknowledged once and for all. We're very susceptible to a nice little game of cards, you know . . . Still and all, that's neither here nor there, that's certainly neither here nor there, my apologies. I talk too much, but, I swear, Varvara Petrovna, he gave me a scare, and part of me was really getting ready to "save" him. Finally I myself felt ashamed. What am I doing, creeping up to him and putting a knife to his throat? Am I some unforgiving creditor, is that it? He writes something here about a dowry. But you don't mean to say you're really getting married, are you, Stepan Trofimovich? Maybe it's just all talk, after all, we talk and talk mostly just to hear ourselves rattle on . . . Varvara Petrovna, I'm really convinced that you are perhaps finding fault with me now, precisely because of my style of speaking?'

'On the contrary, on the contrary, I can see that you've lost patience, and for perfectly good reasons, of course,' Varvara Petrovna rejoined spitefully.

She had listened with spiteful relish to all the 'truthful' verbal outpourings of Pyotr Stepanovich, who was obviously playing a part (what kind I didn't know at the time, but the part was obviously a part, and even too crudely played for words).

'On the contrary,' she continued, 'I'm extremely grateful to you for what you have said; otherwise I would simply not have found out. For the first time in twenty years my eyes have been opened. Nikolay Vsevolodovich, you just said that you were expressly informed too. Stepan Trofimovich didn't write to you in the same vein as well?'

'I received a very innocent letter from him ... and a very honourable one ...'

'You're having a hard time of it, you're searching for words – enough! Stepan Trofimovich, I expect you to do me an extraordinary favour,' she suddenly turned to him with flashing eyes, 'be so kind as to leave us at once, and do not set a foot across the threshold of my house in future.'

I ask you to recall her recent 'exaltation', which had not passed even now. True enough, Stepan Trofimovich was unquestionably guilty! But here's what positively astounded me then: the fact that he stood his ground with surprising dignity, even in the face of Petrusha's 'exposés', without even thinking of trying to interrupt them, and in the face of Varvara Petrovna's 'curse'. Where in heaven's name did he muster up such spirit? One thing I did learn was that he had undoubtedly been deeply offended by this first meeting with Petrusha, specifically by the way they had exchanged embraces. This was a deep and *genuine* sorrow to his heart, at least as he saw it. At that moment he felt another sorrow as well, namely, the sting of his own awareness for having acted like a scoundrel; he later admitted this to me in all frankness. Yet the *genuine*, unambiguous sorrow of even a phenomenally frivolous man is sometimes capable of making him solid and steadfast, albeit for a short time. Moreover, sincere, genuine sorrow has sometimes even made fools wise, also, of course, for a time; such is precisely the nature of sorrow. And if that's the case, then what might conceivably happen with a man like Stepan Trofimovich? A whole radical turnabout – only for a time, of course.

He bowed to Varvara Petrovna with dignity, and didn't utter a word (to be sure, there was nothing for him to say). At that point he simply wanted to be gone, but he couldn't restrain himself and went up to Darya Pavlovna. She seemed to have been anticipating this, because she herself immediately began to speak, all in a flutter, as if hurrying to forestall him.

'Please, Stepan Trofimovich, for heaven's sake, don't say anything,' she began in a rapid patter, with a pained expression on her face, and hastily extending her hand to him, 'rest assured that I respect you as I always have ... and esteem you as I always have, and . . . think well of me too, Stepan Trofimovich, and I will cherish you very, very much . . .'

Stepan Trofimovich bowed to her very low, very low indeed.

'It is up to you, Darya Petrovna, you know that in this matter it is entirely up to you! So it has been and is, both now and in the future,' Varvara Petrovna concluded weightily.

'I see! Why, now I understand everything!' Pyotr Stepanovich struck himself on the forehead. 'But . . . but after this, what an awful position I have been put in! Darya Petrovna, please excuse me! . . . What is it you've done to me after all this, eh?' He turned to his father.

'Pierre, you could have expressed yourself differently to me, couldn't you, my friend?' Stepan Trofimovich said, quite softly.

'Don't shout, please,' said Pierre, with a wave of his hands, 'believe me, it's all your sick old nerves, and it serves no purpose to shout. What you should tell me instead is why you couldn't have imagined that I would start speaking from the very outset, why you couldn't have warned me.'

Stepan Trofimovich looked at him searchingly.

'Pierre, since you know so much of what's going on here, did you really know absolutely nothing about this business, and did you hear nothing about it?'

'Wha-a-at? What sort of people you are! So it's not enough that we're old children, we're spiteful children as well! Varvara Petrovna, did you hear what he's saying?'

An uproar followed, but just then a remarkable incident which absolutely no one could have anticipated suddenly broke upon all of us.

8.

First of all I should mention that in the course of the past two or three minutes, Lizaveta Nikolayevna had been possessed by some new impulse. She was exchanging rapid whispers about something with her mother and with Mavriky Nikolayevich, who was bending over her. Her face showed alarm, but at the same time reflected decisiveness. Finally she rose from her seat, evidently in a hurry to leave and hurrying her mother, whom

Mavriky Nikolayevich was trying to help up from the armchair. But it seemed they were not destined to leave until they had witnessed everything to the end.

Shatov, completely forgotten by everyone in his corner (which wasn't far from Lizaveta Nikolayevna), and who seemingly had no idea himself why he was sitting there and not leaving, suddenly got up from his chair and with an unhurried but firm step made for Nikolay Vsevolodovich on the other side of the room, looking him straight in the face. The latter noticed him approaching while he was still some distance away, and gave a slight smile, but when Shatov came right up to him, he stopped smiling.

When Shatov stopped in front of him, saying nothing, and not taking his eyes off him, everyone suddenly noticed and grew quiet, Pyotr Stepanovich last of all; Liza and her mother stopped in the middle of the room. Some five seconds passed in this way; the expression of puzzled impertinence on Nikolay Vsevolodovich's face was succeeded by anger; he gave a frown, and suddenly . . .

And suddenly Shatov swung his long, heavy arm and hit him on the cheek with all his might. Nikolay Vsevolodovich reeled violently.

Shatov had a special way of delivering the blow, not at all the way a slap on the cheek is usually delivered (provided one can put it that way); not with the palm of the hand, but with the entire fist, and his fist was large, weighty, bony, covered with red hair and freckles. If the blow had landed on the nose, it would have been broken. But it landed on the cheek, and grazed the left corner of the lip and upper teeth, from which blood promptly began to pour.

I think I heard a sudden cry, perhaps it was Varvara Petrovna who cried out – I don't recall, because everything froze again, as it were. However, the entire scene lasted no more than ten seconds or so.

Nevertheless, during these ten seconds an awful lot occurred.

I will again remind the reader that Nikolay Vsevolodovich had the kind of constitution that knew no fear. In a duel he was able to stand cold-bloodedly facing his opponent's shot, then take aim himself and kill him with all the calmness of a beast. If someone had hit him on the cheek, then, or so it seems to me, he wouldn't even have challenged him to a duel, but would have killed the offender right on the spot, without further ado. That was the sort of person he was, and he would have killed with full awareness of what he was doing, and not because he had lost control of himself. It even seems to me that he had never known any of those blinding surges of anger that make rational thought impossible. Even when overcome with boundless rage, as was sometimes the case, he could still maintain full control of himself, and therefore also understand that for a murder not committed during a duel, he would be sentenced to hard labour. Nevertheless, he would still have killed the person who had insulted him, and without the slightest hesitation.

I have been constantly studying Nikolay Vsevolodovich of late, and given the special circumstances, I know a great many facts about him now, as I write this. I would perhaps compare him with some gentlemen of the past, of whom our society keeps alive certain legendary memories. People used to say, for example, of the Decembrist L—n,[21] that he purposely sought out danger all his life, would revel in the sensation of it, would make it a necessary part of his nature. In his youth he would fight a duel for no reason. In Siberia he would go after a bear with just a knife, and in the Siberian forests he loved to come across escaped convicts, who, I will note in passing, were more terrifying than any bear. There is no doubt that these legendary gentlemen were capable of experiencing, and even perhaps to a high degree, a sense of fear; otherwise, they would have been much more calm, and the sense of danger would not have become a necessary part of their nature. But to overcome cowardice in themselves – that, of course, is what proved so seductive. The constant revelling in victory and the awareness that there was no one who could get the better of you – that's what attracted them. This L—n, even before his exile, struggled with hunger for some time, and through arduous labour earned his own bread solely because he had absolutely no desire to submit himself to the demands of his rich father, whom he considered unjust. Therefore, his understanding of struggle had

many sides to it: he valued steadfastness and strength of character in himself, not just in encounters with bears and in duels.

Still and all, many years have passed since then, and the
nervous, tormented and divided nature of the people of our
time doesn't even make the slightest allowance now for the
need of those immediate and undiluted sensations that were
then so sought after by some gentlemen of the good old days,
who were restlessly active. Nikolay Vsevolodovich would perhaps have treated L—n condescendingly, might even have
called him a coward who was constantly showing off, a strutting
cock, though of course he wouldn't have said so aloud. He
would certainly have shot his opponent in a duel, and would
have gone up against a bear, if it were absolutely necessary,
and would have defended himself against a robber in the forest,
just as successfully and fearlessly as L—n, yet without any
sense of enjoyment, and only out of unpleasant necessity, and
unenthusiastically, lackadaisically, even with a feeling of boredom. As far as his rage was concerned, there had been progress
compared with L—n, even with Lermontov.[22] There was more
rage in Nikolay Vsevolodovich, perhaps, than in those other
two put together, but it was a cold, calm and, if one can put it
this way, *rational* rage, and therefore, the most repellent and
most dreadful kind there can be. I repeat: even at that time I
regarded him, and even now (when everything is already over)
I regard him, as precisely the kind of man who, if he had
received a blow in the face or some such equivalent insult,
would immediately have killed his opponent, right on the spot
and without challenging him to a duel.

And yet, in the present situation, something different and
wonderful occurred.

Scarcely had he regained his balance after the shame of reeling
to one side, almost halfway to the floor, from the slap he had
been dealt, and scarcely had the humiliating, sodden-sounding
blow of the fist in his face died away, when he immediately
grabbed Shatov by the shoulders with both hands; but immediately, at virtually the same instant, he jerked both his hands
away and crossed them behind his back. He said nothing, but
merely looked at Shatov, and turned white as a sheet. But

strangely enough, the light in his eyes seemed to be going out. Ten seconds later his eyes had a cold and (I'm sure I'm not lying) calm look to them. The only thing going on was that he was dreadfully pale. Naturally, I don't know what was inside the man, I could see only the outside. It seems to me that if there were a man, for example, who would seize a red-hot iron bar and squeeze it in his hand in order to test his toughness, and then, for a whole ten seconds had tried to overcome the unbearable pain and ended by overcoming it, then this man, it seems to me, would have endured something like what Nikolay Vsevolodovich experienced for these ten seconds.

Shatov was the first to lower his eyes, and evidently because he was compelled to lower them. Then he slowly turned and began to walk out of the room, but in a very different way than he had just walked up to Nikolay Vsevolodovich. He went out quietly, with his shoulders hunched in a peculiarly awkward way, his head lowered, and apparently deep in debate with himself. He seemed to be whispering something. He walked up to the door cautiously, without catching against or overturning anything, opened the door just a crack and slipped through the opening almost sideways. As he was going out, the unruly lock of hair standing straight up on the back of his head was especially noticeable.

Then, before anyone else had a chance to cry out, one dreadful cry rang out. I saw Lizaveta Nikolayevna seize her mother by the shoulder and Mavriky Nikolayevich by the arm and pull at them two or three times as she tried to drag them out of the room, but suddenly she screamed and collapsed on to the floor in a faint. To this day I can still hear the sound of her head hitting the carpet.

PART II

CHAPTER I

Night

1.

Eight days passed. Now, when everything is over and I am writing my chronicle, we know what the situation was; but at that time we knew nothing, and it was natural that various things struck us as being strange. Stepan Trofimovich and I at least shut ourselves up at first and observed things apprehensively from a distance. I for one would still go out here and there, and, as before, bring him various bits of news without which he couldn't survive.

Needless to say, rumours of all different kinds began circulating through the town, concerning, of course, the slap in the face, Lizaveta Nikolayevna's fainting spell, and everything else that had happened on that Sunday. But what surprised us was this: who could have brought all of this to light so quickly and accurately? Not one of the people then present would have had, or so it seemed, any need to expose the secret of what had happened, or anything to gain by doing so. There were no servants there; only Lebyadkin might have blabbed something, not so much from malice, because he had left the room in extreme apprehension (and fear of an enemy eradicates any malice towards him), but only from lack of self-control. But Lebyadkin, along with his sister, had vanished without a trace the very next day; he wasn't to be found in Filippov's house, he had moved somewhere unknown and in effect had vanished. Shatov, whom I wanted to ask about Marya Timofeyevna, had shut himself up and apparently had spent those eight days sitting in his apartment, even abandoning his work in town. He would not receive me. I had gone to his place on Tuesday and knocked at the door. I received no reply, but I was certain, from unmistakable signs, that he was at home, and I knocked a second time. Then, apparently jumping off his bed, he strode up to the door with heavy steps and shouted to me at the top of his voice: 'Shatov is not at home.' With that I left.

Stepan Trofimovich and I, not without trepidation at our bold supposition, but mutually supportive, finally arrived at the same idea: we decided that the one responsible for spreading the rumours was none other than Pyotr Stepanovich, even though sometime later, in the course of a conversation with his father, he insisted that he had already found the story on everyone's lips, primarily in the club, and thoroughly known in its tiniest details to the governor's wife and her spouse. And here's what's remarkable as well: that by the next day, on Monday evening, I ran across Liputin, and he already knew everything, every word of it; so he undoubtedly had been one of the first to find out about it.

Many of the ladies (even from the highest society) were also curious about the 'mysterious cripple', as they called Marya Timofeyevna. There were even those who were intent on seeing her in person and making her acquaintance, so that the gentlemen who had hastened to hide the Lebyadkins away had obviously done the right thing. But the main topic was Lizaveta Nikolayevna's fainting spell, and this was a matter of interest to all of society, if only for the fact that it directly involved Yuliya Mikhaylovna, as Lizaveta Nikolayevna's relative and protectress. And the things they chattered on about! The chattering was fed by the mysterious nature of the situation: both houses were shut up tight; Lizaveta Nikolayevna, as people were reporting, was confined to her bed in a state of delirium; the same thing was affirmed about Nikolay Vsevolodovich as well, with disgusting details about a tooth that supposedly had been knocked out and a swollen, abscessed cheek. In certain little corners it was even said that we would perhaps have a murder, that Stavrogin was not the kind of man to tolerate such an insult, and would kill Shatov, but secretly, as in a Corsican vendetta.[1] This idea had its appeal, but the majority of our fashionable young people listened to all this with contempt and with an air of the most disdainful indifference, which was of course a sham. In general, the ancient enmity that our society felt towards Nikolay Vsevolodovich was clearly evident. Even serious-minded people were eager to accuse him, although of what, they themselves didn't know. It was whispered that he had compromised the honour of Lizaveta Nikolayevna, and that they had had an affair in Switzerland. Cautious people of course held back, but everyone nevertheless listened with relish. Other things were said as well, though not in public, but in private, on rare occasions and almost in secret, extremely strange things, the existence of which I mention merely by way of warning readers, and solely in view of the events that lie ahead in my narrative. Namely, some were saying, knitting their brows and Lord knows on what grounds, that Nikolay Vsevolodovich had some special business in our province, that through Count K. he had made some higher connections in Petersburg, that he was perhaps even in government service and had come all but entrusted with some special mission by someone. When very serious-minded and restrained people smiled at this rumour, sensibly noting that a man who lived for scandal and had begun his stay in town with a swollen cheek didn't look like a government official, people whispered back that he wasn't exactly working in an official capacity, but confidentially,[2] so to speak, and that in such a case the very nature of his work required that the person in question should look as little like a government official as possible. Such an observation produced an effect; it was known in our town that the zemstvo[3] in our province was being watched with some special attention in the capital. Let me repeat: these rumours merely flared up and then disappeared without a trace, when Nikolay Vsevolodovich first came on the scene; but let me note that the cause of many of the rumours was to some extent the few but spiteful words that had been vaguely and abruptly spoken in the club by a retired Guards captain, Artemy Pavlovich Gaganov, who had recently returned from Petersburg. He was a very large landowner in our province and district, a man who circulated in the higher circles of the capital, and the son of the late Pavel Pavlovich Gaganov, the very same respected senior member of

our club, with whom Nikolay Vsevolodovich, more than four
years ago, had had a clash that was extraordinary for its coarseness and unexpectedness, and which I have previously
mentioned, at the beginning of my story.

It immediately became known to all that Yuliya Mikhaylovna
had made a special visit to Varvara Petrovna, and that she was
informed, at the front steps of the house, that 'because of ill
health she could not be received'. It also became known that
two days or so after her visit Yuliya Mikhaylovna sent someone
expressly to inquire about Varvara Petrovna's health. Finally,
she set to 'defending' Varvara Petrovna everywhere, only of
course in the very highest sense, that is, in the vaguest possible
terms. She listened sternly and coldly to all of the initial hasty
insinuations about what had happened on that Sunday, so that
in the days that followed, they were no longer repeated in
her presence. The idea, therefore, became firmly established
everywhere that not only was this mysterious story known
to Yuliya Mikhaylovna in its entirety, but that its mysterious
meaning was also known in its entirety as well, down to the
tiniest detail, and that she had not been an outsider, but an
actual participant. I will note, incidentally, that she had already
begun gradually to exert that lofty influence among us which
she had so unmistakably been striving and thirsting for, and
was already beginning to see herself as 'surrounded' by a circle
of people. One segment of society acknowledged her practical
sense and tactfulness . . . but more about that later. It was her
protection that partly explained the extremely rapid success of
Pyotr Stepanovich in our society – a success which at the time
was astonishing to Stepan Trofimovich.

Perhaps he and I were exaggerating. In the first place, Pyotr
Stepanovich renewed his acquaintance with virtually the entire
town almost immediately in the first four days after his arrival.
He had appeared on a Sunday, and as early as Tuesday I
encountered him sitting in a carriage with Artemy Pavlovich
Gaganov, a proud man, cantankerous and haughty, despite all
his sophistication, whose character made him difficult to get
along with. Pyotr Stepanovich was also hospitably received at
the governor's, so much so that he immediately found himself

in the position of an intimate, or, so to speak, a favoured young man. He dined with Yuliya Mikhaylovna almost every day. He had made her acquaintance while they were in Switzerland, but there was actually something curious about his rapid success in His Excellency's house. After all, he did have the reputation of having once been a revolutionary while abroad, whether true or not, of having participated in some foreign publications and congresses, 'proof of which could be found even in the newspapers', as I was maliciously informed on one occasion by Alyosha Telyatnikov, who is now, alas, a retired clerk, but previously had also been a favoured young man in the house of the former governor. Still and all, this was the plain fact: the former revolutionary had appeared in his beloved fatherland not only without any trouble, but almost with encouragement; therefore, there was probably nothing in it. Liputin had once whispered to me that according to rumour, Pyotr Stepanovich had supposedly repented and received absolution, after providing several other names, and had therefore perhaps now atoned for his guilt by promising to be useful to the fatherland in the future as well. I communicated this venomous remark to Stepan Trofimovich, who, despite being in really no condition to reflect on anything, fell to brooding. Subsequently it emerged that Pyotr Stepanovich had come here with extremely respectable letters of recommendation; at least, he had brought one to the governor's wife from a certain extremely important old lady in Petersburg, whose husband was one of the most distinguished old gentlemen in Petersburg. This old lady, Yuliya Mikhaylovna's godmother, mentioned in her letter that Count K. also knew Pyotr Stepanovich well, through Nikolay Vsevolodovich, treated him with kindness and found him 'a worthy young man, despite his past derelictions'. Yuliya Mikhaylovna set a very high value on her tenuous connections with 'the higher society', which she maintained with such difficulty, and, needless to say, she was happy to receive the letter from the important old woman; yet there was still something rather strange about the whole thing. She even put her husband on an almost familiar footing with Pyotr Stepanovich, which elicited complaints from Mr von Lembke ... but more about that later as well. I will also note for the record that even the great writer himself was very favourably disposed towards Pyotr Stepanovich and immediately invited him to his house. Such haste on the part of a man who was so puffed up about himself cut Stepan Trofimovich to the quick more painfully than anything else; but I had a different explanation for it: by pressing a nihilist to visit him, Mr Karmazinov quite obviously had in mind his relations with the progressive young people of both capitals. The great writer was mortally afraid of the rising generation of young revolutionaries, and imagining, through his ignorance of things, that they held the keys to Russia's future, sucked up to them shamelessly, mainly because they paid absolutely no attention to him.

2.

Pyotr Stepanovich dropped by to visit his father twice, and, unhappily, I was absent both times. He first visited him on Wednesday, that is, only on the fourth day after their first meeting, and on business at that. Incidentally, the matter of their property was somehow settled quietly and unobtrusively. Varvara Petrovna took it all on herself, and paid for everything, acquiring the small piece of land in the process, of course, and merely notified Stepan Trofimovich that everything had been arranged, and Varvara Petrovna's representative, her butler Aleksey Yegorych, had brought him something to sign, which he proceeded to do in silence and with extraordinary dignity. With regard to his dignity, I will note that I scarcely recognized our old man of yore during those days. He behaved as he had never done previously, had become surprisingly taciturn, hadn't even written a single letter to Varvara Petrovna since the Sunday in question, which I regarded as a miracle, and, most important, had become calm. He had fortified himself with some decisive and extraordinary idea that gave him peace, that much was obvious. He had hit upon this idea, and was sitting and waiting for something. At first, however, he was ill, especially on Monday; it was cholerine. He also couldn't rest without news all that time; but no sooner would I move from the bare facts to the heart of the matter and advance some theories than he would immediately begin waving his hands at me to stop. But both meetings with his son had a morbid effect on him, even though they didn't shake his resolve. On both days, after these meetings, he lay on the sofa, with a handkerchief soaked in vinegar wrapped around his head; yet in the highest sense he continued to remain calm.

At times, however, he didn't bother to wave his hands at me. At times it also struck me that his pleasant and mysterious resoluteness was abandoning him, as it were, and that he was beginning to struggle with some new, seductive onrush of ideas. These lasted just moments, but I made a note of them. I suspected that he had a strong desire to emerge from his isolation and declare himself, to put up a fight, to wage a final battle.

'*Cher*, I'd crush them!' This burst forth from him on Thursday evening, after his second meeting with Pyotr Stepanovich, while he was lying stretched out on the sofa with his head wrapped in a towel.

Until that moment he hadn't said a single word to me all day.

'"*Fils, fils chéri*", and so on; I agree that all these expressions are nonsense, part of the vocabulary of kitchen maids; so be it, I can see it for myself now. I didn't give him food or drink, I sent him from Berlin to —sk Province, a babe in arms, by post, and so on and so forth, I agree. "You," he says, "didn't give me anything to drink and you sent me away by post, and what's more you've robbed me here." "But, my unhappy boy," I shouted at him, "I've been heartsick over you my entire life, you know, even if I did send you off by post!" *Il rit*. But I agree, I agree . . . I have to grant that it was by post,' he finished as if in a delirium.

'*Passons*,'[4] he began again five minutes later. 'I don't understand Turgenev. His Bazarov[5] is a fictional character, who never existed; and they were the very first to reject him at the time as something utterly improbable. This Bazarov is some kind of vague mixture of Nozdryov and Byron,[6] *c'est le mot*. Just take a close look at them: they're turning somersaults and squealing with joy like puppies in the sun; they're happy, they've won! What's Byronesque about them! . . . And besides, what a humdrum existence! What irritable vanity, like kitchen maids, what a vulgar little itch to *faire du bruit autour de son nom*, without noticing that *son nom* . . . Oh, what a caricature! "Tell me," I shout at him, "do you really wish to propose yourself, as you are, to people as a substitute for Christ?" *Il rit. Il rit beaucoup, il rit trop*. He has a strange kind of smile. His mother didn't have a smile like that. *Il rit toujours*.'[7]

Again a silence fell.

'They're crafty; on Sunday they'd already come to an understanding . . .' he suddenly blurted out.

'Oh, without a doubt,' I exclaimed, pricking up my ears, 'that all had been agreed on beforehand, and was only too obvious and so badly acted.'

'That's not what I'm talking about. Do you know that it was all deliberately made too obvious so that it could be noticed by those . . . whom it concerned? Do you understand that?'

'No, I don't understand.'

'*Tant mieux. Passons*.[8] I'm very irritable today.'

'But why did you quarrel with him, Stepan Trofimovich?' I said reproachfully.

'*Je voulais convertir*. You may laugh, of course. *Cette pauvre* auntie, *elle entendra de belles choses!* Oh my friend, would you believe that at that point I felt myself to be a patriot! However, I've always been aware that I'm a Russian . . . and a real Russian cannot be anything different from you and me. *Il y a là-dedans quelque chose d'aveugle et de louche*.'[9]

'Most certainly,' I replied.

'My friend, the real truth is always implausible, don't you know that? In order to make the truth more plausible, you mustn't fail to mix a lie in with it. People have always done that. Perhaps there's something here we don't understand. What do you think, is there something here we don't understand, in these triumphant squeals of theirs? I would like there to be. I would like that.'

I said nothing. He also remained silent for a very long time.

'They say that the French mind . . .' he suddenly began babbling as if he had a fever, 'is a lie. That has always been the case. Why slander the French mind? This is nothing but Russian sloth, our humiliating inability to produce an idea, our disgusting parasitism in the ranks of nations. *Ils sont tout simplement des paresseux*, but not the French mind. Oh, the Russians ought to be exterminated for the good of mankind, as harmful parasites! It was not for that, certainly, not at all for that that we strove; I don't understand anything. I've ceased to understand! "Why, do you understand," I shout at him, "do you understand that if you have the guillotine in the foreground and with such enthusiasm too, then it's merely because cutting off heads is the easiest thing of all, while to have an idea is the hardest of all! *Vous êtes des paresseux! Votre drapeau est une guenille, une impuissance*. These carts, or, how do they put it: 'the rumble of carts bringing bread to mankind', are more useful than the Sistine Madonna, or however they put it ... *une bêtise dans ce genre*.[10] But do you understand," I shout at him, "do you understand that besides happiness man needs unhappiness, in exactly the same measure and degree!" *Il rit*. "You're just making witty remarks," he says, "while pampering your limbs" (he put it more obscenely than that) "on a velvet sofa." And note our custom of using the familiar form of address between father and son. It's all right when both are in agreement, but what if they're abusing one another?'

Again we said nothing for a minute or so.

'*Cher*,' he suddenly concluded, raising himself quickly, 'do you know that this will inevitably end with something?'

'Why, of course,' I said.

'*Vous ne comprenez pas*.[11] *Passons*. But ... usually things come to nothing in this world, but in this case there will be an end to something inevitably, inevitably!'

He stood up, walked around the room in extreme agitation and, going up to the sofa again, collapsed on to it in exhaustion.

On Friday morning Pyotr Stepanovich went off somewhere in the district and stayed until Monday. I found out about his departure from Liputin, and somehow in the course of our conversation I learned from him that the Lebyadkins, brother and sister, were both somewhere on the other side of the river, in the suburb of Gorshechnaya. 'I'm the one who took them there,' Liputin added, and, then dropping the subject of the Lebyadkins, he suddenly informed me that Lizaveta Nikolayevna was marrying Mavriky Nikolayevich, and although it had not yet been announced, they were engaged, and everything was settled. The next morning I came across Lizaveta Nikolayevna on her horse in the company of Mavriky Nikolayevich. It was the first time she had been out since her illness. She flashed her eyes at me from a distance, burst out laughing and nodded her head in a very friendly fashion. I conveyed all of this to Stepan Trofimovich; he paid a certain amount of attention only to the news about the Lebyadkins.

And now, having described the puzzling situation we found ourselves in during these eight days, when we as yet knew nothing, I will proceed to give an account of the subsequent events of my chronicle, but now, so to speak, with full knowledge of events as they have now been revealed and explained to us. Specifically, I shall begin with the eighth day after that Sunday, that is, with Monday evening, because that evening essentially marks the beginning of a 'new story'.

3.

It was seven o'clock in the evening. Nikolay Vsevolodovich was sitting alone in his study, a room that had always been his favourite, with its high ceiling, its carpeted floors and its rather heavy, old-fashioned furniture. He was sitting on a sofa in the corner, dressed as if he were about to go out, but apparently not intending to go anywhere. On the table in front of him stood a lamp with a shade. The sides and corners of the large room remained in shadow. His expression was pensive and reflective, and not altogether serene; his face looked tired and rather drawn. Actually, he was suffering from an abscessed tooth; but rumours that a tooth had been knocked out were exaggerated. The tooth had merely come loose, but now it was firmly back in place; the inside of his upper lip had also been badly cut, but this had healed as well. The abscess, on the other hand, had persisted for a whole week only because the sick man had refused to receive the doctor and have the swelling lanced in time, and was waiting until it broke on its own. It was not only the doctor he didn't admit, but his own mother as well, except for a moment once a day and always in early evening, when it was already growing dark and no lights had yet been brought in. He didn't receive Pyotr Stepanovich either, even though he dropped in to visit Varvara Petrovna two and three times a day while he was in town. But on Monday after returning in the morning from his three-day absence, and after running around the entire town and dining with Yuliya Mikhaylovna, Pyotr Stepanovich finally appeared towards evening at Varvara Petrovna's house. She had been impatiently awaiting him. The ban had been lifted; Nikolay Vsevolodovich was receiving. Varvara Petrovna herself led the visitor to the door of the study; she had long been looking forward to their meeting, and Pyotr Stepanovich promised her that he would come directly from Nicolas to her and tell her everything. She gave a timid knock at Nikolay Vsevolodovich's door, and, when she received no reply, ventured to open the door a crack.

'Nicolas, may I bring Pyotr Stepanovich in to see you?' she asked in a soft and reserved voice, straining to make out Nikolay Vsevolodovich behind the lamp.

'You may, you may, of course you may!' Pyotr Stepanovich shouted loudly and cheerfully, opened the door himself and went in.

Nikolay Vsevolodovich had not heard the knock on the door, but only his mother's timid question, and had had no time to reply. Lying before him at that particular moment was a letter he had just finished reading, and to which he was devoting considerable thought. He gave a start when he heard Pyotr Stepanovich's sudden shout, and hastened to cover the letter with a paperweight that happened to be at hand, but wasn't entirely successful: a corner of the letter and almost the entire envelope were visible.

'I made a point of shouting as loud as I could, so that you'd have time to prepare yourself,' Pyotr Stepanovich whispered quickly and with surprising naïveté, as he ran up to the table and promptly clapped his eyes on the paperweight and the corner of the letter.

'And of course you had time to see me hiding a letter from you that I'd just received under the paperweight,' Nikolay Vsevolodovich said calmly, without stirring from his seat.

'A letter? Good Lord, what do I care about you and your letter!' exclaimed the visitor, 'but ... the main thing...' he began whispering again, turning towards the door which was already shut, and nodding in that direction.

'She never eavesdrops,' Nikolay Vsevolodovich coldly observed.

'I don't care whether she eavesdrops or not!' Pyotr Stepanovich instantly shot back, raising his voice cheerfully and settling down in an easy chair. 'I have nothing against that, I'm only dashing in now to have a talk with you alone. Well then, at last I've got in to see you! First of all, how are you feeling? I see you're in splendid health, and perhaps tomorrow you'll put in an appearance, eh?'

'Perhaps.'

'But do deliver them, finally, deliver me!' He began to gesticulate furiously, with a jocular and pleasant air. 'If you only knew the line of twaddle I've had to hand them. But you do know.' He began to laugh.

'I don't know everything. I've only heard from my mother that you've been ... very active.'

'I mean to say that I didn't tell them anything definite,' Pyotr Stepanovich suddenly straightened up, as if defending himself from some terrible attack. 'You know, I put Shatov's wife into circulation, that is to say, the rumours about your liaison with her in Paris, which I of course used to explain the incident on Sunday ... you're not angry?'

'I'm sure you did your very best.'

'Well, that's exactly what I was afraid of. But anyway, what does that mean: "you did your very best"? Why, that's a reproach. However, you do come straight to the point. What I was most afraid of, as I was coming here, was that you wouldn't be willing to come straight to the point.'

'I'm not willing to come straight to the point about anything,' said Nikolay Vsevolodovich with a certain irritability, but he immediately laughed.

'That's not what I'm talking about, not that; make no mistake, not that!' Pyotr Stepanovich began waving his hands, scattering his words like peas and immediately rejoicing in his host's irritability. 'I won't bother you with *our* business, especially in your present situation. I've dropped in only to talk about the incident last Sunday, and only insofar as is absolutely essential, because it's really impossible, you know. I've come with the frankest possible explanations, which I have greater need of than you – that's for your vanity, but at the same time, it's also the truth. I've come in order to be always open and frank from this time forward.'

'That means you weren't open and frank previously?'

'Why, you know that yourself. I've been devious many times . . . you're smiling, I'm very glad to use your smile as an excuse for an explanation; you know, I deliberately coaxed a smile out of you by boasting of being "devious", so that you'd immediately get angry at the thought that I would dare imagine that I could be devious towards you, so that I could explain myself at once. You see, you see how open and frank I've become now? Well then, sir, would you care to hear me out?'

In the expression on Nikolay Vsevolodovich's face, which was scornfully serene and even mocking, despite his visitor's obvious desire to irritate his host with the effrontery of his previously prepared and intentionally crude naïveté, there finally appeared a rather uneasy curiosity.

'Listen here,' Pyotr Stepanovich squirmed more than ever. 'When I was on my way here – that is, here in general, to this town – about ten days ago, I of course made up my mind to take on a role. The very best thing would be to play no role at all, just to show one's own self, isn't that so? There's nothing more devious than one's own self, because no one will believe it. And, I admit I had wanted to play the fool, because a fool is easier than one's own self; but since a fool is an extreme, after all, and an extreme sparks curiosity, then I finally settled on my very own self. Well then, what is my very own self? A golden mean: neither stupid, nor intelligent, without any particular gifts, and "dropped from the moon", as the sensible people here say, isn't that so?'

'Well, all right, perhaps that's so.' Nikolay Vsevolodovich gave a barely perceptible smile.

'Ah, you agree, I'm very glad; I knew in advance that you thought the same way . . . Don't worry, don't worry, I'm not angry and I didn't define myself that way to get you to come up with praise in response. "No," you'd say, "you're not without talent, no," you'd say, "you're intelligent" . . . Ah, you're smiling again! . . . I've been caught again. You wouldn't have said "you're intelligent", let's suppose so, anyway: I grant everything. *Passons*, as papa says, and, in parentheses, don't get angry at my verbosity. By the way, here's an instance: I always talk a great deal, that is, I use a lot of words, and I talk very fast, and nothing ever comes out of me. And why do I use so many words and nothing ever comes out of me? Because I don't know how to talk. Those who do know how to talk well, talk briefly. And so that's a lack of giftedness on my part, isn't that so? But since this gift of not being gifted is already natural to me, then why shouldn't I make use of it in an artificial way? And so I'm making use of it. True enough, as I was planning to come here, I thought at first that I would say nothing; but to say nothing, you know, is a great talent, and therefore unsuitable for me, and in the second place, it's really rather dangerous to keep silent. So then, I finally decided that it was best of all to speak, but just as if I had no gift for it, that is, at length, at great length, at very great length, to be in a great hurry to prove my points, and in the end, by always getting all tangled up in my own attempts to make my points, the listener would walk away from me before I came to the end, throwing up his hands or, even better, dismissing me with contempt. The result would be, in the first place, that you've convinced people of your simplemindedness, bored them to death and been incomprehensible – all three advantages simultaneously! I ask you, who's going to suspect you of harbouring secret designs after that? Why, every one of them will take personal umbrage at anyone who says that I'm harbouring secret designs. And in addition, I'll make them laugh sometimes – and that's really valuable. Why, then they'll all forgive me now just for the fact that the clever fellow who's been issuing manifestos out there turns out, once he's here, to be stupider than they are, isn't that so? By your smile I can see that you approve.'

However, Nikolay Vsevolodovich was not smiling at all, but, on the contrary, was listening with a frown on his face and rather impatiently.

'Eh? What's that? I think you said, "It doesn't matter"?' Pyotr Stepanovich chattered away. (Nikolay Vsevolodovich hadn't said a single word.) 'Of course, of course, I can assure you that the last thing on my mind in coming here is to try to compromise you by association. But you know, you're awfully cantankerous today; I've come running to see you with an open and cheerful heart, and you just pick on every little word of mine. But I can assure you that I won't bring up anything delicate today, I promise, and I agree in advance to all your conditions!'

Nikolay Vsevolodovich maintained a dogged silence.

'Eh? What? Did you say something? I can see, I can see that I seem to have made a fool of myself again. You haven't proposed any conditions, and you won't propose any, I believe it, I believe it, calm down now. I myself know that it's not worth my while offering them, isn't that so? I'm answering for you in advance, and, of course – because I'm not gifted, not gifted and not gifted . . . You're laughing? Eh? What?'

'Nothing.' Nikolay Vsevolodovich finally did laugh. 'I now recall that once I really did call you a man without gifts, but you weren't there then, so someone told you. I'd like to ask you to get to the point as quickly as possible.'

'Why, I *am* at the point, you know, I'm talking specifically about Sunday!' Pyotr Stepanovich began babbling. 'Well, what, what was I on Sunday, in your opinion? Precisely a giftless, average man in a hurry, and I seized control of the conversation in the most giftless way imaginable. But they forgave me everything, because, in the first place, I'd dropped from the moon, that's something they all seemed to have decided on around here; and in the second place, because I told them a nice little story and saved all your necks, isn't that so, isn't that so?'

'Actually, you told it in such a way as to leave doubt in everyone's mind and suggest some secret understanding and juggling of things, whereas there was no secret understanding, and I never asked you to do anything at all.'

'Precisely! Precisely!' Pyotr Stepanovich chimed in almost rapturously. 'I acted as I did so that you would notice the mainsprings of the whole thing, and most importantly, it was for you, you know, that I was putting on my act, because I was trying to catch you and compromise you. And most importantly, I wanted to find out just how afraid you were.'

'I'm curious, why are you being so open now?'

'Don't be angry, don't be angry, don't glare ... However, you're not glaring. You're curious as to why I'm being so open? Why, precisely because everything has changed now, of course, everything is over with and is buried in the sand. I've suddenly changed my mind about you. The old way is completely finished; now I will never again try to compromise you in the old way, now I'll do it in the new way.'

'You've changed your tactics?'

'There are no tactics. Now you are completely free to do whatever you want in every respect, that is, say "yes", and if you want, say "no". Those are my new tactics. But about *our* business I won't breathe a word until you yourself tell me to. You're laughing? Laugh to your heart's content! I'm laughing myself. But now I'm being serious, very serious, very serious indeed, although anyone who's in such a hurry is not gifted, isn't that true? It doesn't matter, even though I'm not gifted, I am serious, very serious.'

In fact he had spoken seriously, in a completely different tone and in a peculiar state of agitation, so that Nikolay Vsevolodovich looked at him with curiosity.

'You say you've changed your mind about me?' he asked.

'I changed my mind about you the moment you took your hands away after Shatov had struck you. But that's enough, enough, please, no more questions, I won't say anything more just now.'

He jumped up, waving his hands, as if waving away questions, but since there were no questions, and there was no reason to leave, he sank back into the armchair, in a somewhat calmer state.

'By the way, parenthetically,' he proceeded to jabber, 'some people around here are babbling that you intend to kill him, and are laying bets on it, so that von Lembke has even thought of putting the police on it, but Yuliya Mikhaylovna has forbidden it ... Enough, enough about that, I bring it up just to keep you informed. By the way again: I moved the Lebyadkins that very same day, you know; did you get my note with their address?'

'I received it that day.'

'I did that not out of a lack of "giftedness", but sincerely, because I wanted to help. If the result showed a lack of giftedness, it nonetheless was sincere.'

'Oh, it was all right, perhaps it was necessary ...' Nikolay Vsevolodovich said thoughtfully. 'Only don't write any more notes to me, I beg you.'

'It couldn't be helped, there was only the one.'

'So Liputin knows?'

'It couldn't be helped; but Liputin, you yourself know, wouldn't dare ... By the way, you ought to go and see our people, that is, *them*, not *our* people, or else you'll be picking at every little thing again. Look, don't worry, it doesn't have to be now, just sometime. It's raining now. I'll let them know, they'll get together and we'll go in the evening. They're just waiting, with their mouths wide open, like baby jackdaws in their nest, to see what treat we've brought them. A hotheaded bunch. They've got their pamphlets out, they're getting ready to quarrel. Virginsky is interested in all mankind, Liputin is a Fourierist, with a strong inclination towards police matters – a man, let me tell you, who's valuable in one respect, but who needs to be treated strictly in all others; and finally, there's the one with the long ears, who'll give a lecture on his own system. And, you know, they're offended that I treat them offhandedly and throw cold water on them, hee, hee! But you absolutely have to go and see them.'

'Have you represented me as some kind of headman to them?' Nikolay Vsevolodovich came out with as casually as possible. Pyotr Stepanovich gave him a quick glance.

'By the way,' he chimed in, as if he had not heard the question and wanted to change the subject as quickly as possible, 'I presented myself to the much-respected Varvara Petrovna two or three times a day, and also had to talk a lot.'

'I can imagine.'

'No, don't imagine, I merely said that you wouldn't kill anyone, and other sweet-sounding things too. And just imagine: the next day she already knew that I'd taken Marya Timofeyevna to the other side of the river. Are you the one who told her?'

'I never thought of doing so.'

'I just knew it wasn't you. But who could it have been besides you? Interesting.'

'Liputin, naturally.'

'N-no, not Liputin,' Pyotr Stepanovich mumbled, with a frown. 'But I do know who. It looks like Shatov. However, it's all nonsense, let's forget about it! It is dreadfully important, though . . . By the way, I kept waiting for your mother to blurt out the important question all of a sudden . . . Oh, yes, at first she was dreadfully out of sorts for days on end, but today, when I arrived, she was suddenly all sunshine. What's going on?'

'She was that way because today I promised her that I would propose to Lizaveta Nikolayevna in five days,' Nikolay Vsevolodovich said suddenly with unexpected openness.

'Oh, well . . . yes, of course,' Pyotr Stepanovich babbled, as if unable to find the right words. 'There are rumours about her engagement, you know? It's true, though. But you're right; she'd come running from the altar, and all you'd have to do is call her. You're not angry that I'm saying this?'

'No, I'm not angry.'

'I notice that it's awfully hard to make you angry today, and I'm beginning to be afraid of you. I'm awfully curious to know how you're going to make your appearance tomorrow. You've probably prepared a thing or two. You're not angry at me for saying this?'

Nikolay Vsevolodovich gave no answer at all, which thoroughly irritated Pyotr Stepanovich.

'By the way, were you serious when you said that to your mother about Lizaveta Ivanovna?' he asked.

Nikolay Vsevolodovich fixed him with a cold and penetrating look.

'Ah, I understand, just to set her mind at rest, why, yes.'

'And if I had been serious?' Nikolay Vsevolodovich asked in a firm tone.

'Well then, God be with you, as they say in such cases, it won't harm the cause (you see that I didn't say "our" cause, you don't like the word "our"), and I . . . I, well, then, I'm at your service, you know that yourself.'

'You think so?'

'I don't think a thing, not a thing,' Pyotr Stepanovich pressed on hurriedly, with a laugh, 'because I know that you yourself have given careful consideration to your affairs ahead of time and that you've got everything well thought out. I'm just saying that I am seriously at your service, always and everywhere and in every case – I mean every single one, do you understand that?'

Nikolay Vsevolodovich yawned.

'You're sick of me,' Pyotr Stepanovich suddenly jumped up, grabbing his brand-new round hat as if he were leaving, while remaining where he was and continuing to talk without stopping, although he was standing, sometimes pacing the room and in the lively parts of the conversation banging his hat against his knee.

'I was thinking of amusing you further with the von Lembkes,' he cried cheerfully.

'No, please; maybe later. But how is Yuliya Mikhaylovna's health?'

'You all have this genteel way about you: you care as much about her health as you do for the health of a grey cat, yet you ask. I find that praiseworthy. She's in good health and she respects you, superstitiously so, and expects a great deal from you, superstitiously so. She is saying nothing about the incident on Sunday, and is convinced that you yourself will overcome everything just by putting in an appearance. I swear, she imagines that you have the ability to do Lord knows what. However, you're an enigmatic and romantic figure now, more so than ever – an extremely advantageous position. It's unbelievable how everyone is waiting for you. When I left, things were hot, but now even more so. By the way, thanks again for the letter. They're all afraid of Count K. Do you know they seem to regard you as a spy? I'm going along with that – you're not angry?'

'It doesn't matter.'

'It doesn't matter; it's essential in the long run. The people here have their own way of doing things. Of course, I'm encouraging them; Yuliya Mikhaylovna is at the head, Gaganov too . . . You're laughing? Why, I'm using tactics, don't you see: I gabble on and on, and suddenly I say an intelligent word, precisely when they're all looking for it. They gather round me, and I start gabbling away again. They've all given me up as hopeless already: "He has talent, they say, but he's dropped from the moon." Von Lembke is inviting me to work in government service, so that I can straighten myself out. You know, I treat him dreadfully, that is, I compromise him, and his eyes simply pop out of his head. Yuliya Mikhaylovna eggs me on. Yes, by the way, Gaganov is dreadfully angry at you. Yesterday at Dukhovo he had the nastiest things to say about you. I told him the whole truth immediately, that is, of course, not the whole truth. I spent a whole day with him at Dukhovo. A wonderful estate, a nice house.'

'So he's really still at Dukhovo even now?' Nikolay Vsevolodovich suddenly heaved himself up, almost jumping out of his chair and making a violent movement forward.

'No, he drove me here this morning, we returned together,' said Pyotr Stepanovich, as if totally oblivious to Nikolay Vsevolodovich's momentary agitation. 'Well, now, I've dropped a book', he bent down and picked up the keepsake that he'd brushed off the table. 'The Women of Balzac, with Illustrations.'[12] He opened it suddenly. 'I haven't read it. Von Lembke also writes novels.'

'Does he?' asked Nikolay Vsevolodovich, as if taking an interest.

'In Russian, on the quiet, of course. Yuliya Mikhaylovna knows and allows it. He's a bit of a simpleton, with his own methods, however; they've got that all worked out. What stick-

lers for form, what self-possession! We could do with something
like that.'

'You're praising the administration?'

'Well, I should certainly say so! It's the only thing in Russia
that's natural and has been successful . . . I won't, I won't . . .'
he suddenly heaved himself up, 'I won't say anything about
that, not a word about something so delicate. But forgive me,
you look rather green.'

'I have a fever.'

'I can believe it, why don't you go and lie down? By the way,
there are castrates[13] in the district here, curious folk . . . Later,
however. Here's another little story for you, though: there's
an infantry regiment stationed in the district here. On Friday
evening I was drinking with the officers in B—tsy. We actually
have three friends there, *vous comprenez*? We were talking
about atheism and, naturally, we were giving God the boot.
They were delighted, they were squealing. By the way, Shatov
assures me that if we're going to start a rebellion in Russia,
then we absolutely have to begin with atheism. Maybe that's
true. An old grey-haired duffer of a captain was sitting there,
sitting, keeping quiet the whole time, not saying a word, and
suddenly he walks into the middle of the room, and, you know,
says aloud, as if to himself: "If there is no God, then what kind
of captain am I after that?"[14] He took his cap, threw up his
arms and walked out.'

'He expressed a rather sound idea,' Nikolay Vsevolodovich
yawned for the third time.

'Really? I didn't understand it; I wanted to ask you. Well
now, what else might I have for you? The Shpigulins' factory
is interesting. There are five hundred workers there, as you
know; it's a hotbed of cholera, hasn't been cleaned for fifteen
years, and the employees are being short-changed. The owners
are millionaires. I assure you that some of the workers have
some understanding of the Internationale.[15] What, you're smiling? You'll see for yourself, just give me a little time, just a
little! I've already asked you for some time, and now I'm asking
you again, and then – however, forgive me, I won't, I won't,
it's not about that, don't scowl. However, goodbye. What's

wrong with me?' He suddenly turned back. 'I completely forgot the most important thing; I've just been told that our box has arrived from Petersburg.'

'Meaning . . . ?' Nikolay Vsevolodovich looked at him, not understanding.

'Meaning your box, your things, your tail-coats, trousers and linen. Has it arrived? Is it true?'

'Yes, I was told something of the sort a while ago.'

'Ah, then, can I get it at once . . . ?'

'Ask Aleksey.'

'Well then, tomorrow, tomorrow? You see, together with your things are also my jacket, frock-coat and three pairs of trousers, from Charmeur's,[16] on your recommendation, do you remember?'

'I've heard that you're playing quite the gentleman here,' Nikolay Vsevolodovich smirked. 'Is it true that you want to take lessons from the riding-master?'

Pyotr Stepanovich gave a crooked smile.

'You know,' he suddenly began speaking much too rapidly, in a trembling and breaking voice, 'you know, Nikolay Vsevolodovich, let's drop all this business of personalities once and for all, shall we? Naturally, you can despise me as much as you like, if you find it so amusing; but still and all, things would be better without personalities for a time, isn't that so?'

'All right, I won't do it any more,' said Nikolay Vsevolodovich. Pyotr Stepanovich smirked, banged his hat against his knee, shifted from one foot to the other and resumed his former expression.

'Some people here even regard me as your rival for Lizaveta Nikolayevna, so how can I fail to look after my appearance?' he laughed. 'But who has been informing on me to you? Hmm. It's exactly eight o'clock. Well, I'm off. I've promised to drop in on Varvara Petrovna, but I'll pass; you lie down and tomorrow you'll be in better spirits. It's rainy and dark outside; however, I have a cab, because I feel uneasy on the streets at night here . . . Ah, how apropos: here in town and in the vicinity a certain Fedka the Convict is roaming about now, a fugitive from Siberia, and my former house-serf; just imagine, my dear father shipped him off to the army[17] some fifteen years ago and took money for him. A very remarkable person.'

'You ... you've spoken with him?' Nikolay Vsevolodovich glanced up.

'I have. He doesn't hide from me. He's someone who's ready for anything, anything; for money, needless to say, but he has convictions too, in his own way, of course. Oh yes, here's another "apropos": if you were serious just now about that plan, you remember, concerning Lizaveta Nikolayevna, then let me renew my assurance once again that I too am someone who's ready for anything, in any form you like, and am completely at your service ... What's this? Are you reaching for your walking stick? Oh, no, you're not after your stick ... Just imagine, it seemed to me that you were looking for your stick.'

Nikolay Vsevolodovich wasn't looking for anything, but he had in fact stood up rather suddenly, his face distorted by some sort of strange expression.

'If you should also need anything concerning Mr Gaganov,' Pyotr Stepanovich suddenly blurted out, nodding straight at the paperweight, 'then, naturally, I can arrange everything, and I'm sure you won't be able to do without me.'

He suddenly went out, not waiting for an answer, but stuck his head through the doorway once more.

'I'm saying this,' he cried in a rush of words, 'because, you see, Shatov, for example, had no right to risk his life on Sunday when he went up to you, isn't that so? I would like you to take note of that.'

He disappeared again, without waiting for an answer.

4.

Perhaps he was thinking, as he disappeared, that once he was alone Nikolay Vsevolodovich would begin to pound the wall with his fists, and he would quite naturally have been very happy to spy on him if that had been possible. But he would have been very disappointed: Nikolay Vsevolodovich stayed calm. For a couple of minutes he remained standing at the table in the same position, evidently deep in thought; but presently a languid, cold smile spread across his lips. He slowly sat down on the sofa, in his previous spot in the corner, and closed his eyes, as if he were tired. A corner of the letter was still peeping from under the paperweight, but he didn't bestir himself even to put it right.

Soon he drifted off completely. Varvara Petrovna, who had tormented herself with worry these past few days, could stand it no longer and after Pyotr Stepanovich, who had promised to look in on her and had not kept his promise, had left, she took the risk of paying Nicolas a visit herself, even though it was not the usual time. She kept imagining that he would finally say something definite to her once and for all. Quietly, as she had done not so long before, she knocked on the door, and again receiving no answer, opened it herself. Seeing that Nicolas was sitting without moving a muscle, she approached the sofa cautiously and with pounding heart. She seemed astonished that he had fallen asleep so quickly and that he could sleep in this position, sitting up so straight and motionless; even his breathing was barely perceptible. His face was pale and stern, but looked utterly frozen and immovable; his eyebrows were drawn together a little and frowning; he certainly looked like a lifeless wax figure. She stood over him for a good three minutes, scarcely breathing, and was suddenly gripped by fear. She went out on tiptoe, paused in the doorway, quickly made the sign of the cross over him and withdrew unobserved, with a new heavy feeling and a new anguish.

He had a long sleep, more than an hour, still in the same state of suspended animation; not a muscle in his face moved, nor did his entire body betray the slightest movement; his eyebrows were still knit in the same stern frown. If Varvara Petrovna had stayed for another three minutes, then most likely she would not have been able to endure the overwhelming feeling created by this lethargy and immobility and would have awakened him. But he suddenly opened his eyes on his own, and without moving, as before, remained sitting for some ten minutes, as if staring intently and curiously at some object in a corner of the room that had struck his attention, although there was nothing new or special there.

Finally the soft, muffled sound of a large wall clock resounded, striking once. With a certain uneasiness he turned his head to look at the clock face, but at almost the same moment the rear door leading into the hallway opened, and the butler Aleksey Yegorovich appeared. In one hand he was carrying a warm overcoat, a scarf and a hat, and in the other a small silver tray on which lay a note.

'Half-past nine,' he announced in a soft voice, and after depositing the articles of clothing he had brought on a chair in the corner, he held out the tray with the note, a small piece of paper, unsealed, with two lines written in pencil. After running his eyes over these lines, Nikolay Vsevolodovich picked up a pencil from the table, added two words at the end of the note and placed it back on the tray.

'Take it back as soon as I go out, and now help me dress,' he said, getting up from the sofa.

Noticing that he had on a light velvet jacket, he thought for a moment and then told the butler to bring him the cloth coat that was used for more ceremonial evening occasions. Finally, having fully dressed and donned his hat, he locked the door through which Varvara Petrovna had come in, and extracting the letter hidden under the paperweight, silently went out into the hallway accompanied by Aleksey Yegorovich. From the hallway they emerged on to a narrow stone back-stairway and went down to an entry-room that led directly into a garden. In a corner of the entry-room stood a small lantern and a large umbrella which had been placed there in advance.

'On account of the unusual amount of rain, the mud in the town streets is unbearable,' Aleksey Yegorovich announced, in an indirect and final attempt to deter his master from making his journey. But the master, after opening the umbrella, silently went out into the damp and wet old garden, which was as dark as a cellar. The wind was howling and rocking the tops of the half-bare trees; the narrow, little sand paths were sodden and slippery. Aleksey Yegorovich went along in what he had been wearing, a frock-coat and no hat, lighting the way about three steps ahead with the small lantern.

'Won't anyone notice us?' Nikolay Vsevolodovich suddenly asked.

'Not from the windows, and besides, everything has already been seen to,' the servant replied quietly and evenly.

'Has mother gone to sleep?'

'The mistress locked herself in, as has been her custom these past few days, at exactly nine o'clock, and now it's impossible for her to find out anything. At what time should I expect you?' he added, making bold to ask the question.

'At one, or one-thirty, no later than two.'

'Yes, sir.'

After making their way along winding paths through the entire garden, which both knew by heart, they came to a stone wall and here, in the very corner, they found a small door, which led out into a narrow and deserted lane, and was almost always locked, but the key to which now appeared in the hands of Aleksey Yegorovich.

'Won't the door creak?' Nikolay Vsevolodovich inquired again.

But Aleksey Yegorovich reported that it had been smeared with grease only yesterday, 'as well as today'. He had already been outside long enough to become soaked through. After opening the small door, he handed the key to Nikolay Vsevolodovich.

'If it pleases you to undertake a distant journey, then I must report being uncertain of the local folk, especially in deserted lanes, and most of all on the other side of the river,' he could not refrain from saying once again. He was an old servant, had been in charge of looking after Nikolay Vsevolodovich as a child and had once dandled him in his arms; a serious and severe man, who liked to listen to matters concerning the divine and do a bit of reading about them as well.

'Don't worry, Aleksey Yegorych.'

'May God bless you, sir, but only in undertaking good deeds.'

'What?' Nikolay Vsevolodovich stopped, although he had already stepped into the lane.

Aleksey Yegorovich repeated his wish in a firm tone; never before had he ventured to express himself aloud in such words to his master.

Nikolay Vsevolodovich locked the door, put the key in his pocket and set off down the lane, sinking three inches into the mud with each step. At last he emerged into a long, empty paved street. The town was as familiar to him as the back of his hand; but Bogoyavlenskaya Street was still quite a distance away. It was after ten o'clock when he finally stopped before the locked gate of the old, dark house of the Filippovs. After the departure of the Lebyadkins, the lower floor now stood completely empty, its windows boarded up, but a light shone in Shatov's quarters in the attic. Since there was no bell, he began pounding on the gate with his hand. A small window opened, and Shatov looked out into the street. It was dreadfully dark, and it was difficult to make anything out. Shatov peered down for quite some time, at least a minute.

'Is that you?' he asked suddenly.

'Yes, it's me,' the uninvited visitor replied.

Shatov banged the window shut, came downstairs and unlocked the gate. Nikolay Vsevolodovich stepped across the high sill and, without saying a word, walked past him and directly into Kirillov's quarters in the small house in the yard.

5.

Everything here was unlocked and the door not even shut. The entryway and the first two rooms were dark, but in the last room, where Kirillov lived and drank his tea, a light was shining and there was the sound of laughter and some strange cries. Nikolay Vsevolodovich began to walk towards the light, but stopped on the threshold without going in. Tea was on the table. Standing in the middle of the room was the old woman, the relative of the landlord, bareheaded, wearing only a skirt and a rabbit-skin jacket, and shoes on bare feet. In her arms she was holding an eighteen-month-old baby wearing nothing but a shirt, with bare legs, its cheeks flushed, its fine white hair tousled, as if just out of its cradle. It must have recently been crying; there were still tears in its eyes; but at that instant it was stretching out its little arms, clapping its hands and laughing the way small children laugh, with a sobbing catch. Kirillov was bouncing a large red rubber ball on the floor in front of it; the ball rebounded to the ceiling, and fell back again, with the child screaming 'Ba, ba'. Kirillov caught the 'ba' and handed it to the child, who now threw it with its own clumsy hands, and Kirillov ran to pick it up again. Finally, the 'ba' rolled under the wardrobe. 'Ba, ba,' the child shrieked. Kirillov lay flat on the floor, and stretched his hand in an attempt to retrieve the 'ba' from beneath the wardrobe. Nikolay Vsevolodovich walked into the room; the child, on catching sight of him, clutched at the old woman and burst into a prolonged, baby's wail; she carried him out immediately.

'Stavrogin?' Kirillov said, half-raising himself from the floor, the ball in his hands, without the slightest surprise at the unexpected visit. 'You want some tea?'

He got to his feet.

'Very much, I won't refuse, if it's warm,' said Nikolay Vsevolodovich, 'I'm soaked through.'

'It's warm, hot even,' Kirillov affirmed with pleasure. 'Have a seat: you're all dirty, it doesn't matter; I'll take care of the floor with a rag later on.'

Nikolay Vsevolodovich settled down and drank his tea almost in one gulp.

'More?' asked Kirillov.

'Thank you.'

Kirillov, who until now had remained standing, immediately sat down opposite him and asked:

'What have you come for?'

'On business. Here, read this letter, from Gaganov. Remember, I told you about him in Petersburg.'

Kirillov took the letter, read it, put it down on the table and looked at him expectantly.

'As you know,' Nikolay Vsevolodovich began to explain, 'I met this Gaganov a month ago in Petersburg for the first time in my life. We ran across each other in public about three times. Without trying to make my acquaintance and without initiating any conversation, he still found an opportunity to be very insolent. I told you about that at the time, but here's what you don't know: as he was leaving Petersburg, before I did, he suddenly sent me a letter, and although it was not like this one, it was still highly improper and all the more peculiar because it contained absolutely no explanation of the reason why it was written. I answered him immediately, also by letter, and told him in complete frankness that he was probably angry at me because of the incident with his father four years ago here in the club, and that on my part I was ready to make every possible apology on the grounds that my action was unintentional and occurred while I was ill. I asked him to take my apologies into consideration. He didn't answer, and left. But now I find him here and in a towering rage. Several remarks he's made about me in public, which are utterly abusive and full of astonishing accusations, have been passed on to me. Finally, this letter arrived today, the likes of which I don't think anyone has ever received, full of abuse and with the expression "your smashed face". I've come in hopes that you won't refuse to be my second.'

'You said that no one has received such a letter,' Kirillov observed. 'It's possible in a rage; people sometimes write like that. Pushkin wrote to Heeckeren.[18] All right, I will. Just tell me how.'

Nikolay Vsevolodovich explained that he wanted it to take place the next day, and that the first step should be a renewal of apologies and even the promise of a second letter of apology, provided, however, that Gaganov, for his part, should promise not to write any more letters. The letter already received would be regarded as not having existed at all.

'Too many concessions; he won't agree,' Kirillov said.

'I've come mainly to find out whether you'd agree to take these conditions to him.'

'I'll take them. It's your affair. But he won't agree.'

'I know he won't agree.'

'He wants to fight. Tell me how you'll fight.'

'The thing is that I would like to get everything out of the way no later than tomorrow. You be at his place about nine o'clock in the morning. He'll hear what you have to say, and won't agree to it, but he'll bring you together with his second – at about eleven, let's say. You'll decide matters with him, and then at one or two o'clock everyone should be on the spot. Please try to see that it's done this way. The weapons are to be pistols, of course, and I ask you in particular to see to it that the barriers are set ten paces apart; then you'll station each of us ten paces from each barrier, and at the given signal we'll begin walking towards each other. Each of us must certainly walk right up to his barrier, but he can fire even earlier, while he's walking. That's all, I think.'

'Ten paces between barriers is close,' Kirillov observed.

'Well then, twelve, but no more; you understand that he wants a serious duel. Do you know how to load a pistol?'

'I do. I have pistols; I'll give my word that you've never fired them. His second will also give his word about his. Two pairs of pistols, and we'll toss for odd or even, to use his or ours?'

'Excellent.'

'Do you want to have a look at the pistols?'

'Please.'

Kirillov squatted down in front of his valise in the corner, which hadn't yet been unpacked, but from which items were extracted as they were needed. From the bottom he took out a palm-wood box, lined with red velvet inside, and from it removed a pair of elegant, extremely expensive pistols.

'Everything's here: powder, bullets, cartridges. I have a revolver too: wait.'

He dived back into the valise and took out another box containing a six-chambered American revolver.

'You have enough weapons, and very expensive ones.'

'Very. Extremely.'

Poor, almost destitute, Kirillov, who, however, had never taken any notice of his poverty, now showed off his treasured weapons, which had undoubtedly been acquired at great sacrifice, with an obvious swagger.

'Are you still of the same mind?' asked Stavrogin after a moment's silence, and with a certain cautiousness.

'Yes,' Kirillov answered curtly, immediately guessing from the tone of voice what was being asked, and he began taking the weapons off the table.

'When, then?' Nikolay Vsevolodovich asked even more cautiously, again after a silence.

Meanwhile, Kirillov had put both boxes back into the valise and taken his seat again.

'That's not up to me, as you know. It'll be when they tell me,' he mumbled, as if somewhat burdened by the question, but at the same time obviously prepared to answer all other questions. He kept looking at Stavrogin without averting his lustreless black eyes, but with a calm, yet kindly and welcoming feeling.

'Of course, I understand shooting yourself,' Nikolay Vsevolodovich began again, frowning somewhat, after a long, reflective three-minute silence. 'I've sometimes imagined doing it myself, and then some new thought always comes to me: if one were to commit an evil deed or, more important, a shameful act, that is, something disgraceful, but very base indeed and . . . absurd, so that people would remember it for a thousand years and hold it in contempt for a thousand years, and suddenly comes the thought: "A single blow in the temple, and after that, nothing". Then what would I care about people and the fact that they'd hold me in contempt for a thousand years, isn't that so?'

'You're calling that a new thought?' Kirillov said after some reflection.

'I'm . . . not calling it . . . once when I thought about it, I felt it a completely new thought.'

'You "felt a thought"?' Kirillov repeated. 'That's good. There are many thoughts which have always existed, and which suddenly become new. That's true. I now see a great deal as if for the first time.'

'Let's suppose you lived on the moon,' Stavrogin interrupted, not listening and continuing his thought. 'Let's suppose you did all those absurd, vile things up there. From here, you know for certain that people up there will laugh at you and hold your name in contempt for a thousand years, eternally, over all the moon. But now you're here and you're looking at the moon from here. From here, what do you care about everything you perpetrated there, and that people up there will be holding you in contempt for a thousand years, isn't that true?'

'I don't know,' Kirillov replied. 'I haven't been on the moon,' he added without any irony, but merely to state a fact.

'Whose child was that just now?'

'The old woman's mother-in-law came – no, daughter-in-law . . . it doesn't matter. For three days. She's sick in bed, with a child; she screams a lot at night, her stomach. The mother sleeps and the old woman brings the child here; I have a ball. The ball is from Hamburg. I bought it in Hamburg, to throw and catch: it makes the back strong. It's a little girl.'

'Do you like children?'

'I do,' Kirillov responded, rather indifferently, however.

'So you love life, too?'

'Yes, I love life, too. What of it?'

'If you should decide to shoot yourself.'

'What do you mean? Why put them together? Life is one thing, and that's another. Life exists, but death doesn't exist at all.'

'You've begun to believe in a future eternal life?'

'No, not in a future eternal life, but in eternal life right here. There are moments, you reach moments, and time suddenly stops and it will become eternal.'

'You hope to reach such a moment?'

'Yes.'

'That's hardly possible in our time,' Nikolay Vsevolodovich responded, also without any irony, slowly and thoughtfully, it seemed. 'In the Apocalypse the angel swears that time will no longer exist.'[19]

'I know. It's very true there – clear and accurate. When all of mankind achieves happiness, then there won't be any more time, because it's not necessary. A very true thought.'

'Where will they hide it, then?'

'They won't hide it anywhere. Time isn't an object, but an idea. It will be extinguished in the mind.'

'Old philosophical commonplaces, one and the same from

the beginning of time,' Stavrogin muttered with a kind of contemptuous compassion.

'One and the same! One and the same from the beginning of time, and never any others!' Kirillov retorted with flashing eyes, as if this idea represented almost a victory.

'You seem very happy, Kirillov.'

'Yes, very happy,' he replied, as if making the most ordinary kind of reply.

'But not so long ago weren't you still very peeved, very angry at Liputin?'

'Hmm . . . I'm not abusing him now. I still didn't know then that I was happy. Have you ever seen a leaf, a leaf from a tree?'

'I have.'

'Not long ago I saw a yellow one, with some green in it, turning brown at the edges. Blown by the wind. When I was ten, I used to close my eyes on purpose in winter and picture a leaf – green and bright with veins in it, and the sun shining. I'd open my eyes and couldn't believe it because it was so very good, and then I'd close them again.'

'What is this, anyway, an allegory?'

'N-no, why should it be? It's no allegory, but just a leaf, nothing but a leaf. The leaf is good. Everything is good.'

'Everything?'

'Everything. Man is unhappy because he doesn't know he's happy; that's the only reason. That's everything, everything! Whoever finds out will become happy right away, this minute. This mother-in-law will die, but the little girl will remain – everything is good. I suddenly discovered it.'

'And someone who dies of hunger, and someone who abuses and dishonours a little girl – is that good?'

'It's good. And someone who bashes in that man's head for the child, that's good too; and someone who doesn't bash in his head, that's good too. Everything is good, everything. It's good for all those who know that everything is good. If they knew it was good for them, then it would be good for them; but as long as they don't know it's good for them, then it won't be good for them. That's the whole thought, all of it, there isn't any more!'

'When was it you found out that you're so happy?'

'Last week, on Tuesday, no, on Wednesday, because it was already Wednesday, at night.'

'What brought it on?'

'I don't remember, it just happened. I was walking around the room. It doesn't matter. I stopped the clock, it was twenty-three minutes to three.'

'As a symbol that time should stop?'

Kirillov said nothing.

'They're not good,' he suddenly began again, 'because they don't know they're good. When they find out, then they won't rape little girls. They have to find out that they're good, and everyone will become good all at once, every last one.'

'So you've found out, then, that you're good?'

'I'm good.'

'With this, I'm in agreement,' Stavrogin muttered with a frown.

'Anyone who teaches that all are good, he will bring about the end of the world.'

'The one who taught that was crucified.'

'He will come, and his name will be Man-God.'

'God-Man?'[20]

'Man-God, there's a difference.'

'Was it you who lit the icon-lamp?'

'Yes, I lit it.'

'You are a believer?'

'The old woman likes the icon-lamp lit . . . but today she had no time,' Kirillov muttered.

'And you yourself don't pray as yet?'

'I pray to everything. You see a spider crawling over the wall, I look and I'm grateful to it for crawling.'

His eyes again began to glow. He kept looking directly at Stavrogin, with a steady and unwavering gaze. Stavrogin kept watching him, with a frowning and distasteful expression, but there was no sneer on his face.

'I'll bet that when I come again, you'll already believe in God,' he said, getting up and picking up his hat.

'Why?' Kirillov stood up as well.

'If you should find out that you believe in God, then you would certainly believe; but since you don't yet know that you believe in God, then you certainly don't believe,' Nikolay Vsevolodovich grinned.

'That's not right,' Kirillov said after some consideration, 'you've turned the thought all around. A society joke. Remember what you've meant in my life, Stavrogin.'

'Goodbye, Kirillov.'

'Come at night. When?'

'Why, you haven't forgotten about tomorrow?'

'Oh, I did forget; don't worry, I won't oversleep. Nine o'clock. I'm able to wake up whenever I want. I go to bed and I think: seven o'clock, and I wake up at seven o'clock. Ten o'clock and I wake up at ten o'clock.'

'You have remarkable qualities,' said Nikolay Vsevolodovich, stealing a glance at his pale face.

'I'll go and open the gate.'

'Don't bother, Shatov will open it for me.'

'Ah, Shatov. All right, goodbye.'

6.

The front door of the empty house in which Shatov lodged wasn't locked, but after gaining access to the entryway, Stavrogin found himself in complete darkness and began to grope for the stairway to the attic. Suddenly a door opened upstairs and there was light; Shatov himself didn't come out, but only opened his door. When Nikolay Vsevolodovich paused in the doorway of the room, he could make him out standing expectantly by the table in the corner.

'Will you receive me on a matter of business?' he asked from the doorway.

'Come in and have a seat,' Shatov replied. 'Lock the door; wait, I'll do it myself.'

He took a key and locked the door, returned to the table, and sat down opposite Nikolay Vsevolodovich. In the course of a week he had grown thin, and now he seemed to be feverish.

'You've been tormenting me,' he said in a soft half-whisper, looking down. 'Why didn't you come?'

'You were so sure that I would come?'

'Yes, but wait, I was delirious . . . maybe I'm delirious now too . . . Wait.'

He got up and took something from the corner of the top of his three bookshelves. It was a revolver.

'One night I was delirious and imagining that you would come and kill me, and early in the morning I bought a revolver from that no good Lyamshin with all the money I had left. I didn't want to give in to you. Then I came to my senses . . . I had neither powder nor bullets; since then it's just been lying on the shelf. Wait . . .'

He stood up and was about to open the vent window.[21]

'Don't throw it out. What for?' Nikolay Vsevolodovich stopped him. 'It costs money, and tomorrow people will start saying that there are revolvers lying about under Shatov's window. Put it back, that's it; sit down. Tell me, why do you seem to be so apologetic about thinking that I was going to come to kill you? Even now I haven't come to make peace, but to talk about something urgent. First of all, explain to me: you didn't hit me because of my connection with your wife?'

'You yourself know that I didn't,' Shatov said, again looking down.

'And not because you believed the stupid gossip about Darya Pavlovna?'

'No, no, of course not! It's stupid! My sister told me from the very beginning . . .' Shatov said impatiently and sharply, even stamping his foot slightly.

'So I guessed and you guessed, too,' Stavrogin went on calmly. 'You're right: Marya Timofeyevna Lebyadkina is my lawful wife, who was married to me about four and a half years ago in Petersburg. Was it perhaps because of her that you struck me?'

Shatov, utterly staggered, listened and said nothing.

'I guessed but didn't believe it,' he finally mumbled, with a strange look at Stavrogin.

'And you struck me?'

Shatov flared up and began mumbling almost disconnectedly:

'I did it because of your degradation . . . because of your lie. I didn't come up to you to punish you. As I was approaching you, I didn't know that I would hit you . . . I did it because you meant so much to me in my life . . . I . . .'

'I understand, I understand, save your breath. I'm sorry you're feverish; I have extremely urgent business.'

'I've been waiting for you too long,' Shatov almost trembled all over and made a move to stand up. 'State your business, I will also say . . . later . . .'

He sat down.

'My business is not in that category,' Nikolay Vsevolodovich began, scrutinizing him with curiosity. 'Because of certain circumstances I was forced to choose this hour today to come to warn you that you are perhaps going to be killed.'

Shatov looked at him wildly.

'I know that my life may be in danger,' he said in measured tones, 'but you – how can that be known to you?'

'Because I also am one of them, like you; and I'm also a member of their society, as you are.'

'You . . . you're a member of the society?'

'I can see from your eyes that you were expecting anything from me, but that,' Nikolay Vsevolodovich gave a barely perceptible smile. 'But excuse me, you mean you already knew that an attempt would be made on your life?'

'The thought never occurred to me. And I don't think so now, despite what you're saying . . . although . . . although who can be certain of anything as far as those fools are concerned!' he suddenly shouted in a fury, banging his fist on the table. 'I'm not afraid of them! I've broken with them. That fellow dropped by four times to tell me that it was possible . . . but,' he glanced at Stavrogin, 'what precisely do you know about it?'

'Don't worry, I'm not deceiving you,' Stavrogin went on rather coldly, with the look of a man who is merely doing his duty. 'You're examining me as to what I know? I know that you entered this society abroad, two years ago, under its old organization at the time, just before your trip to America, and apparently just after our last conversation, about which you wrote to me so much in your letter from America. By the way, pardon me for not sending you a letter in return; I confined myself to . . .'

'To sending some money. Wait a moment.' Shatov stopped talking, hastily pulled a drawer out of the desk and extracted a rainbow-coloured banknote from beneath some papers. 'Here, take it, the hundred roubles you sent me; if it hadn't been for you, I would have died there. I wouldn't have been able to give it back for a long time if not for your mother: these were the hundred roubles she gave me nine months ago because I was so poor, after my illness. But please go on . . .'

He was breathless.

'In America you changed your way of thinking, and after you returned to Switzerland, you wanted to disavow them. They gave you no answer, but entrusted you with taking over a printing press from someone here in Russia until it could be turned over to a person who would come to you from them. I don't know everything in full detail, but I think those are the main points, aren't they? And you, in hope or on condition that this would be their final demand and that after that they would release you entirely, undertook it. All of this, whether it's true or not, I learned not from them but quite by chance. But here's what you don't seem to know as yet: these gentlemen have absolutely no intention of parting company with you.'

'That's absurd!' Shatov howled. 'I told them honestly that I disagreed with them in everything! That's my right, my right of conscience and thought . . . I won't put up with it! There's no power that could . . .'

'You know, you shouldn't shout,' Nikolay Vsevolodovich stopped him very pointedly. 'This Verkhovensky is the sort of little man who perhaps even now is eavesdropping on us, using his own ears or someone else's, right here in your own entryway, perhaps. Even the drunkard Lebyadkin was probably instructed to keep an eye on you, and you perhaps on him, isn't that so? You'd better tell me whether Verkhovensky has now agreed to the points you made or not.'

'He's agreed. He said that I could and that I had the right . . .'

'Well then, he's deceiving you. I know that even Kirillov,

who is hardly one of them at all, has obtained information about you, and they have many agents, even people who have no idea they're serving that society. They've always kept you under surveillance. Pyotr Verkhovensky, incidentally, has come here in order to settle their business with you once and for all, and he has full authorization to do so, namely, to eliminate you at the right moment, as a man who knows too much and is capable of informing on them. I say to you again that this is for certain; and allow me to add that for some reason they are fully convinced that you are a spy and that if you haven't yet informed on them, then you will inform on them. Is that true?'

Shatov twisted his mouth on hearing a question of this sort put in such an ordinary tone.

'Even if I were a spy, who would I inform on them to?' he said angrily, not giving a direct answer. 'No, leave me alone; to hell with me!' he shouted, suddenly snatching at his original thought, which had so shaken him, incomparably more power-fully, by all indications, than the news of the danger to him personally. 'You, you, Stavrogin, how could you dirty yourself by sinking to the level of such shameless, talentless, stupid lackeys! You a member of their society! So this is the magni-ficent exploit of Nikolay Stavrogin!' he shouted almost in despair.

He even clasped his hands, as if nothing could have been more bitter and bleak than this discovery.

'Pardon me,' said Nikolay Vsevolodovich in genuine surprise, 'but you seem to look on me as some shining sun, and on yourself as some tiny insect by comparison. I could see that even in your letter from America.'

'You ... you know ... Oh, better just drop me altogether, altogether!' Shatov suddenly broke off. 'If you can explain something about yourself, then explain it ... Answer my ques-tion!' he repeated feverishly.

'With pleasure. You ask how I could sink into such a den of iniquity. After telling you all this, I even feel obliged to be somewhat open with you about this matter. You see, strictly speaking I don't belong to this society at all, didn't belong to it before and have even a much greater right than you to leave it

because I never did join. On the contrary, from the very beginning I announced that I was no comrade of theirs, and that if I
did happen to help, then it was only as a man who had nothing
else to do. I participated to some extent in the reorganization
of the society according to the new plan, and that was all.
But now they've thought better of it and have decided among
themselves that it's dangerous to release me, and so I'm also
condemned, it seems.'

'Oh, they're always talking about the death penalty and it's
all done by official instructions, on documents with seals on
them, signed by three and a half men. And you believe they're
capable of doing such a thing?'

'In this case you're partly right, partly wrong,' Stavrogin
went on just as indifferently, even languidly as before. 'No
doubt there's a lot of fantasy here, as is always the case in such
situations; a handful of people exaggerate their stature and
significance. If you want my opinion, Pyotr Verkhovensky is
the only real member, and it's very kind of him to regard himself
as a mere agent of his society. However, the basic idea is no
more stupid than others of the same kind. They have connections with the Internationale; they have managed to establish
agents in Russia, they've even hit upon a rather original method
. . . but only theoretically so, of course. As far as their intentions
here, well, the workings of our Russian organization are so
obscure and almost always so unexpected that really anything
can be tried in this country. Note that Verkhovensky is a stubborn man.'

'He's a bedbug, an ignoramus, a buffoon who doesn't understand anything going on in Russia!' Shatov shouted angrily.

'You don't know him very well. It's true that none of them
understands very much of what is going on in Russia, but really
only slightly less than you and I; and besides, Verkhovensky is
an enthusiast.'

'Verkhovensky an enthusiast?'

'Oh, yes. There is a point at which he stops being a buffoon
and turns into . . . a man who's half-demented. I will ask you
to recall one of your very own expressions: "Do you know how
strong one man can be?" Please don't laugh, he's certainly

capable of pulling the trigger. They're convinced that I'm also
a spy. All of them, incapable as they are of running things, are
terribly fond of accusing others of spying.'

'But really, aren't you afraid?'

'N-no . . . I'm not much afraid . . . But in your case it's quite
different. I've warned you so that you can at least bear it in
mind. As I see it, there's no need to be offended that you're in
danger from fools; it's not a question of their intelligence; and
they've raised their hand against people who are better than
you and I. However, it's a quarter past eleven,' he glanced at
his watch and got up from his chair, 'and I would like to put a
question to you that is along completely different lines.'

'For God's sake!' Shatov exclaimed, leaping up from his seat.

'What do you mean?' Nikolay Vsevolodovich looked at him
questioningly.

'Ask your question, ask it, for God's sake,' Shatov repeated
in inexpressible agitation, 'but only provided that I get to put
a question to you. I beg you to permit me . . . I can't . . . ask
your question!'

Stavrogin waited a moment and began.

'I've heard that you've had a certain influence here on Marya
Timofeyevna, and that she likes to see you and listen to you. Is
that so?'

'Yes . . . she used to listen,' Shatov said with some embarrassment.

'Any day now I intend to make a public announcement in
town of my marriage to her.'

'Can that really be?' Shatov whispered almost in horror.

'What do you mean? There are no impediments: the witnesses
to the marriage are on hand. All this happened in Petersburg in
a completely legal and calm fashion, and if it has not come to
light until now, that is because the only two witnesses to the
marriage, Kirillov and Pyotr Verkhovensky, and, last but not
least, Lebyadkin himself (whom I now have the pleasure of
numbering among my relatives) gave their word to say nothing.'

'About that I'm not . . . You are speaking so calmly . . . but
go on! Listen, you weren't forced into this marriage, were you;
you weren't, were you?'

'No, no one forced me into it,' Nikolay Vsevolodovich smiled at Shatov's impassioned haste.

'And why does she keep going on about her baby?' Shatov hurried on, feverishly and disconnectedly.

'She goes on about her baby? Well, well! I didn't know, this is the first time I've heard about it. She had no baby and she could not have: Marya Timofeyevna is a virgin.'

'Ah! That's just what I thought! Listen!'

'What's wrong with you, Shatov?'

Shatov covered his face with his hands, and turned around, but suddenly grabbed Stavrogin firmly by the shoulder.

'Do you know, do you at least know,' he shouted, 'why you have done all this and why you've decided on such a punishment now?'

'Your question is intelligent and painful, but I also intend to surprise you: yes, I do almost know why I got married then, and why I'm deciding on such a "punishment" now, as you put it.'

'Let's leave that . . . about that later, hold off speaking; we'll talk about the main thing, the main thing: I've been waiting two years for you.'

'Yes?'

'I've been waiting for you too long, I've been constantly thinking about you. You're the only man who could have . . . While I was still in America I wrote to you about this.'

'I remember your long letter very well.'

'Too long to be read to the end? I agree: six sheets of note-paper. Keep quiet, keep quiet! Tell me: can you spare me ten minutes more, only now, right this minute . . . I've been waiting for you too long!'

'If you like, I'll spare half an hour, but no more, if that's all right with you.'

'Only provided, however,' Shatov rejoined fiercely, 'that you change your tone. Listen, I am demanding, whereas I ought to plead . . . Do you understand what it means to demand when one ought to plead?'

'I understand that by doing so you rise above all that is ordinary for higher purposes,' said Nikolay Vsevolodovich with the faintest of smiles, 'and I also see to my sorrow that you are feverish.'

'I request respect for myself, I demand it!' Shatov shouted. 'Not for me personally – the devil with that – but for something else, just this once, for the sake of a few words ... We two beings have actually come together in infinity ... for the last time in this world. Drop your tone and adopt a human one! For at least once in your life start speaking in a human voice. I'm saying this not for my sake, but for yours. Do you understand that you should forgive me for hitting you in the face if only because in that way I gave you the opportunity to become aware of your boundless power ... There's that disdainful high-society smile on your face again. Oh, when will you understand me! Just stop being the young master! You must understand that I demand it; I demand it, otherwise I don't want to speak, and I won't do so for anything in the world!'

His frenzy was reaching the point of delirium. Nikolay Vsevolodovich frowned and seemed to turn more cautious.

'Since I have agreed to stay for half an hour,' he said solemnly and seriously, 'when time is so precious to me, then please believe that I intend to listen to you, at least with interest, and ... and I am sure that I will hear a great deal that is new from you.'

He sat down on a chair.

'Have a seat!' Shatov exclaimed, and somewhat suddenly, he himself sat down.

'Permit me, however, to remind you,' Stavrogin suddenly recalled, 'that I was about to ask you a great favour concerning Marya Timofeyevna, one that is very important to her, at least ...'

'Well then?' Shatov suddenly frowned, looking like a man who has been suddenly interrupted at the most important moment, and who, though he is looking at you, hasn't yet had time to grasp your question.

'And you didn't let me finish,' Nikolay Vsevolodovich concluded with a smile.

'Oh, what nonsense – later!' Shatov waved his hand disdainfully, having grasped what Stavrogin was laying claim to, and proceeded directly to his main point.

7.

'Do you know,' he began almost threateningly, leaning forward in his chair, his eyes flashing and the index finger of his right hand raised in front of him (evidently without noticing it himself), 'do you know who on this entire earth is the only "God-bearing" people,[22] destined to renew and save the world in the name of a new God, and to whom alone have been given the keys to life and the new word . . . Do you know who this people is, and what its name is?'

'From the way you put it, I must inevitably conclude, and apparently as quickly as possible, that this is the Russian people.'

'And you're already laughing – oh, what a tribe!' Shatov almost bolted out of his chair.

'Calm down, I beg you: on the contrary, I was expecting something of precisely that sort.'

'Expecting something of that sort? And are these words really unfamiliar to you?'

'They're very familiar; I can see very clearly where you're heading. Your whole choice of words, and even the expression "God-bearing" people, is merely the conclusion of the conversation we had abroad more than two years ago, shortly before your departure for America. At least, as far as I can now recall.'

'It's entirely your choice of words, not mine. It's yours, and not merely the conclusion of our conversation. There was no such thing as "our" conversation: there was a teacher who spouted big words, and there was a pupil who rose from the dead. I am that pupil, and you are the teacher.'

'But if I recall, it was immediately after hearing my words that you went off and joined the society, and only later left for America.'

'Yes, and I wrote to you from America about that; I wrote to you about everything. Yes, I couldn't immediately tear myself away from everything to which I had become attached since childhood – it would have been too bloody – and on which I had lavished all the ecstasies of my hopes and all the tears of my hatred ... It's hard to change gods. I didn't believe you then, because I didn't want to believe, and I clung for the last time to that sewer ... But the seed remained and grew. Seriously, tell me seriously, did you read my letter from America through to the end? Maybe you didn't read it at all?'

'I read three pages of it, the first two and the last, and in addition, I skimmed the middle. However, I kept intending to ...'

'Oh, it doesn't matter; drop it, the devil with it!' Shatov waved his hand dismissively. 'If you've now gone back on what you said about the people then, how could you have come out with it at that time? That's what weighs on me now.'

'I was certainly not joking with you back then; in trying to convince you, I was perhaps more concerned with myself than with you,' Stavrogin stated enigmatically.

'You weren't joking! In America I spent three months lying on straw next to a certain ... unfortunate individual, and I learned from him that at the very same time you were trying to implant God and the motherland in my heart – at that very same time, and perhaps on the very same days, you were poisoning the heart of this unfortunate man, this maniac, Kirillov ... You were validating lies and slander in him, you drove his rational faculties to the point of frenzy ... Go and have a look at him now, he's your creation ... But you have seen him.'

'In the first place, let me observe that Kirillov himself just told me that he is happy and that all is going very well with him. Your supposition that all this occurred at the same time is almost correct; well then, what of it? I repeat: I was not deceiving either one of you.'

'Are you an atheist? Are you an atheist now?'

'Yes.'

'And at that time?'

'Just the same as now.'

'When we began this talk, I wasn't asking you to respect me; with your intelligence you could have understood that,' Shatov grumbled indignantly.

'I didn't get up the moment you began speaking, I didn't put an end to the conversation, I didn't leave you, and I'm still sitting here and quietly answering your questions and ... shouts, and therefore I haven't yet ceased to respect you.'

Shatov interrupted, with a wave of the hand.

'Do you remember your expression: "An atheist cannot be a Russian, an atheist immediately ceases to be a Russian"? Do you remember that?'

'Yes?' Nikolay Vsevolodovich said as if he were asking him to repeat the question.

'Do you have to ask? Have you forgotten? Yet this is one of the surest indications of one of the most essential characteristics of the Russian spirit, which you put your finger on. How could you have forgotten it? There's more, and I'll remind you of it. You also said at that time: "Anyone who is not Orthodox cannot be a Russian."'

'I suppose that's a Slavophile idea.'

'No: today's Slavophiles would disown it. These days the people have grown more intelligent. But you went even further: you believed that Roman Catholicism was no longer Christianity. You asserted that Rome was preaching a Christ who had succumbed to the third temptation of the Devil, and that by proclaiming to the entire world that Christ without an earthly kingdom cannot prevail on earth, Catholicism was thereby preaching the Antichrist and hence had destroyed the entire Western world. You specifically pointed out that if France is in torment, then it's solely the fault of Catholicism,[23] for it has rejected the foul Roman God, and has not found a new one. That's what you were capable of saying then! I remember our conversations.'

'If I believed it, I would undoubtedly repeat it now as well. I wasn't lying when I spoke as a believer,' Nikolay Vsevolodovich stated very seriously. 'But I assure you that this repetition of my past ideas produces an extremely unpleasant impression on me. Can't you stop?'

'If you believed it?' Shatov cried, not paying the slightest attention to this request. 'But wasn't it you who told me that if it were to be mathematically proven to you that the truth existed apart from Christ, then you would rather remain with Christ than with the truth?[24] Did you say that? Did you?'

'But please permit me also to ask, when all is said and done,' Stavrogin raised his voice, 'what is all this impatient and . . . malicious examination leading to?'

'Soon this examination will be over for all eternity, and you will never again be reminded of it.'

'You keep insisting that we stand outside space and time . . .'

'Be quiet!' Shatov suddenly shouted. 'I'm stupid and clumsy, and let my name perish in ridicule! Will you allow me to repeat in your presence your main idea as it was then, in its entirety? Oh, only ten lines, just the conclusion . . .'

'Repeat it, if it's just the conclusion . . .'

Stavrogin almost made a movement to glance at his watch, but restrained himself and did not glance.

Shatov again leaned forward in his chair and for an instant was even on the point of raising his finger again.

'Not a single people,' he began, as if reading line for line and at the same time continuing to look threateningly at Stavrogin, 'not one people has ever yet organized itself according to the principles of science and reason. Never has there been a single example of that, except only for a brief moment, out of stupidity. Socialism, by its very nature, must be atheism, for it has specifically proclaimed, from its very first words, that it is an atheistic construct and is intentionally organized exclusively according to the principles of science and reason. Reason and science in the life of peoples always, now and from the beginning of time, have fulfilled merely a secondary and auxiliary function; and that will be their function until the end of time. Peoples are formed and moved by another force that rules and dominates them, but whose origin is unknown and inexplicable. This force is the force of an unquenchable desire to go on to the end, while at the same time denying the end. This is the force of a ceaseless and tireless affirmation of its own being and the denial of death. It is the spirit of life, as the Scriptures say, "of living water", the drying up of which is threatened in the Apocalypse.[25] It is the aesthetic principle, as the philosophers say, the moral principle, as they also identify it. "The search for God", as I call it more simply. The goal of all movements of peoples, in every people and in every period of its existence, is nothing but a search for God, its own God, unquestionably its own, and faith in him as the only true one. God is the synthesis of the personality of an entire people, taken from its beginning to its end. It has never been the case that all or many peoples have had a single common God, but each has certainly had its own special one. It is a sign of a people's extinction when gods begin to be held in common. When the gods come to be held in common, then the gods die and so does faith in them, along with the peoples themselves. The stronger a people, the more singular its God. There has never yet been a people without religion, that is, without the concept of evil and good. Each people has its own concept of evil and good, and its own evil and good. When many different peoples begin to hold concepts of evil and good in common, then the peoples die out, and then the very difference between evil and good begins to blur and disappear. Reason has never had the power of defining evil and good or separating evil from good, even approximately. On the contrary, it has always mixed them up in a shameful and pitiful fashion, whereas science has found solutions by sheer force. In particular, this is the distinguishing feature of half-science, mankind's most dreadful scourge, worse than plague, famine and war, and it has been unknown until the present century. Half-science is a despot such as has never been seen until now. A despot who has his high priests and his slaves, a despot before whom all have prostrated themselves with love and superstition such as has been unthinkable until now, before which even science itself trembles and to which it shamefully panders. These are all your own words, Stavrogin, excepting the words about half-science. Those are mine, because I myself am only half-science, and therefore I particularly hate it. But in your ideas and even in your very words I have changed nothing, not a single word.'

'I don't think so,' Stavrogin observed cautiously. 'You took it in ardently and modified it ardently without noticing it. Why, the very fact that you've reduced God to a simple attribute of nationality . . .'

He suddenly began to watch Shatov with heightened and particular attention, and not so much his words as the man himself.

'I reduce God to an attribute of nationality?' Shatov shouted. 'On the contrary, I raise the people up to God. Why, has it ever been otherwise? The people are the body of God. Every people is a people only as long as it has its special God and excludes all the other gods in the world without any compromise, as long as it has faith that it will triumph through its own God and will drive all the other gods from the world. That is what everyone has believed from the beginning of time, all the great peoples, at least all those who were in any way singled out, all who stood at the head of humanity. You can't go against facts. The Hebrews lived only in anticipation of the coming of the true God, and they left the true God to the world. The Greeks attempted to deify nature and bequeath their religion to the world, that is, philosophy and art. Rome did deify the people in the form of the state, and bequeathed the state to other peoples. France, in the course of its long history, was merely the incarnation and development of the idea of the Roman god, and if they ended by casting their Roman god into the abyss and going all out for atheism, which they call socialism for the time being, then that's only because atheism is, after all, healthier than Roman Catholicism. If a great people does not have faith that it alone embodies the truth (in itself alone, and in it exclusively), if it does not have faith that it alone has the ability and is called to resurrect all peoples and save them with its truth, then it immediately ceases to be a great people and immediately turns into ethnographic material, and not a great people. A genuinely great people can never reconcile itself to playing a secondary role in humanity or even a primary one, but must stand in the front rank, absolutely and exclusively. If it loses this faith, then it is no longer a people. But there is only one truth, and therefore only one out of all the peoples is capable of having the true God, even though the remaining peoples also have their own special and great gods. The only "God-bearing" people is the Russian people, and ... and ... and really, do you really take me for such a fool, Stavrogin,' he suddenly set up a frenzied howling, 'who is utterly incapable of distinguishing whether his words at this moment are just tired old tommyrot, ground and reground in all the Moscow

Slavophile mills, or an utterly new word, the last word, the sole word of renewal and resurrection, and . . . what do I care for your laughter at this moment! What do I care that you don't understand me in the least, not in the least, not a word, not a sound! . . . Oh, how I despise your proud laughter and the way you're looking at me right now!'

He jumped up from his chair. Foam even appeared on his lips.

'On the contrary, Shatov, on the contrary,' Stavrogin spoke in an unusually serious and restrained manner, without getting up from his chair. 'On the contrary, your impassioned words have revived an extraordinarily large number of memories in me. In your words I recognize my own frame of mind two years ago and now I would no longer tell you, as I just did, that you have exaggerated the ideas I held at that time. It even seems to me that they were even more exclusive, even more absolute, and I assure you for the third time that I would very much like to affirm everything you've been saying just now, down to the last word, but . . .'

'But you need a hare?'

'Wha-a-at?'

'Your own vile expression,' Shatov laughed maliciously, again taking his seat. ' "In order to make sauce from a hare, you need a hare; in order to believe in God, you need a God." You kept saying this in Petersburg, so I'm told, like Nozdryov, who wanted to catch a hare by its hind legs.'[26]

'No, Nozdryov was really boasting that he'd already caught it. By the way, however, allow me to trouble you with a question as well, the more so since it seems to me that I now have a perfect right to ask it. Tell me: has *your* hare been caught, or is it still running around?'

'Don't you dare ask me questions using words like that; use others, others!' Shatov suddenly began to tremble all over.

'All right, then, others.' Nikolay Vsevolodovich looked at him bleakly. 'I merely wanted to find out whether you yourself believe in God or not.'

'I believe in Russia, I believe in her Orthodoxy . . . I believe in the Body of Christ ... I believe that the Second Coming[27] will occur in Russia ... I believe ...' Shatov began to babble in a frenzy.

'And in God? In God?'

'I ... I will believe in God.'

Not a muscle moved in Stavrogin's face. Shatov was directing a fiery, challenging look at him, as if he wanted to scorch him with his eyes.

'Now I did *not* say to you that I don't believe at all!' he finally shouted. 'I'm letting you know, purely and simply, that I'm an unhappy, boring book and nothing more, for the time being, for the time being ... But let my name perish! You're what we're discussing, not me ... I am a man without talent, and all I can do is spill my blood and nothing more, like any man without talent. Let my blood perish as well! I'm talking about you, I've been waiting two years for you here ... I've been dancing around naked for you for half an hour now. You, only you could raise this banner!'

He didn't finish speaking, and leaning his elbows on the table, propped his head in both hands as if in despair.

'I'll only note incidentally and as an oddity,' Stavrogin suddenly interrupted, 'that for some reason everyone is eager to thrust a banner into my hands. Pyotr Verkhovensky is also convinced that I "could also have raised a banner for them", at least that is what I'm told he said. He got the idea in his head that I could have played the part of a Stenka Razin[28] for them "on account of my unusual aptitude for crime" – his words as well.'

'What?' asked Shatov. 'Because of an unusual aptitude for crime?'

'Exactly.'

'Hmm. And is it true that you,' he gave a malicious smirk, 'is it true that in Petersburg you belonged to some secret society that practised bestial carnality? Is it true that the Marquis de Sade[29] could have taken lessons from you? Is it true that you seduced and debauched children? Tell me; don't you dare lie,' he shouted, completely beside himself. 'Nikolay Stavrogin cannot lie in the presence of Shatov, who struck him in the face! Tell me everything, and if it's true, I'll kill you immediately, right here and now!'

'I did say these words, but I didn't harm any children,' Stavrogin pronounced, but only after a very prolonged silence. He had turned pale, and his eyes blazed.

'But you said them!' Shatov continued imperiously, not taking his flashing eyes off him. 'Is it true that you stated you didn't make a distinction between the beauty of any instance of bestial carnality and a heroic deed of any kind, even the sacrifice of one's life for humanity? Is it true that you found equal beauty and identical pleasure in both these extremes?'

'It's impossible to answer like this . . . I don't want to answer,' Stavrogin muttered. He could very easily have stood up and left, but he didn't stand up and leave.

'I also don't know why evil is nasty and good is beautiful, but I do know why the sense of this distinction is erased and lost in gentlemen like the Stavrogins,' Shatov, trembling all over, didn't relent. 'Do you know why you got married then, so shamelessly and vilely? Precisely because it was here that the shamelessness and senselessness reached the point of genius! Oh, don't go sauntering along the brink, but boldly plunge head first. You got married out of a passion for inflicting torment, out of a passion for feeling the pangs of conscience, out of moral carnality. This was an instance of overwrought nerves . . . The challenge to common sense was altogether too seductive! Stavrogin and a pitiful, dim-witted, destitute cripple! When you bit the governor's ear, did you feel a surge of carnality? Did you feel it? You idle, footloose son of a landowner, did you feel it?'

'You're a psychologist,' Stavrogin was growing increasingly pale, 'although you are partly mistaken about the reasons for my marriage . . . However, I wonder who could have given you all this information.' He smiled with difficulty. 'Was it Kirillov? But he didn't take part in . . .'

'You're turning pale?'

'What is it that you want, then?' Nikolay Vsevolodovich finally raised his voice. 'I've been sitting under your knout for half an hour, and you could at least have released me politely

. . . if in fact you had no rational purpose for treating me in such a fashion.'

'Rational purpose?'

'Without a doubt. It was your duty at least to inform me of your purpose eventually. I kept waiting for you to do so, but instead I found only hysterical spite. Please, open the gate for me.'

He got up from his chair. Shatov rushed after him in a frenzy.

'Kiss the earth, drench it in tears, beg forgiveness!' he shouted, grabbing him by the shoulder.

'All the same, I didn't kill you . . . that morning . . . and I pulled both my hands back . . .' Stavrogin said almost in pain, his eyes downcast.

'Finish what you have to say, finish what you have to say! You came here to warn me of danger, you allowed me to speak, and you want to make a public announcement of your marriage tomorrow! Do you think I can't see from your face that some dreadful new idea is taking hold of you? Stavrogin, why am I condemned to believe in you for all eternity? Could I really have spoken as I did with anyone else? I am a chaste man, but I was not afraid of my nakedness, because I was speaking with Stavrogin. I was not afraid to caricature a great idea with my touch, because Stavrogin was listening to me. Do you think I won't kiss your footprints when you've left? I can't tear you out of my heart, Nikolay Stavrogin!'

'I'm sorry that I can't love you, Shatov,' Nikolay Vsevolodovich said coldly.

'I know you can't, and I know you're not lying. Listen, I can put everything right: I'll get the hare for you!'

Stavrogin said nothing.

'You're an atheist because you're a landowner's son, the last son of a landowner. You've lost the distinction between evil and good, because you've stopped recognizing your own people. A new generation is coming, straight from the heart of the people, and neither you, nor the Verkhovenskys, father and son, recognize them in the slightest, nor do I, because I'm also the son of a landowner, the son of Pashka, your serf and footman . . . Listen, acquire God through work. That's it in a nutshell, otherwise you'll disappear, like some nasty mould; acquire him through work.'

'God through work? What kind of work?'

'Muzhik's work. Go and get rid of your riches . . . Ah! You're laughing, you're afraid it might turn out to be a trick?'

But Stavrogin wasn't laughing.

'You suggest that God can be acquired through work, specifically muzhik's work?' he repeated, after some thought, as if he had really encountered something new and serious that was worth pondering. 'By the way,' he suddenly moved on to a new idea, 'you've just reminded me: do you know that I'm not at all rich, so I have nothing to get rid of? I'm hardly in a position even to guarantee Marya Timofeyevna's future . . . And here's something else: I had come to ask you, if possible, not to abandon Marya Timofeyevna in future, since you're the only one who might have some influence on her poor mind . . . I'm saying this just in case.'

'All right, all right, you're talking about Marya Timofey- evna,' Shatov waved one hand dismissively, while holding a candle in the other, 'all right, that's understood . . . Listen, go and see Tikhon.'

'Who?'

'Tikhon. Tikhon, a former bishop, now living in retirement because of ill health, here in town, on the edge of town, in our Yefimyevsky Bogorodsky Monastery.'[30]

'What's this all about?'

'Don't worry. People go and visit him, in carriages and on foot. Go and see him; what will it cost you? Well, what will it cost you?'

'It's the first time I've heard of him, and . . . I've never yet laid eyes on people of that sort. Thank you, I'll go.'

'This way,' Shatov was lighting the stairway. 'Go now,' he opened the gate of the fence on to the street.

'I won't come to see you again, Shatov,' Stavrogin said quietly, stepping through the gate.

Darkness and rain continued as before.

CHAPTER 2

Night (Continuation)

1.

He walked the entire length of Bogoyavlenskaya Street. Finally, the road started to go downhill, his feet slid in the mud, and suddenly there opened before him a broad, misty, seemingly empty stretch – the river. The houses turned into shacks, the street disappeared in numerous jumbled alley-ways. For a long time Nikolay Vsevolodovich made his way along the fences, not moving far from the riverbank, but finding his way unerringly and without even giving it much thought. He was engrossed in something else entirely, and looked round in surprise, when suddenly, coming out of his deep state of preoccupation, he saw that he was in the middle of our long, wet pontoon bridge. There was not a soul anywhere around, so that it seemed strange to him when all of a sudden, almost at his very elbow, he heard the sound of a polite and overly familiar, yet rather pleasant voice, with the honeyed and clearly enunciated tones flaunted by overly refined tradesmen or young, curly-topped sales assistants from the shopping arcade.

'Will you not permit me, kind sir, to use your umbrella in concert with you?'

In fact, a figure slipped, or merely wanted to appear to be slipping, under his umbrella. A tramp was walking beside him, almost 'rubbing elbows', as young soldiers put it. Slowing his pace, Nikolay Vsevolodovich bent down to have a look, insofar as this was possible in the darkness. He was not very tall, and looked something like a petty tradesman out on a spree; his clothing was shabby and not warm; a wet cloth cap with its peak half torn off perched on his shaggy, curly head. He seemed very dark-haired, lean and swarthy. His eyes were large, totally black, with a marked gleam in them and a yellow cast, as with gypsies; this is what could be guessed in the darkness. He must have been about forty years old, and he wasn't drunk.

'Do you know me?' Nikolay Vsevolodovich asked.

'Mr Stavrogin, Nikolay Vsevolodovich. You was pointed out to me Sunday before last at the station, almost as soon as the train stopped. Besides which, I heerd a lot 'bout you before.'

'From Pyotr Stepanovich? You ... you're Fedka the Convict?'

'I was christened Fyodor Fyodorovich. We have our natural mother still livin' in these here parts, an old woman of God, bent over to the ground, she prays to God for us all the time, every day and every night, so's not to waste her old woman's time lyin' on the stove for nothin'.'

'You've escaped from hard labour?'

'I changed my lot in life. I handed in my books and bells and church stuff, because I was sentenced to hard labour, and it was a ver-r-ry long wait for my time to be up.'

'What are you doing here?'

'Day and night come – and twenty-four hours is over and done. Also, our uncle passed away last week in jail here – fake money – so after I went and seen to the wake for 'im, I threw a couple o' dozen stones at the dogs – that's all we was up to so far. Besides which, Pyotr Stepanovich is raisin' my hopes I can get a passport, let's say a merchant's, good for travellin' all over Russia, and so I'm waitin' for his kind attention. Because, he says, "My dad lost you playin' cards in the English club; and I," he says, "find this an unjust act of inhumanity." Would you, sir, have the kindness to favour me with three silver roubles for some tea to warm myself up on?'

'So, you were watching for me here; I don't like that. By whose order?'

'As for an order, there weren't nothin' of the sort from no one. Only reason I done it was I knowed about your love for your fellow man, as is familiar to the whole world. All the likes of us takes in, you know it for yourself, is either a handful o' straw or a poke in the jaw. Friday last I went and stuffed myself on meat-pies, like Martin gobblin' up the soap,[1] and ever since – nothin' to eat one day, waitin' round the next, and the third day nothin' to eat again. The river's got as much water as you want, I started breedin' carp in my belly ... So maybe Your Worship will be real generous-like. I do have a lady friend waitin' not far away from here, but I better not show up there without some roubles.'

'What was it that Pyotr Stepanovich promised I'd give you?'

'He didn't exactly promise nothin', sir, but he was sayin' in his own words that maybe I can be useful to Your Worship, if some bad patch comes up, let's say, but just how, that he didn't explain in any exactitude, 'cause Pyotr Stepanovich, for instance, is puttin' my Cossack patience to the test and don't have no trust in me nohow.'

'But why?'

'Pyotr Stepanych is an astrogolist, and he's learned God's planetations, but even he comes in for criticism. Here I'm standin' before you, sir, like before the One True One, 'cause I heerd lots o' things 'bout you. Pyotr Stepanovich is one thing, but you, sir, maybe are somethin' really different. The way it goes with him, if someone says a man's a scoundrel, then he don't know nothin' more 'bout him 'cept he's a scoundrel. And if it's said he's a fool, ain't no other name for that there man 'cept "fool". But take me, for instance – maybe on Tuesdays and Wednesdays I ain't nothin' but a fool, but on Thursdays I'm a lot smarter than him. Now he knows that I'm really dyin' to get a passport, 'cause in Russia you can't do a damn thing without a document, so here he is thinkin' he's taken my soul prisoner. I tell you, sir, it's real easy for Pyotr Stepanovich to live in this world, 'cause he gets an idea in his head 'bout a man and that's what he lives with. Besides which, he's stingy as hell. He really thinks that without him I wouldn't dare bother you, but here I am standin' before you, sir, like before the One True One, waitin' four nights already for Your Worship on this here bridge, just to show I don't need him to find my own way with my own quiet steps. Better, I think, to bow to a boot than a bast shoe.'[2]

'And who told you that I would be walking across the bridge at night?'

'Well, tellin' you the honest truth, that come out by accident, mostly from Captain Lebyadkin's stupidness, 'cause ain't no way he can hold his tongue. So then, three silver roubles would be owin' from Your Worship, for instance, for three days and three nights, for all that borin' time. And as concerns my wet clothes, well, let's just say that's an offence that we'll just keep quiet about.'

'I'm going to the left, and you're going to the right; here's the end of the bridge. Listen, Fyodor, I want you to understand once and for all what I'm saying: I won't give you even a kopeck, and don't you ever again wait to meet me on the bridge or anywhere else. I have no need for you now and I won't, and if you don't do as I say, I'll tie you up and take you straight to the police. March!'

'Ugh, at least toss me somethin' for keepin' you company; it made things cheerier for you on your walk.'

'Go away!'

'Do you know the way in these here parts, sir? Such twists and turns round here . . . I'd be able to guide you, 'cause this here town's the same as if the Devil himself was carryin' it in a basket and scattered it all over the place.'

'Hey, I'll tie you up!' Nikolay Vsevolodovich turned around menacingly.

'Maybe you'll think it over, sir: it don't take much to do wrong to an orphan.'

'No! You're obviously sure of yourself!'

'I'm sure of you, sir, and not of myself an awful lot.'

'I have absolutely no need of you, I've told you that!'

'But I do have need of you, sir, that's what. I'll be waitin' for you when you come back this way, and that's that.'

'I give you my word of honour: if I meet you, I'll tie you up.'

'Well, then, I'll have a sash ready and on hand. Have a good trip, sir, you did warm an orphan up under your umbrella, and just for that we'll be grateful for the rest of our life.'

He fell behind. Nikolay Vsevolodovich came to his destination feeling worried. This man who had dropped from the sky was utterly convinced that he was indispensable to him, and wasn't slow about announcing it all too insolently. In general, he was being treated unceremoniously. But it could also have been that not everything this tramp had said was a lie, and that he was acting strictly on his own in pushing his services on him, and was really keeping it secret from Pyotr Stepanovich. And that was the most peculiar thing of all.

2.

The house that Nikolay Vsevolodovich had reached stood in a deserted lane between fences, beyond which stretched vegetable gardens, literally on the very edge of town. It was a small, completely isolated wooden house, which had just been built and was not yet covered with planking. In one of the small windows the shutters had deliberately been left unclosed and a candle stood on the window sill, evidently as a beacon to a late-arriving guest who was expected that night. While still thirty or so steps away, Nikolay Vsevolodovich made out the figure of a tall man standing on the front steps, probably the master of the premises, who had come out impatiently to have a look at the road. Then his voice was heard, impatient and rather timid-sounding.

'Is that you, sir? You, sir?'

'It's me,' Nikolay Vsevolodovich responded, but not before walking all the way up to the front steps and rolling up his umbrella.

'At long last, sir!' Captain Lebyadkin began stamping his feet and bustling about, for it was he. 'Please do let me have your umbrella; it's very wet weather, sir; I'll open it here on the floor in the corner, welcome, welcome.'

The door leading from the entryway into a room lit by two candles was wide open.

'If you hadn't definitely promised to come, I would have stopped believing you would.'

'A quarter to one.' Nikolay Vsevolodovich glanced at his watch as he stepped into the room.

'And on top of it, rain and such a long distance . . . I have no clock, and all you can see out of the windows is vegetable gardens, so that . . . you get out of touch with what's happening . . . but actually I'm not saying this to grumble, because I don't dare, I don't dare, but just out of impatience, which has been eating me up all week long, that at last all this should be resolved.'

'What do you mean?'

'To hear my fate, Nikolay Vsevolodovich. Welcome.'

He bowed as he indicated a place at the small table in front of the couch.

Nikolay Vsevolodovich looked around him. The room was tiny and very low, with only the most essential furniture, chairs and a sofa made of wood, also brand new, without upholstery and without cushions, two small lindenwood tables, one by the sofa and the other in a corner, covered with a tablecloth, all of it set with various things and spread on top an extremely clean napkin. In fact, the entire room was obviously kept in a state of great cleanliness. Captain Lebyadkin hadn't been drunk for about eight days now. His face had become rather puffy and yellow, he had a restless, curious and obviously bewildered look about him. It was all too obvious that he himself didn't yet know what tone he should adopt and what course would be most advantageous for him to take.

'As you see, sir,' he waved his hand around, 'I live like Zosima.[3] Sobriety, solitude and poverty – the vow of the knights of yore.'

'Do you suppose that the knights of yore used to take such vows?'

'Maybe I've got it all wrong? Alas, I have no education! I've ruined everything! Would you believe it, Nikolay Vsevolodovich, here for the first time I've recovered from my shameful weaknesses – not a glass, not a drop! I have a corner to live in, and for six days I've been enjoying the blessing of a clear conscience. Even the walls smell of resin, reminding me of nature. And what was I, who was I?

> At night I blow without a place to lie,
> In daytime, though, my tongue stuck out –

as a poet of genius puts it!⁴ But . . . you're soaked all the way
through . . . Wouldn't you like some tea?'

'Don't trouble yourself.'

'The samovar has been on the boil since before eight, but . . .
it's gone out . . . like everything else in the world. Even the sun,
they say, will go out eventually. However, if necessary, I'll start
it going again. Agafya isn't asleep.'

'Tell me, Marya Timofeyevna . . .'

'She's here, she's here,' Lebyadkin whispered in immediate
response, 'would you like to peek in?' He pointed at the slightly
open door to the other room.

'She's not asleep?'

'Oh no, no, how would that be possible? On the contrary,
she's been sitting and waiting since early evening, and as soon
as she learned of it today, she immediately set about making
her toilette.' He was about to twist his mouth into a mocking
little smile, but instantly controlled himself.

'How is she in general?' Nikolay Vsevolodovich asked with
a frown.

'In general? You yourself know that' (he shrugged his shoulders pityingly) 'and now . . . now she sits and tells her fortune
with cards.'

'All right, later. First of all we have to finish with you.'

Nikolay Vsevolodovich settled down in a chair.

The captain didn't dare sit down on the sofa, but immediately
moved another chair up for himself and leaned forward to listen
in anxious anticipation.

'What's that you have there in the corner under the napkin?'
said Nikolay Vsevolodovich, suddenly turning his attention
to it.

'You mean that, sir?' Lebyadkin also turned to look. 'They're
the fruits of your generosity, in the form, so to speak, of a
housewarming, also taking into consideration the very long
journey you've had to take and the fatigue you naturally feel,'
he snickered ingratiatingly, then got up from his chair and on
tiptoe respectfully and carefully removed the napkin from the
small table in the corner. Under it, as it turned out, were *zakuski*
that had been prepared: ham, veal, sardines, cheese, a small

greenish decanter and a tall bottle of Bordeaux. Everything had been laid out neatly, with expertness and almost elegance.

'Was it you who went to the trouble?'

'It was, sir. Since yesterday, and doing everything I could to honour ... As for Marya Timofeyevna, she's indifferent to matters like this, as you yourself know. But the main thing is that it's the result of your generosity, it's all yours, since you, not I, are the master here; while I, so to speak, am only something like your steward, for despite everything, despite everything, Nikolay Vsevolodovich, despite everything, I'm still an independent spirit! Don't you take away this last remaining possession from me!' he finished emotionally.

'Hmm! You'd better sit down again.'

'Mo-o-ost grateful, grateful and independent!' He sat down. 'Ah, Nikolay Vsevolodovich, so much has been seething in this heart of mine that I didn't know how I would wait for you to come! Now you're here to decide my fate and ... the fate of that unfortunate woman, and then ... then, as it was before, in the old days, I'll pour out everything to you, as I did four years ago! You deigned to listen to me then, you read my poems. What if people in those days used to call me your Falstaff from Shakespeare, the point is you meant so much in my life! ... But I have a great deal to be afraid of now, and it's to you alone that I look for advice and illumination. Pyotr Stepanovich is treating me abominably!'

Nikolay Vsevolodovich was listening with curiosity and peering at him. Evidently, Captain Lebyadkin, although he had certainly stopped drinking, nonetheless was far from being in a harmonious state of mind. In the case of drunkards of many years' standing, something incoherent and stultified, blurred, something that seems damaged and deranged finally settles in, although, to be sure, they go on swindling, deceiving and shamming though no worse than anyone else if they have to.

'I see that you haven't changed a bit, Captain, in these four odd years,' Nikolay Vsevolodovich said somewhat more gently. 'Evidently it's true that the entire second half of a man's life is usually composed solely of the habits accumulated during the first half.'

'Lofty words! You've solved the riddle of life!' the captain exclaimed, half-shamming, but half in truly genuine enthusiasm, because he was a great lover of clever words. 'Out of all your sayings, Nikolay Vsevolodovich, one in particular has stuck in my memory, one you came out with while we were still in Petersburg: "One has to be a truly great man in order to know how to hold out even against common sense." There now, sir!'

'And a fool as well.'

'That's so, sir, a fool as well, but you've been a font of witticisms all your life. While the others? Just let Liputin, just let Pyotr Stepanovich try to come out with something like that! Oh, how cruelly I've been treated by Pyotr Stepanovich!'

'Well now, what about you, Captain, how did you yourself behave?'

'A drunken state, and a legion of enemies besides! But now it's all passed, all of it, and I'm renewing myself like a snake. Nikolay Vsevolodovich, do you know that I'm writing my last will and testament and that I've already finished it?'

'That's curious. What are you leaving and to whom?'

'To the fatherland, to mankind and to students. Nikolay Vsevolodovich, I've read the biography of a certain American in the newspapers. He left his entire enormous fortune to factories and to the exact sciences, his skeleton to the students of an academy there, and his skin for a drum, so that the American national anthem could be played on it day and night. Alas, we are pygmies in comparison with the soaring thought of the States of North America. Russia is a freak of nature, but not of intellect. If I should try to bequeath my skin to make a drum, for instance to the Akmolinsk[5] infantry regiment, in which I had the honour to begin my service, so that every day the Russian national anthem could be played on it in front of the regiment, it would be regarded as liberalism, and my skin would be forbidden ... and so I have confined myself to students. I want to bequeath my skeleton to an academy, with the proviso, however, that on its forehead a label should be pasted for all time, reading: "A repentant freethinker". That's what, sir!'

The captain was speaking ardently, and naturally, he already

believed in the beauty of the American's last will, but he was
also a rogue, and he also had a strong desire to entertain
Nikolay Vsevolodovich, with whom he had previously seen
long service in the capacity of a jester. But Stavrogin didn't
smile; on the contrary, he asked, rather suspiciously:

'So you intend to publish your last will while you're still alive
and receive a reward for it?'

'Well, what of it, Nikolay Vsevolodovich, what of it?'
Lebyadkin peered at him cautiously. 'Such is my fate, you see!
I've even stopped writing verses, yet at one time even you were
amused by my little efforts, do you remember, over a bottle?
But I've laid down my pen for good. I've written only one
poem, like Gogol's "Last Story", you remember, where he was
proclaiming to Russia that it had "surged in song" from his
bosom.[6] The same with me: I've sung my song – enough.'

'What poem is that?'

'"In Case She Should Break Her Leg".'

'Wha-a-t?'

That was just what the captain was waiting for. He had an
inordinately great respect and admiration for his own poems,
but also, because of a certain roguish duplicity of character, he
was also pleased that Nikolay Vsevolodovich always used to
enjoy his little verses and laugh heartily at them, sometimes
even holding his sides. Thus two goals were achieved, to be a
poet and to be of service, but now there was also a third
goal, which was special and extremely ticklish: the captain, by
bringing his verses on to the scene, was hoping to justify himself
on one point, which for some reason he was most afraid of,
and where he felt himself most to blame.

'"In Case She Should Break Her Leg", that is, in case she's
out horseback riding. A fantasy, Nikolay Vsevolodovich, ravings, but the ravings of a poet. Once I was struck, as I was
passing, by meeting a lady on horseback, and I put to myself
the weighty question: "What would happen then?" – that is,
just in case. It was quite clear: all her admirers would beat a
retreat, all her suitors would disappear, here today and gone
tomorrow, the poet alone would remain true, his heart crushed
in his breast. Nikolay Vsevolodovich, even a louse, even he

could be in love, there's no law against that even for him. Yet
the person in question was offended by both the letter and the
verses. Even you, they say, were angry; is that so, sir? It's regret-
table. I didn't want to believe it. Come now, who could I possibly
harm with just my imagination? Besides, I swear on my honour,
there was Liputin, saying: "Send it, send it, every man has the
right of correspondence." So I went ahead and sent it.'

'You seem to have put yourself forward as a suitor?'

'Enemies, enemies, enemies!'

'Recite your verses,' Nikolay Vsevolodovich interrupted him
sternly.

'Ravings, mostly ravings.'

Nonetheless he drew himself erect, threw out his arm and
began:

> 'The beauty of beauties has broken her limb,
> Her allure is now doubly enhanced,
> And I, though long since besotted I've been,
> Now find myself doubly entranced.'

'All right, that's enough,' Nikolay Vsevolodovich waved his
hand dismissively.

'I dream of Petersburg,' Lebyadkin quickly skipped to
another topic, as if the poem had never existed. 'I dream of
being reborn . . . Benefactor! May I count on you not to refuse
me the means of making the journey? I've been waiting for you
all week long, like the sun.'

'Why, no, you'll excuse me, but I have almost no means left;
and besides, why should I give you any money?'

Nikolay Vsevolodovich suddenly seemed to grow angry.
He enumerated, dryly and succinctly, all the captain's crimes:
drunkenness, lying, the squandering of the money intended for
Marya Timofeyevna, the fact that she had been removed from
the convent, the insolent letters threatening to make the secret
public, his behaviour towards Darya Pavlovna, and so on and
so forth. The captain rocked back and forth, gesticulated, began
to object, but each time Nikolay Vsevolodovich stopped him
with a commanding gesture.

'And furthermore,' he observed at last, 'you keep writing about "disgrace to the family". What possible disgrace is it for you that your sister is legally married to Stavrogin?'

'But the marriage is hidden under a bushel, Nikolay Vsevolodovich, the marriage is hidden under a bushel, it's a fateful secret. I receive money from you and suddenly people ask me: what's this money for? My hands are tied, and I can't answer; it would damage my sister, damage my family honour.'

The captain raised his voice: he was fond of this topic, and set high hopes on it. Alas, he didn't have the slightest inkling that he was about to come a cropper. Calmly and precisely, as if it were a matter of issuing the most ordinary household instructions, Nikolay Vsevolodovich informed him that in the next few days, perhaps even tomorrow or the day after tomorrow, he intended to make his marriage known everywhere, 'both to the police as well as to society', and therefore the question of family honour would be settled by itself, and with it, the question of subsidies as well. The captain sat goggle-eyed: he didn't even begin to understand; things had to be explained to him.

'But look, isn't she a half-wit? . . .'

'I will make the necessary arrangements.'

'But . . . what about your mother?'

'Well, she can do as she likes.'

'But you will be bringing your wife into your house?'

'Perhaps I will. However, that isn't your business, in the fullest sense of the word, and doesn't concern you in the least.'

'What do you mean, doesn't concern me!' the captain exclaimed. 'And what am I to do, then?'

'Well, naturally, you will not enter the house.'

'But look here, I'm a relative, after all.'

'People run away from such relatives. Why, then, should I give you any money? Just consider that for yourself.'

'Nikolay Vsevolodovich, Nikolay Vsevolodovich, this cannot be, perhaps you'll give it some more thought, you won't want to lay hands on . . . What will people say, what will the world say?'

'Oh, I'm hardly afraid of your world. After all, I did marry your sister then, when I felt like it, after a drunken dinner, on a bet for wine, and now I'm going to proclaim it for all to hear – why not, if it amuses me now?'

He pronounced this in a particular tone of irritation that caused a horrified Lebyadkin to start believing him.

'But look, I, how am *I*, look, the main thing here is *me*! Perhaps you're joking, Nikolay Vsevolodovich?'

'No, I'm not joking.'

'Have it your own way, Nikolay Vsevolodovich, but I don't believe you . . . in that case, I'll submit a petition.'

'You're dreadfully stupid, Captain.'

'That may well be, but after all, that's my only recourse!' The captain was utterly bewildered. 'Before, we were at least given lodging in exchange for her charring work in the corners of the rooms, but now what will happen if you abandon me completely?'

'Why, don't you want to go to Petersburg to take up a new career? Incidentally, is what I hear true, that you intend to go and inform and give the names of all the others in hopes of receiving a pardon?'

The captain stood with his mouth open and his eyes popping, and made no reply.

'Listen, Captain,' Stavrogin suddenly said in an extremely serious tone, leaning slightly over the table. Until this point he had been speaking rather ambiguously, so that Lebyadkin, well practised in the role of jester, was still a trifle uncertain until the very last moment whether the master was truly angry with him or was merely poking fun at him, whether he really had the wild idea of announcing his marriage or was merely toying with him. But now Nikolay Vsevolodovich's uncharacteristically stern look was so convincing that a shudder even ran down the captain's back. 'Listen and tell me the truth, Lebyadkin; have you informed about anything yet or not? Have you actually managed to do anything? Have you sent some letter out of sheer stupidity?'

'No, sir, I haven't had time for anything and . . . I haven't even thought of . . .' the captain was staring at him without moving.

'Come now, you're lying about not having thought about it. That's why you're so eager to get to Petersburg. If you didn't write, then didn't you blurt something out to someone here? Tell me the truth, I've heard something.'

'To Liputin, when I was in a drunken state. Liputin is a traitor. I opened my heart to him,' the poor captain whispered.

'The heart's all well and good, but you really don't have to be a damned fool about it. If you had an idea, you should have kept it to yourself. Nowadays intelligent people keep quiet, and don't have conversations.'

'Nikolay Vsevolodovich!' The captain began to tremble. 'You yourself were not part of anything, after all, and so you really weren't someone I . . .'

'Why, you wouldn't have dared inform on your own milk cow.'

'Nikolay Vsevolodovich, just consider, just consider!' And in despair, in tears the captain began hastily laying out the story of his life for the four years past. It was the extremely stupid story of a fool who had been drawn into something that was not his business and who had virtually no understanding of its importance until the very last minute, on account of his drinking and carousing. He related how while still in Petersburg he had 'got carried away, first off just for friendship's sake, like a real student, although he was not a student', and without knowing anything, 'and not guilty of anything', he distributed various papers on stairways, left them in doorways and on doorbells by the dozens, shoved them in instead of newspapers, took them to theatres, thrust them into hats, stuck them into pockets. And then he also began receiving money from them 'because my financial situation, my financial situation was such, sir!' He distributed 'all sorts of rubbish' throughout the districts of two provinces. 'Oh, Nikolay Vsevolodovich,' he exclaimed, 'what troubled me most of all was that this was completely against all civil laws, and primarily those of the fatherland! Suddenly they would print that people should go out with pitchforks, and remember that he who went out poor in the morning could return home rich in the evening. Just think of it, sir! I was shaking in my boots, but I was distributing them. Or suddenly there would be five or six lines addressed to all of Russia, for no good reason: "Lock the churches as soon as you can, destroy God, violate marriages, destroy the rights of inheritance, take up knives", that's all, and the Devil knows what else. That was the piece of paper, with the five lines, that I was almost caught with, but the officers of the regiment gave me a good beating and then, God bless them, let me go. And then I was almost arrested last year when I passed some counterfeit fifty-rouble French notes to Korovayev. Well, thank God, Korovayev went and drowned in a pond when he was drunk, and they didn't succeed in exposing me. Here, at Virginsky's, I was proclaiming the freedom of the socialist wife. In June I was in —sky District again, distributing leaflets. They say they'll make me do it again. Pyotr Stepanovich suddenly lets it be known that I should obey; he's been threatening me for a long time. Why, look at the way he treated me that Sunday! Nikolay Vsevolodovich, I am a slave, I am a worm, but I'm not God, and that's the only difference between me and Derzhavin.[7] But my financial situation, my financial situation was such!'

Nikolay Vsevolodovich listened to all of this with curiosity.

'There's a great deal I didn't know at all,' he said, 'naturally, anything could have happened to you. Listen,' he said, after some reflection, 'if you want, tell them – well, you know whom – that Liputin lied and that you were only intending to frighten me with a denunciation, on the assumption that I had also been compromised, and so that you could get more money out of me that way . . . You understand?'

'Nikolay Vsevolodovich, my dear fellow, do you really think I'm in such danger? The only reason I've been waiting for you was to ask you.'

Nikolay Vsevolodovich gave a smile.

'They won't, of course, let you go to Petersburg, even if I should give you some money for the trip . . . besides, it's time for me to go to Marya Timofeyevna', and he got up from his chair.

'Nikolay Vsevolodovich, how do things stand with Marya Timofeyevna?'

'Why, just as I was telling you.'

'Is that really the truth?'

'You still don't believe it?'

'Will you really just cast me off like an old worn-out shoe?'

'I'll see,' laughed Nikolay Vsevolodovich. 'All right, let me go in.'

'Wouldn't you like me to stand on the front steps ... so that I don't accidentally overhear anything ... because the rooms are so tiny.'

'That's a good idea: stand on the front steps. Take my umbrella.'

'Is your umbrella ... worthy of the likes of me, sir?' the captain said in a saccharine tone.

'Anyone is worthy of an umbrella.'

'At one stroke you define the minimum of human rights.'

But by now he was babbling mechanically. He was utterly crushed by the news and was completely disoriented. And yet, almost immediately, the minute he walked out on to the front steps and opened the umbrella over his head, the ever-consoling thought once again began to hatch in his frivolous and roguish head that people were deceiving him and lying to him, and if so, then he had nothing to fear, but was the one to be feared.

'If they're lying and deceiving me, then what's really the point of it all?' the question gnawed at him. The announcement of the marriage seemed absurd to him. 'True enough, with a wonder-worker like this, anything can happen; he lives to bring harm to people. Well, what if he himself has been afraid since last Sunday's affront, and in a way he's never been before? He came running to assure me that he himself would announce it, out of fear that I might announce it. Oh, don't slip up, Lebyadkin! And why come at night, like a thief, when he himself wants to make things public? And if he's afraid, then that means he's afraid now, this very moment, and has been for the last several days ... Oh, no false steps, Lebyadkin! ...

'He's trying to frighten me with Pyotr Stepanovich. Oh, it's scary, it's scary; no, here's where it's really scary! And I took it into my head to blab to Liputin. The Devil only knows what these devils have up their sleeve, I've never been able to figure it out. They've started to stir again, like five years ago. Really, who is there I could denounce anyone to? "Didn't you write to someone out of sheer stupidity?" Hmm. So you could write and pretend you were being stupid? Is he perhaps giving me advice? "You're going to Petersburg for that reason." The scoundrel, I'd only dreamed of it, and there he went and figured out my dream! It's as if he himself was egging me on to make the trip. There are probably two things going on here, one or the other: either he's afraid again, because he's up to some major mischief, or . . . or else he's not afraid for himself, but is just egging me on so that I'll tell on all of them. Oh, it's scary, Lebyadkin; oh, you'd better not slip up! . . .'

He became so engrossed in thought that he even forgot to eavesdrop. However, eavesdropping was difficult: the door was thick, of one solid piece, and they were talking very softly; some indistinct sounds reached his ears. The captain even spat and went out again, lost in thought, to whistle on the front steps.

3.

Marya Timofeyevna's room was twice as large as the one occupied by the captain, and was furnished with the same rough and ready furniture. But the table in front of the sofa was covered with an elegant coloured cloth; a lamp was burning on it; a beautiful carpet had been laid over the entire floor; the bed was screened by a long green curtain that ran the length of the room, and, in addition, a large easy chair had been placed by the table, although Marya Timofeyevna never sat in it. In the corner, as in their previous apartment, hung an icon, with a lamp burning before it, and on the table those same essential knick-knacks had been laid out: the pack of cards, the small hand mirror, the songbook, even the sweet roll. In addition, two small books with coloured pictures had made their appearance, one being excerpts from a popular travel book, adapted for adolescent readers, the other a collection of light, edifying stories, mostly about knights, designed for Christmas presents and boarding schools. There was also an album containing a variety of photographs. Marya Timofeyevna was of course waiting for her visitor, as the captain had already forewarned him; but when Nikolay Vsevolodovich went in to see her, she was asleep, half-reclining on the sofa, leaning against a worsted cushion. The visitor closed the door behind him without a sound, and, without moving from where he was standing, began to study the sleeping woman.

In reporting that she had made her toilette, the captain had stretched the truth. She was wearing the same dark dress as on Sunday at Varvara Petrovna's. Her hair was pulled into exactly the same small bun on the nape of her neck; her long, dry neck was bare in exactly the same way. The black shawl, which had been a present from Varvara Petrovna, lay carefully folded on the sofa. As before, she was crudely powdered and rouged. Nikolay Vsevolodovich hadn't been standing there for even a minute when she suddenly woke up, as if she had sensed him looking at her, opened her eyes and quickly sat up. But something strange must have happened to her visitor as well: he remained standing in the same spot by the door, without moving, without speaking, and peered intently and persistently into her face. Perhaps his look was excessively severe, perhaps it showed disgust, even a gloating delight at her fear, unless Marya Timofeyevna just imagined it in her half-awakened state. Yet after almost a minute of expectant waiting, an expression of stark terror suddenly showed on the poor woman's face. It was contorted by spasms; she raised her trembling hands and suddenly burst into tears, exactly like a frightened child; another moment and she would have started screaming. But the visitor recovered himself; in an instant his face underwent a change, and he proceeded to the table with the most affable and tender smile imaginable.

'My apologies, Marya Timofeyevna, for frightening you out of your sleep with my unexpected arrival,' he said, holding out his hand to her.

The sound of these tender words had their effect, her fright vanished, although she continued to look at him fearfully, evidently making an effort to grasp something. She extended her hand fearfully. At last a shy smile stirred on her lips.

'Hello, Prince,' she whispered, peering at him rather strangely.

'You must have been having a bad dream?' He continued to smile even more affably and tenderly.

'And how did you know that I was dreaming *about that*?'

And suddenly she began to tremble, and she recoiled, raising her hand in front of her as if in defence, and preparing to burst into tears again.

'Pull yourself together, enough of this. What are you afraid of? Don't you recognize me?' he said in an attempt to talk her out of it, but on this occasion it took him a long time to do so. She kept looking at him in silence, with that same agonizing incomprehension, with one oppressive thought in her poor head and still trying to think her way through to something. Now she would drop her eyes, then she would suddenly run them over him in a quick glance that took everything in. At last, though she didn't calm down, she seemed to reach some decision.

'Sit down beside me, I beg you, so that I can have a good look at you later,' she said rather firmly, and obviously with some new idea in mind. 'And don't worry, I won't be looking at you now, I'll look down. And don't you look at me either, until I ask you myself. Do sit down,' she added, even impatiently.

A new sensation was evidently beginning to exercise greater and greater control over her.

Nikolay Vsevolodovich took a seat and waited; a rather long silence fell.

'Hmm! All this is strange to me,' she suddenly muttered almost disdainfully, 'of course I've been possessed by bad dreams; except why did I dream of you looking just like that?'

'Come now, let's forget about dreams,' he said impatiently, turning towards her despite her having forbidden it, and there was perhaps a hint of his earlier expression in his eyes. He could see that several times she had the urge, and very much so, to glance at him, but that she was stubbornly controlling herself and looking down.

'Listen, Prince,' she suddenly raised her voice, 'listen, Prince . . .'

'Why did you turn away? Why aren't you looking at me? What's this comedy all about?' he cried, unable to restrain himself.

But it was as if she had not heard a word he said.

'Listen, Prince,' she repeated for the third time in a firm voice, with an unhappy, troubled expression on her face. 'When you told me then in the carriage that the marriage would be announced, I felt frightened right away because the secret would be out. But now I just don't know: I've been thinking it over, and I see clearly that I'm not at all worthy. I would know how to dress well, and I could maybe receive guests too: what's so hard about inviting someone for a cup of tea, especially if there are servants? Still and all, people will be looking at me from outside. Back then, on Sunday morning, I could see a lot going on in that house. That pretty young lady was looking at me all the time, especially when you came in. It was you who came in then, wasn't it? Her mother is just a ridiculous old society woman. My Lebyadkin also distinguished himself. So as not to burst out laughing, I kept looking at the ceiling, they have a beautifully decorated ceiling there. *His* mother should have been a mother superior. I'm afraid of her, even though she gave me her black shawl. They must all have decided then and there that I was something unexpected. I wasn't angry; I was just sitting there and thinking: what sort of relation am I to them? Of course, only spiritual qualities are required of a countess – because for the household ones she has a lot of servants – and some worldly coquettishness besides, so she knows how to receive foreign travellers. But still and all, on that Sunday they were all looking at me as a hopeless case. Only Dasha is an angel. I'm very much afraid that they might distress *him* somehow with careless remarks about me.'

'Don't be afraid and don't be alarmed,' Nikolay Vsevolodovich said with a twist of his mouth.

'However, it won't be so important to me if he's a little ashamed of me, because there's always more pity than shame here, judging of course by the man. And he does know, after all, that I'm the one who should pity them, instead of them pitying me.'

'You seem to have been very offended by them, Marya Timofeyevna?'

'Who, I? No,' she gave a simple-hearted smile. 'Not in the least. I took a look at all of you then: all of you were angry, all of you'd been quarrelling with one other; you don't know how to get together and have a good laugh. So much wealth and so little joy – I find that all disgusting. However, I don't feel sorry for anyone now except for myself.'

'I've heard that you had a bad time living with your brother without me.'

'Who was it told you that? Nonsense; it's much worse now; now my dreams aren't very nice and they've become not very nice because you've arrived. And you, if I may ask, why have you turned up here, tell me, please?'

'Don't you want to go back to the convent?'

'Oh well, I just had a feeling that they would propose the convent again! What's so great about your convent! And why should I go back to it, what would I enter it for now? Now I'm all alone by myself! It's too late for me to begin a third life.'

'You're very angry at something, perhaps you're afraid that I no longer love you?'

'I don't really care a thing about you. I'm just afraid of completely falling out of love with someone.'

She gave a contemptuous grin.

'I must be very guilty before *him* in some very big way,' she suddenly added, as if to herself, 'but I just don't know what I'm guilty of, that's been my whole trouble all along. Always, always, all these five years I've been afraid, day and night, that I'm guilty of something before him. I used to pray and pray and kept thinking about my great guilt before him. And now it's turned out to be true.'

'Why, what is it that's turned out?'

'I'm only afraid there may be something on *his* part,' she went on without answering the question, without even having caught what he said. 'Once again he couldn't get along with such disgusting people. The countess would be happy to eat me alive, even though she did have me sit in her carriage with her. Everyone is in on the conspiracy – is he as well? Has he betrayed me as well?' (Her chin and lips began to tremble.) 'Now, listen: have you read about Grishka Otrepyev,[8] that he was cursed in seven cathedrals?'

Nikolay Vsevolodovich remained silent.

'And by the way, I will turn towards you now, and look at you,' she seemed to have made up her mind quickly, 'and you turn towards me and look at me, only very hard. I want to make sure for the last time.'

'I've been looking at you for a long time now.'

'Hmm,' said Marya Timofeyevna, peering at him sharply, 'you've got very fat.'

She was on the point of saying something else, but suddenly, for the third time, her face was again distorted by the same fear, and she recoiled again, raising her hand before her.

'Why, what's the matter with you?' Nikolay Vsevolodovich cried, almost in a fury.

But her fear continued for only a moment; her face was contorted into a strange smile, suspicious and unpleasant.

'I beg you, Prince, get up and come in,' she suddenly pronounced in a firm and insistent voice.

'What do you mean "come in"? Where will I come into?'

'All these five years the only thing I've done is picture to myself how *he* would come in. Get up right now and go out of the door, into the next room. I'll be sitting here as if I were expecting nothing, and I'll pick up a book, and suddenly you'll come in after being away five years travelling. I want to see how it will be.'

Nikolay Vsevolodovich ground his teeth, and mumbled something that couldn't be made out.

'Enough,' he said, slapping the palm of his hand on the table. 'I ask you, Marya Timofeyevna, to hear me out. Please do me the favour of giving me your full attention, if you can. You aren't completely mad, after all!' he burst out impatiently. 'Tomorrow I shall announce our marriage. You will never live in palaces, disabuse yourself of that. Do you want to live your entire life with me, but very far from here? It's in the mountains, in Switzerland, there's a certain place there ... Don't worry, I'll never abandon you and I won't put you into a madhouse.

I'll have enough money to live without begging. You will have a servant, you won't have to do any work. Everything you can possibly want will be provided for you. You will pray, go where you like and do what you like. I won't touch you. I won't leave the place and go anywhere my whole life either. If you want, I won't speak to you my whole life; if you want, you can tell me your stories every evening, as you used to in the corners of those rooms in Petersburg. I'll read books to you, if you wish. But in exchange for all this, it will be an entire life spent in one place, and a gloomy place at that. Do you want to? Can you make up your mind to do it? You won't regret it, and torment me with tears and curses?'

She listened through to the end with great curiosity and for a long time said nothing while thinking.

'That all seems so improbable to me,' she finally said mockingly and disdainfully. 'So I'll be living maybe forty years in those mountains.' She burst out laughing.

'Well, what of it, then we'll live there forty years,' Nikolay Vsevolodovich gave a fierce frown.

'Hmm. I absolutely refuse to go.'

'Even with me?'

'And what are you that I should go with you? Forty years in a row sitting on a mountain with him – I see what he's up to. And really, people are so patient these days! No, it's impossible that the falcon should become an owl. That's not what my prince is like!' She raised her head proudly and triumphantly.

It suddenly seemed to dawn on him.

'Why do you call me "prince", and . . . who do you take me for?' he asked quickly.

'What? Aren't you really a prince?'

'I've never been one.'

'So you, you yourself, you yourself, go ahead and admit, straight to my face, that you're not a prince!'

'I'm telling you I never have been.'

'Lord!' she clasped her hands, 'I expected anything from *his* enemies, but such insolence – never! Is he alive?' she shrieked in a frenzy, bearing down on Nikolay Vsevolodovich. 'Have you killed him or not, admit it!'

'Who do you take me for?' He jumped up from his chair, his face contorted, but it was now difficult to frighten her. She was triumphant:

'And who knows you, who you really are and where you've sprung from! Only my heart, my heart sensed the entire intrigue, all these five years! And here am I sitting and wondering about this blind owl that's come to me. No, my dear fellow, you're a poor actor, even worse than Lebyadkin. Bow as low as you can to the countess for me and tell her to send someone a bit cleaner than you. Tell me, did she hire you? Does she have you working in her kitchen out of charity? I can see through your whole deception and I understand all of you, every single one!'

He seized her firmly by the arm, above the elbow; she was laughing in his face:

'You look a lot like him, a lot, maybe you're some relative of his – a crafty bunch of people! Only mine is a bright falcon and a prince, and you're just an owl and a filthy little shop-keeper! My hero, if he wants, will bow down to God, and if he wants, he won't, but Shatushka (he's so nice, so dear, my darling!) struck you on both cheeks, my Lebyadkin told me all about it. And what were you so afraid of when you came in that day? Who frightened you then? As soon as I saw your awful face when I fell and you picked me up – it was as if a worm had crawled into my heart: it's not *him*, I thought, not *him*! My falcon would never be ashamed of me in front of a society lady! Oh, Lord! The only thing that made me happy, all those five years, was that my falcon was somewhere out there, far, far away, living and flying and looking at the sun . . . Speak, you impostor, did you take much? Did you agree to it for a lot of money? I wouldn't have given you a penny. Ha, ha, ha! Ha, ha, ha! . . .'

'Ugh, you idiot!' Nikolay Vsevolodovich ground his teeth, still holding her tightly by the arm.

'Get away, you impostor!' she cried imperiously. 'I am the wife of my prince, and I'm not afraid of your knife!'

'Knife!'

'Yes, knife! You have a knife in your pocket. You thought I

was asleep, but I saw that as soon as you came in just now, you
took out a knife!'

'What are you saying, you unfortunate woman, what dreams
you've been having!' he cried out, and pushed her away from
him with all his strength, so that she struck her shoulders and
head painfully against the sofa. He dashed out of the room, but
she instantly leapt up in pursuit, limping and hobbling,
and from the front steps, restrained with all his strength by a
terrified Lebyadkin, she managed to shout after him into the
darkness, screaming and laughing:

'Grish-ka Ot-re-pyev – anathema!'

4.

'A knife, a knife!' he kept repeating in overwhelming anger as
he strode through the mud and the puddles, not even watching
where he was going. To be sure, at moments he had a terrible
desire to burst into loud and insane laughter; but for some
reason he steadied himself and restrained his laughter. He came
to his senses only on the bridge, precisely on the very spot
where he had encountered Fedka earlier that night. And now
none other than Fedka himself was waiting for him there, and,
on catching sight of him, pulled off his cap, bared his teeth
cheerfully, and promptly began to jabber on jauntily and merrily about something. At first Nikolay Vsevolodovich walked
past without stopping, and for some time didn't even listen to
the tramp who was again dogging his footsteps. He was suddenly struck by the thought that he had completely forgotten
about him, and had forgotten precisely when he had been
repeating 'A knife, a knife' to himself over and over. He grabbed
the tramp by the scruff of the neck, and with all the anger that
had built up inside him, flung him against the bridge as hard as
he could. For an instant the tramp considered fighting back,
but immediately deducing that by comparison with his adversary, who had besides launched his attack unexpectedly, he was
no more than something like a wisp of straw, he quieted down
and grew silent, not resisting even in the slightest. On his knees,
pressed to the ground, his elbows twisted behind his back, the

canny tramp calmly waited to see how things would come out, seemingly not believing that he was in the slightest danger.

He wasn't mistaken. With his left hand Nikolay Vsevolodovich had already removed his warm scarf from his neck in order to bind his prisoner's arms but suddenly he let him go for some reason and pushed him aside. In a flash the tramp leaped to his feet, turned around, and a broad, short shoemaker's knife, which had instantly appeared from somewhere, gleamed in his hand.

'Get rid of the knife, put it away, put it away right now!' Nikolay Vsevolodovich ordered him with an impatient gesture, and the knife disappeared just as quickly as it had appeared.

Nikolay Vsevolodovich went on his way again, silent and not turning around; but the persistent rascal still kept pace with him, although now, to be sure, he was no longer jabbering and was even maintaining a respectable distance a whole step behind. In this way, both crossed the bridge and came out on the riverbank, this time turning left, into another long and remote lane, but one which was a shorter distance to the centre of town than the route along Bogoyavlenskaya Street he had taken earlier.

'Is it true what they say, that you robbed a church somewhere here in the district the other day?' Nikolay Vsevolodovich suddenly asked.

'I first of all, that is to say, strictly speaking, went in to say a prayer,' the tramp replied sedately and courteously, as if absolutely nothing had happened, and not even sedately but almost with dignity. There was not the slightest trace of his former 'friendly' familiarity. Evident now was a serious, businesslike man, who, to be sure, had been needlessly offended, but who also knew how to forget offences.

'But as soon as ever the Lord led me in there,' he went on, 'oh, what heavenly abundance, I thought! It was owin' to my lone and orphan state that all this happened, 'cause can't no one in my way of life make out without he gets some good, solid assistance. Well, sir, as God is my witness, I ended up with a loss, the Lord punished me for my sins: I got just twelve roubles, no more, for the little thing you wave, the little container and the deacon's saddle harness. Nikolay the Wonder-Worker's chin-piece, pure silver it was, went for next to nothin', it was plate, they said.'

'Did you cut the watchman's throat?'

'That's to say, that watchman and me, we brung all the stuff together, and later on, towards mornin', by the river, we got to quarrellin' as to who was gonna carry the sack. I sinned, I lightened his burden a bit.'

'Kill some more, steal some more.'

'Pyotr Stepanovich is handin' me that same advice, in them same words as you, 'cause he's a real stingy and hard-hearted man when it comes to givin' assistance. Besides which, he ain't got no belief at all in the heavenly creator, who fashioned us out o' the dust of the earth. He says it's jes' nature made everythin', even down to the last animal, and besides, he ain't got no understandin' that the likes of us jes' can't get along unless we get some beneficial assistance. You start tryin' to explain to him, he stares at you like a sheep at the water, you can't do nothin' but marvel at him. Well now, would you believe it, sir, at Captain Lebyadkin's, sir, where you've jes' been pleased to pay a visit, when he was livin' at Filippov's, sir, sometimes the door's standin' wide open, sir, not locked, all night long, and there he is asleep, dead drunk, and money fallin' out from all his pockets on the floor. Seen it myself with my own eyes, I have, 'cause the way the likes of us is made, no way we can get along without we get some assistance, sir . . .'

'What do you mean "with your own eyes"? Did you go in there at night, or what?'

'Maybe I did go in, only don't nobody know nothin' 'bout it.'

'Why didn't you cut his throat?'

'Takin' everythin' into mind, I steadied myself, sir. 'Cause once I found out for sure I could always pull out a hundred fifty roubles, why should I take on a thing like that when I could pull out the whole thousand and fifty, if I jes' bided my time? 'Cause Captain Lebyadkin (and I heard it with my very own ears, sir) always depended on you a lot when he was in a state of drink, and ain't no tavern establishment hereabouts,

even the nastiest little pot-house,[9] where he ain't declared this
in that same state. So, once I heard about this out o' a lot o'
mouths, I also took to restin' all my hopes on Your Excellency.
I, sir, am like a father or a blood brother to you, 'cause Pyotr
Stepanovich ain't never found out about that from me, nor
has one single soul either. So, jes' three little roubles, Your
Excellency, will you deign or won't you? You'd free me up, sir,
that's to say, if I could know the genuine truth, 'cause no way
the likes of us can make it without we get some assistance.'

Nikolay Vsevolodovich broke out into loud laughter, and
taking out of his pocket a wallet that contained some fifty small
banknotes, he tossed him one bill from the wad, then a second,
a third and a fourth. Fedka tried to grab them as they floated
by, he lunged at them, the notes fluttered down into the mud,
he caught them and kept uttering little cries: 'Ooh, oh!' Finally
Nikolay Vsevolodovich threw the entire wad at him, and continuing to guffaw, set out down the lane, but this time alone.
The tramp remained, groping on his knees in the mud, looking
for notes that had been scattered by the wind and had sunk in
puddles, and for a whole hour after that his sharp little cries
could be heard in the darkness: 'Ooh, oh!'

CHAPTER 3

The Duel

I.

The next day, at two in the afternoon, the proposed duel took place. A quick outcome of the whole matter was made easier by Artemy Pavlovich's unwavering desire to fight no matter what. He couldn't understand his opponent's behaviour, and was in a rage. For a full month now he had been insulting Stavrogin with impunity, and still couldn't make him lose his patience. It was essential for him to be challenged by Nikolay Vsevolodovich, inasmuch as he himself had no direct pretext for issuing a challenge. And for some reason he was ashamed to admit to his secret motives, that is, simply put, his morbid hatred of Stavrogin for the insult to his family honour four years previously. Furthermore, he himself regarded such a pretext as impossible, especially in view of the humble apologies that had been offered by Nikolay Vsevolodovich on two occasions now. He had decided for himself that Stavrogin was a shameless coward; he failed to understand how he could have tolerated a slap in the face from Shatov; and so it was that he at last resolved to send that extraordinarily rude letter which finally prompted Nikolay Vsevolodovich himself to propose a meeting. After dispatching this letter the day before, and waiting in feverish impatience for a challenge, morbidly calculating the chances of receiving one, now hoping, now despairing, he had provided himself, just to be on the safe side, with a second the evening before, namely, Mavriky Nikolayevich Drozdov, his friend, his schoolmate, and a man for whom he had particular respect. So it was that Kirillov, who appeared the next morning at nine o'clock with his message, found the ground already fully prepared. All the apologies and the unprecedented concessions on the part of Nikolay Vsevolodovich were rejected immediately, from the very outset and with extraordinary heat. Mavriky Nikolayevich, who had learned just the day before of the course that this whole matter had taken, opened his mouth in astonishment at such unprecedented proposals, and wanted to insist on a reconciliation then and there, but observing that Artemy Pavlovich, who had an inkling of his intentions, was almost trembling in his seat, kept quiet and said nothing. If he hadn't given his word to his friend, he would have left at once; but he remained, in the sole hope that he could be of some assistance at least in the final outcome of the whole affair. Kirillov conveyed the challenge; all the conditions of the encounter as outlined by Stavrogin were accepted immediately and literally, without the slightest objection. Only one addendum was made: and a very brutal one at that, namely, if the first shots yielded no definite outcome, then they were to take their places a second time; if the second encounter should be inconclusive, they would take their places a third time. Kirillov frowned and began to bargain about the third time, but not getting anywhere, he agreed, with the proviso, however, that 'three times were possible, but four were absolutely impossible'. This was conceded. And so, at two o'clock in the afternoon, the encounter took place in Brykov, that is, in a small suburban grove between Skvoreshniki on the one side and the Shpigulin factory on the other. The previous day's rain had completely stopped, but it was wet, damp and windy. Low, turbid, tattered clouds scudded across the cold sky; the treetops rolled and rustled heavily and their roots creaked; it was a very melancholy morning.

Gaganov and Mavriky Nikolayevich arrived at the designated place in an elegant char-à-banc[1] drawn by a pair of horses, and driven by Artemy Pavlovich. A servant was in attendance. At almost that same moment Nikolay Vsevolodovich and Kirillov appeared as well, not in a carriage, however, but on horseback, and also accompanied by a servant on horseback. Kirillov, who had never mounted a horse, held himself boldly and erectly in the saddle, his right hand clutching the heavy box containing the pistols, which he didn't want to entrust to the servant, and his left, through his lack of experience, constantly twisting and tugging at the reins, which made the horse toss its head and display a desire to rear, which, however, didn't frighten the rider in the slightest. The mistrustful Gaganov, who was easily and deeply offended, regarded their arrival on horseback as a fresh insult to himself, in the sense that it showed his enemies were unduly confident of success if they had not even allowed for the need of a carriage in case a wounded party had to be carried off. He emerged from his char-à-banc yellow with anger, and felt his hands trembling, which he told Mavriky Nikolayevich about. He made no reply at all to Nikolay Vsevolodovich's bow, and turned away. The seconds cast lots: the choice of pistols fell to Kirillov. The barrier was measured off, the opponents were separated, the carriage and horses were sent back some three hundred paces with the servants. The weapons were loaded and handed to the opponents.

It's a pity that the story must be told rather quickly and that there's no time for description; but I can't refrain altogether from making some comments. Mavriky Nikolayevich was gloomy and preoccupied. By contrast, Kirillov was utterly calm and indifferent, very precise in attending to the details of the obligation he had taken upon himself, but without the slightest sign of fuss and virtually without curiosity about the fateful and very imminent outcome of the whole matter. Nikolay Vsevolodovich was paler than usual, and was dressed rather lightly, in an overcoat and a white fur hat. He seemed very tired, frowned from time to time and didn't find it at all necessary to try to hide his unpleasant mood. But at that moment it was Artemy Pavlovich who was the most remarkable of all; consequently, it's quite impossible not to say a few words about him in particular.

2.

Until now we haven't had occasion to mention his appearance. He was a tall man, pale, well-fed (as the common people say), almost plump, with lank blond hair, about thirty-three and perhaps even good-looking. He had retired as a colonel, and if he had stayed in service until he reached the rank of general, he would have been even more imposing, and it is entirely possible that he would have made a good fighting general.

It can't be omitted, in a characterization of the personality of the man, that the chief motive for his retirement had been the thought of the shame to his family, which had dogged and tormented him for so long after the insult visited on his father in the club, four years previously, by Nikolay Stavrogin. In good conscience he considered it dishonourable to prolong his service and felt certain in his own mind that he was tarnishing his regiment and his comrades, although none of them had the slightest idea of what had happened. To be sure, he had wanted to leave the service once before, quite a while ago, long before the insult and for an entirely different reason, but until now he had been hesitating. Strange as it is to write this, his initial reason or, better put, his urge to go into retirement had been the Manifesto of 19 February, regarding the emancipation of the peasants. Artemy Pavlovich, who was the wealthiest landowner in our province, hadn't even lost very much as a result of the Manifesto, and, furthermore, was quite capable of being persuaded of the humane nature of this particular measure and of almost understanding the economic advantages of the reform, suddenly felt himself, after the issuance of the Manifesto, personally insulted somehow. This was something unconscious, more a kind of feeling, but all the stronger because it was instinctive. Until his father's death, however, he had not made up his mind to undertake anything decisive; but in Petersburg he became known for his 'noble' way of thinking to many prominent people, with whom he assiduously maintained ties. He was a man who was withdrawn and removed. Another trait: he belonged to that set of rather strange noblemen, still surviving in Russia today, which deeply cherishes the antiquity and purity of their noble lineage and takes a too serious interest in it. At the same time, he couldn't bear Russian history, and for that matter, regarded Russian customs in general as rather swinish. While still a child in the special military school for pupils from wealthier and more distinguished families, where he had the honour of beginning and completing his education, certain poetic attitudes implanted themselves in him. He developed a fondness for castles, medieval life – its whole oper-atic side – and chivalry; even then he almost wept with shame that a Russian nobleman of the time of the Muscovite rulers could have received corporal punishment from the Tsar,[2] and the comparisons made him blush. This unbending, extremely severe man, who had a remarkably good knowledge of his profession and who carried out his duties, was in his soul a dreamer. People asserted that he could have been a public speaker and that he had a gift for words; be that as it may, he maintained his silence for all of his thirty-three years. Even in the prominent Petersburg milieu where he had been circulating of late, he held himself extraordinarily aloof. His encounter in Petersburg with Nikolay Vsevolodovich, who had recently returned from abroad, nearly drove him mad. At this moment, as he stood at the barrier, he was in a state of dreadful agitation. He kept imagining that the whole business would somehow fail to come off, and the slightest delay threw him into trepidation. A morbid expression appeared on his face when Kirillov, instead of giving the signal for the duel to begin, suddenly began to say – pro forma, to be sure, as he himself announced for all to hear:

'I am speaking only pro forma. Now, when the pistols are already in hand and the command must be given, might you, for the last time, not wish to reconcile? This is the duty of a second.'

As luck would have it, Mavriky Nikolayevich, who had said nothing until now, but who since the previous day had been suffering inwardly for his compliance and indulgence, suddenly picked up on Kirillov's sentiment and also began to speak:

'I fully second the words of Mr Kirillov ... the idea that reconciliation is impossible at the barrier is a prejudice worthy of Frenchmen . . . What's more, I don't see where the insult lies, with all due respect, and I have long wanted to say . . . because all sorts of apologies, after all, have been profered, haven't they?'

He flushed all over. He rarely had occasion to speak so much and with such emotion.

'Once more I affirm my proposal to offer every possible apology,' Nikolay Vsevolodovich chimed in very hastily.

'Can this really be?' Gaganov shouted furiously, turning to Mavriky Nikolayevich and stamping his feet in a fury. 'Explain to this man, if you are my second and not my enemy, Mavriky Nikolayevich,' he thrust his pistol in the direction of Nikolay Vsevolodovich, 'that such concessions only make the insult even worse! He does not find it possible to be insulted by me! He doesn't find it disgraceful to run away from me at the barrier! Who does he take me for after this, in your eyes . . . and you're my second, at that! You're just trying to make me angry so that I'll miss.' Again he stamped his foot and spittle flew from his lips.

'The negotiations are at an end. I ask you to listen for the command!' Kirillov cried at the top of his voice. 'One! Two! Three!'

At the word 'three' the opponents began moving towards each other. Gaganov immediately raised his pistol and after five or six steps, fired. He paused for a second, and after ascertaining that he had missed, quickly walked up to the barrier. Nikolay Vsevolodovich also walked up, raised his pistol, albeit very high, and fired virtually without taking aim. Then he took out a handkerchief and wrapped the little finger of his right hand in it. Only then could one see that Artemy Pavlovich had not missed entirely, but that his bullet had just grazed the soft flesh of the finger joint, without touching the bone. The result was an insignificant scratch. Kirillov promptly announced that the duel, if the opponents were not satisfied, would continue.

'I state,' Gaganov said hoarsely (his throat had gone dry), again turning to Mavriky Nikolayevich, 'that this man' (he again pointed in Stavrogin's direction) 'deliberately fired into the air . . . intentionally . . . This is another insult! He wants to make a duel impossible!'

'I have the right to fire as I wish, as long as everything proceeds according to the rules,' Nikolay Vsevolodovich stated firmly.

'No, he doesn't! Explain it to him, explain it!' Gaganov was shouting.

'I fully share Nikolay Vsevolodovich's opinion,' Kirillov proclaimed.

'Why is he sparing me?' Gaganov raged, without listening. 'I despise his mercy! . . . I spit on it . . . I . . .'

'I give my word that I had absolutely no desire to insult you,' Nikolay Vsevolodovich said impatiently. 'I fired high because I don't want to do any more killing, and whether it's you or someone else, it has no bearing on you personally. True enough, I don't regard myself as having been insulted, and I'm sorry this makes you angry. But I will not permit anyone to interfere with my rights.'

'If he's so afraid of blood, then ask him why he challenged me,' Gaganov wailed, still addressing Mavriky Nikolayevich.

'How could he help but challenge you?' Kirillov put in. 'You didn't want to listen to anything, there was no getting rid of you!'

'I will note only one thing,' Mavriky Nikolayevich said with effort and in a tone of suffering, after gauging the whole matter. 'If an opponent announces ahead of time that he's going to fire into the air, then the duel really cannot continue . . . for delicate and . . . obvious reasons.'

'I certainly didn't announce that I would fire into the air each time!' Stavrogin shouted, now completely losing patience. 'You have absolutely no idea what's in my head and how I'm going to fire the next time . . . I'm not impeding the duel in any way.'

'If that's so, then the contest can continue,' Mavriky Nikolayevich turned again to Gaganov.

'Gentlemen, take your places!' Kirillov commanded.

Again they advanced towards each other, again Gaganov missed and again Stavrogin's shot went high. There could have been a dispute about his firing high: Nikolay Vsevolodovich could have stated flatly that he was firing properly, if he himself hadn't admitted that he had intentionally missed. He hadn't pointed the pistol directly at the sky or at a tree, but had really appeared to be aiming at his opponent, although, to be sure, it had gone an arshin above his hat. The second time his aim was even in fact somewhat lower and somewhat more plausible looking; but by now Gaganov couldn't be convinced otherwise.

'Again!' he said, grinding his teeth. 'It doesn't matter! I've been challenged, and I'm going to take advantage of my right. I want to fire a third time . . . whatever the cost.'

'You have every right,' Kirillov snapped. Mavriky Nikolayevich said nothing. The opponents were separated for a third time, the command was given. This time Gaganov walked right up to the barrier and from the barrier, a distance of twelve paces, began taking aim. His hands were trembling too much for his shot to be accurate. Stavrogin was standing motionless, his pistol lowered, awaiting the shot.

'Your aim is taking too long, too long!' Kirillov cried impulsively. 'Fire! Fi-i-re!' But a shot resounded, and the white fur hat flew off Nikolay Vsevolodovich's head. The shot was rather well placed, the crown of the hat was pierced very low; a quarter of an inch lower, and all would have been over. Kirillov picked up the hat and handed it to Nikolay Vsevolodovich.

'Fire, don't keep your opponent waiting!' Mavriky Nikolayevich cried in extraordinary agitation, seeing that Stavrogin seemed to have forgotten about his shot, as he and Kirillov examined the hat. Stavrogin shuddered, glanced at Gaganov, turned away, and this time without any niceties fired off to the side, into the grove. The duel was over. Gaganov stood there as though crushed. Mavriky Nikolayevich went up to him and began saying something, but Gaganov seemed not to understand. As he was leaving, Kirillov took off his hat and nodded to Mavriky Nikolayevich; but Stavrogin had forgotten his former civility: after firing into the grove, he didn't even turn towards the barrier, but thrust his pistol at Kirillov and headed hastily for the horses. His face expressed anger, and he said nothing. Kirillov also said nothing. They mounted their horses and galloped off.

3.

'Why don't you say anything?' he called impatiently to Kirillov when they weren't far from the house.

'What do you want?' Kirillov replied, almost slipping off his horse, which had reared.

Stavrogin controlled himself.

'I didn't want to insult that ... fool, but I've insulted him again,' he said quietly.

'Yes, you insulted him again,' snapped Kirillov, 'and besides, he's not a fool.'

'However, I did what I could.'

'No.'

'Well, what should I have done?'

'Not challenge him.'

'And put up with getting hit in the face again?'

'Yes, even putting up with getting hit again.'

'I'm beginning not to understand anything!' Stavrogin said angrily. 'Why does everyone expect something from me that they don't expect from other people? Why should I endure something that no one else would endure, and seek out burdens that no one else can bear?'

'I thought you yourself were looking for a burden.'

'I – looking for a burden?'

'Yes.'

'Have you ... seen any evidence of this?'

'Yes.'

'Is it so obvious?'

'Yes.'

They fell silent for a moment. Stavrogin looked very worried, almost stunned.

'I didn't fire because I didn't want to do any more killing, and that's all there was to it, I assure you,' he said quickly and uneasily.

'You didn't have to insult him.'

'What should I have done, then?'

'You should have killed him.'

'Are you sorry I didn't kill him?'

'I'm not sorry for anything. I thought you really wanted to kill him. You don't know what you're looking for.'

'I'm looking for a burden,' Stavrogin laughed.

'If you yourself didn't want bloodshed, why did you give him the chance to kill you?'

'If I hadn't challenged him he would have killed me anyway, without a duel.'

'That's not your concern. Maybe he really wouldn't have killed you.'

'But just beaten me up?'

'That's not your concern. Bear your burden. Otherwise there's no merit.'

'The hell with your merit, I'm not seeking it from anyone!'

'I thought you were seeking it,' Kirillov concluded with dreadful composure.

They rode into the yard of the house.

'You want to come in?' Nikolay Vsevolodovich offered.

'No, home for me, goodbye.' He got off his horse and took his box under his arm.

'At least I trust you're not angry with me?' Stavrogin held out his hand to him.

'Not at all!' Kirillov turned around to shake his hand. 'If my burden is light, because such is my nature, then perhaps your burden is heavier because such is your nature.'

'I know I'm a worthless character, but I'm not trying to be one of the strong ones.'

'And don't try; you're not a strong person. Come and have tea sometime.'

Nikolay Vsevolodovich went into the house, deeply perturbed.

4.

He immediately learned from Aleksey Yegorovich that Varvara Petrovna, very pleased that Nikolay Vsevolodovich had gone out horseback riding – his first time out after eight days of illness – ordered her carriage harnessed up and set out by herself, 'following the example of previous days, to have a breath of fresh air, for it had been eight days since she had remembered what it meant to breathe fresh air'.

'Did she go by herself or with Darya Pavlovna?' Nikolay Vsevolodovich interrupted the old man with a quick question, and frowned deeply when he heard that Darya Pavlovna had 'declined because of ill health to accompany her, and was now in her own rooms'.

'Listen, old man,' he said, as if suddenly making up his mind, 'keep an eye on her all day today, and if you notice that she's coming to see me, stop her at once and tell her that I can't receive her for at least a few days . . . that I myself am asking this of her . . . and that when the time comes, I'll call her myself, you hear?'

'I will tell her, sir,' Aleksey Yegorovich said with sadness in his voice, his eyes lowered.

'However, not before you clearly perceive that she herself is coming to see me.'

'Don't trouble yourself, sir, there will be no mistake. Up to this point, the visits have always taken place through me. I have always been turned to for assistance.'

'I know. However, though, not before she herself comes. Bring me some tea, as quickly as you can.'

The old man had no sooner gone out than the same door opened almost immediately and Darya Pavlovna appeared on the threshold. Her eyes were calm, but her face was pale.

'Where did you come from?' Stavrogin exclaimed.

'I was standing right here and waiting for him to leave, so that I could come in to see you. I heard what you were instructing him to do, and when he went out just now, I hid myself round the corner to the right, and he didn't notice me.'

'I've been meaning to break off with you for a long time, Dasha . . . until . . . for the time being . . . I couldn't receive you last night, despite your note. I wanted to write to you myself, but I don't know what to write,' he added in annoyance, in what even seemed to be disgust.

'I myself have been thinking we should break it off. Varvara Petrovna is highly suspicious of our relationship.'

'Oh, let her be.'

'She shouldn't worry. So then, until the end comes?'

'You're still really expecting the end?'

'Yes, I'm sure of it.'

'Nothing ever comes to an end in this world.'

'There'll be an end in this case. Then you'll call for me and I'll come. Now, goodbye.'

'But what sort of end will there be?' Nikolay Vsevolodovich smiled.

'You're not wounded and . . . you didn't shed any blood?' she asked, without answering his question about the end.

'It was stupid; I didn't kill anyone, don't worry. However, you'll hear everything from everyone today. I feel a bit unwell.'

'I'll leave. There will be no announcement of the marriage today?' she added hesitantly.

'Not today; not tomorrow; day after tomorrow, I don't know; perhaps we'll all be dead, and so much the better. Leave me, leave me now.'

'You won't ruin the other woman . . . the mad one?'

'I won't ruin any mad women, either of them, but it seems I'm going to ruin the sane one: I'm so vile and disgusting, Dasha, that it seems I really will call for you "at the final end", as you put it, and you, despite all your sanity, you'll come. Why are you intent on ruining yourself?'

'I know that in the final analysis I'll be the only one to remain with you, and . . . I'm waiting for that.'

'And if in the final analysis I don't call you but run away from you?'

'That cannot be, you'll call me.'

'There's a great deal of contempt for me in that.'

'You know it's not just contempt.'

'So then, there is contempt all the same?'

'I didn't put it that way. As God is my witness, I would wish with all my heart that you should never have any need of me.'

'One phrase is worth another. I also would wish not to ruin you.'

'You will never be able to ruin me in any way, and you know that better than anyone else,' Darya Pavlovna said rapidly and firmly. 'If I don't come to you, then I'll go to the Sisters of

Mercy, to serve as a nurse and tend to the sick, or to sell books, the Gospels. That's what I've decided. I can't be anyone's wife, I can't even live in houses like this one. I don't want that ... You know everything.'

'No, I've never been able to find out what it is you want. You seem to be interested in me, just as some superannuated sick-nurses for some reason take an interest in one particular patient in preference to others, or, even better, just as some pious little old ladies who totter around from funeral to funeral prefer certain corpses as being easier on the eyes than others. Why are you looking at me so strangely?'

'Are you very ill?' she asked sympathetically, looking at him in some special way. 'Lord! And this man wants to get along without me!'

'Listen, Dasha, I keep seeing ghosts all the time these days. Yesterday on the bridge one little demon offered to kill Lebyadkin and Marya Timofeyevna to solve the problem of my lawful marriage and leave no traces of it behind. He asked for three silver roubles as an advance, but let it clearly be known that the whole procedure would cost no less than fifteen hundred. There's a calculating demon for you! A bookkeeper! Ha, ha!'

'But are you absolutely sure that this was a ghost?'

'Oh no, it was definitely no ghost! It was just Fedka the Convict, a robber who's escaped from hard labour. But that's not the point. What do you think I did? I gave him all the money in my wallet, and he's now utterly convinced that I gave him an advance!'

'You ran across him at night and he made you an offer like that? Can you really not see that they've completely entangled you in their net!'

'Oh, let them! You know, there's a question on the tip of your tongue, I can see it from your eyes,' he added with a malicious and irritated smile.

Dasha grew frightened.

'There's absolutely no question and absolutely no doubts; better that you should keep quiet!' she cried in alarm, as if brushing the question aside.

'In other words, you're certain that I won't get involved in Fedka's little scheme?

'Oh Lord!' she clasped her hands. 'Why do you torment me so?'

'Come now, forgive me for making such a stupid joke, I must be acquiring bad manners from them. You know, ever since last night I've had a dreadful urge to laugh, and keep on laughing, long and loud, without stopping. It's as if I've been loaded with laughter, like a gun . . . Shh! Mother's arrived; I recognize the sound of her carriage stopping by the front steps.'

Dasha seized his hand.

'May God preserve you from your demon and . . . call me, do call me as soon as possible!'

'Oh, it's quite a demon I have! He's simply a small, nasty, scrofulous little demon with a head cold, one of life's failures. And what about you, Dasha, isn't there something else you don't dare say?'

She looked at him with pain and reproach and turned towards the door.

'Listen!' he shouted after her, with a malicious, twisted smile. 'If . . . well, I mean, *if* . . . you understand, even if I should get involved in his little scheme, and call for you afterwards, would you come to me *after* the little scheme?'

She went out without turning around and without answering, covering her face with her hands.

'She'll come even after the little scheme,' he whispered after a moment's thought, and a look of scornful disdain appeared on his face. 'A nurse! Hmm! . . . But maybe I do need something like that after all.'

CHAPTER 4

All Wait Expectantly

I.

The impression produced on our whole society by the story of the duel, which quickly became public, was especially remarkable for the unanimity with which everyone hastened to declare himself unconditionally for Nikolay Vsevolodovich. Many of his former enemies resolutely declared that they were his friends. The main reason for such an unexpected reversal of public opinion was a few unusually felicitous words that were uttered for all to hear by a certain person who until then hadn't spoken out, and which immediately gave the event a significance that proved extraordinarily interesting to the vast majority. This was how it happened. On the very next day after the duel, the entire town gathered at the home of the marshal of the nobility, whose wife was celebrating her name-day. Also present, or rather, presiding, was Yuliya Mikhaylovna, who arrived with Lizaveta Nikolayevna, radiantly beautiful and particularly happy, which on this occasion immediately struck many of our ladies as particularly suspicious. Incidentally, there could no longer be any doubt of her betrothal to Mavriky Nikolayevich. In reply to the joking inquiry that evening of a certain retired but important general, of whom more will be said below, Lizaveta Nikolayevna replied straight out that she was engaged to be married. And what do you suppose? Absolutely none of our ladies wanted to believe in her engagement. They all stubbornly continued to imagine that there had been some romance, some fateful family secret that had played itself out in Switzerland and to which Yuliya Mikhaylovna must have been a party. It's difficult to say why all these rumours, or

even fantasies, so to speak, persisted so stubbornly, and why
the ladies were so resolutely intent on dragging in Yuliya
Mikhaylovna. The minute she walked in, everyone turned to
her with strange looks, filled with expectation. It should be
noted that because the duel and certain circumstances connected with it had occurred so recently, the people present that
evening still spoke of it with a certain caution, and in whispers.
Besides, people as yet knew nothing about what measures the
authorities might take. Neither duellist, as far as was known,
had been bothered.[1] Everyone knew, for instance, that Artemy
Pavlovich had gone off to his estate in Dukhovo early that
morning without any trouble. Meanwhile, everyone naturally
was eager for someone to be the first to speak of it aloud and
thereby open the door for public impatience. Specifically, they
were relying on the above-mentioned general, and they were
not disappointed.

This general, one of the most impressive-looking members of
our club, a not very wealthy landowner, but with an inimitable
way of thinking, and an old-style skirt-chaser, was, among
other things, extraordinarily fond in large gatherings of saying
aloud, with all the weightiness of a general, precisely what
everyone else was still talking about in cautious whispers. This
was what seemed to constitute his, so to speak, special role in our
society. In the process he made his words notably drawling and
mellifluous, having evidently picked up this habit from Russians
who had travelled abroad or from those formerly wealthy
Russian landowners who had been the most thoroughly ruined
after the peasant reform. Stepan Trofimovich even remarked
on one occasion that the more ruined a landowner, the more
mellifluously he lisped and drawled his words. He himself, by
the way, lisped and drawled his words mellifluously, but he
didn't notice this quality in himself.

The general began to speak as a man of authority. Besides
being somehow distantly related to Artemy Pavlovich, although
he had fallen out with him and was even in litigation with him,
he himself had once fought two duels and had been exiled to
the Caucasus and reduced in rank to an ordinary soldier for
one of them. Someone mentioned that it was now the second

day since Varvara Petrovna had begun to go out driving 'after her illness', though strictly speaking, she wasn't the subject, but rather, the splendid matching of her four grey carriage-horses, which had come from the Stavrogin stud-farm. The general suddenly observed that he had encountered 'the young Stavrogin' on horseback that very same day. Everyone immediately fell silent. The general smacked his lips and suddenly proclaimed, twirling a gold presentation snuffbox between his fingers:

'I regret that I was not here several years ago . . . that is, that I was in Karlsbad . . . Hmm. I am very interested in this young man, about whom I heard so many rumours at that time. Hmm. Well then, is it true that he's deranged? Someone said so then. Suddenly I heard that he'd been insulted by some student here, in the presence of his cousins, and that he crawled under a table to get away from him; and yesterday I heard from Stepan Vysotsky that Stavrogin had fought with this . . . Gaganov. And solely with the gallant purpose of exposing himself to a man who was mad with rage, just to shake him off. Hmm. Those are the ways of a Guards regiment of the twenties. Is there anyone he visits here?'

The general stopped talking, as if waiting for an answer. The door of public impatience had been opened.

'What could be simpler?' Yuliya Mikhaylovna suddenly raised her voice, irritated by the fact that everyone suddenly, as if by command, turned their eyes on her. 'Is it really so surprising that Stavrogin fought with Gaganov and paid no attention to a student? After all, he couldn't very well challenge his own former serf to a duel!'[2]

Significant words! A simple and clear thought, but one which, however, hadn't entered anyone's head until now. Words that had unusual consequences. All the scandal and gossip, all the trivia and chitchat were suddenly relegated to the background. A new character had appeared, about whom everyone had been mistaken, a character with almost ideally strict standards. Mortally insulted by a student, that is, by an educated person who was no longer a serf, he held the insult in contempt because the person who had insulted him was his former serf. There had been buzz and gossip about him in society; frivolous society had looked with contempt on a man who had been struck in the face; he had despised the opinion of society, which had not yet developed an understanding of true standards and yet talked about them.

'And meanwhile, you and I, Ivan Aleksandrovich, are sitting and talking about correct standards,' one ancient member of the club was remarking to another in a noble and heated spirit of self-accusation.

'Yes indeed, Pyotr Mikhaylovich, yes indeed,' the other affirmed with pleasure, 'just go and talk about the younger generation after that.'

'It's not the younger generation,' observed a third person who had just come in, 'it's not a question of the younger generation; he's a star, yes, indeed, and not just an ordinary member of the younger generation. That's how this should be understood.'

'That's just the sort of man we need; we're short of such people.'

The main point here was that the 'new man', besides having proved to be a 'genuine nobleman', was, in addition, also the richest landowner in the province, and therefore couldn't fail to lend a helping hand and become actively involved in things. However, I've previously made passing reference to the attitude of our landowners.

They were even getting all worked up.

'It's not only that he didn't challenge the student, he drew his hands back; note that in particular, Your Excellency,' one of them ventured.

'And didn't drag him before one of the new courts,'[3] another added.

'Despite the fact that in a new court he would have been fined fifteen roubles for a *personal* insult to a nobleman, hee, hee, hee!'

'No, I'll tell you the secret of the new courts,' the third person was working himself into a frenzy. 'If someone has been stealing or swindling and has been caught red-handed, better that he should run home while there's still time and kill his mother. In an instant he'll be acquitted of everything, and the ladies will wave their cambric hankies from the gallery, that's the gospel truth!'

'The truth, the truth!'

There was no dispensing with stories. Nikolay Vsevolodovich's connections with Count K. were recalled. Count K.'s severe and solitary opinions of the latest reforms were well known. Also well known was his remarkable activity, which had slowed down somewhat of late. And then everyone suddenly considered it beyond doubt that Nikolay Vsevolodovich was engaged to one of Count K.'s daughters, although there were no grounds for such a rumour. And as for his marvellous adventures in Switzerland and the whole business with Lizaveta Nikolayevna, even the ladies stopped mentioning them. We'll mention in passing that the Drozdovs, at precisely that time, had managed to pay all the visits they had neglected until then. Now there was no question but that everyone had found Lizaveta Nikolayevna to be the most ordinary kind of girl, who 'flaunted' her delicate nerves. Her fainting spell the day Nikolay Vsevolodovich arrived was now explained as nothing but a frightened reaction to the student's outrageous behaviour. They even tried to underscore the prosaic nature of what they previously had attempted to paint with a fantastic coloration; and they finally forgot altogether about a certain crippled woman and were ashamed even to remember it. 'Why, even if there'd been a hundred crippled women, who hasn't been young once!' They trotted out Nikolay Vsevolodovich's respectful attitude towards his mother, looked for various virtues in him and spoke approvingly of the learning he had acquired in four years of study at German universities. Artemy Pavlovich's conduct was declared utterly tactless, 'their own knew not their own'; but Yuliya Mikhaylovna's superior insight was acknowledged without the slightest question.

So it was that when Nikolay Vsevolodovich himself finally put in an appearance, everyone greeted him in the most ingenuously serious manner, and an air of impatient expectation could be read in all the eyes that were directed at him. Nikolay Vsevolodovich promptly retreated into the strictest silence, and thereby of course pleased everyone even more than if he had talked his head off. In a word, he was proving to be a great success, he was in fashion. In provincial society, once someone has made an appearance, there is no way he can hide. As before, Nikolay Vsevolodovich began to fulfil all his provincial obligations to the letter. People did not find him to be a happy man: 'He's a man who's suffered a great deal, a man who's different from others; he has a lot on his mind.' Even the pride and the disdainful aloofness that had made him so hated in our town four years previously were now respected and deemed pleasing.

More than anyone else, Vavara Petrovna felt a sense of triumph. I can't say whether she grieved very much over her shattered dreams for Lizaveta Nikolayevna. Here family pride helped a great deal, of course. One thing was strange: Varvara Petrovna suddenly believed beyond a doubt that Nicolas had actually 'made his choice' at Count K.'s, but, and what was strangest of all, she believed it from the rumours that had reached her, as they had everyone else, out of thin air. She was afraid to ask Nikolay Vsevolodovich herself. On two or three occasions, however, she couldn't resist, and reproached him playfully and slyly for not being very open with her. Nikolay Vsevolodovich would smile and continue to say nothing. His silence was taken as a sign of assent. And yet, for all that, she never forgot about the crippled woman. The thought of her lay on her heart like a stone, like a nightmare, tormenting her with strange spectres and conjectures, and all this along with and at the same time as her fantasies about the daughters of Count K. But of this, we will speak later on. Naturally, people in our society began once again to treat Varvara Petrovna with extreme attentiveness and respect, but she didn't take much advantage of that and went out extremely rarely.

She did, however, make a triumphant visit to the governor's wife. Naturally, no one was more captivated and charmed than she by Yuliya Mikhaylovna's telling words, which we've mentioned above, at the soirée given by the wife of the marshal of the nobility. They had removed much of the anguish from her heart and at the same time had dispelled much of what had tormented her so much ever since that unhappy Sunday. 'I didn't understand that woman!' she intoned, and, with her characteristic impulsiveness, told Yuliya Mikhaylovna straight out that she had come to *thank* her. Yuliya Mikhaylovna was flattered, but kept her distance. By then she had already begun to have a good sense of her worth, perhaps even somewhat too much. For example, she announced, in the middle of the conversation, that she had never heard a thing about the activities and scholarly reputation of Stepan Trofimovich.

'Of course I receive the young Verkhovensky and feel affection for him. He's foolhardy, but he's still young, and has a solid knowledge of things. At least he's not some retired over-the-hill critic.'

Varvara Petrovna immediately hastened to note that Stepan Trofimovich had never been any kind of critic, but, on the contrary, had lived in her house his entire life. He was renowned for the circumstances of his early career, 'which are very well known to the whole world', and most recently, for his studies of Spanish history. He also wanted to write on the situation of the present-day German universities, and apparently something about the Dresden Madonna as well. In a word, Varvara Petrovna didn't want to turn Stepan Trofimovich over to Yuliya Mikhaylovna.

'About the Dresden Madonna? You mean the Sistine Madonna? *Chère* Varvara Petrovna, I spent two hours sitting in front of that picture and went away disillusioned. I understood nothing, and was greatly surprised. Karmazinov also says that it's hard to understand. Nowadays no one finds anything in it, neither Russians nor Englishmen. It's just the old men who've talked it up.'

'A new fashion, you mean?'

'Here's what I think: that our young people shouldn't be neglected either. They shout that they're communists, but in my opinion, they should be treated gently and cherished. I'm now reading everything – all the newspapers, about the communes, the natural sciences – I receive everything, because one does after all have to know where one is living and with whom one is dealing. It's really impossible to live one's entire life on the heights of one's own fantasy. I've reached this conclusion and have made it a rule to treat the young generation with affection and thereby try to keep them from falling into the abyss. Believe me, Varvara Petrovna, only we, our society, are capable, by our wholesome influence and specifically by our kindness, of keeping them from falling into the abyss into which they are being pushed by the impatience of all these little old men. However, I am glad that I've learned about Stepan Trofimovich from you. You've given me an idea: he can be useful at our literary reading. You know, I'm organizing an entire day of festivities, by subscription, to benefit the poor governesses of our province. They're scattered throughout Russia; our district alone numbers at least six; in addition, there are two girls who work in the telegraph office, two who are studying at the academy, and the rest who would like to but haven't the means. The lot of the Russian woman is dreadful,[4] Varvara Petrovna! This matter is now being discussed in the universities, and there has even been a session of the state council. In this strange Russia of ours one can do anything one wants. And therefore, again with nothing but kindness and the warm, direct involvement of our entire society we might be able to direct this great common cause on to the true path. Oh Lord, don't we have a lot of shining personalities among us! Of course we do, but they're scattered. Let's close ranks and we will be stronger. In a word, first I will have a literary morning, then a light lunch, then an intermission, and that same evening a ball. We wanted to begin the evening with *tableaux vivants*,[5] but that seems to entail a lot of expense, and so for the public there will be one or two quadrilles[6] in masks and costumes representing characters from well-known literary movements. This amusing idea was proposed by Karmazinov; he's very helpful to me. You know, he's going to read his most recent work for us, which no one as yet knows. He's abandoning his pen and will write no more; this last article is his farewell to the public. It's a delightful little piece called "Merci". A French title, but he finds this more amusing and even more subtle. I do too, I recommended it. I think Stepan Trofimovich could also read something, if it's a bit shorter and ... not too scholarly. It seems that Pyotr

Stepanovich and someone else too will read something. Pyotr Stepanovich will drop by to see you and tell you about the programme; or better still, permit me to bring it to you myself.'

'And please permit me to put my name on your list too. I will tell Stepan Trofimovich and ask him myself.'

Varvara Petrovna returned home completely bewitched. She was prepared to give full backing to Yuliya Mikhaylovna, and for some reason was now thoroughly angry with Stepan Trofimovich, who, poor man, knew nothing about it as he sat at home.

'I'm charmed with her, and I don't understand how I could have been so wrong about this woman,' she said to Nikolay Vsevolodovich and to Pyotr Stepanovich, who had dropped by that evening.

'Still and all, you have to make peace with the old man,' Pyotr Stepanovich announced, 'he's in despair. You've packed him off to the kitchen in exile. Yesterday he met your carriage and bowed, but you turned away. You know, we'll bring him forward; I have some plans for that, and he can still be useful.'

'Oh, he'll read something.'

'I don't mean just that. I myself wanted to run by and see him today. Shall I let him know?'

'If you want. However, I don't know how you'll arrange it,' she said indecisively. 'I had intended to have a talk with him and I wanted to fix the day and the place.' She frowned deeply.

'Well, it's really not worth fixing the day. I'll just tell him.'

'Tell him if you like. However, do add that I won't fail to fix a day for him. Be sure to add that.'

Pyotr Stepanovich ran off, grinning. In general, as far as I remember, he was especially spiteful at that particular time and even indulged in some extremely short-tempered sallies against virtually everyone. Strangely enough, everyone forgave him for some reason. It became generally accepted that he had to be regarded in a special kind of way. I will note that he reacted to Nikolay Vsevolodovich's duel with extreme anger. It took him unawares; he even turned green when he was told about it. Perhaps it was a question of wounded vanity: he learned of it only the day after, when everyone else already knew about it.

'But you really had no right to fight,' he whispered to
Stavrogin five days later, after he'd happened to meet him at
the club. It's remarkable that during those five days they hadn't
run into each other anywhere, although Pyotr Stepanovich
dropped in to visit Varvara Petrovna almost every day.

Nikolay Vsevolodovich glanced at him in silence, with a
distracted expression, as though he didn't understand what it
was all about, and walked on without stopping. He was passing
through the large hall of the club into the buffet.

'You went to see Shatov too . . . you want to make it public
about Marya Timofeyevna.' He ran after him and grabbed him
by the shoulder as though oblivious to what he was doing.

Nikolay Vsevolodovich shook his hand off suddenly and
turned quickly to him with a menacing scowl. Pyotr Stepanovich glanced at him with a strange and prolonged smile. All
this took but a moment. Nikolay Vsevolodovich moved on.

2.

From Varvara Petrovna's he ran immediately to the old man,
and if he was in such a hurry, then it was only out of anger,
with the purpose of avenging an earlier insult, of which I hadn't
had the slightest idea until then. The situation was this: on the
occasion of their last meeting, specifically on Thursday of the
previous week, Stepan Trofimovich, who was the one who had
started the quarrel, had ended by chasing Pyotr Stepanovich
out with a stick. This fact he concealed from me at the time;
but now, as soon as Pyotr Stepanovich ran in, with his ever-
ready grin, which was so naively condescending, and with his
unpleasantly curious gaze that darted to every corner, Stepan
Trofimovich made a secret sign for me not to leave the room.
And that was how I discovered the nature of their true relationship, since on this occasion I heard their entire conversation
through to the end.

Stepan Trofimovich was sitting stretched out on a small
couch. Since that Thursday he had grown thin and sallow.
Pyotr Stepanovich sat down beside him in an utterly casual
manner, unceremoniously tucking his legs under him and occu-

pying far more space on the couch than respect for his father required. Stepan Trofimovich said nothing, and made room for him in a dignified way.

On the table lay an open book. It was the novel *What Is to Be Done?* Alas, I must admit to a certain strange weakness on the part of our friend: the fantasy that he ought to emerge from his solitude and fight a last battle was taking firmer and firmer hold on his deluded imagination. I concluded that his sole purpose in obtaining the novel and *studying* it was that in the event of an decisive clash with the 'screamers', he would have advance knowledge of their methods and arguments according to their own 'catechism', and thus prepared, would triumphantly refute them all in *her eyes*. Oh, how this book tormented him! At times he would throw it aside in despair, and, jumping up from his seat, would pace about the room almost in a frenzy.

'I agree that the author's basic idea is true,' he said to me feverishly, 'but that's even more dreadful, you know! That's *our* idea, ours: *we, we* were the first to propagate it, we nurtured it, prepared it – why, what could *they* possibly say that's new after us! But, good Lord, how badly it's all been expressed, how distorted and mangled!' he exclaimed, drumming his fingers on the book. 'Are these the conclusions we were striving to reach? Who can detect the original idea in all this?'

'Are you trying to enlighten yourself?' Pyotr Stepanovich smirked, after taking the book from the table and reading the title. 'It's long overdue. I'll bring you something even better if you want.'

Stepan Trofimovich again maintained a dignified silence. I was sitting on the sofa in the corner.

Pyotr Stepanovich quickly explained the reason he had come. Naturally, Stepan Trofimovich was thoroughly astonished, and listened with a mixture of fear and extreme indignation.

'And this Yuliya Mikhaylovna is counting on my coming to her place and reading!'

'That is to say, she really doesn't have any great need of you. On the contrary, the purpose is to be nice to you and thereby suck up to Varvara Petrovna. But it goes without saying that you wouldn't dare refuse to read. And I think you feel like doing so yourself,' he smirked. 'All you old geezers are devilishly ambitious. But listen to me: it shouldn't be too boring. You have something on hand – Spanish history, is it? Give it to me about three days in advance so I can look it over, otherwise you'll most likely put everyone to sleep.'

The brusque and all too blatant rudeness of these gibes was obviously deliberate. The impression was being created that it was impossible to speak with Stepan Trofimovoch using different, more refined language and ideas. Stepan Trofimovich resolutely continued not to notice the insults. But the impression produced on him by the information that was being communicated proved increasingly astonishing.

'And she herself, *herself*, ordered this conveyed to me through . . . *you*?' he asked, turning pale.

'In other words, you see, she wants to fix a time and place for a mutual discussion with you – the last remnants of your sentimentalizing. For twenty years you flirted with her and trained her to handle things in the most amusing ways. But don't worry, that's not what's going on now. Not a moment passes without her saying that she's now just begun to "see through" you. I told her straight out that this whole friendship of yours is nothing but a mutual outpouring of slops. She told me a lot, my friend; ugh, you've been performing the duties of a lackey all this time. I even blushed for you.'

'The duties of a lackey?' Stepan Trofimovich couldn't restrain himself.

'Worse, you were a sponger, that is, a voluntary lackey. You're too lazy to do any work, but you have an appetite for roubles and kopecks. Even she understands all this now; at any rate, it's awful what she said about you. Well now, my friend, what a good laugh I had over your letters to her; it was shameful and disgusting. But you are so depraved, you know, so depraved! There's something about taking charity that depraves a man for all time – you're an obvious example!'

'She showed you my letters!'

'All of them. That is, of course, where else could I have read them? Ugh, the amount of paper you scribbled away on! I think

there must be more than two thousand letters there . . . And
you know, old man, I think there was a moment when she
would have been ready to marry you. You let it slip in the most
stupid way! Of course I'm speaking from your point of view,
but that would still have been better than now, when you
almost got married off for "another man's sins", like a buffoon,
or for amusement, or for money.'

'For money! She, she says it was for money!' Stepan
Trofimovich began to wail in pain.

'Well, what else? What's wrong with you? I was the one who
defended you. That was the only way you could justify yourself.
She herself understood that you needed money, like anyone,
and that you were quite right from that point of view. I proved
to her, like two plus two, that you found it mutually advantageous: she provided the capital, and you were her sentimental
buffoon. However, she isn't angry about the money, even
though you milked her like a nanny goat. She's only furious
because she believed in you for twenty years, and you bam-
boozled her with your elegant ways and forced her to lie for so
long. She'll never admit that she herself lied, but that's something you'll certainly pay double for. I don't understand how
you couldn't figure out that you would have to settle accounts
some day. You did have a brain or two in your head after all.
Yesterday I advised her to put you in an almshouse – now calm
down, a decent one, it wouldn't be any insult – and apparently
that's what she's going to do. Do you remember your last letter
to me in Kh—sk Province, three weeks ago?'

'Did you really show it to her?' Stepan Trofimovich jumped
up in horror.

'Well, of course I did! The first thing. The same one in which
you informed me that she's exploiting you because she's envious
of your talent, and, well, all about "another man's sins" too.
By the way, my friend, your vanity is really something! I had
such a good laugh. In general your letters are very boring; you
have a dreadful style. Often I didn't read them at all, and even
now one is lying around unopened. But that one, that last letter
– that was the height of perfection! What a laugh I had, what
a good laugh!'

'Monster, monster!' Stepan Trofimovich began to wail.

'Ugh, the hell with it, why, it's impossible to have a conversation with you. Listen, are you offended again, the way you were last Thursday?'

Stepan Trofimovich straightened up menacingly.

'How dare you speak to me in such language?'

'What language is that? Simple and clear?'

'But tell me once and for all, you monster, are you a son of mine or not?'

'About that you know better than I. Of course, in such a case any father is inclined to blindness . . .'

'Shut up, shut up!' Stepan Trofimovich began trembling all over.

'You see now, you're shouting and cursing just like last Thursday, when you wanted to raise your stick at me. But you know, I found the document that same day. Out of curiosity I spent the entire evening rummaging through my valise. True enough, there's nothing specific, you can take some comfort in that. It's only a note that my mother sent to that Pole. But, judging by her character . . .'

'One more word and I'll slap your face.'

'What people!' Pyotr Stepanovich suddenly turned to me. 'You see, this has been going on between us ever since last Thursday. I'm glad that now at least you're here and can judge for yourself. First, a fact: he reproaches me for talking that way about my mother, but isn't he the one who put the very same idea into my head? In Petersburg, when I was still in secondary school, wasn't he the one who would wake me up twice during the night, embrace me and weep like a woman, and what do you suppose he told me on those nights? The very same modest stories about my mother! He was the very first one I heard them from.'

'Oh, I did that in the loftiest sense! Oh, you didn't understand me. You understood nothing, nothing.'

'But it was still more ignoble of you than of me, more ignoble, after all, admit it. Don't you see, it's all the same to me, if you like. I'm looking at it from your point of view. From my point of view, don't worry: I'm not blaming my mother; if it's you, it's you, if it's the Pole, it's the Pole; it's all the same to me. I'm not to blame if things worked out so stupidly between you in Berlin. Why, I doubt it could have worked out any more intelligently between you. Well now, aren't you ridiculous people after all that! And isn't it all the same to you whether I'm your son or not? Listen,' he turned to me again, 'he never spent a single rouble on me his whole life, until I was sixteen he didn't know anything about me; then he robbed me here, and now he's shouting that his heart has been aching for me his whole life long; and he's carrying on in front of me like an actor. Why, after all, I'm not Varvara Petrovna, for pity's sake!'

He stood up and took his hat.

'I curse you henceforth in my name!' Stepan Trofimovich, pale as death, stretched a hand above him.

'Well now, what stupidity a man will get himself into!' Even Pyotr Stepanovich was astonished. 'Well, farewell, old boy, I won't come your way again. Deliver your article ahead of time, don't forget, and do try, if you can, to skip the nonsense: facts, facts and more facts, and, most of all, as short as possible. Goodbye.'

3.

However, extraneous factors were also at work here. Pyotr Stepanovich actually did have certain designs on his father. In my opinion, he was counting on driving the old man to despair, thereby pushing him into some public scandal of a certain kind. He needed this to further some remote and unrelated purposes, of which we will speak later. At that time he had amassed an extraordinarily large number of various calculations and plans of this sort – almost all of them fantastic, of course. Besides Stepan Trofimovich, he also had another martyr in mind. In general, he had no small number of martyrs, as proved to be the case subsequently; but on this one he was counting especially, and that was Mr von Lembke himself.

Andrey Antonovich von Lembke belonged to that tribe,[7] so favoured by nature, which in Russia is numbered in the several hundred thousands by the calendar[8] and which perhaps is itself unaware that by its sheer mass, it comprises a single, strictly organized unit within our country. And, it goes without saying, that this unit is not premeditated or fabricated, but exists in its own right within the tribe as a whole, without words and without a formal agreement, as something morally obligatory, and consisting of the mutual support for one another of all the members of this tribe, always, everywhere, and under any imaginable circumstances. Andrey Antonovich had the honour to be educated in one of those Russian higher institutions of learning that are filled with young men from families that are well endowed with connections or wealth. The pupils of this institution, almost immediately on the completion of their course of study, were appointed to rather important positions in one of the departments of the civil service. Andrey Antonovich had one uncle who was a lieutenant colonel of engineers, and another who was a baker; but he managed to make his way into the higher school and there met other members of the tribe who were very much like him. He was a cheerful companion, a rather dull student, but loved by all. And when many of the young men, primarily Russians, who were already in the advanced classes had learned to talk about very lofty contemporary issues, and in such a way that suggested they were only waiting to graduate and then they would find solutions to them all, Andrey Antonovich continued to indulge in the most innocent of schoolboy pranks. He made everyone laugh with antics that were quite unsophisticated, to be sure, though perhaps a bit indecent, but that was precisely what he intended. Now he would blow his nose in some surprising way, when the teacher turned to him with a question during the lecture, and that would make both his companions and the teacher laugh; now, in the dormitory, he would fashion himself into some indecent *tableau vivant*, to the applause of one and all; now he would play (and rather skilfully) the overture to *Fra Diavolo*[9] through his nose, naturally. He was noted for his deliberate untidiness, which for some reason he found funny. In his very last year he became a sometime scribbler of Russian verses. He had a very ungrammatical knowledge of his native tribal language, as did many members of this same tribe in Russia.

This penchant for writing verses threw him in with a companion who was morose and seemed beaten down by something, the son of a poor general, from a Russian family, and who was regarded in the school as a future great man of letters. He treated von Lembke patronizingly. But it so happened that three years after graduating from the school, this gloomy comrade, having abandoned his civil service career for Russian literature and as a consequence now strutting around in torn boots, his teeth chattering from the cold, wearing a summer overcoat in late autumn, suddenly chanced to encounter, by the Anichkov Bridge, his former protégé 'Lembka', as everyone, incidentally, used to call him at school. And what do you think? He didn't even recognize him at first glance, and stopped in astonishment. Before him stood a faultlessly attired young man, with astonishingly well-trimmed side whiskers of a reddish cast, a pince-nez, patent-leather boots, the most immaculate gloves, a roomy greatcoat from Charmeur's and a portfolio tucked under his arm. Von Lembke treated his school chum kindly, gave him his address and invited him to come for a visit some evening. It also turned out that he was no longer 'Lembka', but 'von Lembke'. His school chum did come to see him, however, perhaps only out of spite. On the stairway, which was rather unattractive and certainly not the main entrance, but was covered with red felt, he was met and questioned by the porter. A bell rang loudly upstairs. But instead of the riches that the visitor was expecting to find, he discovered his 'Lembka' in a very small side room, which looked dark and shabby, was divided in two by a large dark-green curtain, and fitted out with furniture which, although comfortable, was a very shabby dark green, with dark-green blinds on the high, narrow windows. Von Lembke was lodging with some very distant relative, a general who was his patron. He greeted his guest hospitably, was serious and elaborately courteous. They chatted about literature as well, but within decent bounds. A servant in a white tie brought in some watery tea and small, round dry biscuits. Out of spite his comrade asked for seltzer water. He got it, but with such a delay that von Lembke grew embarrassed at having to summon the servant yet again and order him to bring it. However, he was the one who suggested that his guest might like a bite to eat, and was visibly gratified when the latter refused and finally left. Simply put, von Lembke was at the beginning of his career, and was sponging off the general, a fellow-tribesman, but an important one.

At that time he was sighing after the general's fifth daughter, and he thought it was reciprocated. Nevertheless, when the time came, Amalia was somehow married off to an old German factory owner, an old comrade of the old general. Andrey Antonovich didn't shed many tears, but proceeded to create a theatre out of paper and paste. The curtain would rise, the actors would come out and gesture with their hands, the audience was sitting in the boxes, the orchestra would move their bows across their violins mechanically, the conductor would wave his baton, and in the stalls, admirers and officers would clap their hands. Everything was made of paper, all devised and executed by von Lembke himself. He had spent six months working on the theatre. The general purposely arranged an intimate evening; the theatre was brought out and shown off; all five of the general's daughters, along with the recently married Amalia, her factory owner and many ladies, young and not so young, along with their German escorts, examined the theatre carefully and praised it; then there was dancing. Von Lembke was very gratified, and quickly found his consolation.

The years passed, and his career was established. He always served in prominent positions, and always under the supervision of fellow-tribesmen, and at last he rose to a rank that was very significant for his age. He had long been wishing to marry, and had long been cautiously looking around. Without a word to his superiors he had sent a story to the editors of a certain magazine, but they didn't publish it. To make up for it, he created an entire railway train from paper and paste, and again the result was a very successful little thing: the public was shown coming out of the station, with valises and bags, with children and small dogs, and getting into the carriages. Conductors and porters were walking back and forth, the bell was ringing, the signal was being given and the train set off on its journey. He spent an entire year working on this piece of ingenuity. Still and all, it was necessary to marry. His circle of acquaintances was rather wide, mostly in German society; but he moved in Russian company as well, in official spheres, it goes without saying. Finally, when he had already turned thirty-eight, he received an inheritance. His uncle, the baker, died, and left him thirteen thousand in his will. The only thing that remained now was the right kind of position. Mr von Lembke, despite the rather lofty style of the official circles in which he worked, was a very modest man. He would have been entirely satisfied with some independent little post in the civil service, with responsibility for ordering and purchasing firewood for official purposes, or some cushy little job of that sort, and would have been happy for the rest of his life. But then, instead of the Minna or Ernestina he had expected, Yuliya Mikhaylovna suddenly turned up. His career immediately rose to a higher level. The modest and precise von Lembke felt that he, too, could be ambitious.

Yuliya Mikhaylovna owned two hundred souls, according to the old way of reckoning, and in addition, she brought highly placed friends with her. On the other hand, von Lembke was handsome, and she was already past forty. Remarkably, he gradually fell in love with her and genuinely so, and little by little he began to feel that he was in fact her fiancé. On the morning of the wedding, he sent her some verses. All this pleased her greatly, even the verses: forty years old is no laughing matter. In short order he received a certain rank and a certain decoration, and was then appointed to our province.

In preparing to come to us, Yuliya Mikhaylovna painstakingly began to work on her spouse. In her opinion, he was not without abilities; he knew how to make an entrance and show himself to best advantage, he knew how to listen with thoughtful attention and how to remain silent, he had picked up a few highly respectable mannerisms, he could even make a speech, he even had some fragments and scraps of ideas, having acquired the essential gloss of the most up-to-date liberalism. Still and all, it bothered her that he was somehow not very receptive to new ideas and that after a prolonged and endless search for a career, he was definitely beginning to feel the need for a rest. She had the urge to infuse him with her own ambition, and he suddenly began assembling a church[10] from paper and paste: the pastor was coming out to deliver his sermon, the congregation was listening, their hands piously folded in front of them, a lady was wiping away tears with her handkerchief, an old man was blowing his nose; finally, the miniature organ, which had been specially ordered and sent from Switzerland, despite the expense, boomed forth. Yuliya Mikhaylovna, even with some trepidation, took the entire project away as soon as she found out about it, and locked it in a box in her own room. In exchange, she allowed him to write a novel, though in secret. Since then, she had begun to rely directly and exclusively on herself, and no one else. The trouble was that there was in her a fair amount of frivolity in all this, and very little sense of proportion. Fate had kept her an old maid too long. Idea after idea now began to flit through her ambitious and rather over-excited mind. She was nurturing plans; she definitely wanted to run the province; she dreamed of immediately becoming the centre of a circle; she adopted a political stance. Von Lembke was even somewhat alarmed, although he soon figured out, with the keen instincts of the civil servant, that he had absolutely nothing to fear when it came to his governorship as such. The first two or three months flowed by very satisfactorily. But then Pyotr Stepanovich turned up, and something strange began to happen.

The fact was that the young Verkhovensky, from the very outset, had displayed a decided lack of respect for Andrey Antonovich and had appropriated some strange rights over him, while Yuliya Mikhaylovna, who had always been so jealous of her husband's position, absolutely refused to take note of this; at least, she attached no importance to it. The young man became her favourite, he ate, drank, and practically slept in their house. Von Lembke tried to defend himself, calling him 'young man' when other people were present, and patronizingly patting him on the shoulder, but he got nowhere with this: Pyotr Stepanovich still seemed to be laughing in his face, even when an apparently serious conversation was under way, and when other people were present, he would say the most unexpected things to him. Once, on returning home, he found the young man in his study, sleeping on the sofa uninvited. Pyotr Stepanovich explained that he had dropped by, but not finding him at home, 'took the opportunity of having a good nap'. Von Lembke was offended, and again complained to his wife, who, risking his irritation, noted acerbically that he himself apparently didn't know how to stand on his own two feet; at least 'this boy' never permitted himself any familiarities with her, and besides, he was 'naive and fresh, albeit outside the conventions of society'. Von Lembke went into a sulk. On that occasion she made peace between them. Pyotr Stepanovich didn't exactly ask forgiveness, but instead got out of it with some coarse joke, which at another time might have been taken as a fresh insult, but in the present circumstances was taken as repentance. The weakness of Andrey Antonovich's position came from the mistake he had made at the very outset, namely, telling him about his novel. Imagining him to be an ardent young man with poetry in his soul, and long dreaming of having an audience, he read him two chapters one evening, still in the early days of their acquaintance. The young man listened through to the end without bothering to conceal his boredom and yawning rudely, and didn't utter a word of praise, but, as he was leaving, asked to borrow the manuscript so that he could form an opinion of it at home at his leisure, and Andrey Antonovich gave it to him. Since then he had not returned the manuscript, even though he dropped in every day, and when questioned about it, his only reply was laughter; in the end, he announced that he had lost it in the street the very day he had borrowed it. When she learned of this, Yuliya Mikhaylovna was dreadfully angry at her husband.

'I suppose you told him about the church as well?' she asked in consternation, almost in fear.

Von Lembke began to think hard about this, but hard thinking was harmful to him and had been forbidden by his doctors. Apart from the fact that there happened to be a great deal of trouble throughout the province, of which we will speak later, this was a special matter, even his heart was suffering, and not just his vanity as a high official. On entering into marriage,

Andrey Antonovich did not in the least entertain the possibility
of family contentions and future conflicts. It was not how he
had imagined his life, as he dreamed of Minna and Ernestina.
He felt that he was in no condition to endure domestic storms.
Finally, Yuliya Mikhaylovna had a frank conversation with him.

'You cannot get angry at him,' she said, 'if only because you
are three times more sensible than he is, and immeasurably
higher on the social ladder. There are still many remnants of
old freethinking ways in this young man, and, as far as I'm
concerned, just plain mischief. But one can't move suddenly; a
gradual approach is what's called for. Our young people must
be cherished; I act with kindness, and keep them from the
abyss.'

'But the Devil only knows what he's saying,' von Lembke
objected. 'I can't treat him with tolerance when he asserts in
public and in my presence that the government is deliberately
plying the people with vodka in order to brutalize them and in
that way keep them from rebelling. Imagine the role I have to
play when I'm forced to listen to this in the presence of others.'

As he said this, von Lembke remembered a recent conversation he had had with Pyotr Stepanovich. With the innocent
aim of disarming him through liberalism, he showed him his
own private collection of manifestos of all sorts, Russian and
foreign, which he had carefully assembled ever since 1859, not
as an admirer, but merely out of commendable curiosity. Pyotr
Stepanovich, having guessed what he had in mind, brusquely
announced that there was more sense in a single line of certain
manifestos than in an entire government office, 'not excluding
even yours, perhaps'.

This grated upon von Lembke.

'But it's too early for us, much too early,' he pronounced
almost pleadingly, pointing at the manifestos.

'No, it's not too early; why, the fact that you're afraid shows
it's not too early.'

'But just a moment, here we see, for example, a call to destroy
churches.'

'Well, why not? You, after all, are an intelligent man, and of
course you yourself aren't a believer, but you understand only

too well that you need faith in order to brutalize the people. Truth is more honest than a lie.'

'I agree, I agree, I agree with you completely, but it's too early for us, too early . . .' von Lembke was wrinkling his brow.

'Well, after that, what sort of government official are you if you yourself agree to smash up churches and move on Petersburg brandishing staves, and the only distinction you make is one of timing?'

After being so crudely caught out, von Lembke was deeply piqued.

'That's not it, not it,' he was getting carried away, his self-esteem increasingly rubbed raw. 'You, as a young man, and, most important, as one who is unacquainted with our goals, are off the mark. You see, my very dear Pyotr Stepanovich, you call us government officials. That is so. Independent officials? That is so. But excuse me, how are we acting? The responsibility is ours, and as a result we are serving the common cause, just as you are. We are merely keeping a firm hand on what you are trying to topple, and what without us would fall completely apart. We are not your enemies, by no means: we say to you: move ahead, make progress, even topple things, that is, everything that's old and subject to refashioning; but when necessary we shall also keep you within the necessary limits and thereby save you from yourselves, because without us, you would simply shake Russia to her foundations and deprive her of all outward decency, while our task is to concern ourselves with outward decency. Dig a little deeper and you will see that we and you are mutually necessary to one another. In England the Whigs and the Tories are also necessary to one another. Well, then: we are Tories, and you are Whigs,[11] that's precisely the way I understand it.'

Andrey Antonovich even waxed passionate. Ever since Petersburg he had enjoyed talking intelligently and liberally, and now the main thing was that no one was eavesdropping. Pyotr Stepanovich was keeping quiet and somehow behaving in an uncharacteristically serious manner. This added more fuel to the orator's fire.

'Do you know that I, as "master of the province",' he

continued, pacing about the study, 'do you know that on account of my many duties I cannot fulfil even one, and on the other hand, I can just as truly say that I have nothing to do here. The whole secret is that here everything depends on the views of the government. Let's suppose the government establishes a republic here, for instance, perhaps for political reasons or to calm passions, and on the other hand, simultaneously strengthens the governor's power; then we, the governors, will swallow up the republic. And not just the republic – we'll swallow anything you like. I at least feel that I am ready . . . In a word, let's suppose the government sends me a telegram proposing that I engage in *activité dévorante*,[12] and I give them *activité dévorante*. I've told everyone here straight to his face: "Gentlemen, to maintain the equilibrium and the health of all provincial institutions, one thing is essential: the strengthening of the governor's powers." You see, all these institutions – whether the zemstvos or the courts of law – should live a double life, so to speak, that is, it's necessary for them to exist (I agree that this is essential), but, well, on the other hand, they ought not to exist. All according to the views of the government. But if the prevailing mood is that the institutions suddenly turn out to be essential, then I immediately have them at hand. If the need for them should pass, no one would be able to find them in my province. That's how I understand *activité dévorante*, and it will not exist without the strengthening of the governor's powers. You and I are speaking in strict secrecy. You know, I've already informed them in Petersburg of the need for a special sentry at the doors of the governor's house. I'm awaiting an answer.'

'You need two,' said Pyotr Stepanovich.

'Why two?' Von Lembke stopped in front of him.

'One is very likely not enough for people to respect you. You need two, without fail.'

Andrey Antonovich made a face.

'You . . . the sort of things you permit yourself to say, Lord knows, Pyotr Stepanovich. Taking advantage of my good nature, you come out with barbs and play the role of some *bourru bienfaisant* . . .'[13]

'Well, that's as you wish,' Pyotr Stepanovich grumbled, 'but still and all, you are paving the way for us, and preparing our success.'

'But who are "us", and what success?' Von Lembke stared at him in astonishment, but received no reply.

Yuliya Mikhaylovna, after hearing an account of the conversation, was very displeased.

'But after all,' said von Lembke in his own defence, 'I can't treat your favourite as if I were his superior, especially when we're speaking in private . . . I might have let something come out inadvertently . . . from the goodness of my heart.'

'From an excess of goodness. I didn't know that you had a collection of manifestos, be good enough to show them to me.'

'But . . . but he begged to take them home for one day.'

'And again you gave them to him!' Yuliya Mikhaylovna said angrily. 'How imprudent!'

'I'll send someone to him immediately to get them back.'

'He won't give them back.'

'I shall demand it!' Von Lembke flew into a rage and even jumped up from his seat. 'Who is he that people should be so afraid of him, and who am I that I shouldn't dare to do something?'

'Sit down and calm yourself,' Yuliya Mikhaylovna stopped him. 'I'll answer your first question: he came to me with excellent recommendations, he has abilities and he sometimes says extraordinarily intelligent things. Karmazinov assured me that he has connections almost everywhere, as well as extraordinary influence on the young people in the capital. And if through him I can attract them all and group them around myself, then I will turn them away from ruin by showing them a new direction for their ambition. He is devoted to me wholeheartedly, and obeys me in every way.'

'But while you're being nice to them, you know, they can . . . Lord knows what they can do. Of course, it's an idea . . .' von Lembke vaguely defended himself, 'but . . . but now I hear that some manifestos have appeared in the —sky District.'

'But look, this rumour was circulating last summer – manifestos, counterfeit money, who knows what else, but so far absolutely nothing has surfaced. Who told you that?'

'I heard it from von Blum.'

'Oh, save me from your Blum and don't you dare mention him ever again!'

Yuliya Mikhaylovna flew into a fury and couldn't even speak for at least a minute. Von Blum was a clerk in the governor's chancellery whom she particularly hated. More about that later.

'Please don't worry about Verkhovensky,' she said, concluding the conversation. 'If he had been party to any mischief, then he wouldn't have talked as he has with you and with others here. Phrasemongers aren't dangerous, and let me say that even if something should happen, I will certainly be the first to find out about it from him. He is fanatically devoted to me, fanatically.'

I will note, in anticipation of events, that if it hadn't been for Yuliya Mikhaylovna's self-importance and ambition, perhaps everything that these wretched little people managed to inflict on us wouldn't have happened. She had a great deal to answer for!

CHAPTER 5

Before the Gala

I.

The day of the gala, which Yuliya Mikhaylovna had planned as a subscription benefit for the governesses of our province, had already been fixed several times in advance and then postponed. Constantly hovering around her were Pyotr Stepanovich; the little clerk Lyamshin, whose job it was to run errands, and who at one time used to visit Stepan Trofimovich and then suddenly found favour in the governor's house for his piano-playing; to some extent Liputin, whom Yuliya Mikhaylovna intended to make the editor of a future independent provincial newspaper; several ladies and young girls, and finally, even Karmazinov, who, though he didn't hover, had announced aloud and with a satisfied air that he would provide a pleasant surprise for one and all when the literary quadrille got under way. An extraordinary number of subscribers and donors declared themselves, all belonging to the select society of the town; but the most unselect were admitted as well, provided they turned up with money. Yuliya Mikhaylovna observed that sometimes a mixing of the classes should even be permitted, 'otherwise who would there be to enlighten them'? An unofficial committee was quietly organized in her house, where it was decided that the celebration would be democratic. The inordinately large number of subscriptions tempted them to increase expenses; they wanted to do something wonderful, and that is why it kept getting postponed. It had not yet been decided where the evening ball would be held: in the enormous house of the wife of the marshal of the nobility, who had made it available for that occasion, or at Varvara Petrovna's house in Skvoreshniki. Skvoreshniki was rather far away, but many members of the committee insisted that it would be 'freer' there. Varvara Petrovna herself would very much have liked for it to be held at her house. It's hard to say why this proud woman almost fawned over Yuliya Mikhaylovna. Perhaps she was pleased that the other woman, in turn, almost grovelled at Nikolay Vsevolodovich's feet and paid court to him, as she did with no one else. I'll repeat once more: Pyotr Stepanovich constantly and tirelessly tried, in whispers, to implant in the governor's house a certain idea that he had put into circulation earlier, that Nikolay Vsevolodovich was a man who had the most mysterious connections in a most mysterious world and was probably here on some mission.

People were in a strange state of mind at the time. Especially among the ladies a certain frivolity was noticeable, and it couldn't be said to have come on gradually. Several extremely unconventional notions seemed to have been floated. There was a heightened gaiety, an air of levity, which I won't say was always pleasant. A certain disorder in people's way of thinking was in fashion. Later, when everything was over, the blame fell on Yuliya Mikhaylovna, her circle and her influence; but Yuliya Mikhaylovna alone was hardly responsible for everything that happened. On the contrary, a great many people at first outdid themselves in praising the new governor's wife for being able to bring society together, and for making everything suddenly more cheerful. A few scandalous incidents even occurred, for which Yuliya Mikhaylovna was certainly not to blame; but everyone at the time merely had a good laugh and was much amused, and there was no one to put a stop to them. True enough, a rather significant group of people stood firm and aloof, with their own particular views on the way things were going; but these people certainly didn't grumble at the time, they even smiled.

I remember that a rather wide circle of people somehow formed by itself at that time, and that its centre was actually located in Yuliya Mikhaylovna's drawing room. In this intimate circle that had crowded around her, among the young people, of course, all kinds of mischief – sometimes actually rather unbridled – was permitted and even became the norm. Several very charming ladies even were members of the circle. The young people arranged picnics and evening parties, sometimes rode through the town in a whole cavalcade, in carriages and on horseback. They were seeking adventures, and even made a point of devising them and carrying them out on their own, solely for the purpose of having a lively story to tell. They treated our town like a kind of Stupidville.[1] They were called scoffers or sneerers because there was little they scorned to do. For instance, it happened that the wife of a local lieutenant, a still very young and pretty brunette, although she looked utterly worn out by the pittance her husband earned, thoughtlessly sat down at an evening party to play whist for high stakes, in hopes of winning enough to buy herself a cloak; but instead of winning she lost fifteen roubles. Afraid of her husband, and having no way of paying what she owed, she remembered how bold she had once been and resolved to borrow some money right then and there on the sly, from the son of our mayor, an extremely nasty young man, who had worn himself out with dissipated living well beyond his years. He not only refused her, but also proceeded, laughing heartily, to tell her husband. The lieutenant, who really was poor, living as he did only on his salary, brought his wife home and proceeded to toy with her to his heart's content, despite the wails, shrieks and supplications for forgiveness that she delivered on her knees. This outrageous affair occasioned nothing but laughter all over town, and although the poor lieutenant's wife certainly didn't belong to the society that surrounded Yuliya Mikhaylovna, one of the ladies of the 'cavalcade', an eccentric and lively individual, who somehow knew the lieutenant's wife, went to her house and quite simply took her off to stay with her. Here she was immediately taken up by our young scamps, cosseted, showered with gifts and kept for some four days without being returned to her husband. She lived with the lively lady and spent her days driving around town with her and with the rest of her roistering company, taking part in their amusements and their dances. They kept egging her on to haul her husband into court and to make a big fuss. They assured her that they all supported her and would go and testify. The husband kept quiet, not daring to fight back. The poor woman finally realized that she had landed herself in a peck of trouble, and nearly dead with fear, she ran away from her protectors back to her lieutenant at twilight on the fourth day. It is not exactly known what happened between the husband and wife, but two shutters of the low little wooden house where the lieutenant was renting an apartment were not opened for two weeks. Yuliya Mikhaylovna was angry at the pranksters when she found out about everything, and was very unhappy with what the lively lady had done, although the lady had introduced the lieutenant's wife to her on the first day after her abduction. However, all this was soon forgotten.

On another occasion, a young man who had come here from another district, a minor official, took in marriage the daughter of another minor official who, to all appearances, was a respectable family man. The girl was seventeen, a beauty, and known to everyone in town. But suddenly it was learned that on the first night of the marriage the young husband treated the young beauty very rudely in revenge for his profaned honour. Lyamshin, who almost witnessed the whole incident, because he had got drunk at the wedding and spent the night in their house, ran around town at daybreak with the joyous news. In an instant a party of some ten men was made up, every last one of them mounted, some on hired Cossack horses, including Pyotr Stepanovich as well as Liputin, who, for all his grey hair, took part in all the scandalous adventures of our flighty young people at that time. When the young couple appeared in the street, in a droshky drawn by two horses, on their way to pay the visits that were prescribed by the inflexible law of custom on the very next day after the wedding, no matter what mishaps might have occurred – this entire cavalcade surrounded the droshky with joyful laughter and accompanied them through town all morning long. To be sure, they didn't go into the houses, but waited by the gates on their horses. They refrained from insulting the groom and bride in any specific way, but nonetheless created a scandal. The entire town started talking. Naturally, everyone had a good laugh. But now von Lembke grew very angry and had another lively scene with Yuliya Mikhaylovna. She was also extremely angry and resolved to bar the pranksters from the house. But on the very next day she forgave them all, as a result of Pyotr Stepanovich's urgings and a few words from Karmazinov, who found the 'joke' rather clever.

'These are our local ways,' he said, 'and in any event characteristic and . . . daring. And look, everyone is laughing; you're the only one who's indignant.'

But some pranks were intolerable, somewhat off-colour.

A woman appeared in town selling the Gospels, a respectable woman, albeit in trade. People began talking about her because some curious reports about book-pedlars[2] had just appeared in the Petersburg newspapers. Once again the same rogue, Lyamshin, with the help of a seminary student who was just hanging around in anticipation of a teaching position in a school, quietly slipped into the book-pedlar's bag, as if they were buying books, a whole packet of indecent and obscene photographs from abroad, which had been specifically donated for that purpose, as was subsequently learned, by a quite respectable old gentleman (whose name I am omitting), who wore a high decoration round his neck and who liked, as he put it, 'healthy laughter and a good joke'. When the poor woman started removing the holy books in our shopping arcade, the photographs fell out as well. There was laughter and murmurs. A crowd gathered round, they began abusing her and she would certainly have been beaten up if the police hadn't arrived in good time. The book-pedlar was put into the lockup, and only that evening, through the efforts of Mavriky Nikolayevich, who was indignant when he learned the intimate details of this sordid story, was she set free and escorted out of town. At this point Yuliya Mikhaylovna would certainly have banished Lyamshin from her house, but that very evening a whole band of our young people brought him to her, with the news that he had specially composed a new piece for the piano, and they talked her into just giving it a hearing. In fact, the piece did prove entertaining, and bore the amusing title of 'The Franco-Prussian War'. It began with the menacing strains of the *Marseillaise*.

Qu'un sang impur abreuve nos sillons![3]

A bombastic summons could be heard, and the intoxication of future victories. But suddenly, along with skilful variations on strains of the national anthem, somewhere from one side, below, in the corner, but very close could be heard the vulgar notes of *Mein lieber Augustin*.[4] The *Marseillaise* didn't notice them, the *Marseillaise* was at the height of intoxication with its own grandeur; but *Augustin* was gaining strength, *Augustin* was growing more and more insolent, and then the strains of *Augustin* somehow began unexpectedly to mingle with the strains of the *Marseillaise*. It was as though the French anthem was beginning to grow angry; finally, it noticed *Augustin*, it wanted to get rid of it, brush it away like some pesky, insignificant fly, but *Mein lieber Augustin* had taken firm hold; it was gleeful and self-assured; and the *Marseillaise* suddenly became dreadfully stupid somehow: it could no longer conceal the fact that it was angry and offended; it was a wail of indignation, it was tears and imprecations with arms outstretched to Providence:

Pas un pouce de notre terrain, pas une pierre de nos forteresses![5]

But by now it was forced to sing in unison with *Mein lieber Augustin*. Its sounds somehow blended into *Augustin* in the silliest way imaginable; it languished and died out. Only occasionally could a snatch of *'qu'un sang impur'* be heard, but it promptly passed back into the trashy little waltz in the most annoying way. Finally, it was completely subdued: it was Jules Favre sobbing on Bismarck's breast and giving everything away, everything ... But at this point *Augustin* turned savage as well: hoarse sounds were heard; there was an atmosphere of measureless quantities of beer being drunk, the fury of self-aggrandizement, demands for billions, fine cigars, champagne and hostages; *Augustin* now became a frenzied roar ... The Franco-Prussian War was coming to an end. Everyone present applauded. Yuliya Mikhaylovna smiled and said, 'Well, but how can we banish him now?' Peace was concluded. This repro-

bate actually did have a modicum of talent. Stepan Trofimovich
once assured me that the greatest artistic talents are capable of
being the most dreadful reprobates and that the one does not
preclude the other. Later it was rumoured that Lyamshin had
stolen this little piece from a talented and modest young man,
a visiting acquaintance of his, who simply remained unknown;
but that's neither here nor there. This scoundrel, who for several
years had been hovering around Stepan Trofimovich, doing
imitations at his evening parties, when called upon, of various
miserable little Jews, the confession of a deaf woman or the
birth of a child, would now sometimes produce killingly funny
caricatures at Yuliya Mikhaylovna's, among them one of
Stepan Trofimovich himself, under the rubric 'A Liberal of the
1840s'.[6] Everyone would roar with laughter, the end result
being that it was absolutely impossible to banish him: he had
become too necessary. Besides, he slavishly fawned on Pyotr
Stepanovich, who in turn had by then acquired a strangely
powerful influence over Yuliya Mikhaylovna.

I wouldn't make a point of speaking specifically about this
scoundrel, and he wouldn't be worth spending any time on,
except for a deplorable incident in which he also took part, or
so they say, and there is no way I can omit this incident from
my chronicle.

One morning news of a shocking and disgraceful sacrilege
quickly spread through the entire town. At the entrance to
our enormous marketplace stands the venerable church of Our
Lady's Nativity, which is a remarkable antiquity in our ancient
town. At the gates of the enclosure, a large icon of the Mother
of God had long ago been set into a wall behind a grating. And
then, one night the icon was stolen, the glass of the icon-case
broken, the grating smashed, and from the crown and the
setting several stones and pearls removed, though I don't know
whether they were very valuable or not. But the main thing
is that besides the theft, a senseless and sacrilegious act of
desecration had been committed: behind the broken glass of
the icon a live mouse was found the next morning, or so they
say. Now, four months later, it's definitely known that the
crime was committed by the convict Fedka, but for some reason

Lyamshin is also said to be involved. At the time no one mentioned Lyamshin and there was absolutely no reason to suspect him, but now everyone asserts that he was the one who let the mouse loose there. I remember that all our authorities rather lost their heads. From early morning a crowd of people had gathered at the scene of the crime. A crowd was constantly in attendance, just how big, Lord only knows, but at least a hundred people. Some were coming, others were going. As people arrived, they crossed themselves and kissed the icon; they began to make offerings, and a collection plate appeared, with a monk standing by the plate, and it was only at three o'clock in the afternoon that the authorities realized that the people could be told not to stand there in a crowd, but to move on, after they had said a prayer, kissed the icon and made a contribution. This unfortunate incident produced the gloomiest of impressions on von Lembke. Yuliya Mikhaylovna, as it was told to me, later said that from that ill-omened morning she had begun to notice in her husband the strange melancholy which subsequently persisted right up to the time of his departure from our town, two months ago, for reasons of ill health, and seems to be still with him even in Switzerland, where he continues to rest after his brief career in our province.

I remember going into the marketplace after twelve o'clock in the afternoon. The crowd was silent, with solemn and gloomy faces. A fat and sallow merchant drove up in a droshky, climbed out of the vehicle, made a low bow, kissed the icon, contributed a rouble, climbed back into the droshky, sighing, and again drove off. A carriage also drove up with two of our ladies accompanied by two of our pranksters. The young men (of whom one was no longer so very young) also stepped out of their vehicle and elbowed their way to the icon, shoving people aside rather unceremoniously. Neither removed his hat, and one perched a pince-nez on his nose. The public began to murmur, indistinctly to be sure, but in an unfriendly way. The young dandy with the pince-nez removed a copper coin from his wallet, which was chock full of banknotes, and threw it on to the plate; both, laughing and talking loudly, turned back to the carriage. At that moment Lizaveta Nikolayevna galloped up, accompanied by Mavriky Nikolayevich. She jumped off her horse, tossed the reins to her companion, who remained on his horse, as she had ordered, and went up to the icon at precisely the moment the kopeck had been tossed. Her cheeks flushed with indignation. She removed her round hat and her gloves, fell on her knees in front of the icon, straight on to the dirty pavement and made three reverential deep bows. Then she took out her purse, but since there proved to be only a few ten-kopeck pieces in it, she instantly removed her diamond earrings and laid them on the plate.

'May I, may I? To ornament the setting?' she asked the monk, in great excitement.

'It is permitted,' he replied, 'any contribution is to the good.'

The people remained silent, without showing either disapproval or approval. Lizaveta Nikolayevna got back on her horse and galloped away in her muddy dress.

2.

Two days following the incident just described I ran across her in a sizeable group of people who were setting out to go somewhere in three carriages surrounded by others on horseback. She beckoned to me, stopped the carriage and insisted that I join their company. A place was found for me in the carriage, and she laughingly introduced me to her companions, elegant young ladies, and explained to me that they were all setting off on an extremely interesting expedition. She was laughing heartily and seemed somehow too happy. Recently she had become lively to the point of exuberance. In fact, the expedition was eccentric: they were all going across the river, to the house of the merchant Sevostyanov. There, in a lodge in the yard, our blessed prophet Semyon Yakovlevich, who was known not only locally but also in the surrounding provinces and even in the two capitals, had been living for about ten years now in peace, comfort and ease. Everyone came to see him, especially visitors to town, who hoped for a word from a saintly fool, as they bowed down to him and made an offering. The offerings, which were sometimes substantial, if they weren't dealt with on the spot by Semyon Yakovlevich himself, would be piously sent to one of God's churches, mainly to our Bogorodsky Monastery. For that purpose a monk from the monastery was constantly on duty at Semyon Yakovlevich's. Everyone was anticipating a lot of fun. No one in this group had yet laid eyes on Semyon Yakovlevich. Only Lyamshin had been at his place sometime previously, and now he was assuring us that the holy man had ordered him driven away with a broom and with his own hand had thrown two large boiled potatoes after him. Among the riders I noticed Pyotr Stepanovich, again on a hired Cossack horse, on which he sat very badly, and Nikolay Vsevolodovich, who was also mounted. On occasion Stavrogin would not abstain from the general merriment, and in such cases always displayed a decently cheerful demeanour, although, as before, he spoke little and seldom. When the expedition had ridden down from the bridge and had drawn up beside the town hotel, someone suddenly announced that the body of a guest who had shot himself had just been discovered in one of the hotel rooms, and that they were waiting for the police. Immediately the idea was floated of having a look at the suicide. The idea found support; our ladies had never seen a suicide. I remember that one of them said aloud, then and there, that 'everything's become so boring that there's no point in being fastidious about one's amusements as long as they were diverting'. Only a few remained outside to wait by the porch, while the rest trooped into the dirty hallway. Among others I saw, to my astonishment, Lizaveta Nikolayevna as well. The room of the person who had shot himself was open, and naturally, no one dared not let us in. He was quite a young boy, of nineteen or so, certainly no more, who must have been very good-looking, with thick blond hair and a regular oval face. He was already stiff, and his small pale face looked as if it had been carved from marble. Lying on the table was a note, in his hand, which said that no one should be blamed for his death and that he had shot himself because he had 'blown' four hundred roubles. The word 'blown' was actually there in the note; and its four lines contained three grammatical errors. Someone, apparently his neighbour, a fat landowner who was staying in

another room for reasons of business, was particularly upset
about him. It turned out, as he told it, that the boy had been
sent by his family – his widowed mother, his sisters and his
aunts – from their village to the town, in order to make various
purchases, under the supervision of a female relative who was
living in the town, for the dowry of his older sister, who was
getting married, which he was then to take home. These four
hundred roubles, which had been saved up over the course of
decades, had been entrusted to him with sighs of trepidation,
and he was seen off with endless, edifying admonishments,
prayers and signs of the cross. Until then the boy had been
decent and reliable. After arriving in town three days previously, he didn't go to his relative's but stayed at the hotel and
went straight to a club, in hopes of finding in some back room
an itinerant gambler or at least a game of cards. But there was
no game that evening, and no one to serve as banker either.
When he returned to his room it was already close to midnight.
He ordered some champagne, some Havana cigars, and a supper of six or seven courses. But he got drunk on the champagne
and sick on the cigars, and so didn't even touch the dishes that
had been brought in, and instead lay down to sleep in an almost
unconscious state. Awakening the next morning, fresh as a
daisy, he immediately set off for the gypsy camp, which was
located in the suburb across the river, and which he had heard
about the day before in the club, and he didn't appear in the
hotel for two days. Finally, at about five o'clock the previous
afternoon, he arrived drunk, immediately went to bed and slept
until ten o'clock that evening. When he woke up he asked for
a cutlet, a bottle of Château d'Yquem[7] and some grapes, as well
as paper, ink and the bill. No one noticed anything out of the
ordinary about him: he was calm, quiet and pleasant. He must
have shot himself at about midnight, although it's strange that
no one heard the shot. They noticed his absence only today at
one o'clock in the afternoon, and, when they received no reply
to their knocking, broke down the door. The bottle of Château
d'Yquem was half empty, and there also remained about half
a plateful of grapes. The shot had been fired from a small
three-chambered revolver directly into the heart. Very little

blood had been lost; the revolver had dropped out of his hands
on to the carpet. The young man was half-reclining in a corner
of the sofa. Death must have occurred instantaneously; there
was no sign of the death agony in his face: his expression was
calm, almost happy, if only he were alive. Everyone in our party
studied him with avid curiosity. Generally speaking, in every
misfortune that befalls one's neighbour there is something that
gladdens the eye of the onlooker, it doesn't make any difference
who you may be. Our ladies studied him in silence, while the
men accompanying them distinguished themselves with clever
remarks and a perfect presence of mind. One observed that this
was the very best way out, and that the young man couldn't
have come up with anything more intelligent than that; another
concluded that though it was only for an instant, he'd had a
good life. A third suddenly blurted: why had people in our
country taken to hanging and shooting themselves so frequently, as if they'd lost their roots, as if the floor had slipped
out from under their feet? The others cast unfriendly looks
at the philosophizer. To lighten the mood, Lyamshin, who
considered himself honoured by his role as a buffoon, pinched
a bunch of grapes off the plate, then a second person, laughing,
did the same, and a third made to reach his hand toward the
Château d'Yquem. But he was stopped by the arrival of a
policeman, who even asked them to 'clear the room'. Since they
all had looked quite long enough, they immediately departed
without any argument, although Lyamshin did begin pestering
the policeman about something. The general merriment, the
laughter and the boisterous conversation became almost twice
as lively during the remaining half of the trip.

We arrived at Semyon Yakovlevich's[8] at exactly one o'clock
in the afternoon. The gate of the merchant's rather large house
stood wide open, and there was easy access to the lodge in the
yard. We learned at once that Semyon Yakovlevich was having
his dinner, but was receiving. Our whole crowd went in
together. The room in which the blessed one was receiving and
having his dinner was rather spacious, with three windows,
and was divided crosswise into two equal parts by a wooden
partition that extended from wall to wall, waist-high. Ordinary

visitors remained on the other side of the partition, but the lucky ones were admitted, at a sign from the blessed one, through the small doors of the partition into his half, and he had them sit, if he wished, on his old leather armchairs and couch, while he himself was invariably ensconced in an ancient, battered Voltaire armchair.[9] He was a rather large, somewhat bloated, sallow-faced man of about fifty-five, fair-complexioned and balding, with thinning hair, clean-shaven, a swollen right cheek and a mouth that was somehow twisted, with a large wart near his left nostril, narrow little eyes and a calm, solid, sleepy expression on his face. He was dressed in the German fashion, in a black frock-coat, but without a waistcoat or a tie. A rather coarse white shirt peeped out from beneath his frock-coat; his feet, which seemed to be ailing, he kept in slippers. I had heard that he was once a civil servant and had some sort of rank. He had just finished eating a light fish soup and had started on his second course, potatoes in their jackets, with salt. He never ate anything else; he just drank a great deal of tea, which he liked very much. Scurrying about him were three servants who were kept by the merchant. One of them wore a tail-coat, the other looked like a member of an artel, the third like a sexton. There was also a lad of about sixteen, who was very lively. There was present besides the servants a venerable grey-haired monk, a little too plump, with a collection box. On one of the tables an enormous samovar stood bubbling away, as well as a tray with almost two dozen glasses on it. On another table, standing just opposite, offerings had been placed: a few loaves and cones of sugar, some two pounds of tea, a pair of embroidered slippers, a foulard scarf, a length of cloth, a piece of linen, etc. The monetary offerings had almost all found their way into the monk's collection box. There were a lot of people in the room: up to a dozen visitors, of whom two were sitting on the other side of the partition with Semyon Yakovlevich. They were a grey-haired little old man, a pilgrim, one of the 'simple' folk, and a small, dried-up little visiting monk, who was sitting modestly with downcast eyes. The other visitors were all stand-ing on the near side of the partition, most of them also of the 'simple' folk, except for one fat merchant who had come here from a district town, sporting a beard, dressed in the Russian fashion, but known to be worth a hundred thousand; an elderly and impoverished woman of the gentry; and a landowner. They were all waiting for their good luck, not daring to utter a word themselves. Four people were on their knees, but the one who attracted the most attention was the landowner, a fat man of about forty-five, who was kneeling right at the partition, for all to see, reverently awaiting a gracious look or word from Semyon Yakovlevich. He had been kneeling for about an hour already, and the holy man had not taken any notice of him.

Our ladies crowded right against the partition, whispering and giggling merrily. They pushed aside or stood in front of all the other visitors except the landowner, who stubbornly remained where he was, even holding on to the partition with his hands. Amused and avidly curious looks were directed at Semyon Yakovlevich, as were lorgnettes, pince-nez and even binoculars; Lyamshin, at least, was surveying the scene through binoculars. Semyon Yakovlevich calmly and languidly cast his little eyes over all of them.

'Comelylooks! Comelylooks!' he deigned to say in a hoarse, soft bass voice that was almost an exclamation.

Everyone in our company began laughing. 'What does "comelylooks" mean?' But Semyon Yakovlevich lapsed into silence and finished eating his potato. At last he wiped his mouth with his napkin, and was given his tea.

He usually didn't drink tea by himself, but poured some for his visitors as well, although by no means for everyone. He himself usually indicated which of them were to be favoured. These instructions always proved surprising in their unexpectedness. Ignoring the rich people and the dignitaries, he would sometimes order a muzhik or some decrepit old crone to be served; another time, ignoring the fraternity of beggars, he would have some fat wealthy merchant served. The tea was also poured out in different ways: some with sugar in the glass, others with a lump of sugar on the side,[10] and others weren't given any sugar at all. On this occasion the favoured ones were the visiting monk, with a glass containing sugar, and the old pilgrim, who was given tea without any sugar. As for the stout monk from the monastery with the collection box, no tea at all was brought to him for some reason, although until then he had been receiving his glassful every day.

'Semyon Yakovlevich, tell me something, I've been yearning to make your acquaintance for ever so long,' crooned the elegant lady from our carriage, smiling and crinkling her eyes; she was the one who just a little while ago had noted that there was no point in being fastidious about one's amusements as long as they were diverting. Semyon Yakovlevich didn't even glance at her. The landowner who was kneeling emitted a sonorous and deep sigh, as if a large pair of bellows had been opened and shut.

'In the glass.' Semyon Yakovlevich suddenly pointed at the merchant worth a hundred thousand, who moved forward and knelt beside the landowner.

'More sugar for him!' Semyon Yakovlevich ordered, after the glass had been filled. Another portion was added. 'More, more for him!' More was added for a third time, and finally for a fourth. The merchant started drinking his syrup unquestioningly.

'Lord!' The people began whispering and crossing themselves. The landowner emitted another sonorous and deep sigh.

'Father! Semyon Yakovlevich!' The voice of the impoverished lady who had been pressed against the wall by our company suddenly rang out, mournful but so strident that it came quite unexpectedly. 'A whole hour it is, dear Father, that I've been waiting for a blessing. Utter a word to me, poor wretch that I am, decide my case.'

'Ask her,' said Semyon Yakovlevich, pointing to the sexton who was serving. He went up to the partition.

'Have you done what Semyon Yakovlevich told you to do last time?' he asked the widow in a soft and measured voice.

'How could I do it, Father Semyon Yakovlevich, how can you do anything with them!' the widow began to wail. 'They're cannibals! They're filing a petition against me in the circuit court, they're threatening to take it to the Senate[11] – and this is all against their own mother!'

'Give it to her!' Semyon Yakovlevich pointed at the loaf of

sugar. The young lad came running, grabbed the loaf and hauled it over to the widow.

'Oh, Father, great is your mercy. And what am I to do with so much?' the widow began to wail.

'More, more!' said Semyon Yakovlevich by way of bestowal.

Another loaf was hauled over to her. 'More, more,' the holy man ordered; a third loaf was brought, and finally a fourth. The widow was surrounded with sugar on all sides. The monk from the monastery heaved a sigh: all this could have gone to the monastery that very day, as it had on previous occasions.

'But what am I to do with so much?' the widow moaned submissively. 'Is this perhaps some prophecy, Father?'

'That's just what it is, a prophecy,' someone in the crowd said.

'Another foont for her, another!' Semyon Yakovlevich was unrelenting.

A whole loaf still remained on the table, but Semyon Yakovlevich indicated that she be given a foont of sugar, and a foont was given to the widow.

'Lord, Lord!' the people sighed and crossed themselves. 'It's obviously a prophecy.'

'First, sweeten your heart with goodness and mercy, and only then come and complain about your own children, flesh of your flesh; that is what one would suppose is meant by this symbol,' the stout monk from the monastery, who had been left out when the tea was served, said quietly and complacently, having taken it upon himself, in an access of wounded vanity, to provide an interpretation.

'Why, what's the matter with you, Father,' the old widow suddenly stormed at him. 'Why, they put a rope around me and dragged me into the flames when the Verkhishin house caught fire. They locked a dead cat in my trunk. In other words, they're prepared to commit any outrage.'

'Get her out of here, get her out!' Semyon Yakovlevich suddenly began waving his arms.

The sexton and the young lad dashed from behind the partition. The sexton took the widow by the arm. She calmed down and shuffled to the door, while looking round at the sugar loaves that had been bestowed on her and were now being dragged out behind her by the young lad.

'Remove one, take it back!' Semyon Yakovlevich commanded the artel-worker who'd remained behind with him. He rushed after the retreating group, and in a little while all three servants returned, carrying back one of the sugar loaves that had just been bestowed on the poor old widow and then taken away. Still and all, she carried three off with her.

'Semyon Yakovlevich,' someone's voice was heard in the back by the door, 'I saw a bird in my dream, a jackdaw, and it flew out of the water and straight into the fire. What does this dream mean?'[12]

'A frost is coming,' Semyon Yakovlevich intoned.

'Semyon Yakovlevich, why won't you answer me? I've been interested in you for so long,' one of our ladies started in again.

'Ask him!' Semyon Yakovlevich, without listening to her, suddenly pointed to the landowner who was kneeling.

The monk from the monastery, who had been ordered to ask him, walked sedately up to the landowner.

'What is the nature of your sin? And were you not told to do something?'

'Not to fight, not to give rein to my hands,' the landowner replied hoarsely.

'Did you do that?' asked the monk.

'I cannot do what I was told, my own strength is too much for me.'

'Out with him, out with him, use the broom, the broom!' Semyon Yakovlevich began waving his arms. The landowner, without waiting for the punishment to be inflicted, jumped up and dashed out of the room.

'He left a gold piece where he was kneeling,' the monk announced, as he picked the five-rouble coin up off the floor.

'There's the one to give it to!' Semyon Yakovlevich jabbed a finger at the merchant who was worth a hundred thousand. The rich man didn't dare refuse it, and took it.

'Gold unto gold,' the monk from the monastery couldn't refrain from saying.

'And sugar in the tea for this one,' Semyon Yakovlevich

suddenly pointed at Mavriky Nikolayevich. A servant poured
the tea and was about to hand it to the fop in the pince-nez by
mistake.

'For the long one, the long one,' Semyon Yakovlevich
corrected him.

Mavriky Nikolayevich took the glass, gave a half-bow in
military fashion and began to drink. I don't know why, but all
our people simply split their sides laughing.

'Mavriky Nikolayevich!' Liza turned to him. 'That man who
was on his knees has left; now you get down on your knees in
his place.'

Mavriky Nikolayevich looked at her in bewilderment.

'I beg you, you'll give me great pleasure. Listen, Mavriky
Nikolayevich,' she suddenly began speaking in an insistent,
obstinate, impassioned patter, 'please do get down, I really
want to see you kneeling. If you don't get down, then don't
come to visit me any more. I really want it, I really do want it!'

I don't know what she meant by this; but she was demanding
it insistently, implacably, as if she were having a fit. As we'll see
later, Mavriky Nikolayevich would interpret these capricious
outbursts of hers, which had become particularly frequent
of late, as flare-ups of blind hatred towards him, not because
of malice – on the contrary, she esteemed, loved and respected
him, and he knew it himself – but because of a particular kind of
morbid, unconscious hatred that she couldn't control at times.

He silently handed his cup to some little old woman who
was standing behind him, opened the door of the partition
and without any invitation, stepped into Semyon Yakovlevich's
private space and in the middle of the room got down on his
knees for all to see. I think that Mavriky Nikolayevich's delicate
and simple soul was utterly shocked by Liza's rude, mocking
sally in full view of everyone. Perhaps the thought crossed
his mind that she would be ashamed of herself on seeing his
humiliation, of which she had made such a point. Of course,
no one but him would have ventured to try to correct a woman
in such a naive and risky way. He was kneeling, his face imperturbable and dignified, long, ungainly, ridiculous. But the
people from our party were not laughing; the unexpectedness

of his action had produced a painful effect on them. Everyone was looking at Liza.

'The holy oil, the holy oil!' Semyon Yakovlevich grumbled.

Liza suddenly turned pale, screamed, exclaimed 'oh' and dashed to the other side of the partition. A brief, hysterical scene then ensued: she tried with all her strength to lift Mavriky Nikolayevich up from his knees, tugging at his elbow with both hands.

'Get up, get up!' she was screaming like a woman possessed. 'Get up immediately, immediately! How dare you kneel!'

Mavriky Nikolayevich got up off his knees. She grasped his arms above the elbows and stared into his face. There was fear in her eyes.

'Comelylooks, comelylooks!' Semyon Yakovlevich repeated once again.

Finally she dragged Mavriky Nikolayevich back outside the partition; a great stir passed through our whole crowd. The lady from our carriage, probably wishing to dispel the impression, asked Semyon Yakovlevich for the third time in a shrill, ringing voice, and, as before, with an affected smile:

'Well then, Semyon Yakovlevich, won't you make some sort of pronouncement for me too? I've been counting on you so much.'

'— you! — you!' Semyon Yakovlevich turned to her and suddenly uttered an extremely indecent word. The words were pronounced savagely and with horrifying clarity. Our ladies squealed and rushed out as fast as they could; the elegant young gentlemen were laughing Homerically. Thus ended our trip to Semyon Yakovlevich.

And yet, they say that another extraordinarily puzzling incident then occurred, and I confess it's precisely for that reason that I've gone to the trouble of mentioning this trip in such detail.

They say that when the whole crowd of people dashed out, Liza, supported by Mavriky Nikolayevich, suddenly bumped into Nikolay Vsevolodovich in the darkness of the doorway. It must be said that they had run across each other more than once since that Sunday morning and her fainting fit, but had never approached each other and hadn't exchanged a word. I saw their encounter in the doorway; it seemed to me that they both paused for a moment and looked at each other in a rather strange way. But I couldn't see clearly in the crowd. People asserted, on the contrary, and entirely seriously, that Liza, on glimpsing Nikolay Vsevolodovich, quickly raised her hand to the level of his face and probably would have struck him if he hadn't contrived to move away. Perhaps she was displeased by the expression on his face or by something in the way he smiled, especially then, after the episode with Mavriky Nikolayevich. I confess that I myself saw nothing, yet everyone insisted they had seen it, although because of the confusion there was no way that absolutely everyone could have seen it, so only some could have seen it. Except at that point I didn't believe it. I remember, though, that Nikolay Vsevolodovich was rather pale all the way back.

3.

At almost the same time, and precisely on that very same day the meeting between Stepan Trofimovich and Varvara Petrovna finally took place, a meeting that she had long been thinking about and had long ago announced to her former friend, but had so far kept putting off for some reason. It took place at Skvoreshniki. Varvara Petrovna arrived at her suburban home all abustle: the day before it had been definitely decided that the forthcoming gala would be given by the wife of the marshal of the nobility. But Varvara Petrovna's quick mind immediately grasped that after the gala nothing would prevent her from giving her own special gala, there at Skvoreshniki, and from convening the entire town again. Then all could see for themselves whose house was better and in which one guests were better received and a ball given with greater taste. In general it was impossible to recognize her. She seemed to have been reborn, and from the unapproachable 'grand lady' of yore (Stepan Trofimovich's expression), she had turned into the most ordinary kind of giddy society woman. However, it might only have seemed so.

After arriving at the empty house, she made a tour of the rooms, accompanied by her old and faithful Aleksey Yegorovich and by Fomushka, a man who had seen a great deal in his time, and was a specialist in interior decoration. Consultations and deliberations got under way: what furniture to bring from the house in town; which objects, which pictures; where they should be placed; the best use to make of the conservatory and the flowers; where to hang new draperies; where to set up the buffet and whether there should be one or two; and so on and so forth. And then, at the height of all this frenzied activity it suddenly occurred to her to send the carriage for Stepan Trofimovich.

He had already been informed long ago, and was ready, and each day he was expecting just this kind of sudden invitation. As he took his place in the carriage, he crossed himself: his fate was being decided. He found his friend in the large hall, sitting on a small couch in a niche, in front of a small marble table, with pencil and paper in hand. Fomushka was measuring the height of the open gallery and the windows, and Varvara Petrovna was herself writing down the numbers and making notations in the margins. Without interrupting her work, she nodded her head in Stepan Trofimovich's direction and, after he had mumbled some kind of greeting, gave him her hand hastily and, without looking, indicated a place next to her.

'I sat and waited a good five minutes, controlling my feelings,' he told me later. 'I saw a different woman from the one I had known for twenty years. The complete conviction that this was the end of everything gave me a strength that astonished even her. I swear, she was surprised by my steadfastness in this final hour.'

Varvara Petrovna suddenly put the pencil down on the table and quickly turned to Stepan Trofimovich.

'Stepan Trofimovich, we need to talk business. I'm sure you've prepared all your highfalutin words and your various aphorisms, but it's best to get directly to the matter at hand, don't you think?'

He winced. She was in too much of a hurry to set the tone; what could possibly be coming next?

'Wait a moment; keep quiet, let me speak, and then you can talk, although I really don't know what you could possibly say by way of an answer,' she continued in a rapid patter. 'The twelve hundred roubles of your pension I consider my sacred obligation to the end of your life. That is, rather than a sacred obligation, let's make it simply an agreement; that will be much more realistic, don't you think? We can put it in writing, if you like. In case of my death, special arrangements have been made. But you're receiving from me now, over and above that, lodging and servants and all your maintenance. Translated into cash, that comes to fifteen hundred roubles, don't you think? I'm putting in an extra three hundred roubles, so the total rounds off to three thousand. Is that enough for you for a year? It doesn't seem too little? In cases of genuine emergency, however, I'll add to that. And so, take the money, send me back my servants and live as you like, where you like, in Petersburg, in Moscow, abroad, or here, only not at my house. Do you understand?'

'Not so long ago a different demand was conveyed to me from those very same lips, just as insistently and just as quickly,' Stepan Trofimovich said slowly and with sad distinctness. 'I humbled myself and danced the *kazachok*[13] to please you. *Oui, la comparaison peut être permise. C'était comme un petit cozak du Don, qui sautait sur sa propre tombe.*[14] Now . . .'

'Stop, Stepan Trofimovich, you're dreadfully long-winded. You didn't dance, you came to see me in a new tie and new linen, wearing gloves, and all pomaded and perfumed. I assure you that you yourself very much wanted to get married; it was written on your face, and believe me, in a far from elegant expression. If I didn't remark on it at the time, it was merely out of delicacy. But you desired it, you desired to get married, despite the vile things you wrote privately about me and about your fiancée. It's completely different now. And why this business of the *cozak du Don* on some tomb of yours? I don't understand the comparison. On the contrary, don't die, but live; live as long as you can, I will be very happy.'

'In the almshouse?'

'In the almshouse? People with three thousand in income

don't go into almshouses. Ah, I remember now,' she grinned, 'in fact Pyotr Stepanovich was once pulling your leg about an almshouse. Why, that was really a special kind of almshouse that's worth thinking about. It's for the most distinguished persons. There are colonels there, a certain general wants to go there even now. If you go into it with all your money, then you'll find peace, contentment, servants. You'll pursue your scholarly work there and can always get up a game of preference.'

'*Passons.*'

'*Passons?*' Varvara Petrovna said with distaste. 'But in that case, that's all: you've been informed, and from now on we are living completely separately.'

'And that's all? All that remains of twenty years? Our last farewell?'

'You are awfully partial to exclamations, Stepan Trofimovich. That's utterly out of fashion these days. People speak rudely, but simply. These twenty years have become an obsession of yours! Twenty years of mutual vanity, and nothing more. Every letter of yours was written not to me but for posterity. You're a stylist, not a friend, while friendship is only a glorified word; in essence – a mutual outpouring of slops.'

'Good Lord, how many borrowed words! Lessons learned by heart! And they've already put their uniform on you! You're also enjoying this; you're also basking in the sun; *chère, chère*, look at the mess of pottage you've sold your freedom to them for!'[15]

'I'm not a parrot, repeating other people's words,' Varvara Petrovna flared up. 'You may be sure that I have an ample supply of my own words. What have you done for me these past twenty years? You've even refused to let me look at the books I've been ordering for you, which pages would still be uncut if the binder hadn't done it. What did you ever give me to read in those first years when I asked you to be my guide? Nothing but Capefigue[16] and more Capefigue. You were even jealous of my intellectual development and took measures. And meanwhile, everyone was laughing at you. I admit I always thought of you as only a critic; you are a literary critic, and

nothing more. When I announced to you on the way to Petersburg that I intended to publish a magazine and devote my entire
life to it, you immediately looked at me ironically and suddenly
became dreadfully supercilious.'

'It was not that, not that . . . we were afraid of persecution
then . . .'

'It was precisely that and there was no way you could have
been afraid of persecution in Petersburg. You remember that
later, in February, when news of the emancipation spread like
wildfire, you suddenly came running to me in a panic and
started demanding that I give you a statement, in the form of a
letter, that the projected magazine had absolutely nothing to
do with you, that the young people were coming to see me, not
you, and that you were just a tutor living in the house because
you hadn't yet been given all your salary, isn't that so? Do you
remember that? You've really distinguished yourself all your
life, Stepan Trofimovich.'

'That was merely a moment of faint-heartedness, a private
moment between us,' he exclaimed mournfully, 'but can you
really, really break off everything because of such trivial impressions? Can it really be that nothing more has survived intact
between us over such a long span of years?'

'You're dreadfully calculating; you want to make everything
come out so that I'm still in your debt. When you returned from
abroad, you stood before me and looked down your nose, and
didn't allow me to utter a word, and when I myself went abroad
and later began to speak with you about my impression of the
Madonna, you didn't hear me out, and began smiling condescendingly into your tie, as if I were incapable of having exactly
the same feelings as you.'

'That wasn't it, that probably wasn't it . . . *J'ai oublié.*'[17]

'No, it was precisely that, and what's more, you had nothing
to boast of in my presence, because it's all nonsense and nothing
but your own invention. Nowadays no one, no one any longer
gets excited about the Madonna or spends any time on it except
old men who are set in their ways. That's been proven.'

'Has it really been proven?'

'The Madonna serves absolutely no purpose. This jug is

useful because you can pour water into it. This pencil is useful because you can write everything down with it; but there's a female face that's uglier than all other faces in nature. Try to draw an apple and place it beside a real apple – which would you take? I dare say you wouldn't make a mistake. This is what all your theories amount to, now that the first light of free inquiry has illuminated them.'

'That's so, that's so.'

'You've got an ironic smirk on your face. And what, for instance, were you telling me about charity? And yet the gratification derived from giving charity is an arrogant and immoral gratification, the gratification a rich man takes in his riches, his power, and the comparison he makes between his importance and the importance of a poor man. Charity corrupts both the one who gives it and the one who receives it, and furthermore, it doesn't achieve its goal, because it only intensifies poverty. Lazy people who don't want to work throng around people who give, like gamblers around the gambling table, hoping to win. And meanwhile, the pitiful coins that are tossed their way are insufficient for even a hundredth of what they need. Have you given away much in your lifetime? Perhaps eighty kopecks, no more, if you stop and think about it. Just try to remember the last time you gave something; it would be a good two years ago, and perhaps four. You're just making a lot of noise and impeding the cause. In today's society charity should definitely be prohibited by law. In the new social order there will be no such thing as poor people.'

'Oh, what an eruption of borrowed words! So it's already come to a new order? God help you, you unfortunate woman!'

'Yes, it's come to that, Stepan Trofimovich. You've tried in vain to hide from me all the new ideas that are now already familiar to everyone, and you've done so solely out of jealousy, in order to have power over me. Now, even this woman Yuliya is a hundred versts ahead of me. But now even I have seen the light. I've tried to defend you, Stepan Trofimovich, as much as I could; you're the one that everyone is blaming.'

'Enough!' He started to get up from his chair. 'Enough! And what else shall I wish you, if not repentance?'

'Sit down for a minute, Stepan Trofimovich, I have something else to ask you. You were given an invitation to read something at the literary matinée; it was arranged through me. Tell me, what precisely will you read?'

'Why, precisely something about that queen of queens, that ideal of humankind, the Sistine Madonna, who, in your opinion, isn't worth a glass or a pencil.'

'So you're not taking anything from history, then?' Varvara Petrovna was sorrowfully surprised. 'But people won't listen to you. You have a bee in your bonnet about this Madonna! What's the point, if you're going to put everyone to sleep? Rest assured, Stepan Trofimovich, that I'm speaking solely in your interest. It would be a different matter if you took some very short but interesting little story from medieval court life, from Spanish history, or, even better, a single anecdote and amplified it with other anecdotes and witty remarks of your own. They had magnificent courts then, such ladies, such poisonings. Karmazinov says that it will be strange if you don't read something interesting from Spanish history.'

'Karmazinov, that fool who's written himself out, is looking for a topic for me!'

'Karmazinov, that almost statesman-like mind! You've too bold a tongue, Stepan Trofimovich.'

'Your Karmazinov is a written-out, embittered old woman! *Chère, chère*, since when have you been so enslaved by them, oh Lord!'

'Even now I can't bear him for the airs he puts on, but I do give him credit for his mind. I repeat, I tried as hard as I could to defend you, as far as I could. And why are you bound and determined to confirm that you're absurd and boring? On the contrary: step out on to the stage with a respectable smile, as a representative of the last generation, and tell them three anecdotes, with all your wit, as only you can sometimes tell them. Granted that you're an old man, granted that you're from an age now past, granted, finally, that you haven't kept up with them; but you yourself will admit all this with a smile in your introductory remarks, and everyone will see that you're a nice, kind, witty old relic . . . In a word, a man with a flavour of the old, and sufficiently advanced that he himself is capable of properly appreciating all the grotesqueness of certain ideas to which he has been subscribing up to now. Now, please do me this favour, I beg you.'

'*Chère*, enough! Don't ask me, I can't. I'll lecture on the Madonna, but I'll raise a storm the likes of which will either crush all of them or strike no one but me!'

'Probably just you, Stepan Trofimovich.'

'Such is my fate. I will talk about that lowly slave, that stinking and depraved lackey who will be the first to climb the ladder, scissors in hand, and slash the divine visage of the great ideal, in the name of equality, envy and . . . digestion. Let my curse thunder forth, and then, and then . . .'

'Off to the madhouse?'

'Perhaps. But in any event, whether I am vanquished or victorious, I'll take up my bag this very evening, my beggar's bag, leave all my belongings, all your gifts to me, all the allowances and promises of future blessings, and will set out on foot, to live out my days as a tutor at some merchant's house, or to die of hunger by some fence. I have spoken. *Alea jacta est!*'[18]

He started to get up again.

'I have been certain,' Varvara Petrovna stood up, her eyes flashing, 'certain for years now that the only thing you ultimately live for is to slander me and my house and bring disgrace on us! What do you mean by being a tutor for some merchant or by dying by a fence? Malice, slander, and nothing more!'

'You have always held me in contempt; but I will end my days as a knight who is true to his lady, for your opinion has always been dearer to me than anything else. From this moment on, I will take nothing, but will honour you disinterestedly.'

'That is really stupid!'

'You have always failed to respect me. I may have had more weaknesses than anyone can count. Yes, I did sponge off you; I am speaking the language of nihilism; but sponging was never the highest principle that guided my actions. It just happened, all by itself, I don't know how. I always thought there was something between us that was higher than sponging, and – never, never was I a scoundrel! And so, I'm on my way, to set things straight! A late journey, it's late autumn outside, mist lies over the fields, the frozen hoar frost of old age covers my future path, and the wind howls in anticipation of a grave in the near future. But on my way, on my way, on a new way:

> Filled with love so true,
> True to a delicious dream . . .[19]

Oh, farewell, my dreams! Twenty years! *Alea jacta est.*'

His face was spattered with a sudden rush of tears. He picked up his hat.

'I don't understand any Latin,' Varvara Petrovna said, trying as hard as she could to control herself.

Who knows, perhaps she, too, felt like weeping, but indignation and capriciousness once again won out.

'I know only one thing, namely, that this is all some childish prank. You have never been in any condition to make good on your threats, which are replete with egoism. You won't go anywhere, not to any merchant, but instead you'll end your days very calmly in my hands, receiving an allowance and bringing your awful friends together on Tuesdays. Goodbye, Stepan Trofimovich.'

'*Alea jacta est!*' He bowed deeply to her and returned home, more dead than alive with agitation.

CHAPTER 6

Pyotr Stepanovich All A-bustle

I.

The day of the gala had definitely been set, and von Lembke was becoming more and more morose and self-absorbed. He was full of strange and ominous forebodings, and this was enormously disturbing to Yuliya Mikhaylovna. True enough, not everything was going well. Our former easygoing governor had left the administration of the province in not altogether good shape; just then cholera was on the rise; in some areas serious outbreaks of cattle plague had appeared; fires raged all summer long in towns and villages, and stupid murmurings about arson were taking firmer hold among the common people. Robberies were twice as frequent as before. But all of this would have been perfectly ordinary, of course, if there hadn't been in addition weightier factors to disturb the peace of the hitherto happy Andrey Antonovich.

What struck Yuliya Mikhaylovna most of all was that with every passing day he was becoming more taciturn and, strangely enough, more secretive. After all, what reason was there for him to be secretive? True enough, he rarely contradicted her and for the most part was utterly obedient. At her insistence, for instance, two or three measures were introduced which were extremely risky and almost illegal, by way of strengthening the governor's powers. There were a few ominous cases where indulgence was shown with the same purpose in mind: for example, people who deserved to be put on trial and sent to Siberia were recommended for awards solely at her insistence. It was decided that certain complaints and inquiries were to be systematically ignored. All this came out subsequently. Von

Lembke not only put his signature to everything, but didn't even discuss the question of the extent to which his wife was involved in carrying out his duties. Yet at times he would suddenly begin to bridle at 'utter trifles' and would surprise Yuliya Mikhaylovna. Of course, after days of being obedient, he felt the need to reward himself with little moments of rebellion. Unfortunately, Yuliya Mikhaylovna, for all her perceptiveness, could not understand this noble nicety in his noble character. Alas! She had no time for that, and many misunderstandings occurred as a result.

It's inappropriate for me to talk about certain things, and what's more, I wouldn't know how. It's also not my business to expatiate on administrative mistakes, besides which I am keeping completely away from the whole administrative side of things. When I began this chronicle, I set other tasks for myself. In addition, much will be revealed by the commission that has just been appointed to investigate our province; we have only to wait a little. Nonetheless, it's still impossible to avoid certain explanations.

But let me continue with Yuliya Mikhaylovna. The poor lady (I'm very sorry for her) could have achieved everything she found so attractive and alluring (renown and all the rest) without any of the drastic and eccentric moves she set her mind to from the very first moment she was here. But whether from an excess of poetry in her soul, or whether from the long, sad failures of her early youth, she suddenly felt, as soon as her fortunes had changed, that she had somehow been specially called, almost anointed, as one 'over whom this tongue of fire had blazed',[1] and it was precisely this tongue that caused all the trouble: after all, it was not a chignon, which can fit any woman's head. But the hardest thing of all is to convince a woman of this truth; on the contrary, anyone who wants to say 'yes' to her will certainly succeed, and people were outdoing themselves to say 'yes' to her. The poor lady immediately became the plaything of all sorts of different kinds of influences, while at the same time imagining herself to be entirely original. Many masters of the game feathered their own nests at her expense and took advantage of her *naïveté* during the short period of her governorship. And the utter chaos that resulted in the guise of independence! She was partial to landownership on a large scale, and to the aristocratic element, and to strengthening the governor's powers, and to the democratic element, and to new institutions, and to order, and to freethinking, and to all sorts of notions about society, and to the austere tone of the aristocratic salon, and to the almost tavern-like casualness of the young people in her circle. She dreamed of *making people happy*, and of reconciling the irreconcilable, or rather, of uniting everyone and everything in the adoration of her own person. She did have her favourites: she especially liked Pyotr Stepanovich, who, incidentally, operated with the crudest sort of flattery. But she liked him for another reason as well, one which was most peculiar and yet portrayed the poor lady's character extremely well: she kept on hoping that he would indicate to her the existence of a real conspiracy against the state! However difficult it is to imagine, that really was the case. It seemed to her for some reason that a conspiracy against the state was definitely lurking in the province. By remaining silent in some cases and dropping hints in others, Pyotr Stepanovich helped this strange idea lodge itself firmly in her mind. And she imagined him to be connected with everything revolutionary in Russia, yet at the same time devoted to her to the point of adoration. The exposure of the conspiracy, the thanks from Petersburg, a career in the future, the influence of 'kindness' on the young people to keep them from falling into the abyss – all this coexisted in complete harmony in her fantastic head. After all, she was the one who had saved Pyotr Stepanovich, the one who had won him over (of this she didn't have the slightest doubt), and she would save others as well. None of them, not one of them would perish, she would save them all; she would sort them out; she would make reports on them accordingly; she would act in the interest of a higher justice, and perhaps history and all of Russian liberalism would even bless her name; and with all that, the conspiracy would be discovered. All the advantages at one stroke.

Still and all, it was necessary that Andrey Antonovich be in a somewhat brighter frame of mind, at least by the time of the gala. He absolutely had to be cheered up and calmed down. With this in mind, she dispatched Pyotr Stepanovich to him, in hopes that he might relieve his despondency with some soothing remedy known only to him. Perhaps even with some information straight from the horse's mouth, so to speak. She had complete faith in his ingenuity. Pyotr Stepanovich had not been in Mr von Lembke's study for a long time. He flew into see him at precisely the moment when the patient was in an especially tense state of mind.

2.

A certain combination of circumstances had come to pass which Mr von Lembke was absolutely unable to disentangle. In the district (the same one in which Pyotr Stepanovich had recently been roistering) a certain second lieutenant was subjected to a verbal reprimand by his immediate superior. This happened in front of the entire company. The second lieutenant was still a young man, recently from Petersburg, chronically taciturn and morose, with an air of importance, although at the same time small, fat and red-cheeked. He couldn't endure the reprimand, and suddenly, with an unexpected yelp that startled the entire company, he flung himself on his superior, his head lowered rather like a wild beast's. He struck his superior and bit him on the shoulder as hard as he could; he could be pulled off only by force. There was no doubt that he had lost his mind; at least, it came out that he had recently been observed doing the strangest and most outlandish things. For example, he threw two of his landlady's icons out of his apartment and chopped one of them up with an axe; in his own room he placed the works of Vogt, Moleschott and Büchner[2] on stands, made to look like three lecterns, and in front of each lectern he lit wax church candles. From the number of books that were found in his quarters it could be concluded that he was a well-read man. If he had had fifty thousand francs, he would perhaps have sailed off to the Marquesas Islands, like the 'cadet' who is mentioned with such good humour by Mr Herzen[3] in one of his works. When he was arrested, a whole bundle of the most desperate manifestos was found in his pockets and in his apartment.

The manifestos, taken by themselves, were of no significance, and, in my opinion, certainly no cause for alarm. We have seen plenty of them. Besides, these were not even new manifestos; exactly the same ones, as was later reported, had recently been distributed in Kh—sk Province, and Liputin, who six weeks earlier had made a trip to the district capital and the neighbouring province, asserted that even then he had seen exactly the same leaflets. But what struck Andrey Antonovich was mainly that at precisely the same time, the director of the Shpigulin factory had delivered to the police two or three bundles of leaflets that were identical to those found on the second lieutenant, which had been dropped at the factory at night. The bundles hadn't even been opened, and none of the workers had had a chance to read a single one. This incident in itself was rather stupid, but it plunged Andrey Antonovich into intense reflection. The whole business presented itself to him in an unpleasantly complicated light.

This Shpigulin factory had just then seen the beginnings of the so-called 'Shpigulin story' that caused such an outcry among us and had found its way into the Petersburg and Moscow newspapers with many variations. About three weeks earlier a worker had been taken ill and died there from Asian cholera; then several people had fallen sick. Everyone in town was terrified, because the cholera was moving in from the neighbouring province. I will note that satisfactory sanitary measures had been taken, as far as possible, to greet the uninvited guest. But somehow the factory of the Shpigulins, who were millionaires and people with connections, had been overlooked. And then everyone suddenly started clamouring that it was precisely there that the source and breeding-ground of the infection lurked, that in the factory itself and especially in the workers' barracks there was such an entrenched lack of cleanliness that if there had been no cholera epidemic at all, it would have started there on its own. Of course, measures were promptly taken, and Andrey Antonovich vigorously insisted on their immediate implementation. The factory was cleaned up in about three weeks, but for some reason the Shpigulins shut it down. One Shpigulin brother lived permanently in Petersburg, and the other left for Moscow after the authorities had given the order for the clean-up. The manager proceeded to pay off the workers, and, as it now turns out, swindled them shamelessly. The workers started grumbling, they wanted a fair settlement, and rather stupidly went to the police, but without any great outcry and without really becoming terribly upset. It was precisely at that particular time that the manifestos were delivered to Andrey Antonovich by the manager.

Pyotr Stepanovich flew into the study without being announced, as a good friend and one of the family, and on an errand from Yuliya Mikhaylovna besides. On seeing him, von Lembke gave a gloomy frown and paused by the table in an unwelcoming way. Until then he had been walking around his study and discussing something confidential with Blum, an official of his chancellery, an extremely clumsy and morose German, whom he had brought with him from Petersburg, despite very strong opposition from Yuliya Mikhaylovna. When Pyotr Stepanovich entered, the official stepped back towards the door, but didn't leave. It even seemed to Pyotr Stepanovich that he had somehow exchanged a significant glance with his superior.

'Aha, I've gone and caught you, you secretive master of the town!' Pyotr Stepanovich cried, laughing, and covered the manifesto that was lying on the table with the palm of his hand. 'This will add to your collection, eh?'

Andrey Antonovich flared up. His face suddenly seemed to twitch.

'Stop, stop right now!' he shouted, trembling with anger, 'and don't you dare, sir . . .'

'Why are you being like this? You seem angry.'

'Permit me to observe, my dear sir, that henceforth I have no intention of tolerating your *sans façon*,[4] and I ask you to remember . . .'

'Oof, damn it all; why, he really means it!'

'Be quiet, I tell you, be quiet!' Von Lembke began to stamp his feet on the carpet, 'and don't you dare . . .'

Lord knows what this would have come to. Alas, apart from
this, yet another circumstance was involved here, which was
completely unknown to Pyotr Stepanovich or even to Yuliya
Mikhaylovna herself. The unhappy Andrey Antonovich had
reached such a distraught state that in the past few days he had
secretly begun feeling jealous of his wife's relationship with
Pyotr Stepanovich. When he was alone, especially at night, he
experienced extremely unpleasant moments.

'And I thought that if a man reads his novel aloud to you
and you alone, for two days running, well past midnight, and
wants to have your opinion, then he has at least put aside
these official relations. Yuliya Mikhaylovna receives me on very
friendly terms; how in the world is a person to make you out?'
Pyotr Stepanovich stated, even with a certain dignity. 'Here's
your novel, by the way.' He lay on the table a large, heavy
notebook rolled into a tube and tightly wrapped in blue paper.

Von Lembke flushed and looked flustered.

'Wherever did you find it?' he asked cautiously, with a surge
of joy that he couldn't hold back, but tried nonetheless to as
hard as he could.

'Just imagine, since it was rolled up, it fell behind a chest of
drawers. I must have been careless enough to toss it on the
chest of drawers when I came in. It was found only the day
before yesterday when the floors were being washed. You really
gave me a good piece of work to do!'

Von Lembke dropped his eyes sternly.

'I didn't sleep for two nights in a row on account of your
kindness. It was found the day before yesterday, and I hung on
to it, reading and reading; there was no time during the day, so
I read it at night. Well, then – I'm not satisfied, it's not my view
of things. But still, who cares? I've never been a critic, but, I
must say, my friend, I couldn't tear myself away, even though
I was dissatisfied! The fourth and fifth chapters are . . . are . . .
are . . . the Devil knows what they are! And there's so much
humour crammed into it, that I just kept laughing. You really
do know how to make fun of things *sans que cela paraisse*![5]
But in the ninth and tenth chapters – well, that's all about
love, which isn't my thing; still, it's effective. I almost began

whimpering over Igrenyev's letter, although you did present him very subtly . . . It's very sensitive, you know, but at the same time you seem to want to present his false side, isn't that so? Have I guessed right or not? But I could just beat you up for the ending. Really, what are you trying to push? Really, this is nothing but the old-fashioned deification of family happiness, the multiplication of children and money, and everyone lives happily ever after, now I ask you! You charm the reader, because I couldn't tear myself away, but that's even worse, you see. The reader is as stupid as ever, it's incumbent on intelligent people to explain things to him, but you . . . Well, enough of that, goodbye. Next time don't be angry. I came to see you because I needed to have a word or two with you, but considering the sort of fellow you are . . .'

Meanwhile, Andrey Antonovich had taken his novel and locked it up in the oak bookcase, having managed to wink at Blum to make himself scarce. He vanished with a long and melancholy face.

'I'm not "the sort of fellow", I'm simply . . . it's all these unpleasant things,' he grumbled and scowled, but now without anger and drawing himself up to the table. 'Sit down and tell me your word or two. I haven't seen you for a long time, Pyotr Stepanovich, only in the future just don't come flying in here with that manner of yours . . . sometimes when I'm busy it's . . .'

'I only have one set of manners . . .'

'I know that, sir, and I believe that you didn't do it intentionally, but sometimes one is busy bustling about . . . Do sit down.'

Pyotr Stepanovich sprawled on the sofa and in a flash tucked his legs under him.

3.

'What's all this bustle about? Surely not about these trifles?' he nodded at the manifesto. 'I can bring you as many leaflets like this as you want, I've already made their acquaintance in Kh—sk Province.'

'You mean to say while you were living there?'

'Well, not in my absence, that stands to reason. There was one that was illustrated – an axe was drawn on top.[6] Allow me.' (He picked up the manifesto.) 'Why, yes, the axe is here too; the very same one, literally.'

'Yes, an axe. You see – it's an axe.'

'What, were you frightened by the axe?'

'It's not the axe that worries me . . . and I wasn't frightened . . . but the whole business . . . the whole business is such, there are circumstances here.'

'What circumstances? That the manifesto was brought from the factory? Hee, hee. But you know, the workers are soon going to start writing manifestos in that factory of yours.'

'What do you mean?' Von Lembke stared at him sternly.

'Just that. Go and take a look at them. You're too soft a man, Andrey Antonovich, you write novels. But here you should act in the old way.'

'What do you mean by the old way, what sort of advice is this? The factory has been cleaned up; I gave the order, and it was cleaned up.'

'But there's rebellion among the workers. Give every last one a good flogging, and there's an end to it.'

'Rebellion? That's nonsense; I gave the order, and it was cleaned up.'

'Oh, Andrey Antonovich, you're a soft man!'

'In the first place, I'm by no means so soft, and in the second place . . .' Von Lembke had been hurt to the quick again. He was speaking to the young man with effort, curious as to whether he would tell him anything new.

'Aha, another old friend!' Pyotr Stepanovich interrupted, taking aim at another piece of paper under a paperweight, which was also like a manifesto, and obviously printed abroad, but in verse. Well now, I know it by heart: "A Radiant Personality"! Let's see: yes indeed, "A Radiant Personality" it is. I've been acquainted with this personality ever since my time abroad. Where did you unearth it?'

'You say you saw it abroad?' Von Lembke said with a start.

'Very definitely! Four months ago, or even five.'

'I'd say you saw a great deal abroad,' von Lembke threw a

sharp look at him. Pyotr Stepanovich, without listening, unfolded the paper and read the verse aloud:

A RADIANT PERSONALITY[7]

> He was not of noble breed,
> The common people were his creed.
> Hunted down by vengeful tsars,
> By spite and envy from boyars,
> He gave himself to painful trials,
> To torments, wounds and torturer's wiles,
> Set forth to tell the news that people
> Should all be one, and free, and equal.
>
> Rebellion he stirred up betimes,
> And then he fled to foreign climes,
> Far from prison, knout and rope.
> The common people, full of hope,
> Were ready to throw off their lot,
> Harsh it was, and dearly bought,
> And so, from Smolensk to Tashkent[8]
> They waited for the young student.
>
> Waited for him, one and all,
> Waited for the battle call
> To settle up with the boyars,
> To put an end to all the tsars,
> To share all property, and wreak
> Vengeance on all of those who seek
> To keep up all the old world's crimes,
> Of marriage, church and family lines!

'They must have taken it from that officer, eh?' Pyotr Stepanovich asked.

'And do you also know that officer?'

'Of course. I spent two days carousing with him. He deserved to lose his mind.'

'Perhaps he really didn't lose his mind.'

'Because he started biting?'

'But tell me, if you saw these verses abroad, and then they turn up here, in this officer's possession . . .'

'What? That's rather intricate! I can see, Andrey Antonovich, that you're giving me an examination. You see, sir,' he suddenly began with uncharacteristic pomposity, 'what I saw abroad I already explained to someone upon my return, and my explanations were found to be satisfactory, otherwise I would not have gladdened this town with my presence. I consider that my business in this sense is concluded, and I'm not obliged to render an account to anyone. And it is concluded not because I am an informer, but because I could not act in any other manner. Those who wrote to Yuliya Mikhaylovna knew about the whole affair, and said that I was an honest man. Still and all, the hell with all that, I came to tell you something very serious, and it's a good thing that you sent your chimney-sweep away. It's a matter of great importance to me, Andrey Antonovich; I have an extraordinary request to make of you.'

'A request? Hmm. Please go on, I'm waiting, and with curiosity, I admit. And in general I will add that you rather surprise me, Pyotr Stepanovich.'

Von Lembke was rather agitated. Pyotr Stepanovich threw one leg over the other.

'In Petersburg,' he began, 'I was open about a great deal, but about some things, for instance, this,' (he tapped his finger against 'A Radiant Personality') 'I held my tongue, in the first place, because they weren't worth talking about, and in the second place, because I spoke out only about what I was asked. In this sense I don't like to get ahead of myself; here I see the difference between a scoundrel and an honest man who, purely and simply, has been caught up by circumstances. Well, in a word, that's neither here nor there. Well, then, sir, and now . . . now when these fools . . . well, when all this came to light and was already in your hands and, as I see, won't escape your notice – because you're a man with eyes in your head and no one can figure you out ahead of time, and meanwhile these idiots are still going on, I . . . I . . . well, yes, I, in a word, I have come to ask you to save a certain person, who is also an idiot, perhaps crazy, for the sake of his youth, his misfortunes, in the name of your humanity ... It's not just in novels of your own making that you're so humane!' He suddenly cut his speech short with impatience and crude sarcasm.

In a word, here was a straightforward individual, but awkward and impolitic, owing to an abundance of humane feelings and perhaps an excess of delicacy, and, mostly, an individual who was not very swift on the uptake, as von Lembke immediately judged him with extraordinary subtlety and as he had already long suspected, especially when, during the past week, alone in his study, he had rained silent curses on him for his inexplicable success with Yuliya Mikhaylovna.

'On whose behalf are you asking, and what does all this really mean?' he inquired grandly, while attempting to hide his curiosity.

'It's ... it's ... damnation! It's not my fault, you know, that I believe in you! Why is it my fault for regarding you as a highly honourable man, and, most importantly, a sensible man ... someone, that is, who's capable of understanding ... damnation!'

Evidently the poor fellow couldn't get hold of himself.

'You, of course, will understand,' he continued, 'you will understand that by giving you his name, I'm actually betraying him to you; I *am* betraying him, isn't that right? Isn't that right?'

'However, how can I possibly guess who it is if you can't make up your mind to speak out?'

'That's it in a nutshell, you always undercut me with that logic of yours, damnation! ... oh, damnation! ... this "radiant personality", this "student" – it's Shatov ... there you are!'

'Shatov? What do you mean it's Shatov?'

'Shatov, he's the "student", the one who's referred to here. He lives here. He's a former serf, and he's the one who delivered the slap.'

'I know, I know!' Von Lembke screwed up his eyes. 'But permit me, exactly what is he being accused of, and, most important, what is it that you are interceding for?'

'Why, I'm asking that he be saved, don't you understand? I

knew him eight years ago, you see, I am or perhaps was a good friend of his, you see.' Pyotr Stepanovich was beginning to lose his temper. 'Actually, I'm under no obligation to give you an account of my previous life.' He waved his hand dismissively. 'That's all of no importance; it's all a matter of three and a half men, and with those living abroad you won't even make a full dozen, but the main thing is that I am relying on your humanity, your intelligence. You will understand and will show the whole matter in its true light, and not as Lord knows what, as the stupid fantasy of a man driven crazy . . . by misfortunes, you see, by a long series of misfortunes, and not as a nonexistent conspiracy against the state, or some such thing!'

He was almost gasping for breath.

'Hmm. I can see that he's guilty of writing the manifestos that have an axe on them,' von Lembke concluded almost majestically. 'But permit me, if there was only one, then how could he distribute them here, and in the provinces, and even in Kh—sk Province, and . . . and, finally, and most importantly, where did he get them?'

'But I'm telling you that there are evidently no more than five men, well, let's say ten, how should I know?'

'You don't know?'

'Why, how should I know, the Devil take it!'

'Still, you did know that Shatov was one of the accomplices?'

'Ugh!' Pyotr Stepanovich waved his hand as if defending himself against the overwhelming perspicacity of his questioner. 'Well then, listen, I'll tell you the whole truth: I know nothing about the manifestos, that is, absolutely nothing, the Devil take it, do you understand what "nothing" means? . . . Well, of course, that second lieutenant, and someone else, and someone else here, and also perhaps Shatov, and someone else too, and that's all of them, the whole sad and sorry lot . . . but I've come to ask you on Shatov's behalf; he must be saved, because this poem is his, his own creation and it was printed abroad through him. That's what I know for sure, but about the manifestos I know absolutely nothing.'

'If the verses are his, then the manifestos probably are too. But what is the evidence that makes you suspect Mr Shatov?'

Pyotr Stepanovich, with the look of a man who has finally lost all patience, pulled a notebook from his pocket, and took a piece of paper out of it.

'Here's the evidence!' he shouted, tossing it on the table. Von Lembke unfolded it. It turned out that the note had been written about six months earlier, from here to some place abroad, and was very short, just a few words:

I cannot print 'A Radiant Personality' here, or in fact anything else. Print it abroad. *Ivan Shatov.*

Von Lembke fixed his eyes on Pyotr Stepanovich. Varvara Petrovna had been correct in remarking that he had the expression of a sheep, especially at certain times.

'You see, this is how it is,' Pyotr Stepanovich hurried on, 'it means that he wrote these verses here, six months ago, but couldn't print them here, in some secret printing shop, for instance, and so he asked for them to be printed abroad . . . Does that seem clear?'

'Yes, of course it's clear, but who was it that he was asking? That's still not clear,' von Lembke observed with very sly irony.

'Why Kirillov, of course, he's the one; the note was written abroad to Kirillov . . . Didn't you really know? Look, it's annoying that you're perhaps just pretending for my benefit and that you've known for ages about these verses and everything else! How, after all, did they turn up on your table? They managed to turn up there somehow! Why are you torturing me, then, if that's the case?'

He produced a handkerchief and mopped the sweat from his forehead with jerky movements.

'Maybe I do know something,' said von Lembke, deftly evasive, 'but who on earth is this Kirillov?'

'Why, he's an engineer who's just come here; he was Stavrogin's second, a maniac, a madman. Your second lieutenant may really just have the d.t.'s[9], but this one is completely mad – completely, I guarantee it. Oh, Andrey Antonovich, if the government knew what sort of people these were, all of them, why, it wouldn't raise a hand against them. They all ought to be locked up in the loony-bin, every last one. I saw more than enough of them in Switzerland and at congresses.'

'That's where the movement here is being directed from?'

'But who is there to direct it? Three and a half men. You know, when you look at them, all you feel is boredom. And what movement is there here? Manifestos, is that it? And just look at who's been recruited, a second lieutenant with the d.t.'s, and two or three students! You're an intelligent man, here's a question for you: why can't they recruit more important people, why is it always students and young oafs of twenty-two? And not even many of those. I'll bet there are a million dogs trying to track them down, but have they found many of them? Seven men. I tell you, all you feel is boredom.'

Von Lembke listened attentively, but with an expression that said: 'Actions speak louder than words.'

'Allow me, however, you stated that the note had been sent abroad, but there's no address here. How did you find out that the note was addressed to Mr Kirillov, and, ultimately, abroad, and ... and ... that it was actually written by Mr Shatov?'

'Well, get hold of a specimen of Shatov's handwriting now, and compare them. You must be able to find a signature of his in your office. And as for its being addressed to Kirillov, why Kirillov himself showed it to me at the time.'

'So you yourself were ...'

'Why yes, of course, I myself was there. They showed me a lot of things. And as for these verses, why supposedly the late Herzen wrote them to Shatov when he was still wandering around abroad, supposedly in memory of their meeting, by way of praise and recommendation, well, damnation ... and Shatov went and distributed them among the young people, as if to say: "This was Herzen's own opinion of me."'

'Well, well, well!' Von Lembke finally grasped the point fully. 'That's what had me baffled: the manifesto, that's understandable, but why the verses?'

'Why, how could you fail to understand it? And the Devil knows why I blabbed everything to you! Listen, give me Shatov, and the Devil take all the rest of them, even Kirillov, who's now shut himself up in Filippov's house, where Shatov is too, and is hiding. They don't like me because I came back . . . but promise me Shatov, and I'll hand them all to you on a platter. I'll be of use, Andrey Antonovich! I estimate this whole pitiful band to number about nine or ten. I'll personally keep track of them, on my own. We already know of three: Shatov, Kirillov and that second lieutenant. The others I'll just *keep an eye on* for the time being . . . I'm not so short-sighted, by the way. It's the way it was in Kh— Province. Two students were arrested there with manifestos, one secondary-school pupil, two twenty-year-old noblemen, one teacher and one retired major, about sixty, dull-witted from drinking; that's all there were, and please believe that's all. It was a real surprise to them that that was all there were. But I need six days. I've already figured it out: six days, no less. If you want results, then don't disturb them for six days, and I'll tie them all up in one bundle for you. But if you disturb them before then, they'll all fly the nest. But give me Shatov. I'm here for Shatov . . . And the best thing would be for you to call him secretly and amicably, here to your office, for instance, and give him a thorough examination, after showing him how things really are. Why, he'll probably throw himself at your feet and start to weep! He's a nervous, unhappy man; his wife is going around with Stavrogin. Be very nice to him, and he'll reveal everything to you on his own, but I need six days . . . But the important thing, the important thing – not a word to Yuliya Mikhaylovna. It's a secret. Can you keep a secret?'

'What?' Von Lembke's eyes were popping. 'Why, you really haven't revealed anything to Yuliya Mikhaylovna?'

'Eh? Why God bless and preserve me! Come now, Andrey Antonovich! Don't you see: I value her friendship too highly and have enormous respect for her . . . and all that sort of thing . . . so I wouldn't make that kind of mistake! I won't contradict her, because to contradict her, as you yourself know, is dangerous. I might have dropped a word or two to her, because she likes that, but that I should give her any names or anything else, as I'm doing with you now – Heaven forbid! Why do you think I'm turning to you now? Because you're a man, after all, a serious person, with long and solid experience as a servant of the state. You've been around. Each step in matters like this, I suspect, is utterly familiar to you from cases when you were still in Petersburg. But if I should tell her these two names, for instance, and if she should start gabbling away ... After all, she wants to make a splash in Petersburg from here. No, she's too hotheaded, she really is.'

'Yes, she does have a streak of fougue,'[10] Andrey Antonovich grumbled, not without pleasure, while at the same time regretting dreadfully that this ignoramus should seemingly have the nerve to speak rather freely about Yuliya Mikhaylovna. But to Pyotr Stepanovich it probably seemed that he hadn't gone far enough, and that he had to raise even more steam in order to flatter and finally conquer 'Lembka' completely.

'Yes, some fougue,' he agreed. 'Granting that she is perhaps a woman of genius, a literary woman, still, she would scare off our sparrows. She wouldn't hold out for six hours, let alone six days. Ah, Andrey Antonovich, don't impose a deadline of six days on a woman! You will admit that I have a certain amount of experience, at least in these matters. I do know something, after all, and you yourself know that I am in a position to know something. I'm not asking you for six days just for the fun of it, but in all seriousness.'

'I've heard,' von Lembke hesitated to express his thought, 'I've heard that when you returned from abroad, you made something like ... an acknowledgement of repentance in the proper quarters.'

'Well, be that as it may.'

'Well, naturally, I don't want to get into it ... but it has seemed to me all along that since you've been here you've been speaking in a completely different style, about Christian faith, for instance, about social institutions, and finally about the government ...'

'I've been saying a great many things. Even now I'm saying the same things, except these ideas shouldn't be carried out the way these fools propose, that's what it's all about. What's the point of biting someone on the shoulder? You yourself, after all, agreed with me, except you said that it was too early.'

'Actually, that's not what I was agreeing with you about or saying that it was too early.'

'Still and all, every word of yours is very carefully weighed, hee, hee! A cautious man!' Pyotr Stepanovich observed cheerfully all of a sudden. 'Listen, my very dear friend, I really had to get to know you, and that's why I spoke in that particular style of mine. That's how I got to know not only you, but many people. Maybe I had to find out what sort of character you have.'

'Why should my character concern you?'

'Well, how should I know why?' (He laughed again.) 'Don't you see, dear and highly respected Andrey Antonovich, you are cunning, but it hasn't yet come to *that*, and probably won't, do you understand? Perhaps you do understand? Although I did provide explanations in the proper quarters after I returned from abroad, and I really don't know why a man with certain convictions shouldn't be able to act in the interests of his sincere convictions ... still, no one *there* has yet ordered me to look into your character, and I've not yet taken on myself any such orders *from there*. Try to think of it this way: I could, after all, have divulged those two names not to you first, but run *there* straightaway, that is, to where I gave my initial explanations. And if I had tried to do that for money or to my own advantage, it would of course have been a miscalculation on my part, because now they will be grateful to you, and not to me. I'm doing it solely for Shatov,' Pyotr Stepanovich added in a noble tone, 'for Shatov alone, for the sake of our former friendship. Well then, perhaps when you take up your pen to notify them *there*, you will praise me, if you want ... I won't object, hee, hee! *Adieu*, however, I've sat here too long, and I shouldn't have carried on so much!' he added not without affability, and got up from the couch.

'On the contrary, I'm very glad that the whole business, so to speak, is being defined,' von Lembke also got up, and with an affable look as well, evidently brought on by the last words. 'I accept your services with gratitude, and you may rest assured that everything that can be done on my part as far as a reference concerning your zeal is concerned ...'

'Six days, that's the main thing, six days, and you shouldn't make a move during this time, that's what I need!'

'So be it.'

'Naturally, I'm not tying your hands, nor would I dare. You can't help but keep an eye on things, but just don't flutter the nest ahead of time; that's where I'm relying on your intelligence and experience. And you must have enough bloodhounds and all sorts of other sleuths of your own in reserve, hee, hee!' Pyotr Stepanovich blurted out cheerfully and thoughtlessly (being a young man).

'That's not quite the case,' von Lembke said pleasantly and evasively. 'Young people have the preconception that a great deal is being held in reserve. Incidentally, though, allow me one small word: if this Kirillov was Stavrogin's second, you see, in that case Mr Stavrogin . . .'

'What about Stavrogin?'

'In other words, if they're such great friends?'

'Oh, no, no, no! Here you're quite off the mark, although you're very clever. And you even surprise me. I'd been thinking, you see, that you weren't without some knowledge of this . . . Hmm, Stavrogin – it's just the opposite, that is, just . . . *Avis au lecteur*.'[11]

'Really! Is that actually possible?' von Lembke declared mistrustfully. 'Yuliya Mikhaylovna told me that according to information she'd received from Petersburg, he is a man with certain, shall we say, instructions . . .'

'I know nothing, I know nothing, nothing at all. *Adieu. Avis au lecteur!*' Pyotr Stepanovich said abruptly and with obvious evasiveness.

He began to fly towards the door.

'Just a moment, Pyotr Stepanovich, just a moment,' von Lembke exclaimed. 'Just one more tiny little piece of business, and I won't hold you.'

He took an envelope out of a drawer in the table.

'Here's just a tiny example in the same category, and I'm showing it to you because I have the utmost trust in you. Here it is. What's your opinion?'

The envelope contained a letter – a strange anonymous letter

that was addressed to von Lembke and had been received by
him only the day before. Pyotr Stepanovich, to his extreme
annoyance, read the following:

Your Excellency!

   For such you are according to rank. Herewith I declare that
an attempt will be made on the lives of personages who are
generals, and on the fatherland; for everything is leading up to
that. I myself have been tirelessly spreading them around for a
good many years. And also godlessness as well. A rebellion is
preparing, and several thousand manifestos, and a hundred men
will run after each one like bats out of hell, if they're not removed
ahead of time by the authorities, for a great deal is promised by
way of a reward, and the simple folk are stupid, and there's
vodka besides. The common people, considering them guilty, are
destroying this one and that, and, fearing both sides, I have
repented of everything in which I have taken no part, for such are
my circumstances. If you want a denunciation for the salvation of
the fatherland, and of churches and icons as well, then I alone
am able to provide that. But only on condition that there is an
immediate pardon by telegraph from the Third Department[12] for
me alone out of all of them, and let the others answer for it. At
seven o'clock every evening place a candle in the porter's window
as a signal. Having seen it, I will believe and will come to bestow
a kiss on the merciful hand from the capital, but on condition
that there is a pension, for how else will I live? And be not
regretful, because you will receive a star for it. One must move
very quietly, otherwise they will wring your neck.

             Your Excellency's desperate servant.
          Who falls at your feet,
                    The Repentant Freethinker Incognito.

Von Lembke explained that the letter had appeared in the
porter's room the day before, when nobody was there.
   'Well, what do you think?' Pyotr Stepanovich asked almost
rudely.
   'I would imagine it's an anonymous lampoon, by way of a gibe.'

'Most probably that's just what it is. There's no deceiving you.'

'Mainly because it's so stupid.'

'And have you received any other lampoons since you've been here?'

'On two occasions, anonymous ones.'

'Well, naturally, they wouldn't be signed. Is the style different? Different handwriting?'

'Different style and different handwriting.'

'And were they buffoonish, like this one?'

'Yes, they were buffoonish, and, you know ... very disgusting.'

'Well, if there were some before, then it's certainly the same thing now.'

'Mainly because it's so stupid. Because these people are educated and probably wouldn't write so stupidly.'

'Yes indeed, yes indeed.'

'And what if this is really a case of someone wanting to make a denunciation?'

'Unlikely,' Pyotr Stepanovich cut him off drily. 'What does he mean by a telegram from the Third Department and a pension? It's obviously a lampoon.'

'Yes, yes,' von Lembke said shamefacedly.

'You know what, why don't you leave it with me? I'll be sure to find out for you. I'll find out sooner than those people will.'

'Take it,' von Lembke agreed, although with a certain hesitation.

'Have you shown it to anyone?'

'No, no one, how could I?'

'Yuliya Mikhaylovna, for instance?'

'Oh, God help us, and for heaven's sake don't you show it to her!' von Lembke exclaimed in a fright. 'She'll be so shaken ... and she'll be dreadfully angry at me.'

'Yes, you'll be the first to get it in the neck; she'll say that you yourself deserved it if people are writing to you like that. We know women's logic. Well, goodbye. Perhaps I'll even present you with the author of this in three days or so. The main thing is our agreement!'

4.

Pyotr Stepanovich was perhaps not a stupid man, but Fedka the Convict got it just right when he said of him that 'he himself goes and invents a man and then lives with him'. He left von Lembke fully convinced that he'd calmed him down for at least six days, and this was the length of time that was absolutely necessary to him. But his idea was false, and was entirely and solely based on his having invented from the very outset an Andrey Antonovich, once and for all, who was a complete and utter simpleton.

As with every morbidly suspicious man, Andrey Antonovich was extremely and happily trustful the moment he emerged from the realm of the unknown. This new turn of events at first presented itself to him in a rather pleasant light, despite certain troublesome complications that were again beginning to appear. At least his old doubts were crumbling into dust. Besides, he had grown so tired over the past few days, he felt himself so exhausted and helpless that his soul could not help but yearn for peace. But alas! He already felt uneasy again. His long sojourn in Petersburg had left ineradicable traces in his soul. The official and even the secret history of the 'new generation' was familiar enough to him – he was a curious man, and a collector of manifestos – but he never understood the first word of this history. And now he seemed to be lost in the woods. Every instinct told him that there was something that simply didn't add up in what Pyotr Stepanovich had said, something beyond all norms and conventions – 'although the Devil only knows what can happen with this "new generation" and the Devil only knows what's going on with them!' he mused, losing himself in his thoughts.

At this point, as luck would have it, Blum again stuck his head into the study. Throughout Pyotr Stepanovich's visit he had been waiting nearby. This Blum was actually a relative of Andrey Antonovich, but a distant one, a fact he had carefully and timidly concealed his entire life. I beg the reader's pardon for devoting just a few words here to this insignificant figure. Blum belonged to the strange genus of 'unfortunate' Germans

– unfortunate certainly not for their utter lack of ability, but for reasons unknown. 'Unfortunate' Germans are not a myth; they actually exist, even in Russia, and form a type of their own. All his life Andrey Antonovich had nursed a deeply touching sympathy for him, and wherever he could, as he himself advanced in government service, would promote him to some small position that was subordinate to and dependent on him, but Blum had no luck anywhere. Sometimes the position was abolished, sometimes a new superior took over and once he was almost dragged into court along with some others. He was thorough, but somehow too much so, and to his detriment needlessly morose; tall, with red hair, stooped, despondent, even sensitive, and for all his submissiveness, stubborn and persistent as an ox, although always at the wrong time. Towards Andrey Antonovich he and his wife and their numerous children had nursed a reverential devotion of many years' standing. Except for Andrey Antonovich, no one had ever liked him. Yuliya Mikhaylovna immediately rejected him, but was unable to overcome her spouse's stubbornness. This was their first quarrel as a married couple, and it occurred immediately after the wedding, during the very first days of the honeymoon, when Blum, who until then had painstakingly been hidden away from her, along with the insulting secret that he was related to her, suddenly stood revealed before her. Andrey Antonovich begged her with clasped hands, and related to her with great emotion the whole story of Blum and of their friendship since earliest childhood, but Yuliya Mikhaylovna considered that she had been disgraced forever, and even resorted to a fainting fit. Von Lembke wouldn't yield an inch to her, and announced that he would not abandon Blum for anything in the world and would not remove him from his presence, so that finally, to her surprise, she was forced to permit Blum to stay. The only thing decided was that the relationship would be concealed even more scrupulously than before, if that were at all possible, and that Blum's first name and patronymic would even be changed, because for some reason he too was called Andrey Antonovich. Blum didn't get to know anyone in our town except for the German pharmacist, never paid visits to anyone and began to

live, as he always had, a miserly and isolated life. He had long
been aware of the literary peccadilloes of Andrey Antonovich.
He was summoned primarily to listen to his novel in secret
readings one on one, and would remain sitting for six hours on
end like a post. He would perspire and summon up all his
strength to avoid falling asleep or smiling. On arriving home,
he would groan, along with his long-legged, skinny wife, over
their benefactor's unfortunate weakness for Russian literature.

Andrey Antonovich cast a look of suffering at Blum as he
came in.

'I beg you, Blum, to leave me in peace,' he began in a nervous
patter, evidently wishing to avoid a renewal of their recent
conversation, which had been interrupted by the arrival of
Pyotr Stepanovich.

'Still and all, this can be arranged in a most delicate way,
completely without publicity. You do have full authority,' Blum
was respectfully but stubbornly insisting on something, stooping and moving closer and closer to Andrey Antonovich with
tiny steps.

'Blum, you are so devoted to me and so obliging that every
time I look at you I am beside myself with fear.'

'You're always saying sharp things and since what you've
said gives you pleasure you fall asleep peacefully, but by the
same token you are hurting yourself.'

'Blum, I've just concluded that it's completely wrong, completely wrong.'

'Isn't it because of what that false, depraved young man,
whom you yourself suspect, has been saying? He won you over
with his flattering praise of your literary talent.'

'Blum, you don't understand anything. Your plan is absurd,
I'm telling you. We won't find anything, and a terrible outcry
will be raised, then laughter, and then Yuliya Mikhaylovna . . .'

'We will undoubtedly find everything we are looking for,'
Blum stepped firmly towards him, placing his right hand on
his heart, 'we will make our inspection suddenly, early in the
morning, observing all the proprieties towards the individual
and all the strictures prescribed by the letter of the law. The

young men, Lyamshin and Telyatnikov, insist that we will find everything we wish. They have visited there many times. No one is favourably disposed towards Mr Verkhovensky. The general's widow, Stavrogina, has openly refused him her bene-factions, and every honest man, if such a person exists in this crude town, is convinced that a source of godlessness and social-ist teachings has always lain hidden there. All the forbidden books are kept there, Ryleyev's *Meditations*,[13] all the works of Herzen . . . Just in case, I have a rough catalogue . . .'

'Good heavens, everyone has these books. How simple you are, my poor Blum!'

'And many manifestos,' Blum moved on, without listening to these remarks. 'We will end by picking up the trail of the manifestos that are being distributed locally. This young Verkhovensky has always seemed very suspicious to me, very.'

'But you're confusing the father with the son. They're at odds; the son openly laughs at his father.'

'That's nothing but a mask.'

'Blum, you've sworn to torment me! Just think, he is after all an eminent person in these parts. He was a professor, he's a well-known man, he'll start screaming to high heaven and everyone in town will begin making fun of us – well, that's all we need. And just think what will happen with Yuliya Mikhaylovna!'

Blum carried on without listening.

'He was only a lecturer, nothing but a lecturer, and his rank was only that of a retired collegiate assessor,'[14] he struck his chest with his hand, 'he has no decorations, he was dismissed from the service on suspicion of plotting against the government. He was under secret surveillance and undoubtedly still is. And in view of the disorders which have now come to light, you are undoubtedly duty-bound. Yet you, on the contrary, are letting your chance for distinction slip away by showing indulgence to a genuine culprit.'

'Yuliya Mikhaylovna! Ge-e-et ou-ou-t, Blum!' von Lembke suddenly shouted, after detecting the voice of his spouse in the next room.

Blum trembled, but didn't yield.

'Allow me, please, allow me,' he importuned, his hands pressed even more tightly to his chest.

'Ge-e-et ou-ou-t!' Andrey Antonovich said through clenched teeth. 'Do as you wish . . . later . . . oh, good heavens!'

The portiere was raised and Yuliya Mikhaylovna appeared. She stopped majestically at the sight of Blum, cast a haughty and offended glance at him, as if the mere presence of this man was an insult to her. Blum made a silent and respectful bow to her and, stooping with respect, moved towards the door on tiptoe, his hands slightly spread.

Whether he actually understood Andrey Antonovich's last hysterical outburst as explicit permission to do what he was asking, or whether he had bent the truth in this case for the immediate good of his benefactor, utterly convinced that the end crowns the work – in any event, as we shall see later, this conversation between a superior and his subordinate gave rise to something totally unexpected, which made many people laugh, received publicity, stirred fierce anger in Yuliya Mikhaylovna, and in all these ways utterly disconcerted Andrey Antonovich, throwing him, at a most critical time, into a state of the most lamentable indecisiveness.

5.

For Pyotr Stepanovich the day turned out to be a busy one. From von Lembke's he quickly hurried to Bogoyavlenskaya Street, but as he was walking along Bykova Street, past the house where Karmazinov was staying, he suddenly halted, grinned and went into the house. 'You are expected, sir,' he was told, which interested him greatly, because he had given absolutely no advance notice of his arrival.

But the great writer actually was expecting him, even as early as the day before and the day before that. Three days earlier he had handed him the manuscript of 'Merci' (which he planned to read at the literary matinée on the day of Yuliya Mikhaylovna's gala), and did so as a kindness, utterly convinced that he would pleasantly flatter the young man's vanity by letting him get to know the great work ahead of time. Pyotr Stepanovich had long noted that this vain and spoiled man, who was insultingly inaccessible to the non-elect, this 'almost statesman-like mind' was, purely and simply, trying to ingratiate himself with him, and even eagerly so. It seems to me that the young man finally figured out that Karmazinov, if he didn't actually regard him as the ringleader of everything that was secretly revolutionary in Russia, at least saw him as one of the people who was most closely initiated into the secrets of the Russian revolution and had an unquestioned influence on young people. The state of mind of the 'cleverest man in Russia' interested Pyotr Stepanovich, but so far he, for certain reasons, had avoided getting into any discussions with him.

The great writer was staying in the house of his sister, a landowner and the wife of a court chamberlain. Both of them, husband and wife, revered their distinguished relative, but on the occasion of his present visit they were both in Moscow, to their great regret, so that the honour of receiving him fell on an old woman, a very distant and poor relation of the court chamberlain, who was living in the house and had long been in charge of all the housekeeping. With Mr Karmazinov's arrival, everyone in the house started walking around on tiptoe. The old woman reported to Moscow almost every day as to how he had slept and what he had had to eat, and once she sent a telegram with the news that after a dinner to which he had been invited at the mayor's, he had been compelled to take a spoonful of a certain medicine. She rarely took the liberty of entering his room, even though he treated her with courtesy, albeit drily, and spoke with her only when he required something. When Pyotr Stepanovich came in, he was eating his morning cutlet, with half a glass of red wine. Pyotr Stepanovich had already visited him before, and had always found him at this morning cutlet, which he proceeded to eat in his presence without once offering him anything. After the cutlet a small cup of coffee was also served. The servant who brought in the food was wearing a tail-coat, soft noiseless shoes and gloves.

'Ah!' Karmazinov rose from the sofa, wiping his lips with a napkin, and with a look of the purest joy sauntered over to

exchange kisses, a characteristic habit of Russians, if they are
very eminent. But Pyotr Stepanovich remembered, from previous experience, that even though Karmazinov was the one
who sauntered up to exchange kisses, he merely offered his
own cheek,[15] and so Pyotr Stepanovich did the same on this
occasion; both of their cheeks met. Karmazinov, showing no
sign of having noticed it, sat back down on the sofa and pleasantly pointed Pyotr Stepanovich to an armchair opposite him,
in which the latter proceeded to sprawl.

'I suppose you haven't . . . You wouldn't like some lunch?'
his host asked, breaking his habit on this occasion, but of
course with an air that clearly suggested a polite refusal. Pyotr
Stepanovich immediately expressed a desire to have lunch. A
shadow of offended surprise darkened the face of the host, but
only for an instant; he nervously rang for the servant, and
despite all his breeding, raised his voice querulously as he gave
orders for another lunch to be served.

'What would you like, a cutlet or some coffee?' he inquired
again.

'A cutlet, and some coffee, and have him bring some wine as
well. I'm dreadfully hungry,' Pyotr Stepanovich replied, examining the host's attire calmly and attentively. Mr Karmazinov
was wearing a short, quilted jerkin, a sort of jacket, with little
mother-of-pearl buttons, but it was much too short and was
therefore anything but becoming to his plump little belly and
his firmly rounded thighs. But tastes do vary. Spread over his
knees, and reaching down to the floor was a checked woollen
plaid, even though it was warm in the room.

'Are you ill, then?'

'No, I'm not ill, but I'm afraid of coming down with something in this climate,' the writer replied in his penetrating voice,
while tenderly declaiming each word in a pleasant, gentlemanly
lisp. 'I've been waiting for you since yesterday.'

'But why? I didn't promise, after all.'

'Yes, but you have my manuscript. Have you . . . read it?'

'Manuscript? Which one?'

Karmazinov was dreadfully surprised.

'But haven't you brought it with you?' He suddenly became

so alarmed that he even stopped eating and looked at Pyotr Stepanovich with frightened eyes.

'Ah, you're talking about "Bonjour", I suppose . . .'

'"Merci".'

'Well, whatever. I completely forgot and didn't read it. I had no time. Perhaps it's in my pocket, I don't know . . . it must be on my table. Don't worry, it'll turn up.'

'No, I'd better send someone to your place right now. It might get lost, or worse, it might be stolen.'

'Well, who needs it! Why, what are you so afraid of? After all, Yuliya Mikhaylovna said that you always have several copies of your things made;[16] one is kept abroad at a notary's, another in Petersburg, a third in Moscow, and then you send one to a bank, don't you?'

'Well, you know, Moscow could burn down, and with it, my manuscript. No, I'd better send someone now.'

'Wait, here it is!' Pyotr Stepanovich extracted a bundle of notepaper from his back pocket. 'It got a little crumpled. Just imagine, ever since I took it from you it's been lying all the time in my back pocket, along with my handkerchief. I forgot.'

Karmazinov eagerly seized the manuscript, looked it over carefully, counted the pages, and for the time being laid it lovingly on a special small table beside him, but in such a way that he could keep an eye on it at every moment.

'You apparently don't read very much?' he hissed, unable to restrain himself.

'No, not very much.'

'And nothing in the way of Russian literature?'

'In the way of Russian literature? Wait, I did read something about a journey . . . *Wayfaring*, or *On the Way*, or *At the Crossways*,[17] or whatever, I don't remember. I read it a long time ago, it must be about five years. I don't have the time.'

An interval of silence followed.

'As soon as I arrived, I assured all of them that you are an extremely intelligent person, and now it seems that everyone here has lost their head over you.'

'I thank you,' Pyotr Stepanovich responded calmly.

Lunch was brought in. Pyotr Stepanovich attacked the cutlet

with extraordinary appetite, consumed it in a flash, drank off the wine and gulped down the coffee.

'This ignoramus,' Karmazinov was surveying him pensively out of the corner of his eye, as he finished the last little piece and drank the last little drop, 'this ignoramus probably felt at once the bite in what I just said . . . and furthermore he did of course read the manuscript, eagerly, and is only lying for show. But it might very well be that he isn't lying, but really is genuinely stupid. I like a man of genius to be somewhat stupid. Perhaps he actually is some sort of genius among them? The Devil take him, though.'

He got up from the sofa and began pacing the floor from one corner of the room to the other, for the sake of exercise, which he always took after lunch.

'Are you leaving here soon?' Pyotr Stepanovich asked from his armchair, lighting a cigarette.

'Actually, I came here to sell my estate and I'm now dependent on my steward.'

'Didn't you really come here because you expected an epidemic to break out there after the war?'

'N-no, not quite for that reason,' Mr Karmazinov continued, good-humouredly declaiming his sentences and jauntily jerking his right foot every time he turned to walk back to the other corner – barely noticeably, however. 'I really do intend,' he grinned not without venom, 'to live as long as possible. There's something in the Russian gentry that wears out extremely rapidly in every respect. But I want to wear out as late as possible, and now I'm moving abroad for good. The climate there is better, and the buildings are made of stone, and everything is sturdier. Europe will last my lifetime, I think. What do you think?'

'How should I know?'

'Hmm. If Babylon really does collapse[18] there, and its fall is great (in which I fully agree with you, although I think that it will last my lifetime), then here in Russia there is nothing to collapse, comparatively speaking. What will fall here is not stones; rather, everything will dissolve into mud. The last thing in the world that Holy Rus is capable of doing is offering resistance to anything. The simple people are still somehow sustained by the Russian God; but the Russian God, according to the latest information, is extremely unreliable and scarcely even held out against the peasant reform, or at least he was severely shaken. And with the railways here, and you here . . . I don't believe in the Russian God in the least.'

'And in the European God?'

'I don't believe in any of them. I've been slandered to the young people of Russia. I have always sympathized with each of their causes. I have been shown the manifestos that are circulating here. People look at them in bewilderment, because everyone is frightened by their form, but everyone nonetheless is convinced of their power, even if they don't admit it to themselves. Everyone has been falling for a long time, and everyone has known for a long time that there is nothing to grab on to. I'm already convinced of the success of this mysterious propaganda, because Russia is now pre-eminently the one place in the whole world where anything you want can happen without the slightest resistance. I understand only too well why Russians with means have all made tracks abroad, and why with every passing year more and more of them dash off abroad. It's simply instinct. If the ship is about to sink, the rats are the first to desert it. Holy Russia is a country made of wood, poverty-stricken and . . . dangerous, the country of vainglorious paupers at its highest levels, and where the vast majority live in wretched little huts on hens' legs.[19] She will be overjoyed at any way out; you only have to explain it to her. Only the government still wants to resist, but it brandishes its cudgel in the darkness and hits its own people. Here everything is doomed and condemned. Russia as it is has no future. I've become a German and I regard that as an honour.'

'But you began by talking about manifestos. Tell me everything – what's your opinion of them?'

'Everyone's afraid of them, therefore they're powerful. They openly expose deceit and prove that we have nothing to grab on to, and nothing to lean on. They speak loudly, while everyone else remains silent. What's most successful about them (despite their form) is the boldness with which they stare truth straight in the face, which has been unheard-of until now. Only one Russian generation commands this ability to look truth straight in the face. No, they're not yet so bold in Europe; there it's a kingdom of stone, there's still something to lean on. As far as I can see and as far as I can judge, the whole essence of the Russian revolutionary idea is contained in the denial of honour. I'm pleased that this is so boldly and fearlessly expressed. No, in Europe they can't yet understand this, but here in Russia this is precisely what they will seize upon. For a Russian, honour is only an unnecessary burden. What's more, it has always been a burden, for his entire history. He can be carried away by an open "right to dishonour"[20] sooner than anything else. I'm of the old generation, and I still stand for honour, I admit it, but it's really only out of habit. The only reason I like the old forms is, let's say, out of faint-heartedness; one really must finish out one's days somehow.'

He suddenly stopped.

'But I'm talking and talking,' he thought, 'while he's saying nothing and watching me. He's come so that I can ask him a direct question. And so I'll ask it.'

'Yuliya Mikhaylovna has asked me to try to find out from you, by some subterfuge, just what surprise you are preparing for the ball the day after tomorrow,' Pyotr Stepanovich suddenly stated.

'Yes, it really will be a surprise, and I'll really astonish them,' Karmazinov said grandly, 'but I won't tell you what the secret is.'

Pyotr Stepanovich didn't press.

'There's a certain Shatov here?' the great writer inquired. 'And just imagine – I haven't seen him.'

'A very nice fellow. What of it?'

'Nothing, really, he's going around saying this and that. Isn't he the one who struck Stavrogin in the face?'

'The same.'

'And what do you think of Stavrogin?'

'I don't know; he's some sort of ladies' man.'

Karmazinov had conceived a hatred of Stavrogin, because the latter had formed the habit of not noticing him at all.

'This ladies' man,' he said, giggling, 'will probably be the first to be strung up on a branch if what's being preached in those manifestos ever comes to pass.'

'Maybe even earlier,' Pyotr Stepanovich suddenly said.

'That's as it should be,' Karmazinov agreed, no longer laughing and in too serious a manner somehow.

'You did say that once before and, you know, I told him about it.'

'What, you really told him?' Karmazinov began to laugh again.

'He said that if he were to be strung up, then it would be enough to flog you, only not as a point of honour, but painfully, the way a muzhik is flogged.'

Pyotr Stepanovich took his cap and got up from his chair. By way of saying goodbye, Karmazinov held out both his hands to him.

'And what,' he suddenly chirped in his mellifluous voice with its peculiar intonation, while continuing to hold Pyotr Stepanovich's hands in his, 'what if everything you are plotting were all set to happen . . . when might that be?'

'How should I know?' Pyotr Stepanovich replied rather rudely. Both were staring each other in the face.

'Roughly? Approximately?' Karmazinov chirped even more sweetly.

'You'll have time to sell your estate and you'll also have time to clear out of here,' Pyotr Stepanovich mumbled even more rudely. They stared even more intently at one another.

A minute of silence passed.

'It will begin in the first few days of May, and everything will be over by the Feast of the Protection,'[21] Pyotr Stepanovich said suddenly.

'I sincerely thank you,' Karmazinov said in a voice filled with emotion, as he pressed his hands.

'You'll have time, you rat, to desert the sinking ship!' Pyotr Stepanovich thought as he walked out on to the street. 'Well, if this "almost statesman-like mind" is inquiring so confidently about the day and the hour and then thanks me so respectfully for the information he's received, we can't have any doubts about ourselves after that.' (He grinned.) 'Hmm. And he's really not stupid and . . . is nothing more than an emigrating rat. Someone like that will never inform on us!'

He dashed off to Bogoyavlenskaya Street, to Filippov's house.

6.

Pyotr Stepanovich first went to Kirillov's. As usual, Kirillov was alone and this time was doing gymnastics in the middle of his room, that is, with his legs spread apart he was twisting his arms above his head in some peculiar way. On the floor lay a ball. On the table his morning tea, now cold, hadn't been cleared away. Pyotr Stepanovich stood for about a minute in the doorway.

'You really take good care of your health, I see,' he said loudly and cheerfully as he entered the room. 'What a splendid ball, look how it bounces. Is it also for your gymnastics?'

Kirillov put on his jacket.

'Yes, also for my health,' he muttered drily. 'Sit down.'

'I've only come for a minute. But I will sit down. Health is all well and good, but I've come to remind you about our agreement. Our time, "in a certain sense", is approaching, sir,' he concluded with an awkward flourish.

'What agreement?'

'What do you mean, "what agreement"?' Pyotr Stepanovich took alarm, even became frightened.

'It's not an agreement and not an obligation, I didn't bind myself in any way; that's a mistake on your part.'

'Listen here, what *are* you doing?' Pyotr Stepanovich now jumped up.

'My own will.'

'And that is?'

'The same as before.'

'But how is that to be understood? Does it mean that you're of the same mind as before?'

'It does. Except there's no agreement and never was, and I didn't bind myself in any way. There was only my own free will, and now there's only my own free will.'

Kirillov's explanation was curt and scornful.

'I agree, I agree, it's your free will, as long as that will hasn't changed.' Pyotr Stepanovich sat down again with a satisfied expression. 'You're getting angry over words. You've somehow become very angry of late; that's why I've avoided visiting you. However, I was quite sure that you wouldn't betray us.'

'I dislike you very much. But you can be quite sure. Although I don't acknowledge betrayal and non-betrayal.'

'However, you know,' Pyotr Stepanovich again took alarm, 'we should have some straight talk so as not to go wrong. The matter requires preciseness, and you're disconcerting me dreadfully. Will you permit me to speak?'

'Speak,' Kirillov snapped, looking into the corner.

'You long ago decided to take your own life . . . that is, you had the idea of doing so. Have I expressed myself correctly, then? There's no mistake?'

'I still have the same idea now.'

'Excellent. And note, moreover, that no one has forced you into this.'

'Of course. How stupidly you talk.'

'All right, granted, I expressed myself very stupidly. It would undoubtedly have been very stupid to try to force you into it. Let me continue: you were a member of the Society under the old organization, and at that time you opened yourself up to one of the members of the Society.'

'I didn't open myself up, I just told him.'

'All right. And it would have been absurd to "open oneself up" to such a thing; what kind of confession would that be? You simply told him, and that's excellent.'

'No, it's not excellent, because you're rambling so. I'm not obliged to give you any accounting, and you can't understand my ideas. I want to take my life because that's my idea, because I don't want to be afraid of death, because . . . because it's none of your business . . . What would you like? Do you want tea? It's cold. Let me bring you another glass.'

Pyotr Stepanovich in fact had grabbed the teapot and was looking for an empty glass. Kirillov went to the cupboard and brought back a clean glass.

'I've just had lunch at Karmazinov's,' his guest observed, 'then I broke out in a sweat listening to him talk, and ran straight here. I've broken out in a sweat again, and I really need something to drink.'

'Drink. Cold tea is good.'

Kirillov again sat down on his chair and again fixed his eyes on the corner.

'In the Society there was the thought,' he continued in the same tone of voice, 'that I could be useful if I killed myself, and that when you cook something up here and they start looking for the culprits, then I'll suddenly shoot myself and leave a letter saying that I did it all, and so it'll be a whole year before they can suspect you of anything.'

'At least a few days; even one day is precious.'

'Good. In this sense they told me I should wait a while, if I wanted. I told them I would wait, until the word comes from the Society as to the time, because it's all the same to me.'

'Yes, but remember you pledged yourself that when you came to write the suicide letter, you wouldn't do so except together with me, and that after you'd arrived in Russia, you would be at my . . . well, in short, at my disposal, that is, in just this one instance, naturally, and in all others you would of course be free,' Pyotr Stepanovich added almost affably.

'I didn't obligate myself, but I did agree because it's all the same to me.'

'And that's excellent, excellent, I have no intention of trying to dampen your spirit of pride, but . . .'

'There's no question of pride here.'

'But remember that a hundred and twenty thalers[22] were collected for your trip, so you've taken money.'

'Not at all,' Kirillov flared up. 'The money wasn't on that condition. People don't take money for that.'

'Sometimes they do.'

'You're lying. I declared in a letter from Petersburg, and in Petersburg I paid you a hundred and twenty thalers, directly to you . . . and they were sent from there, provided you didn't keep them for yourself.'

'All right, all right, I'm not arguing about anything, they

were sent off. The main thing is that you're of the same mind as before.'

'The same. When you come and say, "It's time", then I'll do everything. So, is it to be very soon?'

'Not very many days . . . But remember, we will compose the letter together, that same night.'

'It can be during the day for all I care. You said I have to take responsibility for the manifestos?'

'And for something else.'

'I won't take everything on myself.'

'What is it you're not going to take on?' Pyotr Stepanovich was again alarmed.

'Whatever I don't want to. That's enough. I don't want to talk about it any more.'

Pyotr Stepanovich controlled himself and changed the subject.

'I have something else,' he advised. 'Will you be with us this evening? It's Virginsky's name-day, and we're using that as a pretext to get together.'

'I don't want to.'

'Please do me the favour of being there. It's necessary. It's necessary to impress them with numbers and with a face . . . You have a face . . . well, in short, you have a fateful face.'

'Do you find it so?' Kirillov laughed. 'All right, I'll come, but not for my face. When?'

'Oh, on the early side, half-past six. And you know, you can go in, sit down and not speak with anyone, no matter how many people are there. Only, you know, don't forget to take paper and pencil with you.'

'What for?'

'It's all the same to you, isn't it? This is my special request. All you'll do is sit, talking with absolutely no one, listening and making what look like notes from time to time, even drawing something if you like.'

'What nonsense, what for?'

'Well, since it's all the same to you . . . you do keep saying, after all, that everything's the same to you.'

'No, what for?'

'Here's what for. One member of the Society, a government inspector, has got stuck in Moscow, and I've told someone in the group that a government inspector will perhaps be coming to visit, and they'll think it's you who are the government inspector, and since you've already been here three weeks, they'll be even more surprised.'

'Hocus-pocus. You don't have any government inspector in Moscow.'

'Well, granted that I don't, the Devil take it! What business is it of yours, and why is it a problem for you? You yourself are a member of the Society.'

'Tell them that I'm the government inspector; I will sit and keep quiet, but I don't want any paper or pencil.'

'But why?'

'I don't want them.'

Pyotr Stepanovich got very angry; he even turned green, but again he controlled himself, stood up and took his hat.

'Is *he* with you?' he suddenly asked in a half-whisper.

'He is.'

That's good. I'll soon take him away, don't worry.'

'I'm not worried. He only spends the night. The old woman is in the hospital, her daughter-in-law died; I've been all by myself for two days. I showed him the place in the fence where a board can be removed. He slips through, no one will see him.'

'I'll take him away soon.'

'He says he has many places to spend the night.'

'He's lying, they're looking for him, but here he won't be noticed for the time being. Do you actually talk about things with him?'

'Yes, all night long. He abuses you a lot. At night I've been reading him the Apocalypse and giving him tea. He's been listening closely, very closely, in fact, all night long.'

'Damn it all, why you'll convert him to the Christian faith!'

'He already is of the Christian faith. Don't worry, he'll do the murder. Who do you want to have murdered?'

'No, that's not why he's here, it's for something else . . . And does Shatov know about Fedka?'

'I don't talk to Shatov at all, and I don't see him.'

'Is he angry, or what?'

'No, we're not angry, we just avoid each other. We spent too long a time lying side by side in America.'

'I'll drop in and see him in just a minute.'

'As you wish.'

'Maybe Stavrogin and I will drop in on you from there as well, around nine o'clock.'

'Do come.'

'He and I have to have a talk about something important . . . You know what, let me have your ball; why do you need it now? I'll also use it for gymnastics. Perhaps I'll pay you for it.'

'Just take it.'

Pyotr Stepanovich put the ball in his back pocket.

'And I won't give you anything against Stavrogin,' Kirillov muttered after him, as he saw his visitor out. Pyotr Stepanovich looked at him in surprise, but made no reply.

Kirillov's final words proved highly disconcerting to Pyotr Stepanovich. He hadn't yet had time to take them in, but while still on the stairway to Shatov's, he made an effort to recast his dissatisfied look so that he would present an amiable face. Shatov was at home, and somewhat under the weather. He was lying on his bed, but fully dressed.

'There's a bit of bad luck!' Pyotr Stepanovich exclaimed from the doorway. 'Are you seriously ill?'

The amiable look on his face suddenly disappeared; something malicious flashed in his eyes.

'Not at all,' Shatov jumped up nervously, 'I'm not in the least ill; it's just a headache . . .'

He was quite flustered. The sudden appearance of such a visitor positively frightened him.

'I've come specifically about a matter where you can't be sick,' Pyotr Stepanovich began rapidly and authoritatively, as it were. 'Allow me to sit down,' he sat down, 'and you go and sit on your cot again. That's it. Today, under the pretext of Virginsky's birthday, some of our people are getting together at his place. There's no other meaning to it, however; measures have been taken against that. I am coming with Nikolay Stavrogin. Of course I wouldn't drag you there, knowing your current way of thinking . . . that is, in the sense of not wanting to torment you there, and not because we think that you would inform on us. But as things have turned out, you'll have to come. There you'll meet the very people with whom we will reach a final decision as to how you are to leave the Society and to whom you are to hand over what you have. We'll do it inconspicuously: I'll take you off somewhere into a corner; there will be a lot of people, and not everyone has to know. I admit I've really had to keep my tongue wagging on account of you; but now they also seem to be in agreement, provided, of course, that you turn over the printing press and all the papers. Then you're free to go wherever you please.'

Shatov heard him out, frowning and angry. His recent nervous fear had left him completely.

'I don't recognize any obligation to give an accounting to the Devil knows who,' he said point-blank. 'No one can set me free.'

'Not quite. A great deal was entrusted to you. You had no right to make a clean break. And finally, you never made a clear statement about it, and so you put them in an ambiguous position.'

'As soon as I got here, I stated it clearly in a letter.'

'No, it wasn't clear,' Pyotr Stepanovich calmly begged to differ. 'For instance, I sent you "A Radiant Personality" to be printed here, and copies to be kept somewhere here with you until they were called for, and two manifestos as well. You came back with an ambiguous letter that explained nothing.'

'I refused outright to print it.'

'Yes, but not outright. You said, "I can't", but you didn't explain the reason why. "I can't" doesn't mean "I don't want to." It might have been thought that you weren't able to simply for material reasons. That certainly is how they took it here, and they thought that you were still agreeable to continuing your connection with the Society, and that they could therefore entrust something to you again, and so they have compromised themselves. Now they're saying that you simply wanted to deceive them, so that once you'd received some important piece of news you could inform on them. I defended you as hard as I could, and showed them your two-line written reply as a document in your favour. But I myself must admit that on reading it over again now, those two little lines are unclear and deceptive.'

'And you've been so careful as to keep that letter?'

'Not only have I kept it; I have it with me now.'

'Well, what does it matter, damn it all!' Shatov cried in a frenzy. 'Let your idiot friends think I've informed on them, what do I care! I'd like to see what you can do to me.'

'You'd be a marked man, and hanged the minute the revolution was successful.'

'That's when you seize supreme power and subdue Russia?'

'No need to laugh. I repeat that I tried to vindicate you. One way or another, I nonetheless advise you to put in an appearance today. What good are a lot of idle words for the sake of some kind of false pride? Isn't it better to part amicably? In any case, you know, you'll have to turn over the press and the type and the old papers; that's what we'll have a chat about.'

'I'll come,' Shatov grumbled, hanging his head in thought. From his chair Pyotr Stepanovich studied him out of the corner of his eye.

'Will Stavrogin be there?' Shatov suddenly asked, raising his head.

'He'll definitely be there.'

'Hee, hee!'

Again they said nothing for about a minute. Shatov was smirking contemptuously and irritably.

'And this vile "Radiant Personality" of yours, which I didn't want to print here, has it been printed?'

'It has.'

'To try to make the high-school students think that Herzen himself wrote it in your album?'

'Herzen himself.'

Again they remained silent for some three minutes. Finally, Shatov got up off the bed.

'Get out of my room! I don't want to sit here together with you.'

'I'm going,' Pyotr Stepanovich said, even rather cheerfully, standing up immediately. 'Just one word: is Kirillov all by himself now in his little house, without a servant?'

'All by himself. Get out, I can't stay in the same room with you.'

'Well, you're a fine one now!' Pyotr Stepanovich cheerfully weighed matters as he went out into the street. 'And you'll be a fine one this evening too, and that's just how I need you to be now, and nothing better could be desired, nothing better could be desired! The Russian God himself is helping me!'

7.

He had most likely been very busy that day on various errands, and probably successfully so, which was reflected in the self-satisfied expression on his face when that evening, at exactly six o'clock, he appeared at Nikolay Vsevolodovich's. But he was not admitted right away: Mavriky Nikolayevich had just locked himself in the study with Nikolay Vsevolodovich. This news troubled him for a moment. He took a seat right by the door to the study, in order to wait for the visitor to emerge. A conversation could be heard, but it was impossible to catch the words. The visit didn't last long; soon a noise was heard, then the boom of an extremely loud and sharp voice, after which the door opened and Mavriky Nikolayevich came out, his face deathly pale. He didn't notice Pyotr Stepanovich and quickly walked past him. Pyotr Stepanovich immediately rushed into the study.

I can't pass over a detailed account of this extremely brief meeting of the two 'rivals' – a meeting that was seemingly impossible given the way circumstances had developed, but which took place nonetheless.

This is how it happened. Nikolay Vsevolodovich was dozing on the couch in his study after dinner, when Aleksey Yegorovich reported the arrival of an unexpected visitor. On hearing the name that was announced, he jumped straight up and simply couldn't believe it. But then a smile quickly brightened his lips – a smile of haughty triumph and, at the same time, blank, incredulous astonishment. As Mavriky Nikolayevich came in, he seemed struck by the look of this smile; at least, he suddenly stopped in the middle of the room, as if hesitating whether to proceed further or turn back. The host immediately contrived to change his facial expression and with a look of serious bewilderment, stepped forward to greet him. Mavriky Nikolayevich didn't take the proffered hand, awkwardly pulled up a chair and, without saying a word, sat down even before his host, without waiting for an invitation. Nikolay Vsevolodovich sat himself sideways on the couch, and looking intently at Mavriky Nikolayevich, said nothing and waited.

'If you can, marry Lizaveta Nikolayevna,' Mavriky Nikolayevich said, suddenly making him a present of her, and what was most curious, it was absolutely impossible to tell what this was from the intonation of his voice: a request, a recommendation, a concession or an order.

Nikolay Vsevolodovich maintained his silence; but his visitor had evidently now said everything he had come for, and sat staring as he awaited an answer.

'If I'm not mistaken (however, it's all but certain), Lizaveta Nikolayevna is already engaged to you,' Stavrogin finally said.

'Betrothed and engaged,' Mavriky Nikolayevich confirmed resolutely and clearly.

'You ... have quarrelled? ... Excuse me, Mavriky Nikolayevich.'

'No, she "loves and respects" me – her words. Her words are more precious than anything.'

'There's no doubt about that.'

'But you should know that if she were to be standing at the very altar under the crown, and you were to call her, she would abandon me and everyone else, and go to you.'

'From under the crown?'

'And after the ceremony.'

'Aren't you mistaken?'

'No. From under her relentless hatred of you, which is sincere and absolute, shines love at every moment and ... madness ... the most sincere and boundless love, and – madness! Conversely, from under the love she feels for me, also sincerely, there shines hatred at every moment – the greatest hatred! Until now I could never have imagined all these "metamorphoses".'

'But I'm really surprised, how can you come here and dispose

of Lizaveta Nikolayevna's hand? Do you have the right to do
that? Or did she authorize you to do so?'

Mavriky Nikolayevich frowned and dropped his head for a
moment.

'These are nothing but words on your part, you know,' he
said suddenly, 'vengeful and triumphant words. I'm sure you
understand what's been said between the lines, and is there
really any place for petty vanity here? Isn't this enough satisfaction for you? Is there really any need to spell things out, to dot
the i's? If you like, I'll supply the dots, if you find my humiliation
so necessary. I have no right; no authorization is possible.
Lizaveta Nikolayevna knows nothing about any of this, and
her fiancé has completely lost his mind and is fit for the insane
asylum, and to top it all off, he's the one who's coming to
report all this to you. You're the only one in the whole world
who can make her happy, and I'm the only one who can make
her unhappy. You're contending for her, you're pursuing her,
but, I don't know why, you won't marry her. If it was a lovers'
quarrel that occurred abroad, and if you can put an end to it
by sacrificing me, then do so. She's extremely unhappy, and I
can't bear that. My words don't constitute permission or a
prescription, and therefore there's no insult to your self-esteem.
If you had wanted to take my place at the altar, you could have
done so without any permission from me, and then there would
of course have been no reason for me to come to you with this
madness. Especially since our marriage is absolutely impossible
after the step I've just taken. After all, I can't very well lead her
to the altar when I've been such a scoundrel, can I? What I'm
doing here, and the fact that I'm handing her over to you, who
are perhaps her deadliest enemy, is, in my view, utterly vile and
of course I shall never be able to bear it.'

'Will you shoot yourself while we're getting married?'

'No, much later. Why soil her wedding gown with my blood?
Maybe I won't shoot myself at all, neither now, nor later.'

'In saying that, you probably want to set my mind at rest?'

'You? What can one extra splatter of blood mean to you?'

He turned pale, and his eyes began to flash. A moment of
silence followed.

'Forgive me for the questions I've been asking you,' Stavrogin began again. 'Some of them I had no right to put to you, but to one of them, it seems, I have full rights: tell me, what information made you reach the conclusion you did about my feelings for Lizaveta Nikolayevna? I mean the intensity of these feelings that made you certain enough to come to me and . . . risk such a proposal.'

'What?' Mavriky Nikolayevich even shuddered slightly. 'Haven't you really been trying to get her? Aren't you trying to get her, and don't you want to get her?'

'In general, I can't speak aloud about my feelings for this or any other woman to another party, whoever it might be, except the woman herself. Excuse me, such is the peculiarity of this particular organism. But in exchange I'll tell you the rest of the truth in its entirety: I am married, and it's no longer possible for me to get married or "try to get" someone.'

Mavriky Nikolayevich was so astonished that he recoiled against the back of the chair and looked fixedly at Stavrogin's face for some time.

'Just imagine, I never thought of that,' he mumbled, 'you said then, that morning, that you weren't married . . . I simply believed that you weren't married.'

He was dreadfully pale. Suddenly he banged his fist full force on the table.

'If after admitting such a thing you don't leave Lizaveta Nikolayevna alone, and if you make her unhappy, then I'll beat you to death with a stick, like a dog in a ditch!'

He jumped up and quickly walked out of the room. As Pyotr Stepanovich ran in, he found his host in a most unexpected frame of mind.

'Ah, it's you!' Stavrogin began laughing loudly. He seemed to be laughing merely at the figure of Pyotr Stepanovich, who had run in with such impulsive curiosity.

'Were you listening at the door? Wait, what is it you've come for? I think I did promise you something . . . Ah, yes, I have it! I remember: about going to "our" people. Let's be off, I'm very glad, and you couldn't have thought up anything more appropriate just now.'

He snatched up his cap, and both went out of the house without further ado.

'You're laughing in anticipation of seeing "our" people?' Pyotr Stepanovich was merrily weaving about him, now trying to walk in step with his companion on the narrow brick pavement, now even running into the street, straight into the mud, because his companion was completely oblivious of the fact that he was walking in the very centre of the pavement and was therefore taking all of it up himself.

'I'm not laughing at all,' Stavrogin replied loudly and cheerfully. 'On the contrary, I'm convinced that you have the most serious sort of people there.'

' "Gloomy dunderheads",[23] as you once were pleased to express it.'

'There's nothing merrier than some gloomy dunderhead.'

'Ah, you're talking about Mavriky Nikolayevich! I'm convinced that he came by just now to let you have his fiancée, right? I'm the one who egged him on indirectly, just imagine. But if he won't let you have her, then we'll be the ones to take her away from him, eh?'

Of course, Pyotr Stepanovich knew that he was taking a risk by indulging in such antics, but whenever he was excited, he preferred to risk everything if need be, rather than remain in ignorance. Nikolay Vsevolodovich merely burst out laughing.

'And are you still reckoning on helping me?' he asked.

'If you call on me. But you know what, there's one way that's best.'

'I know your way.'

'Why no, that's a secret for the time being. Just remember that a secret costs money.'

'I know just how much it costs,' Stavrogin grumbled under his breath, but restrained himself and said nothing.

'How much? What did you say?' Pyotr Stepanovich gave a start.

'I said the Devil with you and your secret! Instead, tell me who's going to be there? I know we're going to a name-day party, but who exactly will be there?'

'Oh, a little of this, a little of that, in the highest degree! Even Kirillov will be there.'

'All are members of circles?'

'The Devil take it, what a hurry you're in! Not one circle has been formed here as yet.'

'How did you manage to distribute so many manifestos?'

'Where we're going, there's a total of four members in the circle. The rest are just waiting and are spying on each other as hard as they can, and bring me the results. A reliable bunch of people. All this is raw material that needs to be organized and then we clear out. However, you're the one who wrote the rules, so there's nothing to explain to you.'

'Well then, is it hard going? Any snags?'

'Hard going? Easy as easy can be. Here's something to make you laugh: the first thing that has a tremendous effect is a uniform. There's nothing more powerful than a uniform. I make a point of dreaming up ranks and offices: I have secretaries, secret agents, treasurers, chairmen, registrars, their colleagues – it's a lot of fun and it has really caught on. After that, the second most powerful force is, of course, sentimentality. You know, socialism in Russia is spreading primarily out of sentimentality. But the trouble is all these second lieutenants who go around biting people; every once in a while you run across them. Then come the out-and-out crooks. Well, maybe they're a good bunch of people, sometimes very useful, but a lot of time is spent on them, they require constant watching. Well then, finally there's the most important force, the cement that binds everything: the shame of their own opinion. Now there's a force for you! And who was it that worked so hard, who was this "sweetie-pie"[24] who toiled away so diligently that no one else has a single idea of his own left in his head! They would consider that shameful.'

'But if that's so, then why are you bustling about?'

'But if a fellow's just lying around, gaping open-mouthed at everyone, then why not scoop him up? Don't you really seriously believe that success is possible? Ah, there may be faith, but there has to be desire. Yes, it's precisely with folks like him

that success is possible. I tell you that he'll follow me into the
fire, all you have to do is shout at him that he's not liberal
enough. The fools reproach me for having duped all of them
here with the central committee and "numerous branches".
You yourself once threw this in my teeth, but what sort of
duping is this? The central committee is me and you, and there
will be as many branches as you like.'

'And they're all such a bunch of riff-raff!'

'Raw material. Even they will come in handy.'

'And you're still counting on me?'

'You're the boss, you're a force: I'll merely be at your side,
your secretary. You know, we'll seat ourselves in a barque,
with little oars of maple, silk sails, a beautiful maiden, the fair
Lizaveta Nikolayevna sitting in the stern[25] . . . or how does it
go, damn it, in that song of theirs . . .'

'Got stuck!' Stavrogin began to laugh. 'No, I'd better tell you
the introduction to the tale. Here you are, counting on your
fingers the forces that go to make up circles? All that's just
bureaucracy and sentimentality – all that's good glue, but
there's something that's even better: put four members of a
circle up to bumping off a fifth, on the pretext that he's going
to inform, and the blood that's been spilled will immediately
bind them together in a single knot. They will become your
slaves, they won't dare to rebel or ask for an accounting. Ha,
ha, ha!'

'However, you . . . however, you will have to pay for those
words,' Pyotr Stepanovich thought, 'and as early as this
evening. You allow yourself far too much.'

This is how Pyotr Stepanovich's thoughts must have run, or
something like it. Meanwhile, they were already approaching
Virginsky's house.

'Of course, you've already presented me there as a member
from abroad, connected with the Internationale, as an inspector?' Stavrogin suddenly asked.

'No, not an inspector; you won't be the one who's the inspector. But you are a founding member from abroad, who
knows highly important secrets – that's your role. Of course
you will speak, won't you?'

'Where did you get that idea?'

'You're obliged to speak now.'

Stavrogin stopped in surprise in the middle of the street not far from a lamp-post. Pyotr Stepanovich held his stare arrogantly and calmly. Stavrogin spat and began to walk on.

'And are you going to speak?' he suddenly asked Pyotr Stepanovich.

'No, I'm just going to listen to you.'

'The Devil take you! You're actually giving me an idea!'

'What idea?' Pyotr Stepanovich cried.

'Maybe I'll have a word to say in there, but to make up for it, I'll give you a beating later, and you know, it'll be a proper beating.'

'Incidentally, I told Karmazinov about you earlier, that you said he should be flogged, and not merely for honour's sake, but the way peasants are flogged, painfully.'

'Why, I never said any such thing, ha, ha!'

'That's all right. *Se non è vero* . . .'[26]

'Well thanks, I thank you in all sincerity.'

'You know what Karmazinov also says: that in essence our teaching is a denial of honour and that the easiest way to attract a Russian to us is by openly advocating his right to dishonour.'

'Marvellous words! Golden words!' Stavrogin exclaimed. 'Bull's eye! The right to dishonour – why, everyone will come running to us, there won't be a single one remaining outside! Now listen, Verkhovensky, you're not from the secret police?'

'Why, anyone who even thinks of asking such questions certainly doesn't ask them out loud.'

'I understand, but we're by ourselves.'

'No, so far I'm not from the secret police. Enough, here we are. Put on an appropriate face, Stavrogin. I always do that when I go in to see them. As gloomy as possible, and just that; nothing more is needed. It's a very simple thing.'

CHAPTER 7

Among Our Own

I.

Virginsky lived in his own house, that is, in his wife's house, in Muravinaya Street. It was a wooden one-storey house, and there weren't any lodgers. Under the pretext of the host's birthday, some fifteen guests had gathered; but the party that evening bore absolutely no resemblance to the usual provincial name-day party. From the moment they began their life together, the Virginskys had agreed, once and for all, that it was utterly stupid to invite guests for name-days, and besides, 'there was absolutely nothing to be glad about'. Over a period of several years they had somehow managed to withdraw completely from society. He, although a man with abilities and by no means 'a poor fellow', struck everyone for some reason as an eccentric who liked solitude and, besides that, talked 'in a haughty manner'. As for Madame Virginskaya, she pursued the profession of midwife, and by virtue of that alone stood below everyone else on the social ladder, even lower than the priest's wife, despite the officer's rank held by her husband. But there was not the slightest sign in her of the humility that was appropriate to her calling. And after her utterly stupid and unpardonably open liaison, out of principle, with a certain swindler, Captain Lebyadkin, even the most tolerant of our ladies turned away from her with marked disdain. But Madame Virginskaya took it all as if that was just what she wanted. It was remarkable that these very same stern ladies, if they were in an interesting condition, would turn, if possible, to Arina Prokhorovna (that is, to Virginskaya), ignoring the three other midwives in our town. She was sent for even by the wives of landowners in our district, so great was people's faith in her knowledge, her luck and her skill in critical cases. As a result, she began to practise exclusively in the richest houses; for she had an insatiable love of money. Fully aware of her power, she ultimately made no attempt to restrain her character. When she was in attendance in the grandest houses, she would, perhaps even deliberately, frighten weak-nerved mothers-to-be with some outrageously nihilistic disregard of the proprieties or, even worse, by ridiculing 'all that was holy', and precisely at those moments when the 'holy' might have been the most useful. Our army doctor, Rozanov, who also delivered babies, asserted most emphatically that on one occasion, while a woman in labour was howling and calling out the name of God Almighty, it was actually one of Arina Prokhorovna's freethinking remarks that suddenly, 'like a gunshot', so frightened the patient that it helped free her very quickly from the burden she was carrying. But although she was a nihilist, Arina Prokhorovna, when necessity dictated it, most certainly did not disdain social conventions or even the most ancient prejudices and customs, if they could be of use to her. For instance, nothing in the world would keep her from attending the christening of a baby she had swaddled; and moreover, she would appear in a green silk dress with a train, and would comb her chignon into curls and ringlets, whereas at all other times she would positively revel in her untidiness. And although during the celebration of the sacrament she would always maintain 'a most insolent air', which embarrassed the officiating clergy, after the completion of the rite she was the one who would unfailingly bring out the champagne herself (which is precisely why she appeared and got dressed up), and woe betide anyone who took a glass trying to get away without giving her something by way of a 'tip'.

The guests who had gathered at Virginsky's on this occasion (almost all men) had a kind of casual and urgent look about them. There were no *zakuski* and no cards. In the middle of the large sitting room, which was covered in an excellent old light-blue wallpaper, two tables had been moved together and covered with a large tablecloth, which was not entirely clean, however, and on them two samovars were boiling away. The end of the table was taken up by an enormous tray with twenty-five glasses and a basket with ordinary white French bread cut into a great many chunks, just as in boarding schools for the sons and daughters of the gentry. Tea was being poured by an old maid of thirty, the hostess's sister, browless and flaxen-haired, a taciturn and venomous creature, who, however, shared the latest views, and of whom Virginsky himself was dreadfully afraid in his domestic life. There were altogether three ladies in the room: the hostess, her browless sister and Virginsky's own sister, a maiden lady who had just arrived from Petersburg. Arina Prokhorovna, a striking lady of about twenty-seven, not at all bad-looking, though somewhat dishevelled, wearing an every-day greenish woollen dress, was sitting and taking in the guests with bold eyes, as though in a hurry to say: 'You see, I'm not afraid of anything.' The newly arrived Virginskaya, who was not bad-looking either, a student and a nihilist, rather plump and as round and compact as a little ball, rather short and with very red cheeks, had stationed herself next to Arina Prokhorovna, still almost in her travelling clothes, and was holding a sheaf of papers[1] in her hand and surveying the guests with impatient dancing eyes. Virginsky himself was rather unwell this evening, but he did come out to sit for a while in an armchair at the tea-table. All the guests were also sitting, and this orderly distri-bution of people in chairs around the table created the impres-sion that a meeting was about to take place. Evidently all were waiting for something, and in anticipation were carrying on loud but seemingly irrelevant conversations. When Stavrogin and Verkhovensky appeared, everyone suddenly fell quiet.

But I will allow myself to explain a few things by way of clarification.

I think that all these ladies and gentlemen had really gathered on that occasion in the pleasant hope of hearing something especially curious, and that they had gathered forewarned. They represented the flower of the brightest red liberalism in our ancient town, and had been very carefully chosen by Virginsky for this 'meeting'. I will also note that some of them (very few, however) had never visited him before now. Of course, the majority of the guests had no clear notion of why they had been forewarned. True, all of them on this occasion took Pyotr Stepanovich for an emissary from abroad who had plenipotentiary powers; this idea had immediately taken root somehow and was naturally very flattering. Meanwhile, in this assembled band of citizens, under the guise of a name-day celebration, there were some to whom definite proposals had already been made. Pyotr Stepanovich had succeeded in fashioning a 'group of five' along the lines of the one that had already been established by him in Moscow, and already, as it now turned out, among some army officers in our district. I am told that he also had one in Kh—sk Province as well. This group of five chosen ones was sitting at the common table and had very skilfully succeeded in giving itself the appearance of very ordinary people, so much so that no one could recognize them. They were – inasmuch as this is not a secret now – first of all Liputin, then Virginsky himself, the long-eared Shigalyov (Mrs Virginskaya's brother), Lyamshin and finally, a certain Tolkachenko – a strange individual, a man who was already about forty and was famous for his enormous knowledge of the common people, mainly crooks and thieves, who made a point of frequenting pot-houses (not, however, just to study the people), and who, in our circle, flaunted his bad clothes, his tarred boots, his squinty and cunning eyes, and the folk expressions that he delivered with a flourish. Once or twice before, Lyamshin had brought him to soirées at Stepan Trofimovich's, where, however, he produced no particular impression. He would appear in town from time to time, mainly when he had no job, and he used to work on the railways. Every one of these five operatives formed the first group in the fervent belief that it was merely a unit that linked hundreds and thousands of similar groups of five, just like theirs, scattered throughout Russia, and that everything depended on some huge but secret central organization that, in turn, was organically linked with the universal European revolution. But to my regret, I must admit that even at that time there were signs of discord among them. The thing was that although they had been waiting ever since spring for Pyotr Stepanovich's arrival, which had been announced to them first by Tolkachenko and then by Shigalyov, who had

just come to town, and although they expected extraordinary
miracles from him, and although all of them had immediately
entered the circle, without the slightest criticism and at his very
first summons, still, no sooner had they formed the group
of five than all of them seemed immediately to take offence,
precisely, I suppose, because they had agreed so quickly. They
had joined, of course, out of a high-minded sense of shame, so
that people couldn't say later that they didn't dare join; still
and all, Pyotr Verkhovensky should have appreciated their
noble deed and at least rewarded them by telling them some
really important piece of news. But Verkhovensky had absolutely no desire to satisfy their legitimate curiosity and never
told them anything they didn't need to know. In general, he
treated them with remarkable severity and even offhandedness.
This proved distinctly irritating, and Member Shigalyov was
already egging the others on to 'demand an accounting', but of
course not on this occasion at Virginsky's, where so many
outsiders had gathered.

With regard to the outsiders, I also have an idea that the
members of the first group of five enumerated above were
inclined to suspect the presence among Virginsky's guests that
evening of members of some other groups unknown to them
that had also been established in the town, along the same
secret organizational lines and by the very same Verkhovensky;
the result being that in the final analysis, all those assembled
suspected one another, and struck various poses before one
another, which gave the entire gathering a very confused and
even partly romantic look. However, there were people here
who were certainly above all suspicion. Such, for instance, was
a certain major on active service, a close relative of Virginsky's,
a completely innocent man to whom they hadn't extended an
invitation, but who showed up on his own to greet the name-
day celebrant, so there was no way he couldn't be received. But
the name-day celebrant was nonetheless unperturbed, inasmuch
as 'there was no way the major could inform on them', because,
for all his stupidity, all his life he had enjoyed scampering about
all the places where radical liberals abounded. He himself was
not sympathetic, but he was very fond of listening to them. In

addition, he had even been compromised. It so happened that in his youth whole reams of manifestos and of the *Bell* had passed through his hands, and even though he was afraid even to open them, he would have considered it absolutely dastardly to refuse to distribute them – and that's the way some Russian people are to this very day. The remaining guests represented two types: noble pride that had been crushed to the point of bitterness, or the first and noblest impulse of ardent youth. There were two or three teachers present, one of whom was a lame man of about forty-five, an instructor in a secondary school, a very venomous and conspicuously vain man, and two or three army officers. Of the latter, one was a very young artillery man, who only a few days earlier had come to town from a military academy, a taciturn boy who hadn't yet managed to make any friends, and who now suddenly turned up at Virginsky's, pencil in hand, and although taking practically no part in the conversation, was constantly writing something down in his notebook.[2] Everyone saw it, but for some reason everyone tried to pretend that they didn't notice. There was also a do-nothing seminarian, who had joined Lyamshin in slipping pornographic photographs into the book-pedlar's bag, a sturdy lad with an easygoing yet at the same time mistrustful manner, an accusing smile pasted on his face, yet with a calm look of the triumphant conviction that he embodied perfection. Also present, I don't know why, was our mayor's son, that same nasty boy, dissolute beyond his years, whom I've already mentioned while I was telling the story of the second lieutenant's little wife. He said nothing the entire evening. And finally, in conclusion, a certain high-school student, an extremely hot-tempered and dishevelled boy of about eighteen, who was sitting with the sullen look of a young man whose dignity had been offended and who evidently was suffering for his eighteen years. This scrap of a lad was already the leader of an independent group of conspirators that had been formed in the school's senior class, a fact that subsequently came to light, to the astonishment of all. I haven't mentioned Shatov: he had installed himself right there at a far corner of the table, after moving his chair slightly out of the row, looked at the floor,

maintained a sullen silence, refused tea and bread, and never
let go of his cap, as if wishing in this way to announce that he
wasn't a guest but had come on business, and when he felt like
it, would get up and leave. Kirillov had taken his place not far
from him, and was also very quiet, but wasn't looking at the
floor; on the contrary, he was fixing his steady, lustreless eyes on
everyone who was speaking and listening closely to everything
without the slightest emotion or surprise. Some of the guests
who had never seen him before were surveying him thoughtfully
and stealthily. I can't say whether Madame Virginskaya knew
anything about the existence of the group of five. I suppose she
knew everything, and most probably from her husband. As for
the girl student, she of course took no part in anything, but she
had her own concerns: she was intending to spend only a day
or two visiting, and then move on farther and farther afield, to
all the university towns, in order to 'participate in the sufferings
of the poor students and incite them to protest'. She was carrying with her several hundred copies of a lithographed appeal,
which she had apparently composed herself. Remarkably, the
high-school student conceived an almost murderous hatred for
her at first glance, although this was the first time in his life he
had ever seen her, and she felt the same way about him. The
major was an uncle of hers and that day was the first time he
had seen her in ten years. When Stavrogin and Verkhovensky
came in, her cheeks were as red as cranberries: she had just had
a fierce quarrel with her uncle over his views on the woman
question.

2.

Verkhovensky sprawled with remarkable nonchalance on a
chair at the upper end of the table, having exchanged greetings
with almost no one. He had a scornful and even arrogant look
about him. Stavrogin bowed politely, but despite the fact that
everyone had been waiting only for them, everyone, as if on
command, acted as though they took virtually no notice of
them. The hostess turned sternly to Stavrogin as soon as he had
taken his seat.

'Stavrogin, do you want tea?'

'Give me some,' he replied.

'Tea for Stavrogin,' she ordered the girl who was doing the pouring, 'and do you want some?' (This was now addressed to Verkhovensky.)

'Some tea, of course, who asks guests about such a thing? And give me some cream as well. You always give people such vile stuff instead of tea, and with a name-day party in the house too.'

'What's that, you recognize name-days?' the girl student suddenly began to laugh. 'We were just talking about that.'

'Old stuff,' the high-school student grumbled from the other end of the table.

'What's old stuff about it? It's not old stuff to try to forget old prejudices, however innocent they may be, but on the contrary, to everyone's shame, it's still new to this day,' the girl student declared in a flash. 'Besides, there are no innocent prejudices,' she added fiercely.

'I merely wanted to assert,' said the high-school student in a dreadful state of agitation, 'that prejudices, of course, are old hat and certainly should be eliminated, but name-days, on the other hand, are something that everyone knows to be stupid and too old to waste valuable time on, which has already been wasted by the whole world as it is, so one might make use of one's wits for some topic that's more in need of . . .'

'You're dragging it out, I can't understand a thing,' the girl student shouted.

'It seems to me that everyone has the same right to speak out as anyone else, and if I wish to express my opinion, like anyone else, then . . .'

'No one is taking away your right to speak out,' the hostess herself now broke in sharply, 'you are only being asked not to drone on, because no one can understand you.'

'Permit me to observe, however, that you do not respect me. If I couldn't even finish a thought, it's not because I have no thoughts, but rather because I have too many thoughts,' the high-school student grumbled almost in despair and finally became completely tongue-tied.

'If you don't know how to speak, then keep quiet,' snapped the girl student.

The high-school student jumped up from his chair.

'I merely wanted to state,' he shouted, burning with shame and afraid to look around, 'that you only felt like showing off your cleverness because Mr Stavrogin came in – that's what!'

'You have a dirty and immoral mind, and it shows you're in a primitive stage of development. I ask you to have nothing further to do with me,' the girl student shrilled.

'Stavrogin,' the hostess began, 'just before you came in people here were carrying on about the rights of the family – this officer, for instance.' (She nodded at her relative, the major.) 'And of course I won't trouble you with ancient rubbish that was settled long ago. Still and all, where could the rights and obligations of the family have come from, in the sense of the prejudicial form in which they now exist? That's the question. What's your opinion?'

'What do you mean where could they have come from?' Stavrogin repeated.

'That is to say, we know that the prejudice about God came from thunder and lightning,' the girl student suddenly broke in again, her eyes almost dancing over Stavrogin. 'It's very well known that primitive man, being frightened by thunder and lightning, deified the unseen enemy, aware of how powerless he was before them. But where did the prejudice about the family arise? Where could the family itself have come from?'

'That's not quite the same thing . . .' the hostess tried to stop her.

'I suppose that the answer to such a question is immodest,' replied Stavrogin.

'What's that you say?' The girl student lunged forward.

But giggling was heard in the teachers' group, which was immediately echoed from the other end by Lyamshin and the high-school student, and after them by her relative the major with his hoarse laugh.

'You should write vaudevilles,' the hostess remarked to Stavrogin.

'It doesn't speak well for your honour, whatever your name is,' snapped the girl student in decided indignation.

'Don't you be so uppity!' the major ejaculated. 'You're a young lady, you ought to behave modestly, but it's as if you're sitting on a needle.'

'Kindly be quiet and don't dare address me in such a familiar manner with your nasty comparisons. This is the first time I've ever seen you, and I don't want to know about your relationship to me.'

'But after all, I *am* your uncle; I used to carry you around in my arms when you were still just a baby.'

'What do I care whether you carried me around or not? I didn't ask you to carry me around then, and so that must mean, Mr Impolite Officer, that you derived pleasure from it. And permit me to observe, don't you dare address me in a familiar manner unless it's as a fellow citizen. I forbid you to do so once and for all.'

'That's the way they all are!' The major banged his fist on the table, turning to Stavrogin, who was sitting opposite. 'No, sir, pardon me, but I love liberalism and the modern world and I love to listen to intelligent conversation, but, I warn you – only from men. From women, though, from these flibbertigibbets of today – no, sir, they give me a pain! You, stop fidgeting!' he shouted at the girl student, who was shifting about in her chair. 'No, I also demand to speak; I've been insulted.'

'You're just preventing others from speaking, but you your-self have nothing to say,' the hostess grumbled indignantly.

'No, I'm going to have my say,' said the major heatedly, turning to Stavrogin. I am counting on you, Mr Stavrogin, as someone who has just arrived, although I don't have the honour of knowing you. Without men they would die like flies – that's my opinion. This whole woman's question of theirs is nothing but a lack of originality. And I can assure you that this whole woman's question has been invented for them by men, out of sheer foolishness, and it's a stone around their necks. I just thank God that I'm not married! There's not the slightest diversity in them, sir, they can't invent a simple pattern; it's the men who invent the patterns for them! Look here, sir, I used to carry her in my arms, I used to dance the mazurka[3] with her when she was ten years old; today she arrived, and naturally I flew to give her a hug, and the second thing she had to say to me was that there is no God. It could at least have been the third thing but no, it was the second – she was in such a hurry! Well, let's suppose intelligent people don't believe; well, that's because of their intelligence, but as for you, you little pipsqueak, I say, what do you understand of God? Some student taught you that, you know, and if he'd taught you to light the candle in front of the icon, you would have gone ahead and lit it.'

'You're always telling lies, you're a very spiteful man and I have just demonstrated to you the utter untenability of your views,' the girl student replied scornfully, as if it were beneath her dignity to exchange any further words with such a man. 'Specifically, I was just saying to you that we were all taught, according to the catechism: "If you honour your father and your parents,[4] then you will live a long life and riches will be given to you." That is in the Ten Commandments. If God found it necessary to offer a reward for love, it follows that your God is immoral. It was in precisely those words that I've just proved it to you, and it wasn't the second thing I had to say, but because you had declared your rights. Who is to blame that you're obtuse and still don't understand? You find it insulting and you're angry – there's the whole answer to the riddle of your generation.'

'Stupid girl!' said the major.

'And you're an idiot.'

'Go ahead and call me names!'

'But just a moment, Kapiton Maksimovich, you yourself told me, after all, that you don't believe in God,' Liputin squeaked from the other end of the table.

'Well, supposing I did, it's an entirely different matter for me! Maybe I do believe, but not entirely. Even though I may not fully believe, still, I won't say that God has to be shot. While I was still serving with the Hussars, I used to think a lot about God. It's the accepted thing in all poetry that a Hussar drinks and carouses. Well, sir, maybe I did drink, but believe me, at night I'd jump out of bed in nothing but my socks and start crossing myself in front of the icon so that God would send me faith, because even then I couldn't rest easy: does God exist or not? I had a hard time of it, I can tell you! In the morning, of course, you're distracted, and your faith seems to wane again, and in general I've noticed that faith always does wane somewhat during the day.'

'You don't happen to have some cards around here, do you?' Verkhovensky gave a huge yawn as he turned to the hostess.

'I'm entirely in sympathy with your question, entirely so!' the girl student burst out, aglow with indignation at what the major had been saying.

'Valuable time is being wasted in listening to stupid conversations,' snapped the hostess, and she looked sternly at her husband.

The girl student drew herself up: 'I wanted to inform the meeting about the sufferings and the protests of students, and inasmuch as time is being wasted in immoral conversations . . .'

'There's nothing that is either moral or immoral!' the high-school student promptly said, unable to restrain himself as soon as the girl began to speak.

'I knew that, Mr High-School Student, long before you were taught it.'

'And I declare,' he replied in a fury, 'that you are a child who has just come from Petersburg for the purpose of enlightening us all, while we know things for ourselves. About the commandment "Honour thy father and mother", which you couldn't quote properly, and the fact that it's immoral – everyone in Russia has known that since Belinsky's time.'

'Will this never end?' Madame Virginskaya said firmly to her husband. As the hostess, she was embarrassed by the triviality of the conversations, especially after she had noticed some smiles and even perplexity among the guests who had been invited for the first time.

'Ladies and gentlemen,' Virginsky suddenly raised his voice, 'if anyone would like to initiate a conversation about something more pertinent to the matter at hand, or if he has something to announce, then I propose that we get down to it without wasting any more time.'

'I will be so bold as to ask one question,' said the lame teacher softly. Until now he had remained silent and was sitting with particular decorum. 'I would like to know whether we constitute some sort of meeting, here and now, or are we simply a gathering of ordinary mortals who have come to visit? I'm asking more for form's sake and so as not to remain in ignorance.'

The 'clever' question produced an impression. Everyone exchanged glances, each seemingly awaiting an answer from somebody else, and suddenly everyone, as if by command, turned their eyes on Verkhovensky and Stavrogin.

'I simply propose that we vote to answer the question: "Are we a meeting or not?"' said Madame Virginskaya.

'I subscribe fully to the proposal,' Liputin replied, 'although it *is* rather vague.'

'And I subscribe to it . . . and I,' several voices were heard.

'And it seems to me that there will be greater order,' Virginsky said by way of ratification.

'And so, to the vote!' the hostess announced. 'Lyamshin, please sit at the piano; you can speak from there too when the voting begins.'

'Again!' Lyamshin cried. 'I've banged away enough for you.'

'This is an urgent request. Sit down and play. Don't you want to be useful to the cause?'

'But I can assure you, Arina Prokhorovna, that no one is eavesdropping. It's just your imagination. Besides, the windows are very high, and who could make anything out even if he were eavesdropping?'

'As for us, we just don't understand what's going on,' someone's voice muttered.

'But I'm telling you that precautions are always essential. I'm doing this in case there are spies,' she turned to Verkhovensky by way of explanation, 'let them hear in the street that we're having a name-day party with music.'

'Oh, hell!' Lyamshin cursed, sat down at the piano and began to bang out a waltz recklessly, virtually pounding the keys with his fists.

'I propose that those who want there to be a meeting raise their right hand,' Madame Virginskaya proposed.

Some raised their hands, others didn't. There were some who raised their hands and then lowered them again. Then lowered them and raised them again.

'Ooof, damnation, I didn't understand a thing,' cried an officer.

'And I don't understand it,' cried another.

'No, I understand,' cried a third, 'if it's "yes", then raise your hand.'

'But what does "yes" mean?'

'That means a meeting.'

'No, no meeting.'

'I voted for a meeting,' the high-school student cried, turning to Madame Virginskaya.

'Then why didn't you raise your hand?'

'I kept watching you, you didn't raise yours, so I didn't raise mine.'

'How stupid! The reason I didn't raise mine was that I made the proposal. Ladies and gentlemen, I'm proposing it again, but in reverse: whoever wants a meeting, let him sit still and not raise his hand, and whoever doesn't want it, let him raise his right hand.'

'Who doesn't want it?' the high-school student asked again.

'Are you saying this on purpose, or what?' Madame Virginskaya cried in anger.

'No, wait, is it who wants it or who doesn't want it? This needs to be defined more precisely,' two or three voices cried.

'Whoever doesn't want it, does *not* want it.'

'Well, all right, but what are we to do, raise our hands or not raise them if we *don't* want it?' cried the officer.

'Ugh, we've not yet got used to constitutional procedures,' the major observed.

'Mr Lyamshin, please, you're banging away so hard that no one can hear,' observed the lame teacher.

'Oh, for heaven's sake, Arina Prokhorovna, no one is eavesdropping,' Lyamshin jumped up. 'And I don't feel like playing anyway! I've come here as a guest, not as a piano-banger!'

'Ladies and gentlemen,' Virginsky proposed, 'answer verbally: are we to have a meeting or not?'

'A meeting, a meeting!' was heard from all quarters.

'And if that's the case, there's no need to vote; that's that. Are you satisfied, ladies and gentlemen, do we have to have a vote as well?'

'Not necessary, not necessary, we understand!'

'Perhaps there's someone who doesn't want a meeting?'

'No, no, we all want one.'

'But what is a meeting?' a voice cried. No one answered it.

'We have to elect a president,' came cries from various quarters.

'The host, the host, naturally!'

'Ladies and gentlemen, if that's the case,' began the newly elected Virginsky, 'then I put forth the initial proposal I made earlier: if anyone should wish to begin speaking about something more pertinent to the business at hand, or has something to announce, then let him do so without wasting any more time.'

General silence. Everyone's eyes turned again to Stavrogin and Verkhovensky.

'Verkhovensky, you have nothing to announce?' the hostess asked directly.

'Absolutely nothing,' he stretched in his chair and yawned. 'However, I would like a glass of cognac.'

'Stavrogin, what about you?'

'No thank you, I don't drink.'

'I'm not talking about cognac, but whether you want to speak or not.'

'Speak? About what?'

'You'll be brought some cognac,' she replied to Verkhovensky.

The girl student stood up. She had already jumped up several times.

'I have come to report on the sufferings of unfortunate students and on the efforts being made everywhere to instigate them to protest . . .'

But she stopped short. At the other end of the table a rival had already appeared, and all eyes were turned on him. Long-eared Shigalyov, with his glum and gloomy face had slowly risen from his seat and with a melancholy air had placed a thick and very closely written notebook on the table. He remained standing, saying nothing. Many were looking at the notebook in confusion, but Liputin, Virginsky and the lame teacher seemed to be satisfied with something.

'I request the floor,' Shigalyov announced glumly but firmly.

'You have it,' Virginsky ruled.

The orator sat down, remained silent for about half a minute and then pronounced, in a weighty voice:

'Ladies and gentlemen . . .'

'Here's your cognac!' The hostess's relative, who had been pouring the tea, cut him off contemptuously and disdainfully. She had gone for the cognac, and now set it before Verkhovensky along with a glass, which she brought clasped in her fingers, not on a tray or a plate.

The interrupted orator paused in a dignified manner.

'It's nothing, continue, I'm not listening,' cried Verkhovensky, pouring himself a glass.

'Ladies and gentlemen, addressing myself to your attention,' Shigalyov began again, 'and, as you will presently see, soliciting your help on a point of importance of the first order, I must say something by way of a preface.'

'Arina Prokhorovna, do you have a pair of scissors?' Pyotr Stepanovich suddenly asked.

'What do you want scissors for?' she asked in some astonishment.

'I forgot to trim my nails, I've been meaning to for three days,' he said, serenely surveying his long and unclean fingernails.

Arina Prokhorovna fumed, but Virginsky's sister appeared to be pleased by something.

'I think I saw them here on the window sill not too long ago.' She stood up from behind the table, went over to the window and immediately brought them back with her. Pyotr Stepanovich didn't even look at her; he took the scissors and began to busy himself with them. Arina Prokhorovna understood that there was actually a method to this, and was ashamed at her touchiness. The assembled company exchanged silent glances. The lame teacher was observing Verkhovensky angrily and enviously. Shigalyov resumed.

'Having devoted my energy to the study of the question of the social structure of the society of the future, with which the present one will be replaced, I have come to the conclusion that all creators of social systems, from the most ancient times to our present year of 187–, have been dreamers, spinners of tales and idiots, who have contradicted themselves, understanding absolutely nothing of natural science and of that strange animal that is called man. Plato, Rousseau, Fourier, aluminium columns[5] – all that is fit only for sparrows, and not for human society. But inasmuch as the social form of the future is essential precisely now, when we have all finally assembled to act, in order to stop pondering matters any longer, then I propose my own system for structuring the world. Here it is!' He tapped the notebook. 'I wanted to present my book to this assembly in as compact a form as possible; but I can see that I will still need to add a good many verbal explanations, and therefore the entire presentation will require at least ten evenings, in accordance with the number of chapters in my book.' (Laughter was heard.) 'Besides that, I am announcing in advance that my system is not complete.' (Again laughter.) 'I have become entangled in my own data, and my conclusion stands in direct contradiction to the initial idea from which I started. Proceeding from unlimited freedom, I end with unlimited despotism. I will add, however, that there can be no solution of the social formula except mine.'

The laughter kept increasing in volume, and it was the young and, so to speak, poorly educated guests who were laughing the loudest. A certain annoyance showed on the faces of the hostess, Liputin and the lame teacher.

'If you yourself were unable to fashion your system and are in despair about it, then what is there for us to do with it?' one of the officers observed cautiously.

'You are right, Mr Serving Officer,' Shigalyov turned towards him abruptly, 'and all the more so because you have used the word "despair". Yes, I did despair. Nonetheless, everything that's laid out in my book is indispensable, and there's no other way; nobody will come up with anything. And so I hasten, without wasting time, to invite all of you present here, after you have heard me read my book over the course of ten evenings, to express your opinions. But if the members of the group don't want to listen to me, then let's go our separate ways at the very outset – the men to occupy themselves with service to the state, the women to return to their kitchens, because once they have rejected my book they will find no other way out. Ab-so-lute-ly none! But if they miss this opportunity, they will harm themselves, since they will inevitably return to it later on.'

There was a stir in the audience. 'Is he crazy, or what?' voices were heard.

'So, it's all about Shigalyov's despair,' Lyamshin concluded, 'and the vital question is the following: is he to be in despair or not?'

'How close Shigalyov is to despair is a personal question,' declared the high-school student.

'I propose that we vote on how much Shigalyov's despair bears on the common cause, and at the same time, whether he's worth listening to or not,' the officer cheerfully suggested.

'That's simply not the point,' the lame teacher finally put in his oar. In general, he spoke with the kind of smile that seemed almost mocking, so that it was perhaps difficult to determine whether he was speaking sincerely or was joking. 'That's simply not the point here, ladies and gentlemen. Mr Shigalyov is very seriously devoted to his task and besides he is very modest. His book is familiar to me. He proposes, as a final solution to the question, the division of mankind into two unequal parts. One-tenth is to receive personal freedom and unlimited rights over the remaining nine-tenths.[6] The latter are to lose their individuality and turn into something like cattle, and with this unlimited obedience attain, through a series of regenerations, a primordial innocence, something like the primordial paradise, although they will have to work. The measures proposed by the author for depriving nine-tenths of mankind of their will and refashioning them into a herd by means of the re-education of entire generations are most remarkable, based on the data of nature, and very logical. One may not agree with certain conclusions, but it is difficult to doubt the author's intelligence and knowledge. It's a pity that his condition of ten evenings is completely incompatible with the circumstances, otherwise we could have heard many interesting things.'

'Are you really serious?' Madame Virginskaya addressed the lame teacher, even in some alarm. 'If this man, not knowing what to do with people, turns nine-tenths of them into slaves? I've been suspicious of him for a long time.'

'So you're talking about your dear brother?' asked the lame teacher.

'Family ties? Are you laughing at me or what?'

'And besides to work for aristocrats and obey them as if they were gods – that's unconscionable!' the girl student observed fiercely.

'What I'm proposing is not something unconscionable but paradise, earthly paradise, and there can be no other kind on earth,' Shigalyov concluded imperiously.

'And instead of paradise,' Lyamshin exclaimed, 'I would take this nine-tenths of humanity, if there was really no place to put them, and blow them up, and I would leave only a handful of educated people, who would then begin to live the good life according to scientific principles.'

'Only a buffoon could talk like that!' the girl student spluttered.

'He's a buffoon, but he's useful,' Madame Virginskaya whispered to her.

'And perhaps that would be the very best solution to the problem!' Shigalyov turned to Lyamshin heatedly. 'You, of course, can't begin to know what a profound thing you've managed to express, Mr Cheerful Man. But since your idea is almost unrealizable, we then have to be limited to paradise on earth, if that's what it's called.'

'But this is just plain nonsense!' The words seemed to burst from Verkhovensky. However, he continued trimming his nails with utter nonchalance and without raising his eyes.

'Why do you say nonsense, sir?' The lame teacher picked up on his remark at once, as if he had just been waiting for him to say the first word in order to seize hold of it. 'Why precisely nonsense? Mr Shigalyov is in part a fanatic in his love of mankind; but remember that in Fourier, in Cabet especially, and even in Proudhon[7] himself there are a great many highly despotic and even fantastic attempts to resolve the problem. Perhaps Mr Shigalyov is even resolving the matter in a more sober way than they are. I can assure you that after having read his book, it is almost impossible not to agree with some things. He has perhaps not moved as far away from reality as the others, and his paradise on earth is almost the real one, the same one over whose loss mankind is sighing, provided it ever existed.'

'I just knew I'd run into something like this,' Verkhovensky grumbled again.

'Just a moment, please,' the lame teacher was growing more and more indignant, 'conversations and discussions about the future social structure are almost an urgent necessity for all thinking people of today. That was the only thing Herzen was concerned about his whole life. Belinsky, as I have it on good authority, would spend entire evenings with his friends debating and resolving in advance even the smallest, so to speak, domestic details of the social structure of the future.'

'Some even lose their minds,' the major suddenly noted.

'Still and all, we might at least come to an agreement by talking about it, rather than sitting and remaining silent like dictators,' Liputin hissed as if resolving to go on the attack at last.

'I didn't mean Shigalyov when I said it was nonsense,' Verkhovensky mumbled. 'You see, ladies and gentlemen,' he raised his eyes ever so slightly, 'in my opinion all these books – these Fouriers, these Cabets, all these "rights to work", Shigalyovism – they're all like novels, which can be written in the hundreds of thousands. An aesthetic passing of the time. I understand that you're bored in this dreary little town, so you rush to read any piece of paper with writing on it.'

'Just a moment, please,' the lame teacher began to shift in his chair, 'even though we're provincials, and are therefore quite naturally worthy of pity, still and all, we know very well that so far nothing so new has happened under the sun that would make us weep for having overlooked it. Here they are proposing to us, through various secret pamphlets of foreign manufacture, that we should join ranks and form small groups for the sole purpose of creating mass destruction, under the pretext that since you can't treat the world, you can't cure anything, and that if you're radical enough to cut off a hundred million heads and thereby lighten your burden, you can jump across the ditch more confidently. A beautiful idea, no doubt, but at least as incompatible with reality as "Shigalyovism", which you've just referred to so contemptuously.'

'Well, I didn't come here to engage in discussions,' Verkhovensky blundered in, letting this significant little phrase drop, and as if utterly unaware of his slip, he moved the candle closer, so as to get more light.

'I'm sorry, sir, very sorry that you didn't come here for discussions, and very sorry that you're now so taken up with your grooming.'

'And what's my grooming to you?'

'It's just as difficult to cut off a hundred million heads as to remake the world through propaganda. Perhaps it's even more difficult, especially if it's in Russia,' Liputin ventured again.

'It's precisely on Russia that people are now resting their hopes,' one of the officers said.

'We've heard that they're resting their hopes on it,' the lame teacher interposed. 'We know that the mysterious finger is pointed at our wonderful fatherland as the country that is most capable of accomplishing the great task. Only, consider this: in the event of a gradual resolution of the task through propaganda, I will at least gain something personally, some pleasant chitchat, for instance; I'll receive a promotion from the authorities for services to society. But in the second place, in case of a rapid resolution by means of cutting off a hundred million heads, what actual reward will accrue to me? If you begin to spread propaganda like that, then they might very well cut your tongue out.'

'They'll certainly cut yours out,' Verkhovensky said.

'Well then, you see. And inasmuch as you won't be able to complete a slaughter like that in less than fifty years, or let's say thirty, even under the most favourable circumstances, because people aren't sheep, after all, and they very likely won't allow themselves to be slaughtered, isn't it better to collect one's worldly goods and relocate somewhere to quiet islands beyond quiet seas and serenely close your eyes? Believe me, sir,' he drummed his finger significantly on the table, 'you will only stimulate emigration with such propaganda, and nothing more!'

He finished, visibly triumphant. He was one of the powerful minds of our province. Liputin was smiling insidiously, Virginsky was listening somewhat dejectedly, all the rest were following the discussion with extraordinary attention, especially the ladies and the officers. Everyone understood that the advocate of cutting off a hundred million heads had been pressed to the wall, and were waiting to see what would come of it.

'You've made a good point, though,' Verkhovensky mumbled even more nonchalantly than before, even with what seemed like boredom. 'Emigration is a good idea. But all the same, if, all the obvious disadvantages that you foresee notwithstanding, more and more soldiers turn up every day to serve the common cause, then you can be dispensed with. Now, my friend, a new religion is coming to replace the old one, and that's why so many soldiers will turn up, and the cause is a powerful one. But you go ahead and emigrate! And you know, I advise you to go to Dresden, and not to any quiet islands. In the first place, it's a city that has never experienced any epidemic, and since you are a civilized man, you're probably afraid of death. In the second place, it's close to the Russian border, which means you'll be able to receive income from your beloved fatherland more quickly. In the third place, it contains so-called treasures of art, and you're an aesthetically inclined man, a former teacher of literature, it seems. And last but not least, it contains its own pocket Switzerland,[8] for poetic inspiration, because I'm pretty sure you scribble verses. In a word, a treasure in a snuffbox!'

There was some movement; the officers, in particular, began to stir. Another moment and everyone would have begun talking at once. But the lame teacher irritably snapped at the bait:

DEMONS

'No, sir, perhaps we will not abandon the common cause! This should be understood, sir!'

'What do you mean, you'd really join a group of five if I proposed it to you?' Verkhovensky suddenly blurted out, and he placed the scissors on the table.

Everyone seemed startled. The enigmatic man had suddenly revealed too much of himself. He had even made direct reference to a 'group of five'.

'Everyone feels himself to be an honest man, and doesn't shrink from the common cause,' the lame teacher said with a grimace, 'but . . .'

'No, sir, now it's not a question of *but*,' Verkhovensky interrupted authoritatively and sharply. 'I declare, ladies and gentlemen, that I need a straight answer. I understand very well that having come to town and brought you all together, I owe you some explanations,' (another unexpected revelation) 'but I can't give you any until I know how your thinking runs. All further conversation aside – because we don't have another thirty years to go on babbling, as people have been babbling for the last thirty years – I am asking you what you value more: the slow way, consisting of the writing of social novels and bureaucratic attempts to come to decisions on paper about human destiny for the next thousand years, while despotism swallows up the roasted morsels of meat which would fly into your mouths by themselves and which you are not allowing your mouths to catch; or do you hold to a quick solution, whatever it may consist of, but which will untie people's hands once and for all and will give mankind the freedom to build its own society, and that in fact, not on paper. People cry: "A hundred million heads". That's perhaps just a metaphor, but why be afraid of them, if despotism, with its slow paper daydreams, in a hundred years or so will consume not a hundred but five hundred million heads? Note further that a man who's incurably ill will not be cured no matter what medications are prescribed for him on paper, but on the contrary, if there is any delay, he will begin to rot away so badly that he will infect us as well, will corrupt all the fresh forces we can still count on now, and the result will be that we will all ultimately be doomed. I fully agree that it's extremely pleasant to babble away liberally and eloquently, and that to act is rather painful ... However, I don't know how to speak. I came here with some communications, and therefore I respectfully ask this worthy company not to vote, but to declare, directly and simply, what makes you happier: a tortoise-like procession in the swamp, or crossing the swamp under full sail?'

'I'm absolutely for full sail!' the high-school student cried enthusiastically.

'So am I,' replied Lyamshin.

'Naturally, there's no doubt about the choice,' one of the officers muttered, and then another, and then someone else too. Mainly, all were struck that Verkhovensky had come with 'communications', and that he himself had promised to speak presently.

'Ladies and gentlemen, I see that almost everyone has decided to act in the spirit of the manifestos,' he said, surveying the assembled company.

'Everyone, everyone,' cried a majority of voices.

'I must admit that I'm more for a humane solution,' said the major, 'but since everyone is for yours, then I'll go along with the rest.'

'So, as it turns out, even you have no objections?' Verkhovensky turned to the lame teacher.

'Well, not exactly,' the teacher was on the point of blushing, 'but if I'm in agreement with everyone now, then it's solely because I don't want to violate . . .'

'And that's the way all of you are! He's ready to spend six months arguing to show off his liberal eloquence, and the result is that he goes and votes with everyone else! Ladies and gentlemen, now decide: are all of you truly ready?' (Ready for what? The question was vague, but awfully tempting.)

'Of course, everyone's ready,' came a chorus of declarations. However, they kept glancing at the others.

'Perhaps you'll be sorry afterwards for having agreed so quickly? That, you know, is how it almost always happens with you.'

The assembled company grew agitated for a variety of

reasons, very agitated. The lame teacher pounced on Verkhovensky.

'Permit me to note, however, that the answers to such questions are conditional. If we have in fact made a decision, then note that the question that has been posed in such a strange way is still . . .'

'In what strange way?'

'In a way that such questions are not posed.'

'Explain why, please. And you know, I really was certain that you would be the first to take offence.'

'You extracted from us an answer as to our readiness to take immediate action, but what right, may I ask, did you have to act in such a fashion? What authority do you have to ask such questions?'

'You should have had the wits to ask that earlier! Why did you answer, then? You agreed, and now you want to take it back.'

'And in my opinion, the irresponsible frankness of your main question makes me think that you have no authority at all, no rights, and that you are merely curious for your own purposes.'

'Why, what are you talking about, what?' exclaimed Verkhovensky, apparently in considerable alarm.

'About the fact that affiliations, of whatever kind, are in any case made in private, and not in the company of twenty people one doesn't know!' the lame teacher blurted out. He had expressed everything that was on his mind, but now was much too irritated. Verkhovensky quickly turned to the assembled company with a superbly feigned look of alarm on his face.

'Ladies and gentlemen, I regard it as my duty to declare to all of you that all this is foolishness and that our conversation has gone too far. As yet I have made absolutely no affiliations of anyone to anything, and no one has the right to say of me that I am creating affiliations; we are simply discussing our opinions. Isn't that so? But whether it's so or not, you are alarming me greatly,' he turned again to the lame teacher, 'and I never thought for a moment that here it was necessary to talk privately about such innocent things. Or are you afraid of being denounced? Is it really possible that there's an informer among us here?'

The general excitement increased enormously; everyone began talking.

'Ladies and gentlemen, if that's the case,' Verkhovensky continued, 'then I have actually compromised myself more than anyone else, and therefore I propose that an answer be given to one question – if you wish it, naturally. It's entirely up to you.'

'What question? What question?' A din arose.

'The sort of question that will make it clear, once it's asked, whether we should stay together, or quietly pick up our hats and go our own separate ways.'

'The question, the question?'

'If each of us knew about a political assassination that was being planned, would he go and inform, foreseeing all the consequences, or would he remain at home and wait for things to happen? People can have various views on this. The answer to the question will tell us clearly whether we are to go our separate ways or remain together, and not for just this one evening, either. Permit me to turn to you first,' he addressed the lame teacher.

'Why me first?'

'Because you were the one who started it all. Please don't try to dodge it; it won't do you any good to be nimble here. However, as you wish, it's entirely up to you.'

'Excuse me, but a question of that kind is highly insulting.'

'Come now, can't you be a bit more precise?'

'I have never been an agent of the secret police, sir,' he squirmed even more.

'Please be more precise, don't hold anything back.'

The lame teacher was so angry that he even stopped speaking. Without a word he glared angrily at his tormentor from behind his spectacles.

'Yes or no? Would you inform or wouldn't you?' cried Verkhovensky.

'Of course I would *not* inform!' the lame teacher cried twice as loudly.

'And no one would inform, of course, no one would inform,' cried many voices.

'Let me turn to you, Mr Major, would you inform or would you not?' Verkhovensky continued. 'And observe that I'm turning to you deliberately.'

'I would not inform.'

'Well then, if you knew that someone wanted to kill and rob another person, an ordinary mortal, then would you inform, give warning?'

'Of course, but after all that's a matter of civil law, and we're talking about political denunciation. I have never been an agent of the secret police, sir.'

'Why, no one here has been either,' voices were again heard. 'A pointless question. Everyone has the same answer. There are no informers here!'

'Why is that man getting up?' the girl student cried.

'That's Shatov. Why are you getting up, Shatov?' cried the hostess.

Shatov had in fact stood up; he was holding his hat in his hand and looking at Verkhovensky. He seemed to want to say something to him, but was hesitating. His face was pale and angry, but he held back, didn't say a word and silently began to walk out of the room.

'Shatov, this doesn't do you a bit of good, you know!' Verkhovensky called after him enigmatically.

'But it does you some good, as a spy and a scoundrel!' Shatov shouted from the doorway and went out.

Again, cries and exclamations.

'There it is, that's the test!' cried a voice.

'It's proved useful!' cried another.

'Hasn't it proved useful too late?' observed a third.

'Who invited him? Who admitted him? Who is he? Who is this Shatov? Will he inform or won't he?' the questions poured out.

'If he were an informer, he would have pretended instead of cursing and leaving,' someone remarked.

'There's Stavrogin getting up; Stavrogin didn't answer the question either,' the girl student cried.

Stavrogin had in fact got up, and at the same time at the other end of the table, Kirillov stood up as well.

'Wait a moment, Mr Stavrogin,' the hostess addressed him sharply, 'all of us here have answered the question, while you are leaving without saying anything.'

'I see no need to answer the question that is of interest to you,' Stavrogin grumbled.

'But we've compromised ourselves, while you haven't,' several voices cried.

'And what business of mine is it if you've compromised yourselves?' Stavrogin began to laugh, but his eyes were flashing.

'What do you mean what business is it of yours? What do you mean what business?' came the exclamations. Many jumped up from their chairs.

'Just a moment, ladies and gentlemen, just a moment,' the lame teacher exclaimed, 'why, even Mr Verkhovensky hasn't answered the question; he's only asked it.'

This remark produced a stunning effect. Everyone exchanged glances. Stavrogin laughed loudly in the lame teacher's face and then walked out, with Kirillov following. Verkhovensky ran out after them into the entryway.

'What are you doing to me?' he prattled, grabbing Stavrogin by the hand and squeezing it in his as hard as he could. Stavrogin silently pulled his hand away.

'You go to Kirillov's; I'll come presently . . . it's essential for me, essential!'

'It's not essential for me to be there,' Stavrogin snapped.

'Stavrogin will be there,' Kirillov put an end to the exchange. 'Stavrogin, it is essential for you to be there.'

They went out.

CHAPTER 8

Ivan the Tsarevich

They went out. Pyotr Stepanovich was about to rush back to the 'meeting', to bring order to the chaos, but probably reasoning that there was no point in bothering, he left everything and two minutes later was already flying along the road after the two men. On the way he remembered that the lane would bring him closer to Filippov's house. Sinking up to his knees in mud, he set off down the lane and actually arrived at the very moment when Stavrogin and Kirillov were walking through the gate.

'You're here already?' Kirillov observed. 'That's good. Come in.'

'How is it that you said you live alone?' Stavrogin asked, passing a samovar that had been set up in the entryway and had already come to the boil.

'You'll soon see who I'm living with,' Kirillov muttered. Come in.'

They had hardly gone in when Verkhovensky extracted from his pocket the anonymous letter he had taken from von Lembke earlier, and laid it in front of Stavrogin. All three sat down. Stavrogin read the letter without saying a word.

'Well?' he asked.

'This scoundrel will do just what is written here!' Verkhovensky said by way of clarification. 'Since he's at your disposal, then tell me how to act. I assure you that he may well go to see von Lembke as early as tomorrow.'

'Well, let him go.'

'What do you mean, "let him"? Especially if it can be avoided.'

'You're mistaken; he doesn't depend on me. Well, it's all the same to me. He doesn't threaten me in any way; he threatens only you.'

'And you.'

'I don't think so.'

'But others might not give you any quarter, don't you really understand that? Listen, Stavrogin, this is all just playing around with words. Do you really begrudge the money?'

'And is money really necessary?'

'Absolutely, two thousand or a minimum of fifteen hundred. Give it to me tomorrow or even today, and tomorrow, towards evening, I'll send him on his way to Petersburg for you, that's exactly what he wants. And with Marya Timofeyevna if you want – take note of that.'

Something in him was completely out of kilter; he was speaking without much caution, and ill-considered words were breaking from his lips. Stavrogin was watching him with astonishment.

'I have no reason to send Marya Timofeyevna away.'

'Maybe you don't really want to?' Pyotr Stepanovich gave an ironic smile.

'Maybe I don't really want to.'

'In short, will there be money or not?' he shouted at Stavrogin in angry impatience and rather imperiously. Stavrogin surveyed him with a serious look.

'There will be no money.'

'Eh, Stavrogin! Do you know something or have you already done something? Or are you having a little joke?'

His face became distorted, the corners of his lips quivered and he suddenly burst out in utterly aimless and pointless laughter.

'You did, after all, receive the money for the estate from your father,' Nikolay Vsevolodovich calmly observed. 'Maman gave you six or eight thousand for Stepan Trofimovich. So go ahead and pay the fifteen hundred out of your own money. When all is said and done, I really don't want to pay for other people; I've given away so much as it is, it's beginning to annoy me,' he laughed at his own words.

'Ah, you're beginning to joke . . .'

Stavrogin got up from his chair; Verkhovensky also jumped

up in a flash, and instinctively stood with his back to the door, as if blocking the way out. Nikolay Vsevolodovich had already moved as if to push him away from the door and leave, but suddenly he stopped.

'I won't let you have Shatov,' he said. Pyotr Stepanovich trembled; they were looking at each other.

'I already told you earlier why you need Shatov's blood,' said Stavrogin with flashing eyes. 'It's the glue you want to bind your little groups together. The way you drove Shatov away just now was splendid: you knew very well that he wouldn't say "I won't inform", and he would consider it beneath him to lie to you. But as for me, as for me, what do you need me for now? You've been pestering me almost since you arrived from abroad. And the explanation you've given me so far is just a lot of wild talk. Meanwhile, you're aiming to have me give Lebyadkin fifteen hundred, which in turn would give Fedka the opening to kill him. I know you have the notion that I want my wife killed at the same time. By tying my hands with a crime, you of course think you'll get power over me, don't you? Why do you need the power? Why in the Devil's name do you need me? Take a close look at me, once and for all, and see whether or not I'm your man. And leave me in peace.'

'Did Fedka himself come to you?' Verkhovensky asked breathlessly.

'Yes, he did; his price is also fifteen hundred ... But he'll confirm it himself, he's standing right there.' Stavrogin held out his hand.

Pyotr Stepanovich turned around quickly. A new figure stepped out of the darkness into the doorway – Fedka, in a sheepskin coat but without a hat, as if he were at home. He stood there and chuckled, baring his even white teeth. His black eyes with their yellow cast darted cautiously around the room as he observed the gentlemen. He didn't understand why he was there: evidently he had been brought there just then by Kirillov, who was the focus of his inquiring look. He was standing in the doorway, but didn't want to come into the room.

'He's probably being kept in reserve here so that he can listen to our bargaining or even see the money in our hands, is that it?' Stavrogin asked, and without waiting for an answer, walked out of the house. Verkhovensky caught up with him at the gate, almost in a demented state.

'Stop! Not a step further!' he shouted and seized him by the elbow. Stavrogin tried to jerk his arm away, but didn't succeed. He was overcome with fury: grabbing Verkhovensky by the hair with his left hand, he threw him to the ground as hard as he could and walked through the gate. But he hadn't gone more than thirty steps when he was overtaken again.

'Let's make up, let's make up,' Verkhovensky said to him in an agitated whisper.

Nikolay Vsevolodovich shrugged his shoulders but didn't stop or turn around.

'Listen, I'll bring Lizaveta Nikolayevna to you tomorrow, do you want me to? No? Why aren't you answering me? Tell me what you want and I'll do it. Listen, I'll give you Shatov, do you want me to?'

'So it's true that you've decided to kill him?' cried Nikolay Vsevolodovich.

'Well, what do you need Shatov for? What for?' a frenzied Verkhovensky continued in a breathless patter, constantly running ahead and grabbing Stavrogin by the elbow, probably without even noticing it himself. 'Listen, I'll give him to you, let's make it up. You owe me a lot, but . . . let's make it up!'

Stavrogin finally glanced at him and was stunned. The voice and the look were different from what they always were or had been just now in the room back there; he saw almost a different face. The intonation of the voice was different: Verkhovensky was begging and entreating. This was a man who hadn't yet regained his senses, a man whose most precious thing was being taken away or had already been taken.

'Why, what's the matter with you?' exclaimed Stavrogin. Verkhovensky didn't answer but ran after him and was looking at him with an expression that was imploring, as before, but at the same time adamant as well.

'Let's make it up!' he whispered once again. 'Listen, I have a knife stashed in my boot, just like Fedka does, but I'll make it up with you.'

'But what do you want me for, I ask you, damn it all!' Stavrogin shouted in genuine anger and astonishment. 'Is there some mystery here, or what? Am I some kind of talisman for you?'

'Listen, we're going to create real trouble,' Verkhovensky muttered rapidly and almost as if he were delirious. 'You don't believe we're going to create real trouble? We'll create such trouble that everything will move off its foundations. Karmazinov is right that there's nothing to grab hold of. Karmazinov is very intelligent. All it takes is ten more such small groups throughout Russia, and I'm untouchable.'

'Made up of the same sort of fools,' Stavrogin burst out, unable to control himself.

'Oh, be a bit more stupid, Stavrogin, be a bit more stupid yourself! You know, you're by no means so intelligent that one shouldn't wish that on you. You're afraid, you don't believe in anything, you're frightened by the sheer scale of it. And why do you say they're fools? They're not such fools; nowadays there's no one with a mind of his own. Nowadays there are precious few original minds. Virginsky is the purest of men, ten times purer than people like us; well, enough about him. Liputin is a crook, but he's got one good point. There's no crook who doesn't have his good point. Only Lyamshin is without a single good point, but he's in my hands. A few more such groups, and I'll have passports and money everywhere. Isn't that enough? Isn't that in itself enough? And safe places, and let them search all they want. If they unearth one group, they'll get into a mess with another. We're going to start some real trouble. Don't you really believe that the two of us are quite enough?'

'Take Shigalyov, and leave me in peace . . .'

'Shigalyov is a man of genius! Do you know that he's a genius like Fourier, but bolder than Fourier, stronger than Fourier; I'm going to take him up. He's invented "equality"!'

'He has a fever, and he's raving; something very unusual has happened to him,' Stavrogin looked at him again. Both walked on without stopping.

'It's well put in his notebook,' Verkhovensky continued. 'He's got spying down. He has each member of society watching the others and obliged to inform. Each belongs to all, and all to each. All are slaves, and are equal in their slavery. In extreme cases, there's slander and murder, but the main thing is equality. The first thing is to lower the level of education, science and accomplishment.[1] A high level of science and accomplishment is accessible only to people of high ability, and there's no need for high ability! People of high ability have always seized power and been despots. People of high ability can't help but be despots and have always corrupted more than they have brought benefit; they are sent into exile or executed. Cicero had his tongue cut out, Copernicus had his eyes put out, Shakespeare[2] was stoned – that's Shigalyovism! Slaves should be equal; without despotism there has never yet been either freedom or equality, but there should be equality in the herd, and that's Shigalyovism! Ha, ha, ha. Do you find that strange? I'm for Shigalyovism!'

Stavrogin tried to quicken his pace and get home as quickly as possible. 'If this man is drunk, then when in the world did he have time to get drunk?' the thought occurred to him. 'Could it have been the cognac?'

'Listen, Stavrogin: to level mountains is a good idea, and isn't ridiculous. I'm for Shigalyov! There's no need for education, enough of science! Even without science there's enough material for a thousand years, but obedience has to be established. There's only one thing lacking in the world: obedience. The thirst for education is nothing but an aristocratic thirst. No sooner do we have the family or love than the desire for private property arises. We will kill desire: we will foster drunkenness, gossip, denunciation; we will foster unheard-of depravity; we will stifle every genius in its infancy. Everything reduced to a common denominator, complete equality. "We have learned a trade, and we are honest people, we need nothing else" – that's the answer given recently by the English workers. Only what's essential is essential – that's the motto of the planet from now on. But a shaking up is necessary too: we, the rulers, will take care of that. The slaves ought to have rulers. Complete obedience, a complete lack of individuality, but once every thirty years along comes Shigalyov to shake things up and everyone suddenly begins to devour each other, up to a certain point, only to avoid boredom. Boredom is an aristocratic feeling; in Shigalyovism there will be no desires. Desire and suffering will be for us, and for the slaves – Shigalyovism.'

'Are you excluding yourself?' The words again burst from Stavrogin's lips.

'And you. You know, I've been thinking of handing the world over to the pope. Let him come out barefoot and show himself to the rabble: "This," he'll say, "is what I've been brought to." And everyone will begin to throng after him, even the armies. The pope on top, we all around, and under us Shigalyovism. All that's needed is that the Internationale should come to an agreement with the pope, and that's just what will happen. And the little old man will agree in an instant. For that matter, he has absolutely no other way out, now mark my words, Ha ha, ha. Is it stupid? Tell me, is it stupid or not?'

'Enough,' Stavrogin muttered in annoyance.

'Enough! Listen, I've dropped the pope! The Devil with Shigalyovism! The Devil with the pope! We need something that's up to date, and not Shigalyovism, because Shigalyovism is a piece of jewellery. It's an ideal, it's in the future. Shigalyov is a jeweller, and he's stupid, like any philanthropist. We need manual labour, and Shigalyov despises manual labour. Listen: the pope will be in the West, and we will have – we will have you!'

'Leave me alone, you drunk!' Stavrogin grumbled, and quickened his pace.

'Stavrogin, you're a beauty!' exclaimed Pyotr Stepanovich almost in ecstasy. 'You know, you're a real beauty! What's most precious about you is that you sometimes don't know it. Oh, I've made a close study of you! I often look at you when you're not aware of it! There's even some simple-heartedness and *naïveté* in you, do you know that? There is, there certainly is! You must be suffering, and suffering sincerely, from this simple-heartedness. I love beauty. I'm a nihilist, but I love beauty. Do nihilists really not love beauty? It's only idols they don't love; well, I love idols! You are my idol! You don't insult anyone, and everyone hates you. You look on everyone as an equal, and everyone is afraid of you. No one will come up and pat you on the shoulder. You're a dreadful aristocrat. An aristocrat, when he goes in for democracy, is fascinating! It means nothing for you to sacrifice a life, yours or other people's. You are precisely what is needed. I, I need precisely someone like you. I don't know anyone except you. You are a leader, you are the sun, and I'm your worm . . .'[3]

He suddenly kissed his hand. A chill ran down Stavrogin's spine, and he snatched his hand away in fear. They stopped.

'You're unhinged!' Stavrogin whispered.

'Maybe I'm raving, maybe I'm raving!' he hastened to assent. 'But I've thought up the first step. Shigalyov could never have thought up the first step. There are many Shigalyovs! But one, only one man in Russia invented the first step and knows how to take it. I am that man. Why are you staring at me? You, you are necessary to me, without you I am nothing. Without you I am a fly, an idea in a bottle, Columbus without America.'

Stavrogin stood and stared into his mad eyes.

'Listen, first we'll start some real trouble,' Verkhovensky said in a terrible hurry, constantly grabbing Stavrogin by the left sleeve. 'I've already told you: we will penetrate into the very heart of the people. Do you know that even now we are dreadfully strong? Our people are not only those who kill and burn and fire pistols in the traditional manner or bite others. Such people are only a hindrance. Without discipline I don't understand anything. I'm a scoundrel, actually, not a socialist, ha, ha! Listen, I've counted them all: the teacher who laughs along with the children at their God and at their cradle is already ours. The lawyer who defends an educated murderer on the grounds that he is more highly developed than his victims and that in order to get some money, he couldn't help but kill, he is already ours. The schoolboys who kill a peasant for the thrill of it are ours. Jurors who acquit all criminals without discrimination are ours. The prosecutor in the courtroom who trembles in fear that he is not sufficiently liberal, is ours, ours. Administrators, men of letters, oh, there are many of our people, a tremendous number, and they themselves don't know it! On the other hand, the obedience of schoolboys and fools has reached the highest point; their mentors' gallbladders have burst; everywhere vanity has reached inordinate proportions, there are bestial, unimaginable appetites. Do you know, do you know how much we can take just with ready-made little ideas? When I left, Littré's theory[4] that criminality is insanity was all the rage; then when I returned criminality was no longer insanity, but only common sense and almost a duty, or at least an honourable protest. "Well then, how can a cultured murderer help but kill if he needs money!" But these are only the first-fruits. The Russian God has already given up when it comes to cheap booze. The common people are drunk, the mothers are drunk, the children are drunk, the churches are empty, and in the courts it's "either two hundred lashes, or bring us a bucketful of vodka". Oh, just wait until the present generation grows up! It's only a pity that there's no time to wait, otherwise they could get even drunker! Oh, what a pity there's no proletariat! But there will be, there will be, it's coming to that . . .'

'It's also a pity that we've grown more stupid,' Stavrogin mumbled, and set off in the direction he'd been going.

'Listen, I myself have seen a little boy of six leading his drunken mother home, and she was cursing him with dirty words. Do you think I'm happy about that? When things fall into our hands, maybe we'll find a cure . . . if need be, we'll drive these people into the wilderness for forty years.[5] But one or two generations of debauchery are essential now – unprecedented, utterly vile debauchery, when people turn into nasty, cowardly, cruel, self-centred scum – that's what we need! And with "a little fresh blood" besides, so that they can get used to it. Why are you laughing? I'm not contradicting myself. I'm only contradicting philanthropists and Shigalyovism, but not myself. I'm a scoundrel, and not a socialist. Ha, ha, ha! It's just a pity that there's so little time. I've promised Karmazinov to begin in May, and to finish by the Feast of the Protection. You think that's too soon? Ha, ha! You know what I'm going to tell you, Stavrogin? Until now there's been no cynicism in the

Russian people, although they use dirty words when they abuse each other. Do you know that when they were serfs, they had more self-respect than Karmazinov had for himself? They were flogged, but they stood up for their gods, and Karmazinov didn't stand up for his.'

'Well, Verkhovensky, I'm listening to you for the first time, and I'm listening in astonishment,' said Nikolay Vsevolodovich. 'So you're not really a socialist, but some sort of political . . . self-seeker.'

'A scoundrel, a scoundrel. You're concerned about who I am? I'll tell you presently who I am, I'm leading up to it. It was not for nothing that I kissed your hand. But it's necessary that the common people should come to believe that we know what we want, while the others are merely "brandishing the cudgel and beating up their own". Oh, if only there were time! That's the only trouble – there's no time. We shall proclaim destruction. Why, why? Again, this little idea is so fascinating! But we must, we must stretch our little legs. We'll get fires going. We'll foster legends. Here every mangy little "group" will come in handy. I'll find such enthusiasts for you in these very same groups that they won't shrink from any shooting and will be grateful for the honour besides. Well then, that's when the real trouble will begin! There'll be a shakeup the likes of which the world has never yet seen. Rus will plunge into darkness, the earth will begin to weep for its old gods . . . Well now, at this point we'll trot out . . . who?'

'Who?'

'Ivan the Tsarevich.'[6]

'Who-o-o?'

'Ivan the Tsarevich: you, you!'

Stavrogin reflected for a moment.

'The Pretender?'[7] he asked, looking at this overwrought man in profound astonishment. 'Oho! So there's your plan at last.'

'We'll put it out that he's "in hiding",' Verkhovensky said in a quiet, rather affectionate whisper, as if he really were drunk. 'Do you know what this expression means: "he's in hiding"? But he'll appear, he will appear. We'll spread the legend better than the castrates were able to. He exists, but no one has seen

him. Oh, what a legend we can spread! And most important –
a new force is on the march. And it really is needed, that's what
people are crying out for. Well, what's in socialism? It has
destroyed the old forces, and not introduced any new ones. But
here is a force, and what a force, unprecedented! Just this one
time we'll need it as a lever to raise up the earth. Everything
will rise up!'

'So you really were seriously counting on me?' Stavrogin
asked with a malicious smile.

'Why are you laughing, and so maliciously? Don't try to
frighten me. I'm like a child now, and I can be frightened to
death by just such a smile. Listen, I won't show you to anyone,
to anyone. That's how it should be. He exists, but no one has
seen him; he's in hiding. And you know, he might even be
shown to one person out of a hundred thousand, for instance.
And word will spread across the entire earth: "We've seen
him, we've seen him." And they saw Ivan Filippovich, God of
Sabaoth,[8] ascending to Heaven in his chariot before the people,
"with their very own eyes" they saw him. But you're not Ivan
Filippovich: you're a beauty, proud as a god, seeking nothing
for yourself, surrounded with an aureole of sacrifice, and "in
hiding". The main thing is the legend! You'll conquer them, all
you need do is look at them, and you'll conquer them. He
brings a new truth and "is in hiding". And at this point we'll
hand down two or three Solomonic judgements.[9] We'll have
the small groups, the groups of five – no need for newspapers!
If the request of only one out of ten thousand can be granted,
then they'll all come with requests. In every village every muzhik
will hear the news that somewhere there's a hollow in a tree
trunk where they're supposed to put requests. And the earth
will begin to groan with a great groan: "A new, just law is
coming", and the sea will begin to rage, and the whole carnival
sideshow will collapse, and then we'll think about how to put
up a structure of stone. For the first time! *We* shall do the
building, we, we alone!'

'Madness!' Stavrogin said.

'Why, why don't you want to? Are you afraid? You know, I
seized on you because you're not afraid of anything. You think

that's unreasonable? Well, so far I'm still a Columbus without an America,[10] you know; does a Columbus without an America really make sense?'

Stavrogin remained silent. Meanwhile they had reached his house and stopped by the front entrance.

'Listen,' Verkhovensky leaned over to speak into his ear, 'I'll do it for you for nothing. Tomorrow I'll take care of Marya Timofeyevna ... for free, and tomorrow I'll also bring you Liza. Do you want Liza tomorrow?'

'Has he really gone crazy?' Stavrogin smiled. The front door opened.

'Stavrogin, is America ours?' Verkhovensky seized him by the hand for the last time.

'What for?' Nikolay Vsevolodovich said in a serious and stern voice.

'You don't want to – I just knew it!' Verkhovensky shouted in a mad surge of anger. 'You're lying, you rotten, lecherous, warped little aristocrat, I don't believe you, you've got the appetite of a wolf! You have to understand that you've run up too big an account now, and I absolutely cannot give you up! There's no one else on earth but you! I invented you while I was abroad; I invented it while I was watching you. If I hadn't been watching you on the sly, none of it would have occurred to me!'

Stavrogin went up the steps without answering.

'Stavrogin!' Verkhovensky shouted after him, 'I'm giving you a day – well, two days – three. More than three I can't give you, and then – your account comes due!'

CHAPTER 9

A Search at Stepan Trofimovich's

Meanwhile, an incident occurred in the town which surprised me and shook Stepan Trofimovich. At eight o'clock in the morning Nastasya ran over to see me with the news that the master had been 'searched'. At first I couldn't understand anything: all I could get out of her was that some officials had 'made a search', had come and taken some papers, and a soldier had tied them up in a bundle and 'taken them away in a wheelbarrow'. The news was brutal. I immediately hurried to Stepan Trofimovich.

I found him in a surprising condition: distraught and in great agitation, but at the same time with an unmistakably triumphant air about him. On a table in the middle of the room a samovar was on the boil, and there was a glass of tea that had been poured but remained untouched and forgotten. Stepan Trofimovich was wandering about the table and going into every corner of the room, without being aware of his movements. He was wearing his usual red cardigan, but on seeing me, he hastened to put on his waistcoat and frock-coat, which he had never done before whenever any of his close friends found him in this cardigan. Immediately he seized me warmly by the hand.

'*Enfin un ami!*' (He heaved a deep sigh.) '*Cher*, I sent for you, and no one else, and no one knows anything. We must tell Nastasya to lock the doors and not let anyone in except of course *them . . . Vous comprenez?*'[1]

He looked at me uneasily, as if waiting for an answer. Naturally, I lost no time in asking him all sorts of questions, and from his disconnected account, with interruptions and unnecessary interpolations, I somehow or other learned that at seven o'clock that morning an official from the Governor's office had 'suddenly' turned up at his place.

'*Pardon, j'ai oublié son nom. Il n'est pas du pays*, but I think von Lembke brought him in, *quelque chose de bête et d'allemand dans la physionomie. Il s'appelle Rosenthal.*'[2]

'You don't mean Blum?'

'Blum. That's precisely what he called himself. *Vous le connaissez? Quelque chose d'hébété et de très content dans la figure, pourtant très sévère, roide et sérieux.* A police type, one of those who follows orders, *je m'y connais.* I was still asleep, and just imagine, he asked me if he could "have a look" at my books and manuscripts, *oui, je m'en souviens, il a employé ce mot.* He didn't arrest me, only the books ... *Il se tenait à distance*, and when he began to explain to me why he had come, he looked as though I ... *enfin, il avait l'air de croire que je tomberai sur lui immédiatement et que je commencerai à le battre comme plâtre. Tous ces gens du bas étage sont comme ça* when they deal with a decent man. Of course, I immediately understood everything. *Voilà vingt ans que je m'y prépare.* I opened all the boxes for him and handed over all the keys; I gave them to him myself, I gave him everything. *J'étais digne et calme.* Of the books, he took the foreign editions of Herzen, a bound copy of the *Bell*, four copies of my poem, *et, enfin, tout ça.* Then papers and letters *et quelques-unes de mes ébauches historiques, critiques et politiques.* They carried all this off. Nastasya says that a soldier took them away in a wheelbarrow and covered them with an apron. *Oui, c'est cela,*[3] with an apron.'

He was raving. Who could make anything out of it? I showered him with questions again: Did Blum come alone or not? In whose name? By what authority? How did he dare? How did he explain it?

'*Il était seul, bien seul*, however, someone else was *dans l'antichambre, oui, je m'en souviens, et puis* ... However, I think there was someone else as well, and there was a guard standing in the entrance hall. We'll have to ask Nastasya; she knows all that better than I. *J'étais surexcité, voyez-vous. Il parlait, il parlait* ... *un tas de choses.* However, he said very little, and I just kept on talking ... I told him the story of my life, only of course from that point of view ... *J'était surexcité, mais digne, je vous l'assure.*[4] I'm afraid, however, that I seem to have burst out crying. They took the wheelbarrow from the shopkeeper next door.'

'Oh Lord, how could all this have happened! But for heaven's sake, speak more precisely, Stepan Trofimovich; why, what you're telling me is like a dream!'

'*Cher*, it's as if I myself were dreaming ... *Savez-vous, il a prononcé le nom de Teliatnikoff*, and I think that he was the one hiding in the entrance hall. Yes, I remember, he suggested calling the prosecutor and I think Dmitry Mitrich as well ... *qui me doit encore quinze roubles* that I won at cards, *soi dit en passant. Enfin, je n'ai pas trop compris.* But I outfoxed them, and what do I care for Dmitry Mitrich? I think I began pleading with him to keep it quiet. I pleaded with him, I pleaded very, very earnestly, I'm afraid I even humbled myself, *comment croyez-vous? Enfin, il a consenti.* Yes, I remember he himself was the one who asked whether it would be better to keep it quiet, because he had only come to "have a look around", *et rien de plus*, and nothing more, nothing ... and that if they should find nothing, then nothing would happen. So that we put an end to it all by being *en amis, je suis tout-à-fait content.*'[5]

'Excuse me, but he offered you the procedures and guarantees usual in such cases, and you yourself declined them!' I exclaimed in friendly indignation.

'No, it's better that way, without a guarantee. And why have a scandal? Let it be *en amis* for the time being. You know, in our town, if people find out ... *mes ennemis ... et puis à quoi bon ce procureur, ce cochon de notre procureur, qui deux fois m'a manqué de politesse et qu'on a rossé à plaisir l'autre année chez cette charmante et belle Natalya Pavlovna, quand il se cacha dans son boudoir. Et puis, mon ami,*[6] don't raise any objections and don't dishearten me, I beg you, because there's nothing more unbearable when a man is unhappy and a hundred of his friends proceed to point out what a fool he's made of himself. Take a seat, however, and have some tea. I admit that I'm very tired. Should I lie down and apply some vinegar to my head; what do you think?'

'Absolutely,' I exclaimed, 'and some ice even. You're very distraught. You're pale, and your hands are shaking. Lie down, rest and wait a bit to tell me more. I'll sit beside you and wait.'

He hesitated to lie down, but I insisted. Nastasya brought some vinegar in a cup, I wet a towel and applied it to his head. Then Nastasya stood on a chair and reached up to light the lamp in front of the icon. I observed this with surprise: there had never been a lamp there before, and now one had suddenly appeared.

'I arranged for it a little while ago, as soon as they had left,' Stepan Trofimovich muttered, casting a sly glance at me. '*Quand on a de ces choses-là dans sa chambre et qu'on vient vous arrêter,*[7] that makes an impression, and they do have to report what they have seen . . .'

Finished with the lamp, Nastasya stood in the doorway, pressed her right palm to her cheek and looked at him with a mournful air.

'*Éloignez-la* on some pretext,' he nodded to me from the sofa, 'I can't bear this Russian pity, *et puis ça m'embête.*'[8]

But she left by herself. I noticed that he kept looking round at the door and straining to hear something in the entrance hall.

'*Il faut être prêt, voyez-vous,*' he looked at me significantly, '*chaque moment*[9] they come, they take me, and then – phfft! – a man has disappeared!'

'Lord! Who will come? Who will take you?'

'*Voyez-vous, mon cher*, I asked him directly as he was leaving what will they do with me now?'

'You would have done better to ask where they would send you into exile!' I exclaimed, in the same tone of indignation.

'That's exactly what I meant when I asked the question, but he left and made no reply. *Voyez-vous*: as for linen, clothing, especially warm clothing, well, that's as they themselves wish. If they order me to take them, well, all right; otherwise they might very well ship me off in a soldier's greatcoat. But I quietly slipped thirty-five roubles' (He suddenly lowered his voice, as he looked round at the door through which Nastasya had gone) 'into a slit in my waistcoat pocket, here, feel it . . . I think they'll remove my waistcoat, but for appearance's sake I've left seven roubles in my wallet, "that's all that I have," I'll say. You know, there's some small change and some coppers on the table, so they won't guess that I've hidden money, but will think that this is all. Lord knows where I'll have to spend the night.'

I bowed my head at such madness. It was obvious that it was impossible to arrest or search a man in the way he was describing it, and that of course he was getting everything mixed up. True enough, all this occurred before today's most recent laws had been passed. It was also true that he had been offered (in his own words) a more regular procedure, but that he had 'outfoxed' them and refused. Of course, formerly, that is, not so very long ago, the governor certainly could, in extreme cases . . . But what extreme case could there possibly have been here? That was what was baffling me.

'They probably received a telegram from Petersburg,' Stepan Trofimovich said suddenly.

'A telegram? About you? For Herzen's works and your poem? You've lost your mind; what's there to arrest you for?'

I grew really angry. He grimaced and was evidently offended, not at my outburst, but at the idea that there was nothing to arrest him for.

'Who can know these days what you can be arrested for?' he mumbled mysteriously. A wild and utterly absurd idea flashed through my mind.

'Stepan Trofimovich, tell me as a friend,' I exclaimed, 'as a genuine friend, and I won't betray you: do you belong to any secret society or not?'

And here, to my surprise, even here he was uncertain about whether or not he was a member of some secret society or not.

'Well, it depends on what you regard as, *voyez-vous* . . .'

'What do you mean, "what you regard as"?'

'When you pledge yourself to progress with all your heart and . . . who can say for certain? You think you don't belong, but then you look, and it turns out that you do after all belong to something.'

'How can that be? It's either yes or no.'

'*Cela date de Pétersbourg*,[10] when she and I wanted to found a magazine there. That's the root of it. We slipped away then, and they forgot about us, and now they've remembered. *Cher, cher*, don't you really know?' he exclaimed dolefully. 'In this country of ours they'll take you, stick you in a covered cart, and then – off to Siberia for good, or they'll leave you sitting in some dungeon . . .'

And he suddenly began to weep hot, hot tears. Tears simply gushed from his eyes. He covered his eyes with his red foulard and sobbed, sobbed convulsively for a good five minutes. I was racked with pain, all of me. This man, who had been preaching to us for twenty years, our prophet, our mentor, our patriarch, our Kukolnik, who had held himself so loftily and majestically above all of us, before whom we had bowed with all our hearts, considering it an honour – and suddenly here he was, sobbing, sobbing, like a small, naughty boy waiting for the rod that the teacher has gone to fetch. I became dreadfully sorry for him. He evidently believed as much in the 'covered cart' as he did in the fact that I was sitting beside him, and he expected it to come, that very morning, soon, this minute – and all because of the works of Herzen and some poem of his! Such a complete and utter ignorance of everyday reality was both moving and somehow disgusting.

At last he stopped weeping, got up from the sofa and again began to walk round the room, continuing the conversation with me, but constantly glancing out of the window and straining to hear what was happening in the entrance hall. Our conversation continued, but disconnectedly. All my assurances and attempts to calm him were met by a brick wall. He hardly listened, but even so, he badly needed me to calm him down and to keep on talking with that in mind. I saw that he couldn't get along without me now, and I wouldn't have abandoned him for anything in the world. I stayed, and we remained sitting for two hours and more. As we talked, he remembered that Blum had taken with him two manifestos that he had found in his possession.

'What do you mean, manifestos!' I was foolishly frightened. 'Did you really . . .'

'Oh, they dropped ten of them off here,' he replied in

irritation (He spoke with me now in either an irritated or haughty tone, now in a dreadfully plaintive and humble manner) 'but I'd disposed of eight, and Blum just took two . . .'

And he suddenly flushed in indignation.

'*Vous me mettez avec ces gens-là!* Do you really suppose that I could be involved with those scoundrels, with those clandestine pamphleteers, with my beloved son Pyotr Stepanovich, *avec ces esprits-forts de la lâcheté*![11] Oh, Lord!'

'Well now, haven't they somehow mixed you up with . . . But that's nonsense, that can't be!' I observed.

'*Savez-vous*,' he suddenly burst forth, 'at times I feel *que je ferai là-bas quelque esclandre*. Oh, don't go, don't leave me alone! *Ma carrière est finie aujourd'hui, je le sens.*[12] You know, perhaps I'll throw myself on someone and bite him, like that second lieutenant . . .'

He turned a strange look on me – which was both frightened and at the same time wished to appear frightening. He was actually becoming increasingly irritated at someone and something, while time was passing and the 'covered carts' hadn't appeared; he was even growing angry. Suddenly Nastasya, who had gone from the kitchen into the hallway for some reason, brushed against a clothes-stand and knocked it over. Stepan Trofimovich began to tremble and stood deathly still; but when it became clear what had happened, he practically started screaming at Nastasya and, stamping his feet, chased her back into the kitchen. A moment later he said, looking at me in despair:

'I'm done for! *Cher*,' he suddenly sat down beside me and looked me in the face intently and pitiably, oh so pitiably. '*Cher*, it's not Siberia I fear, I swear to you, oh, *je vous jure*,'[13] (tears even welled up in his eyes) 'it's something else I fear . . .'

I guessed from just his look that he finally wanted to tell me something extraordinary, which he had refrained from telling me until now.

'It's disgrace that I fear,' he whispered mysteriously.

'What disgrace? Why, just the opposite! Believe me, Stepan Trofimovich, everything that's happened today will be explained and resolved in your favour . . .'

'Are you so sure they'll pardon me?'

'Why, what do you mean "pardon"? What words! What did you really do? I do assure you that you've done nothing!'

'*Qu'en savez-vous.*[14] My entire life has been . . . *cher* . . . They will remember everything . . . and if they really do find nothing, then *so much the worse*,' he suddenly added unexpectedly.

'What do you mean "so much the worse"?'

'The worse.'

'I don't understand.'

'My friend, my friend, let it be Siberia, Arkhangelsk,[15] stripped of my rights – let me perish and be done with it! But I fear something else.' Again a whisper, a frightened look and a mysterious air.

'But what, what?'

'That they'll flog me,' he pronounced, and fixed a distracted look on me.

'Who will flog you? Where? Why?' I exclaimed, afraid that he might be losing his mind.

'Where? Why there . . . where it's done.'

'But where is it done?'

'Oh, *cher*,' he whispered almost into my ear, 'the floor suddenly opens up under you, and you're lowered halfway down . . . Everyone knows that.'

'Fairy tales!' I exclaimed, finally getting it. 'Old fairy tales, and you've really believed in them until now?' I burst out laughing.

'Fairy tales! These fairy tales had to come from somewhere! The one who's been flogged won't tell you. I've pictured it ten thousand times in my imagination!'

'But you, you – and for what? Why, you haven't done anything, have you?'

'So much the worse; they'll see that I haven't done anything and they'll flog me.'

'And you're certain they'll ship you to Petersburg for that!'

'My friend, I've already said that I regret nothing, *ma carrière est finie*. Since the moment she bade farewell to me in Skvoreshniki, I've not felt any regret for my life . . . but the disgrace, the disgrace, *que dira-t-elle*,[16] if she finds out?'

He glanced at me in despair, and, poor fellow, flushed all over. I also dropped my eyes.

'She won't find out anything, because nothing will happen to you. It's as if I'm speaking to you for the first time in my life, Stepan Trofimovich, you've surprised me no end this morning.'

'My friend, you should know that this isn't fear. But even if they do pardon me, even if they do bring me back here again and do nothing – even then, I'm done for. *Elle me soupçonnera toute sa vie . . .*[17] me, me, a poet, a thinker, a man whom she bowed down to for twenty-two years!'

'It won't even occur to her.'

'It will,' he whispered with profound conviction. 'She and I talked several times about it in Petersburg, during Lent, just before we left, when both of us feared . . . *Elle me soupçonnera toute sa vie . . .* and how can I convince her otherwise? It will look improbable. For that matter, who in this wretched little town will believe it, *c'est invraisemblable . . . Et puis les femmes . . .*[18] She will be glad. She will be very much distressed, very much so, sincerely, as a true friend, but secretly she will be glad. I'll give her a weapon she can use against me for the rest of my life. Oh, my life is ruined! Twenty years of such complete happiness with her – and look!'

He covered his face with his hands.

'Stepan Trofimovich, shouldn't you let Varvara Petrovna know right away about what's happened?' I suggested.

'Lord, save me!' He trembled and jumped up from the sofa. 'Not for anything, never, not after what was said when we parted at Skvoreshniki, nev-ver!'

His eyes began to flash.

We went on sitting, I think, for another hour or more, all the time expecting something to happen, so obsessed were we with the whole idea. He lay down again, even closed his eyes, and lay there for about twenty minutes, not saying a word, so that I thought he'd fallen asleep or was in a state of reverie. Suddenly he heaved himself up, tore the towel off his head, jumped up from the couch, rushed to the mirror, knotted his tie with trembling hands and shouted for Nastasya in a thunderous voice, ordering her to bring his overcoat, his new hat and his walking stick.

'I can't bear it any longer,' he said in a breaking voice. 'I can't, I can't! . . . I'm going myself.'

'Where?' I also jumped up.

'To see von Lembke. *Cher*, I must, I have an obligation. It's a duty. I am a citizen and a human being, and not a chip of wood; I have rights, I want my rights. I haven't demanded my rights for twenty years, my whole life I've been criminally neglectful of them . . . but now I will demand them. He must tell me everything, everything. He has received a telegram. He won't dare torment me; otherwise, arrest me, arrest me, arrest me!'

His shouting was intermingled with squeals, and a stamping of feet.

'I approve of what you're doing,' I said, deliberately as calmly as possible, although I was very much afraid for him. 'Certainly it's better than sitting in such torment, but I don't approve of your mood. Just see what you look like and what state you'll be in when you get there. *Il faut être digne et calme avec von Lembke.*[19] Now you really are capable of throwing yourself on someone and biting him.'

'I'm giving myself up on my own. I'm walking straight into the jaws of the lion.'

'And I'll certainly go with you.'

'I didn't expect anything less from you, I accept your sacrifice, the sacrifice of a sincere friend, but only as far as the house, only as far as the house: you shouldn't, you have no right to compromise yourself any further by being in my company. *O croyez-moi, je serai calme!* At this moment I feel myself to be *à la hauteur de tout ce qu'il y a de plus sacré . . .'*[20]

'Maybe I'll go into the house with you,' I interrupted him. 'Yesterday I was informed by their stupid committee, through Vysotsky, that they are counting on me and inviting me to tomorrow's gala as one of the stewards, or whatever they're called . . . as one of the six young people who are appointed to keep an eye on the trays, to attend to the ladies, to escort the guests to their places and to wear a rosette of white and crimson ribbons on the left shoulder. I wanted to refuse, but now – why shouldn't I go into the house under the pretext of consulting with Yuliya Mikhaylovna herself? That's how you and I will go in together.'

He listened, nodding his head, but seemed to understand nothing. We were standing in the doorway.

'*Cher*,' he stretched his hand towards the icon-lamp in the corner, '*cher*, I've never believed in all that, but – so be it, so be it!' He crossed himself. '*Allons!*'[21]

'Well, it's better this way,' I thought, going out on to the front steps with him. 'The fresh air along the way will help, and we'll calm down a little, we'll return home and have a little rest . . .'

But I was reckoning without my host. Along the way there occurred an adventure that shook Stepan Trofimovich even more and determined his course irrevocably . . . so that, I confess, I never expected such verve from our friend as he suddenly displayed that morning. Poor friend, good friend!

CHAPTER 10

Filibusters. A Fateful Morning

I.

The incident that occurred on our way was also surprising. But everything has to be told in order. An hour before Stepan Trofimovich and I went out into the street, a crowd of people, workers from the Shpigulin factory, numbering about seventy people, perhaps even more, was walking through the town and being observed with curiosity by many. The crowd was walking with decorum, almost silently, in a deliberately orderly fashion. Some people later asserted that these seventy had been elected from all the factory workers, who numbered as many as nine hundred at the Shpigulin factory, for the purpose of going to the governor and, in the absence of the owners, seeking satisfaction for their grievances against the manager who, in closing down the factory and letting the workers go, had brazenly cheated them all – a fact that is now open to no doubt. Other people to this day reject the whole notion of an election of workers, asserting that seventy would be too many delegates, and that this crowd of people simply consisted of those who felt most aggrieved, and that they were merely coming to petition on their own behalf, so that the 'rebellion' in the factory, which later caused such an uproar, had never existed at all. A third group of people passionately insisted that these seventy men were not mere rebels, but out-and-out political agitators, that is, that they were among the most rebellious, and besides, had been stirred up precisely by the anonymous leaflets. In a word, whether someone's influence or instigation was at work here is still not precisely known. My own personal opinion is that the workers didn't even glance at the anonymous leaflets, and that if they had, they wouldn't have understood one word of them, if for no other reason than that the people who write such things, for all the starkness of their style, write extremely obscurely. But since the factory workers really were having a rough time, and the police, to whom they had turned, didn't want to get involved in their grievance, then what could have been more natural than their idea of going in a group to 'the general himself', if possible with a petition even, drawing themselves up respectfully before his door, and as soon as he made his appearance, all falling down on their knees and crying out as if to Providence itself? As I see it, there was no rebellion here, nor even delegates, for this is an old, historic way of handling things: from time immemorial the Russian people have loved to have a talk with 'the general himself', merely for the sheer pleasure of it, regardless of how the conversation would end.

And that's why I'm utterly convinced that even though Pyotr Stepanovich, Liputin, and maybe someone else, perhaps even Fedka, had scuttled among the factory workers to sound them out (since rather solid evidence of these activities actually exists) and talked with them, though probably with no more than two, three, or maybe five, just to test the waters, nothing had come of these conversations. As far as rebellion is concerned, if the factory workers did understand anything of the propaganda, then they would probably have immediately stopped listening to it as something that was stupid and didn't concern them. Fedka was another matter: he seemed to have had more luck than Pyotr Stepanovich. As has now become unmistakably clear, two factory workers were involved, along with Fedka, in the fire that broke out in town three days later, and then, a month after that, three more former workers were arrested in the district and also charged with arson and robbery. But if Fedka had actually managed to lure them into taking direct, immediate action, then again it was just these five, for nothing of the sort was heard about any others.

Whatever the case may be, the whole crowd of workers finally arrived at the small open area in front of the governor's house and drew themselves up respectfully and silently. Then they stood gaping at the front entrance, and started to wait. I was told as soon as they had taken their places, they proceeded to doff their hats, that is to say, perhaps half an hour before the appearance of the master of the province, who, as luck would have it, happened not to be at home just then. The police promptly showed up, at first individually, and then in as large a contingent as was possible. Naturally, they began in a threatening way, ordering the workers to disperse. But the workers just kept standing there unyieldingly, like a flock of sheep that had come to a fence, and responded laconically that they had come to see 'himself, the general'; stubborn determination was evident. The unnatural shouts ceased; they quickly yielded to ruminations, mysterious whispered instructions and a stern, restless concern, which furrowed the brows of the superior officers. The chief of police preferred to wait for von Lembke himself to arrive. It's nonsense to say that he dashed there full tilt in his three-horse droshky; and that he supposedly began to fight while still in the vehicle. He certainly had a reputation among us for dashing about, and he loved to dash off in his droshky with its yellow back, and as the 'trace-horses driven to debauchery' were growing more and more frenzied, to the utter delight of all the merchants in the shopping arcade, he would rise up in the droshky, stand fully erect, holding on to the strap that had been specially attached to the side, and flinging his right arm out into space, as statues do on monuments, survey the town in this fashion. But in the present situation he didn't fight, and although he couldn't dispense with uttering a strong expression as he bolted from the droshky, he did it only to avoid losing his popularity. It's even greater nonsense to say that soldiers with bayonets were brought in and that a telegram was dispatched somewhere ordering artillery and Cossacks[1] to be sent. These are fairy tales, which now are not believed even by the people who concocted them. It's also nonsense to say that barrels of water were brought from the fire brigade, and that the crowd was drenched. The plain and simple fact was that Ilya Ilyich, in the heat of the moment, shouted that they were all wet behind the ears and nobody would get off scot-free. From this people probably proceeded to invent the barrels, which passed in this form into the newspaper columns of the two capitals. The most accurate version, one must suppose, is that at first all the crowd was cordoned off by the available policemen and a special messenger was sent to von Lembke, an officer of the first precinct, who dashed along the road to Skvoreshniki in the chief of police's droshky, knowing that von Lembke had gone there in his carriage half an hour or so earlier.

But I confess that one question remains unanswered for me: how is it that a nondescript, that is, ordinary crowd of petitioners – seventy men strong, to be sure – was nonetheless, from the very first, the very outset, transformed into a rebellion that threatened to shake society to its foundations? Why did von Lembke himself clutch at this idea, when he appeared twenty minutes later, following the messenger? I would suppose (but again, it's my personal opinion) that Ilya Ilyich, who was on hail-fellow-well-met terms with the factory manager, even found it to his advantage to represent this crowd to von Lembke in this light, specifically to keep him from undertaking a real investigation of the matter, and that von Lembke himself had put the idea into his head. In the two previous days he had had two mysterious and urgent conversations with him, which didn't really get anywhere, but from which Ilya Ilyich could nonetheless see that the governor was obsessed with the manifestos, and with the idea that the Shpigulin workers had been put up to this socialist rebellion by someone, and so obsessed was he that he might well have regretted it if the existence of a plot had turned out to be nonsense. 'He wants to make a name for himself in Petersburg,' our shrewd Ilya Ilyich thought. 'Very well, then, we're at his service.'

But I'm convinced that poor Andrey Antonovich would not have wanted a rebellion even for the sake of making a name for himself. He was an extremely conscientious official, who had remained in a state of innocence until his marriage. Why, was he really to blame that instead of some innocent government job of getting firewood and an equally innocent Minnchen, a forty-year-old princess had raised him up to her level? I know almost for certain that it was precisely that fateful morning which marked the first clear symptoms of the condition that finally brought poor Andrey Antonovich, they say, to the famous special institution in Switzerland, where he is suppos-edly building up his strength. But even granting that clear signs of *something* were evident that morning, then it's possible to grant that manifestations of similar symptoms could well have appeared the day before, although not so clearly. I know from rumours of a most intimate sort (well, you may assume that Yulia Mikhaylovna herself, no longer in triumph but *almost* in repentance, for a woman is never *fully* repentant, subsequently told me a small part of this story), I know that Andrey Anton-ovich had come to his wife very late the previous night, after two o'clock in the morning, had wakened her and demanded that she listen to 'his ultimatum'. His demand was so insistent that she was forced to get up from her bed, in indignation and curling papers, and, seating herself on a couch, to hear him out, willy-nilly, albeit with sarcastic contempt. It was only now that she first understood how far gone Andrey Antonovich was, and she was secretly horrified. She should have come to her senses and relented, but she hid her horror and dug her heels in even more stubbornly than before. She had her way of handling Andrey Antonovich (as every spouse seems to have), which by now she had tested more than once, and it had more than once driven him into a frenzy. Yuliya Mikhaylovna's way consisted of contemptuous silence, for an hour, for two hours, for twenty-four hours and for almost three days – silence no matter what, no matter what he said, no matter what he did, even if he climbed up to throw himself out of a third-storey window. It was a way of operating that was unbearable to a sensitive man!

Whether Yuliya Mikhaylovna was punishing her husband for the blunders he had made over the past three days, and for his envy and jealousy, as governor, of her administrative abilities; whether she was indignant at his criticism of the way she behaved with the young people and with our entire society, without any understanding of her subtle and far-sighted polit-ical purposes; whether she was angry at his stupid and senseless envy of Pyotr Stepanovich – whatever the case may have been, she made up her mind not to relent on this occasion either, even despite the three o'clock hour and Andrey Antonovich's state of agitation, which she had never known to be so intense. As

he paced, distraught, back and forth, here and there over the
carpets of her boudoir, he told her everything, everything, in
utterly disconnected fashion, to be sure, but *everything* that
had boiled up inside him, for – 'it had transcended all limits'.
He began by saying that everyone was laughing at him and
'leading him by the nose'. 'Damn the expression!' – he immediately shrilled, catching her smile – 'even though it's "by the
nose", it's still true!' 'No, madam, the moment has come: you
should know that this is no time for laughter and for the wiles
of female coquettishness. We are not in the boudoir of some
simpering lady, but rather we are like two abstract beings in a
balloon, who have come together to tell the truth.' (Of course
he was confused, and couldn't cast his thoughts, which were
otherwise correct, in the proper form.) 'It's you, you, madam,
who have taken me out of my former situation. I accepted
this post only for you, to gratify your ambition. You smile
sarcastically? Don't look so triumphant, don't be in such a
hurry. You should know, madam, you should know that I
would have been able, that I would have known how to handle
this job, and not just this job, but ten such jobs, because I have
abilities; but you, madam, in your presence I can't manage it;
for in your presence I have no abilities. Two centres cannot
exist, and you have created two – one in my office, and the
other in your boudoir – two centres of power, madam, but I
won't allow that, I won't allow it!! In official work, as in
marriage, there is one centre; two are impossible. How did
you pay me back?' he continued to shout. 'Our marriage has
amounted to nothing more than you constantly and every hour
of the day trying to prove to me that I am worthless, that I'm
stupid and even despicable, and I've been forced, constantly
and every hour of the day and humiliatingly, to try to prove to
you that I am *not* worthless, that I'm anything but stupid and
that I impress everyone with my noble nature. Well now, isn't
that humiliating for both of us?'

Here he began stamping both feet frantically over and over
again on the carpet, and Yuliya Mikhaylovna was forced to get
up, looking stern and dignified. He quickly quieted down, but
then became emotional and started sobbing (yes, sobbing),

striking himself on the chest for almost a full five minutes, increasingly distraught because of Yuliya Mikhaylovna's utterly unbroken silence. Finally, he committed a real blunder by letting it slip that he was jealous of her relationship with Pyotr Stepanovich. Realizing that he had made an utter fool of himself, he began ranting and raving, and shouted that he 'would not permit anyone to deny God'; that he would disband her 'shameless atheistic salon'; that the governor is even obliged to believe in God, 'and therefore, so is his wife'; that he 'would not put up with the young people'; that 'you, you, madam, for the sake of your own dignity, should show concern for your husband and defend his intelligence, even if he has poor abilities (and I certainly don't have poor abilities!), but meanwhile it's you who are the reason why everyone here despises me, you are the one who's turned them all against me!' He shouted that he would get rid of the women's question, that he would smoke out even the faintest trace of it, that he would prohibit and disband the absurd subscription gala for governesses (the Devil with them!) first thing tomorrow; that first thing in the morning he would expel the first governess from the province who crossed his path and 'in the custody of a Cossack!' 'Deliberately, deliberately!' he shrilled. 'Are you aware, are you aware,' he shouted, 'that those scoundrels of yours are stirring people up in the factory, and that I know about it? Are you aware that they're deliberately distributing manifestos, de-lib-er-ate-ly! Are you aware that I know the names of four of those scoundrels, and that I'm losing my mind, I'm losing it for good and all!' But at this point Yuliya Mikhaylovna suddenly broke her silence and announced sternly that she herself had long been aware of those criminal schemes and that it was all rubbish, that he had taken it too seriously and that as far as the pranksters were concerned, she not only knew those four, but all of them (she lied); but that she had no intention of losing her mind over it, and on the contrary, had even more faith in her own intelligence and hoped to bring everything to a harmonious conclusion by encouraging the young people, making them listen to reason, showing them suddenly and unexpectedly that their schemes were known, and then pointing them to new goals for a more rational and luminous form of activity. Oh, what happened to Andrey Antonovich at that moment! After learning that Pyotr Stepanovich had again deceived him and had mocked him so crudely, that he had revealed much more to her than to him, and sooner, and that, finally, Pyotr Stepanovich himself might well be the chief instigator of all the criminal schemes – he flew into a frenzy. 'You should know, you muddle-headed but venomous woman,' he exclaimed, breaking all his chains at one go, 'you should know that I will immediately arrest your unworthy lover, clap him in irons and send him off to the fortress, or I myself will jump out of the window this very moment before your very eyes!' Yuliya Mikhaylovna, green with rage, immediately reacted to this tirade with a pro-longed outburst of ringing laughter that chimed and pealed exactly as it does in the French theatre, when a Parisian actress, who has been hired for a hundred thousand roubles to play a coquette, laughs in the face of her husband for daring to be jealous of her. Von Lembke was on the point of rushing to the window, but he suddenly stopped dead, folded his hands on his chest and, pale as a corpse, cast an ominous look on his laughing wife. 'Do you know, do you know, Yuliya,' he said in a strangled, pleading voice, 'do you know that I, too, really can do something?' But with the fresh, even stronger outburst of laughter that followed these last words, he clenched his teeth, gave a groan and suddenly rushed not to the window, but at his wife, and raised his fist over her! He didn't bring it down upon her – oh no, three times no! – but he was done for there and then. He ran into his study as fast as his legs would carry him, flung himself just as he was, fully dressed, face down on the bed that had been made up for him, in a frenzy wrapped himself, head and all, in a sheet, and lay there for the next two hours or so – not sleeping, not thinking, with a stone weighing on his heart and dull, unwavering despair in his soul. From time to time his whole body would be racked by an agonizing, feverish shudder. He kept remembering some random things that bore no relation to anything: at one moment, for instance, he thought of an old wall clock he'd had some fifteen years earlier in Petersburg and which was missing the minute hand;

then of the unusually cheerful clerk Millebois and how, when together in the Alexander Park, they had once caught a sparrow, and having caught it, they remembered, laughing loudly enough for the whole park to hear, that one of them was already a collegiate assessor. I think he fell asleep about seven o'clock in the morning without noticing it, and slept with enjoyment and with pleasant dreams. On wakening about ten, he suddenly jumped wildly out of bed, instantly remembered everything and smacked the palm of his hand against his forehead. He refused to receive either breakfast, or Blum, or the chief of police, or the official who appeared to remind him that the members of the —— Committee were waiting for him to preside as chairman that morning.

He received no one, he heard nothing and wanted to understand nothing, but ran like a madman to Yuliya Mikhaylovna's part of the house. There Sofiya Antropovna, a little old lady of noble birth, who had long been living with Yuliya Mihkhaylovna, explained to him that at ten o'clock she had set out with a large group of people, in three carriages, to Varvara Petrovna Stavrogina's house at Skvoreshniki, in order to inspect the location of the future gala, the second one, to be held two weeks hence, and that this had been agreed on with Varvara Petrovna herself three days earlier. Stunned by this news, Andrey Antonovich returned to his study, and impulsively ordered horses. He could hardly even wait. His soul yearned for Yuliya Mikhaylovna – just to glance at her, to be near her for five minutes; perhaps she would glance at him, notice him, smile in her same old way, forgive him – ohh! 'What's going on with the horses?' He mechanically opened a thick book that was lying on the table (sometimes he would tell his fortune this way, opening a book at random and reading the third line from the bottom on the right-hand page). The result this time was: '*Tout est pour le mieux dans le meilleur des mondes possibles.*' Voltaire. *Candide.*[2] He spat in disgust and ran to get into the carriage. 'To Skvoreshniki!' The coachman later related that the master kept hurrying him the entire way, but no sooner had they begun to approach the lady's house than he suddenly ordered the coachman to turn the carriage around and take

him back to town. 'Fast as you can, please, fast as you can.'
They hadn't even reached the town wall when 'the master
ordered me to stop again, he got out o' the carriage and walked
'cross the road into the field. I thought it was on account of not
feelin' good, but there he stood lookin' at the flowers, and that's
how he stood for some time. It was strange, it was, and made
me begin to wonder.' That was the coachman's testimony. I
remember the weather that morning: it was a cold and clear
but windy September day. Before Andrey Antonovich, who had
left the road behind, stretched an austere landscape of bare
fields with wheat that had long since been harvested; the howling wind was tossing back and forth some pitiful remnants of
dying yellow flowers. Was he of a mind to compare himself and
his fate to the stunted flowers that had been beaten down by
autumn and frost? I don't think so. I even think it unlikely, and
that he was oblivious to the flowers, despite the testimony of
the coachman and the superintendent of the first precinct who
was approaching just then in the chief of police's droshky, and
who later asserted that he actually found the governor standing
there with a bunch of yellow flowers in his hand. This officer,
an enthusiastic administrative individual, Vasily Ivanovich Filibusterov,[3] was a recent arrival in our town, but had already
distinguished himself and made a name for his inordinate zeal,
for his aggressiveness in every aspect of the execution of his
duties and for his chronically unsober state. After jumping out
of the droshky and not hesitating in the least at the sight of
what the governor was doing, he reported, without drawing a
breath, and with a demented but convinced air about him, that
'there's unrest in the town'.

'Eh? What?' Andrey Antonovich turned a stern face to him,
but without the least surprise or any memory of the carriage
and the coachman, as if they were back home in his study.

'Superintendent of the First Precinct, Filibusterov, Your
Excellency. There's a rebellion in town.'

'Filibusters?' Andrey Antonovich repeated pensively.

'Precisely so, Your Excellency. The Shpigulin men are rebelling.'

'The Shpigulin men!'

The mention of the name 'Shpigulin' seemed to jog his memory. He even gave a start and raised a finger to his forehead: 'The Shpigulin men!' Quietly, but still pensively, he started walking towards the carriage without hurrying, took his seat and ordered it back to town. The superintendent followed him in the droshky.

I imagine that many interesting things vaguely crossed his mind along the way, on many different topics, but he hardly had any firm idea or definite intention when he drove into the open area in front of the governor's house. But as soon as he caught sight of the crowd of 'rebels' drawn up in resolute and orderly fashion, the cordon of policemen, the helpless (and perhaps deliberately helpless) chief of police and the general expectation directed at him, all the blood rushed to his heart. Pale, he stepped out of the carriage.

'Caps off!' he said, barely audibly and in a gasping voice. 'On your knees!'[4] he shrilled unexpectedly, unexpectedly to himself as well, and it was perhaps this very unexpectedness that explains the subsequent turn of events. It was the sort of thing that happens on the hills at Shrovetide: can sleds, as they rush downhill, really just stop in mid-course? To make matters worse, all his life Andrey Antonovich had been marked by a serenity of character, and he never shouted or stamped his feet at anyone. Such people are more dangerous if it ever happens that their sleds start speeding downhill for some reason. Everything began to spin before his eyes.

'Filibusters!' he screamed even more shrilly and absurdly, and his voice broke. He stood there, not yet knowing what he would do, but knowing and sensing with his whole being that he would definitely do something.

'Lord!' came a voice from the crowd. A young lad began crossing himself; three or four men actually did try to get on their knees, but the others moved three steps forward in a great mass and suddenly all set up a din: 'Your Excellency . . . we came on the job for a certain number of days . . . the manager . . . and you can't say,' etc., etc. It was impossible to make out anything.

Alas! Andrey Antonovich couldn't make anything out; he was still holding the flowers in his hands. The rebellion was as obvious to him as the prison carts had been to Stepan Trofimovich earlier. And scurrying amidst the crowd of 'rebels' who were goggling at him he thought he could see Pyotr Stepanovich, who had stirred them up and who hadn't left his mind for a moment since the previous day – Pyotr Stepanovich, the hated Pyotr Stepanovich.

'Birch rods!' he shouted even more unexpectedly.

A dead silence fell.

That's how it happened at the very beginning, to judge by highly reliable information I received and by my own conjectures. But after that the information becomes less reliable, as do my conjectures. Nonetheless, there are some facts.

In the first place, the birch rods appeared rather too quickly: evidently they had been prepared in advance by the resourceful chief of police. However, no more than two men were punished, I don't think that even three were. I stand by that. It's pure fabrication to say that everyone was punished, or at least half the people. It's also nonsense to say that some poor but genteel lady who was just passing by was arrested and immediately flogged for something, and yet I myself later read about this lady in a report in one of the Petersburg papers. Many people in our town were talking about a certain Avdotya Petrovna Tarapygina, who lived in an almshouse by the cemetery, and who supposedly, while returning to the almshouse from a visit and passing through the open square, squeezed between the onlookers, out of natural curiosity, and seeing what was going on, exclaimed: 'What a shame!' and spat in disgust. For that she was supposedly seized and flogged as well. Not only was this incident put into print, but in the town a collection was taken up for her in the heat of the moment. I myself subscribed twenty kopecks. And then what happened? It now turns out that no one named Tarapygina was living in the almshouse at all! I myself went to the cemetery to make inquiries at their almshouse. No one there had even heard of any Tarapygina; what's more, they were very offended when I told them of the gossip that was circulating. In fact, I am mentioning this nonexistent Avdotya Petrovna only because the same thing (in the event that she really did exist) almost happened to Stepan Trofimovich. It may even be that he was somehow responsible for this whole absurd rumour about Tarapygina; that is, the gossip, as it went on developing, proceeded to recast him in the form of some Tarapygina or other. The main thing was that I don't understand how he gave me the slip as soon as we came out on to the square. Having a premonition that something bad was going to happen, I wanted to lead him around the square directly to the governor's front door, but he himself grew curious and stopped for just a minute to ask something of the first person he met, and suddenly I looked and Stepan Trofimovich was no longer beside me. Guided by my instinct I immediately ran to look for him in the most dangerous place; I somehow felt in my bones that his sled too had come careening down the mountain. And in fact, he was now to be found in the very centre of things. I remember that I grabbed him by the arm, but he looked at me quietly and proudly, and, with enormous authority:

'*Cher*,' he uttered in a voice that quivered like a broken string, 'if all of them here in the square are ordering people about so unceremoniously in our presence, then what can one expect from *that one*, for instance ... if he should happen to act independently?'

And trembling with indignation and enormously keen on challenging them, he thrust a threatening finger at Filibusterov, who was standing two steps away and staring wide-eyed at us.

'*That one!*' Filibusterov shouted, blind with fury. 'Which *that one*? And who are you?' he stepped up, clenching his fist. 'Who are you?' he roared ferociously, hysterically and desperately. (I must note that he knew Stepan Trofimovich perfectly well by sight.) A moment more and he would of course have grabbed him by the scruff of the neck; but luckily von Lembke turned his head when he heard the outcry. He looked uncomprehendingly but fixedly at Stepan Trofimovich, as if pondering something, and suddenly began waving his hand impatiently. Filibusterov stopped short. I pulled Stepan Trofimovich away from the crowd. However, he may already have wanted to retreat on his own.

'Home, home,' I kept insisting, 'if they didn't beat us, then it's von Lembke we have to thank, of course.'

'You go, my friend, it's my fault for subjecting you to this.

You have a future and a career of sorts, but I – *mon heure est sonné.*'[5]

He planted a firm foot on the front steps of the governor's house. The porter knew me; I announced that we were both there to see Yuliya Mikhaylovna. We took seats in the reception hall and began to wait. I didn't want to leave my friend, but I couldn't think of anything more to say to him. He had the air of a man who had condemned himself to something like certain death for the fatherland. We didn't sit together, but in different corners. I was closer to the entrance door; he was at the extreme opposite, his head bowed in thought and both hands resting lightly on his walking stick. He was holding his broad-brimmed hat in his left hand. We sat like that for about ten minutes.

2.

Von Lembke suddenly came in with quick steps, accompanied by the chief of police; he glanced at us distractedly, and paying no attention, was about to turn to the right into his study, but Stepan Trofimovich stood up before him and blocked his way. The tall, utterly unique figure of Stepan Trofimovich produced an impression. Von Lembke stopped.

'Who is this?' he grumbled in bewilderment, as if directing his question to the chief of police, but without turning his head towards him in the slightest, and continuing to inspect Stepan Trofimovich.

'Retired Collegiate Assessor Stepan Trofimovich Verkhovensky, Your Excellency,' Stepan Trofimovich replied, with a dignified bow of his head. His Excellency continued to peer at him, but with a very vacant expression.

'About what?' and in the laconic way of authority, he disdainfully and impatiently turned his ear to Stepan Trofimovich, finally taking him for an ordinary petitioner with some written request.

'Today I was subjected to a search at my house by an official who was acting in the name of Your Excellency; therefore, I should like . . .'

'Name? Name?' von Lembke asked impatiently, as if he

had finally put his finger on something. Stepan Trofimovich repeated his name even more grandly.

'Ah-h-h! It's ... it's that hotbed ... My dear sir, you have declared yourself from the point of ... You're a professor? A professor?'

'I once had the honour of delivering a few lectures to the young people of – University.'

'The you-ng-ng-ng people!' Von Lembke seemed to give a start, although, I wager, he still understood little of what was going on, and perhaps even with whom he was speaking. 'My dear sir, I will not permit this,' he suddenly got terribly angry. 'I don't allow young people. It's all these manifestos. They're an attack on society, dear sir, a maritime attack, filibustering ... What is it that you wish to ask?'

'On the contrary, your wife asked me to read at her gala tomorrow. I'm not here to ask for anything, I've come to seek my rights ...'

'At the gala? There will be no gala. I won't allow your gala, sir! Lectures? Lectures?' he shouted in a frenzy.

'I would like it very much if you spoke to me with more civility, Your Excellency, without stamping your feet and shouting at me, as if I were a boy.'

'Do you perhaps understand with whom you are speaking?' Von Lembke flushed.

'Fully,Your Excellency.'

'I am the one who protects society, but you are destroying it. Destroying it! You ... I, however, do have some recollection of you: wasn't it you who were a tutor in the house of General Stavrogin's widow?'

'Yes, I was ... a tutor ... in the house of General Stavrogin's widow.'

'And over the course of twenty years you have been creating a hotbed of everything that has now come to a head ... all the fruits ... I believe I saw you in the square just now. However, you should be afraid, dear sir, you should be afraid; the direction of your ideas is well known. Be assured that I am bearing it in mind. I, dear sir, cannot allow your lectures, I cannot, sir. I am not the one to turn to with such requests.'

He again tried to pass.

'I repeat that you are mistaken, Your Excellency. It is your wife who has asked me to read – not a lecture, but something literary at tomorrow's gala. But now I myself decline to read. My most humble request is that you explain to me, if you can: how, for what reason and why was I subjected to a search today? They took from me certain books, papers, private letters that were dear to me, and they carried them through the town in a wheelbarrow . . .'

'Who conducted the search?' Von Lembke gave a start, recovered himself fully and suddenly flushed all over. He quickly turned to the chief of police. At that moment the stooped, long, awkward figure of Blum appeared in the doorway.

'There's the official himself.' Stepan Trofimovich pointed at him. Blum stepped forward with a guilty but by no means yielding look.

'*Vous ne faites que des bêtises*,'[6] von Lembke hurled at him in annoyance and anger, and suddenly seemed to be totally transformed and completely himself again. 'Pardon me,' he babbled, utterly disconcerted and turning as red as he could. 'That was all . . . that was probably all a blunder, a misunderstanding . . . just a misunderstanding.'

'Your Excellency,' Stepan Trofimovich observed, 'in my youth I witnessed a certain characteristic incident. Once in the theatre, in the corridor, a man walked up quickly to another and gave him a resounding slap in the face, right in public. After immediately perceiving that the injured party was not in fact the one for whom his slap had been intended, but someone else entirely, only rather similar in appearance, he, in anger and haste, like a man who cannot afford to waste precious time, said exactly the same words Your Excellency has just used: "I was mistaken . . . excuse me, it was a misunderstanding, just a misunderstanding." And when the man who had been insulted nonetheless continued to feel insulted and began to shout, the first man said to him, in extreme annoyance: "But I'm telling you that it was a misunderstanding, why are you still shouting?"'

'That . . . that of course is very amusing,' von Lembke gave a crooked smile, 'but . . . but can't you really see how unhappy I am myself?'

He almost cried out and seemed to want to cover his face with his hands.

This unexpected and anguished exclamation, which was almost a sob, was unbearable. This was probably the first moment since the previous day when he was fully and vividly aware of all that had happened, and it was immediately followed by despair – complete, humiliating and palpable. Who knows: a moment longer and he might have filled the whole room with his sobs. At first Stepan Trofimovich gave him a wild look, then he suddenly inclined his head and, in a deeply sympathetic voice, intoned:

'Your Excellency, don't trouble yourself any longer over my peevish complaint, and just order my books and letters returned to me . . .'

He was interrupted. At that same instant Yuliya Mikhaylovna noisily returned with the whole group that had accompanied her. But here I would like to provide as detailed a description as possible.

3.

In the first place, everyone from all three carriages trooped into the reception hall at the same time. The entrance to Yuliya Mikhaylovna's apartments was separate, directly to the left of the front door; but on this occasion everyone went through the reception hall, and, I suppose, precisely because Stepan Trofimovich was there, and because everything that had happened to him, along with everything involving the Shpigulin men, had already been reported to Yuliya Mikhaylovna when she drove into town. Lyamshin, who had been left at home for some offence, and had not joined the expedition, had therefore found out everything before the others, and had given her the news. He had galloped off, with malicious glee, along the road to Skvoreshniki on an old wreck of a hired Cossack horse to greet the returning cavalcade with the happy news. I think that Yuliya Mikhaylovna, for all her lofty resolve, was nonetheless somewhat flustered when she heard such astonishing news, though perhaps only for a moment. The political aspect of the matter, for instance, could not cause her any concern: Pyotr Stepanovich had already tried some four times now to persuade her that the Shpigulin rebels should all be flogged, and Pyotr Stepanovich, for some time now, had really become an extraordinary authority in her eyes. 'But I'll still make him pay for that' is what she was probably thinking to herself, with *he* of course referring to her husband. I will note in passing that on this occasion Pyotr Stepanovich, as luck would have it, was not part of the larger expedition either, and no one had laid eyes on him since that morning. I will also mention in passing that Varvara Petrovna, after receiving her guests, returned with them to town (in the same carriage with Yuliya Mikhaylovna), for the specific purpose of taking part in the final meeting of the committee for the next day's gala. Of course, she should also have been interested in the news that Lyamshin had reported concerning Stepan Trofimovich, and perhaps even have been disturbed by it.

The reckoning with Andrey Antonovich began immediately. Alas, he sensed this the moment he laid eyes on his worthy spouse. With an open manner, with an enchanting smile, she walked briskly up to Stepan Trofimovich, extended her beautifully gloved hand to him and began showering him with highly flattering greetings, as if she hadn't another thing in the world to do that entire morning besides run up to Stepan Trofimovich and be as charming as possible to him because she was finally seeing him in her house. There wasn't a single hint about that morning's search; it was as if she still knew nothing about it. Nor did she utter a single word to her husband, or dart a single glance in his direction; it was as if he were simply not in the room at all. What's more, Stepan Trofimovich was immediately appropriated with great authority and escorted into the drawing room, as if he had had no exchange of words with von Lembke, or, if he had, it was not worth continuing. I repeat again: it seems to me that despite all the loftiness of her tone, Yuliya Mikhaylovna in this case had once again made a major blunder. She was especially helped here by Karmazinov (who had joined the expedition at Yuliya Mikhaylovna's special request and thus, although indirectly, had finally paid a visit to Varvara Petrovna, which absolutely thrilled her, because of her faint-heartedness). While he was still in the doorway (he had come in after the others), he gave a cry on seeing Stepan Trofimovich, and flew towards him with arms outstretched, interrupting even Yuliya Mikhaylovna.

'It's been ages, it's been forever! At long last . . . *Excellent ami*.'

He started exchanging kisses, and of course, presented his own cheek first. A rattled Stepan Trofimovich was forced to press his lips to it.

'*Cher*,' he said to me that evening, as he reminisced about everything that had happened during the day, 'at that moment I thought: which of us is more loathsome? Is it he, who embraced me in order to humiliate me then and there, or is it I, who despised him and his cheek and proceeded to kiss it, even though I could have turned away . . . ugh!'

'Well, tell me then, tell me everything,' Karmazinov babbled and simpered, as if it were really possible just to plunge in and tell him the story of one's life for the past twenty-five years. But this silly piece of frivolity was considered 'high' tone.

'Remember that the last time we saw each other was in Moscow, at a dinner in honour of Granovsky, and that twenty-four years have passed since then,' Stepan Trofimovich began in a very moderate way (and therefore not at all in a high tone).

'*Ce cher homme*,' Karmazinov interrupted him shrilly and familiarly, squeezing his shoulder in too friendly a manner. 'Do take us to your rooms as quickly as possible, Yuliya Mikhaylovna; he'll sit down there and tell us everything.'

'Meanwhile, I was never even remotely close to that cranky old woman,' Stepan Trofimovich, shaking with anger, continued to complain to me that same evening. 'We were both still almost boys, and even then I began to hate him . . . as he did me, naturally . . .'

Yuliya Mikhaylovna's salon quickly filled up. Varvara Petrovna was in an especially excited state, although she was making an effort to appear indifferent, but I caught two or three of the hate-filled looks she directed at Karmazinov, and the irate ones she directed at Stepan Trofimovich – irate in anticipation, irate out of jealousy, out of love. If Stepan Trofimovich were some-how to bungle it this time and allow Karmazinov to cut him down to size in front of everyone, it seems to me that she would have immediately leaped up and flattened him. I forgot to say that Liza was present there as well, and never had I seen her more joyful, more blithe, gay and happy. Naturally, Mavriky Nikolayevich was there, too. Then in the crowd of the young ladies and half-dissipated young people who formed Yuliya Mikhaylovna's usual entourage, and who took such dissipation for high spirits, and cheap cynicism for wit, I noticed two or three new faces: a very flighty Pole who was visiting the town; and a German, a doctor, a sturdy old fellow, who was constantly laughing loudly and with pleasure at his own clever remarks; and a very young prince from Petersburg, an automaton of a figure, with the bearing of a statesman and wearing a dreadfully high collar. But it was obvious that Yuliya Mikhaylovna had a very high opinion of this guest, and was even anxious about the impression her salon was making on him.

'*Cher monsieur Karmazinoff*,' Stepan Trofimovich began to speak, seating himself picturesquely on the sofa and suddenly beginning to simper no less than Karmazinov. '*Cher monsieur Karmazinoff*, the life of a man of our former time and of certain convictions, despite an interval of twenty-five years, must seem monotonous . . .'

The German began laughing loudly and convulsively, as if he were neighing, evidently supposing that Stepan Trofimovich had said something terribly funny. Stepan Trofimovich, in feigned astonishment, looked at him, without, however, pro-ducing any effect on him. The prince also looked, turning his whole collar and his pince-nez at the German, although without the slightest curiosity.

'. . . must seem monotonous,' Stepan Trofimovich deliber-ately repeated, drawing each word out as protractedly and un-ceremoniously as possible. 'Such was my life too over the course of that quarter of a century, *et comme on trouve partout plus de moines que de raison*,[7] and since I am in complete agreement with that, the result was that during this quarter of a century I . . .'

'*C'est charmant, les moines*,'[8] Yuliya Mikhaylovna whispered, turning to Varvara Petrovna, who was sitting beside her.

Varvara Petrovna responded with a proud look. But Karmazinov couldn't endure the success of the French phrase and quickly interrupted Stepan Trofimovich in a loud and penetrating voice.

'As for me, my mind is at rest on that account, and I've already been living in Karlsruhe for the past seven years. And when it was proposed last year by the town council that a new water pipe be laid, I felt in my heart that the issue of the Karlsruhe water pipe was dearer and more precious to me than all the issues of my dear fatherland . . . over the entire period of the so-called reforms that have been carried out here.'

'I'm compelled to sympathize, although it goes against the grain,' Stepan Trofimovich sighed, bowing his head weightily.

Yuliya Mikhaylovna felt a sense of triumph: the conversation was becoming deeper and now had some direction to it.

'Was it a water pipe or a drainpipe?' the doctor asked loudly.

'A water pipe, Doctor, a water pipe, and I even helped them to draw up the plans.'

The doctor burst out in a crackling laugh. Many followed suit, but this time in the doctor's face, although he didn't notice it and was dreadfully pleased that everyone was laughing.

'Permit me not to agree with you, Karmazinov,' Yuliya Mikhaylovna hastened to interject. 'Karlsruhe goes on as usual, but you like to mystify people, and this time we won't believe you. Who among the Russians, among the writers, has presented so many of the most contemporary types, has put his finger on so many of the most contemporary problems, has been responsible for pointing out those major issues of contemporary life that go into the making of the contemporary man of action as a type? You, you alone and no one else. After that just try to convince us of your indifference to your native land and your passionate interest in the Karlsruhe[9] water pipe! Ha, ha!'

'Well, of course,' Karmazinov began to simper, 'in the Pogozhev type I presented all the defects of the Slavophiles, and in the Nikodimov type all the shortcomings of the Westernizers . . .'[10]

'Well, hardly *all* the shortcomings,' Lyamshin whispered very quietly.

'But I do this offhandedly, just to kill the relentless passage of time and . . . to satisfy all the relentless demands of my fellow-countrymen.'

'You probably already know, Stepan Trofimovich,' Yuliya Mikhaylovna continued triumphantly, 'that tomorrow we will have the pleasure of hearing the magnificent lines of one of Semyon Yegorovich's latest and most elegant literary inspirations; it is called "Merci". He announces in this piece that he will write no more, and will not do so for anything in the world, even if an angel from heaven, or, better put, all of the best society should beg him to change his mind. In short, he is laying down his pen for the remainder of his life, and this graceful "Merci" is addressed to the public in gratitude for the constant enthusiasm with which it has welcomed for so many years his constant service to honest Russian thinking.'

Yuliya Mikhaylovna was at the height of bliss.

'Yes, I am taking my leave; I will say my "Merci" and depart, and there . . . in Karlsruhe . . . I shall close my eyes,' Karmazinov began gradually to run out of energy.

Like many of our great writers (and we have a lot of great writers), he couldn't resist praise and immediately began to weaken, despite his wit. But I think this is forgivable. It's said that one of our Shakespeares, in a private conversation, actually blurted out that 'we *great people*[11] cannot do otherwise', and so on, and didn't even notice it.

'There, in Karlsruhe, I shall close my eyes. All that's left for us great people, once we have finished our work, is to close our eyes as quickly as possible, without seeking any reward. That is what I shall do too.'

'Give me your address, and I'll come and visit your grave in Karlsruhe,' the German roared with laughter.

'Nowadays dead bodies are also shipped by rail,' one of the insignificant young people said.

Lyamshin simply began to squeal with delight. Yuliya Mikhaylovna frowned. Nikolay Stavrogin came in.

'I've been told that you were taken to the police station?'

he said loudly, addressing first of all Stepan Trofimovich.

'No, it was only an *arresting* instance,' Stepan Trofimovich punned.

'But I hope it won't have the slightest influence on my request,' Yuliya Mikhaylovna again put in, 'and I hope that you, regardless of this unfortunate unpleasantness, of which I had no idea until now, will not disappoint our heartiest expectations and will not deprive us of the pleasure of listening to your reading at the literary matinée.'

'I don't know, I . . . now . . .'

'Really, I'm so unhappy, Varvara Petrovna . . . and imagine, just when I was so eager to get to know personally one of the most remarkable and independent Russian minds, and all of a sudden, Stepan Trofimovich goes and announces his intention to withdraw from us.'

'Your praise is uttered so loudly that of course I should pretend not to have heard it,' Stepan Trofimovich said clearly and distinctly, 'but I don't believe that my poor self is so essential to your gala tomorrow. However, I . . .'

'Why, you're spoiling him!' Pyotr Stepanovich exclaimed, as he came running quickly into the room. 'I've only just taken him in hand, and suddenly, in one morning – a search, an arrest, a policeman grabs him by the scruff of the neck, and now the ladies are coddling him in the governor's salon! Why, every bone in his body is aching with ecstasy now; he's never seen such a benefit performance even in his dreams. Any minute now he'll begin denouncing the socialists!'

'That cannot be, Pyotr Stepanovich. Socialism is too great an idea for Stepan Trofimovich not to recognize it,' said Yuliya Mikhaylovna, vigorously taking his part.

'The idea is great, but those who profess it are not always giants, *et brisons-là, mon cher*,'[12] Stepan Trofimovich concluded, turning to his son and rising handsomely from his seat.

But at this point a most unexpected circumstance arose. Von Lembke had been present in the salon for some time now, but was seemingly unnoticed by anyone, although everyone had seen him come in. Yuliya Mikhaylovna, still intent on her previous idea, continued to ignore him. He stationed himself by the door, and with a stern face listened glumly to the conversations. Having caught mention of the morning's events, he began shifting uneasily, first fixing his stare on the prince, obviously struck by the heavy forward thrust of his starched collar; then he suddenly seemed to give a start, as he heard the voice of Pyotr Stepanovich and saw him running in, and as soon as Stepan Trofimovich had succeeded in expressing his sentiment about socialists, he suddenly walked up to him, in the process knocking against Lyamshin, who jumped aside in a deliberately exaggerated gesture of surprise, rubbing his shoulder and pretending that he had been injured very painfully.

'Enough!' said von Lembke, energetically seizing the frightened Stepan Trofimovich by the hand and squeezing it as hard as he could in his. 'Enough, the filibusters of our time have been identified. Not a word more. Measures have been taken . . .'

He had spoken loudly, for the whole room to hear, and concluded energetically. The impression produced was painful. Everyone sensed that something wasn't right here. I saw Yuliya Mikhaylovna turn pale. To complete the effect, a stupid accident occurred. After announcing that measures had been taken, von Lembke turned around sharply and began to walk quickly out of the room, but after two steps he tripped on the carpet, stumbled forward and nearly fell. He stopped for a moment, looked at the spot he had tripped against and, saying 'Fix it', walked out of the door. Yuliya Mikhaylovna ran after him. As soon as she had gone out, a din arose, in which it was difficult to make out anything. Some said he was 'deranged', others that he was 'susceptible'. Still others pointed their fingers to their foreheads; in the corner, Lyamshin stuck two fingers above his forehead.[13] Hints were dropped about certain domestic incidents, all in a whisper, naturally. No one picked up his hat; all were waiting. I don't know what Yuliya Mikhaylovna managed to accomplish, but in about five minutes she returned, trying as best she could to appear composed. She replied evasively that Andrey Antonovich was somewhat agitated, but that it was nothing, that he had been that way since childhood, that she knew 'much better' and that tomorrow's gala would of course cheer him up. Then came a few more flattering (but only for pro-

priety's sake) words for Stepan Trofimovich, and a loud invitation for the members of the committee to begin their meeting
then and there. Only then did those who weren't members of
the committee start getting ready to go home; but the painful
adventures of this fateful day were not yet at an end.

At the very moment when Nikolay Vsevolodovich came in, I
noticed that Liza gave him a quick and intent look and then
didn't take her eyes off him for a long time – so long that it
finally attracted attention. I saw Mavriky Nikolayevich bend
over her from behind, seemingly wanting to whisper something
to her, but evidently he changed his mind and quickly straightened up, looking round at everyone with a guilty air. Nikolay
Vsevolodovich stirred curiosity too: his face was paler than
usual, and he looked unusually distracted. After hurling his
question at Stepan Trofimovich when he came in, he seemed to
have promptly forgotten about him, and, indeed, it seems to
me that he even forgot to go up to his hostess. He didn't glance
at Liza once, not because he didn't want to, but because – and
I'm sure of it – he simply didn't notice her either. And suddenly,
after a period of silence that followed Yuliya Mikhaylovna's
invitation to open the final meeting without wasting any more
time, the ringing, intentionally loud voice of Liza was heard.
She called to Nikolay Vsevolodovich.

'Nikolay Vsevolodovich, some captain who calls himself
your relative, the brother of your wife, Lebyadkin by name,
keeps writing me indecent letters, complaining about you in
them and proposing to reveal to me some secrets about you. If
he really is your relative, tell him to stop insulting me and spare
me such unpleasantness.'

A desperate challenge could be heard in these words, everyone understood that. The accusation was clear, although perhaps she herself hadn't expected it. It was like the situation
where a man shuts his eyes and throws himself off the roof.

But Nikolay Vsevolodovich's reply was even more astonishing.

In the first place, it was certainly strange that he was not in
the least surprised, and listened to what Liza had to say with
utterly calm attention. Neither confusion nor anger showed in

his face. He answered the fateful question simply, firmly, even with an air of complete readiness.

'Yes, I have the misfortune of being the relative of this man. It will soon be five years since I became the husband of his sister, whose maiden name is Lebyadkina. Rest assured that I will convey your demands to him in the shortest possible time, and I guarantee that he will not bother you any more.'

I will never forget the horror that registered on Varvara Petrovna's face. She got up from her chair with a deranged look, raising her right hand before her, as if to defend herself. Nikolay Vsevolodovich looked at her, at Liza, at the spectators, and suddenly smiled with infinite haughtiness; he walked out of the room unhurriedly. All saw Liza jump up from the sofa as soon as Nikolay Vsevolodovich turned to leave, and she made an obvious movement to run after him, but thought better of it and didn't, but quietly walked out, also not saying a word to anyone and not glancing at anyone, but accompanied, naturally, by Mavriky Nikolayevich, who had rushed after her.

I won't mention the uproar and the tittle-tattle in the town that evening. Varvara Petrovna shut herself up in her town house, while Nikolay Vsevolodovich, they say, drove straight to Skvoreshniki without seeing his mother. Stepan Trofimovich sent me that evening to '*cette chère amie*' to beg her for permission to visit her, but I was not received. He was dreadfully affected, he wept. 'Such a marriage! Such a marriage! Such a horror in the family,' he repeated constantly. However, he also remembered Karmazinov and abused him dreadfully. He was energetically rehearsing for tomorrow's reading, and – the artistic temperament! – was preparing himself in front of the mirror and calling to mind all the witticisms and little puns that he'd uttered over the course of his entire life, which had been written down in a special notebook to insert into his reading the next morning.

'My friend, I am doing this for the sake of a great idea,' he said to me, obviously in self-justification. '*Cher ami*, I've moved from the place where I've been stuck for twenty-five years, and I've suddenly set out – where, I don't know, but I've set out . . .'

PART III

CHAPTER I

The Gala. First Part

1.

The gala took place despite all the confusions of the preceding 'Shpigulin' day. I think that even if von Lembke had died that very night, the gala would still have taken place the next morning, so special was the significance that Yuliya Mikhaylovna had attached to it. Alas, until the last minute she remained in a state of blindness and didn't understand the public's frame of mind. Ultimately no one believed that the festive day would pass without something happening on a colossal scale, without a 'denouement', as some people put it, rubbing their hands in anticipation. Many, to be sure, tried to assume a disapproving or politic air, but generally speaking, the Russian is inordinately delighted by any tumultuous social scandal. True enough, we sensed something even more serious than merely an eagerness for scandal: there was a general feeling of irritation, something relentlessly malevolent. Everyone seemed to be fed up with everything. The prevailing mood was one of confused cynicism, forced cynicism, stretched beyond its limits, as it were. Only the ladies weren't confused, focused as they were on one point: a merciless hatred of Yuliya Mikhaylovna. Ladies of every shade of opinion were of one mind here. But the poor thing suspected nothing; to the last moment she remained convinced that she had an 'entourage' and that everyone was still 'fanatically devoted' to her.

I've already mentioned that various low types of people had appeared among us. In troubled times, times of uncertainty or transition, various low types of people always and everywhere appear. I'm not talking about those so-called 'advanced' people who are always rushing ahead of everyone else (their main concern), albeit very often with a purpose that's extremely stupid, but is nonetheless more or less definite. No, I'm talking here only about the riff-raff. The riff-raff that exists in every society rises to the surface in any time of transition, and is utterly devoid not only of any goal, but even the slightest indication of an idea, and merely gives expression to restlessness and impatience as forcefully as it can. Meanwhile, the riff-raff, without being aware of it, almost always falls under the sway of that small band of 'advanced people' which acts with a definite goal, and which points all this rabble in whatever direction they please, provided that they in turn don't consist of utter idiots as well, which, however, also happens. Now that everything is over, people in our town are saying that Pyotr Stepanovich was controlled by the Internationale, and that Pyotr Stepanovich controlled Yuliya Mikhaylovna, who in turn directed, at his command, all manner of riff-raff. The more sensible of our intellects are amazed at themselves now: how could they have suddenly made such a blunder then? What our time of troubles consisted of, and what we were making a transition from and to, I don't know, and no one else knows, I think, except perhaps for certain of our visitors from outside. And meantime, the lowest of low types suddenly gained predominance, and began loudly criticizing all that was sacred, whereas previously they hadn't dared open their mouths, and the leading people, who until then had blithely had the final say, suddenly began listening to them while keeping quiet themselves, and some began tittering in a most disgraceful manner. Certain Lyamshins, Telyatnikovs, landowner Tentetnikovs,[1] home-grown snivelling Radishchevs, nasty little Jews with mournful but arrogant smiles, guffawing travellers just passing through, poets from the capital with political agendas, poets in peasant coats and tarred boots instead of an agenda and talent, majors and colonels who made fun of the foolishness of their profession and who, for an extra rouble, were ready then and there to unbuckle their swords and slip off to become railway clerks; generals scuttled away into the ranks of the lawyers; intellectually developed mediators and petty merchants who were still developing; countless seminary students, women who embodied the woman question – all these suddenly got the upper hand in our town, and over whom, I may ask? Over the club, over the respected elder statesmen, over the generals on wooden legs, over the very severe and very unapproachable ladies of our society. If Varvara Petrovna, right up to the catastrophe involving her own dear son, was practically running errands for all this riff-raff, then other Minervas[2] among us can be partially forgiven for their state of stupefaction at the time. Now people, as I've already said, are ascribing everything to the Internationale. This notion has become so firmly lodged that it is even reported to visiting outsiders. Not too long ago Councillor Kubrikov, a man of sixty-two and wearing the Order of St Stanislav[3] around his neck, came forward quite voluntarily and announced in an emotional voice that for three whole months he had undoubtedly been under the influence of the Internationale. But when, with all due respect for his years and his services, he was invited to provide a more satisfactory explanation, he was utterly unable to produce any evidence beyond saying that 'he had felt it with all his senses', but nonetheless stood firmly by his statement, so that he was no longer questioned.

I repeat again. A small group of cautious people which had withdrawn at the very beginning and even locked themselves in, still remained. But what lock can stand against natural law? In the most cautious of families young girls grow up in exactly the same way, and yet they find it essential to dance. And so all these individuals also ended by subscribing to the fund for the governesses. It was assumed that the ball would be so brilliant, so without precedent; wonders were told about it; rumours were circulating about visiting princes with lorgnettes, about the ten stewards, all young gallants with rosettes on their left shoulders; about certain movers and shakers from Petersburg; about the fact that Karmazinov, to increase the collection, had agreed to read 'Merci' aloud dressed in the costume of a governess of our province; about the fact that there would be a 'literary quadrille', also entirely in costume, and that each costume would represent some particular mode of thought. Finally,

something called 'honest Russian thought' would dance in costume too – which in itself was a complete novelty. How could
one not subscribe? Everyone subscribed.

2.

According to the programme, the festive day was divided into
two parts: a literary matinée,[4] from noon until four, and then
a ball, from ten o'clock on through the night. But this particular
arrangement already contained the seeds of disorder. In the first
place, from the very beginning a rumour had become firmly
established among the public that there would be a luncheon
immediately after the literary matinée or even during it, with
an interval devoted expressly to it – a free luncheon, naturally,
which would be part of the programme, and with champagne.
The enormous cost of the ticket (three roubles) helped confirm
the rumour. 'As if I would subscribe for nothing? The gala
is supposed to go on for twenty-four hours, so they'll feed us;
people will get hungry' – that's how people reasoned. I must
confess that Yuliya Mikhaylovna herself was responsible for
implanting this pernicious rumour through her own heedless-
ness. About a month earlier, while under the initial spell of her
great plan, she was babbling about her gala to anyone she
happened to meet, and she even sent a notice to one of the
newspapers in the capital about the toasts that would be proposed for the occasion. She was then mainly attracted by the
idea of these toasts; she herself wanted to propose them and
kept composing them in anticipation. They were to elucidate
our main motto (what was it? I'll bet the poor lady hadn't
composed anything at all), which would then go to the newspapers in the two capitals as coming from a provincial correspondent, intrigue and fascinate the higher authorities, and then
spread throughout all the provinces, inspiring wonderment and
emulation. But for toasts champagne is necessary, and since it's
impossible to drink champagne on an empty stomach, then, it
went without saying, luncheon became necessary as well. Later,
when a committee was formed through her efforts and the
matter was addressed more seriously, then it was immediately

and clearly proved to her that if they were to think of banquets, very little would be left for the governesses, even if the collection were very large. And so there were two ways out of the problem: either a Belshazzar's feast[5] with toasts, and about ninety roubles for the governesses, or the raising of a substantial sum of money, with the gala only a matter of form, so to speak. The committee, however, only wanted to give her a scare, and of course devised a third solution, which reconciled the first two and was reasonable, that is, a very decent gala in all respects, only without champagne, and therefore with a very respectable sum remaining, much more than ninety roubles.

But Yuliya Mikhaylovna didn't agree; by nature she despised the philistine middle way. She proposed forthwith that if the first idea couldn't be realized, then they should rush to the opposite extreme immediately and wholeheartedly, that is, raise an enormous subscription that would be the envy of all the other provinces. 'The public really must understand once and for all,' she concluded her fiery speech to the committee, 'that the achievement of universal human goals is incomparably loftier than ephemeral corporeal pleasures; that the gala in essence is only the proclamation of a great idea, and one therefore ought to be content with the most economical little German ball, merely as a symbol, and only if we can't dispense with this intolerable ball altogether!' – so great was the hatred she had suddenly conceived for it. But they finally calmed her down. It was then, for instance, that they finally devised and proposed a 'literary quadrille' and other aesthetic things as substitutes for corporeal pleasures. It was then that Karmazinov finally and definitely agreed to read 'Merci' (until then he had been tormenting them with his shilly-shallying), thereby eradicating the very idea of food in the minds of our irrepressible public. And so it was that the ball once more became a magnificent triumph, although not in the same way. And to avoid floating off into the clouds altogether, they decided that tea with lemon and small round biscuits could be served at the beginning of the ball, then orgeat[6] and lemonade, and towards the end even ice cream, but that was all. And for those who were always, everywhere and invariably hungry, and, most importantly, thirsty, a special buffet would be opened at the end of a suite of rooms, and Prokhorych (the head chef at the club) would be in charge of it, and – though under the strictest supervision of the committee – anything anyone liked would be served, but for a separate price, and for that purpose a notice would be posted on the doors of the hall, to the effect that the buffet was not included in the programme. But in the morning they decided not to open the buffet at all, so as not to disturb the reading, even though the buffet was to be located five rooms away from the White Hall, where Karmazinov had agreed to read 'Merci'. It was curious that enormous significance seemed to have been attached to this event by the committee, that is, to the reading of 'Merci', and by even its most practical members. And as far as the poetic people were concerned, the wife of the marshal of the nobility, for one, informed Karmazinov that after the reading she would immediately order a marble plaque fixed to the wall of her White Hall, with a gold inscription that read that on such-and-such a date in such-and-such year, here, on this very spot, a great Russian and European writer, on laying down his pen, had read 'Merci', and thereby had for the first time taken leave of the Russian public in the persons of the representatives of our town, and that everyone could then read this inscription at the ball, that is, a mere five hours after the reading of 'Merci'. I know for a fact that it was mainly Karmazinov who demanded that under no circumstances should there be a buffet that morning, while he was reading, despite observations from some members of the committee to the effect that this was not quite our way of doing things.

This was the state of affairs, while people in town continued to believe in a Belshazzar's feast, that is, in a buffet provided by the committee; they went on believing until the very last moment. Even the young ladies were dreaming of lots of sweets and jam and things even more wonderful. Everyone knew that a very sizeable amount of money had been collected, that the entire town would be breaking down the doors, that people would be coming in from the outlying districts and that there wouldn't be enough tickets. It was also known that over and above the fixed price there had been considerable contributions as well: Varvara Petrovna, for instance, had paid three hundred roubles for her ticket and had donated all the flowers from her greenhouse to decorate the hall. The wife of the marshal of the nobility (a member of the committee) had provided her house and the lighting; the club had furnished the music and the servants, and had released Prokhorych for the entire day. There were other contributions as well, although by no means so large, so that there was even some thought of reducing the initial price of a ticket from three roubles to two. In fact, the committee at first was afraid that the young ladies wouldn't come for three roubles each, and proposed that a system of family tickets be somehow established, namely, that each family should pay for only one young lady, and that all the other young ladies who were members of a particular family, even if there were as many as ten, should be admitted at no charge. But all fears proved groundless: on the contrary, it was precisely the young ladies who did appear. Even the poorest of the clerks brought their girls, and it was abundantly clear that if they hadn't had girls, it wouldn't have occurred to them for a moment to subscribe. One highly insignificant little secretary brought all seven of his daughters, not to mention, of course, his wife, as well as a niece, and each of these persons was holding a three-rouble ticket of admission in her hand. One can just imagine, then, the revolution that swept through the town! Just take the fact that since the gala was divided into two segments, each lady needed two costumes – a morning one for the reading, and a ball gown for the dancing. Many from the middle class, as it later turned out, had pawned everything for that day, even the family linen, even the sheets and almost the mattresses, to our Jews, who, as if on purpose, had entrenched themselves in our town in awfully large numbers over the past two years, with more of them arriving as time went on. Almost all the clerks had taken an advance on their pay, and some landowners had sold livestock they couldn't do without, all just so they could bring their young ladies dressed as marquises, and be no worse than anyone else. The magnificence of the costumes on this occasion was unheard of in our parts. For the past two weeks the town had been awash in funny stories about various families, all of which were promptly conveyed to the court of Yuliya Mikhaylovna by our local wits. Caricatures of families began to pass from hand to hand. I myself saw several drawings of this kind in Yuliya Mikhaylovna's album. All this became known only too well to the people who were the source of the funny stories; that's why, I think, hatred of Yuliya Mikhaylovna had increased so much of late in those families. Now everyone curses and gnashes his teeth when they remember it. But it was clear even beforehand that if the committee should fail to please in some way, or if something should go wrong at the ball, there would be an unprecedented explosion of indignation. That's why everyone secretly expected a scandal; and if people were actually expecting it, how could it fail to come to pass?

Precisely at noon the orchestra struck up. Being one of the stewards, that is, one of the twelve 'young men with rosettes', I myself saw with my own eyes how this day, which is so shameful to remember, began. It began with an incredible crush at the entrance. How did it happen that everything went wrong from the very first moment, beginning with the police? I don't blame the real public. The fathers of families not only didn't crowd each other or anyone else, despite their rank, but, on the contrary, it was said that they had been upset while they were still outside at the sight of the crowd's pushing and shoving, which was unusual in our town, as it besieged the entrance and taking it by storm instead of simply going in. Meanwhile, carriages kept pulling up and finally blocked the street. Now, when I'm writing, I have solid grounds to affirm that several of the worst specimens of riff-raff in our town were simply brought in by Lyamshin and Liputin without tickets, and perhaps by others as well who, like me, were serving as stewards. In any case, some utterly unknown individuals, who had come in from the outlying districts and from other places as well, made their appearance. These savages, as soon as they set foot in the hall, immediately wanted to know, in one voice (as if they had been coached), where the buffet was, and on learning there was no buffet, began to curse, without any sense of propriety and with an insolence that had scarcely ever been heard before then

among us. To be sure, some of them arrived drunk. Several
were struck, like savages, by the magnificence of the marshal's
hall, since they had never seen anything like it, and as they went
in, they fell silent for a moment and looked around open-
mouthed. This large White Hall, although by now rather old
and decrepit, was in fact magnificent: of enormous dimensions,
with two rows of windows, a ceiling decorated in the old-
fashioned way and trimmed with gold, with galleries, mirrors
between the windows, red and white draperies, marble statues
(undistinguished, but statues all the same), with heavy antique
furniture of the Napoleonic period, white and gold and
upholstered in red velvet. At the time I'm describing, a high
platform had been erected at the end of the hall for the men of
letters who were scheduled to read, and the entire hall, like the
parterre of a theatre, was completely filled with chairs, with
wide aisles for the public. But after the initial surprise, the most
senseless questions and statements began. 'Maybe we don't
want any reading yet . . . We've paid our money . . . The public
has been brazenly cheated . . . We're the ones in charge here,
not the Lembkes!' In short, it was as if they had been let in
precisely for this purpose. I especially remember one clash, in
which the young prince with the stand-up collar and the face
of a wooden doll, who had arrived the day before and had
been at Yuliya Mikhaylovna's yesterday morning, distinguished
himself. He had also agreed, at her insistent request, to pin the
rosette to his left shoulder and become a steward along with
the rest of us. It turned out that this mute wax figure on springs
knew how if not to speak, then to act in his fashion. When a
gigantic, pockmarked retired captain, supported by a whole
band of all sorts of riff-raff crowding behind him, began to
pester him by asking how to get to the buffet, the prince winked
at a policeman. The hint was immediately taken: despite the
cursing of the drunken captain, he was dragged out of the
hall. Meanwhile, the 'real' public finally began to appear and
stretched in three long lines down all three aisles between the
chairs. The unruly element began to quiet down, but the public,
even the 'cleanest' of them, had a dissatisfied and startled look;
and some of the ladies were simply frightened.

Finally, people took their seats; and the music stopped. People began blowing their noses and looking about. They were waiting with too solemn an air, which was already a bad sign in itself. But as yet there were no 'Lembkas'. Silks, velvets, diamonds sparkled and glowed on all sides; fragrance wafted through the air. The men were wearing all their decorations, and the little old men were even in uniform. At last the marshal's wife appeared, together with Liza. Liza had never yet been so dazzlingly lovely as on that morning and in such elegant attire. Her hair had been done up in curls, her eyes were sparkling, a smile shone on her face. She visibly produced an impression; people were inspecting her, and whispering about her. They were saying that her eyes were seeking out Stavrogin, but neither Stavrogin nor Varvara Petrovna was there. I didn't understand the expression on her face just then: why was there so much happiness, joy, energy, strength in this face? I remembered the incident of the day before, and didn't know what to make of it. But still and all, the 'Lembkas' hadn't yet appeared. This was a great mistake. I later learned that until the last moment Yuliya Mikhaylovna was waiting for Pyotr Stepanovich, without whom recently she had been unable to take a step, even though she would never have admitted it. I will note parenthetically that the night before, at the final meeting of the committee, Pyotr Stepanovich had refused to put on a steward's rosette, which had offended her, even to the point of tears. To her surprise, and then to her extreme embarrassment (of which I will have something to say later), he disappeared for the entire morning, and didn't show up for the literary reading at all, and no one ran across him until that evening. Finally, the public began to display obvious impatience. No one appeared on the platform either. In the back rows they began to clap, as in a theatre. The old men and young ladies frowned; the 'Lembkas' were obviously putting on airs. Even among the more respectable members of the public an absurd whispering began to the effect that there would perhaps be no gala at all, that von Lembke himself was perhaps really unwell, and so on and so forth. But thank heaven von Lembke finally appeared. He was leading her by the arm; I myself admit that I was dreadfully worried that they might not appear. But the fact was that the fairy tales were evaporating, and the truth was coming into its own. The public seemed to relax. Von Lembke himself seemed to be in perfect health, as, I remember, everyone else also concluded, because you can imagine how many eyes were turned on him. I will mention, by way of characterizing our society, that in general there were very few in the upper ranks who supposed that von Lembke was at all ill; they found his actions perfectly normal, and even looked approvingly on yesterday morning's incident in the square. 'That's how it should have been done from the start,' said the worthies. 'Otherwise if they come as philanthropists, they'll end up the same way, without noticing that it's necessary from a philanthropic standpoint to begin with.' That at least was how the thinking went in the club. The only fault they found was that he had lost his temper in the process. 'Something like that has to be done more coolly, but he's new at the job,' said those in the know. All eyes turned to Yuliya Mikhaylovna with the same eagerness. Of course, no one has the right to demand of me, the narrator, extremely precise details concerning one point: there's a mystery involved here, there's a woman involved. But I know only one thing: the evening of the previous day she went into Andrey Antonovich's study and stayed with him well past midnight. Andrey Antonovich was forgiven and consoled. The spouses agreed on everything, everything was forgotten and when, at the conclusion of their discussion, von Lembke did kneel before her, as he remembered with horror the main and final episode of the previous night, his spouse's charming little hand, and after it her lips, checked the impassioned outpourings of the contrite speeches of a man who was chivalrously delicate but weakened by emotion. Everyone could see happiness on her face now. She walked with an open expression and was magnificently turned out. She seemed to be at the pinnacle of her desires; the gala – the goal and crown of her diplomacy – had come into being. As they proceeded to their places, directly in front of the platform, both von Lembkes were bowing and responding to bows. They were instantly surrounded. The marshal's wife got up to greet them. But at this point a nasty misunderstanding occurred: the orchestra, for no earthly reason, struck up a flourish – not a march, but simply a flourish of the kind that is played in our club when someone's health is being drunk at the dinner table. I now know that Lyamshin was responsible for this in his capacity as a steward, supposedly in honour of the 'Lembkas' as they were making their entrance. Of course, he could always have excused himself by saying that he'd done it out of stupidity or excessive zeal. Alas, I didn't yet know at the time that they no longer cared for excuses, and that that day marked the end of all such things. But the flourish wasn't the end of it: along with the annoyance, perplexity and smiles of the public came a sudden shout of 'hurrah' at the end of the hall and in the gallery, also supposedly in honour of von Lembke. There were not many voices, but I confess they continued for some time. Yuliya Mikhaylovna flushed, and her eyes began to flash. Von Lembke stopped by his seat, and turning in the direction of those who were shouting, surveyed the hall majestically and sternly. He was quickly shown to his seat. Again I noticed with apprehension the same dangerous smile on his face that he'd worn yesterday morning as he stood in his wife's drawing room looking at Stepan Trofimovich before going up to him. It seemed to me that now, too, there was a sinister expression on his face and, what was worse, a rather comic one – the expression of a being who was bent on sacrificing himself merely to serve his wife's lofty purposes.

Yuliya Mikhaylovna quickly beckoned me to come to her, and whispered that I should run to Karmazinov and beg him to begin. And then, no sooner had I turned around when another disgraceful incident occurred, except that it was much nastier than the first. On the platform, on the empty platform, to which all eyes and all expectations had been directed until that moment, and where the only things to be seen were a small table, a chair in front of it, and on the table a glass of water on a silver tray – on the empty platform there suddenly appeared out of the blue the gigantic figure of Captain Lebyadkin in a tail-coat and white tie. I was so astonished that I couldn't believe my eyes. The captain seemed to be confused and

remained standing at the back of the platform. Suddenly someone from the audience shouted 'Lebyadkin! Is that you?' At
this, the captain's stupid red face (he was dead drunk) spread
into a broad, vacant smile. He raised his hand, wiped his forehead with it, shook his shaggy head and, as if throwing caution
to the winds, took two steps forward and suddenly snorted
with laughter, which, though not loud, was pealing, prolonged
and merry, and set his whole corpulent mass to heaving and his
little eyes to squinting. Nearly half the audience began to laugh
at this sight, and twenty people began to applaud. The serious
members of the audience exchanged gloomy glances; however,
it all lasted less than half a minute. Suddenly Liputin, with his
steward's rosette and accompanied by two servants, rushed on
to the platform. They carefully grabbed the captain under the
arms, and Liputin whispered something to him. The captain
frowned and muttered: 'Oh, well, if that's the way it is', waved
his hand dismissively, turned his enormous back to the audience
and disappeared with his escorts. But a moment later Liputin
again leaped out on to the platform. His lips wore the very
sweetest of his perpetual smiles, which were especially reminiscent of vinegar mixed with sugar, and in his hand he held a
sheet of notepaper. With small but quick steps he approached
the edge of the platform.

'Ladies and gentlemen,' he addressed the audience, 'because
of an oversight a comic misunderstanding has occurred, which
has now been cleared up, but full of hope, I have taken on
myself the commission, and the sincere, most respectful request
of one of our local poets from these parts . . . Suffused with a
human and lofty purpose . . . despite my appearance . . . with
that very purpose which has brought all of us together . . . to
wipe away the tears of the poor educated young ladies of our
province . . . this gentleman, that is, I mean this local poet . . .
desiring to remain incognito . . . would very much like to see
his poem read out before the commencement of the ball . . .
that is, I mean to say the commencement of the reading. Although this poem is not part of the programme, and does not
enter . . . because it was delivered only half an hour ago . . .
but it seemed to *us*' (what 'us'? I'm quoting this disconnected

and inconsistent speech word for word) 'that because of the remarkable *naïveté* of feeling that is also conjoined with a remarkable joyfulness, the poem might well be read, that is, not as something serious, but as something that is appropriate to these festivities . . . In short, to the idea . . . The more so since several lines . . . and I wanted to ask the permission of a most indulgent audience.'

'Read it!' roared a voice at the back of the hall.

'Shall I read it, then?'

'Read it, read it!' came many voices.

'I'll read it, then, with the permission of the audience,' Liputin again twisted his face into the same sugary smile. Still, he seemed unable to make up his mind, and it even struck me that he was agitated. For all the brazenness of such people they do nonetheless stumble sometimes. A seminary student, however, wouldn't have stumbled, but Liputin did, after all, belong to the previous generation.

'I warn you, that is, I have the honour of warning you that this is actually not the kind of ode that used to be written on festive occasions, but is almost a joke, so to speak, yet it indubitably has feeling conjoined with playful gaiety and, so to speak, is suffused with real and genuine truth.'

'Read it, read it!'

He unfolded the paper. Naturally, no one had time to stop him. Besides, he was standing there wearing his steward's rosette. In a ringing voice he declaimed:

'To a local governess of the Fatherland from a poet at the gala:

> 'Governess! I kiss your hand,
> Joy to you, we're in your debt,
> Reactionary or George Sand.
> It matters not, enjoy this fête.'

'Why, that's Lebyadkin's! That's by Lebyadkin!' several voices exclaimed. There was an outburst of laughter and even applause, though scanty.

> 'Teaching French to snivelly kids,
> You'd be glad to take the hand
> Of even a sexton if he rids
> You of that lethal, boring band.'

'Hurrah, hurrah!'

> 'But in our age of great to-do,
> Even a sexton won't look your way,
> Unless you have a rouble or two,
> Else – back to the primer, day after day!'

'That's right, that's right, that's realism, you can't take a step without a rouble or two!'

> 'But now that our gala's power
> Has yielded us such capital,
> We're sending each of you a dower
> From this festive, jubilant hall.

> Reactionary or George Sand
> It matters not, enjoy this fête.
> Now that you're dowered, as we've planned,
> Spit in triumph on all you've met.'

I confess I couldn't believe my ears. This was such brazen insolence that it was impossible to excuse Liputin even on the grounds of stupidity. And Liputin was certainly by no means stupid. The intention was obvious, at least to me: they seemed to be in a hurry to throw things into disorder. Several stanzas of this idiotic poem, for example the very last, were of such a nature that no amount of stupidity could have allowed them. Liputin himself seemed to feel that he had gone too far: after accomplishing his bold deed, he was so taken aback by his own brazenness that he didn't even leave the platform, but stood there as if wishing to add something more. He probably imagined that the result would be different, but even the little band of hooligans who had been applauding during this escapade suddenly fell silent, as if they were also taken aback. The stupidest thing of all was that many of them took the whole escapade seriously, that is, not at all as a lampoon, but actually as a true statement about a governess, as a poem with a political message. But the sheer cheekiness of the verses finally struck even them. As far as the audience as a whole was concerned, the entire hall was not only scandalized, but visibly offended. I'm not mistaken about the impression I'm reporting. Yuliya Mikhaylovna later said that if it had gone on for another minute, she would have fainted. One of the most highly respected little old men helped his wife to her feet, and they both walked out of the hall accompanied by the anxious looks of the audience. Who knows, their example might have inspired others as well if Karmazinov himself hadn't appeared on the platform at that moment, in tail-coat and white tie, notebook in hand. Yuliya Mikhaylovna looked at him ecstatically, as if he were a saviour. But I was already backstage; I needed to get hold of Liputin.

'You did that deliberately!' I said, grabbing him indignantly by the arm.

'I swear, I had no idea,' he winced, immediately beginning to lie and pretending to be unhappy. 'The poem was brought to me just a few minutes ago, and I really thought it was just an amusing joke . . .'

'You thought no such thing. Do you really regard this talentless rubbish as an amusing joke?'

'Oh yes, I do.'

'You're simply lying, and it wasn't brought to you just a few minutes ago. You and Lebyadkin composed it together, perhaps yesterday, just to create a scandal. The last stanza is certainly yours, maybe the business of the sexton as well. Why did he come on stage in a tail-coat? You must have meant him to read it too, if he hadn't got dead drunk.'

Liputin looked at me coldly and sarcastically.

'Really, what business is it of yours?' he suddenly asked, strangely composed.

'What do you mean "what"? You're also wearing a rosette. Where's Pyotr Stepanovich?'

'I don't know, around here somewhere – what of it?'

'Because I see through everything now. This is simply a plot against Yuliya Mikhaylovna, to turn the day into a scandal.'

Liputin again gave me a sideways glance.

'Really, what do you care?' he smirked, shrugged his shoulders and walked off to the side.

I was simply staggered. All my suspicions were confirmed. And yet I went on hoping that I was wrong! What was I to do? It occurred to me to ask Stepan Trofimovich's advice, but he was standing in front of a mirror, trying on various smiles and constantly struggling with the piece of paper on which he had made some notes. It was his turn to go out on to the platform immediately after Karmazinov, and he was no longer in any condition to talk to me. Should I run to Yuliya Mikhaylovna? But it was too early for that: she needed a much harsher lesson if she was to be cured of her conviction that she had an 'entourage' and was surrounded by 'fanatically devoted' people. She wouldn't have believed me and would have considered me deluded. Besides, how could she have helped? 'Oh well,' I thought, 'really and truly, what business is it of mine? I'll just take off my rosette and go home *when it begins*.' That's just what I said, 'when it begins', I remember that.

But I had to go and listen to Karmazinov. Looking around backstage for the last time, I noticed that a rather sizeable number of outsiders, even women, were flitting about, going in and out. This 'backstage' was a rather narrow space, fully screened from the audience by a curtain, and connected to other rooms at the back by a corridor. There the people who were scheduled to read awaited their turn. But I was especially struck at that moment by the speaker who was to follow Stepan Trofimovich. He was also some sort of professor (even now I don't know precisely who he was), who had voluntarily retired from some institution after some incident involving the students and for some reason had ended up in our town just a few days earlier. He had also been recommended to Yuliya Mikhaylovna and she had received him worshipfully. I know now that he had been at her house on only one evening before the reading, had sat silently throughout that evening, had smiled ambiguously at the jokes and tone of the company assembled around

Yuliya Mikhaylovna and had produced an unpleasant impression on everyone with his manner, which was haughty and at the same time timorous and hypersensitive. It was Yuliya Mikhaylovna herself who had recruited him to read. Now he was pacing from corner to corner and whispering to himself, just like Stepan Trofimovich, but looking at the floor, and not into a mirror. He was not trying on smiles, although he did smile frequently and lustfully. It was clear that he was someone who could not be talked to either. He was short of stature, about forty, completely bald, with a small greyish beard, and decently dressed. But most interesting of all was that every time he turned, he raised his right fist, shook it in the air above his head and suddenly brought it down, as if he were smashing some opponent to smithereens. He repeated this performance again and again. I became terrified. I ran off as quickly as I could to listen to Karmazinov.

3.

Again there was a sense in the hall that something wasn't quite right. I will declare in advance that I bow before the greatness of genius, but why on earth do these great geniuses of ours, at the end of their years of glory, sometimes act just like little boys? What did it matter that he was Karmazinov and came out swaggering like five court chamberlains rolled into one? Can the attention of an audience like ours be held for a whole hour by the reading of a single article? In general, I have observed that even a genius of the highest order cannot hold an audience's attention for more than twenty minutes at a light literary reading without paying a price. To be sure, the entrance of the great genius was greeted with enormous respect. Even the severest of the little old men expressed approval and curiosity, and the ladies even showed a certain enthusiasm. The applause, however, was rather brief, not unanimous somehow, and ragged. On the other hand, there wasn't a single instance where anyone acted up in the back rows until the moment when Mr Karmazinov began to speak, and even then, nothing especially bad happened, just something that seemed to be more a misunderstanding. I have already mentioned earlier that he had a very shrill voice, even rather feminine, and with it, a genuinely aristocratic lisp. He had no sooner uttered a few words than suddenly someone permitted himself a loud laugh – probably some inexperienced little fool who hadn't yet seen anything of the world, and who was inclined to find everything amusing anyway. But there wasn't the slightest hint of a demonstration; on the contrary, the fool was hissed at, and that shut him up. But then Mr Karmazinov, mincing and simpering, announced that 'at first I did not agree to read under any circumstances' (as if he really needed to announce that!). 'There are,' he said, 'lines that sing so straight out from the heart that they cannot be spoken, and such a sacred object cannot be brought out before the public,' (well, then, why did he bring it out?) 'but inasmuch as he had been begged to do so, then he did bring it out, and since, in addition, he was laying down his pen forever and had vowed never to write another line, then he had gone ahead and written this final piece; and since he had vowed never again to read anything in public under any circumstances, then he would go ahead and read this final piece in public', and so on and so forth – all in the same vein.

But all that would have made no difference. Who isn't familiar with authors' introductory remarks? Although I will observe that considering the scanty education of our public and the irritability of those in the back rows, all this could have had its effect. Why, wouldn't it have been better to read a small piece of prose fiction, a very short story such as he had often written in the past, that is, polished and mannered, to be sure, but showing some signs of wit? That would have saved everything. No, indeed, that was not to be! A veritable oration got under way![7] Heavens, what didn't it contain! I will say without hesitation that even an audience in the capital, let alone ours, would have been reduced to a state of stupefaction. Just imagine almost thirty pages of the most mannered and useless babble. In addition, the gentleman in question also read it rather condescendingly, in a melancholy tone, as if bestowing a favour, and as a result it all proved insulting to our public. The theme . . . but who could make it out, this theme? It was an account of certain impressions, certain reminiscences. But of what? And about what? No matter how fiercely our provincial foreheads frowned for a good half of the reading, we could make nothing of it, and as a result went on listening to the second half only out of politeness. To be sure, a great deal was said about love, about the love of a genius for some person, but I admit that it all came out rather awkwardly. In my view, it was not quite appropriate for the small, plumpish figure of a writer of genius to tell us about his first kiss. And, what was again offensive, these kisses somehow occurred rather differently from the majority of mankind. Invariably gorse was growing all around (inevitably gorse or some such plant that has to be looked up in a botany text). At the same time, there was invariably a kind of violet tint in the sky, which, of course, no mortal had ever noticed, that is to say, everyone had of course seen it, but had never really noticed it, 'and so,' he says, 'I've looked at it and I'm describing it to you fools, as if it were a most ordinary thing'. The tree beneath which an interesting couple was seated was invariably of some orange colour. They were sitting some-where in Germany. Suddenly they saw Pompey or Cassius on the eve of battle and both were pierced by a chill of ecstasy. A water nymph began to squeak in the bushes. Gluck[8] began to play his violin in the reeds. The title of the piece he was playing was spelled out *en toutes lettres*,[9] but was not familiar to any-one, and had to be looked up in a musical dictionary. Mean-while, a fog began to swirl, and it swirled and swirled so that it was more like a million pillows than a fog. And suddenly everything disappeared, and the great genius was crossing the Volga in winter, during a thaw. Two and a half pages were given to the crossing, but he still fell through a hole in the ice. The genius sank, but do you think he drowned? It didn't even occur to him: the only reason all that happened was that when he was already in the process of drowning and sputtering, an ice floe suddenly appeared before him. A tiny little ice floe, small as a pea, but clear and transparent, 'like a frozen teardrop', and reflected in this ice floe was Germany, or rather, the sky of Germany, and the rainbow play of colours in this reflection reminded him of that very tear which, 'you remember, coursed down your cheek when we were sitting beneath the emerald tree and you joyfully exclaimed: "There is no crime!" "Yes," I replied through my tears, "but if that's so, then there are no righteous people either." We began to sob and parted forever.' She went somewhere to the seashore, and he went off to some caves; and there he descended, descended, for three years he descended beneath the Sukharev Tower[10] in Moscow, and suddenly in the very bowels of the earth, in a cave he found an icon-lamp and in front of the lamp a hermit. The hermit was praying. The genius bent his ear to the tiny barred window and suddenly heard a sigh. Do you think it was the hermit who sighed? Much need he has of your hermit! No indeed, plainly and simply this sigh 'reminded him of her first sigh, thirty-seven years previously', when, 'you remember, in Germany, we were sitting beneath an agate tree, and you said to me: "What is the purpose of loving? Look, ochre is growing everywhere around, and I love you; but the ochre will cease to grow, and I will cease to love you."' Then the fog began to swirl again, Hoffmann appeared, the water nymph whistled something from Chopin, and suddenly out of the fog, in a laurel wreath, over the roofs of Rome appeared Ancus Marcius.[11] 'A shiver of ecstasy ran down our spines, and we parted forever', and so on and so forth. Perhaps I haven't conveyed it correctly, and perhaps I don't know how to convey it, but the meaning of all this babble was something of the sort. And in the end, what a shameful passion our great minds have for clever talk in the higher sense! A great European philosopher, a great scholar, an inventor, a toiler, a martyr – all these people who toil and are heavy laden[12] are, for our great Russian genius, nothing more than cooks in his kitchen. He is the master, and they appear before him with toques in hand and await his orders. To be sure, he also mocks Russia superciliously, and he finds nothing more pleasant than to declare to the great minds of Europe that Russia is bankrupt in all respects, but as far as he himself is concerned, no indeed, he has already risen above these great minds of Europe; for him they are all just material for his clever talk. He takes someone else's idea, tacks its antithesis on to it, and the quip is ready. There is crime, there is no crime; there is no truth, there are no

righteous men;[13] atheism, Darwinism, the bells of Moscow ...
But alas, he no longer believes in the bells of Moscow; Rome,
laurels ... but he doesn't even believe in laurels ... Then there's
a routine attack of Byronesque melancholy, a grimace from
Heine,[14] something from Pechorin – and the machine starts up
and moves along with a whistle ... 'But do praise me, do praise
me, I'm dreadfully fond of that, you know; I'm only saying that
I'm laying down my pen, you know; just wait, I'll bore you
three hundred times more, you'll grow tired of reading ...'

Naturally, it didn't end so smoothly as that. But the trouble
was that it all started with him. For some time people had been
shuffling their feet, blowing their noses, coughing and doing all
those things they do when an author, whoever he may be, holds
an audience more than twenty minutes at a literary reading.
But the writer of genius didn't notice any of that. He continued
to lisp and mumble, without paying the slightest attention to
the audience, with the result that everyone began to grow indignant. Suddenly in the back rows a solitary but loud voice was
heard:

'Good Lord, what rubbish!'

This escaped involuntarily, and without any attempt at a
demonstration, I'm sure. The man was simply tired. But Mr
Karmazinov paused, looked at the audience sarcastically and
suddenly began to lisp in the dignified manner of a highly
offended court chamberlain:

'I seem to have bored you dreadfully, ladies and gentlemen?'

His mistake here lay in having spoken first; for in challenging
the audience to reply in this way, he made it possible for the
riff-raff to have their say, too, and even legitimately, so to
speak, whereas if he had restrained himself, then people would
just have gone on blowing their noses, and everything would
have passed off somehow. Perhaps he was waiting for applause
in response to his question, but there was no applause; on the
contrary, everyone seemed to become frightened, shrink into
themselves, and fall quiet.

'You never did see Ancus Marcius, that's all just a lot of talk,'
an irritated, even pained voice suddenly rang out.

'Exactly,' another voice immediately chimed in. 'There are

no ghosts these days, just the natural sciences. Deal with the natural sciences.'

'Ladies and gentlemen, I anticipated such objections least of all,' said Karmazinov, dreadfully surprised. In Karlsruhe the great genius had grown quite unaccustomed to his fatherland.

'In our time it's shameful to say that the world rests on three fishes,'[15] the voice of a young girl suddenly crackled. 'Karmazinov, you couldn't possibly have walked down a ladder into a hermit's cave. Besides, who talks about hermits these days?'

'Ladies and gentlemen, what surprises me most of all is that you're taking all this so seriously. However . . . however, you're quite right. No one respects actual truth more than I.'

Even though he was smiling ironically, he was severely shaken. The expression on his face plainly said: 'I'm really not the person you think, I'm really on your side; just praise me, praise me more, as much as possible, I like that very much.'

'Ladies and gentlemen,' he cried at last, now thoroughly wounded, 'I see that my poor little poem didn't hit the mark. And I seem not to have hit the mark either.'

'He aimed at a crow and hit a cow,' some fool shouted at the top of his voice. He must have been drunk, and of course no notice should have been taken of him. To be sure, a disrespectful laugh was heard.

'A cow, you say?' Karmazinov immediately shot back. His voice was becoming shriller. 'With respect to crows and cows, ladies and gentlemen, I will permit myself to refrain. I have too much respect even for any audience to permit myself comparisons, innocent though they may be; but I thought . . .'

'However you, dear sir, shouldn't be so . . .' someone from the back rows shouted.

'But I had supposed that in laying down my pen and bidding farewell to my reader, I would receive a hearing . . .'

'No, no, we want to listen, we do,' came a few voices from the first row that had finally summoned up the courage.

'Read, read!' a few ecstatic female voices chimed in, and finally there was a burst of applause, sparse and scattered, to be sure. Karmazinov gave a crooked smile and got up from his seat.

'Believe me, Karmazinov, everyone regards it as an honour . . .' even the marshal's wife couldn't restrain herself.

'Mr Karmazinov,' suddenly cried a fresh young voice from the depths of the hall. It was the voice of a very young teacher in the district school, a splendid young man, quiet and honourable, who had come to town only recently. He even got up from his chair. 'Mr Karmazinov, if I had experienced the happiness of loving in the way you've described it to us, I would certainly not put anything about my love in an article that was intended to be read in public . . .'

He even blushed all over.

'Ladies and gentlemen,' Karmazinov cried, 'I have finished. I am omitting the ending and withdrawing. But permit me to read you just the final six lines.

'Yes, dear reader, farewell!' he began at once from the manuscript, no longer seated in his chair. 'Farewell, reader; I do not even insist that we part friends; what is really the point of troubling you? Even abuse me, abuse me all you like, if it gives you any pleasure. But it's best if we forget each other forever. And if all of you, dear readers, should suddenly become so kind as to get on your knees and begin to beg tearfully: "Write, oh write for us, Karmazinov – for the fatherland, for posterity, for laurel wreaths", even then I would reply to you, after thanking you, of course, with all due courtesy: "No, really, we have had enough to do with each other, dear fellow-countrymen, *merci*! It's time for us to go our separate ways! *Merci, merci, merci!*"'

Karmazinov bowed ceremoniously, and red all over, as if he had been boiled, proceeded backstage.

'Well, no one is going to get on his knees; that's just a wild fantasy.'

'That's vanity for you!'

'It's just humour,' someone a bit more sensible begged to differ.

'No, spare us your humour.'

'But this is just impertinence, ladies and gentlemen.'

'At least he's finally had his say.'

'After boring us all to tears!'

But all these ignorant outbursts from the back rows (though

not just the back) were drowned out by the applause of the other part of the audience. They were calling Karmazinov back. A few ladies, headed by Yuliya Mikhaylovna and the marshal's wife, crowded at the foot of the platform. In Yuliya Mikhaylovna's hands there appeared a magnificent laurel wreath on a white velvet cushion, inside another wreath of live roses.

'Laurels!' Karmazinov exclaimed with a subtle and rather sarcastic smile. 'Of course I am touched, and it is with genuine emotion that I accept this wreath, which was prepared earlier but has not yet had time to wither. But I assure you, *mesdames*, I have suddenly become such a realist that in our day I regard your wreaths as being much more appropriate in the hands of a skilful cook than in mine . . .'

'Well, a cook's more useful,' cried the same seminary student who had been at the 'meeting' at Virginsky's. Order was somewhat disrupted. People jumped up from a number of rows to watch the ceremony with the laurel wreath.

'I'd give another three silver roubles for a cook right now,' another voice loudly chimed in, even too loudly, insistently loudly.

'Me too.'

'Me too.'

'Is there really no buffet here?'

'Ladies and gentlemen, this is simply a fraud.'

However, it must be admitted that all these ladies and gentlemen, however unrestrained, still stood very much in fear of our high officials, and of the chief of police, who was present in the hall. Within about ten minutes, all had somehow taken their places again, but the previous sense of order was never restored. And it was just this incipient chaos that poor Stepan Trofimovich stumbled into.

4.

However, I had again run backstage to see him and, beside myself, had time to warn him that in my opinion everything had collapsed and that it was better for him not to go on at all, but instead to go home immediately, using his cholerine as an excuse, and that I would also pull off my rosette and leave with him. At that moment he was already heading for the platform, but he suddenly stopped, surveyed me haughtily from head to toe and intoned majestically:

'Why is it, dear sir, that you regard me as capable of such a low act?'

I stepped back. I was as convinced as twice two makes four that he wouldn't get out of here without a disaster. While I was standing there utterly dejected, my eye again caught the figure of the visiting professor whose turn it was to go out after Stepan Trofimovich, and who earlier had kept raising his fist and bringing it down with all his might. He was still pacing back and forth in the same way, preoccupied and mumbling something to himself with a spiteful but triumphant smile. Somehow, almost without intending to (what could have possessed me just then?), I went up to him as well.

'You know,' I said, 'there are many instances where if a reader tries to hold his audience for more than twenty minutes, they stop listening to him. There's not even a celebrity who can pull it off for half an hour . . .'

He suddenly stopped and even seemed to tremble all over with resentment. Infinite haughtiness was reflected in his face.

'Don't worry,' he mumbled disdainfully, and walked past me. At that moment Stepan Trofimovich's voice sounded in the hall.

'Oh, the hell with you all!' I thought, and ran into the hall.

Stepan Trofimovich had seated himself in the chair, amid the disorder that still persisted. He was evidently met by unfriendly looks from the front rows. (In the club they had recently seemed to stop liking him for some reason, and respected him much less than before.) However, it was already a good sign that they didn't hiss at him. Since the previous day I had had a strange idea: I kept thinking that they would boo as soon as he appeared. However, with the disorder that still prevailed they hardly even took any notice of him now. But what could this man hope for if they had treated Karmazinov the way they had? He was pale; he hadn't appeared before the public for about ten years. From his agitation and from what I knew all too well about him, it was clear to me that he himself believed that his present appearance on the platform would decide his fate, or something like it. That's exactly what I was afraid of. This man was dear to me. And what came over me when he opened his mouth and I heard his first sentence!

'Ladies and gentlemen!' he suddenly intoned, as if having resolved to venture all, yet in a voice that was almost breaking. 'Ladies and gentlemen! This very morning one of the illegal pamphlets that has recently been distributed here was lying before me, and for the hundredth time I asked myself the question: "What is its secret?"'

The entire hall instantly fell silent; all eyes turned on him, some in fear. Needless to say, he knew how to stir interest with his very first words. Two heads even protruded from backstage: Liputin and Lyamshin were eagerly listening. Yuliya Mikhaylovna again began to wave her hand at me.

'Stop him, stop him at all costs!' she whispered in alarm. I only shrugged my shoulders; was it really possible to stop a man who had *ventured all*? Alas, I understood Stepan Trofimovich.

'Aha, it's about the manifestos!' came a whispering from the audience. The entire hall began to stir.

'Ladies and gentlemen, I have solved the whole mystery. The whole secret of their effect lies in their stupidity!' (His eyes began to flash.) 'Yes, ladies and gentlemen, if this were deliberate stupidity, simulated and calculated, oh, even that would be a stroke of genius! But they must be given full credit: they didn't simulate anything. This is the baldest, the most naive, the narrowest kind of stupidity – *c'est la bêtise dans son essence la plus pure, quelque chose comme un simple chimique*. If this had been expressed just a trifle more cleverly, anyone could have immediately seen all the poverty of this narrow little piece of stupidity. But as things are now, everyone stands there bewildered: no one can believe that this was so stupid to begin with. "It can't be that there was nothing more here," everyone says to himself, and looks for the secret, sees a mystery, wants to read between the lines – the effect is achieved! Oh, never yet has stupidity received such a splendid reward, despite the fact that it has so often deserved it . . . For, *en parenthèse*,[16] stupidity, like the loftiest of geniuses, is equally useful to the destiny of mankind . . .'

'The old word-games of the 1840s,' came someone's voice, albeit very shyly, but after that everything seemed to break loose, as a general din and uproar ensued.

'Ladies and gentlemen, hurrah! I propose a toast to stupidity!' Stepan Trofimovich shouted, now in an utter frenzy, in defiance of the hall.

I ran up to him on the pretext of pouring him a glass of water.

'Stepan Trofimovich, let it be, Yuliya Mikhaylovna begs you . . .'

'No, you let it be, you empty young man!' he attacked me at the top of his voice. I ran off. '*Messieurs*!' he continued, 'what is this to-do, what are these shouts of indignation that I hear? I have come with an olive branch. I have brought the last word, for in this matter I possess the last word – and we will be reconciled.'

'Down with him!' some people shouted.

'Quiet, let him speak, let him have his say,' another segment of the audience cried out. The young teacher was especially agitated: having once summoned up the courage to speak, he seemed no longer able to stop himself.

'*Messieurs*, the last word in this matter is general forgiveness. I, an outmoded old man, I declare triumphantly that the spirit of life breathes as before and that the life force has not dried up in the younger generation. The enthusiasm of today's youth is as pure and bright as it was in our time. Only one thing has happened: a shift of goals, the replacement of one beauty with another! The entire misunderstanding lies merely in the question of which is more beautiful: Shakespeare or a pair of boots, Raphael or petroleum?'

'Is this a denunciation?' some grumbled.

'Compromising questions!'

'Agent provocateur!'

'And I declare,' squealed Stepan Trofimovich, throwing all caution to the winds, 'and I declare that Shakespeare and Raphael are of higher value than the emancipation of the peasants, of higher value than the national principle, of higher value than socialism,[17] of higher value than the younger generation, of higher value than chemistry, of higher value than almost all mankind, for they are already the fruit, the real fruit of mankind, and perhaps the most precious fruit there can possibly be! The ultimate form of beauty has already been achieved, and without that achievement I would perhaps not agree to go on living . . . Oh, Lord!' he clasped his hands, 'ten years ago I was shouting exactly the same thing from a platform in Petersburg, in exactly the same words, and in exactly the same way they understood nothing, they laughed and hissed, as you are doing now. Narrow little people, what do you lack in order to understand? Do you know, do you know that mankind can still continue to live without the Englishman, can continue without Germany, can continue all too well without the Russian, can continue without science, can continue without bread – it is only without beauty that we cannot continue, for there will be nothing at all to do in the world! That's where the whole secret lies, that's where the whole of history lies! Science itself would not last a minute without beauty – do you know about that, you who are laughing now? – it would turn into loutishness, you wouldn't even be able to invent the nail! . . . I won't yield!' he cried absurdly in conclusion and banged his fist on the table with all his might.

But while he was squealing away without any sense or order, order in the hall was disintegrating as well. Many people jumped up from their chairs, some surged forward to get closer to the platform. In general, all this happened much more quickly than I'm describing it, and there was no time to take any measures. And perhaps there was no desire to do so.

'It's all very well and good for those of you who have everything, you spoiled creatures!' the same seminary student howled at the very foot of the platform, baring his teeth in pleasure at Stepan Trofimovich. The latter noticed and ran up to the very edge.

'Haven't I, haven't I just stated that the enthusiasm of the younger generation is just as pure and bright as it was, and that it is coming to grief only because it is mistaken about the forms of the beautiful? Isn't that enough for you? And if you take into consideration that the man who has proclaimed this is a crushed and abused father, then surely, oh you narrow little people, then surely one can rise to greater heights of impartiality and serenity? . . . Ungrateful . . . unjust . . . why, why then don't you want to make peace?'

And he suddenly began to sob hysterically. He wiped his flowing tears with his fingers. His shoulders and chest heaved with sobs. He was oblivious to everything around him.

The audience was suddenly overcome with panic. Almost all got up out of their seats. Even Yuliya Mikhaylovna jumped up quickly, after grabbing her husband by the arm and pulling him up. A complete and utter scandal ensued.

'Stepan Trofimovich!' the seminary student howled in joy. 'In the town and the surrounding areas here, Fedka the Convict, a fugitive from hard labour, is wandering about. He's robbing people and has just recently committed another murder. Let me ask you: if you hadn't sent him off to the army fifteen years ago to pay off a gambling debt, that is to say, if you hadn't simply lost him at cards – tell me, would he have ended up doing hard labour? Would he be murdering people, as he's doing now, in his struggle for existence? What do you have to say to that, Mr Aesthete?'

I decline to describe the scene that followed. In the first place, there was a burst of mad applause. Not everyone applauded, only about one-fifth of the hall, but they applauded madly. All the rest of the audience streamed towards the exit, but since the applauding part of the audience kept pressing forward towards the platform, the result was general confusion. The ladies began to shriek, some of the girls began crying and asking to go home. Von Lembke, who was standing by his chair, kept looking wildly about him. Yuliya Mikhaylovna lost her head completely, for the first time in her career among us. As for Stepan Trofimovich, for a moment he seemed literally crushed by the words of the seminary student; but suddenly he raised both hands, as if extending them over the audience, and began to wail:

'I shake the dust off my feet and curse you[18] . . . The end . . . the end.'

And turning round, he ran backstage, waving his hands threateningly.

'He's insulted our society! . . . Verkhovensky!' the frenzied members of the audience roared. They even wanted to rush in pursuit of him. It was impossible to calm them down, at least at that moment, and – suddenly the final disaster burst like a bomb over the assembly and exploded in their midst: the third reader, the maniac who had been waving his fist offstage,[19] suddenly ran out on to the platform.

He had a completely mad look about him. With a broad, triumphant smile, full of boundless self-confidence, he surveyed the agitated hall and seemed to be glad of the disorder. It did not disconcert him in the least that he had to read amid such chaos; on the contrary, he was visibly pleased. This was so obvious that he immediately attracted attention.

'What's this now?' came the questions. 'Who's this now?' 'Shh! What does he want to say?'

'Ladies and gentlemen!' The maniac shouted as loud as he could, standing at the very edge of the platform, his voice almost as shrill and effeminate as Karmazinov's, but without the aristocratic lisp. 'Ladies and gentlemen! Twenty years ago, on the eve of war with half of Europe, Russia stood as an ideal in the eyes of all state and privy councillors. Literature served at the pleasure of the censorship; close-order drill was taught in the universities;[20] the army was turned into a ballet company; and the common people paid their taxes and remained silent under the knout of serfdom. Patriotism had turned into the extraction of bribes from the living and the dead. Those who did not take bribes were regarded as rebels, because they were disturbing the harmony of things. Birch groves were stripped to help maintain order. Europe was trembling . . . But in all the senseless thousand years of its life, Russia has never sunk to such depths . . .'

He raised his fist, waved it ecstatically and menacingly over his head, and suddenly brought it down savagely, as if he were smashing an enemy into smithereens. A frenzied howling echoed from all quarters, and there was a deafening burst of applause. Now almost half the hall was applauding; the most innocent among them were being carried away; Russia was being dishonoured for all to hear, publicly, so how could they not howl in ecstasy?

'That's it! That's the way to go!' 'Hurrah! No, this is no longer aesthetics!'

The maniac went on ecstatically:

'Since then twenty years have passed. Universities have opened and increased in number. Close-order drill has passed into legend; we lack thousands of officers to fill the ranks of our military. Railways have eaten up all the capital and have spread all over Russia like a spider's web, so that in fifteen years or so, it will perhaps be possible to go anywhere and back. Bridges burn only rarely, while towns burn down properly, in established order by turns, during the fire season. Solomonic judgements are rendered in the courts, and jurors take bribes only because they are struggling for existence, when they are threatened with starvation. The serfs have been freed, and now they flog one another with birch rods instead of being flogged by the former landowners. Seas and oceans of vodka are drunk up in support of the budget, and in Novgorod, opposite the ancient and useless Cathedral of St Sophia, a colossal bronze globe has been erected to commemorate a thousand years[21] of disorder and chaos, now past. Europe is frowning and growing uneasy again. Fifteen years of reform! And yet never has Russia, even in the most grotesque periods of its senseless existence, descended to . . .'

The final words couldn't even be heard over the roar of the crowd. He could be seen raising his arm again and triumphantly bringing it down once more. Ecstasy passed all limits. People were howling, clapping their hands, and even some of the ladies were shouting: 'That's enough! You can't say anything better than that!' They were like drunkards. The orator was sweeping his eyes over all of them and seemed to be melting away in his own triumph. I caught a glimpse of von Lembke pointing something out to someone in indescribable agitation. Yuliya Mikhaylovna, deathly pale, was hastening to say something to the prince who had run up to her. But at this moment a crowd of some six men, officials most of them, burst from backstage on to the platform, seized the orator and dragged him backstage. I don't understand how he could have broken away from them, but he did. He again dashed up to the very edge of the platform and managed to shout at the top of his voice, brandishing his fist:

'But never yet has Russia descended . . .'

But again he was dragged away. I saw perhaps fifteen men or so dash backstage to try to free him, though not across the platform but from the side, breaking the flimsy barrier, which proceeded to fall. Then I saw, though I could hardly believe my eyes, that the girl student (Virginsky's relative) suddenly leaped on to the platform with the same bundle under her arm, dressed the same, just as red-faced, just as plump, surrounded by two or three women and two or three men, and accompanied by her mortal enemy the high-school student. I even managed to hear the sentence:

'Ladies and gentlemen, I have come to inform you of the sufferings of the unfortunate students, and stir them to protest, one and all.'

But I ran off. I hid my rosette in a pocket and by a back stairway that I knew about managed to make my way out of the house and on to the street. First of all, of course, to Stepan Trofimovich's.

CHAPTER 2

The End of the Gala

I.

He didn't receive me. He'd locked himself in and was writing. To my repeated knocking and calling, he answered through the door:

'My friend, I've finished with everything. Who can ask anything more of me?'

'You haven't finished with anything, but have only helped everything collapse. For heaven's sake no clever words, Stepan Trofimovich. Open the door. Measures must be taken; they might still come here and insult you . . .'

I considered myself entitled to be strict and even severe. I was afraid that he might undertake something even more insane. But to my surprise, I met with an unusual firmness.

'Don't you be the first to insult me. I thank you for all you have done in the past, but I repeat that I'm completely finished with people, both good and bad. I'm writing a letter to Darya Pavlovna, whom I've neglected so unforgivably until now. You can deliver it tomorrow, if you wish, but for now, *merci*.'

'Stepan Trofimovich, I assure you that the matter is more serious than you think. Do you think you annihilated anyone there? You didn't annihilate anyone, but you shattered yourself like an empty bottle.' (Oh, I was rude and impolite, I remember that with chagrin!) 'There's absolutely no reason for you to write to Darya Pavlovna . . . and where will you go now without me? What do you understand about practical matters? Are you perhaps plotting something else? You'll only come to grief again if you're plotting something again . . .'

He rose and walked right up to the door.

'You haven't been with them very long, but you've become infected with their language and their tone. *Dieu vous pardonne, mon ami, et Dieu vous garde*. But I have always observed the rudiments of decency in you, and perhaps you'll think better of it – *après le temps*, of course, like all of us Russian people. As for your observation about my lack of practicality, I will remind you of an idea I've had for a long time: that here in Russia there's a whole mass of people who are concerned with nothing more than attacking other people's impracticality as savagely as they can, with the annoying persistence of flies in summer, finding each and every one to blame for it except themselves. *Cher*, remember that I am in a state of agitation, and don't torment me. Once more, *merci* to you for everything, and let us part with one another as Karmazinov did with his public, in other words, let us forget one another as magnanimously as we can. He was a sly old fox when he so earnestly begged his former readers to forget him; *quant à moi*, I am not so vain and I mostly rest my hopes on the youth of your inexperienced heart. Why should you remember a useless old man for very long? "Live more", my friend, as Nastasya wished me on my last name-day (*ces pauvres gens ont quelquefois des mots charmants et pleins de philosophie*).[1] I don't wish you much happiness – it will get boring; I don't wish you misfortune either; but in keeping with the philosophy of the simple folk, I will simply repeat: "Live more", and try somehow not to be too bored; this futile wish I'll add on my own. Well, farewell, and farewell for good. And don't stand at my door, I won't open it.'

He walked away, and I got nothing more out of him. Despite his 'agitation', he had been speaking fluently, unhurriedly and with authority, and was evidently trying to make an impression. Of course, he was somewhat vexed with me and was indirectly taking his revenge, perhaps, for yesterday's 'prison carts' and 'floors that suddenly open up'. But this morning's public tears, despite a victory of a certain sort, placed him, and he knew it, in a rather comic position, and there wasn't a man who cared so much about the beauty and strictness of form in his relations with his friends as Stepan Trofimovich. Oh, I don't blame him!

But it was precisely this punctiliousness and sarcasm, which hadn't left him despite all the shocks he'd suffered, that actually reassured me at the time: a man who had changed so little from what he had always been would not of course have been disposed at that moment to do anything tragic or unusual. That's how I reasoned then, and good heavens, how wrong I was! I had lost sight of too much.

In anticipation of events to come, I will cite a few of the opening lines of his letter to Darya Pavlovna, which she actually received the following day:

'*Mon enfant*, my hand is trembling, but I have finished with everything. You were not present during my final wrangle with the people; you did not come to this "reading", and you did well not to. But you will be told that in our Russia, which is so sorely lacking in men of character, one bold man stood up and, despite the mortal threats that rained down on him from all sides, he told these little fools the truth about themselves, namely, that they are little fools. *O, ce sont des pauvres petits vauriens et rien de plus, des petits fools – voilà le mot!*[2] The die is cast; I am leaving this town forever, and I don't know where I'm going. Everyone I loved has turned away from me. But you, you, a pure and naive creature, you, a meek being, whose fate was almost linked with mine, by the will of a capricious and autocratic heart, who perhaps looked on disdainfully while I shed my cowardly tears on the eve of our marriage that came to nought; you, who perhaps cannot, no matter who you may be, look at me otherwise than as a comic figure – oh, to you, to you I send the final cry of my heart, my final duty, to you alone! But I cannot leave you forever thinking that I am an ungrateful fool, ignoramus and egotist, as is perhaps being affirmed to you about me daily by an ungrateful and cruel heart, which, alas, I cannot forget . . .'

And so on and so forth, for a total of four large pages.

After banging my fist on the door three times in response to his 'I won't open it', and shouting after him that he would send Nastasya to fetch me three times that very day, but that I would be the one to refuse to come, I left him and ran to Yuliya Mikhaylovna's.

2.

Here I was unwittingly witness to a disgraceful scene: the poor woman was being deceived to her face, and I could do nothing. In fact, what could I say to her? I had already managed to recover my senses somewhat and to consider that all I had were some feelings and some suspicious presentiments, and really nothing more. I found her in tears, almost in hysterics, with eau-de-cologne compresses and a glass of water. Standing before her was Pyotr Stepanovich, who talked nonstop, and the prince, who remained silent, as if he had been put under lock and key. With tears and outcries she was reproaching Pyotr Stepanovich for his 'apostasy'. I was immediately struck that she ascribed the entire failure, the entire shame of that morning, in short, everything, entirely to the absence of Pyotr Stepanovich

But I noticed one very important change in him: he seemed to be extremely preoccupied with something, and almost serious. Normally he never appeared serious, he was always laughing, even when he was angry, and he was often angry. Oh, he was angry now as well; he was speaking coarsely, carelessly, with annoyance and impatience. He was trying to assure her that he had fallen ill with a headache and an attack of vomiting in Gaganov's apartment, where he had happened to drop by early that morning. Alas, the poor woman still so wanted to be deceived! The main issue that I found under discussion was the following: should there be a ball or not, that is, the entire second half of the gala? Yuliya Mikhaylovna flatly refused to appear at the ball after the 'recent insults', in other words, she was desperately longing to be compelled to do just that, and precisely by him, Pyotr Stepanovich. She looked on him as an oracle, and I really think that if he had left just then, she would have taken to her bed. But he hadn't the slightest desire to leave: he himself desperately needed the ball to take place that evening, and for Yuliya Mikhaylovna to be present at it.

'Now, now, what are you crying for? Do you really want a scene? To vent your wrath on someone? Well, then, vent it on me, but be quick about it, because time is passing and you have to make up your mind. We spoiled it with the reading, but we'll fix it with the ball. The prince here is of the same opinion. Yes, indeed, if it hadn't been for the prince, then how would it all have ended for you?'

At first the prince was against the ball (that is, against Yuliya Mikhaylovna's appearance at the ball; the ball itself must be held at all costs), but after two or three such references to his opinion, he gradually began to mumble as a sign of his assent.

I was also surprised by the highly unusual rudeness of Pyotr Stepanovich's tone. Oh, I indignantly reject the low gossip that later spread about some supposed liaison between Yuliya Mikhaylovna and Pyotr Stepanovich. There was nothing of the sort, nor could there be. He had gained ascendancy over her merely because from the very beginning he agreed whole-heartedly with her dreams of exerting an influence on society and on the ministry, entered into her plans, even devised them for her himself, operated with the coarsest flattery, wove a web around her from head to toe and became as necessary to her as breathing.

On catching sight of me, she cried, with flashing eyes:

'You just ask him, he didn't abandon me for a moment either, just like the prince. Tell me, isn't it obvious that this is all a plot, a low, cunning plot, to do everything bad they could possibly do to me and Andrey Antonovich? Oh, they had agreed on it! They had a plan. It's a political party, a genuine political party!'

'You're really wide of the mark, as usual. You've always got some fantasy in your head. But I'm glad that Mr . . .' (he pretended he'd forgotten my name) 'he'll give us his opinion.'

'My opinion,' I hastened to reply, 'is that I'm in agreement with Yuliya Mikhaylovna's opinion in every respect. The plot is only too obvious. I've brought you these rosettes, Yuliya Mikhaylovna. Whether the ball will take place or not – that of course is not my business, because it's not within my power. But my function as a steward is over. Excuse my ardour, but I'm unable to act to the detriment of common sense and personal conviction.'

'You hear, you hear?' She clasped her hands.

'Indeed, I do hear, and this is what I have to say to you,' he turned to me. 'I imagine that all of you have eaten something that's made you all delirious. In my opinion, nothing has happened, absolutely nothing that hasn't happened before and couldn't have happened at any time in this town. What plot? It was all very ugly, shamefully stupid, but where's the plot in all of it? Is it against Yuliya Mikhaylovna, who spoiled them, protected them, forgave them all their schoolboy pranks for no reason at all? Yuliya Mikhaylovna! What have I been drumming into your head ceaselessly this whole month? What have I been warning you about? Why, why did you need to have all these common people here? You had to go and hook yourself up with riff-raff! Why, what for? To bring society together? Do you really think they can be brought together, have mercy on us!'

'When did you ever warn me? On the contrary, you encouraged me, you even demanded . . . I confess I'm so surprised . . . You yourself used to bring a lot of strange people to see me.'

'On the contrary, I argued with you, I didn't encourage you, and as for bringing you people – well, I did bring them, but after they'd started flocking here by the dozens and then only very recently, to make up the "literary quadrille". You couldn't have brought it off without these louts. But I'll just bet that today a dozen and more of the same sort of louts were let in without tickets.'

'Undoubtedly,' I confirmed.

'There, you see, you're agreeing already. Remember what sort of tone has prevailed around here of late, that is, in the whole of this wretched little town? Why, it's turned into nothing but impudence, shamelessness; why, it's been a scandal with all the bells ringing at full tilt. And who has been encouraging them? Who has shielded them with her authority? Who has thrown everything into confusion? Who has upset all the smallfry? Why, all the local family secrets are recorded in your album here. Weren't you the one who patted your poets and caricaturists on the head? Wasn't it you who let Lyamshin kiss your hand? Wasn't it in your presence that the seminary student cursed the actual state councillor and ruined his daughter's dress with his huge tarred boots? Why, then, are you so surprised that the public is set against you?'

'But it was actually all you, no one but you! Oh, my God!'

'No, indeed, I cautioned you, we quarrelled, do you hear, we quarrelled!'

'Why, you're lying to my face.'

'Well, of course it's easy for you to say that. You need a victim now, someone to vent your wrath on. Well, then, vent it on me, I've told you that. I'd better turn to you, Mr . . .' (He still couldn't remember my name.) 'Let's count on our fingers. I maintain that except for Liputin there was no plot, none at all! I will prove it, but first let's analyse Liputin. He came out on to the platform with the poem of that fool Lebyadkin. What sort of plot is that, in your opinion? Why, do you know that it could simply have struck Liputin as being witty? Seriously, seriously – witty. He simply came out with the purpose of amusing everyone and making them laugh, and above all, his protectress, Yuliya Mikhaylovna, that's all. You don't believe it? Well, wasn't it in keeping with everything that's gone on here for the past month? And if you want, I'll tell everything: I swear, under different circumstances it would perhaps have gone off very well! It was a coarse joke, even a salty one, if you like, but it was amusing, wasn't it?'

'What! You consider that what Liputin did was clever?' Yuliya Mikhaylovna exclaimed, dreadfully indignant. 'Such idiocy, such tactlessness, this vile, disgusting display, this deliberate insult – oh, you're saying all this on purpose! You must be in on the plot with them!'

'Of course, I was sitting in the back, hiding, and setting in motion the entire little mechanism! Why, if I had taken part in the plot – and you will certainly understand this! – it would by no means have ended with just Liputin! And so, in your view, I also made an arrangement with Papa so that he would deliberately create such a scandal? Well now, who's to blame for allowing Papa to read? Who tried to stop you yesterday, just yesterday, yesterday?'

'Oh, *hier il avait tant d'esprit*,[3] and I was so counting on him, and besides he has such good manners. I thought that he and Karmazinov . . . and look what happened!'

'Yes, indeed, and look what happened. But despite all his *tant d'esprit*, my papa made a mess of it, and if I myself had known ahead of time that he would make such a mess of it, then, as a participant in this supposed plot against your gala, I would certainly not have started yesterday trying to talk you out of letting the goat loose into the vegetable garden, would I? And yet I did try to talk you out of it yesterday, I did try because I had a premonition. Naturally, it wasn't possible to foresee everything: he himself probably didn't know what he would do a minute before he blasted away. Do you really think these nervous little old men are like other people! But things can still be saved: tomorrow, to satisfy the public, send two doctors to him, by administrative order and with all the trappings, to ascertain his health, even today if possible, and have him taken straight to the hospital, with cold compresses. At least everyone will laugh and will see there's nothing to be offended at. I'll announce it at the ball tonight, since I'm his son. Karmazinov is another matter, he turned out to be a perfect ass, and dragged his article out for a whole hour – that's the one who's undoubtedly in the plot with me! Let me do something disgusting as well, he says, to harm Yuliya Mikhaylovna!'

'Oh, Karmazinov, *quelle honte!*[4] I burned, burned with shame for our audience!'

'Well, I wouldn't have burned, but I would have roasted him alive. The audience, after all, was right. And again, who's to blame for Karmazinov? Did I force him on you or not? Did I take part in his deification or not? Oh well, the Devil with him, but the third maniac, the political one, that's a different story altogether. Here everyone slipped up, it wasn't just my plot.'

'Oh, don't mention it, it's dreadful, dreadful! For that I, I alone am to blame!'

'Of course you are, but here I'll excuse you. Oh, who will keep an eye on them, these candid people! There's no getting away from them even in Petersburg. He was recommended to you, after all, he certainly was! So you must agree that you're now even obliged to appear at the ball. This is an important matter, you know, you yourself put him on the platform, you know. You absolutely must now announce publicly that you have nothing in common with him, that this fine fellow is already in the hands of the police, and that you were deceived in some inexplicable way. You should announce indignantly that you were the victim of a madman. Because he really is a madman, and nothing more. That's how you should refer to him. I can't bear these people who bite. Perhaps I myself say even worse things, but not from the lecture platform. And they're now shouting about a senator.'

'About what senator? Who's shouting?'

'You see, I myself understand nothing. You have no knowledge of any senator, Yuliya Mikhaylovna?'

'A senator?'

'You see, they're convinced that a senator has been appointed here, and that Petersburg is replacing you. I've heard it from many people.'

'And I've heard it,' I confirmed.

'Who's been saying this?' Yuliya Mikhaylovna flared up.

'You mean who said it first? How should I know? They're just saying it. The ordinary people have been saying it. Yesterday in particular they were saying it. They're all very serious about it somehow, although you can't make anything out of it. Of course, those who are more intelligent and competent aren't saying it, but even among them there are those who are listening.'

'How vile! And . . . how stupid!'

'Well then, you really must put in an appearance, just to show these fools.'

'I admit I myself feel that I'm somewhat obliged, but . . . what if another disgrace awaits me? What if people don't come? No one will come, you know, no one, no one!'

'Such fervour! Do you really think they won't come? What about the dresses that have been sewn, and the girls' costumes? Why, after that I give up on you as a woman. So much for a knowledge of human beings!'

'The marshal's wife won't be there, she won't!'

'Well, what happened there when all is said and done! Why won't they come?' he finally exclaimed, angry and impatient.

'Infamy, shame – that's what happened. I don't really know what to call it, but after that, it's impossible for me to go.'

'Why? What are you to blame for, after all? Why are you taking the blame on yourself? Isn't the audience to blame instead, your distinguished old men, your heads of families? They should have restrained the scoundrels and good-for-nothings, because it was just good-for-nothings and scoundrels, nothing serious. You can never control things with just the police in any society, anywhere. Every one of us, when he goes in, demands that a special policeman be assigned to protect him. They don't understand that society protects itself. And what do our heads of families, our worthies, our wives, our young girls do in such circumstances? They say nothing and just pout. There's not even enough social initiative to restrain the pranksters.'

'Oh, that's the gospel truth! They say nothing, they pout and . . . they look around.'

'And if it is the truth, then you need to say so then and there, aloud, proudly, firmly. Just to show that you're not beaten. And specifically to these little old men and mothers. Oh, you'll know how, you have the gift when your head is clear. You'll bring them all together and say so aloud, aloud. And then you'll write a letter to the *Voice* and the *Stock Exchange Gazette*.[5] Wait, I'll see to it, I'll arrange everything for you. Of course, as much attention as possible must be paid, an eye must be kept on the buffet; the prince must be asked, Mr — must be asked . . . You really can't leave us, *monsieur*, just when we have to start everything all over again. And then, of course, you'll make your entrance arm-in-arm with Andrey Antonovich. How is Andrey Antonovich's health?'

'Oh, how unjustly, how unfairly, how insultingly you've always judged that angel of a man!' Yuliya Mikhaylovna suddenly exclaimed in an unexpected outburst and almost in tears, raising her handkerchief to her eyes. At first Pyotr Stepanovich was even at a loss for words.

'For heaven's sake, I . . . why, what have I . . . I always . . .'

'You never did, never! You never gave him his due!'

'There's no understanding a woman!' Pyotr Stepanovich grumbled, with a crooked smile.

'He's the most upright, the most considerate, the most angelic man! The kindest of men!'

'For heaven's sake, but as for his kindness . . . I've always given him his due as far as kindness is concerned . . .'

'Never! But let's leave it at that. I've been too clumsy in my defence of him. This morning that Jesuit of a marshal's wife also dropped some sarcastic hints about what happened yesterday.'

'Oh, she has no time now for hints about yesterday, she has today to think about. And why are you so worried that she won't come to the ball? Of course, she won't come after getting involved in such a scandal. Maybe she really isn't to blame, but she does have her reputation to think of: her hands are dirty.'

'What do you mean, I don't understand: how are her hands dirty?' Yuliya Mikhaylovna looked at him in bewilderment.

'To put it another way, I really can't confirm it, but the town is already ringing with the news that she was the one who brought them together.'

'What do you mean? Whom did she bring together?'

'Ah, you really don't know yet?' he exclaimed in well-feigned surprise. 'Why, Stavrogin and Lizaveta Nikolayevna.'

'What? How?' we all exclaimed.

'So you really don't know! Phew! Why, there are a couple of real tragic romances going on here. Lizaveta Nikolayevna went straight from the carriage of the marshal's wife and took a seat in Stavrogin's carriage and slipped off with him to Skvoreshniki in broad daylight. It was just an hour ago, not even an hour.'

We were flabbergasted. Naturally, we fell all over ourselves trying to find out more, but to our surprise, although he himself had been a witness 'by accident', he could give us no details at all. Supposedly this was the way it had happened: when the marshal's wife had driven Liza and Mavriky Nikolayevich from the 'reading' to the house of Liza's mother (whose legs were still giving her trouble), someone's carriage was waiting not far from the front steps, about twenty-five paces away, off to the side. When Liza jumped out, she ran straight to this carriage. A door opened and banged shut; Liza shouted to Mavriky Nikolayevich, 'Spare me', and the carriage sped off to Skvoreshniki at full tilt. To our hurried questions – 'Had there been an arrangement here? Who was sitting in the carriage?' – Pyotr Stepanovich replied that he knew nothing; that there had of course been an arrangement, but that he hadn't spotted Stavrogin himself in the carriage; perhaps the butler, old Aleksey Yegorych, had been sitting there. To the questions 'How did you happen to find yourself there? And how do you know for sure that she went to Skvoreshniki?' he replied that he happened to be there because he was passing by, and on catching sight of Liza, he even ran up to the carriage (and even so couldn't tell who was in the carriage, for all his curiosity!), and that Mavriky Nikolayevich not only didn't set off in pursuit, but didn't even try to stop Liza, and even laid a restraining hand on the marshal's wife, who was shouting at the top of her lungs: 'She's going to Stavrogin's, she's going to Stavrogin's!' At this point I lost patience and in a frenzy began shouting at Pyotr Stepanovich:

'You're the one, you scoundrel, who arranged everything! That's what you spent the morning doing. You were helping Stavrogin, you came in the carriage, you helped her into it – you, you, you! Yuliya Mikhaylovna, here's your enemy, he will ruin you as well! Take care!'

And I ran headlong out of the house.

To this day I don't understand why I shouted at him then, and I am surprised at myself. But I had figured things out in their entirety: everything had happened almost as I had told him, and subsequently was proved to be the case. Above all, the obviously false way in which he had broken the news was all too clear. When he came into the house, he didn't tell us immediately, as the first and most important piece of news, but instead acted as if we already knew anyway – which was impossible in such a short period of time. And even if we had known, we would in any case not have been able to keep quiet until he began to speak about it. He also couldn't have heard

that the town was already 'ringing' with the news of the
marshal's wife, again on account of the short period of time.
Besides, as he was telling us about it, he smiled once or twice
in a disgusting and empty-headed way, probably regarding us
as fools who had already been completely taken in. But I no
longer had time for him: I believed the central fact, and I was
beside myself as I ran out of Yuliya Mikhaylovna's. The disaster
had struck me to the very heart. I was pained almost to the
point of tears; yes, perhaps I was even crying. I had absolutely
no idea what to do. I rushed to Stepan Trofimovich's, but again
the annoying fellow would not open the door. Nastasya assured
me in a reverential whisper that he had lain down to take a
rest, but I didn't believe her. In Liza's house I managed to
question the servants; they confirmed that she had fled, but
knew nothing more. The house was in turmoil; the sick mistress
had begun having fainting fits, but Mavriky Nikolayevich was
with her. I didn't think it possible to send for Mavriky Nikolayevich. In response to my inquiries about Pyotr Stepanovich,
it was confirmed that he had been darting in and out of the
house for the past few days, sometimes twice a day. The servants
were glum, and spoke of Liza with a kind of special respect.
That she was ruined, utterly ruined I had no doubt, but I had
absolutely no understanding of the psychological aspect of the
matter, especially after yesterday's scene between her and Stavrogin. To run around town and make inquiries in the houses
of gloating acquaintances, where of course the news would
already have spread by now, struck me as disgusting, and
demeaning to Liza besides. But strangely enough I ran to Darya
Pavlovna's, where, however, I was not received (no one had
been received in the Stavrogin house since the day before). I
didn't know what I could have said to her, and why I had run
to see her. From there I went to her brother's. Shatov heard me
out, gloomy and silent. I will note that I found him in an even
more sullen mood than ever; he was dreadfully preoccupied
and listened to me as if it were an effort. He said almost nothing,
and began walking back and forth, from one corner to another
of his little box of a room, stamping his feet more than usual.
But while I was already making my way down the stairs, he

shouted out to me that I should drop in to see Liputin: 'There you'll learn everything.' But I didn't go to Liputin's. Instead, even though I was well on my way, I returned to Shatov's, and, half-opening the door, without going in, asked him laconically and without any explanation whether he was going to visit Marya Timofeyevna that day. Shatov responded with a curse, and I left. I'm writing this down so as not to forget that on that same evening he made a point of walking to the outskirts of town to Marya Timofeyevna's, whom he hadn't seen for a long time. He found her in the best possible health and mood, and Lebyadkin dead drunk, asleep on the sofa in the first room. This was at exactly nine o'clock. So he told me the next day, when he happened to run across me on the street. Sometime after nine o'clock that night I decided to go to the ball, not in the capacity of 'a young man serving as steward' (besides, my rosette was still at Yuliya Mikhaylovna's), but out of an irresistible curiosity to listen in on what was happening (without asking any questions): how were people in our town in general talking about all these events? Besides, I wanted to have a look at Yuliya Mikhaylovna, if only from a distance. I reproached myself heartily for having run out of her house not so long before.

3.

That entire night, with its almost absurd happenings and the dreadful 'denouement' the next morning, still haunts me like an ugly nightmarish dream and comprises – at least, for me – the most painful part of my chronicle. Although I arrived late at the ball, I did in any event arrive before it was over, though it was destined to end quickly. It was already past ten when I reached the front steps of the marshal's house, where the same White Hall in which the readings had taken place had already been tidied up, despite the brief span of time, and made ready, as had been proposed, to serve as the main ballroom for the entire town. But no matter how unfavourably disposed I had been about the ball that morning, I still had no inkling of the full truth. Not one family from the higher circles had appeared;

even officials holding positions of any importance at all had
stayed away, and that was an extremely striking feature. As far
as the ladies and girls were concerned, the earlier calculations
of Pyotr Stepanovich (which were now obviously perfidious)
had proved completely wrong. Very few people had come; for
every four men there was scarcely even one lady, and what
ladies, besides! Wives 'of a sort' of regimental middle-rank
officers and of various petty officials from the post office and
the civil service, three doctors' wives with their daughters, two
or three impoverished landowners' wives, the seven daughters
and one niece of the secretary I happened to mention earlier,
merchants' wives – is that what Yuliya Mikhaylovna was
expecting? Even half the merchants didn't turn up. As for the
men, they were there in large numbers, despite the total absence
of our entire nobility, but they created an ambiguous and suspicious impression. Of course, a few extremely quiet and deferential officers were present with their wives, and a few of the
most docile fathers of families, like that same secretary, the
father of seven daughters. All these humble, unimportant folk
appeared, so to speak, 'out of inevitability', as one of these
gentlemen expressed it. But on the other hand, the mass of
lively characters and, in addition, the mass of those whom Pyotr
Stepanovich and I suspected of having been admitted without
tickets that morning, seemed to have grown larger than before.
They were all sitting in the buffet for the time being; as they
arrived, they passed directly into the buffet, as if it was the
place they had agreed on earlier. So, at least, it seemed to me.
The buffet was located at the end of a suite of rooms, in a
spacious hall, where Prokhorych had installed himself with all
the enticements of the club's kitchen and with a tempting display of *zakuski* and drinks. Here I noticed some individuals
in frock-coats that were practically ragged, attire that was
extremely dubious and entirely unsuitable for a ball. They
had obviously been sobered up with extraordinary difficulty
and certainly wouldn't remain so for long, and were not local
people, though Lord knows where they'd been found. I knew,
of course, that in keeping with an idea of Yuliya Mikhaylovna's,
it had been proposed to throw the most democratic ball pos-

sible, 'without refusing even the tradespeople, if it should happen that some of them should pay for a ticket'. She was able to say these words boldly to her committee, in full confidence that it wouldn't occur to any of the tradespeople of our town, all of whom were poor, to buy a ticket. But in any event I doubted that these sullen people in frock-coats that were almost ragged would have been admitted, all the democratic sentiments of the committee notwithstanding. But who admitted them, and with what purpose? Liputin and Lyamshin had already been deprived of their stewards' rosettes (although they were present at the ball and took part in the 'literary quadrille'); but Liputin's place had been taken, to my surprise, by the seminary student who had created the greatest scandal that morning by his tussle with Stepan Trofimovich, and Lyamshin's place by Pyotr Stepanovich himself. What could one possibly expect in such a case? I made an effort to listen in on the conversations. Some of the opinions expressed were striking for their wildness. In one little group, for instance, people were asserting that Yuliya Mikhaylovna had masterminded the entire affair between Stavrogin and Liza, and that she had taken money for it from Stavrogin. They even named the amount. They asserted that she had even organized the gala with that in mind; therefore, they said, half the town didn't bother to put in an appearance once they'd learned what was up, and von Lembke himself was so stunned that 'his reason was unhinged', and she was now 'leading him about' like a madman. There was also much guffawing as well, hoarse, wild and sly. Everyone criticized the ball savagely, and abused Yuliya Mikhaylovna without any ceremony. In general, the babble was disorderly, disconnected, drunken and agitated, so that it was hard to make any sense of it or get any meaning out of it. People who simply wanted to have a good time also found refuge here in the buffet, and there were even several ladies, very agreeable and in high spirits, whom nothing could surprise or frighten, mostly all officers' wives, with their husbands. They had arranged themselves in groups at separate small tables and were drinking tea in an extremely jolly mood. The buffet had turned into a warm refuge for almost half of the assembled public. Still and all, within a short period of time this entire mass of people would have to stream into the hall; it was dreadful even to think about it.

Meanwhile, in the White Hall three scanty little quadrilles had been formed with the help of the prince. The young ladies were dancing, and their parents were beaming at them. But even then, many of these respectable people were already beginning to wonder how, after allowing their girls to enjoy themselves, they would get away in good time, and not later, when 'things would begin to happen'. All without exception were certain that something was bound to happen. It would be difficult for me to describe Yuliya Mikhaylovna's state of mind. I hadn't been able to speak to her, although I did walk up rather close to her. She didn't respond to my bow when I entered, since she hadn't noticed me (she really hadn't noticed). Her face had a pained expression, her eyes scornful and haughty but restless and troubled. She was trying to control herself though she was visibly suffering – for what and for whom? She should certainly have left and, most importantly, taken her husband with her, but she was staying! Just a look at her face showed that her eyes had been 'fully opened', and that there was no need for her to wait any longer. She didn't even summon Pyotr Stepanovich (he himself seemed to be avoiding her; I saw him in the buffet, and he was in an extremely good mood). Still and all, she was remaining at the ball and not letting Andrey Antonovich leave her side for an instant. Oh, until the last possible moment she would have rejected, with utterly sincere indignation, any hint about the state of his health, even earlier that day. But now her eyes must have been opened too in that respect. As for me, it seemed to me at first glance that Andrey Antonovich looked worse than earlier that day. He struck me as being in a state of oblivion and not entirely aware of where he was. Sometimes he suddenly looked around in unexpected severity, for instance, at me a couple of times. Once he tried to say something; he began audibly and loudly, and didn't finish, almost throwing a fright into a meek old clerk who happened to be standing beside him. But even the meek half of the public that was present in the White Hall kept sullenly and fearfully clear of Yuliya Mikhaylovna, while casting extremely strange glances at her husband, glances that in their intensity and candour didn't at all go with the apprehensive behaviour of these people.

'This was what particularly struck me, and I suddenly began to figure out what was going on with Andrey Antonovich,' Yuliya Mikhaylovna confided in me later.

Yes, she was guilty again! Earlier in the day, when I had run off, when she and Pyotr Stepanovich had decided that there must be a ball and that she must attend the ball, she probably went into Andrey Antonovich's study, after he had been 'shaken' at the 'reading', again employed all her blandishments and persuaded him to come along with her. But how she must have been suffering now! And yet she was making no move to leave! Whether she was tormented by pride or had simply lost her head, I don't know. For all her haughtiness, she did try, with humiliation and smiles, to strike up a conversation with some of the ladies, but they immediately became flustered, escaped with monosyllabic and wary 'yes, ma'am' and 'no, ma'am', and were obviously trying to avoid her.

Of the undisputed dignitaries in our town only one appeared at the ball – that same pompous retired general whom I've already characterized on one occasion and who, after Stavrogin's duel with Gaganov, 'opened the door to public impatience' at the house of the marshal's wife. He strode importantly through the rooms, looked and listened closely, and endeavoured to give the impression that he had come more to observe morals than for his own personal pleasure. He ended by attaching himself to Yuliya Mikhaylovna and not moving a step away from her, obviously trying to cheer her up and reassure her. Without a doubt this man was kindness itself, of very exalted rank and so old that one could even put up with his compassion. But for her to admit to herself that this old windbag was venturing to take pity on her and almost to protect her, and to understand that he was doing her an honour with his presence, was very irritating. But the general didn't leave her and kept babbling away without stopping.

'A city, they say, cannot stand without seven righteous men[6] ... seven, I think, though I do not remember the prescribed

number. I do not know how many of these seven ... those in
our town who are in-dub-it-ably righteous ... have had the
honour to attend your ball, but, despite their presence, I am
beginning to feel myself unsafe. *Vous me pardonnerez,
charmante dame, n'est-ce pas?* I am speaking sym-bol-ic-ally,
but I did go to the buffet, and I am glad that I returned in one
piece ... Our priceless Prokhorych is out of place there, and it
seems that his stall will probably be pulled down by morning.
However, I am jesting. I am waiting only to see how the "literary
quadrille" will turn out, and then – to bed. Forgive a gout-
ridden old man, but I go to bed early, and I would also advise
you to "go sleepy-bye", as they say *aux enfants.*[7] But I've
actually come for the beautiful young girls, whom I, of course,
cannot meet anywhere in such large numbers as here. They are
all from the other side of the river, and I do not go there. The
wife of one officer – a chasseur,[8] I think – is even not at all
bad-looking, very ... and ... and she herself knows it. I was
having a conversation with the sweet little rogue; perky and ...
well, the young girls are fresh-looking too, but that is all, they
have nothing but freshness. However, it is a pleasure for me.
There are some sweet little buds, except their lips are too thick.
In general, there is little regularity in the Russian beauty of the
ladies' faces, and ... and they end up looking rather like pan-
cakes ... *Vous me pardonnerez, n'est-ce pas* ... with pretty
little eyes, however ... laughing little eyes. These sweet little
buds are char-ming for a couple of years when they are young,
even for three ... and then, well, they spread out forever ...
producing in their husbands that sad in-dif-fer-ence, which
so promotes the development of the woman question ... if I
understand that question correctly ... Hmm. The hall is attractive; the rooms are not decorated badly. It could have been
worse. The music could be much worse ... I will not say that
it should be. It makes a bad impression that there are generally
so few ladies. I won't say a word about the way people are
dressed. It's too bad that that man in grey trousers is so openly
permitting himself to dance the cancan. I forgive him if he is
doing it for the fun of it, and since he is the local apothecary
... but before eleven o'clock is still early even for an apothecary

... In the buffet back there two people got into a fight and were not escorted out. Before eleven, people ought to be escorted out for fighting, whatever the customs of the public are ... I won't say after two – then one has to make concessions to public opinion, and only if this ball keeps going until after two. Varvara Petrovna did not keep her word, though, and she did not contribute any flowers. Hmm, she cannot be bothered with flowers, *pauvre mère*![9] And poor Liza, have you heard? They say it is a mysterious story and ... and again Stavrogin is in the arena. Hmm. I should leave and go to bed ... I am beginning to nod off. And when will this "li-ter-a-ry quadrille" take place?'

Finally, the 'literary quadrille'[10] got under way. Of late, whenever conversation in town turned to the forthcoming ball, it immediately focused on the 'literary quadrille', and since no one could imagine what this was, it succeeded in arousing inordinate curiosity. Nothing could have been more dangerous for its success, and – what a disappointment it turned out to be!

The side doors of the White Hall, which until then had been locked, were opened, and suddenly several maskers appeared. The public eagerly gathered round them. The entire buffet, down to the last person, burst into the hall as one. The maskers took their positions for the dance. I managed to squeeze to the front, and installed myself directly behind Yuliya Mikhaylovna, von Lembke and the general. At this point Pyotr Stepanovich, who had been absent so far, trotted up to Yuliya Mikhaylovna.

'I've been in the buffet all this time, observing,' he whispered, with the look of a guilty schoolboy, although it was purposely put on in order to irritate her even more. She flushed with anger.

'You could at least stop deceiving me now, you insolent man!' burst from her lips, almost loud enough for the public to catch. Pyotr Stepanovich trotted off, extremely pleased with himself.

It would have been difficult to imagine a more pitiful, more tasteless, more talentless and vapid allegory than this 'literary quadrille'. No one could have devised anything less suitable for our public; and yet it was devised, they say, by Karmazinov. To be sure, Liputin arranged it, in consultation with that same lame teacher who had been at the Virginskys' evening meeting. Nonetheless, Karmazinov had come up with the idea and, they say, even wanted to dress himself up and take some special solo part in it. The quadrille consisted of six pathetic pairs of maskers – really not even maskers, because they were wearing the same kinds of clothes as everyone else. So, for instance, an elderly gentleman, short and in a tail-coat – in fact, dressed the same as everyone else – and with a respectable grey beard that had been tied on (this constituted his entire costume), was trotting away in place as he danced, a stolid expression on his face, taking tiny and rapid steps in one and the same spot. He was making some sounds in a subdued but hoarse bass, and it was this hoarseness of voice that was supposed to represent one of the well-known newspapers. Opposite this masker two giant X and Z were dancing, and these letters had been pinned on their tail-coats, but what the X and Z stood for remained unspecified. 'Honest Russian thought' was represented in the form of a middle-aged gentleman wearing spectacles, a tail-coat, gloves and – fetters (real fetters). Tucked under this idea's arm was a portfolio with some 'case' in it. Peeping out of one pocket was an unsealed letter from abroad, which contained a certificate attesting, for the benefit of all doubters, to the honesty of 'honest Russian thought'. All of this was spelled out verbally by the stewards, since the letter sticking out of the pocket could certainly not have been read. In his raised right hand 'honest Russian thought' was holding a glass, as if he wished to propose a toast. On either side of him two close-cropped nihilist girls danced in mincing steps, and vis-à-vis danced another elderly gentleman, in a tail-coat, but with a heavy cudgel in his hand, apparently representing a formidable publication, although not from Petersburg, entitled 'One Bash – You're Just Hash'. But despite his cudgel, he simply couldn't endure the spectacles of 'honest Russian thought' that were trained on him, and he was trying to look away, and when he was doing a *pas de deux*, he twisted and turned and didn't know where to go, so much did his conscience pain him, apparently. However, I won't mention any more of these stupid little contrivances; everything was in the same vein, so that I finally became painfully ashamed. And then this very same expression of what seemed like shame was reflected on the faces of the entire public, even the most gloomy ones that had appeared from the buffet. For some time everyone remained silent and looked on in angry bewilderment. A man who is ashamed usually begins to grow angry and is inclined to cynicism. Little by little our public began to buzz.

'What is this, anyway?' a devotee of the buffet began grumbling in one of the small groups.

'Some piece of stupidity.'

'Some piece of literature. They're criticizing the *Voice*.'

'Well, what's it to me?'

From another group:

'Asses!'

'No, they're not asses, we're the asses.'

'What makes you an ass?'

'Why, I'm not an ass.'

'Well, if you're not an ass, then I'm even less so.'

From a third group:

'Give their behinds a good kicking and send them all to the Devil!'

'Shake up the whole hall!'

From a fourth:

'How is it the von Lembkes aren't ashamed to watch?'

'Why should they be ashamed? After all, you're not ashamed, are you?'

'I'm certainly ashamed, but he's the governor.'

'And you're a pig.'

'I've never in my life seen such a common ball,' came the venomous words of a lady standing next to Yuliya Mikhaylovna, obviously desiring to be overheard. This lady was about forty, solidly built and thickly rouged, in a bright silk dress. Almost everyone in town knew her, but no one received her. She was the widow of a state councillor, who had left her a wooden house and a meagre pension, but she lived well and kept her own horses. A couple of months before, she had been the first to call on Yuliya Mikhaylovna, who didn't receive her.

'Well, it certainly could have been foreseen,' she added, staring brazenly into Yuliya Mikhaylovna's eyes.

'And if you could foresee it, then why did you bother to come?' Yuliya Mikhaylovna couldn't help but remark.

'Because I'm naive,' the perky lady snapped back instantly, and got all armed and ready (she was dreadfully keen to take the hostess on); but the general stepped between them.

'*Chère dame*,' he bent over to Yuliya Mikhaylovna, 'we really should leave. We are only inhibiting them, and without us they will enjoy themselves enormously. You have accomplished everything, you have opened the ball for them; better now to leave them in peace . . . Besides, Andrey Antonovich does not appear to be in an entirely sat-is-fac-to-ry state of health . . . What if some misfortune should occur?'

But it was already too late.

Throughout the quadrille, Andrey Antonovich had been watching the dancers in a kind of wrathful bewilderment, and when the comments from the public began, he started looking around nervously. Then for the first time he was struck by certain individuals from the buffet; his eyes expressed extreme surprise. Suddenly there was a burst of laughter at one of the antics in the quadrille: the publisher of the 'menacing periodical not from Petersburg', who had been dancing with a cudgel in his hands, and who finally had come to feel that he couldn't endure the spectacles of 'honest Russian thought' staring at him, and not knowing where to go to escape them, in the final turn, suddenly began to walk upside down towards the spectacles, which, incidentally, was supposed to signify the constant turning upside down of common sense in the 'menacing periodical not from Petersburg'. Since only Lyamshin knew how to walk upside down, he had undertaken to represent the editor with the cudgel. Yuliya Mikhaylovna had absolutely no idea that someone was going to walk upside down. 'They concealed it from me, they concealed it,' she later repeated to me in despair and disgust. The roar of laughter from the crowd came of course not in reaction to the allegory, which no one cared anything about, but merely at seeing someone walking upside down in a coat with tails. Von Lembke began to seethe and tremble.

'Scoundrel!' he cried, pointing at Lyamshin. 'Seize the villain, turn him . . . turn his feet . . . his head . . . put his head on top . . . on top!'

Lyamshin jumped to his feet. The laughter grew louder.

'Kick out all the villains who are laughing!' Von Lembke suddenly ordered. The crowd began to buzz and rumble.

'That can't be done, Your Excellency.'

'You shouldn't abuse the public, sir.'

'You're a fool yourself,' came a voice from somewhere in the corner.

'Filibusters!' shouted someone from the opposite corner.

Von Lembke spun around on hearing the shout and turned deathly pale. A vacant smile appeared on his lips, as if he had suddenly remembered and understood something.

'Ladies and gentlemen,' Yuliya Mikhaylovna turned to the advancing crowd, meanwhile drawing her husband after her, 'ladies and gentlemen, you will excuse Andrey Antonovich. Andrey Antonovich is not well . . . excuse him . . . forgive him, ladies and gentlemen!'

I heard exactly what she said: 'forgive him'. The scene moved very quickly. But I definitely remember that part of the public had already rushed out of the hall at that same moment, as if in fright, directly after these words of Yuliya Mikhaylovna's. I even recall a hysterical woman's tearful cry:

'Oh, it's like this morning all over again!'

And suddenly, in the midst of what was almost the beginning of a crush, another bombshell went off, and it was 'like this morning all over again'.

'Fire! All of Zarechye[11] is on fire!'

I just don't remember where this dreadful cry first came from: whether from the hall, or whether, more likely, someone ran in from the stairway leading to the entrance hall, but it was followed by such a commotion that I won't even attempt to describe it. More than half the public that had assembled for the ball was from Zarechye – owners of the wooden houses there, or those who lived in them. People rushed to the windows, pulled the drapes apart in an instant, tore down the blinds. Zarechye was burning. To be sure, the fire had only just begun, but it was burning in three separate places – and that's what was frightening.

'Arson! The Shpigulin workers!' the crowd howled.

I recall a few highly characteristic exclamations:

'I felt in my heart there would be arson; all this time I've felt it!'

'The Shpigulin workers, the Shpigulin workers, no one else!'

'We were brought together here on purpose so that the fire could be set there!'

This last and most surprising cry was a woman's, the spontaneous, involuntary cry of a Korobochka who has been burned out. Everyone surged towards the exit. I won't try to describe the crush in the entrance hall while fur coats, shawls and cloaks were being sorted out, the shrieks of terrified women, the weeping of young ladies. I doubt that anything was stolen, but it's not surprising that given such chaos some people simply left without warm clothing, not having found their own, a fact that occasioned discussion in the town long afterwards, with legends and embellishments. Von Lembke and Yuliya Mikhaylovna were almost crushed by the crowd in the doorway.

'Stop everyone! Don't let a single person leave!' von Lembke howled, stretching his hand out menacingly towards the people who had crowded together. 'The strictest search of each and every one, immediately!'

A flood of violent oaths poured from the hall.

'Andrey Antonovich! Andrey Antonovich!' Yuliya Mikhaylovna exclaimed in utter despair.

'Arrest her first!' he shouted, pointing his finger at her menacingly. 'Search her first! The ball was arranged so that there could be a fire . . .'

She let out a shriek and fell into a faint (oh, a real faint, of course). I, the prince and the general flew to her aid; there were others, too, who helped us at this difficult moment, even some of the ladies. We carried the unfortunate woman from this hell into the carriage; but she came to just as we were driving up to the house, and her first cry was again about Andrey Antonovich. With the collapse of all her fantasies, only Andrey Antonovich remained to her. The doctor was sent for. I waited at her house for a whole hour, as did the prince. The general, in an access of magnanimity (even though he himself was extremely frightened), didn't want to leave 'the unfortunate woman's bed' all night, but in ten minutes he had fallen asleep in an armchair in the hall, still waiting for the doctor, and we simply left him there.

The chief of police, hurrying from the ball to the fire, had managed to escort Andrey Antonovich out after us, and had tried to seat him in the carriage next to Yuliya Mikhaylovna, attempting as best he could to persuade His Excellency to 'take some rest'. But – and I don't understand why – he didn't insist. Of course, Andrey Antonovich wouldn't hear of resting, and was eager to get to the fire, but that wasn't a good enough reason. It ended with the chief of police taking him to the fire in his own droshky. Later, people said that von Lembke was making wild gestures during the whole trip and 'shouting out ideas that couldn't be implemented because they were so unusual'. Subsequently it was simply announced that at those moments His Excellency was in a state of delirium as the result of 'a sudden shock'.

There's no need to relate how the ball ended. A few dozen revellers, and with them even several ladies remained in the hall. There were no police. They wouldn't let the musicians go, and beat up the players who tried to leave. Towards morning they pulled down Prokhorych's stall, drank themselves senseless, danced the Komarinsky unexpurgated,[12] made a filthy mess of the rooms, and only at dawn did part of this gang, completely drunk, arrive at the scene of the fire, which was already dying down, to create new disorders. The other part simply spent the night in the hall, on velvet sofas and on the floor, dead drunk, with all the consequences. In the morning, as soon as possible, they were dragged by their feet into the street. So ended the festivities for the benefit of the governesses of our province.

4.

The fire terrified those members of our audience who lived across the river because it was obviously arson. It's worth noting that the first cry of 'Fire!' was immediately followed by the cry that 'the Shpigulin workers are setting it on fire'. Now we know only too well that in fact three Shpigulin workers were involved in the arson, but only three; all the rest from the factory have been completely exonerated both officially and by public opinion. Besides those three scoundrels (of whom one has been caught and has confessed, and two are still at large), Fedka the Convict undoubtedly was involved in the arson as well. That's all that's known so far in detail about the origin of the fire; conjectures are a completely different matter. What motivated these three scoundrels? Had they received orders from someone or not? It's very difficult to give answers to all this even now.

Thanks to the strong wind, the predominantly wooden buildings of Zarechye and, finally, the three different points at which it had been set, the fire spread rapidly and engulfed the whole area with incredible intensity (however, it's more accurate to say that the fire was set in two places; the third was caught and extinguished almost as soon as it flared up – of which more later). But the newspapers in the capitals nonetheless exaggerated our misfortune: no more than a quarter (and perhaps less) of all Zarechye burned down, approximately speaking. Our fire brigade, though inadequate for the extent and population of the town, acted, however, with great efficiency and self-sacrifice. But it would have accomplished little, even with the friendly cooperation of the inhabitants, if it hadn't been for a shift in the wind, which suddenly died down just before dawn. When I made my way into Zarechye only an hour after I'd fled the ball, the fire was at its height. An entire street parallel to the river was in flames. It was bright as day. I won't undertake to paint a detailed picture of the fire: who in Russia isn't familiar with it? In the side streets closest to the one in flames unbelievable confusion and congestion prevailed. There they were definitely expecting the fire, and the residents were hauling out their belongings, but were still not abandoning their dwellings, and were sitting in anticipation on trunks and feather beds that they had dragged out, each under his own windows. Part of the male population was engaged in heavy work, mercilessly cutting down fences and even pulling down whole huts that were located close to the fire and downwind. Nobody except the babies who had been awakened were crying, and the women who had already managed to drag out their possessions were howling and keening. Those who hadn't yet managed to do so were in the process of dragging them out, vigorously and in silence. Sparks and embers were flying far in all directions; people were putting them out as best they could. At the scene of the fire itself, there were crowds of onlookers who had run there from all parts of the town. Some were helping to put out the flames; others were gawking like tourists. A large fire at night always creates an exciting and exhilarating impression. That explains the appeal of fireworks; but there the fires are arranged in elegant, symmetrical patterns, and because they are completely harmless, they produce a playful and happy impression, like a glass of champagne. A real fire is another matter: here the horror and a certain sense of personal danger, coupled with the exhilarating impression created by a night-time fire, produces in the onlooker (not, of course, in the house-holder who has been completely burnt out) a certain concussion of the brain, and a challenge, as it were, to his own destructive instincts, which – alas! – lurk in every heart, even in the heart of the meekest titular councillor[13] with a loving family. This gloomy feeling is almost always intoxicating. 'Indeed, I don't know whether one can look at a fire without a certain pleasure.' This, word for word, was said to me by Stepan Trofimovich after he had returned on one occasion from a night-time fire he had just happened upon, and while still under the first impression of the spectacle. Of course, that same admirer of a night-time fire will throw himself into the fire to save a child or an old woman who is in danger; but that, after all, is an entirely different proposition.

Following close behind the curious crowd, I managed, without asking any questions, to make my way to the most important and most dangerous place, where I finally spotted von Lembke, whom I was looking for at Yuliya Mikhaylovna's behest. His position was surprising and extraordinary. He was standing on the ruins of a fence; to his left, about thirty steps away, jutted the black skeleton of a two-storey wooden house which had almost completely finished burning now, with holes instead of windows in both storeys, with a roof that had collapsed and with a flame that was still snaking its way around the charred beams here and there. Deep inside the courtyard, about twenty steps from the burnt-out house, a smaller building, also of two storeys, was beginning to burn, and the firemen were doing the very best they could with it. To the right some firemen and ordinary people were fighting to save a rather large wooden building that had not yet burned but had already caught fire several times, and was inevitably fated to burn down. Von Lembke was shouting and gesticulating as he faced the smaller building, and kept issuing orders, which no one obeyed. It occurred to me that he had simply been abandoned there and was being utterly ignored. At least the thick and extraordinarily varied crowd that surrounded him, in which gentlemen and even the archpriest from the cathedral mingled with all kinds of people, was listening to him with curiosity and surprise, but not one of them struck up a conversation with him or made any attempt to escort him away. Von Lembke, pale and with piercing eyes, was saying the most surprising things; what's more he was not wearing a hat, having lost it some time ago.

'It's all arson! This is nihilism! If anything's burning, it's nihilism!' I heard almost in horror, and although there was no longer anything to be surprised at, graphic reality always has something staggering about it.

'Your Excellency,' a policeman materialized beside him, 'if you would be pleased to try to rest at home . . . Otherwise it is dangerous for Your Excellency even to be standing here.'

This police officer, as I learned later, had specifically been assigned to Andrey Antonovich by the chief of police, in order to keep an eye on him and try as best he could to take him home, and in case of danger, even to act with force – an assignment that was evidently beyond the powers of the man who was supposed to carry it out.

'They will wipe away the tears of those who have been burnt out, but will burn down the town. It's those four scoundrels, four and a half. Arrest that scoundrel! He's here alone, and the four and a half have been slandered by him. He worms his way into the honour of families. He used the governesses to set the houses on fire. That's vile, that's vile! Oh, what's he doing!' he exclaimed, suddenly noticing a fireman on top of the blazing small house in the back, the roof already burned through under him, and the flames leaping round him. 'Pull him down, pull him down, he'll fall through, he'll catch fire, put him out . . . What's he doing there?'

'He's putting out the fire, Your Excellency.'

'That's impossible. The fire is in people's minds, and not on the roofs of houses. Pull him down and leave everything! Better to leave everything, better to leave everything! Let it go out by itself somehow! Oh, who's that crying? An old woman! An old woman's crying, why have they forgotten the old woman?'

In fact, on the ground floor of the smaller burning building an old woman, forgotten, was crying out, an eighty-year-old relative of the merchant who owned the burning house. But she hadn't been forgotten: she herself had returned to the burning house while it was still possible, with the insane purpose of dragging her feather bed out of a tiny box of a corner room that had so far been untouched. She was choking from the smoke and screaming from the heat, because the little room had caught fire too, but even so she was trying as hard as she could to push her feather bed through a broken window with her decrepit hands. Von Lembke rushed to help her. Everyone saw him run up to the window, grab the corner of the mattress and try with all his might to pull it through the window. As luck would have it, at that very moment a broken board fell off the roof and struck the unfortunate man. It didn't kill him, since only a corner grazed his neck as it fell, but Andrey Antonovich's career was over, at least in our town. The blow knocked him off his feet, and he fell unconscious.

At last a gloomy, sullen dawn broke. The fire had died down;

a sudden silence fell after the wind, and then a light, slow rain
began to fall, as if through a sieve. I was already in another
part of Zarechye, far from the place where von Lembke had
fallen, and I heard some rather strange conversations in the
crowd there. A curious fact had come to light: on the very
outskirts of the quarter, on a piece of empty ground, beyond
the vegetable gardens, no less that fifty paces from the other
buildings, stood a small wooden house that had just been built,
and this isolated house had caught fire almost before all the
others, at the very beginning of the conflagration. If it had in
fact burned down, the fire could not have spread to any of the
other buildings because of the distance, and, conversely, if all
of Zarechye had burned down, then this house alone would
have survived, whether there was a wind or not. As it turned
out, the house had caught fire on its own and independently,
and therefore suspiciously. But the main thing was that it had
not actually burned down, and inside it, towards dawn, surprising things were discovered. The owner of this new house, a
tradesman who lived nearby, rushed over to it as soon as he
saw it in flames, and with the help of the neighbours managed
to save it by throwing aside the burning logs that had been
stacked against the side wall. But there were tenants in the
house – a captain who was well known in the town, his sister
and an aged servant of theirs; and these tenants – the captain,
his sister and the servant – all three of them had had their
throats cut during the night, and had evidently been robbed.
(This is where the chief of police had dashed off to while von
Lembke was trying to save the feather bed.) By morning the
news had spread, and a huge crowd of all kinds of people and
even those who had been burned out of Zarechye had surged
to the new house on the empty plot of land. It was hard to get
through, so densely packed were the people. I was immediately
told that the captain had been found with his throat cut, on a
bench, fully dressed, and that he had probably been murdered
while dead drunk, so that he had heard nothing, and that the
blood had gushed out of him 'like from a bull'; that his sister,
Marya Timofeyevna, had been 'stabbed all over' with a knife,
and was lying on the floor in the doorway, so that she probably

had been awake and had struggled and fought back with her killer. The servant, who had also probably woken up, had had her skull completely smashed. As the owner told it, the captain on the previous morning had come to see him in a drunken condition, had boasted and shown him a lot of money, as much as two hundred roubles. The captain's tattered old green wallet had been found empty on the floor; but Marya's trunk hadn't been touched, nor had the silver frame of the icon; and all of the captain's clothing appeared to be intact. It was evident that the thief was in a hurry, was a person who had been familiar with the captain's affairs, and had come just for the money and knew where it was kept. If the owner hadn't dashed up at just that moment, the wood, which had caught fire, would probably have burned the house down, 'and it would have been difficult to ascertain the truth from the charred corpses'.

This was how the whole business was reported. Another piece of news was added to it: that this apartment had been rented for the captain and his sister by Mr Stavrogin himself, Nikolay Vsevolodovich, the son of Stavrogina, the general's widow, that he himself had come to rent it and had to be very persuasive because the owner didn't want to let it out and had intended the house to be a tavern, but Nikolay Vsevolodovich was willing to pay anything, and had given six months' rent in advance.

'The fire was no accident,' could be heard from the crowd.

But most of the people said nothing. Their faces were gloomy, but I didn't notice a great deal of obvious anger. However, people all around were continuing to tell stories about Nikolay Vsevolodovich: that the murdered woman was his wife; that the day before he had, 'in dishonourable fashion', lured a young girl away from the best house in town, the daughter of the widow Drozdova; and that a complaint would be lodged against him in Petersburg; and that his wife had evidently been murdered so that he could marry the Drozdova girl. Skvoresh-niki was no more that two and a half versts away, and I remem-ber being struck by the thought: shouldn't I let them know there? However, I didn't notice that anyone in particular was egging the crowd on; I don't want to speak ill of anyone, although I did catch a glimpse of two or three of the bunch from the buffet, who had turned up at the fire towards morning and whom I immediately recognized. But I especially remember a thin, tall young man, a tradesman, hollow-cheeked, curly-headed, who looked as if he had been smeared with soot – a locksmith, as I learned subsequently. He wasn't drunk, but in contrast to the crowd that was gloomily standing around, he seemed to be beside himself. He kept addressing the ordinary people, although I don't really remember his exact words. All he said that was coherent was little more than: 'Brother, what is this? Is it really going to be like this?' and this was accompanied by him waving his arms.

CHAPTER 3

A Romance Is Ended

1.

From the great hall at Skvoreshniki (the same one in which the final meeting between Varvara Petrovna and Stepan Trofimovich had taken place) the fire could be plainly seen. At dawn, around six in the morning, Liza was standing by the window to the far right and looking at the dying glow. She was alone in the room. She was wearing the dress from the day before, her best one, in which she had appeared at the reading – elegant, light green, covered in lace, but now crumpled and donned hastily and carelessly. She suddenly noticed that the bodice hadn't been properly fastened, and she blushed, hastily adjusted the dress, snatched up the red shawl that she had thrown on the armchair when she had come in the day before and threw it round her neck. Some loose curls of her luxuriant hair had come loose on to her right shoulder and crept from under the shawl. Her face looked tired and preoccupied, but her eyes glowed beneath her knitted brows. She went up to the window again and rested her burning forehead against the cold glass. The door opened, and in came Nikolay Vsevolodovich.

'I've sent a messenger on horseback,' he said. 'In ten minutes we'll know everything, and meanwhile people are saying that part of Zarechye has burned down, closest to the river bank, on the right side of the bridge. It caught fire some time after eleven; it's dying down now.'

He didn't go up to the window, but stopped three steps behind her; she didn't turn towards him.

'According to the calendar it was supposed to be getting light an hour ago, but it's still almost like night,' she said irritably.

'Calendars always lie,'[1] he noted with an amiable laugh, but then was ashamed of himself and hastened to add: 'It's boring to live by the calendar, Liza.'

And he subsided into silence, annoyed at the fresh platitude he had come up with. Liza gave a crooked smile.

'You're in such a melancholy mood that you can't even find words to talk to me. But don't worry: what you said is to the point: I always live by the calendar, my every step is calculated according to the calendar. Are you surprised?'

She quickly turned away from the window and sat down in an armchair.

'You sit down too, please. We don't have long to be together, and I want to tell you everything that's on my mind . . . Why shouldn't you also say everything that's on yours?'

Nikolay Vsevolodovich sat down beside her, and quietly, almost apprehensively took her hand.

'What's the meaning of such words, Liza? Where is it suddenly coming from? What is the meaning of "we don't have long to be together"? This is the second puzzling thing you've uttered since you woke up half an hour ago.'

'Are you undertaking to count the puzzling things I say?' she laughed. 'But do you remember that when I came in yesterday I said I was a dead woman? And you've found it necessary to forget that. To forget or not to notice.'

'I don't remember, Liza. Why a dead woman? We must live . . .'

'And you had nothing to say? You've completely lost your eloquence. I've lived my time on this earth, and that's enough. Do you remember Khristofor Ivanovich?'

'No, I don't,' he frowned.

'Khristofor Ivanovich, in Lausanne? You found him a dreadful bore. He would open your door and always say: "I'm here for just a minute", and then he'd stay all day. I don't want to be like Khristofor Ivanovich and stay all day.'

A painful expression appeared on his face.

'Liza, I find this contorted way of speaking very painful. This affectation costs you very dear. What's it for? Why are you doing it?'

His eyes began to glow.

'Liza,' he exclaimed, 'I swear, I love you more now than yesterday, when you came to me!'

'What a strange confession! Why are you bringing in yesterday and today, why these two particular measures?'

'You won't leave me,' he continued, almost in despair. 'We'll go away together, today, all right? All right?'

'Oh, don't squeeze my hand so painfully! Where are we to go away together today? Somewhere to "be resurrected"? No, I've had enough experiments . . . and it's too slow for me; and I'm incapable of it, it's too lofty for me. If we're to go somewhere, then let's go to Moscow, and pay visits there and receive visitors ourselves – that's my ideal, you know. I never concealed from you, even in Switzerland, the kind of person I am. Since it's impossible for us to go to Moscow and pay visits, because you're married, there's no point in talking about it.'

'Liza! What happened yesterday?'

'What happened, happened.'

'That's impossible! That's cruel!'

'Well, all right, then, it's cruel; just put up with it if it's cruel.'

'You're taking revenge on me for yesterday's whim . . .' he muttered with a malicious smile. Liza flushed.

'What a vulgar thought!'

'Well then, why did you give me . . . "so much happiness"? Do I have the right to know?'

'No, you'll have to get along without rights somehow. Don't try to crown the vulgarity of your supposition with stupidity. You're not lucky today. By the way, aren't you afraid of society's opinion, and that you will be judged for that "so much happiness"? Oh, if that's so, for heaven's sake don't worry about it. You're not the cause of anything here, and you won't have to answer to anyone for it. When I opened your door yesterday, you didn't even know who was coming in. It was only my whim, as you just put it, and nothing more. You can look everyone in the eye boldly and triumphantly.'

'Your words, this laughter of yours, they've been giving me chills of horror for the past hour now. This "happiness" that you talk about so brutally is worth . . . everything to me. Can

I really lose you now? I swear, I loved you less yesterday. Why, then, are you trying to take everything away from me today? Do you know what it's cost me, this fresh hope? I've paid for it with a life.'

'Yours or someone else's?'

He stood up quickly.

'What does that mean?' he said, staring at her.

'Have you paid with your life or with mine – that's what I wanted to ask. Or have you completely lost all powers of understanding now?' Liza flushed. 'Why did you jump up so suddenly? Why are you looking at me that way? You're frightening me. What are you so afraid of all the time? I noticed some time ago that you're afraid, right now, right at this very moment . . . Lord, how pale you've turned!'

'If you know something, Liza, I swear *I* don't know . . . I certainly wasn't talking about *that* just now when I said that I paid with a life . . .'

'I don't understand you at all,' she said in a halting and apprehensive voice.

At last a slow, thoughtful smile appeared on his lips. He sat down quietly, rested his elbows on his knees and covered his face with his hands.

'A bad dream and delirium . . . We've been talking about two different things.'

'I have absolutely no idea what you're talking about. Yesterday didn't you really know that I would leave you today – did you know that or not? Don't lie, did you know that or not?'

'I knew it,' he said quietly.

'Well then, what more do you want? You knew and you reserved that "moment" for yourself. What scores do we have to settle now?'

'Tell me the whole truth,' he exclaimed in a voice filled with profound suffering. 'When you opened my door yesterday, did you yourself know that you were opening it for just one hour?'

She looked at him with hatred.

'It's true that the most serious person can ask the most surprising questions. And why are you so anxious? Could it be your vanity because a woman threw you over first, instead of your throwing her over? You know, Nikolay Vsevolodovich, while I've been with you I've become convinced, among other things, that you're terribly generous towards me, and that's precisely what I can't endure from you.'

He stood up and took a few steps around the room.

'Very well, let it end this way . . . But how could this all have happened?'

'What do you care! The main thing is that you know it all by heart and that you understand it better than anyone in the world and were counting on it yourself. I am a young lady, and my heart has been brought up on the opera; that's where it all began, that's the explanation of it all.'

'No.'

'There's nothing here that can wound your vanity, and it's all absolutely true. It began with a beautiful moment that I could not endure. The day before yesterday, when I "insulted" you in front of everyone and you responded so gallantly, I came home and immediately realized that you were running away from me because you were married, and not at all because you despised me, which I, as a young lady of society, feared more than anything else. I understood that it was me, fool that I was, that you were protecting by running away. You see how I value your generosity. Then Pyotr Stepanovich trotted up and proceeded to explain everything to me. He told me that you were having strong doubts about some great idea, and that he and I were absolutely nothing in comparison, but that even so I was in your way. He included himself here as well; he insisted that the three of us should be in it together, and said the most fantastic things, about a boat and maple oars, from some Russian folk song. I praised him, told him he was a poet, and he accepted it as if it were pure gold. And since I've known for a long time anyway that I have only enough in me for one moment, then I went ahead and made up my mind. Well, that's all, and it's enough, and no more explanations, please. Perhaps we'll quarrel again. Don't be afraid of anyone; I'm taking every-thing on myself. I'm bad, I'm capricious; I've been seduced by that operatic barque; I'm a young lady. But you know, even so I've been thinking that you were terribly in love with me. Don't despise me for being a fool, and don't make fun of the tear that's just fallen. I'm very fond of crying "out of self-pity". Well, enough, enough. I'm not capable of anything, and you're not capable of anything. We've given each other a couple of little flicks on the face, and let's be satisfied with that. At least our vanity hasn't suffered.'

'Dream and delirium!' cried Nikolay Vsevolodovich, wringing his hands and pacing about the room. 'Liza, you poor thing, what have you done to yourself?'

'I burned myself on a candle, nothing more. Surely you're not crying too? You should behave properly and be less sensitive . . .'

'Why, why did you come to me?'

'But don't you really understand the comic position you're putting yourself in as far as society is concerned by asking such questions?'

'Why did you ruin yourself in such an ugly and stupid way, and what are you going to do now?'

'And this is Stavrogin, "the bloodsucker Stavrogin", as a certain lady around here who's in love with you calls you! Listen, I've already told you, you know: I've given my life in exchange for just one hour, and I'm at peace. You should give your life in exchange as well . . . however, there's no need for you to do so; you will still have many different "hours" and "moments".'

'Just as many as you have. I give you my solemn word, not an hour more than you!'

He kept on pacing and didn't see her quick, penetrating look, which suddenly seemed to light up with hope. But the ray of light went out that same instant.

'If only you knew the price I have to pay for my present *impossible* sincerity, Liza, if only I could reveal to you . . .'

'Reveal? You want to reveal something to me? God save me from your revelations!' she interrupted, almost in fear.

He stopped and waited anxiously.

'I must confess to you that when we were still in Switzerland, I was nagged by the thought that you had something terrible, dirty and bloody on your soul, and . . . at the same time, something that puts you in a very ridiculous light. Beware of revealing anything to me, if that's the case: I'll ridicule you. I'll laugh at you your whole life long. Oh, you're turning pale again? I won't, I won't, I'm leaving now.' She jumped up from the chair in a movement of disgust and contempt.

'Torment me, punish me, vent your anger on me,' he cried in despair. 'You have every right! I knew I didn't love you, and I ruined you. Yes, "I reserved a moment for myself"; I have had hope . . . for a long time now . . . a last hope . . . I couldn't hold out against the light that illuminated my heart when you came to me yesterday, you yourself, alone, before I came to you. I suddenly believed . . . Perhaps I believe even now.'

'For such noble candour I will pay you back in kind. I don't want to be a sister of mercy to you. Maybe I really will become a nurse, if I happen not to die this very day; but if I do, it won't be as your nurse, although you are worth as much as anyone without legs or arms. It always seemed to me that you would carry me off to some place where a huge evil spider as big as a man lives, and we would spend our entire lives looking at him and being afraid of him.[2] That's how our mutual love would pass. Talk to Dashenka; why, she'll go with you wherever you want.'

'And you can't help thinking of her even now?'

'Poor little doggie! Give her my regards. Does she know that even when you were in Switzerland you had already assigned her to your old age? What thoughtfulness! What foresight! Oh, who's that?'

At the other end of the room a door opened ever so slightly. Someone's head was thrust in and hastily withdrawn.

'Is that you, Aleksey Yegorych?' asked Stavrogin.

'No, it's just me.' Pyotr Stepanovich thrust himself halfway in again. 'Greetings, Lizaveta Nikolayevna; in any event, good morning. I knew that I'd find both of you in this room. Really I'm here for just a moment, Nikolay Vsevolodovich – I've hurried here to have a couple of words with you, no matter what . . . essential words . . . just a couple!'

Stavrogin moved towards him, but when he'd gone three steps he turned back to Liza.

'If you hear anything now, Liza, you should know that I'm to blame.'

She gave a start and looked at him fearfully. But he went out hurriedly.

2.

The room from which Pyotr Stepanovich had looked in was the great oval front hall. Aleksey Yegorych had been sitting there before he came in, but was sent away. Nikolay Vsevolodovich closed the door behind him tightly and stood waiting. Pyotr Stepanovich examined him rapidly and searchingly.

'Well?'

'Well then, if you already know,' Pyotr Stepanovich prattled away, his eyes looking as if they wanted to plumb the depths of Stavrogin's soul, 'then, it stands to reason that none of us is guilty of anything, least of all you, because there's such a confluence . . . a coincidence of events . . . in short, you can't be touched legally, and I flew here to let you know.'

'Have they been burnt? Their throats cut?'

'Their throats have been cut, but they haven't been burnt, and that's too bad, but I give you my word of honour that I'm not to blame there, no matter how much you might suspect me – because you do perhaps suspect me, eh? If you want the whole truth, the thought really did cross my mind, you see – you were the one who suggested it to me, not seriously, but teasingly (because you wouldn't really suggest such a thing seriously); but I couldn't make up my mind to do it, and I wouldn't make up my mind to do it for anything in the world, not for a hundred roubles – why, there are no advantages to it, that is, for me, for me . . .' (He was in a dreadful hurry and was chattering away.) 'But just look at the coincidence of circumstances: out of my own money (you hear, out of my own, there wasn't one rouble of yours, and the main thing is that you yourself know it), I gave that drunken idiot Lebyadkin two hundred and thirty roubles the day before yesterday, in the evening. You hear, the day before yesterday, and not yesterday after the "reading", take note of that: that's a very importance coincidence, because

I didn't know anything for certain at the time, you see, whether Lizaveta Nikolayevna would come to you or not. And I gave my own money solely because the day before yesterday you distinguished yourself by taking it into your head to announce your secret to everyone. Well, I'm not going into . . . it's your business . . . you gallant knight . . . but I admit I was as surprised as if I'd been hit on the head with a cudgel. But since these tragedies have bored me exceeding much – and note that I'm speaking seriously, even though I'm using an archaic expression – since all this ultimately works against my plans, then I promised myself to send the Lebyadkins off to Petersburg at all cost and without your knowledge, the more so since he himself was itching to go there. One mistake: I gave him the money in your name. Was that a mistake or not? Maybe it wasn't a mistake, eh? Now listen to me, listen to how all this turned out.' In the heat of all this talk he had walked right up to Stavrogin and was about to grab him by the lapel of his frock-coat (I swear, perhaps deliberately). Stavrogin struck him on the arm with a vigorous gesture.

'Come now, what are you doing? . . . enough . . . you'll break my arm that way . . . Here the main thing is the way it turned out . . .' he began to chatter again, not in the least surprised at the blow. 'I handed over the money to him that evening, so that he and his sister could set out the next morning at dawn. I entrusted this simple little task to that scoundrel Liputin, getting them on the train and seeing them off. But that scoundrel Liputin felt the need to play his schoolboy pranks on the audience – perhaps you've heard? At the "reading"? Now listen, listen: both were drinking and writing the poem, half of which is Liputin's, who dresses Lebyadkin up in a tail-coat, while assuring me in the meantime that he'd already sent him off that morning, meanwhile he was actually keeping him somewhere in a back room so that he could push him out on to the platform. But Lebyadkin quickly and unexpectedly has far too much to drink. Then follows the well-known scandal, and then he is delivered home half-dead, and Liputin quietly takes two hundred roubles from him, leaving just some small change. But unfortunately, it turned out that Lebyadkin that same morning had also taken these two hundred roubles out of his pocket, bragged about them and showed them around where he shouldn't have. And since that was exactly what Fedka was waiting for, and since he'd heard something at Kirillov's (you remember your hint?), he made up his mind to take advantage of it. That's the whole truth. I'm glad at least that Fedka didn't find the money – the scoundrel was counting on a thousand, you know! He was in a hurry, and he was frightened by the fire, it seems. Believe me, that fire hit me like a blow to the head. No, the Devil knows what sort of thing that is! It's taking matters into your own hands. There, you see, since I expect so much from you, I won't hide anything from you. Well, yes, the nice little idea of having a fire had been ripening in my mind for a long time, since it's something so popular and so dear to the common people. But you know, I was saving it for a critical time, for the precious moment when we would all rise up and . . . And they suddenly took it into their heads to act on their own and without orders, now, at precisely the moment when they should have been lying low and keeping quiet! No, that's really taking things into their own hands! In a nutshell, I don't know anything yet, the talk around here now is about two Shpigulin workers, but if *our people* are involved in it as well, if even one of them warmed his hands – then woe betide him! Now you see what it means to let things get out of hand even a tiny bit! No, this democratic riff-raff with their groups of five is a poor foundation. What's needed is one single magnificent, despotic will, like an idol, that rests on something fundamental yet external . . . Then even the groups of five will put their tails between their legs and obey, and will prove useful in their servile way when needed. But in any event, even though everyone out there is now loudly trumpeting the news that Stavrogin had to have his wife burnt to death and that's why the town was burnt down as well, still . . .'

'Are they really trumpeting the news?'

'Well, not yet, really, and I admit I've heard absolutely nothing, but what can you do with ordinary people, especially the ones who've been burnt out? *Vox populi vox dei.*[3] Does it take very long to send the most stupid rumour floating through the air? But you know, basically you have absolutely nothing to fear. You're completely clear from the legal point of view, and as far as your conscience goes as well. After all, you didn't want this to happen, did you? Did you? There's no evidence, just coincidence. Maybe Fedka will happen to remember what you said so carelessly that night at Kirillov's (and why did you say it then?), but that proves absolutely nothing, you know, and we'll take care of Fedka. I'll take care of him this very day . . .'

'And the bodies didn't burn at all?'

'Not at all. That rabble couldn't do anything right. But I'm glad at least that you're so calm . . . because even though you're not guilty of anything in this case, not even in thought, still and all . . . And besides, you must agree that all this wraps your affairs up very nicely: you're suddenly a free widower and you can marry a beautiful girl with an enormous fortune this very minute, one who's already in your hands to boot. That's what a simple, crude coincidence of circumstances can do – eh?'

'Are you threatening me, you stupid man?'

'Enough, enough, now you're calling me a stupid man, what sort of tone is that? You should be glad, but instead . . . I rushed here on purpose to alert you as quickly as possible . . . Besides, what can I threaten you with? Much use you'd be to me if it were only the result of some threats! I need your goodwill, and not because you're afraid. You are the light and the sun . . . I'm the one who's deathly afraid of you, not you of me! I'm not Mavriky Nikolayevich, after all. And just imagine, I flew here in a racing droshky, and there was Mavriky Nikolayevich sitting by your garden fence, in the back corner of your garden, in his greatcoat, soaked through; he must have been sitting there all night! What wonders! Amazing how insane people can get!'

'Mavriky Nikolayevich? Is that true?'

'It's true, it's true. He's sitting by the garden fence. From here – about three hundred paces from here, I think. I walked by him as quickly as I could, but he saw me. You didn't know? In that case, I'm very glad I didn't forget to tell you. Now, someone like this is more dangerous if he has a revolver with him, and then, when you think of the night, the slush, his natural irritability – because look at his circumstances, after all, ha, ha! What do you think, why is he sitting there?'

'He's waiting for Lizaveta Nikolayevna, naturally.'

'So that's it! But why should she go out to see him? And in such rain. What a fool he is!'

'She'll go out to him presently.'

'Aha! That's news! And so . . . But listen, her situation is completely different now. Why should she need Mavriky now? Aren't you a free widower and in a position to marry her tomorrow? She doesn't know yet. Let me handle it, I'll arrange everything for you immediately. Where is she? She needs cheering up.'

'Cheering up?'

'Absolutely. Let's go.'

'And you think she won't figure out what's happened to those bodies?' Stavrogin squinted in a peculiar way.

'Of course, she won't figure it out,' Pyotr Stepanovich responded like a perfect fool, 'because legally, you see . . . Oh, you! And what if she did figure it out! All this kind of thing is so easily erased from the minds of women; you don't know women yet! Besides, it's to her full advantage to marry you because she's the one who's disgraced herself; and besides, I was the one who gave her all that stuff about the "barque": I saw right away that one could have an effect on her with the "barque" business, and so that's the calibre of girl she is. Don't worry, she'll step across those bodies tra-la-la, the more so since you're completely, completely innocent, isn't that so? Except that she'll save up those corpses to needle you with later on, maybe in the second year of your marriage. Every woman, when she goes to the altar, stores up something of this sort from her husband's past, but then, you know – what can happen in a year or so? Ha, ha, ha!'

'If you've come in a racing droshky, then drive her to Mavriky Nikolayevich at once. She's just said that she can't stand me and is leaving me, and of course she won't accept a carriage from me.'

'That's interesting! But is she really leaving? How could

that have happened?' Pyotr Stepanovich looked at him rather obtusely.

'She somehow guessed during the night I don't love her at all, though of course she had always known it.'

'Why, do you really not love her?' Pyotr Stepanovich rejoined, with a look of infinite surprise. 'And if that's the case, then why did you let her stay when she came in yesterday, and, as an honourable man, why didn't you let her know straightaway that you didn't love her? That's horribly vile of you; and how utterly vile you make me look in her eyes.'

Stavrogin suddenly began to laugh.

'I'm laughing at my monkey,' he promptly explained.

'Ah! You guessed that I was clowning around.' Pyotr Stepanovich also burst into terribly bright laughter. 'I did it to amuse you! Imagine, when you came out to see me, I immediately guessed by your face, you know, that you'd had a "misfortune". Even perhaps a complete failure, eh? Well, I'll just bet,' he exclaimed, almost choking with delight, 'that you two spent the whole night in the room sitting side by side on chairs, wasting valuable time arguing about lofty and noble matters. But forgive me, forgive me, it's none of my concern. Even yesterday I knew for certain, you see, that it would all end in something foolish between you two. I brought her to you simply to give you a bit of amusement and to demonstrate that you wouldn't be bored with me; I can prove useful for this sort of thing three hundred times. In general, I like to please people. But if you don't need her now – as I calculated would be the case – then I've come to . . .'

'So you brought her here just for my amusement?'

'Well, what else?'

'Not to make me kill my wife?'

'So-o-o, did you really kill her? What a tragic fellow!'

'It doesn't matter. You killed her.'

'Did I really kill her? I'm telling you, I didn't have a thing to do with it. However, you're beginning to worry me . . .'

'Go on. You said: "If you don't need her now, then . . ."'

'Then leave it to me, of course! I'll happily marry her off to Mavriky Nikolayevich, who, by the way, I certainly did not plant in your garden, don't get that into your head! I'm afraid of him now, you see. You said something about "your racing droshky", but I simply scooted past him . . . really, what if he'd had a revolver? It's a good thing I brought mine along. Here it is.' (He pulled a revolver out of his pocket, showed it and immediately put it back again.) 'I brought it because of the length of the trip. However, I'll fix things up for you in a jiffy. Her tender little heart is aching for Mavriky Nikolayevich right now; at least it should be aching . . . and you know . . . I swear, I even feel a bit sorry for her! I'll get her together with Mavriky, and she'll immediately start remembering you – praising you to him, and abusing him to his face – the heart of a woman! There you are, laughing again! I'm terribly glad that you find all this so amusing. Well then, let's go. I'll begin straightaway with Mavriky, and about them . . . about those who were murdered . . . you know, shouldn't we keep quiet for now? She'll find out later anyway.'

'What will she find out about? Who's been murdered? What did you say about Mavriky Nikolayevich?' Liza suddenly opened the door.

'Ah! You were eavesdropping?'

'What were you just saying about Mavriky Nikolayevich? Has he been murdered?'

'Ah, so you didn't really hear! Calm down, Mavriky Nikolayevich is alive and well, which you can verify in just a moment, because he's here, by the road, at the garden fence . . . and he seems to have sat there all night. He's in his greatcoat, soaked through . . . I was driving, and he saw me.'

'That's not true. You said "murdered". Who's been murdered?' she kept insisting in an agony of mistrustfulness.

'The only ones murdered are my wife, her brother Lebyadkin and their servant,' Stavrogin announced firmly.

Liza shuddered and turned dreadfully pale.

'A brutal, strange case, Lizaveta Nikolayevna, an utterly stupid case of robbery,' Pyotr Stepanovich immediately began rattling away, 'just robbery, taking advantage of the fire. It's the fault of Fedka the Convict and that fool Lebyadkin, who was showing his money to everyone . . . I came flying here to tell you . . . it hit me like a rock on the head. Stavrogin could hardly keep on his feet when I told him. We were discussing it here: whether to tell you now or not?'

'Nikolay Vsevolodovich, is he telling the truth?' Liza could hardly speak.

'No, it's not true.'

'What do you mean "not true"?' Pyotr Stepanovich shuddered. 'What do you mean by that?'

'Lord, I'm going to lose my mind!' Liza exclaimed.

'At least you should understand that he's insane now!' Pyotr Stepanovich shouted as loud as he could. 'Because his wife really has been murdered. Look how pale he is . . . Why, he stayed with you all night, he didn't leave you for a moment – how can you possibly suspect him?'

'Nikolay Vsevolodovich, tell me before God whether you're guilty or not, and I swear I'll believe your words as if they were God's, and I'll follow you to the end of the earth, oh, I'll follow you! I'll follow you like a dog . . .'

'Why do you torment her so, you fantastic intellect!' Pyotr Stepanovich shouted in a fury. 'Lizaveta Nikolayevna, really and truly, you can grind me in a mortar, but he's innocent; on the contrary, he's been crushed and is raving, as you can see. He's not guilty of anything, of anything, even in thought! It's all the doing of robbers who will certainly be found in a week and punished by flogging. It's all the fault of Fedka the Convict and the Shpigulin workers; the whole town is chattering about it, and that's why I am too.'

'Is that so? Is that so?' Liza was waiting, all atremble, for the final verdict.

'I didn't kill them and I was against it, but I knew they would be killed, and I didn't stop the killers. Step away from me, Liza,' Stavrogin said, and he went into the drawing room.

Liza covered her face with her hands and went out of the house. Pyotr Stepanovich was on the point of rushing after her, but he immediately turned back into the drawing room.

'So that's how it's to be? So that's how it's to be? So you're not afraid of anything?' He fell upon Stavrogin in an absolute fury, muttering incoherently, almost incapable of finding words and foaming at the mouth.

Stavrogin stood in the middle of the drawing room and didn't say a word. With his left hand he gently tugged at a lock of hair and smiled distractedly. Pyotr Stepanovich pulled him hard by the sleeve.

'So it's all over for you, is that it? So that's what you've set your mind to? You'll inform on everyone, and then you'll go off to a monastery or to the Devil . . . But you know, I'll get rid of you anyway, even though you're not afraid of me!'

'Oh, are you still chattering away?' Stavrogin finally noticed him. 'Run,' he suddenly came to his senses, 'run after her, order the carriage, don't abandon her . . . Run, go ahead and run! Take her home, so no one knows and so she doesn't go there . . . to the bodies . . . to the bodies . . . put her in the carriage by force. Aleksey Yegorych! Aleksey Yegorych!'

'Stop, don't shout! She's already in Mavriky's arms. Mavriky won't get into your carriage . . . Stop, I say! There's something more precious here than a carriage!'

He pulled out his revolver again. Stavrogin looked at him seriously.

'Well, go ahead, kill me,' he said quietly, in almost a conciliatory way.

'Ugh! Damn it all, what a bunch of lies a man dumps on himself!' Pyotr Stepanovich began to tremble. 'I swear, you should be killed! She should really have spit on you! What sort of "barque" are you, you're just an old wooden barge full of holes, ready to be demolished! It's time for you to come to your senses now, if only out of spite, if only out of spite! Ugh! Why, it wouldn't make the least bit of difference to you since you're asking for a bullet in the head.'

Stavrogin gave a strange smile.

'If you weren't such a buffoon, maybe I'd say "yes" now. If you were just a smidgen more intelligent . . .'

'I am indeed a buffoon, but I don't want you, as my better half, to be a buffoon! Do you understand me?'

Stavrogin understood, but perhaps he was the only one to do

so. But Shatov had been astonished when Stavrogin told him that Pyotr Stepanovich did have enthusiasm.

'Leave me now and go to the Devil, and by tomorrow I'll have wrung something out of myself. Come tomorrow.'

'Yes? Yes?'

'How should I know! . . . Go to the Devil, go to the Devil!'

And he walked out of the room.

'Well, maybe it's for the best,' Pyotr Stepanovich muttered to himself as he put away the revolver.

3.

He rushed to try to overtake Lizaveta Nikolayevna. She hadn't yet gone far, just a few steps from the house. She had been delayed by Aleksey Yegorych, who was following her now, a step behind, in tail-coat and without a hat; he bowed respectfully. He persisted in entreating her to wait for the carriage; the old man was frightened and almost crying.

'Go, the master is asking for some tea, there's no one to serve it,' Pyotr Stepanovich pushed him aside and proceeded to take Liza by the arm.

She didn't pull her arm away, but she hadn't yet come to her senses, seeming not quite aware of what was going on.

'In the first place, you're not going the right way,' Pyotr Stepanovich began babbling, 'we should go this way and not past the garden. And in the second place, there's no question of going on foot, it's three versts to your house, and you don't have the proper clothes. If only you'd wait just a little while, I've got a racing droshky; you see, the horse is here in the yard. I'll bring it in just a minute, put you in and deliver you, so that no one will see.'

'How kind you are,' Liza said affectionately.

'Think nothing of it. In a case like this any humane person in my place would do the same.'

Liza looked at him and was surprised.

'Oh, my heavens, and I thought that old man was still standing here!'

'Listen, I'm awfully glad you're taking it this way, because that's all just a deplorable convention, and since it's come to that, wouldn't it be better if I told that old man to get the carriage ready; it would only take ten minutes, and we'll go back and wait beneath the porch, eh?'

'First I want to . . . Where are these murdered people?'

'There you go again imagining things! That's what I was afraid of. No, we'd better leave that nonsense alone; besides, there's nothing for you to look at there.'

'I know where they are, I know the house.'

'Well, what does it matter that you know! Please, it's raining, it's foggy. (This is really some sacred obligation I've got myself into!) Listen, Lizaveta Nikolayevna, you have one of two choices: either you come with me in the droshky, in which case you must wait here, and not take another step, because if you go about twenty steps further, then you'll certainly be seen by Mavriky Nikolayevich.'

'Mavriky Nikolayevich! Where? Where?'

'Well, if you want to see him, then perhaps I'll escort you a bit further and point out where he's sitting, and let it go at that: I don't want to approach him just now.'

'He's waiting for me, heavens!' She suddenly stopped, and her face was suffused with colour.

'But after all, he's surely no slave to convention! You know, Lizaveta Nikolayevna, none of this is any of my business; I'm a complete outsider here, and you know that yourself; but still, I do wish you well . . . If our "barque" didn't succeed, if it turned out that it was nothing more than an old, rotten barge, fit only to be demolished . . .'

'Oh, that's wonderful!' Liza exclaimed.

'Wonderful, but tears are streaming down your face. You need courage here. You mustn't yield to a man in any way. In our times, when a woman . . . oh, the Devil!' (Pyotr Stepanovich almost spat in disgust.) 'And the most important thing is that there is nothing to regret; maybe things really will turn out marvellously. Mavriky Nikolayevich is a man . . . in short, a sensitive man, although not very talkative, which, however, is also a good thing, provided of course that he isn't bound by convention.'

'Wonderful, wonderful!' Liza began laughing hysterically.

'Oh, well, damn it . . . Lizaveta Nikolayevna,' Pyotr Stepanovich suddenly said in a pique, 'actually, I'm here for your sake . . . I myself have no need . . . I did you a good turn yesterday when you yourself wanted it, but today . . . Well, you can see Mavriky Nikolayevich from here, he's sitting over there, he can't see us. You know, Lizaveta Nikolayevna, have you read *Polinka Saks*?'[4]

'What's that?'

'There's a novel called *Polinka Saks*. I read it when I was still a student. It's about some official named Saks, very wealthy, who had his wife arrested at their summer place for infidelity. Oh, well, damn it, forget about it! Just you wait, Mavriky Nikolayevich will propose to you even before you get home. He still can't see us.'

'Oh, I hope he doesn't see us!' Liza suddenly gave a mad cry. 'Let's go away, let's go away! Into the woods, into the fields!'

And she began to run back.

'Lizaveta Nikolayevna, that's just cowardice!' Pyotr Stepanovich ran after her. 'And why don't you want him to see you? On the contrary, look him straight and proudly in the eyes . . . If you're concerned about *that* . . . the virginity business . . . why, that's a convention, so out-of-date . . . But where are you going anyway, where are you going? Oh, she can run! Let's go back to Stavrogin's, let's take my droshky . . . But where are you going? There's a field there . . . oh, she's fallen!'

He stopped. Liza had been flying like a bird, not knowing where, and Pyotr Stepanovich was already lagging about fifty steps behind her. She tripped over a knoll and fell. At that same moment, behind them and off to the side, came a dreadful cry; it came from Mavriky Nikolayevich, who had seen her running and falling, and was running towards her across the field. In a flash Pyotr Stepanovich retreated through the gate of Stavrogin's house and got into his droshky as quickly as possible.

And Mavriky Nikolayevich, greatly alarmed, was already standing beside Liza, who had got to her feet, bending over her and holding her hand in his. He couldn't think straight, given all the improbable circumstances of this encounter, and tears were streaming down his face. He had seen the one whom he held in such reverence madly running across the field, at such an hour, in such weather, wearing only a gown, the elegant gown that was now rumpled and muddy from her fall. He couldn't say a word, but took his greatcoat and with trembling hands began covering her shoulders. Suddenly he cried out, as he felt her lips touching his hand.

'Liza!' he cried. 'I'm no good for anything, but don't chase me away!'

'Oh, yes, let's get away from here as fast as we can; don't leave me!' And grabbing him by the hand, she pulled him after her. 'Mavriky Nikolayevich,' she suddenly lowered her voice in fear, 'I kept pretending to be brave in there, but out here I'm afraid of death. I'm going to die, I'm going to die very soon, but I'm afraid, I'm afraid of dying,' she whispered, squeezing his hand tightly.

'Oh, if only there were someone here,' he looked around in despair, 'if only there were someone passing by! You'll get your feet wet, you'll . . . lose your mind!'

'It's nothing, it's nothing,' she said reassuringly. 'That's it, I feel less afraid with you; hold me by the hand, lead me. Where are we going now? Home? No, first I want to see the people who were murdered. People say they cut his wife's throat, and he says that he cut her throat himself; why, that's not true, is it? I want to see the murdered people for myself . . . for myself . . . because of them he fell out of love with me last night . . . I'll see them and I'll find out everything. Faster, faster. I know the house . . . there was a fire there . . . Mavriky Nikolayevich, my friend, don't forgive me, I'm not an honorable woman! Why should I be forgiven? Why are you crying? Give me a slap in the face and kill me right here in the field, like a dog!'

'No one is your judge now,' Mavriky Nikolayevich stated firmly, 'may God forgive you; I'm less worthy than anyone of being your judge!'

But it would be strange to try to describe their conversation. Meanwhile they walked hand in hand, rapidly, hurriedly, as if they were half mad. They were making their way directly to the fire. Mavriky Nikolayevich still had not lost hope of perhaps coming across a cart, but no one came along. A fine drizzle was enveloping everything around them, swallowing up every reflection and every hue, and turning everything into a smoky, leaden-grey, featureless mass. It had long since been daylight, but it seemed as if dawn had not yet broken. And suddenly out of this smoky, cold mist a figure took shape, strange and awkward, walking towards them. Imagining it now, I don't think I would have believed my eyes, even if I had been in Lizaveta Nikolayevna's place; but meanwhile she let out a shout of joy and immediately recognized the approaching man. It was Stepan Trofimovich. How he had gone off, how the insane idea of flight came to be realized – about that, later. I will merely mention that he already had a fever that morning, but even illness didn't stop him: he was making his way firmly over the wet ground; it was obvious that he had planned his venture as best he could, given all his armchair inexperience. He was dressed 'for the road', that is, in a greatcoat with sleeves and a wide patent-leather belt with a buckle, along with new high boots with his trousers tucked into the tops. He had probably been imagining himself as a travelling man for a long time now, and several days ago had acquired the belt and the high boots with their shiny hussar tops in which he could hardly walk. The broad-brimmed hat, the worsted scarf that was snugly wound round his neck, a stick in his right hand, and in his left an extremely small but overpacked travelling bag completed his outfit. In addition, this same right hand held an unfurled umbrella. These three objects – the umbrella, the stick and the travelling bag – had been very awkward to carry the first verst of the way, and burdensome beginning with the second.

'Is that really you?' Liza exclaimed, looking him over in sorrowful surprise, which had replaced her initial involuntary surge of joy.

'Lise!' Stepan Trofimovich exclaimed as well, rushing towards her almost in delirium too. '*Chère, chère*, is it you too ... in such a fog? You see: a glow! *Vous êtes malheureuse, n'est-ce pas?* I can see, I can see, don't tell me, but don't ask me either. *Nous sommes tous malheureux, mais il faut les*

pardonner tous. Pardonnons, Lise, and we shall be free forever.
To be rid of the world and become completely free – *il faut
pardonner, pardonner et pardonner!*'⁵

'But why are you on your knees?'

'Because in saying farewell to the world, I want to say farewell
to my entire past in your person!' He began to weep, and raised
both her hands to his tearful eyes. 'I fall on my knees before
everything that was beautiful in my life; I kiss you and thank
you! Now I have broken myself in two: back there is the madman, with his dreams of soaring into the heavens, *vingt-deux
ans*! Here is the shattered and frozen old tutor . . . *chez ce
marchand, s'il existe pourtant ce marchand* . . . But you're
absolutely drenched, Lise!' he cried, scrambling to his feet,
feeling that his knees had also become soaked through on the
wet ground, 'and how is it possible, you in such a dress? . . .
and on foot, and in a field like this . . . Are you crying? *Vous
êtes malheureuse?* Well yes, I did hear something . . . But where
are you coming from now?' He looked at her timidly as the pace
of his questions quickened, and he kept glancing at Mavriky
Nikolayevich in profound perplexity. '*Mais savez-vous l'heure
qu'il est!*'⁶

'Stepan Trofimovich, have you heard something back there
about people who've been murdered? . . . Is it true? Is it true?'

'These people! I saw the glow of what they'd done all night
long. They couldn't come to any other end.' (His eyes began to
flash again.) 'I'm running away from delirium, away from a
feverish dream, I'm running to seek out Russia, *existe-t-elle la
Russie? Bah, c'est vous, cher capitaine!*⁷ I never had any doubt
that I would meet you somewhere engaged in some lofty exploit.
But take my umbrella and – why must you go on foot? For
heaven's sake, at least take the umbrella, and I'll hire a carriage
somewhere in any event. The reason I'm on foot, you see, is
that Stasie (that is, Nastasya) would have burst out screaming
for all to hear if she had found out that I was driving off, and
so I slipped away as *incognito* as possible. I don't know: the
Voice writes about robberies⁸ that are going on everywhere,
but I thought it surely wasn't possible that as soon as I set out
on my way there'd be a robber standing there. *Chère* Lise, I

think you said that someone has killed someone? *O mon Dieu*, you're not feeling well!'

'Let's go, let's go,' Liza screamed almost in hysterics, again pulling Mavriky Nikolayevich behind her. 'Wait a minute, Stepan Trofimovich,' she suddenly turned to him, 'wait a minute, you poor man, let me make the sign of the cross over you. Perhaps it would be better to tie you up, but I'll do even better by making the sign of the cross over you. And in turn you should pray for "poor" Liza[9] – well, just a little, don't take too much trouble over it. Mavriky Nikolayevich, give this child back his umbrella, give it back to him. That's it. Let's go then! Let's go!'

Their arrival at the fatal house occurred precisely at the moment when the large crowd gathered before the house had heard a great deal about Stavrogin and about how it was to his advantage to murder his wife. But still and all, I repeat, the vast majority continued to listen in silence and without moving. The only people who were out of control were loud-mouthed drunkards and 'unhinged' types like that tradesman who was waving his arms. Everyone knew him as a quiet man, but he would suddenly become rather unhinged and fly off on a tangent if something struck him in a certain way. I didn't see Liza and Mavriky Nikolayevich arrive. Stunned with amazement, I first noticed Liza already standing in the crowd at some distance from me, but in the beginning I didn't even discern Mavriky Nikolayevich. I think there must have been a moment when he fell a couple of steps behind her, or was pushed back. Liza, who was trying to press her way through the crowd, not seeing or noticing anything around her, like someone in a fever, like someone who had escaped from a hospital, very quickly of course attracted attention: people began talking loudly and then howling. Suddenly someone shouted: 'It's Stavrogin's woman!' Then: 'It's not enough for them to commit murder, they have to come and look!' Suddenly I saw someone's hand raised above her head from behind, and then it came down; Liza fell. Mavriky Nikolayevich let out a dreadful cry and rushed to help her, hitting with all his strength a man who was trying to block his way. But at that very instant the tradesman grabbed him from behind with both hands. For some time it was impossible to make anything out in the scuffle that ensued. Liza seemed to get up, but fell again from another blow. Suddenly the crowd parted, and a small empty circle formed around the prostrate Liza with the bloody, crazed Mavriky Nikolayevich standing over her, shouting, crying and wringing his hands. I don't remember with absolute accuracy what happened then; I remember only that Liza was suddenly carried away. I ran after her; she was still alive and perhaps still conscious. The tradesman and three other men in the crowd were seized. To this day these three deny any part in the evil deed, stubbornly insisting that they were arrested by mistake; perhaps they are actually right. The tradesman, though clearly guilty, is a man of limited understanding, and to this day cannot give a coherent explanation of what happened. As an eyewitness, albeit a distant one, I had to give evidence at the inquest: I stated that everything had happened quite accidentally, the work of people who, though perhaps incited, were scarcely aware of what they were doing as they were drunk and disorderly. I hold this opinion even now.

CHAPTER 4

A Final Decision

I.

That morning Pyotr Stepanovich was seen by many people.
Those who saw him remembered that he was in an extremely
excited state. At two o'clock in the afternoon he ran off to visit
Gaganov, who had arrived from the country just the day before,
and whose house was full of visitors, who were talking heatedly
and at length about the events that had just occurred. Pyotr
Stepanovich talked more than anyone else, and made himself
heard. He had always been considered locally as a 'garrulous
student with a hole in his head', but now he was talking about
Yuliya Mikhaylovna, and given the general commotion, the
topic was gripping. In his capacity as her recent and highly
intimate confidant, he revealed many completely new and
unexpected details about her. Inadvertently (and of course
indiscreetly) he revealed some of her personal remarks about
people known to everyone in town, thereby wounding their
vanity. He related all this in a vague and inconsistent way, like
a man who wasn't clever, but who had been faced, as an honest
man, with the painful necessity of explaining a whole mass of
misunderstandings all at once; one who, in his naive awkwardness, didn't himself know where to begin and where to stop.
He also let it slip rather indiscreetly that Stavrogin's entire
secret was known to Yuliya Mikhaylovna, and that she was
the one who had masterminded the whole intrigue. And she
supposedly had deceived him, Pyotr Stepanovich, because he
himself was in love with the hapless Liza, and meanwhile he'd
been 'twisted round' to the point where he'd *almost* escorted
her to Stavrogin's carriage. 'Yes, yes, it's all very well for you

to laugh, ladies and gentlemen, but if I had only known, if I had only known how this would end!' he concluded. To various alarmed questions about Stavrogin he stated straight out that the disaster that had befallen Lebyadkin in his opinion was purely accidental, and that Lebyadkin himself was to blame for everything, since he had shown people his money. He explained that especially well. One of his listeners happened to observe that it did him no good to 'present himself' this way: he had eaten, drunk, almost slept in Yuliya Mikhaylovna's house, and now he was the first to blacken her name, and that was not as pretty a thing as he supposed it to be. But Pyotr Stepanovich immediately sprang to his own defence: 'I ate and drank there not because I had no money, and I'm not to blame that I kept being invited there. Permit me to judge for myself how grateful I am to be for that.'

The general impression was in his favour. 'Granted he's an absurd fellow and, of course, without substance, but after all, how is he to blame for Yuliya Mikhaylovna's foolishness? On the contrary, it turns out that he actually tried to stop her . . .'

About two o'clock the news suddenly spread that Stavrogin, about whom there had been so much talk, had abruptly left for Petersburg on the afternoon train. This proved very interesting; many people frowned. Pyotr Stepanovich was so stunned that they say his face even lost colour and he cried out strangely: 'Why, who could possibly have let him go?' He immediately left Gaganov's in a hurry. However, he was later seen in two or three other houses.

Around dusk he found an opportunity to get in to see Yuliya Mikhaylovna, although with great difficulty, because she definitely didn't want to receive him. It was only three weeks later that I learned about this from her own lips, before her departure for Petersburg. She didn't tell me the details, but observed with a shudder that he 'had astounded her beyond all measure'. I suppose he simply frightened her by threatening to identify her as an accomplice in case she should take it into her head to talk. But the need to throw a scare into her was closely linked with his plans at the time, which, naturally, were unknown to her, and only later, about five days after that, did she figure out why he had such doubts about her silence and was so afraid of fresh outbursts of her indignation . . .

Between seven and eight that evening, when it had already grown completely dark, *our people* assembled, all five of them, on the edge of town, in Fomin Lane, in a crooked little house, in the tiny apartment of Ensign Erkel. This general meeting had been fixed by Pyotr Stepanovich himself, but he was inexcusably late, and the other members had already been waiting an hour for him. This Ensign Erkel was the same visiting officer who during the evening at Virginsky's had sat the whole time with a pencil in hand and a notebook in front of him. He had recently arrived in town, had rented a room in a solitary, out-of-the-way lane from two sisters, old tradeswomen, and was supposed to be leaving soon. A meeting at his place was least conspicuous of all. This strange lad was distinguished by unusual taciturnity: he could sit for ten evenings in a row in noisy company with the most unusual conversations going on, not saying a word himself, yet concentrating hard on following the speakers with his childlike eyes and listening. He had a pretty little face, and even appeared to be intelligent. He didn't belong to the group of five; our people supposed that he had some special instructions from somewhere, of a purely executive nature. Now it's known that he had no instructions at all, and, what's more, that he barely understood his position. It was just that he worshipped Pyotr Stepanovich, having met him not too long before. If he had encountered some prematurely depraved monster who, on some social and romantic pretext, put him up to forming a band of robbers and ordered him as a test to kill and rob the first muzhik he came across, he wouldn't have hesitated to obey and would have gone and done it. He had an ailing mother somewhere, to whom he sent half of his meagre pay – and how she must have kissed this poor little blond head, worried about it, prayed for it! I'm going on at such length about him because I feel very sorry for him.

Our people were excited. The events of the previous night had astonished them, and they seemed to have lost their nerve. The simple, albeit well-planned scandal in which they had been so eagerly taking part hadn't turned out as they'd expected.

The night fire, the murder of the Lebyadkins, the violence of the crowd towards Liza – those were all surprises for which their plan of action had made no provision. They heatedly accused the hand that directed them of despotism and a lack of candour. In short, while they were waiting for Pyotr Stepanovich, they worked each other into such a state that they again resolved to demand a categorical explanation from him, and if, as before, he evaded it once more, then they would even break up the group, but with the proviso that in its place a new secret society would be founded 'for the propagation of ideas' – their own – and based on principles of equality and democracy. Liputin, Shigalyov and the expert on the common people lent particularly strong support to this idea; Lyamshin said nothing, although he looked as if he agreed. Virginsky hesitated and first wanted to hear what Pyotr Stepanovich had to say. They agreed to hear Pyotr Stepanovich out, but he still hadn't shown up; such negligence poisoned the atmosphere even more. Erkel remained totally silent and only took charge of serving the tea, which he brought from his landladies with his own hands, in glasses and on a tray, but without bringing in the samovar or letting the servant woman enter.

Pyotr Stepanovich appeared only at half past eight. With quick steps he walked up to the round table in front of the sofa, around which the group had arranged itself. He kept his hat in his hands, and refused tea. He looked angry, stern and haughty. He must have noticed immediately from the faces that they were 'rebelling'.

'Before I open my mouth, say what you have to say; I can see you're all wound up,' he observed, running his eyes over their faces, with a malicious smile.

Liputin began 'on behalf of everyone', and in a voice quivering with resentment announced that 'if we are to continue this way, then we could very well smash our own heads, sir'. Oh, they were certainly not afraid to smash their own heads and were even prepared to do so, but solely and purely for the common cause. (A general stir of approval.) And so, let him be open with them as well, so that they would always know in advance, 'or else what would happen?' (Again a stir, and a few guttural sounds.) 'To act like this was demeaning and dangerous. We are certainly not saying this because we are afraid, but if one person acts, and the rest are just pawns, then that one might slip up and everyone get caught.' (Exclamations: 'Yes! Yes!' General support.)

'Damn it all, what do you want?'

'What relation to the common cause,' Liputin began to seethe, 'do Mr Stavrogin's little intrigues have? Let's suppose he does have some relationship to the centre, in some mysterious way, provided this fanciful centre actually exists, though we certainly don't want to know about it. Meantime, a murder has been committed, the police are on the alert; they'll find the string and follow it to the ball.'

'You and Stavrogin will be caught, and we'll be caught,' added the expert on the common people.

'And it's utterly useless for the common cause,' Virginsky concluded mournfully.

'What rubbish! The murder was purely a matter of chance, perpetrated by Fedka for the sake of robbery.'

'Hmm. A strange coincidence, nonetheless,' Liputin grimaced.

'If you wish, it came about through you.'

'What do you mean through you?'

'In the first place, you, Liputin, took part in this intrigue yourself, and in the second place and most important, you were ordered to send Lebyadkin away and you were given money to do it, and what did you do? If you had sent him away, then absolutely nothing would have happened.'

'Well, weren't you the one who came up with the idea that it would be a good thing to let him go out and read poetry?'

'An idea is not an order. The order was to send him away.'

'The order. A rather strange word . . . On the contrary, you specifically ordered his sending away to be stopped.'

'You were mistaken, and have shown stupidity and self-will. But the murder is Fedka's doing, and he acted alone, for the sake of robbery. You heard people gossiping, and you believed it. You got cold feet. Stavrogin isn't so stupid, and the proof is that he left at twelve o'clock noon, after a meeting with the vice governor. If something had been wrong, they wouldn't have let him go to Petersburg in broad daylight.'

'But look, we're certainly not asserting that Mr Stavrogin himself committed the murders,' Liputin rejoined, venomously and boldly. 'He might not even have known, sir, any more than I did; and you yourself know perfectly well that I knew nothing at all, although I fell right into it like a sheep into a pot.'

'Who is it you're accusing then?' Pyotr Stepanovich looked at him sullenly.

'Those people who find it necessary to burn down towns, sir.'

'The worst thing is that you're trying to squirm out of it. However, would you mind reading this and showing it to the others? It's only for purposes of information.'

He took Lebyadkin's anonymous letter to von Lembke out of his pocket and handed it to Liputin, who read it through, obviously surprised, and, with a thoughtful expression on his face, handed it to his neighbour. The letter quickly made the rounds.

'Is this really Lebyadkin's handwriting?' Shigalyov wondered.

'Yes, it is,' declared Liputin and Tolkachenko (that is, the expert on the common people).

'I'm showing it to you only for purposes of information and because I know how deeply attached you were to Lebyadkin,' Pyotr Stepanovich repeated, taking the letter back. 'And so, gentlemen, one Fedka has saved us, completely by chance, from a dangerous man. That's what chance means sometimes! It's instructive, isn't it?'

The members of the group exchanged quick glances.

'And now, gentlemen, it's my turn to ask questions,' said Pyotr Stepanovich, with an air of dignity. 'Permit me to know your reasons for setting fire to the town without permission?'

'What! We, we set fire to the town? Now that's really putting the blame on someone else!' they exclaimed.

'I understand that you got carried away with the game,' Pyotr Stepanovich went on stubbornly, 'but you know, this isn't a question of petty little scandals with Yuliya Mikhaylovna. I've brought you together here, gentlemen, to explain to you the degree of the danger which you've so stupidly brought on yourselves and which threatens a great deal besides yourselves.'

'Just a moment, we, on the contrary, were intending to inform *you* now of the degree of the despotism and inequality that was shown in taking such a serious and at the same time strange measure without the members' knowledge,' Virginsky, who had remained silent until then, announced almost with indignation.

'And so you deny it? And I maintain that you did burn it down, you alone and no one else. Gentlemen, don't lie, I have precise information. Because of your self-will you even exposed the common cause to danger. You are nothing but one knot in the endless network of knots, and you owe blind obedience to the centre. Meanwhile three of you put the Shpigulin men up to setting the fire, without having any instructions whatsoever to do such a thing, and there was a fire.'

'Which three? Which three of us?'

'The day before yesterday, between three and four in the morning, you, Tolkachenko, were putting Fomka Zavyalov up to it in the Forget-Me-Not.'

'Just one moment,' Tolkachenko jumped up. 'I hardly said a word, and even then without intending anything, and only because he had been flogged that morning, and I immediately let it drop – I could see that he was too drunk. If you hadn't reminded me, I wouldn't have remembered it at all. Words don't cause fires.'

'You're like a man who is surprised that a tiny spark can blow up an entire gunpowder factory.'

'I was speaking in a whisper, and in the corner, into his ear; how could you find out?' Tolkachenko suddenly wondered.

'I was sitting there under the table. Don't worry, gentlemen, I know every step you take. Is that a spiteful smile on your face, Mr Liputin? Well, I know, for example, that three days ago you gave your wife a good pinching all over, at midnight, in your bedroom, as you were getting ready to go to bed.'

Liputin's mouth fell open and he turned pale.

(Subsequently it became known that he had found out about Liputin's heroic deed from Agafya, the Liputins' servant, to whom he had been paying money from the very beginning to be a spy; this became clear only later.)

'May I verify a fact?' Shigalyov suddenly stood up.

'Yes, you may.'

Shigalyov sat down and composed himself.

'As far as I understand it, and it's impossible not to understand it, you yourself, at the beginning and then again, very eloquently – albeit too theoretically – have been developing a picture of a Russia covered with an endless network of knots. For their part, each of the active groups, by proselytizing and branching out ad infinitum, has the task, through systematic denunciatory propaganda of constantly undermining the authority of the local authorities, creating confusion in the villages, fostering cynicism, scandals and an utter lack of belief in anything at all, a burning desire for something better, and finally, using fires as a measure that appeals primarily to the common people, to throw the country, at a designated moment, if necessary, even into a state of despair. Are those your words, which I have tried to recall literally? Is that your programme of action, which you have communicated in your capacity as a representative of the central committee, an organization that to this day remains completely unknown to us and is almost mythical?'

'Correct, but you're really dragging it out.'

'Everyone has a right to speak his mind. In leaving us to guess that there are now up to several hundred individual knots in the overall web already covering Russia, and in developing the proposition that if each individual does his job successfully, then all of Russia, by the given date and at the signal . . .'

'Oh, the Devil take it; there's enough to be done without you!' Pyotr Stepanovich turned in his chair.

'Well, all right, I'll keep it short and will end with just a question: we have already seen scandals, we have seen the dissatisfaction of the population, we have been present at and taken part in the fall of the local administration, and finally, we have seen the fire with our own eyes. What, then, are you dissatisfied with? Isn't this your programme? What can you blame us for?'

'For self-will!' Pyotr Stepanovich shouted savagely. 'While I am here, you shouldn't dare to act without my permission. Enough. The denunciation is ready, and perhaps tomorrow or tonight you will be arrested. There you have it. The information is reliable.'

At this point everyone's jaws dropped.

'You will be arrested not only as instigators of arson, but as a group of five. The informer knows the whole secret of the network. Look at the mess you've made of everything!'

'Stavrogin most likely!' Liputin cried.

'What ... why Stavrogin?' Pyotr Stepanovich suddenly seemed to be at a loss for words. 'Oh, damn,' he promptly recovered, 'it's Shatov! I think you all know already that Shatov in his time belonged to the cause. And I must tell you that by having him followed by individuals he doesn't suspect I've learned, to my surprise, that even the organization of the network is no secret to him ... and, in short, everything. To save himself from accusations of having once been a member of it, he will denounce everyone. Until now he's been wavering, and I've spared him. Now you've untied his hands, thanks to this fire. He's shaken, and is no longer wavering. Tomorrow we'll be arrested as incendiaries and political criminals.'

'Is that true? How does Shatov know?'

The agitation was indescribable.

'It's all completely true. I am not authorized to explain my methods and how I discovered it, but here's what I can do for you for the time being: through a certain individual I can act on Shatov so that he will delay the denunciation, without suspecting it in the least – but no longer than twenty-four hours. I can't manage it for more than twenty-four hours. And so you can consider yourselves secure until the morning after next.'

Everyone remained silent.

'Why, he should be packed off to the Devil!' Tolkachenko was the first to exclaim.

'And it should have been done a long time ago!' Lyamshin put in maliciously, banging his fist on the table.

'But how is it to be done?' Liputin grumbled.

Pyotr Stepanovich immediately took up the question and

outlined his plan. It consisted of luring Shatov, so that he could
hand over the secret printing press (that was in his possession),
to the isolated spot where it was buried, tomorrow, at nightfall,
and 'take care of things then and there'. He went into many
necessary details, which we are omitting here, and he clarified
at length Shatov's currently ambiguous relations to the central
society, of which the reader is already aware.

'That's all very well,' Liputin noted tentatively, 'but since this
is yet another . . . a fresh adventure of the same sort . . . it will
attract too much attention.'

'Undoubtedly,' Pyotr Stepanovich confirmed, 'but that's
been foreseen as well. There is a way of averting suspicion
completely.'

And with the same attention to detail, he told them about
Kirillov, about his intention to shoot himself and how he had
promised to wait for the signal, and, just before his death, to
leave a note taking responsibility for everything they dictated
to him. (In short, everything that is already familiar to the
reader.)

'His firm intention to take his life – a philosophical one, and
in my opinion, an insane one – has become known *there*.' (Pyotr
Stepanovich went on with his explanation.) '*There* not a hair
or a speck of dust is overlooked; everything is put to the service
of the common cause. Foreseeing his usefulness, and convinced
that his intention is utterly serious, they offered him the means
of travelling to Russia (for some reason Russia was the place
he wanted to die), gave him a mission, which he pledged himself
to complete (and did complete), and in addition, bound him
with the promise, of which you are already aware, to do away
with himself only when he was told to. He promised everything.
Note that he belongs to the cause on special grounds, and wants
to be useful; I can't reveal any more to you. Tomorrow, *after
Shatov*, I will dictate the note to him, saying that he is the cause
of Shatov's death. That will be very plausible: they were close
friends and went to America together, but had a falling out
there, and all that will be explained in the note . . . and . . . and
. . . if circumstances permit, it might be possible to dictate
something else to Kirillov – for instance, about the manifestos

and perhaps in part the fire. However, I'll give it some thought. Don't worry, he has no prejudices; he'll sign anything.'

There was a flurry of doubt. The story struck them as fantastic. However, they had all heard something about Kirillov, Liputin more than the rest.

'What if he changes his mind and doesn't want to?' said Shigalyov. 'One way or another, he's still crazy, and so it's a pretty slim hope.'

'Don't worry, gentlemen, he'll want to,' snapped Pyotr Stepanovich. 'According to our agreement, I'm obliged to let him know the day before, that is, today. I invite Liputin to go with me to see him now and make sure, and when he returns, gentlemen, he'll let you know today, if necessary, whether I've told you the truth or not. However,' he suddenly broke off, in extreme irritation, as if he suddenly felt that it did too much honour to such lowly people to try to persuade them, 'however, do as you like. If you decide not to, then the union is dissolved, but only by the fact of your insubordination and treachery. From that moment on, we each go our own way. But you should know that in this case, besides the unpleasantness of Shatov's denunciation and its consequences, you are bringing on yourselves another little unpleasantness, which you were apprised of in no uncertain terms when the union was formed. As for me, I'm not really very afraid of you, gentlemen ... Don't imagine that I actually have any ties to you ... However, that doesn't matter.'

'No, we're ready to act,' Liputin announced.

'There's no other way out,' Tolkachenko mumbled, 'and if Liputin will confirm about Kirillov that . . .'

'I'm opposed. With all my soul I protest against such a bloody decision!' Virginsky got up from his chair.

'But?' Pyotr Stepanovich asked.

'What do you mean *but*?'

'You said *but* ... and I'm waiting.'

'I don't think I said *but* ... I only wanted to say that if the others decide on it, then . . .'

'Then?'

Virginsky fell silent.

'I think one can ignore danger to one's own life,' Erkel suddenly opened his mouth, 'but if the common cause suffers, then I think one shouldn't dare ignore danger to one's own life.'

He grew flustered and turned red. Preoccupied as they all were with their own ideas, everyone still looked at him in astonishment, so little did they expect that he, too, could venture an opinion.

'I'm for the common cause,' Virginsky suddenly intoned.

Everyone rose from his chair. It was decided that they would communicate again the next day at noon, although they would not all get together, and come to a final agreement. It was announced where the printing press was buried, and roles and duties were assigned. Liputin and Pyotr Stepanovich immediately set out together for Kirillov's.

2.

That Shatov would denounce them, all of them believed; but that Pyotr Stepanovich was playing with them like pawns they also believed. And yet they all knew that tomorrow they would nevertheless come in a group to the spot in question, and that Shatov's fate had been decided. They felt that they had suddenly fallen like flies into a huge spider's web; they were angry, but they shook with fear.

Pyotr Stepanovich was undoubtedly guilty of treating them badly: everything would have gone off more harmoniously and *easily* if he had taken the trouble to embellish reality just a whit. Instead of presenting the facts in a respectable light, as something reminiscent of Roman civic ideals or the like, he merely proffered raw fear and the threat to their own skins, which was simply uncouth. Of course, the struggle for existence[1] goes on everywhere, and there is no other principle, everyone knows that, but still and all . . .

But Pyotr Stepanovich had no time to dredge up the Romans: he himself had been thrown off balance. Stavrogin's flight had stunned and crushed him. He lied in saying that Stavrogin had had an interview with the vice governor. The whole point was that he had left without seeing anyone, even his mother, and it was truly strange that he hadn't even been disturbed. (Subsequently, the authorities were forced to account for that in particular.) Pyotr Stepanovich had been making inquiries the whole day, but so far he had learned nothing, and he had never been so alarmed. Why, could he, could he really give up Stavrogin just like that, all at once? That's why he was unable to treat our people too tenderly. Besides, they were tying his hands: his mind was already made up to go rushing after Stavrogin, but meanwhile he was being delayed by Shatov. He had to solidify the group of five once and for all, just in case. 'No need to discard it for nothing, maybe it'll come in handy.' That, I suppose, was his reasoning.

As far as Shatov was concerned, Pyotr Stepanovich was utterly convinced that he would denounce them. He lied when he told *our people* about the denunciation: he had never seen any evidence or heard anything about a denunciation, but was convinced of it as surely as two times two equals four. And he felt certain that Shatov would never be able to bear what was happening just then – the death of Liza, the death of Marya Timofeyevna – and would finally make up his mind right now. Who knows, perhaps he had some grounds for supposing so. It was also well known that he hated Shatov personally: there had been a quarrel between them at one time, and Pyotr Stepanovich never forgave an insult. I am even convinced that this was in fact the overriding reason.

The pavements of our town are very narrow and made of brick, or else just planks. Pyotr Stepanovich was striding down the middle of the pavement, taking up all of it and not paying the slightest attention to Liputin, who had no room to walk beside him, and therefore to keep up either had to walk a step behind him or run off into the muddy street if he wanted to walk beside him and converse. Pyotr Stepanovich suddenly remembered that not too long ago he had had to pick his way through the mud in the same fashion in order to keep up with Stavrogin, who was striding down the middle, as he was now, taking up the entire pavement. He remembered this whole scene, and was gasping with rage.

But Liputin, too, was gasping with resentment. Let Pyotr

Stepanovich treat *our people* as he liked, but him? After all, he *knew* more than all of our people, he was closer to the cause, he was more intimately associated with it, and so far had taken an active part in it, indirectly but constantly. Oh, he knew that Pyotr Stepanovich even now could destroy him *if worst came to worst*. But he had long since conceived a hatred for Pyotr Stepanovich, not because of the danger he posed, but for the arrogance of his manner. Now, when it had become necessary to decide on such a matter, he was angrier than all the rest of our people put together. Alas, he knew that 'like a slave' he would unfailingly be first on the spot tomorrow, and would also bring the others, and if he could now, before tomorrow, have somehow killed Pyotr Stepanovich, he would certainly have killed him.

Absorbed in his feelings, he remained silent and trudged along behind his tormentor. Pyotr Stepanovich seemed to have forgotten about him; from time to time he merely poked him with his elbow carelessly and rudely. Suddenly Pyotr Stepanovich came to a stop in the most prominent of our streets, and went into a tavern.

'Where are you going?' Liputin flared up. 'Why, this is a tavern.'

'I want some beefsteak.'

'But wait a minute, it's always full of people.'

'So what?'

'But . . . we'll be late. It's already ten o'clock.'

'It's impossible to be late there.'

'But I'll be late, you know! They're waiting for me to come back.'

'Well, let them; except that it's stupid of you to go there. What with all your to-do, I've had no dinner today. And the later you go to Kirillov's, the better your chances of finding him in.'

Pyotr Stepanovich took a private room. Liputin angrily and resentfully sat down in an armchair off to the side and watched him eat. A half hour and more passed. Pyotr Stepanovich didn't hurry; he ate with relish, he rang, asked for a different kind of mustard, then some beer, and still didn't say a word. He was deeply absorbed in something. He could do two things – eat with relish and be deeply absorbed. Liputin ended up hating him so much that he hadn't the strength to tear himself away. It was something like an attack of nerves. He counted every piece of beefsteak that Pyotr Stepanovich directed into his mouth, hated him for the way he opened it, the way he chewed, the way he savoured and smacked his lips over the pieces that had a bit more fat; he hated the beefsteak itself. Finally, things seemed to blur before his eyes; he became slightly dizzy; and fever and chills ran by turn up and down his spine.

'You're not doing anything, read this,' Pyotr Stepanovich suddenly tossed him a piece of paper. Liputin drew up to the candle. The paper was closely written in a wretched hand and with corrections in every line. By the time he had figured it out, Pyotr Stepanovich had already paid the bill and was leaving. On the pavement Liputin handed him back the paper.

'Keep it; I'll tell you about it later. What do you have to say about it, though?'

Liputin shuddered all over.

'In my opinion ... a manifesto of that sort ... is just an amusing absurdity.'

His anger broke through; he felt as if he had been caught up and carried along.

'If we decide,' he was trembling lightly all over, 'to distribute manifestos of this sort, we will make ourselves contemptible for our stupidity and lack of understanding of the cause.'

'Hmm. I don't think so,' Pyotr Stepanovich was striding along resolutely.

'And I do. Did you really compose this yourself?'

'That's none of your business.'

'I also think that "A Radiant Personality" is just doggerel, the worst excuse for poetry imaginable, and could never have been written by Herzen.'

'You're talking nonsense; it's good poetry.'

'I'm also surprised, for instance,' Liputin kept rushing along, his words jumping ahead impetuously, 'that people are proposing that we should act in such a way that everything collapses into ruins. In Europe it's natural to want everything to collapse, because they have a proletariat, but here we are just amateurs, and, in my opinion, we're just raising dust.'

'I thought you were a Fourierist.'

'That's not what Fourier says, not at all.'

'I know it's nonsense.'

'No, Fourier isn't nonsense . . . Excuse me, I just can't believe that there will be an uprising in May.'

Liputin was so hot that he even unbuttoned his coat.

'All right, enough. And now, before I forget,' Pyotr Stepan-ovich jumped to another topic with frightening coolness, 'you must set up the type for this leaflet and print it with your own hands. We'll dig up Shatov's printing press, and you'll take it tomorrow. In the shortest time possible you will set up and run off as many copies as possible, and then distribute them throughout the winter. The means for doing so will be provided. We need as many copies as possible, because you'll get requests for them from other places.'

'No indeed, excuse me, but I can't take on myself such a . . . I refuse.'

'Still and all, you will take it on. I am acting on instructions from the central committee, and you must obey.'

'And I believe that our foreign centres have forgotten what Russia is really like, have broken all ties with it and are there-fore living in a fantasy world . . . I even think that instead of many hundreds of groups of five in Russia we are the only one, and that there is no network at all,' Liputin finally gasped for breath.

'It's all the more contemptible of you that you don't believe in the cause, yet you run after it . . . and you're running after me now, like a mangy little cur.'

'No indeed, I'm not. We have every right to break off and form a new society.'

'You fool!' Pyotr Stepanovich suddenly thundered menac-ingly, his eyes flashing.

Both stood facing each other for some time. Pyotr Stepan-ovich turned around and continued confidently on his way.

It flashed like lightning through Liputin's mind: 'I'll turn around and go back: if I don't turn around now, I'll never go back.' This thought occupied him for exactly ten steps, but on the eleventh, a new and desperate thought blazed in his mind: he didn't turn around and didn't go back.

They came to Filippov's house, but before reaching it, they took a side street, or, rather, an imperceptible path that ran beside a fence, and for some time had to make their way along the steep slope of a ditch that afforded no sure footing and made it necessary for them to hold on to the fence. In the darkest corner of the dilapidated fence, Pyotr Stepanovich pulled out a board; this created a gap through which he promptly climbed. Liputin was surprised, but he also climbed through; then the board was returned to its former position. This was the same secret passage through which Fedka had crawled to see Kirillov.

'Shatov mustn't know we're here,' Pyotr Stepanovich whispered sternly to Liputin.

3.

Kirillov, as always at this time of day, was sitting on his leather sofa, drinking tea. He did not stand up to greet them, but seemed to stiffen to attention and looked at them in alarm as they came in.

'You're not mistaken,' Pyotr Stepanovich said, 'I've come for *that*.'

'Today?'

'No, no, tomorrow . . . at about this time.'

And he hastened to sit down at the table, observing Kirillov's alarm with a certain uneasiness. Kirillov, however, had already calmed down, and looked his usual self.

'These people simply refuse to believe it. You're not angry that I've brought Liputin?'

'Today I'm not angry, but tomorrow I want to be alone.'

'But not before I come, and so, in my presence.'

'I would prefer it not to be in your presence.'

'You remember that you promised to write and sign anything I dictate to you.'

'It doesn't matter. And will you be staying long now?'

'I have to meet with a certain person, and I have about half an hour left, so no matter what, I'm going to sit here for the next half hour.'

Kirillov said nothing. Meanwhile, Liputin found room for himself off to one side, under the bishop's portrait. The desperate thought that had struck him earlier increasingly took possession of his mind. Kirillov paid virtually no attention to him. Liputin was already familiar with Kirillov's theory and had always made fun of it before; but now he kept silent and looked around him gloomily.

'I wouldn't say no to some tea,' said Pyotr Stepanovich, moving closer. 'I've just eaten a beefsteak and I was really counting on finding some tea at your place.'

'Have some, please.'

'You yourself used to offer it to me,' Pyotr Stepanovich observed acidly.

'It doesn't matter. Liputin can have some too.'

'No, indeed, I . . . I can't.'

'You don't want to or you can't?' Pyotr Stepanovich whirled around.

'I won't have any here,' Liputin refused pointedly. Pyotr Stepanovich gave a frown.

'This smells of mysticism; the Devil only knows what sort of people you all are!'

No one answered him; they said nothing for a whole minute.

'But I know one thing,' he suddenly added sharply. 'No prejudices are going to stop each of us from fulfilling his obligation.'

'Has Stavrogin left?' Kirillov asked.

'He has.'

'It's good that he's done so.'

Pyotr Stepanovich's eyes flashed in anger, but he restrained himself.

'It's all the same to me what you think, as long as each person keeps his word.'

'I will keep my word.'

'However, I was always certain that you would discharge your duty, as an independent and progressive person.'

'You're funny.'

'That may well be; I'm very happy to amuse you. I'm always glad to be of service.'

'You want very much for me to shoot myself, and you're afraid if I suddenly don't do so?'

'That is, you see, you yourself connected your plan with our actions. Relying on your plan, we have already undertaken certain things; so there's no way you could refuse, because you'd be letting us down.'

'You had absolutely no right.'

'I understand, I understand; it's your own free will entirely, and we have nothing to say – as long as this free will of yours is carried out.'

'And I'm supposed to take all your vile actions on myself?'

'Listen, Kirillov, you aren't getting cold feet, are you? If you want to back out, then say so right now.'

'I'm not getting cold feet.'

'I'm saying this because you're asking a lot of questions.'

'Are you leaving soon?'

'Another question?'

Kirillov surveyed him with contempt.

'Now, you see,' Pyotr Stepanovich went on, getting more and more angry and worried, and not finding the proper tone, 'you want me to leave so that you can be alone, so that you can concentrate; but these are dangerous signs for someone like you, for someone like you above all. You want to think a lot. As I see it, it would be better not to think, but just to do it. And you really worry me.'

'There's only one thing I feel very bad about, that at that moment I'll have a reptile like you beside me.'

'Well, that doesn't matter. Perhaps when the time comes I'll go out and stand on the porch. If you're dying and are so indifferent, then . . . all this is very dangerous. I'll step out on to the porch, and you can imagine that I understand nothing and that I'm a man who's immeasurably lower than you.'

'No, not immeasurably: you have abilities, but there's a great deal you don't understand, because you're a low person.'

'I'm very glad, very glad. I've already said that I'm very glad to provide entertainment . . . at such a moment.'

'You understand nothing.'

'That is, I . . . in any event, I'm listening respectfully.'

'You can't do anything. You can't even conceal your petty malice now, although it's not to your advantage to show it. You'll make me angry, and then I'll suddenly want another six months.'

Pyotr Stepanovich looked at his watch.

'I never understood anything about your theory, but I do know that you didn't devise it for us, and so, you will act on it even without us. I also know that you haven't consumed the idea but that you have been consumed by the idea, and so you won't be able to relinquish it.'

'What? I've been consumed by the idea?'

'Yes.'

'And I'm not the one who's consumed the idea? That's good. You have a little intelligence. Except you're teasing, and I'm proud.'

'Wonderful, wonderful. That's exactly what's needed, for you to be proud.'

'Enough. You've had your tea, now leave.'

'The Devil take it, I suppose I'll have to.' Pyotr Stepanovich got up. 'However, it's still early. Listen, Kirillov, will I find that man at Myasnichikha's? You understand? Or did she lie as well?'

'You won't find him, because he's here, and not there.'

'What do you mean "here", the Devil take it, where?'

'He's sitting in the kitchen, eating and drinking.'

'Why, how dare he?' Pyotr Stepanovich flushed with anger. 'He was supposed to wait . . . nonsense! He doesn't have a passport or any money!'

'I don't know. He came to say goodbye, all dressed and ready. He's leaving and not coming back. He said that you're a scoundrel, and he doesn't want to wait for your money.'

'A-a-ah! He's afraid that I . . . Well, even now I can, if . . . Where is he? In the kitchen?'

Kirillov opened a side door leading into a tiny dark room. From this room they took three steps down into the kitchen, directly into that partitioned-off little closet where the cook's cot was usually set up. And there, in a corner, under the icons, sat Fedka at a bare plank table. On the table before him stood a pint bottle, on a plate there was some bread, and on an earthenware dish, a slice of cold beef and potatoes. He was having a leisurely snack and was already half drunk, but he was sitting there in a sheepskin coat and evidently was all ready for a journey. Behind the partition the samovar was on the boil, but not for Fedka, though he had taken it upon himself to blow on the coals and set it up every night, for a week or more now, for 'Aleksey Nilych, 'cause he's got very used to havin' his tea of a night'. I'm strongly of the opinion that Kirillov himself, for lack of a cook, had prepared the beef and potatoes for Fedka that same morning.

'What have you been up to?' Pyotr Stepanovich barrelled down the steps. 'Why didn't you wait where you were told to?'

And he raised his fist and banged the table.

Fedka stood on his dignity.

'You just stop it, Pyotr Stepanovich, just stop it,' he said, enunciating each word like a fop. 'The first thing you gotta understand is you're payin' an honourable visit to Mr Kirillov, Aleksey Nilych, whose boots you could always clean, 'cause compared to you, he's got an educated mind, and you're just – pah!'

And he made a gesture of spitting foppishly to one side. There were signs of haughtiness, decisiveness and a certain highly dangerous, albeit assumed, calm moralizing that might precede a sudden explosion. But Pyotr Stepanovich was no longer in a state to notice any danger; moreover, it didn't fit with his view of things. The events and disasters of the day had made his head spin. Liputin was looking down curiously from the three steps leading from the dark little room.

'Do you or do you not want to have a valid passport and good money to go where we agreed? Yes or no?'

'You see, Pyotr Stepanovich, you begun to fool me right from the very beginning, so you come out lookin' to me like a real scoundrel. You're jes' the same as some unclean human louse – that's what I think you are. You promised me big money for innocent blood, and swore an oath that it was for Mr Stavrogin, even though it turns out it was nothin' but your own bad manners. As things worked out, I didn't get a drop of nothin' out of it, let alone fifteen hundred, and Mr Stavrogin slapped you in the face the other day, which fact is already knowed to us. Now here you are threatenin' me again and promisin' money, but what for, you won't say. And I'm not so sure in my mind but that you're sendin' me to Petersburg to take out your own anger by getting revenge on Mr Stavrogin with whatever you've got, trustin' in my gullible nature. And that means you're the murderer first and foremost. And do you know what you deserved by just the one fact that you stopped believin' in God, the true creator, on account o' your depravity? It's all the same as bein' an idol-worshipper, and standin' in the same line as a Tartar or a Mordvinian.[2] Aleksey Nilych, bein' a philosopher, has explained the real God to you many a time, the maker and creator, and about the creation of the world, along with what's fated in the future and the transformation of every creature and every beast from the book of the Apocalypse. But you're jes' a brainless idol, you keep on with your deafness and dumbness and have brung Ensign Erkel to the very same thing, as that same evildoer and seducer as is called an atheist . . .'

'Oh, you drunken slob! He's the one who strips an icon, and yet preaches about God!'

'You see, Pyotr Stepanovich, I'm tellin' you true that I did strip it; but I only took out the pearls, and how do you know, maybe my tear was transformed in the furnace of the Almighty that very instant, for some offence against me, being as I'm nothin' but an orphan, without no daily bread nor place to rest my head. Do you know by the books that once in olden times a certain merchant, he stole a pearl from the halo of the Most Holy Virgin, with jes' such tears and sighs and prayers, and then he returned the whole amount to the foot of the icon, in public and on bended knee, and the Mother Protector in front of all the people shadowed him over with her veil, so on account of that object a miracle happened even then, and everything was ordered written down in the official books by the authorities, word-for-word jes' like it happened. But you let a mouse in, so you done an outrage to the very finger of God. And if you wasn't my natural master, who I used to carry in my arms when you was still a youngster, I'd settle your hash this very instant, not even movin' from this spot!'

Pyotr Stepanovich flew into a tremendous rage.

'Tell me, did you meet with Stavrogin today?'

'Don't you ever dare question me. Mr Stavrogin is surprised as can be by you, and he didn't have no part in it even as far as desirin' it, not to speak of orderin' nothin' or payin' out no money. You dared me.'

'You'll get the money, and you'll also get the two thousand, in Petersburg, on the spot, all of it in its entirety, and you'll get more.'

'You're lyin', old pal, and I even think it's funny to see how easy you fall for things. Mr Stavrogin is standin' on a ladder in front of you, and you're lower than he is, like a stupid little puppy-dog, yappin'away, and there he is standin' above you and thinkin' it's a big honour to spit on you.'

'And do you know,' said Pyotr Stepanovich in a rage, 'that I won't let you move a step from here, you scoundrel, and I'll turn you over to the police straightaway?'

Fedka leaped to his feet, his eyes fiercely flashing. Pyotr Stepanovich pulled out his revolver. A rapid and disgusting scene then ensued. Before Pyotr Stepanovich could aim the revolver, Fedka, in a flash, dodged him and then struck him as hard as he could on the face. In an instant a second dreadful blow was heard, then a third, and then a fourth, all on the face. Pyotr Stepanovich, in a daze and wide-eyed, muttered something and suddenly crashed full length on to the floor.

'There he is, he's all yours!' Fedka shouted with a triumphant flourish. In an instant he had grabbed his cap and the bundle from beneath the bench, and was off. Pyotr Stepanovich lay gasping and unconscious. Liputin even thought that a murder had been committed. Kirillov dashed headlong into the kitchen.

'Water!' he shouted, and dipping an iron ladle into a bucket, poured it on his head. Pyotr Stepanovich stirred, raised his head, sat up and looked blankly straight ahead.

'Well, are you all right?' Kirillov asked.

Pyotr Stepanovich stared at him, still not recognizing him; but on catching sight of Liputin, who had leaned out from the kitchen, he gave his nasty smile and suddenly jumped up, scooping the revolver off the floor.

'If you have any idea of trying to run away tomorrow like that scoundrel Stavrogin,' he swooped down on Kirillov in a frenzy, deathly pale, stammering and garbling his words, 'then I'll find you, even at the other end of the world ... I'll hang you ... like a fly ... I'll squash you ... you understand!'

And he aimed the revolver straight at Kirillov's forehead; but at almost that same moment he came fully to his senses, pulled his hand away, stuck the revolver back in his pocket and, without saying another word, ran out of the house. Liputin went after him. They climbed through the gap and again walked along the slope, hanging on to the fence. Pyotr Stepanovich began to walk rapidly down the lane, so that Liputin could scarcely keep up. He suddenly stopped at the first crossroads.

'Well?' He turned to Liputin challengingly.

Liputin remembered the revolver and was still trembling from the scene that had just occurred. But a reply somehow tripped from his tongue by itself, suddenly and irrepressibly:

'I think ... I think that "from Smolensk to Tashkent they're not so impatiently awaiting the student".'[3]

'Did you see what Fedka was drinking in the kitchen?'

'What he was drinking? He was drinking vodka.'

'Well, you should know that he was drinking vodka for the last time in his life. I recommend that you keep that in mind for future consideration. And now get the hell out of here, you're not needed until tomorrow. But watch out: don't do anything stupid!'

Liputin ran home as fast as he could.

4.

He had long been holding in reserve a passport under a different name. It's preposterous even to think that this most particular of men, a petty family tyrant, a civil servant in any event (albeit a Fourierist), and, finally, first and foremost a capitalist and a moneylender, had long ago conceived the fantastic idea of holding this passport in reserve just in case, so that he could use it to slip across the border, *if* . . . he did admit the possibility of this *if!* Although he himself could never clearly formulate precisely what this *if* might mean.

But now it had suddenly formulated itself, and in the most unexpected way. The desperate idea with which he had gone in to see Kirillov, after that 'fool' he had heard from Pyotr Stepanovich on the pavement, consisted of his abandoning everything at dawn the very next day and expatriating himself! Anyone who doesn't believe that such fantastic things happen in our ordinary reality even now should take a look at the lives of all the Russian emigrants who are currently abroad. Not one had a more intelligent or realistic reason for running away. It's still the same old unbridled realm of phantoms and nothing more.

After running home, he began by locking himself in, taking out his bag and beginning to pack frantically. His main worry was money, how much he would manage to salvage – specifically, to salvage, for as he saw it, he could not linger for even an hour, and must be on his way as soon as it got light. He also didn't know where he would get the train. He vaguely decided to get on at the second or third large station from town, and to make his way there on foot if necessary. And so he busied himself with his bag, instinctively and mechanically, his head whirling with thoughts, and – suddenly he stopped, dropped everything and stretched out on the sofa with a deep groan.

He clearly sensed and was suddenly aware that he might very well succeed in running away, but that to decide the question of whether he had to run away *before* or *after* Shatov was now utterly beyond his powers; that now he was only a crude, insensate body, an inert mass, but that he was being moved by a dreadful outside force and that although he had a passport to go abroad, although he could even run away from Shatov (otherwise, why be in such a hurry?), he was running away not before Shatov, not from Shatov, but precisely *after* Shatov, and that it had been already so decided, signed and sealed. In unbearable anguish, constantly trembling and surprised at himself, in turn moaning and inert with terror, he somehow survived, locked in and lying on the sofa until eleven o'clock the next morning, when suddenly there came the anticipated jolt that suddenly gave direction to his resolution. At eleven o'clock, as soon as he had unlocked the door and gone out to see the members of his household, he suddenly learned that the brigand, the escaped convict Fedka, who had thrown such fear into everyone, the plunderer of churches, the recent murderer and arsonist, whom our police had been following but couldn't catch, had been found that morning at daybreak murdered, seven versts from town, at the turn-off from the main road into the country lane to Zakharino, and that the whole town was already talking about it. He immediately ran from the house as fast as he could to try to learn the details, and he learned, first of all, that Fedka, who had been found with his head bashed in, had by all indications been robbed, and, in the second place, that the police already had strong suspicions and even certain solid evidence to conclude that his murderer had been the Shpigulin worker Fomka, the same one with whom he had undoubtedly committed the murder and arson at the Lebyadkins, and that a quarrel had arisen between them on the road because of the large amount of money that had been stolen from Lebyadkin and supposedly hidden by Fedka. Liputin also ran to Pyotr Stepanovich's lodgings and managed to learn at the back door, on the sly, that Pyotr Stepanovich had in fact returned home the day before, about one o'clock or so in the morning, and he saw fit to rest quietly at home the rest of the night, right up to eight o'clock that morning. Naturally, there could be no doubt that there had been absolutely nothing unusual about the death of the brigand Fedka, and that endings of this sort do in fact happen very often in the case of such careers, but the coincidence of the fateful words 'that Fedka was drinking vodka for the last time in his life that evening' with the immediate fulfilment of the prophecy was so significant that Liputin suddenly stopped hesitating. The jolt had been administered: it was if a stone had fallen on him and crushed him forever. On returning home, he silently pushed his bag under the bed with his foot, and that evening was the first to appear at the designated place for the meeting with Shatov, albeit with his passport in his pocket.

CHAPTER 5

A Woman Traveller

1.

The disaster that had befallen Liza and the death of Marya Timofeyevna had produced an overwhelming impression on Shatov. I have already mentioned that I encountered him in passing that morning, and he struck me as being not quite in his right mind. Incidentally, he told me that the night before, at about nine o'clock (in other words, two hours before the fire), he had been at Marya Timofeyevna's. He had gone there the next morning to have a look at the bodies, but as far as I know, on that morning he gave absolutely no evidence anywhere. Meanwhile, by the end of the day a veritable storm had arisen in his heart and . . . and I think I can say positively that there was a certain moment at dusk when he wanted to get up, go and speak out about everything. What exactly this *everything* was – only he himself knew. Naturally, he would have achieved nothing, but would simply have betrayed himself. He had no evidence that would throw light on the evil deed that had just been committed, and what's more, he himself could make only vague surmises about it which were tantamount for him alone to complete conviction. But he was prepared to doom himself provided he could 'crush the scoundrels' – his own words. Pyotr Stepanovich was partly right in guessing that this impulse lay within him and knew that he was taking a great risk in postponing the execution of his dreadful new plan until the next day. Here, as usual, he had a great deal of self-confidence and contempt for all these 'petty little people', and for Shatov in particular. He had long held Shatov in contempt for his 'whining idiocy', as he himself characterized it while he was still abroad, and had every expectation of dealing with such a guileless man, that is, by not letting him out of sight that whole day and stopping him in his tracks at the first sign of danger. However, the 'scoundrels' were saved for a short time yet by a certain unexpected circumstance that they had utterly failed to foresee . . .

At some time between seven and eight in the evening (that was precisely the time when *our people* had gathered at Erkel's and were awaiting Pyotr Stepanovich, and feeling indignant and upset), Shatov was lying stretched out on his bed, with a headache and a slight chill, in the darkness with no candlelight. He was tormented by a sense of bewilderment; he was peeved; he was trying to decide on something but could come to no final decision and cursed as he sensed that it would lead to nothing anyway. Little by little he subsided into a light sleep and he had something like a nightmare: he dreamt that he was tied down to his bed with ropes, was bound all over and couldn't move, and meanwhile there resounded throughout the house a frightful banging – at the fence, at the gate, at his door, at Kirillov's little house, making the whole house shake, and some distant, familiar, but tormenting voice was plaintively calling out to him. He suddenly came awake, and raised himself off his bed. To his surprise, the banging at the gate continued, and although it was by no means as loud as it had been in his dream, it was frequent and insistent, and a strange and 'tormented' voice, although by no means plaintive, but, on the contrary, impatient and irritated, kept echoing from the gate below and alternated with another more restrained and ordinary voice. He jumped up, opened the window and thrust his head out.

'Who's there?' he called out, literally numb with fright.

'If you're Shatov,' came the abrupt and firm reply from below, 'then please be kind enough to state directly and honestly whether you're willing to let me in or not.'

Just as he thought: he recognized the voice!

'Marie! Is that you?'

'It is, it's me, Marya Shatova, and I assure you I can't keep the driver one moment longer.'

'Just a minute. Let me get a candle,' Shatov exclaimed feebly. He then rushed around looking for matches. As is usual in such cases, no matches could be found. He dropped the candlestick and the candle on to the floor, and as soon as he heard the impatient voice from below again, he dropped everything and flew as fast as he could down his narrow stairway to open the gate.

'Please be good enough to hold the bag while I settle up with this blockhead,' Marya Shatova met him downstairs and thrust into his hands a rather light, cheap canvas bag with bronze studs, of Dresden manufacture. Then she laid into the driver in irritation.

'I make bold to assure you that you're asking too much. If you've dragged me around these dirty streets here for a whole extra hour, then you're the one to blame, seeing that you, after all, were the one who didn't know where this stupid street and this idiotic house were located. Please take your thirty kopecks and rest assured that you won't receive anything more.'

'Why, dear lady, you yourself said Voznesenskaya Street, and this is Bogoyavlenskaya:[1] Voznesenskaya is way over that way. You got my gelding all lathered up.'

'Voznesenskaya, Bogoyavlenskaya – you should know all these stupid names better than I do, since you live here, and what's more, you're not being fair: the first thing I did say was Filippov's house, and you specifically said that you knew it. In any case you can lodge a complaint against me tomorrow at the Justice of the Peace, but for now I ask you to leave me alone.'

'Here, here's another five kopecks!' Shatov was quick to pull a five-kopeck piece out of his pocket and hand it to the driver.

'Be so kind, I beg of you, don't dare do that!' Madame Shatova was on the point of boiling over, but the driver started the 'gelding', and Shatov, grabbing her by the arm, guided her through the gate.

'Hurry up, Marie, hurry up . . . this is all nonsense and – how wet you are! Careful, we go up here – what a pity there's no light – the stairway is narrow, hold on tight, tight – here's my closet. Excuse me, I have no light . . . Here we are!'

He picked up the candlestick, but took a long time finding the matches. Madame Shatova stood waiting in the middle of the room, saying nothing and not moving.

'Thank God, at last!' he exclaimed happily, when the room was lit up. Marya Shatova gave the lodgings a cursory glance.

'I was told that you lived badly, but I still didn't think it was this bad,' she pronounced squeamishly and made for the bed.

'Oh, I'm so tired!' she sat down on the hard bed, looking utterly exhausted. 'Please, put the bag down and take a seat. However, as you like, but you're looming in front of me. I'll be with you temporarily, until I get some work, because I know nothing about the situation here and I have no money. But if I'm in your way, be so kind, I beg of you again, as to tell me immediately, which you are obliged to do if you're an honest man. After all, I can sell something tomorrow and pay for a hotel, but you will be so good as to escort me to the hotel yourself . . . Oh, I'm just so tired!'

Shatov simply began to tremble all over.

'There's no need, Marie, no need for a hotel! What hotel? What for? What for?'

He clasped his hands imploringly.

'Well, if I can get along without a hotel, then I still have to explain what's going on. You remember, Shatov, that we lived together in Geneva as man and wife for two weeks and several days, and it's been three years since we broke it off, without any particular quarrel, however. But don't imagine that I've come back to renew all that old idiocy. I've returned to look for work, and if I came straight to this town, then it was because it just didn't matter to me. I didn't come to repent of anything; be so kind as not to imagine anything as stupid as that.'

'Oh, Marie, there's no point in this, no point at all!' Shatov mumbled vaguely.

'Well, if that's so, if you are sufficiently developed to under-stand even this, then I'll permit myself to add that if I've turned directly to you and have come to your lodgings, then it's partly because I always regarded you as anything but a scoundrel and perhaps much better than the other . . . reprobates!'

Her eyes began to flash. She must have put up with a great deal from certain 'reprobates'.

'And please rest assured that I certainly wasn't making fun of you just now when I told you that you were kind. I was speaking straightforwardly, without any eloquence, which by the way I can't stand. However, that's all nonsense. I have always hoped that you were sufficiently intelligent not to be boring . . . Oh, enough, I'm so tired!'

And she gave him a long, tormented, tired look. Shatov was standing before her, across the room, five steps away, and was listening to her shyly but somehow renewed, with a certain glow to his face that had never been there before. This strong and rough man, whose feathers were constantly being ruffled, had suddenly softened and brightened. Something unusual and entirely unexpected had begun to stir in his soul. Three years of separation, three years of a broken marriage had dislodged nothing from his heart. And perhaps every day of those three years he had dreamed of her, of the beloved being who had once said 'I love you' to him. Knowing Shatov, I can say for certain that he would never have allowed himself even to dream that any woman could say 'I love you' to him. He was fiercely chaste and modest, regarded himself as a dreadful freak, hated his own face and character, compared himself to some monster who was fit only to be taken around and exhibited at fairs. As a consequence of all this, he valued honesty above all things and dedicated himself to his convictions to the point of fanaticism; he was sullen, proud, quick to anger and sparing with words. But now this single being who had loved him for two weeks (he had always, always believed that!), this being whom he had always regarded as immeasurably superior to himself despite his utterly sober understanding of her faults; this being whom he could forgive everything, *everything* (of which there could be absolutely no question, for just the opposite was actually true, so that in his eyes he himself was guilty of everything before her), this woman, this Marya Shatova, was suddenly again in his house, before him again . . . this was almost impossible to understand! He was so startled, this event contained

within it so much that was somehow terrible and at the same
time so much happiness that he was, of course, unable to come
to his senses, and perhaps didn't wish to and was afraid to. It
was a dream. But when she directed this tormented look at
him, he suddenly understood that this being, so beloved, was
suffering and perhaps had been wronged. His heart sank. He
scrutinized her features in anguish: the first bloom of youth had
long ago vanished from this tired face. True, she was still pretty
– and in his eyes, as before, a beauty. (In point of fact she was
a woman of about twenty-five, rather powerfully built, taller
than the average – taller than Shatov – with luxuriant dark-
brown hair, a pale oval face and large dark eyes which were
now glittering feverishly.) But her lighthearted, naive and spontaneous energy of old, so familiar to him, had now given way
to a sullen irritability, a kind of cynical disappointment to
which she had not yet become accustomed and which she herself
found burdensome. But the main thing was that she was sick,
he could see that clearly. Despite all the fear he felt in her
presence, he suddenly went up to her and seized her by both
hands.

'Marie . . . you know, perhaps you're very tired, for heaven's
sake, don't get angry . . . If only you'd agree to a spot of tea,
for instance, eh? Tea is very strengthening, eh? If only you'd
agree!'

'What's to agree to; of course I'll agree; what a baby you are,
just as you used to be. Give me some tea if you can. How
cramped it is in here! How cold it is in here!'

'Oh, I'll bring some wood right away, some wood – I have
firewood!' He started pacing about. 'Firewood . . . that is, but
. . . still and all, I'll bring you some tea right away', and he
waved his hand in a kind of desperate resolve, and snatched up
his cap.

'Where are you off to? Does this mean there's no tea in the
house?'

'There will be, there will be, there will be, there will be
everything right away . . . I . . .' He pulled his revolver down
off the shelf.

'I'll go and sell this revolver right now . . . or pawn it . . .'

'Don't be silly, that will take such a long time! Here's my
money, take it if you have nothing; there are eighty kopecks
here, I think; that's all. It's like living in a madhouse here.'

'I don't need your money, I don't need it; I'll be right back,
in just a second, and I can do it without the revolver . . .'

And he dashed straight off to Kirillov's. This was probably
about two hours before Kirillov was visited by Pyotr Stepanovich and Liputin. Shatov and Kirillov, though they shared a
yard, almost never saw each other, and whenever they did meet,
they didn't exchange bows and didn't speak: they had spent far
too much time 'lying about' together in America.

'Kirillov, you always have tea; do you have tea and a
samovar?'

Kirillov, who was pacing about his room (as was his habit,
all night long, from corner to corner), suddenly stopped and
stared at the man who had run in, though without any particular surprise.

'There's tea, there's sugar and there's a samovar. But a samovar isn't necessary, the tea is hot. Have a seat and just drink
some.'

'Kirillov, we lay around together in America . . . My wife has
come back . . . I . . . Give me some tea . . . I need a samovar.'

'If there's a wife, then you need a samovar. But we'll deal
with the samovar later. I have two. And now take the teapot
off the table. It's hot, very hot. Take everything: take sugar, all
of it. Bread – there's a lot of bread; all of it. There's veal. One
rouble cash.'

'Let me have it, friend, I'll give it back tomorrow. Ah,
Kirillov!'

'This is the wife who was in Switzerland? That's good. And
the fact that you ran in now is also good.'

'Kirillov!' Shatov exclaimed, seizing the teapot by the
handle, and the sugar and bread in both hands. 'Kirillov! If
only . . . if only you could give up your dreadful fantasies
and drop your atheistic ravings . . . oh, what a man you'd be,
Kirillov!'

'It's obvious you love your wife after Switzerland. That's
good if it's after Switzerland. When you need some tea, come

again. Come anytime all night long, I don't sleep at all. There
will be a samovar. Take the rouble, here. Go to your wife, I'll
stay here and I'll think about you and your wife.'

Marya Shatova was obviously pleased at the haste with which
her husband made his return, and addressed herself to the tea
almost greedily, but there was no need to run and get a samovar:
she drank only half a cup and swallowed only a tiny piece of
bread. She refused the veal with disgust and irritation.

'You're ill, Marie, all this is a sign of illness in you,' Shatov
shyly observed as he shyly waited on her.

'Of course I'm ill. Please sit down. Where did you get the tea
if you didn't have any?'

Shatov told her about Kirillov, just a little, briefly. She had
heard something about him.

'I know that he's mad; please, enough about him; aren't there
enough fools already? So you were in America? I heard, you
wrote.'

'Yes, I . . . wrote to Paris.'

'Enough, and please, let's talk about something else. Are you
a Slavophile by conviction?'

'I . . . I, well, not exactly . . . Because it's impossible to be a
Russian, I became a Slavophile,' he grinned crookedly, with the
effort of someone who's made an inappropriate and strained
witticism.

'And you're not a Russian?'

'No, I'm not a Russian.'

'Well, that's all just stupid. Please, once and for all, do sit
down. Why do you keep wandering back and forth? You think
I'm delirious? Perhaps I will be delirious. You say that there are
only two of you in the house?'

'Two . . . downstairs . . .'

'And both so intelligent. What's downstairs? You said downstairs?'

'No, nothing.'

'What do you mean "nothing"? I want to know.'

'I only meant that now there are two of us in the yard, but
the Lebyadkins used to live downstairs.'

'She's the one whose throat was cut last night?' she suddenly gave a start. 'I heard. As soon as I got here, I heard. You had a fire?'

'Yes, Marie, yes, and perhaps I'm doing a dreadfully vile thing at this moment in forgiving the vile people who were involved.' He suddenly got up and began pacing about the room, his hands raised as if in a frenzy.

But Marie didn't understand him fully. She was listening to his answers absentmindedly; she was asking questions, but not listening.

'Wonderful things you've got going on here. Oh, how vile everything is! How vile everyone is! Once and for all do sit down, I beg you, oh, how you irritate me.' And she dropped her head on to the pillow in exhaustion.

'Marie, I won't . . . Perhaps you would like to lie down for a while, Marie?'

She didn't answer, and closed her eyes in exhaustion. Her pale face became like a dead woman's. She fell asleep almost at once. Shatov looked around, adjusted the candle, again looked at her face uneasily, clasped his hands tightly in front of him and went out of the room into the entryway on tiptoe. At the top of the stairway he pressed his face into a corner and remained standing there like that for about ten minutes, without speaking or moving. He would have stood even longer, but suddenly quiet, cautious steps were heard below. Someone was walking up the stairs. Shatov remembered that he had forgotten to lock the front gate.

'Who's there?' he asked in a whisper.

The unknown visitor kept walking up the stairs without hurrying and without replying. Once he reached the top, he stopped. It was impossible to see him in the darkness. Suddenly a cautious question was heard:

'Ivan Shatov?'

Shatov identified himself, and immediately held out his hand in order to stop him; but the stranger grabbed his hand and Shatov gave a start, as if he had touched some horrible reptile.

'Stay here,' he whispered rapidly, 'don't come in, I can't receive you now. My wife has come back to me. I'll bring a candle out.'

When he returned with the candle, a very young-looking army officer was standing there. Shatov didn't know his name, but he had seen him somewhere.

'Erkel,' the young man introduced himself. 'You saw me at Virginsky's.'

'I remember. You were sitting and writing. Listen.' Shatov suddenly boiled over, walked up to him in a frenzy, but continued to speak in a whisper. 'You just gave me a sign when you took my hand. But you should know that I don't give a damn about all these signs! I don't recognize them . . . I don't want to . . . I could throw you down the stairs this very moment, do you know that?'

'No, I know nothing about that, and I have absolutely no idea why you're so angry,' the visitor replied mildly and almost ingenuously. 'I merely have to tell you something and that's why I've come, the main thing being that I don't want to waste any time. You have a printing press that doesn't belong to you and that you're responsible for, as you know yourself. I have been ordered to request that you hand it over no later than tomorrow, at exactly seven o'clock in the evening, to Liputin. In addition, I have been ordered to inform you that nothing more will ever again be required of you.'

'Nothing?'

'Absolutely nothing. Your request is being granted, and you are dismissed forever. I have been ordered to communicate this to you.'

'Who ordered you to inform me?'

'Those who gave me the sign.'

'Are you from abroad?'

'That . . . that, I think, is a matter of indifference to you.'

'Oh, damnation! And why didn't you come earlier if you were ordered to do so?'

'I was following certain instructions and I was not alone.'

'I understand, I understand that you were not alone. Oh, damnation! And why didn't Liputin come himself?'

'And so, I'll be here to fetch you tomorrow at exactly six o'clock in the evening, and we'll go there on foot. There will be no one apart from the three of us.'

'Will Verkhovensky be there?'

'No, he won't. Verkhovensky is leaving town tomorrow morning at eleven o'clock.'

'That's just what I thought,' Shatov whispered fiercely and struck his hip with his fist. 'He's run away, the swine!'

He sank into agitated thought. Erkel kept staring at him, saying nothing and waiting.

'How are you planning to take it? After all, it's not something you can just pick up and carry away.'

'Why, it won't be necessary. You just indicate the place, and we'll simply verify that it really is buried there. We only know the approximate location, you see, but we don't know the exact location. Have you ever shown anyone the place?'

Shatov looked at him.

'You, you, you're such a little boy, such a stupid little boy. Are you also up to your ears in it, like a silly sheep? Oh, that's just what they need, some fresh young blood! All right, get out of here! O-oh! That scoundrel has taken you all in and has run away.'

Erkel looked at him serenely and calmly, but didn't seem to understand.

'Verkhovensky has run away, Verkhovensky!' he said savagely through clenched teeth.

'But he's still here, he hasn't left. He's not leaving until tomorrow,' Erkel observed in a soft and persuasive tone. 'I invited him specially to be present as a witness; all my instructions pertained to him.' (He was being outspoken like a very young and inexperienced boy.) 'But unfortunately, he didn't agree, on the grounds that he was leaving; and in fact he's in a hurry for some reason.'

Shatov threw another pitying look at the young simpleton, but suddenly waved his hand dismissively, as if thinking: 'Is he really worth pitying?'

'All right, I'll come,' he suddenly snapped, 'and now clear off, march!'

'And so, I'll be here at precisely six o'clock,' Erkel bowed politely and began to walk down the steps in a leisurely way.

'You stupid little fool!' Shatov couldn't help shouting after him from the top of the stairs.

'What's that?' Erkel replied, now from below.

'Nothing, clear out!'

'I thought you said something.'

2.

Erkel was the sort of 'stupid little fool' who was short on sense of the higher sort, but he had enough sense for an underling, even to the point of cunning. Fanatically, childishly devoted to the 'common cause', and specifically to Pyotr Stepanovich, he acted according to his instructions, which had been given him at the meeting of *our people*, when they had come to an agreement and parcelled out the roles for the following day. In assigning him the role of envoy, Pyotr Stepanovich had managed to take him aside and chat with him for about ten minutes. This shallow, mindless nature, which constantly thirsted to subordinate itself to another person's will, had a need to see orders through – oh, for no other reason, of course, than for the sake of a 'common' or 'great' cause. But even this didn't matter, because petty fanatics like Erkel are utterly incapable of understanding service to an idea other than by conflating it with the very individual who, as they understand it, gives expression to this idea. Sensitive, affectionate and kind, Erkel was perhaps the most unfeeling of the murderers who plotted against Shatov, and he would be present at his killing without the slightest personal hatred, and without batting an eye. Among other things he had been ordered, for instance, to look closely at Shatov's situation while he was carrying out his mission, and when Shatov met him on the stairway and blurted out in the heat of the moment, most likely without being aware of it, that his wife had returned to him, Erkel immediately had the instinctive cunning not to display further curiosity of any kind, even though it dawned on him that the fact of the return of a wife had great significance for the success of their undertaking.

And so it was in reality: this fact alone saved the 'scoundrels' from what Shatov intended, and at the same time helped them 'get rid of' him. In the first place, it disturbed him, threw him off balance and robbed him of his usual perspicacity and caution. Any idea of danger to him personally was the last thing now to enter his head, taken up as it was with something completely different. On the contrary, he fervently believed that Pyotr Verkhovensky would run away the next day: this fell in so perfectly with his suspicions! After returning to his room, he sat down in a corner, propped his elbows on his knees and covered his face with his hands. He was tormented by bitter thoughts . . .

And then he would raise his head again and tiptoe over to have a look at her. 'Lord! Why, by tomorrow she'll certainly develop a fever, by morning; maybe it's already begun! Of course she's caught cold. She's not used to this horrible climate, and then there was the third-class railway carriage, the strong winds, rain, a cloak that wasn't at all warm, a flimsy little dress . . . And then to leave her, to abandon her without help! And that bag of hers, that bag, so tiny, so light, so crumpled, weighing all of ten pounds! Poor thing, she's so worn out, she's endured so much! She's so proud, that's why she doesn't complain at all. But she's irritable, so irritable! That's her illness: even an angel would be irritable if ill. How dry and hot her forehead must be, what dark circles under her eyes, and . . . still and all, how beautiful the oval of her face and these luxuriant tresses, how . . .'

And he would quickly avert his eyes and walk away in haste, as if afraid of the very idea of seeing in her something other than an unfortunate, worn-out being who needed help. 'What *hopes* could there possibly be here! Oh, how low, how vile human beings are!' And he would again go back to his corner, sit down, cover his face with his hands and again fall to dreaming and remembering . . . and again hopes would glimmer before him.

'Oh, I'm so tired, oh, I'm so tired' – he would remember her exclaiming in her weak, broken voice. 'Lord! To abandon her now, and she with all of eighty kopecks. She had held out her purse, old and tiny as it was! She had come here to look for a job. Why, what did she understand about jobs, what did they understand about Russia? Why, they're like irresponsible children; everything is their own fantasies that they've made up all by themselves. And she gets angry, poor thing, that Russia isn't like their little foreign dreams! Oh, what unfortunates, what innocents! . . . Still and all, it really is cold in here.'

He remembered that she had complained, and that he had promised to light the stove. 'There's firewood here; I can bring it in as long as I don't wake her. Still, I can do that. And what should I decide about the veal? She'll get up and perhaps want something to eat . . . Well, I'll take care of that later; Kirillov doesn't sleep all night. What should I cover her with, she's sleeping so soundly, but she must be cold, oh, so cold!'

And he went to have a look at her again. Her dress had pulled up slightly, and half her right leg was bare to the knee. He turned away suddenly, almost in fright, removed his own warm overcoat and, standing there in nothing but a tattered old frock-coat, covered the bare spot, trying not to look at it.

The lighting of the firewood, the tiptoeing around, the inspection of the sleeping woman, the daydreaming in the corner and once again the inspection of the sleeping woman all took a great deal of time. Two to three hours passed. And that was precisely the time when Verkhovensky and Liputin managed to visit Kirillov. At last he too began to doze in the corner. A sudden moan came from her; she had woken up and was calling to him; he jumped up like a criminal.

'Marie! I was just about to fall asleep . . . Oh, what a vile human being I am, Marie!'

She sat up, looked around in surprise, as if not recognizing where she was, and was suddenly all aquiver with indignation and anger:

'I took your bed, I fell asleep because I was so dead tired; how dare you not wake me? How did you have the nerve to think that I intend to be a burden to you?'

'How could I wake you, Marie?'

'You could have! You should have! There's no other bed for you here, and I've taken yours! You shouldn't have put me in a false position. Or do you think I've come here to take advantage of your charity? Please take your bed at once, and I'll lie down in the corner on some chairs . . .'

'Marie, there aren't that many chairs, and there's nothing to make them up with either.'

'Well then, I'll just lie down on the floor. Otherwise you'll have to sleep on the floor yourself. I want to sleep on the floor, at once, at once!'

She got up, tried to take a step, but suddenly what seemed like a violent spasm of pain took away all her strength and all her resolve at once, and she fell back on to the bed with a loud groan. Shatov ran over to her, but Marie, hiding her face in the pillows, seized his hand and began pressing and squeezing it as hard as she could. This lasted about a minute.

'Marie, dear heart, if you need it, there's a Doctor Frenzel here, my friend, a very . . . I could run and fetch him.'

'Nonsense!'

'What do you mean "nonsense"? Tell me, Marie, where does it hurt? Maybe we could put hot compresses . . . on your stomach, for instance . . . That I can do without a doctor . . . Or maybe mustard plasters.'

'What's this all about?' she asked strangely, raising her head and looking at him fearfully.

'What do you mean, Marie?' said Shatov uncomprehendingly. 'What are you asking me? Oh, Lord, I'm completely at a loss, Marie. Forgive me for not understanding anything.'

'Oh, stop it, it's not your business to understand. And it would be very funny if you did,' she smiled bitterly. 'Talk to me about something. Walk about the room and talk. Don't stand next to me and don't look at me, I particularly ask you that for the five hundredth time!'

Shatov began to walk about the room, looking at the floor and making every effort to avoid glancing at her.

'Here – don't get angry, Marie, I beg you – there's some veal here, not far away, and tea . . . You had so little to eat before . . .'

She waved her hand with disgust and anger. Shatov bit his tongue in despair.

'Listen, I intend to open a bookbindery here, on rational

cooperative principles.² Since you live here, what do you think:
will it be successful or not?'

'Ah, Marie, people here don't read books, and there just
aren't any. So why would he take to binding books?'

'Who's "he"?'

'The local reader, and the local inhabitant generally, Marie.'

'Well, speak more clearly, then, otherwise there's no knowing
what and who "he" is. You don't know grammar.'

'It's in the spirit of the language, Marie,' Shatov muttered.

'Oh, get along with your "spirit", I'm tired of it. Why won't
the local inhabitant or reader think of binding books?'

'Because to read a book and to bind it represent two entirely
different periods of development, and huge ones at that. At first
he learns to read just a little – over the course of centuries,
naturally – but he tears the books and throws them around,
regarding them as something that's not serious. But binding
signifies respect for the book; it means that not only has he
learned to love reading, but he has recognized it as something
worthwhile. Russia as a whole hasn't developed to that stage
yet. Europe has been binding books for a long time.'

'That's rather pedantic, but at least not stupidly put and
reminds me of three years ago: you were sometimes rather witty
three years ago.'

This was said in the same dismissive tone as all her earlier
capricious remarks.

'Marie, Marie,' Shatov turned to her tenderly, 'oh, Marie! If
you only knew how much has passed and gone forever in these
three years! I heard later that you despised me for changing
my convictions. But whom did I abandon? The enemies of
living life – the outmoded little liberals who were afraid of
their own independence, the lackeys of thought, the enemies
of individuality and freedom, the decrepit proponents of everything dead and rotten! What did they have? Senility, the golden
mean, the most philistine and vile mediocrity, envious equality,
equality without personal dignity, equality as a lackey conceives
it or as it was conceived by a Frenchman in 1793³ ... But the
main thing is the scoundrels, scoundrels and more scoundrels
everywhere!'

'Yes, there are a lot of scoundrels,' she said haltingly and morbidly. She was lying stretched out and still, as if afraid to move, her head thrown back on the pillow, somewhat to the side, with a fatigued but feverish look directed at the ceiling. Her face was pale, her lips dry and parched.

'You acknowledge it, Marie, you acknowledge it!' Shatov exclaimed. She wanted to shake her head in denial, but suddenly she was racked by the same sort of spasm. Again she hid her head in the pillow and again for a full minute she squeezed as hard as she could the hand of Shatov, who had run over to her in a panic.

'Marie, Marie! Why, this could be very serious, Marie!'

'Be quiet . . . I don't want you to, I don't want you to,' she cried almost in a frenzy, again turning her face upwards, 'don't you dare look at me, with your pity! Walk about the room, say something, say . . .'

Like a lost man, Shatov was on the point of mumbling something again.

'What kind of work do you do here?' she asked, interrupting him contemptuously and impatiently.

'I work in a certain merchant's office. If I particularly wanted to, Marie, I could even make good money here.'

'So much the better for you . . .'

'Ah, don't think that way, Marie, I just said it . . .'

'And what else do you do? What do you preach? After all, you can't help but preach – that's the kind of character you have!'

'I preach God, Marie.'

'In whom you yourself don't believe. I never could understand such an idea.'

'Let's leave that for later, Marie.'

'What sort of person was this Marya Lebyadkina?'

'We'll talk about that later too, Marie.'

'Don't you dare speak to me that way! Is it true that her death can be attributed to the evil deeds . . . of these people?'

'Absolutely,' Shatov said through clenched teeth.

Marie suddenly raised her head and cried out in agony:

'Don't you dare speak to me any more about that, ever, ever!'

And she again fell back on to the bed in an attack of the same painful spasm. This was now the third time, but this time her moans had become louder, and had turned into screams.

'Oh, you intolerable man! Oh, you unbearable man!' She thrashed about, no longer sparing herself, and pushing away Shatov, who was standing over her.

'Marie, I'll do whatever you want . . . I'll walk around and talk . . .'

'But can't you really see that it's begun?'

'What's begun, Marie?'

'How should I know? You think I know anything about it? . . . Oh, curses on me! Oh, curse everything beforehand!'

'Marie, if you'd only tell me *what*'s beginning . . . otherwise I . . . what can I make of it?'

'You're an abstruse, useless windbag. Oh, curse everything in the world!'

'Marie! Marie!'

He seriously thought that she was beginning to lose her mind.

'Why, can't you really see, when all is said and done, that I'm having labour pains?' She raised herself up, looking at him with a strange, morbid anger that distorted her entire face. 'May he be cursed beforehand, this child!'

'Marie,' Shatov exclaimed, finally figuring out what was going on, 'Marie . . . But why didn't you say so before?' He suddenly collected his wits, and snatched up his cap with forceful determination.

'Well, how was I to know when I came here? Do you really think I would have come to you? I was told that I had another ten days! Where are you going? Where is it you're going? Don't you dare!'

'For the midwife! I'll sell my revolver; what's needed now is money first and foremost!'

'Don't you dare do anything, don't you dare bring a midwife. Just a peasant woman, an old woman; I have eighty kopecks in my purse . . . After all, village women give birth without midwives . . . And if I die, so much the better.'

'I'll get a midwife, and an old woman. Except how can I, how can I leave you alone, Marie!'

But realizing that it was better to leave her alone now, despite all her frenzy, than to leave her without any help later on, he dashed down the stairs as fast as he could, without listening to her moans or her enraged exclamations, and relying on his own legs, rushed headlong down the stairs.

3.

He went first to see Kirillov. It was about one o'clock in the morning. Kirillov was standing in the middle of his room.

'Kirillov, my wife is giving birth!'

'What do you mean?'

'She's giving birth, to a child!'

'You're . . . not mistaken?'

'Oh, no, no, she's having labour pains! . . . I need a peasant woman, some old woman, right now, without fail . . . Can you get one for me? You used to have a lot of old women around . . .'

'It's a great pity I'm not able to give birth,' Kirillov replied thoughtfully, 'that is, not that I'm not able to give birth, but not able to do something to make childbirth . . . I don't know how . . . or . . . No, I don't know how to say it.'

'In other words, you can't help with childbirth yourself. But that's not what I'm talking about – I'm asking for an old woman, an old woman, a peasant woman, a nurse, a servant!'

'You'll have an old woman, only perhaps not right away. If you want, instead I . . .'

'Oh, that's impossible. I'll go to Virginskaya now, to the midwife.'

'A disgusting woman!'

'Oh yes, Kirillov, yes, but she's the best! Oh yes, it will all be without reverence, without joy, with contempt, with swearing, with blasphemy – in the presence of such a great mystery, the appearance of a new being! Oh, even now she's cursing it!'

'If you want, I . . .'

'No, no, meanwhile I'll be on my way (oh, I'll drag Virginskaya here!), but you come to the bottom of my stairway now and then, and listen carefully and quietly, but don't dare go in, you'll frighten her; don't go in for any reason, just listen

. . . in case anything dreadful happens. And if anything unusual does happen, then go in.'

'I understand. I have another rouble. Here. I wanted a chicken tomorrow, but I don't want it now. Run as fast as you can, run as hard as you can. There's a samovar all night.'

Kirillov knew nothing about what was intended for Shatov now, nor had he known earlier the full extent of the danger that threatened him. He knew only that he had some old accounts to settle with 'those people', and although he actually had been partly implicated in this matter by virtue of the instructions that had been sent him from abroad (even though they were very superficial, for he had never been intimately involved in anything), but recently he had dropped everything, all his assignments, and had completely distanced himself from all causes, primarily from the 'common cause', and had devoted himself to a contemplative life. Although at the meeting Pyotr Verkhovensky had summoned Liputin to go with him to Kirillov's to ascertain whether Kirillov would take the 'Shatov matter' on himself at the given moment, he had not said a word about Shatov in his discussions with Kirillov, even by way of a hint. He probably considered it impolitic and Kirillov even unreliable, and he put it off until the following day when everything would have been done and when it would therefore 'make no difference' to Kirillov. At least, that was Pyotr Stepanovich's reasoning about Kirillov. Liputin was also very much aware that not a word had been said about Shatov, despite Pyotr Stepanovich's promise, but Liputin was too upset to protest.

Shatov ran like the wind to Muravinaya Street, cursing the distance and seeing no end to it.

He had to knock on Virginsky's door for a long time: everyone had long been asleep. But Shatov began to bang on a shutter as hard as he could and without any ceremony. A dog chained up in the yard lunged at him and let loose with angry barking. All the dogs on the street chimed in; a canine din was raised.

'Why are you knocking and what do you want?' the voice of Virginsky himself at last came from the window, sounding too soft to correspond with the 'offence'. The shutter opened partway, and the vent window all the way.

'Who's there, what sort of scoundrel is this?' shrieked a female voice, that of the old maid who was Virginsky's relative, now completely in keeping with the offence.

'It's me, Shatov, my wife has come back to me and she's now in childbirth . . .'

'Well, let her give birth; clear out of here!'

'I've come for Arina Prokhorovna, I won't leave without Arina Prokhorovna!'

'She can't go to just anyone. Night-time practice is a special category . . . Take yourself off to Mashkeyeva and don't you dare make any more noise!' the enraged female voice rattled on. Virginsky could be heard trying to stop her, but the old maid kept pushing him away and wouldn't desist.

'I won't go away!' Shatov shouted again.

'Wait, just wait!' Virginsky finally bellowed, having over-come the old maid's resistance. 'I beg you, Shatov, wait five minutes, I'll wake Arina Prokhorovna, and please, don't knock and don't shout . . . Oh, how dreadful this all is!'

After five endless minutes Arina Prokhorovna appeared.

'Your wife has come back to you?' her voice was heard from the vent window, and, to Shatov's surprise, it wasn't angry, but merely imperious as usual; but Arina Prokhorovna couldn't speak in any other way.

'Yes, my wife, and she's giving birth.'

'Marya Ignatyevna?'

'Yes, Marya Ignatyevna. Of course, Marya Ignatyevna!'

A silence ensued. Shatov waited. There was whispering in the house.

'Has she been here long?' Madame Virginskaya asked again.

'This evening, at eight o'clock. Please, come right away.'

Again there was whispering; again they seemed to be con-sulting with each other.

'Listen, you're not mistaken? Did she herself send for me?'

'No, she didn't send for you; she wants a peasant woman, a simple peasant woman so as not to burden me with expenses, but don't worry, I'll pay.'

'All right, I'll come, whether you pay or not. I always valued Marya Ignatyevna's independent way of thinking, although she perhaps doesn't remember me. Do you have the most essential things at your place?'

'There's nothing, but there'll be everything, there will be, there will be . . .'

'There's a generosity of spirit in these people, too!' Shatov thought, as he made his way to Lyamshin's. 'Convictions and a human being – these seem to be two things different in many respects. Perhaps I am guilty of a great deal before them! All are guilty, all are guilty, and . . . if only everybody were convinced of that! . . .'

He didn't have to knock on Lyamshin's door for long. To his surprise, Lyamshin instantly opened the vent window, after jumping out of bed barefoot and in his underclothes, risking a cold, even though he was very much a hypochondriac and was constantly concerned about his health. But there was a special reason for such watchfulness and haste: as a result of the meeting of *our people*, Lyamshin had been trembling all evening and was far too upset to get to sleep: he kept picturing the visit of certain uninvited and certainly unwanted guests. The news that Shatov was denouncing them tormented him more than anything else . . . And now suddenly, as though by design, there had come such a dreadfully loud knocking on the window!

On catching sight of Shatov, he was so terrified that he immediately slammed the vent window shut and ran off to his bed. Shatov set up a frenzied knocking and shouting.

'How dare you knock like that in the middle of the night?' Lyamshin shouted menacingly, but petrified with fear when, after at least two minutes, he ventured to open the vent window again to make certain finally that Shatov had come alone.

'Here's your revolver. Take it back, and give me fifteen roubles.'

'What is this? Are you drunk? This is highway robbery; I'll catch cold. Wait a minute, I'll just throw a plaid over me.'

'Give me fifteen roubles now. If you don't, I'll keep on knocking and shouting till dawn, and smash the window frame.'

'And I'll shout for the police, and you'll be taken off to the lock-up.'

'And am I mute or what? You don't think I'll shout for the police? Who has more to fear from the police, you or me?'

'And you can entertain such vile thoughts . . . I know what you're hinting at . . . Wait, wait, for heaven's sake, don't knock! I ask you, who has money at night? Well then, what do you need money for if you're not drunk?'

'My wife has come back to me. I've knocked off ten roubles for you; I haven't fired it even once. Take the revolver, take it this very minute.'

Lyamshin mechanically reached his hand through the vent window and took the revolver. He waited a moment and then suddenly thrust his head through the vent and babbled, as if he were unaware of what he was doing, and with a chill running up and down his spine:

'You're lying, your wife hasn't come back to you at all. It's . . . it's just that you want to run off somewhere.'

'You're a fool, where is there for me to run? Let your Pyotr Verkhovensky run away, not me. I've just been at Virginskaya's house, the midwife, and she's agreed to come to my place right away. You can ask. My wife is in labour; I need money; give me some money!'

Ideas burst forth like a whole display of fireworks in Lyamshin's resourceful head. Everything immediately took a different turn, but he was still too afraid to think straight.

'But how is it . . . why, you're not living with your wife?'

'I'll smash your head for asking such questions.'

'Oh, my God, forgive me, I understand, I was just stunned . . . But I understand, I understand. But . . . but – will Arina Prokhorovna really come? You just said that she's gone to your place. You know, that's just not true. You see, you see, you see how at every step you say things that aren't true.'

'She's probably sitting with my wife right now; don't hold me up; it's not my fault that you're stupid.'

'It's not true, I'm not stupid. Pardon me, there's no way I can . . .'

And, now utterly flustered, for a third time he began shutting the window again, but Shatov began howling so loudly that he promptly stuck his head out again.

'But this is a complete infringement of my privacy! What is it you want from me, well, what, what? State it clearly! And note, note well, in the middle of the night like this!'

'I want fifteen roubles, you mutton-head!'

'Well, maybe I just don't want to take the revolver back. You have no right. You bought the thing, and that's that, and you have no right. There's no way I can come up with money like that in the middle of the night. Where will I get money like that?'

'You always have money. I've knocked off ten roubles for you, but everybody knows you're a nasty little Jew.'

'Come back the day after tomorrow – you hear, day after tomorrow in the morning, at exactly twelve o'clock, and I'll give you everything, everything, is that all right?'

For the third time Shatov set up a frenzied banging on the window frame:

'Give me ten roubles, and the other five first thing in the morning.'

'No, five the day after tomorrow, but tomorrow, I swear, I can't. Best that you don't come at all, best that you don't come.'

'Give me ten; oh, you bastard!'

'Why are you swearing so? Just a minute, I have to have some light here. You've gone and broken the glass ... Who swears like that at night? There!' He handed a banknote through the window.

Shatov snatched it – it was a five-rouble note.

'I swear, I can't, you can cut my throat but I can't. The day after tomorrow I can give you all of it, but today I can't do a thing.'

'I won't leave!' Shatov bellowed.

'Well then, take this, here's some more, and see here's some more, but I won't give you anything beyond that. Even if you yell at the top of your lungs I won't give you anything more, no matter what happens, I won't give you more, I won't, I won't, I won't!'

He was in a state of frenzy, in despair, in a sweat. The two banknotes he had just handed over were for a rouble each. Shatov now had a total of seven roubles.

'Oh, the hell with you, I'll come tomorrow. I'll beat you within an inch of your life, Lyamshin, if you don't have eight roubles ready for me.'

'Well, I won't be at home, you fool!' Lyamshin thought quickly to himself.

'Wait, wait!' he shouted in a fury after Shatov, who had already begun to run off. 'Stop, come back! Tell me, please, was it true what you said, that your wife has come back to you?'

'Fool!' Shatov spat and ran home as fast as his legs would carry him.

4.

I will note that Arina Prokhorovna knew nothing about the plans that had been formulated during the previous day's meeting. On returning home, Virginsky felt stunned and weak, and didn't dare tell her about the decision that had been taken. Still and all, he couldn't keep himself from revealing half of it – that is, all the information communicated by Verkhovensky about Shatov's definite intention to denounce them; but he went on to declare that he didn't completely trust the information. Arina Prokhorovna was terribly frightened. That's why, when Shatov ran to see her, she immediately decided to come, even though she was exhausted from having spent the whole of the previous night with a woman giving birth. She had always been convinced that 'a piece of trash like Shatov was capable of vile acts against society', but the arrival of Marya Ignatyevna put the whole matter in a different light. Shatov's apprehensions, the desperate tone of his requests, his entreaties for help marked a drastic change in the traitor's feelings: a man who had resolved even to betray himself for the sole purpose of ruining others would presumably look and sound differently than his appearance suggested. In short, Arina Prokhorovna resolved to examine everything for herself, with her own eyes. Virginsky was very pleased with her decisiveness – it was as if five poods had been lifted from him! He even felt a quickening of hope: Shatov's whole appearance struck him as incompatible with Verkhovensky's supposition.

Shatov hadn't been mistaken: on returning home he found
Arina Prokhorovna already with Marie. She had just arrived,
and had scornfully chased away Kirillov, who had been hanging
about at the foot of the stairs. She quickly introduced herself
to Marie, who didn't recognize her as someone she had already
met; she found her in a 'very bad state', that is, querulous,
distraught, and 'in the most craven despair', and in something
like five minutes she had established the upper hand as far as
her patient's objections were concerned.

'Why were you going on about not wanting an expensive
midwife?' she was saying just as Shatov was coming in. 'It's utter
nonsense, false ideas as the result of your abnormal situation. If
you'd got the help of some simple old woman, a peasant midwife, you'd have a fifty-fifty chance that things would end badly,
and in addition, you'd have more fuss and bother and more
expense than with an expensive midwife. How do you know
that I'm an expensive midwife? You can pay later, I won't take
anything extra from you and I can guarantee success. In my
hands you won't die, I've seen worse cases. And what's more
I'll send the baby to a foundling home tomorrow for you, and
then to the country to be raised, and that'll be the end of it.
And then you'll get your health back, you'll undertake some
sensible work and in very short order you'll pay Shatov back
for the lodging and the expenses, which certainly won't be all
that much.'

'That's not the point . . . I have no right to be a burden . . .'

'Rational and civic feelings, but believe me, Shatov will spend
practically nothing if only he'll stop playing the eccentric and
turn himself, even ever so slightly, into a man of true ideas. All
he needs is not to do anything stupid, not go banging his drum,
not go running through the town like a madman. If we don't
keep him in tow, he'll probably stir up all the local doctors by
morning; after all, he stirred up all the dogs in my street. There's
no need for doctors, I've already told you that I vouch for
everything. An old woman can perhaps be hired as a servant,
that doesn't cost anything. However, he himself can be good
for something besides doing stupid things. He has hands, he
has feet, he can run to the pharmacy without offending your

feelings with his charity. What the Devil kind of charity is that! Isn't he the one who got you into this situation? Isn't he the one who made you quarrel with the family where you were governess, for the egotistic purpose of marrying you? We've heard, you see . . . However, he himself just now ran to our place like a crazy man and shouted for the whole street to hear. I'm not forcing myself on anyone, and I've come here just for you, on the principle that all of our people are bound by solidarity; I told him this even before I left the house. If you think I don't need to be here, then forgive me, but you never know what trouble you might get into, and it could so easily be avoided.'

And she even got up from her chair.

Marie was so helpless, was suffering so much and, to tell the truth, was so frightened of what lay before her that she didn't dare dismiss Virginskaya. But this woman suddenly became hateful to her: she was talking about the wrong thing entirely, that was not at all what lay in Marie's heart! But what Virginskaya had prophesied about the possibility of death at the hands of an inexperienced midwife overcame her revulsion. But to make up for it, from that moment on she became even more demanding, even more merciless towards Shatov. Things finally reached the point where she forbade him not only to look at her, but even to stand facing her. Her pains grew more intense. Her curses, even her abuse became more savage.

'Ah, well, we'll send him out,' snapped Arina Prokhorovna. 'He looks dreadful, he's only scaring you; he's pale as a corpse! What's it to you, you funny, ridiculous man, please tell me that? There's a comedy for you!'

Shatov made no reply; he had resolved to say nothing.

'I've seen some stupid fathers in such cases, who lose their minds too. But you know, at least they . . .'

'Stop it, or leave me alone so that I can die! Don't say another word! I don't want you to, I don't want you to!' Marie started shouting.

'It's impossible not to say another word unless you have lost your reason; that's what I understand to be the case in your situation. At the very least we need to get down to business.

Tell me, has anything been prepared here? You answer, Shatov, she's not up to it.'

'Tell me, what precisely is needed?'

'That means nothing has been prepared.'

She ticked off everything that was absolutely essential, and, to give her her due, she limited herself to the barest of bare essentials. Some things were found in Shatov's room. Marie produced a key and handed it to him, so that he could look in her bag. Since his hands were shaking, he spent more time than necessary fumbling around as he tried to unlock the unfamiliar catch. Marie flew into a rage, but when Arina Prokhorovna jumped up to take the key away from him, Marie was not about to permit her to look into the bag, and with impulsive cries and tears insisted that Shatov himself should be the one to open it.

For the other things it was necessary to run down to Kirillov's. No sooner had Shatov turned to go than Marie immediately began calling him back frantically, and she calmed down only when Shatov dashed back from the staircase and explained to her that he was going out only for a minute, for the most essential things, and that he would come back right away.

'Well, you're a hard one to please, my lady,' Arina Prokhorovna laughed. 'First it's stand with your face to the wall and don't dare look at me, then it's don't you dare leave me even for a second or else you'll start crying. He might start getting some ideas if you keep that up. Now, now, don't start carrying on, stop sulking, I'm just making fun.'

'He wouldn't dare get any ideas.'

'Tsk, tsk, tsk, if he weren't in love with you like a sheep, he wouldn't be running around the streets like a madman and wouldn't be stirring up all the dogs in town. He broke my window frame.'

5.

Shatov found Kirillov still pacing from corner to corner, so distracted that he had even forgotten about the arrival of Shatov's wife, and listened to him without understanding anything.

'Oh, yes,' he suddenly remembered, as if tearing himself away with effort and only for a moment, from some idea that had absorbed him ... 'Yes, the old woman ... A wife or an old woman. Wait: both a wife and an old woman, right? I remember: I was walking: the old woman will come, only not right away. Take a pillow. What else? Yes ... Wait, do you ever have moments of eternal harmony, Shatov?'

'You know, Kirillov, you must put a stop to not sleeping at night.'

Kirillov snapped out of it and, strangely enough, began to speak much more coherently than he usually did; it was evident that he had already formulated all of this long before, and had perhaps written it down.

'There are seconds – they come only five or six at a time – when you suddenly feel the presence of an eternal harmony that has been fully attained. This is not something earthly. I'm not saying that it's heavenly, but that man in his earthly form cannot endure it. He must change physically or else die. It is a clear and unambiguous feeling. It's as if you suddenly have a sense of nature as a whole, and you suddenly say: yes, this is true. God, when he was creating the world, said at the end of each day of creation: "Yes, this is true, this is good."[4] This ... this is not deep emotion, but is simply joy. You don't forgive anything, because there's no longer anything to forgive. You don't really love – oh, this is higher than love! If it lasts longer than five seconds, your soul can't endure it and must disappear. In these five seconds I live an entire lifetime, and for them I will give my entire life, because it's worth it. In order to endure ten seconds, one must change physically. I think that man should stop giving birth. Why have children, why have evolution if the goal has been attained? In the Gospels it is said that in the resurrection there will be no childbirth, but all will be like God's angels.[5] It's a hint. Is your wife giving birth?'

'Kirillov, does this happen often?'

'Once every three days, once a week.'

'You don't have epilepsy?'[6]

'No.'

'That means you will. Take care, Kirillov, I've heard that's precisely how epilepsy begins. An epileptic gave me a detailed description of these sensations just before an attack, precisely as you did: he specified exactly five seconds, and said that more could not be endured. You remember Mohammed's pitcher that didn't spill while he was flying all over paradise on his horse.[7] The pitcher is those same five seconds; it is highly reminiscent of your harmony, and Mohammed was an epileptic. Take care, Kirillov, epilepsy!'

'It won't spill,' Kirillov softly laughed.

6.

The night was passing. Shatov was sent off, cursed, summoned. Marie was more afraid for her life than she had ever been. She shouted that she wanted to live, 'absolutely, absolutely!' and that she was afraid of dying. 'No, don't, no, don't!' she kept repeating. If it hadn't been for Arina Prokhorovna, things would have been very bad. Little by little she established complete domination over the patient. Marie began obeying her every word, her every order, like a child. Arina Prokhorovna got her way with strictness, not with kindness, but she worked masterfully. It began to grow light. Arina Prokhorovna suddenly imagined that Shatov had just run out on to the staircase and was praying to God, and she began to laugh. Marie also began to laugh, spitefully and bitterly, as if that sort of laughter made her feel better. Finally, Shatov was chased out altogether. A damp, cold morning broke. He leaned his face against the wall, in the corner, just as he had been doing the night before when Erkel came in. He was trembling like a leaf and was afraid to think, but his mind would catch at everything that presented itself, as is the case when one is dreaming. Daydreams were constantly distracting him and constantly breaking off like rotten threads. Finally, what came from the room was no longer moaning, but dreadful, sheer animal cries, unbearable, impossible. He thought of stopping up his ears, but couldn't do so, and fell on his knees, unconsciously repeating: 'Marie, Marie!' And then there finally came a cry, a new cry, which made

Shatov start and jump up from his knees. The cry of an infant, weak and broken. He crossed himself and dashed into the room. In Arina Prokhorovna's arms was a small, red, wrinkled creature, crying and waving its arms and legs, terribly helpless, and as vulnerable as a speck of dust to the first puff of wind, but crying and giving notice of itself as if it also had every right to life. Marie was lying there seemingly insensible, but a moment later she opened her eyes and looked at Shatov strangely, ever so strangely: her look was somehow utterly new, though in precisely what way, he was incapable of understanding, but never before had he seen or remembered such a look on her face.

'A boy? A boy?' she asked Arina Prokhorovna in a suffering voice.

'A little boy!' came the reply, as the baby was being swaddled.

After she had swaddled him, and was looking to lay him crosswise on the bed between the two pillows, she handed him to Shatov to hold for a moment. Marie nodded to him on the sly, as if she were afraid of Arina Prokhorovna. Shatov understood and brought the baby to show her.

'So . . . handsome,' she whispered feebly with a smile.

'Ugh! See how he looks!' a triumphant Arina Prokhorovna said with a happy laugh, glancing at Shatov's face. 'What a face he has on him!'

'Be happy, Arina Prokhorovna . . . It's a great joy,' Shatov babbled with an idiotically blissful look on his face, all aglow after the two words Marie had said about the baby.

'What's the point of such great joy anyway?' Arina Prokhorovna said happily, bustling about, tidying up and working like a convict.

'The mystery of the appearance of a new being, a great and inexplicable mystery, Arina Prokhorovna, and what a pity you don't understand it!'

Shatov was muttering incoherently, ecstatically, in a kind of stupor. Something seemed to be dislodging itself in his head and pouring out of his soul all on its own, apart from his will.

'There were two, and suddenly there's a third person, a new

spirit, whole and finished as human hands couldn't make him, a new thought and a new love – it's even terrifying . . . And there's nothing higher in the world!'

'Oh, listen to him going on! It's simply the further development of the organism, and nothing more, no mystery,' Arina Prokhorovna was guffawing sincerely and happily. 'Otherwise any old fly is a mystery. But here's what I think: superfluous people shouldn't be born. First of all everything should be recast so they won't be superfluous, and then you proceed to bring them into the world. As things stand, he should be taken to the foundling home the day after tomorrow . . . However, that's as it should be.'

'He will never leave me for any foundling home!' Shatov pronounced firmly, his eyes fixed on the floor.

'Are you adopting him?'

'He *is* my son.'

'Of course, he's a Shatov, a Shatov by law, and there's no need for you to represent yourself as a benefactor of the human race. People can't get along without fine phrases. Well, well, that's all very fine, my friends, but here's what,' she finally finished tidying up, 'it's time for me to go. I'll come again in the morning and in the evening if necessary, and now, since everything went so very well, I've got to run off to attend to others, who've been expecting me for a long time now. I hear you've got some old woman sitting somewhere, Shatov; an old woman is all well and good, but don't you go and leave her, good little husband that you are. Sit beside her, maybe you'll be useful for something. I don't think Marya Ignatyevna will chase you away . . . now, now, I'm just joking.'

At the gate, to which Shatov had escorted her, she added, now for his ears only:

'You've given me enough to laugh about for the rest of my life. I won't take any money from you; I'll go on laughing in my sleep. I've never seen anything funnier than you tonight.'

She left entirely satisfied. Shatov's appearance and conversation made it clear as day that this man 'was getting ready for all this father stuff, and was a complete doormat'. She made a point of dashing home to tell Virginsky about all this, although it would have been more direct and closer for her to go to another patient.

'Marie, she told you to wait a bit before you go to sleep again, even though I can see that it's awfully hard for you,' Shatov began timidly. 'I'll sit here by the window just in case you need something, all right?'

And he took a seat by the window, behind the sofa, so that she couldn't see him at all. But no more than a minute had passed when she called out to him and in a tone of disgust asked him to adjust her pillow. He began setting it to rights. She was looking angrily at the wall.

'Not that way, oh, not that way . . . You're all thumbs!'

Shatov adjusted it again.

'Bend down towards me,' she suddenly said fiercely, trying as best she could not to look at him.

He trembled, but bent down.

'Lower . . . not that way . . . closer,' and suddenly her left hand snaked around his neck, and on his forehead he felt her firm, moist kiss.

'Marie!'

Her lips were quivering, she was trying to hold back, but suddenly she raised herself and, with flashing eyes, said:

'Nikolay Stavrogin is a scoundrel!'

And with no strength left, she fell face first into the pillow, as if cut down at the roots, tightly squeezing Shatov's hand in hers.

From that moment on, she no longer let him leave her side; she demanded that he sit by the head of her bed. She could not speak much, but she kept looking at him and smiling at him like someone blessed. She suddenly seemed to have turned into a silly little girl. It was as if everything had been transformed. Shatov at one moment was crying like a little boy, and at the next saying God knows what, in a wild, stunned and inspired way. He was kissing her hands; she was listening to him in ecstasy, perhaps without understanding, but tenderly fingering his hair with a feeble hand, stroking it, admiring it. He talked to her about Kirillov, about their beginning to live now 'again and forever', about the existence of God, about how everyone is good . . . Rapturously, they again took the baby out to have a look at him.

'Marie,' he exclaimed, as he held the baby in his arms, 'the old ravings, the shame and the decay are all over and done with! Let's work hard and set out on a new path, the three of us, yes, yes! . . . Oh, yes: what are we going to name him, Marie?'

'Him? What shall we name him?' she repeated with surprise, and suddenly a terrible sadness showed on her face.

She clasped her hands, looked reproachfully at Shatov and threw herself face down on the pillow.

'Marie, what's wrong with you?' he exclaimed in sorrow and fright.

'And how could you, how could you . . . Oh, you ungrateful man!'

'Marie, forgive me, Marie, I was simply asking what to name him. I don't know . . .'

'Ivan, Ivan,' she raised her flushed and tear-drenched face, 'can you really imagine that I would choose some other *dreadful* name?'

'Marie, calm down; oh, how upset you are!'

'More rude behaviour! What do you attribute my upset condition to? I'll bet that if I'd said to name him . . . that dreadful name, you'd have gone right ahead and agreed, you wouldn't even have noticed! Oh, ungrateful people, low people, everyone, everyone!'

A minute later they had of course made peace. Shatov talked her into going to sleep. She fell asleep, but still not releasing his hand from hers, would wake up often and glance at him as if afraid that he would leave, and then she would fall asleep again.

Kirillov sent an old woman to 'congratulate' them, and some hot tea besides, some freshly cooked cutlets, and bouillon and white bread for Marya Ignatyevna. The sick woman greedily drank up the bouillon, the old woman swaddled the baby, and Marie forced Shatov to have a cutlet as well.

Time was passing. An exhausted Shatov proceeded to fall asleep on his chair, with his head on Marya's pillow. That was how Arina Prokhorovna found them. She had kept her word, cheerfully woke them up, began to talk about what needed talking about with Marie, looked the child over and again ordered Shatov not to go away. Then, after making a joke about the 'married couple' with a certain tinge of contempt and superiority, she left just as satisfied as she had been earlier.

It had already grown completely dark when Shatov woke up. He hurried to light a candle and ran after the old woman, but he had hardly stepped on to the stairway when he was struck by the quiet, unhurried steps of some person who was climbing up in his direction. Erkel came in.

'Don't come in!' Shatov whispered, and impulsively seizing him by the hand, dragged him back to the gate. 'Wait here, I'll be right out, I completely forgot about you, completely! Oh, but how you've brought it all back!'

He was in such a hurry that he didn't even run to Kirillov's house, but only summoned the old woman. Marie became despairing and indignant that he 'could even think of leaving her alone'.

'But,' he shouted in ecstasy, 'this is now absolutely the last step! And then a new path, and we shall never ever again think of the old horror!'

He managed somehow to persuade her, and promised to return at exactly nine o'clock. He kissed her hard, kissed the baby and quickly ran down to Erkel.

Both set out for the Stavrogin park in Skvoreshniki, where, about a year and a half earlier, in an isolated place, on the very edge of the park, just where the pine forest begins, he had buried the printing press that had been entrusted to him. The place was wild and deserted, quite inconspicuous, at some distance from the Stavrogin house. From Filippov's house they had to walk about three and a half versts, perhaps four.

'Do we really have to go the whole way on foot? I'll hire a cab.'

'I beg you in all earnestness not to do that,' Erkel objected, 'they insisted on it specifically. The cab driver would be a witness.'

'Oh, well . . . the Devil with it! It doesn't matter, as long as it's over with, over with!'

They began to walk very rapidly.

'Erkel, you're still a little boy,' Shatov shouted, 'have you ever been happy?'

'You seem to be very happy right now,' Erkel observed with curiosity.

CHAPTER 6

A Night of Many Difficulties

I.

In the course of the day Virginsky took two hours to run around to all of *our people* and notify them that Shatov would probably not denounce them, because his wife had returned to him and a baby had been born, and, 'knowing the human heart', it was impossible to suppose that he could be dangerous at such a time. But to his bewilderment he found almost no one at home except Erkel and Lyamshin. Erkel heard him out silently, and looked him brightly in the eyes. But to the direct question of 'whether he would come at six o'clock or not', he replied with the brightest of smiles that 'of course he would come'.

Lyamshin was lying down, apparently very seriously ill, with his head wrapped in a blanket. He grew frightened when Virginsky came in, and as soon as Virginsky began talking, he suddenly waved his arms from beneath the blanket, begging that he be left in peace. However, he listened to all that was said about Shatov, and for some reason was extraordinarily astonished by the news that no one was at home. It also turned out that he already knew (through Liputin) about Fedka's death and he told Virginsky about it in a hasty and disconnected way, which in turn astonished Virginsky. But to Virginsky's direct question, 'Do we have to go or not?' he suddenly began to plead again, waving his arms, that it was 'none of his concern, that he knew nothing, and that he should be left in peace'.

Virginsky returned home depressed and highly agitated. It also weighed on his mind that he was supposed to conceal everything from his family; he was accustomed to telling his wife everything, and if a new idea had not kindled in his fevered

brain at that very moment, a certain new conciliatory plan
for further activity, then perhaps he would have taken to his
bed, like Lyamshin. But his new idea bucked him up, and
what's more, he even began to await the appointed time with
impatience, and went off to the meeting place even earlier than
necessary.

It was a very gloomy place,[1] at the end of the Stavrogins'
huge park. Later I made a point of going to have a look at it.
How dismal it must have seemed on that harsh autumn evening.
The old forest preserve began here: huge, ancient pine trees
stood as gloomy and vague shapes in the gloom. The gloom
was such that at a distance of two steps it was almost impossible
to make one another out, but Pyotr Stepanovich, Liputin and
then Erkel had brought lanterns. No one knew for what purpose
and in what remote time a rather ridiculous grotto had been
built here out of natural unhewn stones. A table and benches
inside the grotto had long ago rotted and fallen apart. Some
two hundred paces to the right the park's third pond came to
an end. These three ponds, which began at the house itself,
stretched, one after the other, for more than a verst, to the very
end of the park. It was hard to imagine that any noise, shout
or even shot could reach the inhabitants of the Stavrogins'
deserted house. With yesterday's departure of Nikolay Vsevolodovich and with the absence of Aleksey Yegorych no more
than five or six servants remained living in the entire house, all
of an old and retired nature, so to speak. In any event, it could
be supposed with almost complete certainty that even if shrieks
and cries for help were to be heard by any of these isolated
inhabitants, the reaction would be only fear, but not one of
them would have stirred from their warm stoves and heated
stove-benches to offer any help.

At twenty minutes past six almost everyone except Erkel,
who had been dispatched to fetch Shatov, had turned up at the
meeting place. On this occasion Pyotr Stepanovich wasn't late;
he arrived with Tolkachenko. Tolkachenko was frowning and
preoccupied; all his simulated and arrogantly boastful decisiveness had vanished. He virtually didn't leave Pyotr Stepanovich's side and seemed suddenly to have become boundlessly

devoted to him; he made a point of frequently creeping closer to exchange whispers with him, but Pyotr Stepanovich scarcely answered him or else mumbled something in irritation to get rid of him.

Shigalyov and Virginsky had appeared even a little earlier than Pyotr Stepanovich, and when he turned up they immediately withdrew slightly to one side, in profound and obviously prearranged silence. Pyotr Stepanovich raised the lantern and examined them with unceremonious and insulting attentiveness. 'They want to speak,' flashed through his head.

'Lyamshin isn't here?' he asked Virginsky. 'Who said that he was sick?'

'I'm here,' Lyamshin replied, suddenly stepping out from behind a tree. He was wearing a warm coat and was snugly wrapped up in his plaid, so that it was hard to make his face out even with the help of the lantern.

'So Liputin's the only one who's not here?'

Liputin too silently stepped out from behind the grotto. Pyotr Stepanovich again raised the lantern.

'Why did you hide in there? Why didn't you come out?'

'I suppose we've all retained the right to the freedom . . . of our movements,' Liputin began to grumble, though probably not fully understanding what he wanted to express.

'Gentlemen,' Pyotr Stepanovich raised his voice, speaking for the first time in more than a half-whisper, which produced an effect. 'I think you understand very well that we have no time to rehash things now. Everything was said and chewed over yesterday, straightforwardly and to the point. But as I can see from your faces, someone wants to say something; in that case, I ask that it be done as quickly as possible. The Devil take it, there's little time, and Erkel may bring him at any moment . . .'

'He will definitely bring him,' Tolkachenko interjected for some reason.

'If I'm not mistaken, we'll begin with handing over the printing press?' Liputin inquired, again seeming not to understand why he was asking the question.

'Well, naturally, we don't want to lose the thing,' Pyotr Stepanovich raised the lantern to his face. 'But look, yesterday we all agreed that we don't actually need to take possession of it. Let him just show us the place where he's buried it; we can dig it up ourselves later. I know it's ten paces somewhere from some corner of this grotto . . . But damn it all, how could you possibly have forgotten that, Liputin? It was agreed that you should meet him alone, and that we would come out later . . . It's strange that you're asking, or are you just asking for the sake of asking something?'

Liputin maintained a gloomy silence. Everyone kept silent. The wind was swaying the tops of the pines.

'However, I hope, gentlemen, that everyone will do his duty,' Pyotr Stepanovich broke in impatiently.

'I know that Shatov's wife has come back and has had a baby,' Virginsky suddenly said, excitedly and hurriedly, barely articulating his words and gesticulating. 'Knowing the human heart . . . we can rest assured that he won't denounce us now . . . because he's a happy man . . . So I went to see everyone this morning and found no one at home . . . so perhaps there's no need to do anything at all now . . .'

He stopped; his breath caught in his throat.

'If you, Mr Virginsky, should suddenly become happy,' Pyotr Stepanovich took a step towards him, 'would you forget about – not a denunciation, there's no question of that – but some risky heroic deed as a citizen, which you had planned before your happiness came and which you regarded as your duty and obligation, despite the risk and the loss of happiness?'

'No, I wouldn't forget about it! I wouldn't forget about it for anything in the world!' Virginsky said in a ridiculously heated tone, gesticulating with his whole body.

'You would rather become unhappy again than a scoundrel?'

'Yes, yes . . . even quite to the contrary . . . I'd rather be an utter scoundrel . . . that is, no . . . although certainly not a scoundrel, but, on the contrary, utterly unhappy, rather than be a scoundrel.'

'Well, you should know that Shatov regards his denunciation as his heroic deed as a citizen, an expression of his highest conviction, and the proof is that he himself is at some risk in the eyes of the government, although he will of course be forgiven a great deal for his denunciation. A man like that will certainly never renounce anything. No manner of happiness will win out: in a day he'll come to his senses, reproach himself and go and do his duty. Besides, I can't see where there's any happiness in the fact that his wife, after three years, has come to his house to give birth to Stavrogin's child.'

'But after all, no one has seen any denunciation,' Shigalyov said suddenly and insistently.

'*I* have seen the denunciation,' Pyotr Stepanovich shouted, 'it exists, and all this is dreadfully stupid, gentlemen!'

'And I,' Virginsky suddenly flared up, 'I protest . . . I protest as vigorously as I can . . . I want . . . This is what I want: when he gets here, I want all of us to come out and ask him. If it's true, then we accept his repentance, and if he gives his word of honour, then we let him go. In any case, we'll have a trial; we'll have a trial; we'll act only after a trial. And not us hiding, and then falling upon him.'

'To put the common cause at risk because of someone's word of honour is the height of stupidity! Damn it all, that's just plain stupid now, gentlemen! And what role are you proposing to assume at the moment of danger?'

'I protest, I protest,' Virginsky kept repeating.

'At least don't shout, we won't hear the signal. Shatov, gentlemen . . . (Damn it all, how stupid this all is now!) I've already told you that Shatov is a Slavophile, in other words, one of the most stupid people . . . However, damn it, that's neither here not there, and the hell with it! You're just trying to throw me off the track! . . . Shatov, gentlemen, was an embittered man, but since he belonged to the society, whether he wanted to or not, I was hoping until the last minute that he could be of service to the common cause and be used as an embittered man. I looked after him and spared him, despite the most precise instructions . . . I spared him a hundred times more than he deserved! But he ended by denouncing us, so damn him, to hell with him! . . . And just let somebody try to wriggle out of it now! Not one of us has the right to abandon the cause! You can exchange kisses with him if you want, but you don't have the right to stake the common cause on someone's word of honour! That's the way swine and people in the pay of the government behave!'

'Who here has been bribed by the government?' Liputin again tried to ascertain.

'You, perhaps. You'd do better to keep quiet, Liputin, you're only saying that out of habit. The people in the pay of the government, gentlemen, are the ones who get cold feet at the moment of danger. You can always find some fool who's frightened and at the last minute runs off and shouts: "Oh, forgive me, I'll betray them all!" But you should know, gentlemen, that you'll no longer be forgiven for any denunciation. Even if they lighten your sentence in court, each of you will still be sent to Siberia, and besides that, you won't escape another sword either. And the other sword is much sharper than the government's.'

Pyotr Stepanovich was in a fury and had said too much. Shigalyov took three resolute steps towards him.

'Since yesterday evening I have given the matter a great deal of thought,' he began confidently and methodically, as he always did (and it seems to me that if the ground had given way beneath him, even then he wouldn't have raised his voice or changed one iota of anything in his methodical presentation). 'Having given the matter a great deal of thought, I have decided that the proposed murder is not only a waste of valuable time, which could be used in a more essential and relevant way, but above and beyond that, it represents the sort of pernicious deviation from the normal path that has always done the utmost harm to the cause and has sidetracked its successes for decades, by subordinating itself to the influence of frivolous and primarily political people, instead of pure socialists. I have appeared here solely to protest against the proposed undertaking, for general edification, and then to remove myself from the present moment, which you, I don't know why, call your moment of danger. I am leaving – not because I'm afraid of this danger, and not out of any sentiment for Shatov, whom I have absolutely no desire to kiss, but solely because this whole business, from beginning to end, literally stands in contradiction to my programme. As far as my denouncing you and being in the pay of the government, you can rest fully assured: there will be no denunciation.'

He turned and began walking away.

'Damn it all, he'll run across them and warn Shatov!' Pyotr Stepanovich cried out and grabbed his revolver. The click of the gun being cocked could be heard.

'You can rest assured,' Shigalyov turned around again, 'that when I do meet Shatov on the way I may very well exchange bows with him, but I won't warn him.'

'And do you know what the penalty is for that, Mr Fourier?'

'I beg you to note that I am not Fourier. By confusing me with that sentimental, abstract mumbler, you merely prove that even though you held my manuscript in your hands, it's utterly unfamiliar to you. As far as your revenge is concerned, I will tell you that it's pointless to cock the gun; at this moment it's not at all in your interest. But if you threaten me tomorrow or the day after, then again, you'll gain nothing for yourself by shooting me except unnecessary trouble. You'll kill me, but sooner or later you'll come round to my system. Goodbye.'

At that instant, some two hundred paces away, from the park, in the direction of the pond, a whistle was heard. Liputin promptly answered, also with a whistle, as they had agreed the day before (he didn't rely on his rather toothless mouth for this purpose, but had bought at the bazaar that morning a child's clay whistle for a kopeck). Erkel had managed to warn Shatov along the way that there would be whistles, so that no doubt would creep into his mind.

'Don't worry, I'll go round them on the other side, and they won't notice me at all,' Shigalyov announced in a loud whisper, and then, without hurrying or quickening his step, he set out for home through the dark park.

Now it is fully known, down to the smallest details, how this dreadful event occurred. At first Liputin met Erkel and Shatov right at the grotto. Shatov didn't bow to him and didn't offer his hand, but immediately held forth, hastily and loudly:

'Well then, where's your spade, and don't you have another lantern? Don't be afraid, there's absolutely no one here, and they can't hear anything in Skvoreshniki, even if you should fire off a cannon. It's here, right here, in this very spot . . .'

And indeed he proceeded to stamp his foot ten paces from the rear corner of the grotto, in the direction of the forest. At that very moment Tolkachenko rushed from behind a tree and jumped on him from the rear, and Erkel also grabbed him from behind by the elbows. Liputin lunged forward. All three immediately knocked him off his feet and pressed him to the ground. Then Pyotr Stepanovich ran up with his revolver. They say that Shatov managed to turn his head towards him and so could make him out and recognize him. Three lanterns illuminated the scene. Shatov suddenly let out a brief and despairing shout, but they didn't let him go on: Pyotr Stepanovich pressed the revolver tightly and firmly, point-blank, against his forehead, and pulled the trigger. Apparently the shot wasn't very loud; at least, nothing was heard in Skvoreshniki. Shigalyov, who had barely managed to get some three hundred paces away, of course heard it – he heard both the shout and the shot, but according to his own testimony, he didn't turn around and didn't even stop. Death occurred almost instantaneously. Pyotr Stepanovich was the only one who remained in full possession of his faculties ·· I don't think it was actually cold-bloodedness. Squatting down, he rummaged in the dead man's pockets quickly but with a firm hand. There wasn't any money (Shatov's wallet was still under Marya Ignatyevna's pillow). Two or three pieces of paper of no importance were found: a note from his office, the title of some book and an old bill from a tavern abroad, which, Lord knows why, had been preserved for two years in his pocket. Pyotr Stepanovich transferred the papers into his pocket, and suddenly noticing that everyone had crowded around, looking at the corpse and not doing anything, he began berating and pushing them to act, angrily and rudely. Tolkachenko and Erkel snapped to, ran off and in an instant brought from the grotto the two stones that had been put there that morning, each weighing about twenty pounds, and already prepared, that is, tightly and securely tied with cord. Since the corpse was destined to be carried to the nearest (the third) pond and sunk in it, they began tying these stones to him, to his feet and his neck. Pyotr Stepanovich did the tying, while Tolkachenko and Erkel only held the stones and passed them to him each in turn. Erkel passed him the first one, and while Pyotr Stepanovich, growling and cursing, was tying the corpse's feet with rope and attaching this first stone to him, Tolkachenko, throughout all this rather protracted business, kept holding on to his stone with drooping arms, his entire body bent sharply forward in a seemingly respectful attitude, in order to hand it over without delay at the first request, and not once did he think of lowering his burden to the ground in the meantime. When both stones had finally been tied on, and Pyotr Stepanovich had got to his feet to scrutinize the faces of those present, then suddenly something strange happened, completely unexpected, and surprising to almost everyone.

As has already been said, almost all of them were standing and doing nothing, with the partial exception of Tolkachenko and Erkel. Although Virginsky rushed at Shatov when all the others did, he didn't grab Shatov and didn't help hold him down. As for Lyamshin, he joined the group only after the shot had been fired. Then during the entire course of this fussing with the corpse, which lasted perhaps ten minutes, they all seemed to be only partially conscious. They grouped themselves around and rather than any uneasiness or alarm, seemed to feel nothing but surprise. Liputin was standing in front, right by the corpse. Virginsky was behind him, peering over his shoulder with peculiar and seemingly detached curiosity, even standing on tiptoe to have a better look. And Lyamshin had hidden behind Virginsky and would peer out from behind him occasionally and apprehensively, and then immediately hide himself again. But when the stones were tied on and Pyotr Stepanovich stood up, Virginsky began to quiver all over, clasped his hands, and shouted mournfully at the top of his voice:

'This isn't right, it isn't right! No, it's absolutely not right!'

He perhaps would have added something more to his very belated outcry, but Lyamshin didn't let him finish: suddenly he wrapped his arms around him with all his might and squeezed him from behind and began to shriek in an inhuman way. There are powerful moments of fear, for instance, when a person suddenly begins to scream in an unnatural voice, one that you could never before have imagined to be his, and that's sometimes even a very terrifying thing. Lyamshin began to scream in a voice that wasn't human, but animal-like. Squeezing Virginsky with his hands tighter and tighter from behind, convulsively, he kept shrieking incessantly and without pause, his eyes goggling at everyone and his mouth wide open, his feet pounding on the ground as if they were beating a drum. Virginsky was so frightened that he himself began screaming like a madman, and in a kind of frenzy so vicious that Virginsky was the last person you'd expect it of, he began to wrench free of Lyamshin's arms, scratching and pounding him as much as he could with his hands behind his back. Finally, Erkel helped him pull Lyamshin away. But when the terrified Virginsky leaped some ten steps to the side, then Lyamshin, on seeing Pyotr Stepanovich, suddenly began howling again and went straight for him. Tripping over the corpse, he fell across it on to Pyotr Stepanovich and gripped him so tightly in his arms, with his head pressed against his chest, that neither Pyotr Stepanovich nor Tolkachenko nor Liputin was able to do anything at first. Pyotr Stepanovich was shouting, cursing, beating him on the head with his fists; finally, somehow pulling loose, he seized the revolver and pointed it straight into the wide-open mouth of Lyamshin, who was still howling, and whose arms by now were being tightly held by Tolkachenko, Erkel and Liputin; but Lyamshin went on shrieking, even despite the revolver. Finally, Erkel, somehow wadding his foulard into a ball, deftly shoved it into his mouth, and so the shouting stopped. Meanwhile, Tolkachenko tied his hands with the remaining piece of rope.

'That's very strange,' Pyotr Stepanovich said, inspecting the madman in alarmed surprise.

He was visibly shaken.

'I expected something quite different from him,' he added thoughtfully.

They left Erkel with him for the time being. They had to

hurry up with the dead man: there had been so much shouting
that it might have been heard. Tolkachenko and Pyotr Stepanovich raised their lanterns and grabbed the corpse by the head;
Liputin and Virginsky took the feet and began to carry it. With
two stones the burden was heavy, and the distance was more
than two hundred paces. Tolkachenko was the strongest one
there. He tried to advise them to move in step, but no one
responded, and they set off walking any which way. Pyotr
Stepanovich walked on the right and, bent over double, was
carrying the dead man's head on his shoulder, supporting the
stone from below with his left hand. Since it never occurred
to Tolkachenko for a good half of the way to help with the
stone, Pyotr Stepanovich finally shouted a curse at him. It
was a sudden, solitary shout. They all continued to carry the
body in silence, and only when they had reached the pond did
Virginsky, stooped under the load and seemingly exhausted by
its weight, suddenly exclaim again, in precisely the same loud
and querulous voice:

'It's not right, no, no, it's absolutely not right!'

The place where this third, rather large Skvoreshniki pond
ended, and to which they had carried the murdered man, was
one of the most isolated and unfrequented places in the park,
especially at such a late time of year. The pond at this end
was overgrown with grass along the bank. They set down the
lanterns, swung the corpse and threw it into the water. A
muffled and protracted sound followed. Pyotr Stepanovich
raised his lantern, and they all leaned forward, looking on with
curiosity as the dead man disappeared under the water, but
now nothing could be seen. The body and the two rocks had
immediately sunk. The large ripples that had begun to spread
over the surface of the water quickly died away. The business
was over.

'Gentlemen,' Pyotr Stepanovich turned to them all. 'Now
we'll go our separate ways. Undoubtedly you should now be
feeling that proud sense of freedom that is associated with the
fulfilment of an obligation freely undertaken. But if you are
now unfortunately too upset to experience such feelings, you
will undoubtedly feel them tomorrow, when it would be a

672   DEMONS

shame not to feel them. I agree to regard Lyamshin's extremely
shameful state of agitation as delirium, the more so since they
say he really has been ill since this morning. And as for you,
Virginsky, one moment of free reflection will show you that in
view of the interests of the common cause it was impossible to
act on someone's word of honour, but that we had to do
precisely as we did. Subsequent events will show that there was
a denunciation. I am willing to forget your cries of protest. As
for danger, none is foreseen. It won't even enter anyone's head
to suspect any of us, especially if you manage to behave yourselves. So the main thing still depends on you yourselves and
on your complete conviction, which I hope you will find confirmed by tomorrow. And that is why, by the way, you have
closed ranks in a separate organization freely assembled from
like-minded people: so that in the common cause you share in
your efforts at a given moment, and, if need be, observe and
keep an eye on one another. Each of you is accountable to a
higher authority. You are called upon to renew a cause that has
become decrepit and has begun to reek of stagnation. Always
keep that before your eyes to encourage yourselves. Your every
step now should be taken in order to bring about the collapse
of everything, both the state and its moral code. Only we shall
remain, we who have destined ourselves to take power; we shall
join the intelligent ones to ourselves and ride roughshod over
the fools. You must not be embarrassed by this. We must
re-educate a generation in order to make it worthy of freedom.
There are still many thousands of Shatovs in our future. We
shall organize ourselves in order to seize control of the direction
in which things are moving. It's a shame not to grab hold of
what is lying idle and staring open-mouthed at us. Now I'm
going to go to Kirillov's, and by morning there will be the
document in which he, as he is dying, by way of explanation to
the government takes it all on himself. Nothing could be more
plausible than such a stratagem. In the first place, he had a
falling out with Shatov: they lived together in America, and so
they had time to quarrel. It's known that Shatov changed his
convictions; and enmity prompted by convictions and by fear
of denunciation is the most unforgiving kind. All this will be

written down just like that. Finally, keep in mind that Fedka lodged with him, in Filippov's house. And so, all this will completely lift any suspicion from us, because it will throw all these mutton-heads off track. Tomorrow, gentlemen, we won't see each other: I'm going off to the country for a very short time. But the day after tomorrow you will hear from me. I would advise you, as a matter of fact, to stay at home tomorrow. Just now we'll leave in two different directions. I'll ask you, Tolkachenko, to look after Lyamshin and take him home. You might have some influence on him and, most of all, explain the extent to which he'll be the first to harm himself with his cowardice. Mr Virginsky, I don't want to have any doubts about your relative Shigalyov, any more than I do about you: he won't denounce us. All that remains is to regret his actions; still and all, he hasn't yet announced that he's leaving the society, and therefore it's still too early to bury him. Well then, let's hurry up, gentlemen. They may be mutton-heads out there, but caution still doesn't hurt.'

Virginsky set off with Erkel. In the process of handing Lyamshin over to Tolkachenko, Erkel had managed to bring him to Pyotr Stepanovich and he announced that he had regained his senses, was contrite, asked forgiveness and didn't even remember what had happened to him. Pyotr Stepanovich set out alone, going around the ponds on the other side, skirting the park. That way was the longest. To his surprise, Liputin caught up with him when he had gone almost halfway.

'Pyotr Stepanovich, Lyamshin will denounce us, you know!'

'No, he'll come to his senses and figure out that he'll be the first to go to Siberia if he does denounce us. Now no one will denounce us. And you won't either.'

'And you?'

'Don't think for a moment that I won't get rid of all of you the moment you make a move to betray us, and you know it. But you won't betray us. Is this what you ran two versts after me for?'

'Pyotr Stepanovich, Pyotr Stepanovich, why, we may never see each other again!'

'Wherever did you get that?'

'Just tell me one thing.'

'Well, what? However, I want you to clear off.'

'Answer me one thing, but truthfully: are we the only group of five in the world, or is it true that there are several hundred such groups? I'm asking this because it's of the greatest importance, Pyotr Stepanovich.'

'So I see by your wild excitement. Do you know, Liputin, that you're more dangerous than Lyamshin?'

'I know, I know, but – the answer, your answer!'

'What a stupid man you are! Why, it would seem that now of all times it wouldn't matter to you whether there's one group of five or a thousand.'

'So, there's one! I just knew it!' Liputin exclaimed. 'I knew all the time, all along, that there was only one.'

And without awaiting a further reply, he turned and quickly disappeared in the darkness.

Pyotr Stepanovich reflected on this a little.

'No, no one will denounce us,' he said decisively. 'But the group must remain a group and obey, or else I'll ... What a miserable bunch of people they are, though!'

2.

At first he went to his own place, and neatly and leisurely packed his suitcase. An express train was due to leave at six o'clock in the morning. This early express train ran only once a week, and had been established very recently, only as an experiment so far. Although Pyotr Stepanovich had advised *our people* that he was going off to the country for a while, it turned out later that his intentions were quite different. With his suitcase packed, he settled up with the landlady, who had previously been given notice, and took a cab to Erkel's, who lived not far from the station. And after that, close to one o'clock in the morning, he directed his steps to Kirillov's, and again got in through Fedka's secret passage.

Pyotr Stepanovich was in a dreadful mood. Besides other dissatisfactions that were extremely important to him (he still could learn nothing about Stavrogin), it would seem that he –

for I can't confirm it definitely – had received secret information during the course of the day from somewhere (most probably from Petersburg) about a certain danger that awaited him in the near future. Of course, a great many legends concerning this particular time are now circulating in our town, but if anything is actually known for sure, then it's only to those whose business it is to know. All I can do is surmise, on my part, that Pyotr Stepanovich could have had business somewhere else besides our town, and could actually have received some information. I'm even convinced, despite Liputin's cynical and despairing doubts, that he could actually have had two or three other groups of five besides ours, for example, in the two capitals, and if not groups, then ties and connections, and perhaps even very curious ones. No more than three days following his departure an order from the capital was received in our town for his immediate arrest – for precisely what activities, ours or others, I don't know. This order arrived just in time to heighten the overwhelming sense of almost mystical fear that suddenly overcame our authorities as well as our society (which until then had been stubbornly frivolous), after the discovery of the mysterious and extremely significant murder of the student Shatov – a murder that was the climax of our stupidities – and of the highly enigmatic circumstances that accompanied this incident. But the order came too late: Pyotr Stepanovich by then was already in Petersburg, under a different name, where, after sniffing out what was going on, he instantly slipped across the border. However, I've run awfully far ahead of myself.

He went in to Kirillov with an angry and ill-tempered look. Besides the main business at hand, he seemed to want to get back at Kirillov for something personal, to vent his anger on him. Kirillov seemed to be glad that he had come; it was obvious that he had been expecting him for an awfully long time and with morbid impatience. His face was paler than usual, and his black eyes had a heavy, fixed look to them.

'I thought you weren't coming,' he said gravely from the corner of the sofa, from which, however, he didn't move to greet him. Pyotr Stepanovich stood in front of him, and before saying a word, stared intently into his face.

'So, everything's in order, and we aren't backing down from our intention, bravo!' He gave an insultingly patronizing smile. 'Well, what of it?' he added in an offensively joking manner. 'If I was late, you have nothing to complain about: I gave you an extra three hours.'

'I don't want extra hours as a gift from you, and you can't give them to me . . . you fool!'

'What?' Pyotr Stepanovich almost gave a start, but instantly controlled himself. 'You're so touchy! Hey, are we going to fly into a rage?' he said, pronouncing each syllable distinctly, in the same offensively supercilious way. 'At a time like this calmness is what's called for. The best thing is for you to regard yourself as a Columbus now, and to look on me as a mouse, and not to take offence at me. I recommended that yesterday.'

'I don't want to look on you as a mouse.'

'What's that, then, a compliment? By the way, the tea's cold; that means everything's topsy-turvy. No, something's not quite right here. Aha, I notice something there on the window sill, on a plate.' (He went up to the window.) 'Oho, boiled chicken and rice! But why haven't you started in on it yet? So, we were in such a mood that even chicken . . .'

'I've eaten, and it's none of your business, so shut up!'

'Oh, of course, and besides, it makes no difference. But for me it does make a difference. Just imagine, I had practically no dinner and so, if this chicken, as I imagine, is no longer needed . . .'

'Eat it if you can.'

'I thank you very much, and then I'll have some tea.'

In a flash he had established himself at the table on the other end of the sofa and fell upon the food with extraordinary greediness; but at the same time he was observing his victim every moment. Kirillov kept his eyes fixed on him with angry loathing, as if incapable of tearing himself away.

'However,' Pyotr Stepanovich suddenly straightened up, while continuing to eat, 'however, what about the business at hand? So we won't back out, eh? And the little piece of paper?'

'I determined tonight that it's all the same to me. I'll write it. About the manifestos?'

'Yes, about the manifestos as well. However, I'll dictate to you. After all, it's all the same to you what you say. Could you possibly be disturbed by the contents at such a time?'

'It's none of your business.'

'Of course it's not. However, just a few lines: that you and Shatov distributed the manifestos, and incidentally with the help of Fedka, who was hiding in your apartment. This last point about Fedka and the apartment is extremely important, even the most important one. You see, I'm being completely open with you.'

'And Shatov? Why Shatov? I won't say a word about Shatov.'

'You must be joking, what's it to you? You can't harm him any longer.'

'His wife has come to him. She woke up and sent someone to ask me where he is.'

'She sent someone to you for information? Hmm, that's too bad. Maybe she'll send someone again; no one must know that I'm here ...'

Pyotr Stepanovich began to grow uneasy.

'She won't find out; she's sleeping again. She has a midwife, Arina Virginskaya.'

'That's just the problem ... and she won't overhear, I suppose? You know, you ought to lock the front door.'

'She won't overhear anything. And if Shatov does come, I'll hide you in that room.'

'Shatov won't be coming. And you will write that you quarrelled over his treachery and his denunciation ... this evening ... and are the reason for his death.'

'He's dead!' Kirillov cried, leaping up from the sofa.

'Today after seven o'clock in the evening, or rather, yesterday after seven o'clock in the evening, since it's already after midnight.'

'You're the one who killed him! ... And I foresaw it yesterday!'

'How could you fail to foresee it! And with this revolver here.' (He took out the revolver, evidently to show it, but this time he didn't put it away, and continued holding it in his right hand, as if keeping it in readiness.) 'However, you're a strange man, Kirillov, you yourself knew, after all, that it had to end this way with this stupid man. What was there to foresee here, after all? I spelled it all out for you a number of times. Shatov was preparing a denunciation; I was watching him; things couldn't be left as they were. What's more, you were given instructions to watch him; you yourself informed me about three weeks ago . . .'

'Shut up! You did this because he spat in your face in Geneva!'

'For that and for something else as well. For a great deal else: however, without any malice. Why jump up? Why this posturing? Oho! So that's how we are!'

He jumped up and raised his revolver in front of him. What had happened was that Kirillov had suddenly grabbed his revolver from the window sill, which had been ready and loaded since morning. Pyotr Stepanovich got into position and aimed his weapon at Kirillov, who began to laugh maliciously.

'Admit it, you bastard, you took up your revolver because I'm going to shoot you . . . But I won't shoot you . . . although . . . although . . .'

And he again aimed his revolver at Pyotr Stepanovich, as if testing it, as if incapable of resisting the pleasure of imagining how he would shoot him. Pyotr Stepanovich, still in position, was waiting, waiting until the last moment, not pulling the trigger, running the risk of receiving a bullet in his own forehead before that: anything was possible with a 'maniac'. But the 'maniac' finally lowered his arm, panting and unable to speak.

'You've had your little game, and that's enough,' Pyotr Stepanovich also lowered his weapon. 'I just knew that you were playing a game, except, you know, it was a risky one: I could have fired.'

And he sat down on the sofa rather calmly and poured himself some tea, though his hand was trembling slightly. Kirillov put the revolver on the table and began walking back and forth.

'I won't write that I killed Shatov . . . and now I won't write anything. There will be no piece of paper!'

'There won't?'

'There won't.'

'How vile and how stupid!' Pyotr Stepanovich turned green with anger. 'However, I had a feeling this would happen. You should know that you're not taking me by surprise. As you wish, however. If I could make you do it by force, then I'd make you do it. However, you're a scoundrel,' Pyotr Stepanovich was increasingly unable to hold himself back. 'You asked us for money then and promised us all sorts of things . . . But in any event I won't leave here without getting some result; at the very least I'll see you blow your brains out.'

'I want you to get out of here immediately,' Kirillov said, standing firmly opposite him.

'No, that's not how it's going to be.' Pyotr Stepanovich again seized his revolver. 'Maybe you'll take it into your head now to postpone everything out of anger and cowardice and go and denounce us tomorrow, in order to get a little bit of money again – after all, they pay for that sort of thing. Damn you to hell – there are enough nasty little people like you who are ready for anything! Except don't worry, I've foreseen everything: I won't leave before I've blown your brains out with this revolver, just like I did to that scoundrel Shatov, if you get cold feet and put off what you were intending. The Devil take you!'

'Do you really want to see my blood as well?'

'It's not out of anger, understand that; I personally don't care. I'm doing it to rest easy about our cause. You can't rely on people, you yourself can see that. I don't understand anything about your fantasy of destroying yourself. I'm not the one who thought that up for you; you yourself first announced it not to me, but to our members abroad, before I came on the scene. And note that none of them was trying to pry anything out of you, not one of them was even aware of your existence; you yourself came to bare your soul, out of sheer sentimentality. Well then, what is to be done if a certain course of action for things here and now, which it's no longer possible to change, was based on this then with your full agreement and at your suggestion (take note of that: your suggestion!). You've now put yourself in a position where you know too much that you don't need to. If you start acting stupidly and go off to denounce us tomorrow, that may very well be to our disadvantage, what do you think of that? No, indeed: you assumed an obligation, you gave your word, you took money. There's no way you can deny that . . .'

Pyotr Stepanovich was in a highly excited state, but Kirillov had long since stopped listening. He was again pacing about the room deep in thought.

'I'm sorry for Shatov,' he said, stopping before Pyotr Stepanovich.

'Well, perhaps I'm sorry too, you know, and is it possible that . . .'

'Shut up, you scoundrel!' Kirillov bellowed, making a terrible and unambiguous movement, 'I'll kill you!'

'Now, now, now, I lied, I agree, I'm not sorry at all; enough now, enough!' Pyotr Stepanovich jumped up in alarm, thrusting his arm out in front of him.

Kirillov suddenly quieted down and again began pacing.

'I won't put it off; I want to kill myself right now: they're all scoundrels!'

'Now that's an idea; of course they're all scoundrels, and since a decent man finds it loathsome to live in this world, then . . .'

'You fool, I'm as much a scoundrel as you are, as everyone is, and not a decent man. There's never been a decent man anywhere.'

'At long last he's figured it out. Haven't you really understood yet, Kirillov, with your intelligence, that everyone is exactly the same, that there's no better or worse, but only more intelligent and more stupid, and that if they're all scoundrels (which, however, is nonsense), then it follows that there shouldn't be any non-scoundrels?'

'Ah! Why, are you actually not joking?' Kirillov looked at him with some surprise. 'You're speaking heatedly and simply . . . Can it be that people like you have convictions?'

'Kirillov, I've never been able to understand why you want to kill yourself. I only know that it's out of a conviction – a firm conviction. But if you feel the need to pour yourself out, so to speak, then I'm at your service. Except we have to keep the time in mind . . .'

'What time is it?'

'Oho, exactly two.' Pyotr Stepanovich looked at his watch and lit a cigarette.

'I think we can still come to an understanding,' he thought to himself.

'I have nothing to say to you,' Kirillov grumbled.

'I remember that there was something about God . . . you tried explaining it to me once, you know, even twice. If you do shoot yourself, then you will become God. That's how it goes, I think?'

'Yes, I will become God.'

Pyotr Stepanovich didn't even smile; he was waiting. Kirillov looked at him subtly.

'You are a political trickster and intriguer, you want to lead me off into philosophy and ecstasy and bring about a reconciliation, to dispel my anger, and when I'm reconciled with you, to prevail on me to give you a note saying that I killed Shatov.'

Pyotr Stepanovich answered with an artlessness that sounded almost natural:

'Well, let's grant that I am such a scoundrel, except that in your last minutes isn't it all the same to you, Kirillov? What are we quarrelling over, tell me, please? You're a particular kind of man, and I'm a particular kind of man, and what of it? And both of us, besides . . .'

'Are scoundrels.'

'Well, yes, scoundrels, perhaps. You know, don't you, that these are just words.'

'My whole life I've wanted them not to be just words. The reason I've lived is that I kept wanting it not to be. Even now every day I want it not to be words.'

'Well then, everyone seeks to be where it's best. A fish . . . that is, each one of us seeks his own sort of comfort, that's all. That's been known for an extraordinarily long time.'

'Comfort, you say?'

'As if it's worth quarrelling over words.'

'No, you put it well; let it be comfort. God is necessary, and therefore he must exist.'

'Now, that's splendid.'

'But I know that he doesn't exist and cannot exist.'

'That's more likely.'

'Don't you really understand that a man with two such ideas can't go on living?'

'Must shoot himself, you mean?'

'Don't you really understand that he can shoot himself just because of that one thing? You don't understand that there can be such a man, one man out of the thousands of your millions, one who won't want that and won't tolerate it.'

'The only thing I understand is that you're wavering ... That's very bad.'

'Stavrogin was also consumed by an idea.' Kirillov hadn't noticed Pyotr Stepanovich's remark as he gloomily paced around the room.

'What?' Pyotr Stepanovich pricked up his ears. 'What idea? Did he himself say something to you?'

'No, I guessed it myself. If Stavrogin believes, then he doesn't believe that he believes. But if he doesn't believe, then he doesn't believe that he doesn't believe.'

'Well, Stavrogin has something else on his mind, cleverer than that,' Pyotr Stepanovich muttered peevishly, as he uneasily followed the turn of conversation and observed Kirillov's pale face.

'Damn it all, he won't shoot himself,' he thought, 'I always had a feeling about that. It's a mental quirk and nothing more; what garbage these people are!'

'You're the last person to be with me; I wouldn't want to part with you on bad terms,' Kirillov suddenly conceded.

Pyotr Stepanovich didn't answer immediately 'Damn it all, what is it now?' he thought again.

'Believe me, Kirillov, I have nothing against you personally as a man, and I always ...'

'You're a scoundrel and a false mind. But I'm the same as you, and I'm going to shoot myself, while you'll remain alive.'

'That is, you wish to say that I'm so low I'll want to remain among the living.'

He still couldn't decide whether it was to his advantage or not to continue such a conversation at such a moment, and he made up his mind to 'yield to circumstances'. But the tone of superiority and the chronic contempt for him that Kirillov made no effort to disguise had always irritated him before this, and now for some reason even more than before. Perhaps because Kirillov, who was due to die in an hour or so (at any rate, Pyotr Stepanovich still kept that in mind), now seemed to him something like a half-man, something that he no longer could permit to be arrogant.

'You seem to be boasting to me about shooting yourself?'

'I've always been surprised that everyone goes on living,' Kirillov didn't catch his remark.

'Hmm, let's suppose that's an idea, but . . .'

'You ape, you're yesing me so as to get the better of me. Shut up, you can't understand anything. If there is no God, then I am God.'

'You know, I never was able to understand this particular point of yours: why should *you* be God?'

'If God exists, then all will is his, and I can't escape his will. If he does not exist, then all will is mine, and I am obliged to proclaim self-will.'

'Self-will? And why are you obliged?'

'Because all will has become mine. Can it really be that no one on this entire planet, once having put an end to God and having developed a belief in self-will, will dare to proclaim self-will, in the fullest possible sense? It's like a poor man who's received an inheritance and is frightened by it and doesn't dare come near the bag full of money, regarding himself as too feeble to possess it. I want to proclaim self-will. Even if I'm the only one, I'll do it.'

'So go ahead and do it.'

'I am obliged to shoot myself because my self-will in the fullest possible sense is for me to kill myself.'

'But look, you're not the only one to kill yourself; there are many suicides.'

'With good reason. But to do it without any reason, and solely for self-will – I'm the only one.'

'He won't shoot himself,' again flashed through Pyotr Stepanovich's mind.

'You know what,' he observed irritably, 'if I were in your place, to show self-will I would kill someone else, and not myself. You could become useful. I'll show you who, if you're not afraid. Then perhaps you won't have to shoot yourself today. We could reach an understanding.'

'To kill someone else would be the lowest point of my self-will, and that's where you reveal who you are completely. I'm not you: I want the highest point, and I'll kill myself.'

'He's worked this out all by himself,' Pyotr Stepanovich muttered angrily.

'I am obliged to proclaim disbelief,' Kirillov was walking about the room. 'For me there is no higher idea than the non-existence of God. Human history is behind me. Man has done nothing but invent God in order to live without killing himself; that's the essence of world history to this point. I am the only one in world history who hasn't felt like inventing God for the first time. Let people find that out once and for all.'

'He won't shoot himself,' an alarmed Pyotr Stepanovich was thinking.

'Well, who is there to find out about it?' he egged Kirillov on. 'There's you and me here; you mean Liputin?'

'All are to find out; all will find out. There is nothing secret that will not become manifest.[2] That is what *He* said.'

And in a fever of ecstasy he pointed to an icon of the Saviour before which a lamp was burning. Pyotr Stepanovich flew into a rage.

'And so you still do believe in *Him* and you've lit the lamp. Isn't that an instance of "just in case"?'

Kirillov remained silent.

'You know what, in my opinion, your belief is even stronger than a priest's.'

'In whom? In *Him*? Listen.' Kirillov stopped pacing, and stared straight before him with a fixed and ecstatic look. 'Listen to a great idea. There was a certain day on earth, and in the centre of the earth stood three crosses. One man on a cross believed to such an extent that he said to another: "Today you will be with me in paradise."[3] The day ended, both died, they went and they found nothing – neither paradise nor resurrection. What had been said proved unjustified. Listen: this man was the highest on the entire earth, he comprised that which allowed it to live. The entire planet, with everything on it, is nothing but madness without that man. There has never been one like *Him*, either before or after, even by virtue of a miracle. The miracle is that there never has been nor will there be another such man, ever. And if that's so, if the laws of nature didn't spare even *This One*, didn't even spare his miracle, but compelled even *Him* to live amidst a lie and to die for a lie, then it follows that the entire planet is a lie and rests on a lie and on a stupid joke. It follows that the very laws of the planet are a lie and a farce put on by the Devil. What's there to live for, answer me, if you are a man?'

'That is a different matter entirely. It seems to me that you've confused two different causes here, and that's very dangerous. But allow me to ask, well then, what if you are God? If the lie were ended, and you realized that the whole lie was the result of there having been that former God?'

'At long last you've understood!' Kirillov cried in ecstasy. 'And so it can be understood, if even someone like you has understood! You understand now that the salvation for all depends on proving this idea to all. Who will prove it? Me! I don't understand how an atheist could reach this point knowing that God does not exist and not kill himself immediately. To realize that God does not exist, and not to realize at the same time that you yourself have become God is absurd. Otherwise you'd certainly kill yourself. If you realize it, you are a tsar and you will no longer kill yourself, but will live in the greatest glory. But one man, the one who is first, must kill himself without fail; otherwise who will begin and prove it? I will kill myself without fail in order to begin and prove it. Now I am still only God against my will, and I'm unhappy, because I'm *obliged* to proclaim self-will. All are unhappy because all are afraid to proclaim self-will. Man until now has been so unhappy and impoverished, because he has been afraid to proclaim the most important aspect of self-will and has shown his self-will in marginal ways, like a schoolboy. I'm dreadfully unhappy because I'm dreadfully afraid. Fear is the curse of man . . . But

I am proclaiming self-will, and I am obliged to believe that I don't believe. I'll begin and end and thus open the door. And I'll bring salvation. That is the only thing that will save all people and will cause them to be reborn in the next generation; for in his present physical form, as far as I have been thinking about it, it's impossible for man to be without his former God altogether. I have been looking for the attribute of my godhood for three years, and I have found it: the attribute of my godhood is – Self-Will! This is the only way I can show, in its main aspect, my independence and my terrible new freedom. For it is very terrible. I am killing myself in order to show my independence and my new terrible freedom.'

His face was unnaturally pale, the look in his eyes unbearably heavy. He seemed to be feverish. Pyotr Stepanovich almost thought that he was about to fall to the floor.

'Give me the pen!' Kirillov suddenly cried completely unexpectedly, in a burst of resolute inspiration. 'Dictate, and I'll sign. And I'll sign that I killed Shatov. Dictate, while I still find it funny. I'm not afraid of the ideas of arrogant slaves! You will see for yourself that everything that's hidden will become manifest! And you will be crushed ... I believe! I believe!'

Pyotr Stepanovich leaped out of his chair and in a flash handed Kirillov the ink-pot and some paper, and began to dictate, seizing the moment and trembling for its success.

'I, Aleksey Kirillov, declare ...'

'Stop! I don't want that! Who am I declaring to?'

Kirillov was shaking as if he had a fever. This declaration and the sudden peculiar idea of it seemed to have absorbed him completely, as if it were an outlet towards which his tormented spirit had rushed headlong, if only for a moment.

'Who am I declaring to? I want to know, who?'

'To no one, everyone, the first person who reads it. Why try to define it? To the whole world!'

'To the whole world? Bravo! And just so there's no need for repentance. I don't want there to be any repentance, and I don't want it addressed to the authorities!'

'Why, certainly not, there's no need; to hell with the author-

ities! Come now, write, if you're serious!' Pyotr Stepanovich
raised his voice hysterically.

'Wait! On the top of the paper I want an ugly face with its
tongue stuck out.'

'Oh, nonsense!' Pyotr Stepanovich exclaimed angrily. 'You
can express all that in the tone, without a drawing.'

'The tone? That's good. Yes, by the tone, the tone! Dictate
in the right tone.'

'I, Aleksey Kirillov,' Pyotr Stepanovich dictated in a firm
and commanding voice, leaning over Kirillov's shoulder and
following every letter that he was tracing in a hand trembling
with emotion, 'I, Kirillov, declare that today, the –th of
October, in the evening, between seven and eight o'clock, I
killed the student Shatov in the park for being a traitor and for
his denunciation about the manifestos and Fedka, who secretly
stayed with both of us and spent ten nights in Filippov's house.
And today I am killing myself with a revolver not because I
repent and am afraid of you, but because even while abroad
I had the intention of putting an end to my life.'

'Is that all?' Kirillov exclaimed with surprise and indignation.

'Not a word more!' Pyotr Stepanovich waved his hand
dismissively, trying to pull the document away from him.

'Stop!' Kirillov put his hand firmly on the paper. 'Stop! Nonsense! I want to say who I killed him with. Why Fedka? And
the fire? I want everything and I also want to curse them in the
tone, the tone!'

'Enough, Kirillov, I assure you it's enough!' Pyotr Stepanovich was almost pleading, and trembling lest he should tear
up the paper. 'For them to believe it, it has to be as vague as
possible, just the way it is, with just hints. You have to show
only a corner of the truth, just enough to pique them. They'll
always tell themselves a taller tale than ours, and will of course
believe themselves more than they do us, and that's best of all,
you know, best of all! Give it to me; it's fine just as it is; give it
to me, give it to me!'

And he kept trying to pull the paper away. Kirillov, wide-
eyed, listened and seemed to be trying to make sense of it, but
apparently he was beyond understanding.

'Oh, damn!' Pyotr Stepanovich suddenly grew angry. 'Why, he hasn't even signed it yet! Why are you sitting there wide-eyed, sign!'

'I want to curse them,' Kirillov muttered, though he did take the paper and sign it. 'I want to curse them.'

'Write: *Vive la république*, and let it go at that.'

'Bravo!' Kirillov almost howled in ecstasy. ' "*Vive la république démocratique, sociale et universelle ou la mort!*" . . . No, no, that's not right. "*Liberté, égalité, fraternité ou la mort!*"[4] There, that's better, that's better', and he wrote it with delight under his signature.

'Enough, enough,' Pyotr Stepanovich kept repeating.

'Wait, just a bit more . . . you know, I'm going to sign it again in French: "*de Kiriloff, gentilhomme russe et citoyen du monde.*" Ha, ha, ha!' He burst out in malicious laughter. 'No, no, no, wait, I've found the best thing of all, eureka! "*Gentilhomme-séminariste russe et citoyen du monde civilisé!*"[5] That's better than anything.' He jumped up from the sofa and suddenly with a quick gesture snatched the revolver from the window sill, ran into the next room with it and shut the door tightly behind him. Pyotr Stepanovich stood there for a moment, reflecting, and looking at the door.

'If he does it now, then maybe he'll shoot himself, but if he begins to think – nothing will happen.'

Meanwhile he picked up the paper, sat down and looked it over once more. He was again pleased by the wording of the declaration.

'What's needed for the time being? What's needed is to throw them off the track and distract their attention. The park? There's no park in town, but they'll figure out for themselves that it's in Skvoreshniki. While they're figuring that out, time will pass, while they're looking, still more time, and when they discover the body that'll mean that the note is telling the truth: that'll mean everything is true, it'll mean that it's true about Fedka. And what's the significance of Fedka? Fedka is the fire, the Lebyadkins: it means that everything came from here, from the Filippov house, and that they saw absolutely nothing, and that they overlooked everything – that'll put their heads in a complete spin! It won't even occur to them to think of *our people*. It'll be just Shatov and Kirillov and Fedka and Lebyadkin, and why they killed each other – that'll pose a nice little question for them. Oh, damn, I still haven't heard a shot!'

Although he was reading and admiring the wording, he kept listening all the time, in painful anxiety, and suddenly he flew into a rage. He looked at his watch uneasily; it was getting rather late; about ten minutes had passed since Kirillov had left. Picking up the candle, he walked to the door of the room in which Kirillov had shut himself. Just at the door it occurred to him that the candle in his hand was very low and that in twenty minutes or so it would burn out entirely, and there wasn't another one. He took hold of the latch and listened very carefully to see whether he could hear the slightest sound; he suddenly opened the door and raised the candle. Something gave a howl and rushed at him. He slammed the door shut as hard as he could and pressed against it, but everything had already grown quiet, and again there was dead silence.

For a long time he stood indecisively with the candle in his hand. During the second the door had been open he could make out very little, but nonetheless he had glimpsed the face of Kirillov, who was standing deep inside the room by the window, and the animal-like rage with which he suddenly hurled himself forward. Pyotr Stepanovich shuddered, quickly set the candle down on the table, cocked his revolver and sprang back on tiptoe to the opposite corner, so that if Kirillov opened the door and made a sudden move towards the table with his revolver, he would still have time to aim and pull the trigger before Kirillov did.

By now Pyotr Stepanovich didn't believe in the suicide at all! 'He was standing in the middle of the room and thinking' – this whirled through Pyotr Stepanovich's head. 'Besides, it was a dark and horrible room. He gave a howl and threw himself at me. There are two possibilities here: either I disturbed him at the very second he was about to pull the trigger, or ... or he was standing and trying to figure out how to kill me. Yes that's it, he was trying to figure out how. He knows that I won't leave without killing him if he gets cold feet, so he has to kill me first,

so that I won't kill him. The nasty thing about it is that he
believes in God more than any priest . . . there's no way he'll
shoot himself! Now there are swarms of people who've
"worked it out for themselves". Swine! Ugh, damn it, the
candle, the candle! It'll definitely burn out in the next quarter
of an hour. I have to put an end to this, put an end to it no
matter what . . . Well then, I could kill him now . . . With this
paper they'll never think I killed him. He can be laid out and
arranged on the floor with the discharged revolver in his hand,
and they'll certainly think that he himself . . . Oh, damn, how's
he to be killed? I'll open the door and he'll come rushing at
me again, and he'll shoot before I do. Oh, damn, and he'll miss
for sure!'

And so he agonized, trembling at the inevitability of the plan
and at his own indecision. Finally, he took the candle and
walked over to the door again, with the revolver raised and
ready; and with his left hand, in which he was holding the
candle, he pressed down on the handle of the latch. But he had
made a clumsy move: the handle gave a click, there was a sound
and a squeak. 'He'll go ahead and shoot!' flashed through Pyotr
Stepanovich's mind. He pushed the door with his foot as hard
as he could, raised the candle and held out the revolver; but
neither a shot nor a shout came . . . There was no one in the
room.

He gave a start. There was no other way out of the room, no
other exit; there was no way to escape. He raised the candle
even higher and looked around carefully: absolutely no one.
He called Kirillov's name in a soft voice, then a second time
more loudly; no one responded.

'Could he possibly have escaped through the window?'

In fact, the vent was open in one window. 'That's ridiculous,
he couldn't have escaped through the vent.' Pyotr Stepanovich
walked across the room directly to the window. 'There's no
way he could have done that.' Suddenly he turned around
quickly, and was shaken by something extraordinary.

Against the wall opposite the window, to the right of the
door, stood a wardrobe. To the right of this wardrobe, in the
corner formed by the wall and the wardrobe, stood Kirillov,

and he was standing there in an awfully strange way – not moving, drawn up erect, his arms held at his sides, his head raised and pressed tightly against the wall, as far into the corner as he could get, looking as if he wanted to sink into obscurity and disappear. By all indications he was hiding, but it was somehow impossible to believe that. Pyotr Stepanovich was standing somewhat at an angle to the corner and could see only the projecting parts of the figure. He still could not bring himself to move to the left in order to see the whole of Kirillov and understand what was going on. His heart began to pound violently . . . And suddenly he was gripped by utter fury: he tore himself away from where he was standing, began to shout and, stamping his feet, rushed to the terrible place in a frenzy.

But once he had got there, he stopped again as if rooted to the spot, even more struck with horror. What struck him most of all was that the figure, despite his shouts and his furious attack, hadn't even stirred, hadn't moved a single limb, as though it were made of stone or wax. The pallor of the face was unnatural, the black eyes were completely fixed and were staring at some point in space. Pyotr Stepanovich moved the candle up and down and then up again, illuminating it from all points and scrutinizing this face. He suddenly noticed that although Kirillov was looking somewhere in front of him, he could see him out of the corner of his eye and perhaps was even watching him. Then the thought occurred to him to lift the flame straight to the face of 'this scoundrel', burn it and see what he would do. Suddenly he imagined that Kirillov's chin had moved and that a mocking smile had passed across his lips – as if Kirillov had guessed what he was thinking. He began to tremble and, unaware of what he was doing, grabbed Kirillov by the shoulder.

Then something so hideous happened so quickly that afterwards Pyotr Stepanovich could never put his recollections into any sort of order. Scarcely had he touched Kirillov when the latter quickly dipped his head and knocked the candle out of his hand with his head. The candleholder clattered to the floor and the candle went out. At that same moment he felt a dreadful pain in the little finger of his left hand. He cried out, and the only thing he remembered was that he was beside himself and had struck as hard as he could three times with the revolver the head of Kirillov, who had fallen on him and bitten his finger. Finally, he pulled his finger away and rushed headlong out of the house, trying to find his way in the darkness. He was pursued by terrible cries coming from the room:

'Now, now, now, now . . .'

About ten times. But he kept on running and was already in the entryway when he suddenly heard a loud shot. He promptly stopped in the dark entryway and weighed matters for some five minutes; finally he went back into the rooms. But he had to find the candle. All he needed to do was search on the floor to the right of the cupboard for the candleholder that had been knocked out of his hand; but what could he light the stub with? Suddenly a vague memory flashed through his mind: he recalled that the day before, when he had run into the kitchen to attack Fedka, he seemed to have noticed in passing a large red box of matches. He felt his way to the left, towards the kitchen door, found it, crossed the landing and went down the stairway. On a shelf, precisely in the spot he had just recalled, he felt for and found in the darkness a full unopened box of matches. Without lighting one, he hurried back upstairs, and then only by the cupboard, in the same place where he had used the revolver to hit Kirillov for biting him, did he suddenly remember his bitten finger and at that very moment felt an almost unbearable pain. Gritting his teeth, he somehow lit the candle stub, stuck it in the holder again and took a look around. By the small window with the open vent lay the body of Kirillov, his feet pointing to the right-hand corner. The shot had been fired at the right temple and the bullet had exited at the top on the left side, shattering the skull. Splashes of blood and brains could be seen. The revolver remained in the suicide's hand, which lay stretched out on the floor. Death must have occurred instantaneously. After examining all this in minute detail, Pyotr Stepanovich stood up and went out on tiptoe, left the door ajar, set the candle on the table in the first room, thought for a moment and decided not to extinguish it, figuring that it couldn't start a fire. With another glance at the document that lay on the table, he grinned mechanically and only then, still on tiptoe for some reason, walked out of the house. He again slipped through Fedka's passage, and again carefully closed it up behind him.

3.

At exactly ten minutes to six, at the railway station, Pyotr Stepanovich and Erkel were walking up and down beside a rather long line of coaches. Pyotr Stepanovich was leaving, and Erkel was seeing him off. The luggage had been checked, and his bag had been carried to the seat he had chosen in a second-class coach. The first bell had already rung, and they were waiting for the second. Pyotr Stepanovich was openly looking round, observing the passengers who were getting into the coaches. But no close acquaintances were encountered; only on two occasions did he have to nod his head – once to a merchant whom he knew slightly, and then to a young village priest who was travelling to his parish two stations away. In these final moments Erkel evidently wished to talk about something important, although perhaps he himself may very well not have known about what; but he couldn't bring himself to begin. He kept thinking that Pyotr Stepanovich found his presence burdensome, and was waiting impatiently for the second and third bells.

'You're looking at everyone so openly,' Erkel observed with a certain diffidence, as if wishing to warn him.

'And why not? I can't go into hiding yet. It's too soon. Don't worry. The only thing I'm afraid of is that the Devil might send Liputin in this direction. He'll sniff things out and come running.'

'Pyotr Stepanovich, they're unreliable,' Erkel stated decisively.

'Liputin?'

'All of them, Pyotr Stepanovich.'

'Nonsense, now they're all bound by what happened yesterday. Not one of them will betray us. Who will go to certain destruction if he hasn't lost his reason?'

'But, Pyotr Stepanovich, they will lose their reason.'

This thought had evidently already entered Pyotr Stepanovich's head as well, and so Erkel's remark angered him even more:

'Are you getting cold feet as well, Erkel? I'm relying on you more than all the rest of them. I've now seen what each of them is worth. Tell them everything today, in your own words; I'm entrusting them to you. Go round to all of them this morning. Read them my written instructions tomorrow or the day after, when you've all assembled and they're capable of hearing what you're saying . . . but believe me, they'll be capable of that tomorrow, because by then they'll be scared to death and they'll become as pliable as wax. The main thing is for you not to lose heart.'

'Ah, Pyotr Stepanovich, it would be better if you weren't going away!'

'Why, it's only for a few days; I'll be back before you know it.'

'Pyotr Stepanovich,' Erkel uttered cautiously but firmly, 'even if you were really going to Petersburg, do you think I don't understand that you're only doing what's necessary for the common cause?'

'I actually didn't expect anything less of you, Erkel. If you figured out that I was going to Petersburg, then you are capable of understanding that I really couldn't tell them yesterday, at that moment, that I was going so far away, so as not to frighten them. You yourself could see what a state they were in. But you understand that I'm doing it for the cause, for the central and so important cause, for the common cause, and not to sneak away, as some Liputin might suppose.'

'Pyotr Stepanovich, even if you were to go abroad, I would certainly understand. I would understand because you have to look after your person, because you are everything, and we are nothing. I would understand, Pyotr Stepanovich.'

The poor boy's voice was even trembling.

'I thank you, Erkel. Ouch, you touched my sore finger.' (Erkel had clumsily shaken his hand; the sore finger had been nicely wrapped in black taffeta.) 'But I'm telling you definitely once more that I'm going to Petersburg only to get the lay of the land and perhaps just for twenty-four hours, and then immediately coming back here. When I return, I'll settle down with Gaganov in the country, for appearances' sake. If they suspect there's danger anywhere, I'll be the first to stand out in front and share it. But if I'm delayed in Petersburg, then I'll let you know immediately . . . in the usual way, and you'll tell them.'

The second bell rang.

'Ah, that means there's only five minutes until the train leaves. You know, I wouldn't like the group here to break up. I'm not afraid, don't worry about me; I have enough of these knots in the general network, and there's no need for me to set store by any one in particular, but an extra knot wouldn't hurt at all. I feel quite at ease about you, even though I'm leaving you almost alone with these freaks. Don't worry, they won't inform, they wouldn't dare. Oh, you're travelling today too?' he suddenly shouted in a completely different, cheerful voice to a very young man, who had cheerfully come up to greet him. 'I didn't know that you were going by the express train, too. Where are you heading, to see your mother?'

The young man's mother was a very rich landowner in a neighbouring province, and the young man was a distant relative of Yuliya Mikhaylovna and had been visiting our town for about two weeks.

'No. I'm going a bit farther, I'm going to R—. I have about eight hours in the train to look forward to. You're going to Petersburg?' the young man laughed.

'What makes you think I'm going to Petersburg anyway?' Pyotr Stepanovich laughed even more openly.

The young man shook an elegantly gloved finger at him.

'Well, yes, you've guessed it,' Pyotr Stepanovich whispered to him mysteriously, 'I'm going with letters from Yuliya Mikhaylovna and I have to call on three or four people there, you know the kind, may the Devil take them, frankly speaking. A devil of a duty!'

'But what is she in such a funk about, tell me?' the young man whispered back. 'Yesterday she wouldn't even let me in to see her. In my opinion, she has no reason to fear for her husband; on the contrary, he fell down so nicely at the fire, so to speak, ready to sacrifice his life.'

'Well then, there you are,' laughed Pyotr Stepanovich. 'She's afraid, you see, that people have already written from here . . . that is, certain gentlemen . . . In short, Stavrogin's the main one here, or I should say, Prince K. Oh, that's a whole other story. Maybe I'll tell you some of it along the way, though only as far as chivalry permits . . . This is a relative of mine, Ensign Erkel, who lives in the district here.'

The young man, who had been taking sidelong glances at Erkel, touched his hat; Erkel gave a bow.

'You know, Verkhovensky, eight hours in a railway carriage is a dreadful fate. But Berestov is travelling in first class with us – a very amusing colonel, our neighbour in the country. He's married to Garina (née de Garine), and you know, he's a decent sort. He even has ideas. He's been here only two days. Absolutely crazy about whist. How about our giving it a try, eh? I've already spotted a fourth: Pripukhlov, our merchant from T—, with a beard, a millionaire, I mean, a genuine millionaire, I'm telling you. I'll introduce you, he's a very interesting old moneybags; we'll have a good laugh.'

'Whist, with the greatest pleasure, and I'm awfully fond of it on the train, but I'm in second class.'

'Come on, that won't do! Come sit with us. I'll have you switched to first class immediately. The head conductor will do what I say. What do you have, a bag? A plaid?'

'Wonderful, let's go!'

Pyotr Stepanovich took his bag, plaid and book, and immediately moved to first class with the greatest alacrity. Erkel lent a hand. The third bell rang.

'Well, Erkel,' Pyotr Stepanovich, hastily and with a preoccupied look, held out his hand for the last time, from the window of the coach, 'I'm actually going to sit down and play cards with them.'

'But why do you need to explain to me, Pyotr Stepanovich? I do understand, I understand everything, Pyotr Stepanovich!'

'Well, till we meet,' he suddenly turned away in response to the voice of the young man, who called him to meet his partners. And Erkel never saw his Pyotr Stepanovich again!

He returned home very sad. It was not that he was afraid that Pyotr Stepanovich had suddenly abandoned them, but . . . but he had turned away from him so quickly when he was called by the young fop, and . . . he could have said something else to him besides 'till we meet', or . . . or at least shaken his hand more warmly.

This last thing was actually the most important. Something else was beginning to claw at his poor heart, and he himself didn't yet understand that it was something connected with the previous evening.

CHAPTER 7

Stepan Trofimovich's Last Wandering

I.

I'm convinced that Stepan Trofimovich was very much afraid as he felt the time for his mad venture approaching. I'm convinced that he was suffering terribly from fear, especially the night before, that dreadful night. Nastasya later mentioned that he had gone to bed very late, and had slept. But that doesn't prove anything: people condemned to death, they say, sleep very soundly even the night before their execution. Although he did set out when it was already daylight, when a nervous man always takes heart somewhat (the major, Virginsky's relative, used to stopped believing in God as soon as night had passed), I'm still convinced that never before could he have imagined himself alone on the high road and in such a situation without a feeling of horror. Of course, at first a certain desperation in his thoughts most likely cushioned the full force of that terrible sense of solitude that he suddenly faced as soon as he had left Stasie and his comfortable, warm place of twenty years. But it didn't matter: even with the clearest apprehension of all the horrors that awaited him, he would still have set forth on the high road and begun his journey along it! There was something about it that stirred his pride and delighted him, despite everything. Oh, he could have accepted Varvara Petrovna's conditions and remained beholden to her charity '*comme un* simple hanger-on'! But he hadn't accepted her charity and hadn't remained. And here he was leaving her on his own and raising 'the banner of a great idea' and walking along the high road to die for it! That's precisely how he must have felt, precisely how his actions must have struck him.

I was struck by another question more than once: why was he actually running away, that is, running with his feet, in the literal sense, and not simply going away by horse and carriage? At first I tried to explain this by the impracticality of a fifty-year-old man and a fantastic divergence of his thinking under the influence of powerful feelings. It seemed to me that the thought of hiring a series of post-horses (even if they had bells) must have struck him as too simple and prosaic; on the contrary, a pilgrimage on foot, even if with an umbrella, was much more picturesque and much more in keeping with the spirit of love and revenge. But now, when it is all over, I suppose that everything happened in a much simpler way. In the first place, he was afraid of hiring horses, because Varvara Petrovna might find out and stop him by force, which she would certainly have done and he would certainly have submitted – and then, farewell to the great idea forever. In the second place, in order to hire a series of post-horses, you at least have to know where you are going. But knowing this was precisely the greatest source of suffering for him at this juncture: he couldn't for the life of him name and settle on a place. For, if he should decide on some town, his venture would instantly become both absurd and impossible in his own eyes; he felt that very keenly. And what exactly would he do in one particular town and not in another? Look for *ce marchand*? But what *marchand*? This second and even most terrible question came to the fore at this point. At bottom, there was nothing more terrible for him than *ce marchand*, whom he had so suddenly rushed off to look for as fast as he could, and whom, quite naturally, he was actually most afraid of finding. No, the high road was really the best thing; it was so simple to set off on it, and walk along it and not think of anything, as long as it was possible not to think. The high road is something eternally long, long, and no end in sight. It's like human life, like human dreams. An idea is contained in the high road; but what idea is contained in a series of post-horses? Post-horses are the end of an idea ... *Vive la grande route*,[1] and then it's what God will provide.

After his sudden and unexpected meeting with Liza, which

I have already described, he set off again in an even greater state of oblivion. The high road ran half a verst from Skvoreshniki, and strangely enough, he didn't even notice at first how he had come to be on it. It was unbearable for him just then to think anything through or even to be clearly aware of anything. The fine rain now stopped, now began again; he didn't even notice the rain. Nor did he notice that he had thrown the bag over his shoulder and that made it easier for him to walk. He must have gone something like a verst or a verst and a half when he suddenly stopped and looked around. The old, black and rutted road stretched before him in an unbroken thread, with white willows planted on either side. To the right there was an utterly bare spot, where the harvest had long ago been reaped; to the left were bushes, and beyond them a wooded area. And in the distance, in the far distance, the barely perceptible line of the railway ran crosswise, and on it the faint smoke of some train, but no sound could be heard. Stepan Trofimovich quailed somewhat, but only for a moment. After sighing for no particular reason, he set his bag by a willow tree and sat down to rest. As he moved to sit down, he felt a chill and wrapped himself in his plaid; then, suddenly noticing the rain, he opened his umbrella over himself. He remained sitting for a rather long time like this, moving his lips now and then and firmly gripping the umbrella handle in his hands. Various images scudded before him in a feverish train, one rapidly succeeding the other in his mind. 'Lise, Lise,' he thought, 'and with her, *ce* Maurice . . . Strange people . . . Well, wasn't that a strange fire, and what were they talking about, and what people were murdered? . . . I think Stasie hasn't had time to find out anything yet and is still waiting for me with a cup of coffee . . . A game of cards? Did I actually lose to some people at cards? Hmm . . . in this Russia of ours, during the time of so-called serfdom . . . Oh, my God, and Fedka?'

He gave a frightened start, and looked about: 'Well, what if this Fedka is sitting here somewhere behind a bush; they do say that he has a whole band of brigands somewhere on the high road. Oh, my God, then I . . . I'll tell him the whole truth then, that I'm to blame . . . and that *for ten years* I suffered for him, more than he did as a soldier, and . . . and that I'll give him my wallet. Hmm, *j'ai en tout quarante roubles; il prendra les roubles et il me tuera tout de même.*[2]

Out of fear he closed his umbrella for some unknown reason, and laid it down beside him. In the distance, on the road leading from the town, a cart appeared; he began peering at it anxiously.

'*Grace à Dieu*, it's a cart and it's moving at a walking pace; it can't be dangerous. It's those worn-out nags that we have around here . . . I always said about the breed . . . Though it was Pyotr Ilych who spoke about the breed in the club, and I took him at cards, *et puis*, but what's that in the back and . . . looks like a woman in the cart. A peasant man and woman – *cela commence à être rassurant*. The woman in back, and the man in front – *c'est très rassurant*. A cow is tied to the back of the cart by its horns, *c'est rassurant au plus haut degré.*'[3]

The cart drew even with him, a rather sturdy and decent peasant cart. The woman was sitting on a tightly stuffed bag, and the man on the driver's seat, with his legs hanging in Stepan Trofimovich's direction. Behind, there actually was a red cow plodding along, tied by her horns. The muzhik and the woman were staring open-eyed at Stepan Trofimovich, and Stepan Trofimovich was staring at them in precisely the same way, but by the time he had let them get about twenty paces ahead, he suddenly stood up and hurried to catch up with them. Naturally, it seemed safer to him to be in the vicinity of the cart, but once he had caught up with it, he promptly forgot about everything, and again became absorbed in his fragmented thoughts and notions. He was walking along and, needless to say, didn't suspect that for the muzhik and the woman he was at that moment the most puzzling and curious object that one could possibly meet on the high road.

'You, what sort might you be, I mean if it ain't too rude o' me to ask?' the wench finally couldn't resist when Stepan Trofimovich looked at her absent-mindedly. The wench was about twenty-seven, plump, black-browed and ruddy-cheeked, with pleasantly smiling red lips, behind which sparkled white, even teeth.

'You ... are you addressing me?' muttered Stepan Trofimovich with deplorable surprise.

'Must be from the merchants,' said the muzhik confidently.
He was a strapping man of about forty, with a broad and not
stupid face and a full and thick reddish beard.

'No, I'm not really a merchant, I ... I ... *moi c'est autre
chose*,'⁴ Stepan Trofimovich managed to counter, and just to
be on the safe side he dropped slightly behind, so that he now
began to walk alongside the cow.

'From the gentry, must be,' the muzhik decided, having heard
the foreign words, and he tugged at the little horse.

'That's why we was lookin' at you, maybe you went out to
take a walk?' the wench again asked curiously.

'You ... are you asking me?'

'Foreign folk come to these here parts on a different sort of
road, the iron one, and your boots don't look like they're from
around here ...'

'Military boots,' the muzhik offered complacently and significantly.

'No, I'm not exactly a military man, I ...'

'Such an inquisitive wench,' Stepan Trofimovich raged
inwardly, 'and how they look me over ... *mais, enfin* ... In a
word, it's strange that I seem to feel guilty before them, and
I'm not guilty of anything before them.'

The wench was exchanging whispers with the muzhik.

'If it don't put you out none, we could give you a ride, if it's
agreeable to you.'

Stepan Trofimovich suddenly collected his wits.

'Yes, yes, my friends, I accept with great pleasure, because
I'm very tired; except how do I get in?'

'How extraordinary,' he thought to himself, 'I've been walking alongside this cow all this time and it didn't occur to me
to ask them to let me sit with them ... This "real life" has
something very distinctive about it.'

The muzhik, however, did not bring the horse to a stop.

'Where might you be headin'?' he inquired, with a certain
mistrustfulness.

Stepan Trofimovich didn't understand immediately.

'To Khatovo, mebbe?'

'To Khatov? No, not to Khatov . . . I'm not really acquainted with him, although I've heard of him . . .'

'The village of Khatovo, it's a village, about nine versts from here.'

'A village? *C'est charmant*, yes, I seem to have heard of it . . .'

Stepan Trofimovich kept on walking; they still hadn't let him get onboard. An ingenious guess flashed through his head:

'Perhaps you think that I . . . I do have my passport with me and I am a professor, that is, if you want, a teacher . . . but a head one. I'm a head teacher. *Oui, c'est comme ça qu'on peut traduire.*[5] I would very much like to sit down, and I'll buy you . . . for that I'll buy you a pint of vodka.'

'That'll be fifty kopecks, sir; the road's a hard one.'

'Or else we'll be mighty put out,' the wench interjected.

'Fifty kopecks? All right, fifty kopecks. *C'est encore mieux, j'ai en tout quarante roubles, mais . . .*'[6]

The muzhik stopped the cart. And Stepan Trofimovich was dragged into it by their joint efforts and seated on the bag, beside the wench. He was still caught up in a whirlwind of thoughts. At times he sensed that he was somehow dreadfully absent-minded and was not thinking right about things, and he was amazed at that. His awareness of the morbid weakness of his mind was very oppressive to him at moments, and even unbearable.

'How . . . how is it you've got a cow behind?' he suddenly asked the wench.

'What's that, sir, ain't you never seen one?' The wench began to laugh heartily.

'We bought her in town,' the muzhik interjected. 'Our own cattle, you see, went and died last spring – the plague. They was droppin' all 'round us, all of 'em; no more than half was left, 'twas enough to make yer howl.'

And again he lashed the little horse, which had got stuck in a rut.

'Yes, that happens in this Russia of ours . . . and in general we Russians . . . well, yes, it happens,' Stepan Trofimovich didn't finish.

'If you're a teacher, what are you goin' to Khatovo for? Or are you goin' some place further on?'

'No . . . that is, I'm not going anywhere farther on . . . *C'est à dire*,[7] I'm going to see a certain merchant.'

'To Spasov, must be?'

'Yes, yes, to Spasov, exactly. However, that doesn't matter.'

'If you was goin' to Spasov, and on foot, you'd ha' been walkin' a whole week in them boots o' yours,' the wench laughed heartily.

'That's so, that's so, and it doesn't matter, *mes amis*, it doesn't matter,' Stepan Trofimovich cut her short impatiently.

'Dreadfully inquisitive people; the wench, though, speaks better than he does, and I notice that since the 19th of February their speech has changed somewhat, and . . . why should they care whether I go to Spasov or don't go to Spasov? However, I shall pay them, so why are they pestering me?'

'If it's Spasov, then you need to go on the boat,' the muzhik didn't let up.

'That's right as rain,' the wench put in with animation, ' 'cause if you go along the riverbank with horses, it'll be 'bout thirty versts the long way 'round.'

'Forty it'll be.'

'Tomorrow by two o'clock you'll be right on time to catch the boat in Ustyevo,' the wench chimed in. But Stepan Trofimovich maintained a stubborn silence. His questioners fell silent as well. The muzhik kept tugging at the nag; the woman exchanged rare and brief remarks with him. Stepan Trofimovich began to doze. He was dreadfully surprised when the woman, with a laugh, shook him and he found himself in a rather large village by the front entrance of a peasant hut with three windows.

'You had a little doze, sir?'

'What is this? Where am I? Ah, I see! Well, it doesn't matter,' Stepan Trofimovich gave a sigh and got down from the cart.

He looked around him sadly; the village scene seemed strange and somehow terribly foreign to him.

'The fifty kopecks, I completely forgot!' He turned to the muzhik with a quick gesture that was somehow exaggerated. Evidently he was afraid to part with them.

'You can settle up inside, come in please,' the muzhik invited him.

'It's nice here,' said the wench approvingly.

Stepan Trofimovich stepped on to the rickety little porch.

'Why, how can this possibly be?' he whispered in profound and timid bewilderment, yet he went into the hut. '*Elle l'a voulu.*'[8] Something pierced his heart, and he again suddenly forgot about everything, even that he had gone into the hut.

It was a bright, rather clean peasant hut with three windows and two rooms; it wasn't so much a coaching inn as a hut for travellers, where, by ancient custom, acquaintances passing through would stay. Stepan Trofimovich, without any embarrassment, proceeded to the nearest corner, sat down and fell to thinking. Meanwhile, after three hours of dampness on the road an extraordinarily pleasant sense of warmth suddenly suffused his entire body. Even the chill itself, which kept running sharply and spasmodically up and down his spine, as is always the case when especially nervous people have a fever, suddenly struck him as strangely agreeable the moment he made the abrupt transition from the cold into the warmth. He raised his head, and the delicious smell of hot blini, which the mistress of the house was busy making on the stove, tickled his nose. With a childlike smile, he leaned towards the mistress of the house and suddenly began to babble:

'What's that? Are those blini? *Mais . . . c'est charmant.*'

'Would you like some, sir?' the woman offered immediately and politely.

'I would, I would very much, and . . . I would ask you for some tea besides,' Stepan Trofimovich livened up.

'Should I put on the samovar? That would be our great pleasure.'

The blini appeared on a large plate with a bold blue pattern on it – the famous thin peasant blini, made half of wheat flour, drenched in hot fresh butter, extremely tasty blini. Stepan Trofimovich sampled them with delight.

'How buttery they are, and how tasty! And if only I could have *un doigt d'eau de vie.*'[9]

'And it wouldn't be some vodka you would like, sir?'

'Precisely, precisely, just a little, *un tout petit rien*.'[10]

'Five kopecks' worth, you mean?'

'Yes. Five – five – five – five, *un tout petit rien*,' Stepan Trofimovich affirmed with a blissful little smile.

Ask a man of the common people to do something for you, and, if he can and wants to, he'll oblige you diligently and cordially. But if you ask him to fetch some vodka for you, his normal calm cordiality suddenly turns into a cheerful readiness to please, almost a brotherly solicitude for you. The one who goes for the vodka – even though you, not he, will be the one drinking it, and he knows this in advance – still feels a sense of participation in your future pleasure. No more than three or four minutes later (the pothouse was just two steps away) a half-bottle, along with a large greenish glass, turned up on the table before Stepan Trofimovich.

'And that's all for me!' He was extremely surprised. 'I've always drunk vodka, but I never knew that you could get so much for five kopecks.'

He poured out a glassful, got up and with a certain air of triumph walked across the room to the other corner, where his travelling companion on the bag was installed, the black-eyed wench, who had pestered him so with questions on the road. The wench was embarrassed, and started to refuse, but having said all that was prescribed by decorum, she at last stood up, drank it off politely in three sips, as women do, and with a look of extraordinary suffering on her face, handed back the glass and bowed to Stepan Trofimovich. He gave a dignified bow in return and went back to his table with a proud expression on his face.

All this occurred as if by some inner inspiration; he himself, even a second before, had no idea that he would go and offer the glass to the wench.

'I know how to deal with the common people perfectly, perfectly, and I've always told them that,' he thought complacently, as he poured himself the vodka that remained in the bottle. Although it amounted to less than a glass, the vodka warmed him and perked him up, and even went a little to his head.

'*Je suis malade tout à fait, mais ce n'est pas trop mauvais d'être malade.*'[11]

'Would you care to purchase something?' came a soft woman's voice from beside him.

He raised his eyes and, to his surprise, saw before him a lady – *une dame et elle en avait l'air*[12] – already past thirty, very modest in appearance, dressed like a town woman, in a darkish dress and with a large grey shawl around her shoulders. There was something very welcoming in her eyes, which immediately proved pleasing to Stepan Trofimovich. She had just then come back into the hut, where her things had been left on a bench, right beside the spot that Stepan Trofimovich was occupying – among them a portfolio, at which, he now remembered, he had looked with curiosity when he came in, and a not very big oilskin bag. From this bag she extracted two small, beautifully bound books with crosses stamped on the binding and held them up for Stepan Trofimovich to see.

'Eh . . . *mais je crois que c'est l'Évangile*; with the greatest of pleasure . . . Ah, now I understand . . . *Vous êtes ce qu'on appelle*[13] a book-pedlar; I've read about that more than once . . . Fifty kopecks?'

'Thirty-five kopecks each,' replied the book-pedlar.

'With the greatest of pleasure. *Je n'ai rien contre l'Évangile, et . . .*[14] I've long wanted to reread it . . .'

It flashed through his mind at that moment that he hadn't read the Gospels for at least thirty years, except perhaps for a bit he had recalled some seven years before when reading Renan's book, *La Vie de Jésus*.[15] Since he had no change, he proceeded to pull out his four ten-rouble notes – everything he had. The mistress of the house undertook to give him change, and only at that point did he notice, on looking closely, that rather a lot of folk had assembled in the hut and that they had been observing him for a long time now, and seemed to be talking about him. They were also discussing the fire in the town, especially the owner of the cart with the cow, since he had just returned from town. They were talking about arson and about the Shpigulin workers.

'Well, he certainly didn't say anything about the fire to me when he was giving me a ride, but he talked about everything else,' it occurred to Stepan Trofimovich for some reason.

'Stepan Trofimovich, is it you I see, sir? That's somethin' I didn't expect no-how! . . . Or didn't you recognize me?' exclaimed a rather elderly fellow, who had the look of an old-time house-serf about him, his face clean-shaven and wearing a greatcoat with a long turned-back collar.

On hearing his name, Stepan Trofimovich became frightened.

'Excuse me,' he muttered, 'I don't quite remember you . . .'

'You've forgotten! Why, I'm Anisim, Anisim Ivanov. I was in service at the late Mr Gaganov's and used to see you, sir, many times with Varvara Petrovna at the late Avdotya Sergeyevna's. I used to come with books from her and two times brought you Petersburg sweets from her.'

'Oh, yes, I remember you, Anisim,' Stepan Trofimovich smiled. 'Are you living here?'

'Near Spasov, sir, in a village by the V— Monastery, at Marfa Sergeyevna's, the sister of Avdotya Sergeyevna, mebbe it pleases you to remember. She broke her leg jumpin' out of a carriage, goin' to a ball. Now she lives near the monastery, and I'm in service with her; and now, if it pleases you to see, here I am on my way to the town to see my kinfolk . . .'

'Oh yes, yes.'

'When I saw you, I was so glad; you was always so kind to me, sir,' Anisim gave an ecstatic smile. 'But where are you headin' for now, sir, all alone and on your own, it seems . . . Seems to me you never went nowhere all on your own before, did you?'

Stepan Trofimovich gave him an apprehensive look.

'You wouldn't be comin' to us in Spasov, would you, sir?'

'Yes, I'm going to Spasov. *Il me semble que tout le monde va à Spassof . . .*'[16]

'And it wouldn't be to Fyodor Matveyevich's, would it? They'll be so glad to see you. Why, they used to respect you so much in the old days. Even now they remember you often.'

'Yes, yes, I'm going to see Fyodor Matveyevich.'

'That's as it should be, that's as it should be. The muzhiks here are wonderin', sir; they say they met you on the high road and you was walkin' on foot. Stupid people, sir.'

'I . . . this I . . . You know, Anisim, I made a bet, the way the English do, that I would go there on foot, and I . . .'

His forehead and his temples broke out in a sweat.

'That's as it should be, that's as it should be,' Anisim stood listening closely with merciless curiosity. But Stepan Trofimovich couldn't endure it any longer. He was thrown into such confusion that he wanted to get up and leave the hut. But the samovar was brought in, and at that same moment the book-peddler, who had gone out somewhere, came back. With the gesture of a man who was trying to save himself, he turned to her and offered her tea. Anisim yielded and walked away.

Indeed, the muzhiks were showing signs of perplexity.

'What sort of man is this? They found him walkin' on the road; he says he's a teacher, he's wearin' foreign clothes on him, but he's got the brains of a little boy; he answers vague-like, like he ran away from someone, but he's got money!' People began to think of notifying the authorities, ' 'cause on top of everythin' else ain't no real quiet in the town'. But Anisim straightened things out in a minute. Going into the entryway, he informed everyone who would listen that Stepan Trofimovich wasn't really a teacher, but 'a man with a lot o' book-learnin' and workin' hard on big questions of learnin'; and used to be a landowner in these parts and had been livin' twenty-two years now at Stavrogina's, the full general's widow, in place of the most important man in the house; and has real high respect from everyone in the town. In the nobles' club he used to drop fifty and a hundred roubles in one night; and he had the rank of councillor, same as a military lieutenant colonel, that would be just one rank below full colonel. And the fact that he had money, well, he had more than anyone could count through Stavrogina, the full general's widow', and so on and so forth.

'*Mais c'est une dame, et très comme il faut,*' said Stepan Trofimovich, recovering from Anisimov's onslaught, as he observed with pleasant curiosity his neighbour the book-peddler, who, however, was drinking tea out of a saucer with a piece of sugar in her mouth. '*Ce petit morceau de sucre ce n'est rien* . . . There's something noble and independent about her, and at the same time quiet. *Le comme il faut tout pur*,[17] except in rather a different way.'

He soon learned from her that her name was Sofya Matveyevna Ulitina, and that she actually lived in K—, that she had one widowed sister there, a tradeswoman. She herself was also a widow, and her husband, who had been promoted from sergeant major to ensign for meritorious service, had been killed at Sevastopol.

'But you're still so young, *vous n'avez pas trente ans*.'[18]

'Thirty-four, sir,' Sofya Matveyevna smiled.

'What, you understand French as well?'

'Just a little. I spent four years living in a noble house and picked up a bit from the children.'

She told him that after being left a widow at only eighteen, she was in Sevastopol for a time 'as a nurse', and then she lived in various places, and now she travelled around selling the Gospel.

'*Mais mon Dieu*, wasn't it you who had a strange, even a very strange adventure in our town?'

She blushed; it turned out that she was the one.

'*Ces vauriens, ces malheureux!*'[19] he was about to begin in a voice trembling with indignation. A morbid and hateful memory echoed painfully in his heart. He seemed to forget himself for a minute.

'There, she's left again.' He snapped out of it, noticing that again she was not by his side. 'She goes out often, and she's busy with something; I notice that she's even agitated . . . *Bah, je deviens égoïste* . . .'[20]

He raised his eyes and again saw Anisim, but this time in highly threatening surroundings. The whole hut was filled with muzhiks, and Anisim had evidently dragged all of them in there with him. Here was the owner of the hut, and the muzhik with the cow, two more muzhiks of some sort (they turned out to be coachmen), some other little half-drunken man, who was dressed like a muzhik yet was clean-shaven and looked like a tradesman who had succumbed to drink and who was talking more than anyone else. And absolutely all of them were discussing him, Stepan Trofimovich. The muzhik with the cow was holding his ground, maintaining that if he went along the riverbank it would be a good forty versts out of the way, and that it was absolutely necessary to go by boat. The half-drunk tradesman and the owner objected heatedly:

'Because, good brother, of course it's closer for His High Excellency to go across the lake on the boat; that's all well and good; but the boat, considerin' the time o' year, mebbe won't even come.'

'It'll get here, it'll get here, it's runnin' for another week,' Anisim was more impassioned than the others.

'That may well be! But it don't come on schedule, 'cause it's late in the year; sometimes they have to wait for it three days in Ustyevo.'

'It'll be here tomorrow, tomorrow it'll come on time, right at two o'clock. And you'll get to Spasov before evenin' and right on the dot, sir,' Anisim was getting all worked up.

'*Mais qu'est ce qu'il a cet homme*,'[21] Stepan Trofimovich was trembling as he fearfully awaited his fate.

The coachmen also stepped forward and began to bargain with him; they wanted three roubles to take him to Ustyevo. The others shouted that it wasn't at all bad, that it was a fair price and that people were taken from here to Ustyevo all summer long for that price.

'But ... it's nice here, too ... And I don't want ...' Stepan Trofimovich began to mumble.

'Very good, sir, you're right, it's really nice at Spasov just now, and Fyodor Matveyevich will be so glad to see you.'

'*Mon Dieu, mes amis*, all this is so unexpected.'

Finally, Sofya Matveyevna returned. But she sat down on the bench so crushed and sad.

'I'm not going to get to Spasov!' she said to the woman of the house.

'What, you're going to Spasov too?' cried Stepan Trofimovich with a start.

It turned out that a certain landowner, Nadezhda Yegorovna Svetlitsyna, had asked her the day before to wait for her in

Khatovo and promised to drive her to Spasov, but then had not come.

'What am I going to do now?' Sofya Matveyevna kept repeating.

'*Mais, ma chère et nouvelle amie,*[22] why, I can also drive you there just as well as that landowner, to this village, what do you call it, for which I've hired a coach, and tomorrow – well, tomorrow we'll go to Spasov together.'

'Are you really going to Spasov, too?'

'*Mais que faire, et je suis enchanté!*[23] I will take you along with the greatest pleasure. Those men over there want it, and I've already hired them ... Which of you did I hire?' Stepan Trofimovich suddenly wanted terribly to get to Spasov.

A quarter of an hour later they were already taking seats in a covered britska: he very lively and utterly content; she beside him with her bag and a grateful smile. Anisim was helping them in.

'Have a good trip, sir,' he bustled about the britska as energetically as he could. 'We were so very glad to see you!'

'Goodbye, goodbye, my friend, goodbye.'

'You'll see Fyodor Matveyevich, sir ...'

'Yes, my friend, yes ... Fyodor Matveyevich ... but goodbye.'

2.

'You see, my friend, you will permit me to call myself your friend, *n'est ce pas?*' Stepan Trofimovich began rapidly, as soon as the britska had begun to move. 'You see, I ... *J'aime le peuple, c'est indispensable, mais il me semble que je ne l'avais jamais vu de près. Stasie ... cela va sans dire qu'elle est aussi du people ... mais le vrai peuple,*[24] that is, the real common people who are on the high road seem to me to be concerned only with where I'm actually going ... But there's no point in taking offence. I seem to be rambling a bit, but I think that's from being in a rush ...'

'You seem to be unwell, sir,' Sofya Matveyevna was keeping a sharp but respectful eye on him.

'No, no, I just have to wrap myself up; the wind is a bit brisk, very brisk, in fact, but we'll forget about it. That's not what I really wanted to say. *Chère et incomparable amie*,[25] it seems to me that I'm almost happy, and the cause of that is you. Happiness is not to my advantage, because I immediately make a point of forgiving all my enemies . . .'

'What do you mean, why, that's very good, sir.'

'Not always, *chère innocente. L'Évangile . . . Voyez-vous, désormais nous le prêcherons ensemble*, and I will sell your beautiful little books with pleasure. Yes, I feel that this is perhaps an idea, *quelque chose de très nouveau dans ce genre*. The common folk are religious, *c'est admis*, but they don't yet know the Gospel. I will expound it to them . . . In an oral account one can correct the mistakes in this remarkable book, which, it goes without saying, I am ready to treat with the utmost respect. I shall be useful on the high road as well. I have always been useful, as I've always told *them et à cette chère ingrate*.[26] Oh, let us forgive, let us forgive, let us first of all forgive everyone everywhere . . . We will hope that they will forgive us as well. Yes, because each and every one of us is guilty as far as others are concerned. All are guilty!'

'I think you've managed to put that very well, sir.'

'Yes, yes . . . I feel that I am speaking very well. I will speak to them very well, but . . . but what is the main thing I wanted to say? I keep losing my train of thought and not remembering . . . Will you permit me not to part company with you? I feel that your views and . . . I am even surprised at your manner: you are simple-hearted, you use the word "sir", and you turn your cup upside down on your saucer . . . along with that ugly little piece of sugar; but there's something delightful about you, and I can see from your features . . . Oh, don't blush and don't be afraid of me as a man. *Chère et incomparable, pour moi une femme c'est tout*. I can't live without a woman nearby, but only nearby . . . I'm dreadfully, dreadfully confused . . . I just can't remember what I wanted to say. Oh, blessed is he to whom God always sends a woman, and . . . and I also think that I'm in a certain state of ecstasy. There is a lofty idea in the open road as well! There, that's what I wanted to say – about the idea, I've just remembered it, and I couldn't quite hit on it. And why have they taken us farther? It was nice there too, but here – *cela devient trop froid. Á propos, j'ai en tout quarante roubles et voilà cet argent*,[27] take it, take it, I don't know what to do with it, I'll lose it and they'll take it away from me, and . . . I think I feel like sleeping; something's spinning in my head. Spinning, spinning, spinning. Oh, how kind you are, what is this you're covering me with?'

'You must have a high fever, sir, and I've covered you with my blanket, but about the money I'd . . .'

'Oh, for heaven's sake, *n'en parlons plus, parce que cela me fait mal*,[28] oh, how kind you are!'

He broke off talking rather quickly, and almost immediately fell into a feverish, shivering sleep. The country road by which they covered these seventeen versts was not the smoothest, and the carriage jolted them about cruelly. Stepan Trofimovich would wake up frequently, quickly raise himself off the small pillow that Sofya Matveyevna had slipped under his head, seize her by the hand and inquire: 'Are you here?' as if afraid that she had left him. He also declared that he had dreamed of gaping jaws with teeth, and that he found this very repulsive. That made Sofya Matveyevna very uneasy about him.

The coachman drove them straight to a large peasant hut with four windows and with additional rooms in outbuildings in the yard. Stepan Trofimovich, who was now awake, hurried in and proceeded directly into the second, more spacious and better room of the house. His sleepy face took on a very restless expression. He promptly explained to the landlady, a tall and thick-set peasant woman of about forty, with very black hair and the beginnings of a moustache, that he required the entire room for himself 'and that the room should be locked and no one else allowed in, *parce que nous avons à parler*'.

'*Oui, j'ai beaucoup à vous dire, chère amie*.[29] I'll pay you, I'll pay!' he said with a wave of his hand to the landlady.

Although he was in a hurry, he found it difficult to move his tongue. The landlady listened to him in an unfriendly manner, but kept quiet as a token of her agreement, in which, however, there was a hint of something menacing. He noticed nothing of this, and hastily (he was in a dreadful hurry) asked her to leave and bring them some dinner as soon as possible, 'without a moment's delay'.

At this point the woman with the moustache could endure it no longer.

'This ain't some coachin' inn, sir; we don't do dinners for travellers. I can boil some crayfish or put on the samovar, but we don't have nothin' else. There won't be fresh fish until tomorrow.'

But Stepan Trofimovich began waving his arms and repeating, irate and impatient: 'I'll pay, only make it quick, make it quick.' They decided on fish chowder and roasted chicken. The landlady stated that it was impossible to find chicken anywhere in the village; however, she agreed to go and look, but with an air of doing him an enormous favour.

As soon as she had left, Stepan Trofimovich sat down in an instant on the sofa and seated Sofya Matveyevna beside him. The room contained a sofa and chairs, but they looked dreadful. In general the entire room, which was rather spacious (with a compartment behind a partition, where a bed stood), with old, torn yellow wallpaper, dreadful mythological lithographs on the walls, a long row of icons and folding bronze ones in the front corner, and a strange collection of furniture, all represented an unattractive mixture of something from the urban and traditionally peasant styles. But he didn't so much as glance at all this, didn't so much as look out of the window at the enormous lake that began ten sazhens from the hut.

'Finally, we're alone, and we won't let anyone in! I want to tell you everything, everything from the very beginning.'

Sofya Matveyevna stopped him, looking very uneasy:

'Do you know, Stepan Trofimovich . . .'

'*Comment, vous savez déjà mon nom?*'[30] he smiled happily.

'I heard it from Anisim Ivanovich this morning when you were talking to him. And now I'll be so bold as to tell you, on my part . . .'

And she quickly began whispering to him, glancing round at the closed door lest anyone be eavesdropping, that here, in this village, there was real trouble. That all the local muzhiks,

though fishermen, actually earned their living during the summer by extracting from travellers whatever payment they fan-
cied. This village was not on a through road, but was a dead
end, and people came here only because the boat stopped here,
and that when the boat didn't come – all it took was a little
bad weather and it definitely wouldn't come – then over the
course of several days it would become very crowded, and then
all the huts in the village were filled, and that's just what the
owners were waiting for: they would charge three times the
usual price for each item, and the landlord here was proud and
arrogant because he was very rich by local standards; his fishing
net alone was worth a thousand roubles.

Stepan Trofimovich was looking into Sofya Matveyevna's
extraordinarily animated face almost reproachfully, and several
times gestured in an attempt to stop her. But she held her
ground and said what she had to say: according to her, she
had been here before in the summer with a 'very genteel lady,
sir' from the town, and they had also spent the night, waiting
for the boat, and even two whole days after that, sir, and the
grief they'd had to put up with was a dreadful memory. 'You
were pleased to ask for this room just for yourself, Stepan
Trofimovich . . . I'm mentioning it just to warn you . . . There,
in the next room, there are already some travellers, an older
man and a young man, and a lady with children, and by tomorrow the whole hut will be filled to overflowing before two
o'clock, because the boat, since it hasn't come for two days,
will most likely come tomorrow. And so, for a private room,
and for what you asked them to prepare for your dinner, sir,
and for the inconvenience to all the other travellers, they will
charge you a price that would be utterly unheard of in Moscow
and St Petersburg, sir . . .'

But he was suffering, truly suffering.

'Assez, mon enfant, I beg you; nous avons notre argent, et
après – et après le bon Dieu. And I'm even surprised that you,
considering the high level of your understanding of things . . .
Assez, assez, vous me tourmentez,'[31] he exclaimed hysterically.
'Our whole future lies before us, and you . . . you're trying to
frighten me about the future.'

He immediately proceeded to lay out his entire history, in such haste that at first it was even hard to understand him. It continued for a very long time. The fish chowder was brought in, the chicken was brought in and finally a samovar was brought in, and he kept on talking . . . Everything was coming out rather strangely and morosely, but after all, he was ill. This was a sudden overtaxing of his mental powers, which, of course – and Sofya Matveyevna had foreseen this with anguish throughout his account – was bound to take its toll immediately afterwards in an extraordinary physical decline of his already weakened organism. He began virtually with his childhood, when he 'ran through the fields with a happy heart'; an hour later he had only come to his two marriages and his life in Berlin. However, I wouldn't dream of making fun of him. There was something highly important for him in all this, and to use the latest expression, almost a struggle for existence. Before him he saw the one whom he had already chosen for his future journey, and he hastened to consecrate her, so to speak. His genius must no longer remain a secret to her. Perhaps he was grossly exaggerating in the case of Sofya Matveyevna, but he had already chosen her. He couldn't be without a woman. He himself could clearly see from her face that she didn't understand virtually anything he was saying, even what was most important.

'*Ce n'est rien, nous attendrons*,'[32] and meanwhile she can understand through intuition . . .'

'My friend, all I need from you is just your heart!' he exclaimed, interrupting his story, 'and also this dear, enchanting look that you're now bestowing on me. Oh, don't blush! I've already told you . . .'

A great deal remained foggy to poor, entrapped Sofya Matveyevna when Stepan Trofimovich moved on to what amounted to an entire dissertation about how no one had ever been able to understand him, and how 'talents are perishing here in Russia'. It was 'all so terribly intellectual', she later reported despondently. She listened with obvious suffering, her eyes wide open. But when Stepan Trofimovich ventured into humour and highly witty barbs directed against our 'progressives and lords and masters', she tried out of desperation, once or twice, to laugh in response to his laughter, but the result was worse than tears, to the point where Stepan Trofimovich was finally even embarrassed himself and hit out at the nihilists and the 'new people' with still greater rancour and malice. Here he simply frightened her, and she got some respite, albeit only a most deceptive respite, when the story of his great romance began. A woman is a woman, even if she be a nun. She smiled, shook her head, and promptly blushed furiously and dropped her eyes, which in turn brought Stepan Trofimovich to the point of ecstasy and so inspired him that he even began to embroider a great deal. Varvara Petrovna was now transformed into a most charming brunette ('who enchanted Petersburg and a great many capitals of Europe'), and her husband had died after being 'struck down by a bullet at Sevastopol', only because he felt himself unworthy of her love and yielded to his rival, that is, to none other than Stepan Trofimovich. 'Don't be embarrassed, my gentle one, my Christian,' he exclaimed to Sofya Matveyevna, almost believing himself that everything he was saying was true. 'It was something lofty, something so subtle that not once did either of us ever discuss it our entire lives.' As the story went on, the reason for such a state of affairs was now a blonde (if not Darya Pavlovna, then I have absolutely no idea whom Stepan Trofimovich had in mind). This blonde owed everything to the brunette, and, in her position as a distant relative, grew up in her house. The brunette, finally noticing the blonde's love for Stepan Trofimovich, withdrew into herself. The blonde, for her part, noticing the brunette's love for Stepan Trofimovich, also withdrew into herself. And so all three, pining away from mutual magnanimity, remained silent for twenty years, withdrawn into themselves. 'Oh, what a passion that was, what a passion that was!' he exclaimed, sobbing in the most sincere ecstasy. 'I saw the full flowering of her beauty (the brunette's), I saw daily, with a "festering in my heart", how she would walk by me as if ashamed of her beauty.' (Once he said 'ashamed of her plumpness'.) Finally, he ran away, abandoning this whole delirious twenty-year dream. '*Vingt ans!*' And now on the high road . . . Then, in what must have been an inflamed condition of the brain, he undertook to explain to Sofya Matveyevna what must have been the meaning of their 'so unexpected and so fateful meeting today, for all eternity'. In dreadful embarrassment Sofya Matveyevna finally got up from the sofa; he even attempted to fall on his knees before her, making her burst out weeping. The twilight was thickening; both had now spent several hours in the locked room.

'No, it would be better if you let me go into the other room, sir,' she prattled, 'otherwise, what are people going to think, sir?'

At last she tore herself away; he let her go, after promising her that he would go to bed. As they parted, he complained that he had a bad headache. Sofya Matveyevna, as soon as she had come in, had left her bag and her things in the first room, with the intention of spending the night with the landlords; but she didn't manage to get any rest.

During the night Stepan Trofimovich had an attack of cholerine, which was all too familiar to me and to all his friends – the usual outcome for him of nervous tension and moral shock. Poor Sofya Matveyevna didn't sleep all night. Since looking after the sick man made it necessary for her to go in and out of the hut rather frequently through the landlords' room, the landlady and the travellers who were sleeping there grumbled and even ended by cursing when she decided to put on the samovar towards morning. Throughout his attack Stepan Trofimovich was in a state of semi-consciousness; sometimes he seemed to imagine that the samovar was being readied, that he was being given something to drink (raspberry tea), that his stomach and chest were being warmed with something. But he felt almost every minute that *she* was there beside him; that she was coming in and going out, lifting him off the bed and laying him down again. About three o'clock in the morning he felt better. He sat up, let his legs down from the bed and, without thinking of anything in particular, fell on the floor at her feet. He was not kneeling as he had done earlier; he simply fell at her feet and kissed the hem of her dress.

'Enough, sir, I'm not worthy, sir,' she babbled, trying to lift him back on to the bed.

'My saviour,' he reverently folded his hands before her. '*Vous êtes noble comme une marquise!*[33] I – I am a scoundrel! Oh, I have been dishonest my entire life . . .'

'Calm yourself,' Sofya Matveyevna entreated.

'I told you a pack of lies earlier – to glorify myself, to make it sound good, because I lack substance – everything was a lie, every last word; oh, what a scoundrel I am, what a scoundrel!'

And so the cholerine had developed into another attack, one of hysterical self-condemnation. I have already mentioned these attacks in speaking of his letters to Varvara Petrovna. He suddenly recalled Lise, his encounter with her the previous morning: 'That was so dreadful and she was probably very unhappy, and I didn't ask, I didn't find out! I was thinking only of myself! Oh, what's become of her, do you know what's become of her?' he begged Sofya Matveyevna.

Then he swore that he would 'not betray her', that he would return to *her* (that is, to Varvara Petrovna). 'We will go up to her front steps every day' (that is, always with Sofya Matveyevna) 'when she's getting into her carriage for her morning drive, and we'll watch very quietly . . . Oh, I want her to strike me on the other cheek; I will delight in it! I will turn my other cheek to her *comme dans votre livre!*[34] Only now, only now have I understood what it means to turn the other cheek. I never understood that before!'

Then came two of the most terrible days in Sofya Matveyevna's life; even now she remembers them with a shudder. Stepan Trofimovich fell so seriously ill that he couldn't leave on the boat, which on this occasion appeared precisely at two o'clock in the afternoon. She couldn't bring herself to leave him alone, so she didn't go to Spasov either. As she told it, he was even very happy that the boat had left.

'Well, that's marvellous, that's wonderful,' he muttered from his bed, 'I was so afraid that we would have to go. It's so nice here, it's better here than anywhere . . . You won't leave me? Oh, you haven't left me!'

'Here', however, was not all that nice. He didn't want to know anything about her difficulties; his head was filled with fantasies. He regarded his own illness as something temporary, as a mere trifle, and gave no thought to her at all, but thought only of how they would go out and sell 'these little books'. He asked her to read him the Gospel.

'I haven't read it for a long time . . . in the original. What if someone should ask and I made a mistake; one must be prepared, after all.'

She sat down beside him and opened the book.

'You read beautifully,' he interrupted her after the very first line. 'I can see, I can see that I was not mistaken,' he added obscurely but ecstatically. And in general he was in a state of chronic ecstasy. She read the Sermon on the Mount.

'*Assez, assez, mon enfant*, enough . . . Don't you really think *that's* enough!'

And he closed his eyes in exhaustion. He was very weak, but hadn't yet lost consciousness. Sofya Matveyevna made to get up, imagining that he wanted to go to sleep. But he stopped her:

'My friend, I've told lies all my life. Even when I was speaking the truth. I never said anything for the sake of truth, but only for myself. I knew that before, but only now do I see it . . . Oh, where are those friends whom I have offended with my friendship my whole life? And it's all of them, all of them! *Savez-vous*, perhaps I'm lying even now; I'm probably lying even now. The main thing is that I believe myself when I lie. The hardest thing in life is to live and not lie . . . and . . . and not to believe your own lies, yes, yes, that's it precisely! But wait a moment, more of that later . . . We're together, together!' he added with enthusiasm.

'Stepan Trofimovich,' Sofya Matveyevna asked timidly, 'shouldn't we send to town for a doctor?'

He was dreadfully taken aback.

'What for? *Est-ce que je suis si malade? Mais rien de sérieux.*[35] And why should we have any outsiders? They'll find out, and then what will happen? No, no, no outsiders, just the two of us together, together!'

'You know,' he said, suddenly silent, 'read me something else, whatever you like, wherever your eye happens to fall.'

Sofya Matveyevna opened the book and began to read.

'Wherever it opens, wherever it happens to open,' he repeated.

' "And to the angel of the church in Laodicea write . . ." '[36]

'What's that? What? Where's that from?'

'It's from the Apocalypse.'

'*O, je me souviens, oui, l'Apocalypse. Lisez, lisez*,[37] I'll use the book to predict our future, and I want to know how it comes out. Read from the angel, from the angel . . .'

' "And to the angel of the church in Laodicea write: The words of the Amen, the faithful and true witness, the beginning of God's creation. I know your works: you are neither cold nor hot. Would that you were cold or hot! So, because you are lukewarm, and neither cold nor hot, I will spew you out of my mouth. For you say, I am rich, I have prospered and I need nothing; not knowing that you are wretched, pitiable, poor, blind and naked." '

'That . . . and that's in your book!' he exclaimed, his eyes flashing as he raised himself up from the head of the bed. 'I never knew this great passage! Just listen: better to be cold, cold, than lukewarm, than *only* lukewarm. Oh, I'll prove it. Only don't leave me, don't leave me alone! We will prove it, we will prove it!'

'Why, I certainly won't leave you, Stepan Trofimovich, I'll never leave you, sir!' She seized his hands and clasped them in hers, and pressed them to her heart as she looked at him with tears in her eyes. ('I became very sorry for him at that moment,' she told us later.) His lips began to tremble, almost convulsively.

'Even so, Stepan Trofimovich, what are we to do, when all is said and done? Shouldn't we let some of your friends know, or perhaps your relatives?'

But at this point he became so terribly frightened that she was sorry that she'd mentioned it again. Trembling and shaking, he begged her not to summon anyone and not to undertake anything. He made her give her word, and kept insisting: 'No one, no one! We are by ourselves, by ourselves, *nous partirons ensemble*.'[38]

It was a very bad thing, too, that the landlords were also beginning to be concerned, were grumbling and pestering Sofya

Matveyevna. She paid them, and made certain to show them her money. This mollified them for a time, but the landlord demanded Stepan Trofimovich's 'documents'. The sick man pointed to his small bag with a supercilious smile; in it Sofya Matveyevna found the certificate that verified his resignation, or something of the sort, which had served as an identity card all his life. The landlord didn't relent, and said that 'he has to be taken in someplace else, 'cause we ain't no hospital, and if he dies, who knows what might come of it; we've had a lot to put up with'. Sofya Matveyevna tried to talk with him about getting a doctor, but it turned out that if they were to send to town, then it would cost such a huge sum of money that of course any thought of having a doctor had to be abandoned. She returned to her invalid in anguish. Stepan Trofimovich had grown progressively weaker and weaker.

'Now read me another passage . . . about the swine . . .' he suddenly declared.

'What's that, sir?' Sofya Matveyevna was thoroughly startled.

'About the swine . . . it's in there as well . . . *ces cochons*[39] . . . I remember the demons entered the swine and they all were drowned. You must read me this passage; I'll tell you why later. I want to recall it literally. I must recall it literally.'

Sofya Matveyevna knew the Gospels well and immediately found in Luke the passage that I placed as an epigraph to my chronicle. I will quote it here once again:

' "Now a large herd of swine was feeding there on the hillside; and they begged him to let them enter these. So he gave them leave. Then the demons came out of the man and entered the swine, and the herd rushed down the steep bank into the lake and were drowned. When the herdsmen saw what had happened, they fled, and told it in the city and in the country. Then people went out to see what had happened, and they came to Jesus, and found the man from whom the demons had gone, sitting at the feet of Jesus, clothed and in his right mind; and they were afraid. And those who had seen it told them how he who had been possessed with demons was healed." '

'My friend,' Stepan Trofimovich intoned, with great emotion, '*savez-vous*, this marvellous . . . and unusual passage has been a stumbling block for me all my life . . . *dans ce livre* . . . and I have remembered this passage since I was a child. And now I have an idea: *une comparaison*. A great many ideas are coming to me now: you see, it's just like our Russia. These demons who come out of the sick man and enter the swine – these are all the sores, all the contagions, all the uncleanness, all the demons, large and small, who have accumulated in our great and beloved sick man, our Russia, over the course of centuries, centuries! *Oui, cette Russie, que j'aimais toujours*. But she will be protected by a great idea and a great will from on high, just like that madman possessed by demons, and all these demons, all the uncleanness, all this filth that has festered on the surface . . . all this will beg to enter the swine. And perhaps they have already entered them! That's us, us and them, and my son Petrusha . . . *et les autres avec lui*, and I perhaps am the first, standing at the very head; and we shall throw ourselves, the madmen and the possessed, from a rock into the sea and we shall all drown, and that's no more than we deserve, because that's precisely what we're fit for. But the sick man will be healed and "will sit at the feet of Jesus", and all will look at him in astonishment. My dear, *vous comprendrez après*, but now this excites me very much . . . *Vous comprendrez après . . . Nous comprendrons ensemble*.'[40]

He began to rave, and finally lost consciousness. And so it continued for all of the following day. Sofya Matveyevna sat beside him and wept, hardly slept at all for a third night, and avoided showing herself to the landlords who, she suspected, were already beginning to plot something. Deliverance came only on the third day. In the morning Stepan Trofimovich came to, recognized her and reached his hand out to her. She crossed herself hopefully. He wanted to look out of the window: '*Tiens, un lac*,'[41] he said, 'oh, my God, I hadn't seen it till now . . .' At that moment a carriage rattled up to the entrance of the hut, and an extraordinary hubbub arose in the house.

3.

It was none other than Varvara Petrovna, who had arrived in a four-seater carriage with two footmen and Darya Pavlovna. This miraculous event had come about simply: Anisim, who had been dying of curiosity, arrived in town and the following day stopped by Varvara Petrovna's house, where he told the servants that he had run across Stepan Trofimovich alone in the village, that muzhiks had seen him walking along the high road alone, on foot, and that he had set out for Spasov by way of Ustyevo, now in the company of Sofya Matveyevna. Since Varvara Petrovna, for her part, was already dreadfully alarmed and was searching for her runaway friend as best she could, she was immediately informed about Anisim. After hearing him out, and, more important, the details of Stepan Trofimovich's departure for Ustyevo together with a certain Sofya Matveyevna in the same britska, she immediately got ready and proceeded to drive off to Ustyevo in hot pursuit. As yet she had no idea about his illness.

Her stern and imperious voice rang out; even the landlords quailed. She had only stopped to make inquiries and ask the way, certain that Stepan Trofimovich was already long since in Spasov; but on learning that he was lying ill right there, she stepped into the hut in agitation.

'Well, where is he? Ah, it's you!' she exclaimed, on catching sight of Sofya Matveyevna, who happened to appear in the doorway of the second room at precisely that moment. 'I can guess from your shameless face that it's you. Away with you, you horrible creature! Let no trace of her remain in the house! Kick her out, or else, my dear woman, I'll have you put in jail for life. Have her watched in some other house for the time being. She's already been in jail in town once, and she'll do some more time there. And I ask you, landlord, not to dare let anyone in while I'm here. I am the widow of General Stavrogin, and I'm occupying the entire house. And you, my dear woman, are going to give me an account of everything.'

The familiar sounds shook Stepan Trofimovich. He began to tremble. But she had already stepped behind the partition. With

flashing eyes, she pulled up a chair with her foot, and leaning
back in it, shouted at Dasha:

'Be off with you now; stay with the landlords. Why such
curiosity? And close the door after you as tight as you can.'

She stood in silence for some time, scrutinizing his frightened
face with a kind of predatory look.

'Well, how are you doing, Stepan Trofimovich? Did you have
a nice little romp?' This suddenly burst from her with savage
sarcasm.

'*Chère*,' Stepan Trofimovich began prattling, unaware of
what he was saying, 'I have learned about real Russian life . . .
Et je prêcherai l'Évangile . . .'[42]

'Oh, shameless, ungrateful man!' she shrieked suddenly,
clasping her hands. 'It's not enough for you to shame me,
you've got yourself mixed up with . . . Oh, you brazen old
libertine!'

'*Chère . . .*'

His voice broke, and he could say nothing more, but only
looked, his eyes open wide with fear.

'Who is *she*?'

'*C'est un ange . . . C'était plus qu'un ange pour moi*,[43] all
night long she . . . Oh, don't shout, don't frighten her, *chère,
chère . . .*'

Varvara Petrovna suddenly jumped up from the chair with a
clatter, and her frightened shout was heard: 'Water, water!'
Although he'd come to, she, still pale and trembling with fear,
was looking at his distorted face: only now for the first time
did she guess the extent of his illness.

'Darya,' she suddenly began whispering to Darya Pavlovna,
'send for a doctor at once, for Saltzfisch; have Yegorych go
immediately; let him hire horses here and take another carriage
from town. He must be here by nightfall.'

Darya hurried to do as she was told. Stepan Trofimovich was
looking on with the same wide, frightened eyes; his pale lips
were trembling.

'Just a moment, Stepan Trofimovich, just a moment, my
dear!' She was coaxing him as if he were a child. 'Come now,
wait just a moment, wait, Darya will return soon and . . . Oh,

my God, landlady, landlady, at least you can come in here, my dear woman!'

In her impatience she herself ran to the landlady.

'Bring *that woman* back immediately, right away. Get her back, get her back!'

Fortunately, Sofya Matveyevna hadn't yet had time to make her escape from the house and was just going out through the gate with her bag and bundle. She was brought back. She was so frightened that even her legs and hands were trembling. Varvara Petrovna seized her by the hand, as a hawk does a chicken, and forcibly dragged her to Stepan Trofimovich.

'Well, here she is for you. I really didn't eat her alive. You thought I'd eaten her alive.'

Stepan Trofimovich seized Varvara Petrovna by the hand, raised it to his eyes and burst into tears, sobbing morbidly and hysterically.

'Calm yourself, now, calm yourself, my dear, dearest fellow! Oh, my God, just calm yourself!' she shouted in a frenzy. 'O tormentor, tormentor, eternal tormentor mine!'

'My dear,' Stepan Trofimovich finally prattled, turning to Sofya Matveyevna, 'do stay out there, my dear, there's something I want to say in here . . .'

Sofya Matveyevna immediately hastened to leave.

'*Chérie, chérie,*' he gasped.

'Wait before you speak, Stepan Trofimovich, wait just a little until you've had some rest. Here's some water. Now wait just a little!'

She sat down on the chair again. Stepan Trofimovich was holding her tightly by the hand. For a long time she didn't permit him to speak. He raised her hand to his lips and began kissing it. She clenched her teeth, looking off somewhere into the corner.

'*Je vous aimais!*'[44] finally broke from him. She had never heard such a phrase from his lips, pronounced in such a way.

'Hmm,' she mumbled by way of reply.

'*Je vous aimais toute ma vie . . . vingt ans!*'[45]

She still said nothing – for a good two or three minutes.

'Well, that didn't prevent you from spraying yourself with

perfume when you were getting ready to propose to Dasha,'
she said suddenly in a terrible whisper. Stepan Trofimovich was
dumbfounded.

'You put on a new tie . . .'

Again, silence for a good two minutes.

'Do you remember the cigar?'

'My friend,' he murmured in horror.

'The cigar, in the evening, by the window . . . the moon was
shining . . . after the summerhouse . . . in Skvoreshniki? Do you
remember, do you remember?' She jumped up from her chair,
seized his pillow by both corners and shook it with his head still
on it. 'Do you remember, you empty, empty, ignominious, lily-
livered, forever, forever empty man!' she hissed in a frenzied
whisper as she tried to restrain herself from shouting. Finally, she
let him go and fell back into the chair, covering her face with her
hands. 'Enough!' she snapped, sitting erect. 'Twenty years have
passed, there's no bringing them back; I'm a fool as well.'

'*Je vous aimais*,' he again folded his hands.

'But why do you keep at me with your *aimais* and *aimais*!
Enough!' She jumped up again. 'And if you don't go to sleep
now, then I . . . You need rest; sleep now, sleep, close your eyes.
Oh, my God, maybe he wants to have something to eat! What
are you eating? What is he eating? Oh, my God, where's that
woman? Where is she?'

A commotion was in the making. But Stepan Trofimovich
babbled in a weak voice that he really would sleep for *une
heure*, and then – *un bouillon, un thé . . . enfin, il est si heureux*.[46] He lay down and really did seem to go to sleep (he was
probably pretending). Varvara Petrovna waited a moment and
then tiptoed out from behind the partition.

She took a seat in the landlords' room, chased the landlords
out and ordered Dasha to bring *that woman* to her. A serious
interrogation got under way.

'Tell me all the details now, my good woman; sit beside me,
that's it. Well?'

'I met Stepan Trofimovich . . .'

'Stop, be quiet. I warn you that if you lie or conceal anything,
I'll dig you up out of the ground. Well?'

'I came across Stepan Trofimovich . . . as soon as I arrived in Khatovo, ma'am,' Sofya Matveyevna said, almost in a gasp.

'Stop, be quiet, wait a moment: what's all this jabbering? First of all, what sort of creature are you, anyway?'

The other woman told her something about herself, as briefly as possible, to be sure, beginning with Sevastopol. Varvara Petrovna heard her out silently, sitting erect on her chair, looking sternly and stubbornly straight into her eyes.

'Why are you so frightened? Why are you looking at the floor? I like people who look me straight in the eye and argue with me. Continue.'

The other woman finished telling her about their meeting, about her books, about how Stepan Trofimovich had treated the peasant woman to some vodka.

'That's it, that's it, don't leave out the slightest detail,' Varvara Petrovna said approvingly. Finally, about how they set off and how Stepan Trofimovich had kept on talking, though he was 'now quite ill, ma'am', and had told her about his whole life, from the very beginning, and had even spent several hours in the telling.

'Tell me about his life.'

Sofya Matveyevna suddenly hesitated and came to a complete impasse.

'Here I can't tell you anything, ma'am,' she offered, almost crying, 'because I understood almost nothing.'

'You're lying – as if you couldn't understand anything.'

'He went on for a long time about some high-born, black-haired lady.' Sofya Matveyevna blushed violently, having noticed, however, Varvara Petrovna's blonde hair and her utter lack of resemblance to the 'brunette'.

'Black-haired? What's that all about? Well, tell me!'

'About how this high-born lady was very much in love with him, ma'am, her whole life, twenty whole years, but she didn't dare declare herself to him and was ashamed, because she was very plump, ma'am.'

'What a fool he is!' Varvara Petrovna snapped thoughtfully, but decisively.

Sofya Matveyevna was now crying her eyes out.

'I can't tell anything very well here, because I myself was terribly afraid for him and couldn't understand, because he's such an intelligent man . . .'

'It's not for a crow like you to judge his intellect. Did he offer his hand?'

The other woman began to tremble.

'Did he fall in love with you? Speak! Did he offer his hand?' Varvara Petrovna shouted menacingly.

'It almost amounted to that, ma'am,' she sniffled. 'Only I didn't take it seriously, on account of his illness,' she added firmly, raising her eyes.

'What's your name? Your first name and patronymic?'

'Sofya Matveyevna, ma'am.'

'Well then, Sofya Matveyevna, you should know that this is the most worthless, most empty and vile little man . . . Good Lord! Do you take me for a dreadful woman?'

The other woman looked at her wide-eyed.

'For a dreadful woman, for a tyrant, who's ruined his life?'

Varvara Petrovna actually had tears in her eyes.

'Well then, sit down, sit down, don't be frightened. Look me in the eyes again, straight in the eyes: why are you blushing? Dasha, come here, look at her: what do you think, does she have a pure heart?'

And to Sofya Matveyevna's surprise, and perhaps to her even greater alarm, she suddenly patted her on the cheek.

'It's just a pity that you're a fool. You're too old to be such a fool. All right, my dear, I'll take you in hand. I can see that this is all nonsense. Stay here nearby for the time being; they'll rent you a room, and you'll receive board and everything from me, until I send for you.'

Sofya Matveyevna stammered in fright that she had to hurry off.

'There's no need for you to hurry. I'll buy all your books, and you just sit here. Keep quiet, no excuses. After all, if I hadn't come, you wouldn't have left him in any case?'

'I wouldn't have left him for anything in the world, ma'am,' Sofya Matveyevna stated quietly and firmly, wiping her eyes.

Dr Saltzfisch arrived by carriage when it was already late at night. He was a highly respectable old man and a rather experienced practitioner, who had recently lost his official post in our town as the result of some quarrel over a matter of principle with his superior. From that moment on, Varvara Petrovna began to 'protect' him as much as she possibly could. He examined the sick man carefully, asked some questions and cautiously informed Varvara Petrovna that the condition of the 'sufferer' was highly dubious, as a result of complications of his illness, and that it was necessary to 'expect even the worst'. Varvara Petrovna, who in twenty years had grown unaccustomed to the thought of anything serious and decisive happening as far as Stepan Trofimovich personally was concerned, was profoundly shaken, and even turned pale.

'Is there really no hope?'

'Can we really ever say that there is absolutely no hope, but . . .'

She didn't go to bed all night, and could hardly wait for morning. As soon as the sick man had opened his eyes and come to his senses (he was still conscious, although he was growing weaker by the hour), she went up to him with a very decisive look on her face.

'Stepan Trofimovich, one must be prepared for everything. I have sent for a priest. You are obliged to do your duty . . .'

Knowing his convictions, she was very much afraid that he would refuse. He looked at her in surprise.

'Nonsense, nonsense!' she cried out, thinking that he was already refusing. 'It's no time for games now. There's been quite enough tomfoolery.'

'But . . . am I really so ill?'

He gave his thoughtful consent. And on the whole it was with great surprise that I later learned from Varvara Petrovna that he didn't have the slightest fear of death. Perhaps he simply didn't believe that he would die, and continued to look on his illness as something insignificant.

He made his confession and received communion very willingly. Everyone, including Sofya Matveyevna, and even the servants, came to congratulate him on receiving the holy sacraments. Everyone without exception was crying as they looked at his sunken and wasted face and his pale, quivering lips.

'*Oui, mes amis*, and I'm just surprised that you are making such a . . . fuss. Tomorrow I will probably get up and we . . . will set out . . . *Toute cette cérémonie* . . .[47] to which I, of course, render full credit . . . was . . .'

'I ask you, Father, to be sure to stay with the patient,' Varvara Petrovna stopped the priest, who had already removed his vestments. 'As soon as tea has been served to everyone, I ask you to begin speaking immediately about divine matters, in order to strengthen his faith.'

The priest began to speak. Everyone was sitting or standing around the sick man's bed.

'In our sinful time,' the priest began smoothly, a cup of tea in his hands, 'faith in the Most High is the sole refuge of the human race in all the sorrows and trials of life, as well as in the hope of eternal bliss which has been promised to the righteous . . .'

Stepan Trofimovich seemed to gain a new lease on life; a subtle smile played on his lips.

'*Mon père, je vous remercie, et vous êtes bien bon, mais* . . .'[48]

'No *mais* about it at all, absolutely no *mais*!' exclaimed Varvara Petrovna, leaping up from her chair. 'Father,' she turned to the priest, 'this is the kind of man, the kind of man . . . you'll have to hear his confession all over again in an hour! That's the kind of man he is!'

Stepan Trofimovich gave a restrained smile.

'My friends,' he announced, 'God is necessary to me because he is the only being who is capable of eternal love . . .'

Whether he had actually come to believe, or whether the majestic ceremony of the sacrament that had just been administered had shaken him and awakened the artistic receptivity of his nature, still, he did utter several words firmly and, they say, with great feeling, that went directly against many of his former convictions.

'My immortality is necessary if only because God would not want to commit an injustice and utterly quench the flame of love for him once it has been kindled in my heart. And what is more precious than love? Love is higher than existence, love is the crown of being, and how is it possible that existence is not subordinate to it? If I have come to love him and have taken joy in my love, is it possible that he should extinguish both me and my joy and turn us into nothing? If God exists, then I am immortal too! *Voilà ma profession de foi!*[49]

'God exists, Stepan Trofimovich, I assure you that he exists,' Varvara Petrovna said imploringly. 'Renounce, abandon all your stupid notions at least once in your life!' (She seemed not to have fully understood his *profession de foi*.)

'My friend,' he was becoming more and more animated, although his voice often broke, 'my friend, when I understood ... this business of turning the other cheek, I ... I at once understood something else as well ... *J'ai menti toute ma vie*,[50] my entire, entire life! I would like ... However, tomorrow ... tomorrow we'll all set out.'

Varvara Petrovna began to cry. His eyes were searching for someone.

'Here she is, she's here!' She seized Sofya Matveyevna by the hand and brought her up to him. He gave a tender smile.

'Oh, I would very much like to live again!' he exclaimed with an extraordinary surge of energy. 'Every minute, every instant of life ought to be a blessing to man ... they ought to be, they definitely ought to be! It is the duty of man himself to see to it; this is his law, which is hidden but which definitely exists ... Oh, I would love to see my son Petrusha ... and all of them ... and Shatov!'

I will observe that neither Darya Pavlovna nor Varvara Petrovna nor even Saltzfisch, who had been the last to come from town, as yet knew anything about Shatov.

Stepan Trofimovich was growing more and more agitated, painfully so, beyond his strength.

'Just the constant thought that something exists that is immeasurably more just and happier than I am already fills my entire being with immeasurable tenderness and – glory – oh, whoever I may be, whatever I might have done! It is much more necessary for man to know his own happiness and to believe, every moment, that perfect and serene happiness exists somewhere, for all people and for everything . . . The entire law of human existence consists merely in the fact that man has always been able to bow down before something immeasurably great. If people are deprived of what is immeasurably great, they will cease to live and will die in despair. The immeasurable and infinite are just as necessary to man as is this small planet on which he lives . . . My friends, everyone, all of you: long live the Great Idea! The eternal, immeasurable Idea! Every man, whoever he is, needs to bow down before the Great Idea! Even the most stupid of men needs something great. Petrusha . . . Oh, how I yearn to see them all again! They don't know, they don't know that this same eternal Great Idea is contained within them!'

Dr Saltzfisch had not been present at the ceremony. He came in abruptly, was horrified and dispersed the assembly, insisting that they should not excite the patient.

Stepan Trofimovich passed away three days later, but by then he had become completely unconscious. He just went out quietly, like a guttering candle. After having the funeral service performed there, Varvara Petrovna had the body of her poor friend taken to Skvoreshniki. His grave is in the churchyard, and is already covered with a marble slab. The inscription and the railing have been left until spring.

Varvara Petrovna's absence from the town lasted a total of eight days. Sofya Matveyevna returned with her, in the same carriage, and settled down with her apparently for good. I will note that no sooner had Stepan Trofimovich lost consciousness (that same morning) than Varvara Petrovna again made Sofya Matveyevna leave the hut altogether, and tended the sick man herself, alone with him until the end. And the moment he had given up his soul, she immediately summoned her back. Sofya Matveyevna was dreadfully frightened by the proposal (rather, the order) to settle in Skvoreshniki for good, but Varvara Petrovna didn't want to hear any objections from her.

'All nonsense! I myself will go with you to sell the Gospel. Now I have no one else in the world!'

'But you do have a son,' Saltzfisch ventured.

'I have no son!' snapped Varvara Petrovna – and it was like a prophecy.

CHAPTER 8

Conclusion

I.

All the outrages and crimes that had been committed came to light with extraordinary rapidity, much more rapidly than Pyotr Stepanovich had supposed. It all began when the unfortunate Marya Ignatyevna, the night of her husband's murder, woke up before dawn, found that he wasn't there and became indescribably agitated when she didn't see him beside her. A servant woman Arina Prokhorovna had hired to spend the night with her was unable to calm her down, and as soon as it began to grow light, she ran to fetch Arina Prokhorovna herself, after assuring the sick woman that the midwife knew where her husband was and when he would return. Meanwhile, Arina Prokhorovna was also in a state of some anxiety: she had already found out from her husband about the nocturnal exploit in Skvoreshniki. He had returned home after eleven, his appearance and state of mind were dreadful; wringing his hands, he threw himself down on the bed and kept repeating, convulsed with sobbing: 'It's not right, not right. It's absolutely not right!' Arina Prokhorovna confronted him, and naturally, the result was that he confessed everything to her – but to her alone of all the people in the house. She left him in bed, sternly insisting that 'if he wanted to be a baby about it then he should howl into his pillow, so that no one would hear, and that he would be a fool to show any sign of it on his face the next day'. Still and all, she gave it some thought, and immediately began to tidy up, just in case: she managed to hide or completely destroy any papers they didn't need, books, and even perhaps manifestos. Yet despite everything, she didn't think that she,

her sister, her aunt, the young woman student and perhaps even
her lop-eared brother had very much to fear at all. When the
nurse ran in to fetch her in the morning, she went off to Marya
Ignatyevna without giving it another thought. However, she
was dreadfully anxious to find out whether it was true what
her husband had told her the night before, in a frightened,
demented and almost delirious whisper, about Pyotr Stepanovich counting on Kirillov in the interests of the common cause.

But it was too late by the time Virginskaya got to Marya
Ignatyevna's. Having sent the nurse away, Marya Ignatyevna
remained alone, and unable to bear it any longer, got up from
her bed and throwing on whatever clothing came to hand,
apparently something light and inappropriate to the season, she
set out to Kirillov's part of the house, figuring that he perhaps
would give her a more accurate account of her husband than
anyone. One can just imagine how the new mother was affected
by what she saw there. Remarkably, she didn't read Kirillov's
final note, which was lying on the table in plain view, having
of course overlooked it in her panic. She ran back to her attic,
snatched up the baby and walked out of the house with him
and down the street. It was a damp morning and there was fog.
No passers-by were encountered in such an out-of-the-way
street. She kept on running, out of breath, through the cold and
sticky mud, and finally began to bang on the doors of houses.
In one house no one answered the door; in another, they took
their time in coming to the door: she gave up impatiently and
began banging on the door of a third house. This was the house
of our merchant Titov. Here she raised a great commotion,
shrieking and insisting incoherently that 'her husband had been
killed'. The people at Titov's knew something about Shatov
and his story; they were horror-struck that, as she told it, she
had given birth only the day before and was now running
around through the streets dressed like that in such cold
weather, with a baby in her arms who was barely covered. At
first they were inclined to think that she was simply delirious,
the more so since they were utterly unable to ascertain who had
been killed: Kirillov or her husband. Realizing that they didn't
believe her, she was about to run further, but they stopped

her forcibly, and, people say, she screamed and fought back dreadfully. They set off for Filippov's house, and in two hours Kirillov's suicide and his final note had become known to the entire town. The police began questioning the new mother, who was still conscious, upon which it turned out that she hadn't read Kirillov's note, and they couldn't get out of her precisely why she had concluded that her husband had been killed. All she did was scream that 'if he's been killed, then my husband's been killed; they were together!' Towards midday she fell into an unconsciousness from which she never recovered, and about three days later she died. The baby, who had caught cold, died before her. Arina Prokhorovna, not finding Marya Ignatyevna or the baby at home, and realizing that all was not well, was about to run home, but she stopped at the gate and sent the nurse 'to inquire of the gentleman in the annexe whether Marya Ignatyevna was there, and whether he knew anything about her'. The nurse returned, hysterically screaming for all to hear. After persuading her to stop screaming and not to tell anyone, using the well-known argument 'it'll be your neck', she slipped out of the yard.

It goes without saying that she was questioned that very same morning, as the former midwife of the new mother, but they got little out of her: she related everything that she had seen and heard at Shatov's very efficiently and coolly, but to questions about what had happened, she responded that she knew and understood nothing about it.

One can imagine the hullabaloo that arose in the town. A new 'incident', another murder! But now there was something else: it was becoming clear that there was, there really was a secret society of murderers, revolutionaries, arsonists and rebels. The dreadful death of Liza, the murder of Stavrogin's wife, Stavrogin himself, the arson, the ball for the governesses, the dissoluteness surrounding Yuliya Mikhaylovna ... People were even eager to see something mysterious in the disappearance of Stepan Trofimovich. An inordinate amount of whispering went on about Nikolay Vsevolodovich. By the end of the day people had also learned of the absence of Pyotr Stepanovich, and, strangely enough, he was the least talked about. But most of the talk that day was about 'the senator'. A crowd remained standing outside Filippov's house almost the entire morning. The authorities indeed had been misled by Kirillov's note. They had come to believe that Shatov had been murdered by Kirillov and that the 'murderer' had committed suicide. However, even though the authorities were at a loss, they were not completely in the dark. The word 'park', for instance, which had been so vaguely inserted into Kirillov's note, didn't fool anyone, as Pyotr Stepanovich had reckoned. The police immediately rushed to Skvoreshniki, not only because there was a park there, and there wasn't another one in the vicinity, but they also had a certain instinctive reaction, since all the horrors of the past few days had been linked directly or partially with Skvoreshniki. At least, that's the conclusion I draw. (I will note that Varvara Petrovna, early in the morning and unaware of anything, had driven off to try to catch Stepan Trofimovich.) The body was discovered in the pond that same day, towards evening, after several clues had turned up: on the very spot where the murder had been committed, Shatov's cap was found, having been left behind because of the extraordinary careless-ness of the murderers.[1] The external appearance of the body and the medical examination, along with certain conjectures, awakened the suspicion from the very outset that Kirillov could not have failed to have accomplices. The existence of a Shatov–Kirillov secret society, connected to the manifestos, came to light. But who were these accomplices? As yet, there was no idea that any of *our people* was involved. It was learned that Kirillov lived as a recluse and was so isolated that it was poss-ible, as the note explained, for Fedka to lodge with him for so many days, while he was being sought everywhere. The main thing that troubled everyone was that it was impossible to derive any general principle or connecting link from all this muddle. It's hard to imagine what conclusions and what a chaos of hypotheses our utterly panic-stricken society would finally have reached if everything had not finally been explained all at once, the very next day, thanks to Lyamshin.

He couldn't endure it. What happened to him was what even Pyotr Stepanovich towards the end had begun to suspect. After

being turned over to Tolkachenko, and then to Erkel, he spent
all of the next day lying in bed, apparently calm, facing the wall
and not saying a word, virtually not answering if anyone tried
to talk to him. And so he learned nothing about what was
happening in the town that whole day. But towards evening,
Tolkachenko, who had found out everything that had happened, took it into his head to abandon the role of keeping an
eye on Lyamshin that had been assigned him by Pyotr Stepanovich, and left the town for the district seat, that is, he simply
ran away. They really were losing their minds, as Erkel predicted about all of them. I will note in passing that Liputin also
disappeared from town that very same day, well before noon.
But in his case it somehow happened that his disappearance
became known to the authorities only the following day
towards evening, when they arrived to ask direct questions of
his family, who were terrified by his absence but had remained
silent out of fear. But let me continue about Lyamshin. As soon
as he was alone (Erkel, relying on Tolkachenko, had left for his
own place earlier), he immediately ran out of the house, and,
naturally, very soon learned how things stood. Without even
returning home, he also tried to run away without caring where.
But the night was so dark, and the effort so terrible and fraught
with difficulties, that after passing two or three streets, he went
back home and locked himself in for the whole night. Towards
morning, apparently, he made an attempt at suicide but didn't
succeed. However, he remained locked in until almost noon
and suddenly ran off to the authorities. They say he crawled on
his knees, sobbed and screamed and kissed the floor, shouting
that he was unworthy of even kissing the boots of the worthies
who were standing before him. They calmed him down and
even treated him nicely. The interrogation dragged on, they
say, for about three hours. He revealed everything, everything,
told them the whole truth, everything he knew, all the details;
he got ahead of himself, was quick to confess, imparted even
what was not necessary and what had not been asked of him.
It turned out that he knew enough and presented it rather well:
the tragedy with Shatov and Kirillov, the fire, the deaths of the
Lebyadkins, and so on, were relegated to second place. In first

place stood Pyotr Stepanovich, the secret society, the organization, the network. To the question of why so many murders,
scandals and vile acts had been committed, he answered with
feverish haste that it was for the purpose of 'systematically
shaking the foundations, systematically undermining society
and all principles; for the purpose of demoralizing everyone
and throwing everything into chaos, and then, once society had
begun to totter as a result – and was sick and weakened, cynical
and devoid of beliefs, yet still yearning for some guiding idea
and self-preservation – they would suddenly take it into their
hands, raising the banner of rebellion and relying on a complete
network of groups of five, which would all be active at the same
time, recruiting and making practical efforts to search out all
the means and all the weak spots that could be exploited'.
He concluded that here, in our town, Pyotr Stepanovich had
organized only the first experiment in such systematic disorder,
a programme, so to speak, of further actions, and even for all
the groups of five – and that this was his (Lyamshin's) own
thought, his own conjecture, and that 'they should definitely
remember and keep in mind how openly and willingly he had
explained the whole business, and that he could therefore be of
service to the authorities even in the future'. To the direct
question of whether there were many groups of five, he replied
that there was a countless number, that all of Russia was
covered with a network, and although he didn't offer any proof,
I think he answered sincerely. He offered only the printed
programme of the society, which had been published abroad,
and a plan for the development of a system of further activity,
which existed only in draft form, but was in Pyotr Stepanovich's
handwriting. It turned out that Lyamshin was quoting the
business of the 'shaking the foundations' from this piece of
paper, including even the full stops and commas, although
he insisted that this was only his own notion. About Yuliya
Mikhaylovna he got ahead of himself and said in a wonderfully
amusing way and even without any prompting that 'she was
innocent and they'd simply made a fool of her'. But remarkably
enough he completely exonerated Nikolay Stavrogin from any
participation in the secret society, and from any agreement with

Pyotr Stepanovich. (Lyamshin had no idea of Pyotr Stepanovich's cherished and highly amusing hopes for Stavrogin.) The deaths of the Lebyadkins, in his words, had been arranged by Pyotr Stepanovich alone, without any help from Nikolay Vsevolodovich, with the cunning purpose of implicating him in the crime and thereby making him dependent on Pyotr Stepanovich; but instead of gratitude, on which he had undoubtedly and naively been counting, Pyotr Stepanovich merely aroused utter indignation and even despair in the 'noble' Nikolay Vsevolodovich. He ended his account of Stavrogin, also in haste and without any prompting, with an evidently deliberate hint that he was probably an extremely important personage, but that there was some secret about him: that he had been living among us incognito, so to speak, that he had instructions and that it was very possible that he would again come here from Petersburg (Lyamshin was certain that Stavrogin was in Petersburg), but in that case only in a completely different guise and under different circumstances, and in the company of persons of whom we would perhaps hear soon, and that he had heard all this from Pyotr Stepanovich, 'Nikolay Vsevolodovich's secret enemy'.

Let me add a note here. Two months later Lyamshin admitted that he had deliberately shielded Stavrogin then, hoping for his protection and that Stavrogin would manage to obtain in Petersburg a reduction in his sentence by two degrees, and would provide him with money and letters of recommendation in exile. It's evident from this admission that he had a truly exaggerated view of Nikolay Stavrogin.

On the very same day Virginsky was arrested, naturally, and in the heat of the moment, his entire household as well. (Arina Prokhorovna, her sister and aunt, and even the girl student were released long ago; people also say that supposedly even Shigalyov is definitely scheduled to be set free in the very near future, since he doesn't fit into any of the categories of those who've been accused; however, this is still only talk.) Virginsky immediately confessed to everything; he was sick in bed and feverish when he was arrested. They say that he was almost glad: 'A weight dropped from my heart', was how he supposedly put it. One hears that he's now giving evidence without constraint, albeit with a certain dignity, and isn't retreating from a single one of his 'bright hopes', while at the same time cursing the political direction (in contrast to the social) into which he was so unexpectedly and naively enticed 'by the whirlwind of concurrent circumstances'. His behaviour at the time of the murder has been seen in a mitigating light, and apparently he, too, can count on a certain mitigation of his sentence. That, at least, is what is maintained here in town.

But there is scarcely any possibility that Erkel's fate will be lightened. From the moment of his arrest he either maintained silence or did his best to pervert the truth. Not one word of repentance has been extracted from him so far. And yet even in the most severe judges he has awakened a certain sympathy for himself – on account of his youth, his helplessness, the evidence that makes it clear that he is only the fanatical victim of political circumstances, and most of all, the evidence that has come to light of his treatment of his mother, to whom he used to send virtually half of his paltry salary. His mother is now living in town; she is a weak and sick woman, old before her time; she weeps and grovels as she begs for her son. Whatever may happen, many of us feel sorry for Erkel.

Liputin was arrested in Petersburg, where he had been living for two weeks. Something well nigh improbable happened to him, which is even difficult to explain. They say that he had a passport in another name, and every chance of slipping across the border, and a considerable sum of money on his person, and yet he remained in Petersburg and went nowhere. He spent some time trying to find Stavrogin and Pyotr Stepanovich, and suddenly began to drink and lead a life of debauchery without any restraint, like a man who had completely lost his common sense and any understanding of his situation. He was arrested somewhere in Petersburg in a brothel, far from sober. It is rumoured that he's not yet lost heart, that he tells lies when he gives evidence and is preparing for the forthcoming trial with a certain sense of triumph and hope (?). He even intends to speak out at the trial. Tolkachenko, who was arrested somewhere in the district seat, about ten days after making his escape, is conducting himself with incomparably greater decorum; he doesn't lie, he doesn't prevaricate, he tells everything he knows, doesn't try to justify himself; he blames himself with all modesty, but is also inclined to make eloquent-sounding speeches; he says a great deal perfectly willingly, but when it comes to his knowledge of the common people and the revolutionary (?) elements among them, then he even strikes poses and is eager to make an effect. One hears he also intends to speak out at his trial. In general, he and Liputin are not very frightened, and that is even strange.

I repeat, the whole business is far from over. Now, three months later, our society has rested, recovered and relaxed, and has its own opinion, to the point where even Pyotr Stepanovich is regarded as almost a genius, or at least possessed of 'the capacities of a genius'. 'Organization, you know!' they say in the club, raising a finger. However, all that is very innocent, and not many people are saying such things. Others, on the contrary, don't deny that he has keen abilities, yet at the same time point to a complete ignorance of reality, a terrible abstractness, a development that is one-sided, deformed and obtuse, and as a result of all that an extreme superficiality. Regarding his moral characteristics all are in agreement; there is no argument.

I really don't know who else to mention, if I'm not to forget anyone. Mavriky Nikolayevich has gone off somewhere for good. Old Madame Drozdova has grown senile. However, I still have to tell another very sombre story. I will confine myself to the facts.

After returning from Ustyevo, Varvara Petrovna stayed at her house in town. All this accumulated news came crashing like a flood upon her all at once and shook her terribly. She shut herself up alone in her house. It was evening; everyone was tired and went to bed early.

The next morning the maid, with a mysterious look, handed Darya Pavlovna a letter. According to her, this letter had arrived the night before, but late, when everyone was already sleeping and she didn't dare wake them up. It came not through the mail but to Aleksey Yegorych at Skvoreshniki, through someone unknown. And Aleksey Yegorych had at once delivered it to her last night, and had immediately gone back again to Skvoreshniki.

Darya Pavlovna, her heart pounding, looked at the letter for a long time and didn't dare open it. She knew who it was from: the author was Nikolay Stavrogin. She read what was written on the envelope: 'To Aleksey Yegorych, to be given to Darya Pavlovna, in secret'.

Here is the letter, word for word, without the slightest correction to the style of a Russian nobleman who never fully learned to write proper Russian, despite all his European education:

Dear Darya Pavlovna,

At one time you wanted to be my 'nurse' and made me promise to send for you when I needed you. I'm going in two days and I won't be back. Do you want to come with me?

Last year, like Herzen, I became a citizen of the Canton of Uri,[2] and no one knows that. I've already bought a small house there. I still have twelve thousand roubles; we'll go and live there forever. I don't ever want to go anywhere else.

It's a very boring place, a gorge. The mountains cramp one's sight and thought. It's very sombre. I went there because the small house was for sale. If you don't like it, I'll sell it and buy another in another place.

I'm not in good health, but I hope the air there will get rid of my hallucinations. It's physical; about the moral you know everything; but is it everything?

I've told you much about my life. But not everything. Not even you! By the way, I affirm that I am guilty in my conscience for the death of my wife. I didn't see you after that, and so I'm affirming it here. I'm also guilty before Lizaveta Nikolayevna; but this you know; you predicted almost everything.

It's best if you didn't come. The fact that I'm summoning you is awfully vile of me. And why should you bury your life along with me? You're dear to me, and in my misery, I felt good beside you; only with you, you alone, could I speak about myself out loud. But nothing comes of that. You defined it yourself – a 'nurse'. That's your expression. What's the point of sacrificing so much? Understand, too, that I don't feel sorry for you if I summon you, and I don't respect you, if I'm waiting for you. And yet, I both summon and wait. In any case, I need your answer, because I must go very soon. In that case, I'll leave by myself.

I don't expect anything of Uri; I'm simply going. I didn't choose a gloomy place on purpose. In Russia I'm not tied by anything; here everything is just as foreign as everywhere else. True enough, I haven't liked living in it any more than in any other place, but even here I can't bring myself to hate anything!

I've tried my strength everywhere. You recommended this, 'so as to get to know yourself'. In the tests that I set for myself and for show, as has always been the case throughout my life, my strength proved boundless. Before your very eyes I endured a slap in the face from your brother; I acknowledged my marriage publicly. But what to apply this strength to – that's something I've never seen, I don't see it even now, despite your encouraging words in Switzerland, which I believed. I am still, as I have always been, capable of wanting to do a good deed and I take pleasure in this; at the same time I want evil as well, and I also feel pleasure. But both feelings are too shallow, as always before, and they are never enough. My desires are too weak; they can't guide me. You can cross a river on a log, but not on a chip of wood. This is so you don't think I'm going to Uri with any hopes.

As before, I don't blame anyone. I've experienced great debauchery and have exhausted my energy on it; but I don't like debauchery and don't want it. You've been watching me recently. Do you know that I've even been looking at our negative people with malice, out of envy of their hopes? But you were needlessly afraid; I couldn't be their comrade, because I didn't share anything. And I also couldn't do it out of ridicule, out of malice, and not because I fear ridicule – I can't be afraid of ridicule – but because I still have the habits of a decent man and I felt disgusted. But if I'd had more malice and envy towards them, then maybe I would have gone with them. Just judge to what extent it was easy for me, and how much I've been tossed about!

Dear friend, tender and magnanimous creation which I divined! Perhaps you dream of giving me so much love and pouring out on to me so much that is beautiful from your beautiful soul that you hope thereby to establish some goal for me at last? No, it's best for you to be cautious: my love will be as shallow as I am myself, and you will be unhappy. Your brother told me that he who loses ties with his earth, also loses his gods, that is, all his goals. One can argue endlessly about everything, but from me only negativity has poured forth, without any magnanimity and without any strength. Not even negativity has poured forth from me. Everything is always shallow and flaccid. The magnanimous Kirillov couldn't tolerate the idea and he shot himself; but I really do see that he was magnanimous because he was not in his right mind. I will never lose my mind and will never believe an idea to the same extent as he did. I can't even devote myself to an idea to that extent. Never, never shall I shoot myself!

I know I should kill myself, wipe myself from the face of the earth like a nasty insect; but I'm afraid of suicide, because I'm afraid of showing magnanimity. I know that it will be another deception – the final deception in an endless series of deceptions. What's the use of deceiving oneself just to play at being magnanimous? There can never be indignation and shame in me; and therefore, no despair either.

Forgive me for writing so much. I've come to my senses, and that's unexpected. A hundred pages are too little and ten lines is enough. Ten lines is also enough to summon you as a 'nurse'.

Since I left, I've been living at the sixth station on the line, with the stationmaster. I became friendly with him during a spree five or so years ago in Petersburg. No one knows I'm here. Write to me care of him. I enclose the address.

Nikolay Stavrogin.

Darya Pavlovna immediately went and showed the letter to Varvara Petrovna. She read it and asked Darya to leave, so that she could read it again by herself, but for some reason she called her back very soon.

'Are you going?' she asked almost timidly.

'I'm going,' Dasha replied.

'Then get ready! We'll go together!'

Dasha looked at her inquiringly.

'And what am I to do here now? Does it make any difference? I will also register as a citizen of Uri and live in the gorge. Don't worry, I won't be in the way.'

They began to pack quickly, in order to make the noon train. But no more than a half hour passed when Aleksey Yegorych appeared from Skvoreshniki. He reported that Nikolay Vsevolodovich had 'sudddenly' arrived that morning, by the early train, and was now at Skvoreshniki, but 'in such a state that he doesn't answer questions, he's walked through all the rooms and has locked himself in his half of the house'.

'Regardless of his orders I decided to come and report to you,' Aleksey Yegorych added with a very significant look.

Varvara Petrovna looked at him closely and didn't question him. The carriage was brought up at once. She went with Dasha. On the way there they say that she crossed herself often.

The doors in 'his half' were open, and Nikolay Vsevolodovich was nowhere to be found.

'Is he perhaps in the mezzanine?' Fomushka said cautiously.

It was noteworthy that several servants came in and followed Varvara Petrovna to 'her half', while the remaining servants all waited in the hall. Before this they would never have permitted themselves such a breach of etiquette. Varvara Petrovna saw it and said nothing.

They climbed up to the mezzanine as well. There were three rooms there; but they found no one in any of them.

'Perhaps he went up there?' Someone pointed at the door to the attic. In fact, the door to the attic, which was always closed, now stood wide open. They had to go up almost under the roof along a long, very narrow and terribly winding wooden stairway. There was also a small room up there.

'I won't go up there. Why would he climb up there?' said Varvara Petrovna, dreadfully pale, as she looked round at the servants. They looked at her and said nothing. Dasha was trembling.

Varvara Petrovna rushed up the stairs, Dasha behind her, but no sooner had she entered the attic than she gave a cry and fell senseless.

The citizen of the Canton of Uri was hanging right there behind the door. On a small table lay a scrap of paper with the words in pencil: 'No one is to blame, I did it.' Also lying on the table were a hammer, a piece of soap and a large nail, which had evidently been kept in reserve as a spare. The strong silk cord with which Nikolay Vsevolodovich had hanged himself had evidently been prepared and chosen ahead of time, and was thickly soaped. Everything pointed to premeditation and awareness until the last moment.

After the autopsy, our medical men rejected insanity completely and resolutely.

APPENDIX

'At Tikhon's'

At the end of the opening chapter of Part II, Shatov advises Stavrogin to go to see Tikhon, a former bishop who is living in retirement in a local monastery, and the part as it was then conceived was to end with the powerful chapter 'At Tikhon's' (Chapter 9). However, it was rejected by Mikhail Katkov, the editor of the *Russian Herald*, the journal in which the novel was being serialized. Katkov objected to the shocking revelations that Dostoyevsky considered essential, and as he wrote in a letter to Katkov's assistant, when sending the revised chapter: 'Everything very obscene has been thrown out; the main thing has been shortened; and this whole half-insane escapade has been sufficiently indicated, but will be indicated even more strongly subsequently. I swear to you that I could not omit the essence of the matter; this is a whole social type . . . a Russian, a person . . . who has lost everything native and most importantly, faith; a degenerate *out of ennui* . . . Along with the nihilists this is a serious phenomenon' (March–April 1872, *Complete Letters*, tr. David Lowe, vol. 4 (Ann Arbor: Ardis Publishers, 1991), p. 23). Nevertheless, Katkov remained firm in his objections and Dostoyevsky was forced to abandon Stavrogin's confession altogether, and make several changes elsewhere in his manuscript to compensate somewhat. When the novel was published in book form, Dostoyevsky did not reinstate the chapter, which in any case would have entailed removing the alterations. The chapter resurfaced among Dostoyevsky's papers in 1921 and was published the following year. The text survives in two versions, both of which are incomplete: the author's proofs for the December 1871 issue of the *Russian Herald*, and a copy made by Dostoyevsky's wife,

Anna Grigoryevna, which represents a fair copy of the proofs and takes into account the author's revisions. Since the chapter 'At Tikhon's', which is also known in English as 'Stavrogin's Confession', was never reinstated by the author in the novel, it has become customary, in both Russian editions and English translations, to print the text as an appendix.

At Tikhon's

I.

Nikolay Vsevolodovich didn't sleep that night and spent it sitting on the sofa, often staring at one point in the corner by the chest of drawers. His lamp burned all night long. At about seven in the morning he fell asleep sitting up, and when Aleksey Yegorovich, according to the custom that had been established for all time, came in at exactly half-past nine with his morning cup of coffee and woke him by simply appearing, he opened his eyes and seemed unpleasantly surprised that he could have slept so long and that it was already so late. He quickly drank his coffee, quickly dressed and hurriedly left the house. To Aleksey Yegorovich's cautious question – 'Will there be any orders?' – he made no reply. He walked along the street, looking at the ground, deep in thought and only by raising his head now and then, did he sometimes betray a vague but intense anxiety. At a crossroads not far from his house, his path was crossed by a crowd of muzhiks, some fifty men or more. They were walking with dignity, almost in silence, in a deliberately orderly fashion. At a small shop where he was forced to wait for a moment, someone said that they were the 'Shpigulin workers'. He hardly paid any attention to them. Finally, at about half-past ten, he reached the gates of our Spaso-Yefimyevsky Bogorodsky Monastery,[1] on the edge of town, by the river. Only here did he suddenly seem to remember something; he paused, hastily and anxiously felt for something in his side pocket, and grinned. Entering the enclosure, he asked the first lay brother he encountered how to find Bishop Tikhon, who was living in retirement in the monastery. The lay brother began bowing and immediately led the way. By a little flight of steps, at the end of the long, two-storey monastery building, they were met by a stout, grey-haired monk who took him over from the lay brother in an authoritative and efficient manner, and began to lead him down a long, narrow corridor, also constantly bowing (although because of his corpulence he couldn't bow low but only jerked his head frequently and abruptly); he kept inviting Stavrogin to follow him, although Stavrogin was walking behind him anyway. The monk kept asking questions and talking about the Father Archimandrite,[2] but receiving no replies, he became even more deferential. Stavrogin noted that everyone here knew him, although, as far as he could remember, he had only been here as a child. When they came to a door at the very end of the corridor, the monk opened it with what seemed like an authoritative hand, inquired familiarly of the novice who trotted up whether they might come in, and, without even waiting for an answer, flung the door all the way open and, after bowing, let the 'dear' visitor pass by. After receiving his thanks, he quickly disappeared, as if he had run away. Nikolay Vsevolodovich stepped into a small room, and at almost the same moment a tall and gaunt man appeared in the door to the next room, a man of about fifty-five, wearing a simple ordinary cassock and appearing to be rather ill, with a vague smile and a strange, rather shy look in his eyes. This was none other than Tikhon, whom Nikolay Vsevolodovich had heard about for the first time from Shatov, and about whom he had since managed to collect some information.

The information was varied and contradictory, but had one common feature, namely, that those who loved and those who didn't love Tikhon (and there were such) somehow had little to say about him – those who didn't love him perhaps out of contempt, and his devotees, and even the passionate ones, out of a certain modesty, as if they wanted to conceal something about him, some weakness, perhaps holy folly.[3] Nikolay Vsevolodovich had found out that he had been living in the monastery for about six years now, and that his visitors included not only the simplest folk, but also distinguished personages; that even in distant Petersburg he had his ardent admirers, primarily women. By contrast, he had heard from one of the dignified old men in our club, and a devout one at that, that 'this Tikhon is practically insane, at least he is a completely talentless creature and undoubtedly fond of a drop or two'. I will add for myself, looking ahead, that the last part of this statement was utter rubbish: it was only a chronic rheumatic complaint in the legs, and from time to time nervous twitches of some sort. Nikolay Vsevolodovich also found out that the retired Bishop, whether from a weakness of character or 'an unpardonable absent-mindedness that was not appropriate to his rank', had been unable to inspire any particular respect towards himself within the monastery. Rumour had it that the Father Archimandrite, a man who was severe and strict when it came to his duties as a superior, and, in addition, who was well known for his learning, supposedly even harboured hostile feelings towards him and condemned him (not to his face, but indirectly) for his careless way of living and almost for heresy. The monastery brother-hood also supposedly treated the sick prelate not so much offhandedly as familiarly, so to speak. The two rooms that comprised Tikhon's cell were also done up in a rather strange way. Alongside the clumsy, ancient, worn-out leather furniture there were three or four elegant little pieces: a very luxurious easy chair, a large writing table of excellent finish, an elegant carved bookcase, small tables, étagères[4] – all of them gifts. There was an expensive Bukhara carpet, and some mats next to it. There were engravings on 'secular' and mythological subjects, and in the corner, a large case with icons gleaming with gold and silver, one of which was from ancient times and contained saintly relics. The library too, people said, was also composed of varied and contradictory items: next to the works of the great prelates and heroes of Christianity could be found theatrical works, 'and perhaps even worse'.

After the initial greetings, which for some reason were delivered with obvious awkwardness on both their parts, hastily and even indistinctly, Tikhon escorted his guest into his study and seated him on a sofa, in front of a table, and installed himself in a wicker armchair nearby. Nikolay Vsevolodovich was still in a state of profound distraction as the result of some oppressive inner agitation. It was as if he had resolved to do something, which was extraordinary and incontestable, and at the same time almost impossible for him. For about a minute he looked around the study, obviously without seeing what he was looking at; he was thinking and of course he didn't know what about. He was roused by the silence, and it suddenly seemed to him that Tikhon was looking down bashfully and even with an unnecessarily amused smile. This momentarily stirred a feeling of disgust in him; he wanted to get up and leave, the more so since Tikhon, in his opinion, was unquestionably drunk. But Tikhon suddenly raised his eyes and fastened on him a gaze so firm and thoughtful and at the same time so unexpected and enigmatic that he almost gave a start. For some reason it seemed to him that Tikhon already knew why he had come, had already been forewarned (although no one in the whole world could have known the reason), and that if he himself didn't speak first, then it was to spare him, for fear of humiliating him.

'Do you know me?' Stavrogin suddenly asked in a jerky voice. 'Did I introduce myself to you or not when I came in? I'm so absent-minded . . .'

'You did not introduce yourself, but I had the pleasure of seeing you once, some four years ago, here in the monastery . . . by chance.'

Tikhon spoke in a very unhurried and even manner, in a soft voice, enunciating his words clearly and distinctly.

'I wasn't in this monastery four years ago,' Nikolay Vsevolodovich said, even somewhat rudely. 'I was here only as a child, when you weren't yet here at all.'

'Perhaps you have forgotten?' Tikhon observed cautiously and without insisting.

'No, I haven't forgotten, and it would be funny if I hadn't remembered,' Stavrogin insisted rather extravagantly. 'Perhaps you have only heard of me and formed some impression, and therefore you are wrong about having seen me.'

Tikhon remained silent. Here Nikolay Vsevolodovich observed that a nervous twitch sometimes passed over his face, the sign of an old nervous debility.

'I only see that you are not well today,' Stavrogin said, 'and it would perhaps be better if I left.'

He even made a move to get up from his seat.

'Yes, today and yesterday I've had sharp pains in my legs and I slept very little last night . . .'

Tikhon stopped talking. His guest suddenly lapsed again into his earlier vague state of reverie. The silence lasted a long time, about two minutes.

'Have you been observing me?' Stavrogin suddenly asked, alarmed and suspicious.

'I have been looking at you and recalling the features of your mother's face. For all the lack of outward similarity, there is much inner, spiritual similarity.'

'There's no similarity, especially spiritual. Ab-so-lute-ly none!' Nikolay Vsevolodovich again grew alarmed, and unnecessarily and extravagantly insistent, not knowing why himself. 'You're saying this out of compassion for my position and it's nonsense,' he suddenly blurted out. 'Oh well, I see: does my mother come to visit you?'

'She does.'

'I didn't know. I've never heard her say so. Often?'

'Almost every month, and sometimes more often.'

'I never, never heard her say so. I simply haven't heard. And of course you've heard from her that I'm insane,' he suddenly added.

'No, not really that you're insane. However, I have heard this notion put forth, but by other people.'

'You must have a very good memory if you can recall such trifles. And have you heard about the slap in the face?'

'I've heard something.'

'In other words, everything. You have an awful lot of spare time. And about the duel?'

'And about the duel.'

'You've heard a great deal here. This is one place where there's no need for newspapers. Did Shatov warn you about me? Eh?'

'No. However, I do know Mr Shatov, but I haven't seen him for a long time.'

'Hmm . . . What sort of map is that you have there? Oh, a map of the last war! Why do *you* have that?'

'I was consulting the map in connection with this text. A most interesting description.'

'Show me. Yes, that's not a bad account. However, it's strange reading for you.'

He pulled the book towards him and took a quick glance at it. It was a lengthy and skilful account of the circumstances of the last war, though not so much from a military point of view as a purely literary one. He turned the book over, and suddenly tossed it aside impatiently.

'I really don't know why I've come here,' he said disdainfully, looking Tikhon straight in the eye, as if expecting him to come up with an answer.

'You also seem to be unwell?'

'Yes, I'm unwell.'

And suddenly, albeit rather briefly and disconnectedly, so that some of it was even difficult to grasp, he recounted that he was subject, especially at night, to hallucinations of a sort, that he sometimes saw or felt some sort of evil being beside him, mocking and 'rational', 'in various guises and with various personalities, but always one and the same, and I always get angry . . .'

These revelations were wild and incoherent, and actually did seem to be the product of a deranged mind. But even so, Nikolay Vsevolodovich spoke with such strange candour and such simple-heartedness, both absolutely uncharacteristic of him, that the former self seemed suddenly and unexpectedly to disappear completely. He was not at all ashamed to show fear as he spoke of his apparition. But all this was only momentary, and disappeared just as suddenly as it had come.

'That's all rubbish,' he said quickly and in embarrassed annoyance, catching himself. 'I'll go to the doctor.'

'By all means go,' Tikhon affirmed.

'You say that so confidently . . . Have you ever seen people like me, with such visions?'

'I have, but very rarely. I remember only one such case in my life, a military officer, after he had lost his wife, who was his irreplaceable life companion. I've only heard of one other. Both were cured abroad ... And have you been afflicted with this for long?'

'About a year, but that's all rubbish. I'll go to the doctor. And it's all rubbish, dreadful rubbish. It's just me in different guises, and nothing more. Since I just now added this last ... phrase, you probably think that I'm still doubtful and unsure whether it's me, and not actually a demon?'

Tikhon looked at him questioningly.

'And ... you actually see him?' he asked, thereby removing all doubt that this was undoubtedly a false and morbid hallucination. 'Do you really see some image?'

'It's strange that you keep insisting on this, when I've already told you that I do. Stavrogin's irritation grew with every word. 'Of course I see it, I see it just as I see you ... and sometimes I see it and I'm not sure that I see it, although I do see it ... and sometimes I'm not sure that I see it, and I don't know if it's true. I or it ... that's all rubbish. And you, can't you really imagine it's a demon?' he added, beginning to laugh in a way that shifted too abruptly into a mocking tone. 'After all, wouldn't that be more in keeping with your profession?'

'It's more likely that it's illness, although ...'

'Although what?'

'Demons undoubtedly exist, but the understanding of them can vary greatly.'

'You just lowered your eyes again,' Stavrogin chimed in with irritated sarcasm, 'because you're ashamed of me, ashamed that I believe in demons, and that under the guise of not believing, I was cunning enough to ask you the question: do they actually exist or not?'

Tikhon gave a vague smile.

'And you know, it doesn't become you at all to lower your eyes: it's artificial, ridiculous and mannered, and in order to make up for my rudeness to you, I will say seriously and boldly: I believe in demons, I believe canonically in a personal demon, not an allegorical one, and I don't need to try to find out about him from anyone, that's all I have to say to you. You ought to be terribly happy ...'

He began to laugh nervously and artificially. Tikhon was
looking at him with curiosity, his eyes soft and seemingly
rather shy.

'Do you believe in God?' Stavrogin suddenly burst forth.

'I do believe.'

'Well, it's said that if you believe and you order a mountain
to move,[5] it will move itself . . . however, that's nonsense. But
I'm still curious to know: can you move a mountain or not?'

'If God commands it, I will move it,' Tikhon pronounced
with quiet restraint, again beginning to lower his eyes.

'Well, that's the same as if God himself moves it. No, what
about you, you, as a reward for your belief in God?'

'Perhaps I couldn't move it after all.'

' "Perhaps"? That's not bad. But why do you doubt it?'

'My faith is imperfect.'

'What? Your faith is imperfect? Not absolute?'

'No, perhaps not perfect.'

'Well! At least you do believe that you can move a mountain
if only with God's help, and that's no small thing, you know.
That's still somewhat more than the très peu[6] of a certain man
who was also an archbishop, under the threat of the sword, to
be sure. You, of course, are also a Christian?'

'Lord, let me not be ashamed of thy cross,' Tikhon almost
whispered, in a kind of passionate whisper and bowed his head
even lower. The corners of his lips began to twitch nervously
and rapidly.

'And is it possible to believe in the demon without fully
believing in God?' Stavrogin laughed.

'Oh, very possible, it happens all the time,' Tikhon raised his
eyes and almost smiled.

'And I'm sure you find such faith more respectable, after all,
than a complete lack of faith . . . Oh, you priest!' Stavrogin
burst out laughing. Tikhon again smiled at him.

'On the contrary, complete atheism is more respectable than
secular indifference,' Tikhon rejoined merrily and ingenuously.

'Oho, so that's what you think.'

'The complete atheist stands on the next-to-last highest rung
leading to the fullest and most complete faith (he may take that

step, or he may not), but the indifferent man has no faith at all, except an ugly fear.'

'However, you . . . have you read the Apocalypse?'

'I have.'

'Do you remember "Unto the angel of the church of the Laodiceans write"?'

'I do. Delightful words.'

'Delightful? A strange expression for a bishop, and in general you're an odd fellow. Where do you have the book?' Stavrogin became strangely impatient and alarmed, as his eyes searched for the book on the table. 'I want to read it to you . . . do you have a Russian translation?'

'I know it, I know the passage, I remember it very well,' Tikhon said.

'You remember it by heart? Recite it!'

He quickly lowered his eyes, rested the palms of his hands on his knees and impatiently prepared to listen. Tikhon recited, recalling it word for word: '"And to the angel of the Church in Laodicea write: These things saith the Amen, the faithful and true witness, the beginning of God's creation. I know your works, you are neither cold or hot! Would that you were cold or hot! So, because you are lukewarm, and neither cold nor hot, I will spue you out of my mouth. For you say, I am rich, I have prospered, and I need nothing; not knowing that you are wretched, pitiable, poor, blind and naked . . ."'[7]

'Enough,' Stavrogin cut him short. 'This is for the average ones, for the indifferent ones, isn't that so? You know, I love you very much.'

'And I love you,' Tikhon responded in a low voice.

Stavrogin fell silent and suddenly lapsed once again into a reverie, as before. This happened fitfully, as it were, and now for the third time. And he said 'I love you' to Tikhon almost in a kind of fit, at least without expecting it himself. More than a minute passed.

'Don't be angry,' Tikhon whispered, barely touching his finger to Stavrogin's elbow and seemingly shy about doing so. Stavrogin gave a start and glowered in anger.

'How did you know that I was angry?' he said quickly.

Tikhon was about to say something, but Stavrogin suddenly interrupted him, unaccountably agitated:

'Why exactly did you suppose that I was bound to get angry? Yes, I was angry, you're right, and precisely because I told you "I love you." You're right, but you're a crude cynic; you have a low opinion of human nature. There might have been no anger if only it had been anyone else, and not me . . . However, it's not a matter of just any person, but of me. Even so, you're an eccentric and a holy fool . . .'

He was growing more and more irritated, and strangely enough, he wasn't ashamed to speak out.

'Listen, I don't like spies and psychologists, at least those who try to creep into my soul. I don't invite anyone into my soul; I don't need anyone; I can get along on my own. Do you think I'm afraid of you?' He raised his voice and looked up challengingly. 'You're utterly convinced that I've come to you to reveal a "dreadful" secret and you're waiting for that with all the monkish curiosity that you're capable of. Well, you should know that I'm not going to reveal anything to you, no secret, because I have absolutely no need of you.'

Tikhon took a hard look at him:

'You were struck by the fact that the Lamb has greater love for the cold man than for one who is merely lukewarm,' he said, 'and you don't want to be *merely* lukewarm. I have an inkling that some extraordinary resolve, perhaps a dreadful one, is locked in a struggle with you. If that is so, then I implore you not to torment yourself and to tell me everything that you've come here for.'

'And you knew for certain that I came here for something?'

'I . . . guessed from your face,' Tikhon whispered, lowering his eyes.

Nikolay Vsevolodovich was rather pale, his hands were trembling slightly. For several seconds he looked, motionless and silent, at Tikhon, as if coming to a final decision. At last he took some sheets of printed paper out of the side pocket of his frock-coat and laid them on the table.

'Here are some papers that are intended for distribution,' he said in a somewhat tremulous voice. 'If even one man reads them, then you should know that I won't conceal them after that, and everyone will read them. That's been decided. I have absolutely no need of you, because I've decided everything. But read them ... While you're reading, don't say anything, but when you've finished reading, then say anything you want ...'

'Should I read them?' Tikhon asked hesitantly.

'Read them. I've felt at ease about this for a long time now.'

'No, I can't make it out without my glasses; the print is small and foreign.'

'Here are your glasses.' Stavrogin picked them up off the table and handed them to him, and leaned against the back of the sofa. Tikhon immersed himself in reading.

2.

The print indeed was foreign – three sheets of print on ordinary, small-format notepaper, stitched together. It must have been printed secretly by some Russian printing press abroad, and at first glance the pages very much resembled a manifesto. The heading read: 'From Stavrogin'.

I am incorporating this document into my chronicle verbatim. One must suppose that it's already known to many people by now. The only liberty I've allowed myself is to correct spelling mistakes, which are rather numerous and which even surprised me somewhat, inasmuch as the author, after all, was an educated man and even well-read (relatively speaking, of course). I have made no changes at all in the style, despite some irregularities and even obscurities. In any event, it is obvious that the author is not first and foremost a man of letters.

FROM STAVROGIN.

I, Nikolay Stavrogin, a retired army officer, was living in Petersburg in 186– and devoting myself to dissipation, in which I took no pleasure. I then had three different apartments for a certain period of time. In one of them I lived by myself in rooms with board and service, and Marya Lebyadkina, now my lawful wife, was staying there as well. As for my other two apartments, I rented them at that time by the month, for trysts. In one I used to receive a certain lady who loved me, and in the other her housemaid, and for a time I was very preoccupied with the intention of bringing them together, so that mistress and maid-servant should meet in the presence of my friends and the husband. Knowing both their characters, I anticipated that I would derive much pleasure from this stupid joke.

While preparing at leisure for this encounter, I was obliged to pay frequent visits to one of these apartments, which was located in a large house on Gorokhovaya Street, since the housemaid in question used to come there. Here I had only one room, on the fourth floor, which I rented from some Russians of the lower middle class. They themselves lived next door in another room, which was more cramped, so much so that the door dividing us always stood open, which was precisely what I wanted. The husband worked in an office, and was away from morning till night. The wife, a woman of about forty, was always cutting and sewing something old to make it new, and was also often away from the house delivering what she had made. I remained alone with their daughter, who was about fourteen, I think, and still nothing more than a child by the looks of her. Her name was Matryosha. Her mother loved her, but would often beat her and scream at her dreadfully, as such women have the habit of doing. This girl waited on me and tidied up behind the screen. I declare that I have forgotten the number of the house. Now, after inquiring, I know that the old house has been torn down and resold, and where two or three houses once stood there is now one, new and very large. I have also forgotten the surname of my landlords (perhaps I didn't know it even then). I remember that the wife was called Stepanida, and her patronymic was Mikhaylovna, I think. His I don't remember. Who they were, where they came from and where they've gone now I have no idea. I suppose that if one were to begin searching for them in earnest, and make thorough inquiries of the Petersburg police, then some trace of them might be found. The apartment was on the courtyard, in the corner. It all happened in June. The house was painted a bright sky-blue.

One day my penknife, which I had absolutely no need of and

which was just lying around, disappeared from the table. I told the landlady, not thinking for a moment that she would thrash her daughter. But she had just been screaming at the child (I lived simply, and they stood on no ceremony with me) because some rag had disappeared, and she suspected that the girl had swiped it, and even pulled her hair. But when this very same rag was found under the tablecloth, the girl chose not to utter a word of reproach, and just looked at her mother in silence. I took note, and it was at this very moment that for the first time I had a good look at the child's face, which until then had merely been a vague presence. She was fair-haired and freckled, with a face that was ordinary but had much in it that was childlike and gentle, extremely gentle. The mother was not pleased that her daughter had failed to reproach her for being beaten for nothing, and she brandished her fist at the girl, but didn't hit her. At precisely this moment the question of my missing knife came up. In fact, besides the three of us, no one was present, and the little girl was the only one who would come into my room behind the screen. The woman flew into a rage, because the first time she had beaten the girl unjustly; she rushed for the broom, tore some twigs from it and thrashed the girl until she raised welts, before my very eyes. Matryosha didn't cry out from the thrashing, but with each blow she emitted a strange kind of sobbing. And later she gave full vent to her sobbing, for a whole hour.

But before that this is what happened: at the very moment when the landlady rushed for the broom to tear some twigs from it, I found the knife on my bed, where it had somehow fallen from the table. It immediately occurred to me not to say anything, so that the girl would be thrashed. My decision was instantaneous: at such moments, my breath always catches in my throat. But I'm determined to relate everything in the bluntest possible words, so that absolutely nothing remains hidden.

Every situation in my life in which I have ever happened to find myself, however unspeakably shameful, utterly degrading, vile and, most importantly, ridiculous, has always aroused both boundless anger and unbelievable pleasure in me. Precisely the same has also been true in moments when I was committing a crime, and in moments when my life was in danger. If I was stealing something, then while I was perpetrating the theft, my awareness of the depths of my vileness would send me into ecstasy. It was not vileness that I loved (here my reason remained fully intact), but rather, the ecstasy I derived from the tormenting awareness of having fallen so low that was so gratifying. By the same token, every time I stood facing my opponent in a duel, waiting for him to fire, I would experience the same feeling of shame and frenzy, and on one occasion, extremely strongly. I admit that I myself often sought it out, because for me it is the strongest of all such feelings. Whenever I was slapped in the face (and that has happened twice in my life), this feeling was present then as well, despite my dreadful anger. But suppressing my anger on those occasions would heighten the pleasure beyond anything you could imagine. I never spoke about this to anyone or even hinted at it, and hid it as a shame and a disgrace. But once, when I was painfully beaten up in a tavern in Petersburg and dragged by the hair, I did not experience this feeling, but only incredible anger; since I wasn't drunk, I merely fought back. But when I was abroad, if I had been grabbed by the hair and pulled down by that Frenchman, the vicomte, who struck me on the cheek and whose lower jaw I shot off for doing so, then I would have felt a sense of ecstasy, and perhaps I would not even have felt any anger. So it seemed to me at the time.

I am telling all this so that everyone knows that this feeling never gained full control over me, and that my mind always remained fully aware (and indeed, it was precisely on awareness that everything was based!). And although this feeling would possess me to the point of irrationality, it never reached the point where I forgot myself. Although it would reach the intensity of a raging fire within me, I could at the same time subdue it completely, even stop it at its height, only I myself never wanted to stop it. I am convinced that I could live my whole life as a monk, despite the sweet animal carnality with which I am endowed, and which I have always managed to summon up. Until the age of sixteen I gave myself over, with extraordinary abandon, to the vice that Jean-Jacques Rousseau confessed to.[8] I stopped the moment I decided that I wanted to, in my seventeenth year. I have always been master of myself when I have wanted to be.

And so, let it be known that I do not want to look at environment or illnesses for the causes of my irresponsibility when I commit crimes.

When the punishment was done with, I put the knife in my waistcoat pocket, went out and threw it away in a street far from the house, so that no one would ever find out. Then I bided my time for two days. The girl, after a good cry, became even more silent; but I am convinced that she harboured no angry feelings towards me. However, she most likely felt a certain shame for having been punished in such a manner in my presence. She hadn't screamed but only sobbed as she was being whipped, because, of course, I was standing there and could see everything. But being a child, she probably blamed only herself for her shame. Until that time, perhaps, she had only been afraid of me, not as a person but as a lodger, a stranger, and she seemed to be very timid.

It was precisely then, during these two days, that I asked myself whether I could just drop the plan I intended to pursue and walk away, and I immediately felt that I could, that I could at any time and at that very moment. At about that same time, I wanted to kill myself, because I was suffering from the disease of indifference; however, I don't really know if that was the reason. And during these two or three days (since it was absolutely essential to bide my time, so that the girl would forget everything) I – probably to distract myself from my incessant daydreaming or just for the fun of it – I committed a theft in the rooms. That was the only theft of my life.

Many people had found lodgings in these rooms. Among them lived a certain clerk, with his family, in two small furnished rooms. He was about forty, not altogether stupid, and with a respectable look about him, but poor. I never became friends with him, and he was afraid of the company that surrounded me there. He had just received his pay, thirty-five roubles. What mainly impelled me to do it was that at that particular moment I really needed money (although I did receive some through the mail four days later), so that I was stealing out of need, as it were, and not just as a joke. It was done brashly and with no attempt at concealment. I simply walked into his room while he, his wife and his children were eating their dinner in the other little closet of a room. His uniform lay folded on a chair right by the door. The idea suddenly flashed upon me while I was still in the hallway. I thrust my hand into the pocket and extracted a wallet. But the clerk heard a rustling and glanced out of his little closet. He seemed to have seen something at least, but not everything, so he of course refused to believe his eyes. I told him that as I was walking through the hallway, I had stopped in to see what time it was by his clock. 'It's stopped, sir,' he replied, upon which I walked out.

At that time I was drinking a great deal, and I had a whole gang of people in my rooms, including Lebyadkin. I threw away the wallet with the small change, but kept the banknotes. There were thirty-two roubles, three red ones and two yellow ones. I immediately changed a red one and sent out for champagne; then I dispatched another red one, and after that, the third as well. About four hours later, in the evening, the clerk was waiting for me in the hallway.

'Nikolay Vsevolodovich, when you dropped by a bit earlier, did you perhaps inadvertently knock my uniform off the chair – the one lying by the door?'

'No, I don't remember. Your uniform was lying there?'

'Yes, sir, it was lying there.'

'On the floor?'

'First on the chair, and then on the floor.'

'Well then, did you pick it up?'

'I did.'

'Well, what do you want then?'

'Why, if that's the case, then nothing, sir . . .'

He didn't dare finish, and he didn't dare tell anyone else in the house. That's how timid these people are. Besides, everyone in the other rooms was dreadfully afraid of me and showed me respect. Subsequently I enjoyed exchanging glances with him a couple of times in the hallway. But that soon bored me.

As soon as the three days were up, I returned to Gorokhovaya Street. The mother was getting ready to go out somewhere with a bundle; her husband, needless to say, was not at home. Matryosha and I were left alone. The windows were open. It was mostly artisans who lived in the house, and all day long the tapping of hammers or singing could be heard from every floor. We'd been there for about an hour. Matryosha was sitting in her tiny room, on a small bench, with her back to me, and was doing something with a needle. Then she suddenly began to sing softly, very softly; she did that occasionally. I took out my watch and looked at the time; it was two o'clock. My heart began to pound. But then I suddenly asked myself again: can I stop? And I immediately answered myself: I can. I stood up and began creeping towards her. There were many pots of geraniums on the window sills, and the sun was shining terribly brightly. I quietly sat down on the floor next to her. She gave a start and at first was incredibly frightened and jumped up. I took her hand and kissed it gently, sat her back down on the bench, and began looking into her eyes. The fact that I had kissed her hand suddenly made her laugh, like a child, but only for a second, because she leaped up a second time, now so frightened that a spasm crossed her face. She looked at me, her eyes staring in terror, and her lips began to twitch, as if she were on the verge of tears, but nevertheless she didn't cry out. I began kissing her hands again, took her on to my knees and kissed her face and feet. When I kissed her feet, she drew away from me, and smiled as if from shame, but with a kind of crooked smile. Her whole face flushed in shame. I kept whispering something to her. Finally, something so strange occurred that I shall never forget it, something that astonished me: the girl threw her arms around my neck and suddenly began kissing me furiously. Her face wore an expression of utter rapture. This struck me as so unpleasant in such a tiny child that I almost got up and left out of pity. But I overcame my sudden feeling of fear and stayed.

When it was all over, she was embarrassed. I didn't try to reassure her and I stopped caressing her. She looked at me, timidly smiling. Suddenly her face looked stupid to me. She was becoming more and more embarrassed with every passing moment. Finally, she covered her face with her hands and went to stand in the corner with her face to the wall, without moving. I was afraid she would become frightened again, as she had been earlier, and I left the house without saying a word.

I suppose everything that had happened must ultimately have struck her as an utter outrage, a mortal horror. Despite all the Russian oaths she must have heard since she was an infant, and all sorts of strange conversations, I am fully convinced that as yet she had no understanding of anything. Most likely she thought, when all was said and done, that she had committed an unspeakable crime and a mortal sin – that 'she had killed God'.

That was the night I had the fight in the tavern, which I have mentioned in passing. But I woke up in my own room the next morning; Lebyadkin had brought me back. My first thought on awakening was whether she had told anyone or not; this was a moment when I felt genuine fear, although it was still not really very strong. I was very happy that morning and dreadfully kind to everyone, and my whole gang was very pleased with me. But I left them all and set out for Gorokhovaya Street. I ran across her downstairs in the entryway. She was coming from the shop where she had been sent for some chicory. On seeing me, she shot up the staircase, dreadfully frightened. When I came in, her mother had already slapped her on the cheek twice for dashing into the apartment 'at breakneck speed', which concealed the real reason why she was so frightened. And so everything was calm for the time being. She had hidden herself away somewhere and didn't come in all the time I was there. I stayed for about an hour and left.

Towards evening I again experienced a sense of fear, now incomparably more intense. Of course, I could have denied everything, but they certainly could have found me out. I was haunted by the spectre of hard labour. I had never felt fear, and except for this one instance in my life, I was never afraid of anything, either before or after. And certainly not of Siberia in particular, although I could have been exiled there on more than one occasion. But this time I was frightened, and I really did feel fear – I don't know why – for the first time in my life. It was a very tormenting sensation. Besides, that evening, in my rooms, I conceived such hatred for her that I resolved to kill her. The main reason for my hating her was the memory of her smile. Contempt and overwhelming revulsion welled up within me because she had rushed into the corner afterwards and covered herself with her hands. I was seized by an inexplicable fury, followed by a chill, and when I began to run a fever towards morning, I was again overcome by fear, now so strong that I have never known any torment that was stronger. But I no longer hated the little girl; at least, it did not reach the point of paroxysm as it had the evening before. I have noticed that strong fear utterly dispels hatred and the feeling of revenge.

I woke around midday, now feeling fine, and was even surprised at some of my feelings of the day before. Yet I was in a bad mood, and was once again compelled to go to Gorokhovaya Street, despite all the disgust I felt. I remember that at that moment I felt desperately like having a quarrel with someone, provided it was a really serious one. But once I reached Gorokhovaya Street, I suddenly found Nina Savelyevna, the housemaid, in my room; she had been waiting for me for about an hour. I didn't love this young woman at all, and she herself was somewhat afraid that I would be angry at the unexpected visit. But suddenly I was very glad to see her. She was not bad looking, but modest and with the kind of manners that the lower middle class likes, so that my landlady had been singing her praises to me for a long time. I found them both having coffee, with the landlady exceptionally pleased at their nice conversation. In the corner of their tiny room I noticed Matryosha. She was standing and staring at her mother and the visitor. When I came in, she didn't hide, as she had before, and didn't run away. All that struck me was that she had grown very thin and that she had a fever. I was affectionate to Nina and locked the door to the landlady's quarters, which I hadn't done for a long time, and as a result, Nina left in a very happy mood. I saw her out myself, and didn't return to Gorokhovaya Street for two days. I was already tired of it.

I resolved to put an end to everything, give up the apartment and leave Petersburg. But when I came to give up the apartment, I found the landlady anxious and worried: Matryosha had been sick for three days running, she was in bed with a fever and was raving at night. Naturally, I asked what she was raving about (we were talking in whispers in my room). She whispered to me that she was raving about 'dreadful things': ' "I killed God," she says.' I offered to bring in a doctor at my expense, but she didn't want that: 'God grant it will just pass; she's not in bed all the time; she does go out during the day, just now she's run to the shop.' I resolved to catch Matryosha alone, and since the landlady let slip that she had to go to the Petersburg Side[9] by five o'clock, I decided to come back that evening.

I had my dinner in a tavern. Precisely at a quarter past five I returned. I always used my own key to get in. No one was there except Matryosha. She was lying in the tiny room on her mother's bed behind the screens and I saw her look out; but I pretended I hadn't noticed. All the windows were open. The air was warm, it was even hot. I walked round the room a while and sat on the sofa. I remember everything to the very last moment. It gave me distinct pleasure not to get into conversation with Matryosha. I waited and kept sitting for a whole hour, and suddenly she jumped out from behind the screens. I heard her two feet hit the floor when she jumped out of the bed, then some rather quick steps, and she was standing in the doorway of my room. She looked at me without speaking. In the four or five days that had elapsed, during which I had never once seen her closely, she really had grown very thin. Her face seemed to have shrivelled, and she was most likely feverish. Her eyes had grown big and were staring at me with a kind of dull curiosity, or so it seemed to me at first. I was sitting in a corner of the sofa, looking at her and not moving. And then suddenly I felt hatred again. But I very quickly noticed that she had absolutely no fear of me, and perhaps was instead delirious. But she wasn't delirious either. She suddenly began shaking her head rapidly at me, as people do when they are reproaching you in earnest, and suddenly she raised her tiny fist at me and began to threaten me from where she was standing. At first this gesture seemed ridiculous to me, but then I couldn't bear it any longer: I stood up and moved towards her. There was such despair on her face, something unbearable to see on the face of a child. She kept waving her tiny fist at me in a threatening gesture, and kept shaking her head by way of reproach. I moved up close to her and began to speak cautiously, but perceived that she wouldn't understand. Then she suddenly and impulsively covered her face with both hands, as she had done before, moved away and stood by the window, with her back to me. I left her, returned to my room and sat down, also by the window. I simply can't understand why I didn't leave then, instead of remaining there as if waiting for something. Before long I heard her hurried steps again; she went out through the door on to the wooden gallery, from which a staircase led down, and I immediately ran to my door, opened it a crack and had time to see Matryosha stepping into a tiny closet of a room, like a hen-coop, next to the privy. A strange thought flashed through my mind. I left the door ajar and went to the window. Needless to say, it was still impossible to believe the fleeting thought ... 'and yet' ... (I remember everything.)

A minute later I looked at my watch and noted the time. Evening was coming on. A fly was buzzing round my head and kept lighting on my face. I caught it, held it in my fingers and released it through the window. Down below a wagon drove very loudly into the yard. In a corner of the courtyard a craftsman, a tailor, was at his window singing very loudly (and had been doing so for some time). He was sitting at his work, and I could see him. It occurred to me that since no one had seen me as I was coming through the gate and climbing the stairs, then there was of course no reason why I should be seen going down the stairs, and I moved the chair away from the window. Then I picked up a book, but put it down and began watching a tiny red spider on a geranium leaf and forgot where I was. I remember everything to the very last moment.

Suddenly I pulled out my watch. Twenty minutes had passed since she had gone out. My guess was assuming the appearance of probability. But I resolved to wait for another quarter of an hour. It also kept entering my head that she might have come back and that I had perhaps failed to hear her, but that could simply not have been the case: it was deathly quiet, and I could hear the buzzing of every tiny insect. Suddenly my heart began to pound. I took out my watch: three minutes remained, and I waited them out, even though my heart was pounding painfully. At this point I stood up, put on my cap, buttoned up my coat and looked round the room to see whether everything was where it had been before, whether there were any traces of my presence remaining there. I moved the chair closer to the window, where it had been. Finally, I opened the door quietly, locked it with my key and walked to the tiny closet-like room. It was shut but not locked; I knew that it didn't lock, but I didn't want to open it, and I stood on tiptoe and looked through a crack. At the very moment when I was standing on tiptoe, I remembered that when I was sitting by the window and looking at the tiny red spider and forgetting myself, I was thinking how I would stand on tiptoe and put my eye to this crack. By inserting this trifle here, I want to demonstrate beyond all doubt the degree to which I was clearly in possession of my mental faculties. I took a long look through the crack; it was dark inside, but not completely. Finally I made out what was necessary . . . I wanted to be absolutely sure.

I finally decided that I could leave, and I walked down the stairs. I saw no one. Three hours or so later, we were all in our shirtsleeves in my rooms, drinking tea and playing cards with an old pack, while Lebyadkin was reciting poetry. We were telling a lot of stories, and, as it turned out, with great success and much laughter, and not stupidly, as was so often the case. Kirillov was there as well. No one was drinking, and even though there was a bottle of rum on the table, only Lebyadkin was tippling. Prokhor Malov observed that 'when Nikolay Vsevolodovich is content and not depressed, then all of us are jolly and talk cleverly'. I committed that to memory then and there.

But at about eleven o'clock the caretaker's little girl came running from the landlady's in Gorokhovaya Street to let me know that Matryosha had hanged herself. I set out with the girl and saw that the landlady herself did not know why she had sent for me. She was wailing and throwing herself about, there was a commotion, lots of people, the police. I stood in the entryway for a while and then left.

The police hardly bothered me, although they did ask the usual questions. But besides the fact that the girl had been sick and delirious in her final days, and that I had offered to call in a doctor at my expense, there was absolutely nothing I could provide by way of evidence. They questioned me about the knife as well; I said that the landlady had given her a thrashing, but that it was not serious. No one had found out about my having come back that evening. About the results of the medical examination, I heard nothing.

I didn't go back there for about a week. I returned only long after she had been buried, in order to give up the apartment. The landlady was still crying, although she had already gone back to fussing with her rags and her sewing as before. 'It was all because of your knife that I made her feel bad,' she said to me, but without any particular reproach. I paid up, and gave as an excuse that I really couldn't stay in such an apartment and receive Nina Savelyevna there after what had happened. She praised Nina Savelyevna once again as we were saying goodbye. As I was leaving I gave her five roubles over and above what I owed for the apartment.

In general my life just then was stupefyingly boring. Once the danger had passed, I would have almost completely forgotten the incident on Gorokhovaya Street, along with everything else that had happened then, if I hadn't been so furious whenever I remembered, as I kept doing for some time, just how cowardly I had been. I vented my fury on anyone I could. It was at that time, but certainly not coincidentally, that I conceived the idea of crippling my life somehow, but only in the most disgusting way imaginable. A year or so earlier, I had contemplated shooting myself; but something rather better presented itself. On one occasion, as I was looking at the lame Marya Timofeyevna Lebyadkina, who occasionally came in to tidy up the rooms, and was not yet insane but merely an ecstatic idiot, and madly and secretly in love with me (our people had found that out), I suddenly resolved to marry her. The thought of Stavrogin marrying such a hopeless creature set my nerves tingling. Nothing more grotesque could possibly have been imagined. But I won't venture to decide whether my resolve was affected even unconsciously (unconsciously, it goes without saying!) by my anger at the abject cowardice that held me in its grip after the business with Matryosha. Actually, I don't think so; but in any event I became a married man not just on 'a bet on a bottle of wine after a drunken dinner'. The witnesses to the marriage were Kirillov and Pyotr Verkhovensky, who happened to be in Petersburg just then, and last but not least, Lebyadkin himself and Prokhor Malov (who is now dead). No one else ever found out about it, and they promised to keep it quiet. Such silence has always seemed odious to me, but it has remained unbroken until now, although I did actually intend to announce it. I am announcing it now along with everything else.

After the wedding, I left for the country to visit my mother. I went to distract myself, because things had become unbearable. I left our town with the notion that I was crazy – a notion that remains firmly entrenched and has undoubtedly done me harm, as I will explain below. Then I went abroad and stayed for four years.

I was in the East, on Mount Athos I stood through night vigils that lasted eight hours; I was in Egypt, I lived in Switzerland, I was even in Iceland. I spent a whole academic year studying at Göttingen. In my final year I became very friendly with a certain distinguished Russian family in Paris and with two Russian girls in Switzerland. About two years ago, in Frankfurt, as I was passing by a stationer's, I noticed, among the photographs for sale, a small picture of a young girl dressed in an elegant child's outfit, and very much resembling Matryosha. I immediately bought the picture, and, on reaching my hotel, placed it on the mantelpiece. There it simply lay untouched for about a week, and I didn't glance at it even once, and on departing from Frankfurt I forgot to take it with me.

I bring this in precisely to show the degree to which I was master over my own memories and had grown indifferent towards them. I would reject them all at once, in a mass, and the entire mass would obediently disappear each time I wanted it to. It was always boring for me to call up the past, and I was never able to talk about the past, as almost everyone else does. As far as Matryosha is concerned, I even left her picture on the mantelpiece.

About a year ago, in the spring, as I was travelling by train through Germany, I absent-mindedly went past the station where I was supposed to change on to the main route, and ended up on a different branch. They let me off at the next station. It was between two and three in the afternoon, on a clear day. It was a tiny German town. A hotel was pointed out to me. I had some time to wait: the next train came through at eleven o'clock at night. I was even pleased by the adventure, because I was in no hurry to get anywhere. The hotel proved to be shabby and small, but it was set amid greenery and completely surrounded by flower beds. I was given a cramped little room. I had a glorious meal, and since I had been travelling all night, I quickly fell asleep after dinner at about four o'clock in the afternoon.

I had a dream that I didn't in the least expect, because I had never dreamed anything like it before. In the Dresden Gallery there is a painting by Claude Lorrain, which is listed in the catalogue, I think, as 'Acis and Galatea',[10] but I always called it 'The Golden Age', I really don't know why. I had seen it before, and now, some three days earlier, I noticed it again as I was passing through. It was precisely this painting that I dreamed of, not as a painting, however, but as if it were real.

Here was a small corner of the Greek archipelago; sky-blue, caressing waves, islands and rocks, a flowering strip of coastline, a magical panorama in the distance, an inviting sunset – you can't describe it in words. This is what the peoples of Europe remembered as their cradle; here unfolded the first scenes of mythology, here was their earthly paradise. Here lived beautiful people! They got up and went to sleep happy and innocent; the groves were filled with their joyous songs, their great excess of untapped energies went into love and artless joy. The sun bathed these islands and the sea in its rays, rejoicing in its beautiful children. A wondrous dream, a sublime illusion! A vision, more incredible than any that has ever existed, for which mankind throughout its whole existence has given all its energies, for which it has sacrificed everything, for which men have died on crosses and prophets have been killed, without which nations do not want to live and cannot even die. I seemed to have lived through all these sensations in this dream; I don't know precisely what I dreamed, but the rocks and the sea and the slanting rays of the setting sun – all this I still seemed to see when I woke up and opened my eyes, which for the first time in my life were literally wet with tears. A feeling of happiness, as yet unknown to me, passed through my heart until it hurt. Evening had already come; through the window of my small room a whole sheaf of the bright slanting rays of the setting sun was bursting through the greenery of the geraniums standing on the sill and bathing me in light. I quickly closed my eyes again, as if desperate to bring back the now vanished dream, but suddenly, as if in the very midst of the dazzling light, I saw a tiny dot. It assumed a kind of shape, and suddenly a tiny red spider appeared to me distinctly. I immediately remembered it as it had been on the geranium leaf, when the slanting rays of the setting sun were pouring down in just the same way. It was as though something had pierced me. I raised myself up and sat on the bed . . . (That's how it all happened then!)

Before me I saw (oh, not in actuality! If only, if only it had been a genuine apparition!), I saw Matryosha, emaciated and with feverish eyes, exactly as she had been then, when she was standing in my doorway, shaking her head and brandishing her tiny little fist at me. And never have I found anything so torment-ing! The pitiful despair of a helpless ten-year-old creature[11] whose mind had not yet been formed, threatening me (with what? What could she do to me?), but of course blaming only herself! Nothing like that had ever happened to me. I sat until nightfall, not moving and oblivious of time. Is this what is called pangs of conscience or repentance? I don't know and to this day I can't say. Perhaps even to this very day I don't find the memory of what I did loathsome, perhaps even now this memory contains something that gratifies my passions. No, the only thing that is unbearable to me is this image, standing right in the doorway, with her tiny fist raised and threatening, only the way she looked just then, only that particular minute, only that shaking of the head. That's what I can't bear, because since then it has appeared to me almost every day. It doesn't appear by itself; I myself summon it up and I can't help but summon it up, even though I simply can't live with it. Oh, if only I could see her in reality some time, even if in a hallucination!

I have other old memories that perhaps are even somewhat better than this one. Towards one woman I acted worse, and she died as a result. In duels I deprived two people of their lives, even though they had done nothing to me. On one occasion I was mortally insulted and I did not take revenge on my adversary. I have one poisoning to my credit, which was deliberate and successful and known to no one. (If need be, I'll tell everything.)

But why is it that not one of these memories awakens anything comparable in me? Nothing but hatred, and even that is summoned up by the situation I now find myself in, whereas formerly I could cold-bloodedly forget about it and keep it at a distance.

After that I wandered about for nearly a whole year and tried to find something to do. I know that I could dismiss this little girl from my mind even now, whenever I feel like it. I have full mastery of my will, as before. But the whole point is that I never wanted to do so, that I don't want to now and that I will not want to; that is something I do know. And so it will continue right up to the point where I lose my mind.

In Switzerland, two months later, I was able to fall in love with a girl, or, to put it better, I experienced an attack of the same kind of passion accompanied by the same kind of violent outburst that used to occur only a long time ago, early on. I felt a terrible temptation to commit a new crime, that is, bigamy (because I was already married); but I ran away, on the advice of another girl to whom I confided almost everything. Besides, this new crime would not in any way have saved me from Matryosha.

And so, I have resolved to have these pages printed and have them conveyed to Russia in three hundred copies. When the time comes, I will send them off to the police and the local authorities; simultaneously, I will send them to the editors of all the newspapers, with a request that they be made public, and to many of the people who know me in Petersburg and in Russia. Likewise, they will appear in translation abroad. I know that legally I will perhaps not be disturbed, at least not significantly; I alone make this declaration about myself, and I have no accuser; besides, there is no evidence, or extremely little. Finally, there is the deep-seated idea that I am not in my right mind, and most likely the efforts of my relatives who will take advantage of this notion and suppress any legal proceeding that represents a danger to me. I am announcing this, by the way, to show that I am in full possession of my mental faculties and that I understand my situation. But for me there will remain those who will know everything and will look at me, and I at them. And the more of them, the better. Whether that will make things easier for me, I don't know. I am falling back on it as a last resort.

Once again: if a thorough search is made in the records of the Petersburg police, then perhaps something might well be found. The girl's parents are perhaps in Petersburg even now. They will of course remember the house. It was a bright sky-blue. I will certainly not go off anywhere, and for some time (a year or two) I can always be found at Skvoreshniki, my mother's estate. But if need be, I will appear anywhere.

                                                             Nikolay Stavrogin

The reading went on for about an hour. Tikhon read slowly and perhaps reread several passages a second time. During all this time Stavrogin sat silent and unmoving. Strangely enough, the hint of impatience, distraction and something like delirium that had been on his face that entire morning had almost disappeared now, to be replaced by serenity and something resembling sincerity, which almost gave him an air of dignity. Tikhon took off his glasses and spoke, first with a certain cautiousness.

'Would it not be possible to make some corrections in this document?'

'What for? I was sincere in what I wrote,' replied Stavrogin.

'Perhaps in the style a little.'

'I forgot to warn you that all your words would be in vain, I won't postpone carrying out my intention. Don't go to the trouble of trying to dissuade me.'

'You didn't forget to warn me earlier, before I read it.'

'It doesn't matter, I repeat again: however strong your objections may be, I'm not going to back down from my intentions. Note that by employing this infelicitous or felicitous phrase – think what you like – I'm certainly not suggesting that you should immediately start raising objections and trying to prevail on me,' he added, as if unable to restrain himself and suddenly reverting for a moment to his former tone once again; but he immediately smiled sadly at his own words.

'I certainly could not possibly object or try especially to prevail on you to put aside what you intend. This idea is a great idea, and a Christian idea could not have found fuller

expression. Repentance can go no further than the astonishing
heroic deed that you have contemplated, if only . . .'

'If only what?'

'If only it is truly repentance and truly a Christian idea.'

'These are quibbles, it seems to me; isn't it all the same? I
was sincere in what I wrote.'

'You seem deliberately to wish to present yourself more
coarsely than your heart would desire.' Tikhon was growing
bolder and bolder. Obviously the 'document' had produced a
strong impression on him.

'"Present"? I repeat: I wasn't "presenting myself", and in
particular, I wasn't posturing.'

Tikhon quickly lowered his eyes.

'This document comes straight from the need of a heart that
has been mortally wounded – do I understand it correctly?' He
went on insistently and with unusual heat. 'Yes, this is repentance and the natural need for it that has got the better of you,
and you have entered upon a great path, an unprecedented
path. But you already seem to hate everyone in advance who
will read what has been described here, and you are challenging
them to a fight. You have not been ashamed to admit a crime,
why are you ashamed of repentance? Let them look at me, you
say; well, and what about *you*, how will you look at them?
Some passages in your account are stylistically heightened, as
if you're admiring your own psychology and are grasping at
every tiny detail, in order to astonish the reader with your
insensitivity which is not a part of you. What is this if not the
proud challenge of a guilty man to his judge?'

'Where do you see a challenge? I eliminated all personal
arguments.'

Tikhon said nothing. Some colour even suffused his pale
cheeks.

'Let's leave it at that,' Stavrogin abruptly cut him off. 'Permit
me to ask you a question of my own. It's now been five minutes
that we've been talking about this' (he nodded at the pages)
'and I don't see any sign of revulsion or shame in you. You
don't seem to be disgusted!'

He didn't finish, and grinned.

'In other words, you would prefer me to express my scorn for you as quickly as possible,' Tikhon finished for him in a firm voice. 'I won't conceal anything from you; I was horrified by the enormous waste of energy that has deliberately been expended on vileness. As for the crime itself, there are many people who are guilty of the same sins, but they live with their conscience in peace and serenity, even regarding them as the inevitable peccadilloes of youth. There are also old men who sin in the same way, and even imperturbably and playfully. The whole world is filled with such horrors. But you have felt all the depth of your sins, which happens very rarely to this degree.'

'You certainly haven't begun to respect me after what you've read?' Stavrogin gave a crooked grin.

'I will not give a direct answer to that. But naturally, there is not, nor can there be a greater or more dreadful crime than the one you committed with this maiden.'

'Let's stop measuring it so precisely. I am rather astonished by your opinion of other people and of the frequency of a crime of this kind. Perhaps I'm not suffering nearly as much as I've described it here, and perhaps I really have told a lot of lies about myself,' he added unexpectedly.

Tikhon fell silent again. Stavrogin didn't even consider leaving; on the contrary, he again began to sink for moments at a time into a deeply pensive state.

'And this girl,' Tikhon again began shyly, 'with whom you broke off relations in Switzerland, if I may venture to ask, is . . . where, at this moment?'

'Here.'

Again a silence.

'I may have told you a lot of lies about myself,' Stavrogin repeated insistently once more. 'However, what does it matter that I am challenging them with the crudeness of my confession, if you yourself have noticed the challenge? I will make them hate me even more, that's all. That will make it easier for me, you see.'

'In other words, their hatred will evoke yours, and hating them will make it easier for you than if you accepted their pity?'

'You're right. You know,' he suddenly began to laugh,

'people will perhaps call me a Jesuit and a pious hypocrite, ha, ha, ha! Isn't that so?'

'Of course, there certainly will be such a reaction. And do you plan to act on your intention soon?'

'Today, tomorrow, the day after tomorrow – how should I know? But very soon. You're right: I think it's certainly bound to happen that I'll suddenly make it public, and precisely at a moment of revenge and hatred, when I'll be feeling the greatest hatred for them.'

'Answer one question, but sincerely, and to me alone, only to me: if someone should forgive you for this' (Tikhon indicated the pages) 'and not any of those whom you respect or fear, but some unknown person, a person whom you will never know, silently, while reading your terrible confession – would this thought make it easier for you, or wouldn't it matter?'

'Easier,' Stavrogin answered in a low voice, dropping his eyes. 'If you were to forgive me, I would find it much easier,' he added unexpectedly and in a half-whisper.

'Provided you also forgave me,' Tikhon uttered in a voice full of emotion.

'For what? What have you done to me? Ah yes, this is some monastic formula.'

'For my voluntary and involuntary sins.[12] In sinning, each person has already sinned against all, and each person is in some way guilty for another person's sin. There is no isolated sin. I am truly a great sinner, and perhaps greater than you.'

'I will tell you the whole truth: I wish you to forgive me, and with you, one or two others, but as for everyone – it would be better if everyone hated me. But I wish it in order to bear it with humility . . .'

'But universal compassion for you – you wouldn't be able to bear that with the same humility?'

'Perhaps I wouldn't. It was very subtle of you to detect that. But . . . why are you doing this?'

'I sense the degree of your sincerity, and, of course, I am very much at fault in that I don't know how to approach people. I have always felt that it's my greatest shortcoming,' Tikhon said sincerely and from the heart, looking Stavrogin straight in the eye. 'I am doing this only because I'm afraid for you,' he added, 'an almost unbridgeable abyss lies before you.'

'That I won't hold out? That I won't endure their hatred with humility?'

'Not just their hatred.'

'Well, what else?'

'Their laughter.' The words burst from Tikhon with apparent effort and in a half-whisper.

Stavrogin was flustered. Anxiety showed on his face.

'I anticipated that,' he said. 'That means you find me very comical after reading my "document", despite all the tragedy? Don't worry, don't be embarrassed . . . I myself anticipated it, you see.'

'The horror will be widespread, and of course more false than sincere. People are fearful only of whatever threatens their personal interests. I'm not talking about pure souls: they will be horrified and will blame themselves, but they will not be noticed. But laughter will be universal.'

'And add the observation of the thinker that we always find something pleasing in someone else's misfortune.'

'A fitting thought.'

'However, you . . . you yourself . . . I'm surprised at the poor opinion you have of people, the disgust you feel,' Stavrogin declared with a certain air of bitterness.

'But would you believe that I said it more by way of judging myself than about other people!' Tikhon exclaimed.

'Really? And perhaps there is a little something in your soul that delights you about my misfortune?'

'Who knows, perhaps there really is. Oh, perhaps there really is!'

'Enough. Show me then what exactly is so ridiculous about my manuscript. I know what it is, but I want you to put your finger on it. And tell me as cynically as you like, tell me with all the sincerity of which you are capable. And I will repeat to you again that you are an awful eccentric.'

'Even the form of a great act of repentance like this one does have something ridiculous about it. Oh, don't believe that you won't prevail!' he exclaimed almost in ecstasy. 'Even this form will prevail' (he pointed at the pages) 'if only you will sincerely accept being slapped and spat upon. The end result has always been that the most shameful cross becomes a great glory and a great power, if the great deed has been sincerely humble. Perhaps you will find consolation even in your lifetime!'

'And so, what you find ridiculous is just in the form, in the style?'

'And in the substance. The ugliness will kill it,' Tikhon whispered, lowering his eyes.

'What's that? Ugliness? Where's the ugliness?'

'Of the crime. There are crimes that are truly ugly. In crimes, of whatever kind, the more blood and horror there is, the more appealing they are, or, so to speak, picturesque. But there are shameful crimes, disgraceful ones that transcend any horror, so to speak, even too inelegant, actually . . .'

Tikhon did not finish speaking.

'In other words,' an agitated Stavrogin picked up his thought, 'you find that I cut a highly ridiculous figure when I kissed the foot of the dirty little girl . . . and everything I said about my temperament, and . . . well, and everything else . . . I understand. I understand you very well. And you despair of me precisely because it's not pretty, it's disgusting – no, not so much disgusting as shameful and ridiculous, and you think that's what I won't be able to bear most of all?'

Tikhon said nothing.

'Yes, you know people, that is, you know that I, precisely I won't be able to bear it. I understand why you asked about the young lady from Switzerland, whether she's here or not.'

'You're not prepared, not hardened,' Tikhon whispered shyly, lowering his eyes.

'Listen, Father Tikhon: I want to forgive myself, and that's my main purpose, my entire purpose!' Stavrogin suddenly said with a look of gloomy ecstasy in his eyes. 'I know that only then will the apparition disappear. That's precisely why I'm seeking boundless suffering, seeking it myself. So don't try to frighten me.'

'If you believe that you can forgive yourself and can achieve this forgiveness for yourself in this world, then you believe in everything!' Tikhon exclaimed ecstatically. 'How could you have said that you don't believe in God?'

Stavrogin made no reply.

'God will forgive you for your lack of belief, for you honour the Holy Spirit, without knowing him.'

'By the way, Christ won't forgive me, will he?' Stavrogin asked, and in the tone of his question could be heard a slight touch of irony. 'For it is stated in the Book: "For whoso shall offend one of these little ones"[13] – you remember? According to the Gospel, there is no greater crime, nor can there be. It's all there in this book!'

He pointed at the Gospel.

'I bring you joyful news about this,' Tikhon said with emotion, 'even Christ will forgive you if only you can reach the point of forgiving yourself . . . Oh, no, no, don't believe me, I have uttered blasphemy. Even if you don't achieve reconciliation with yourself and forgiveness of yourself, even then he will forgive you for your intention and for your great suffering . . . for there are neither words nor thought in human language to express *all* the ways and means of the Lamb, "until his ways are made manifest[14] to us". Who can embrace him, the unembraceable, who can understand *all of him*, the infinite!'

His lips began to twitch, as they had earlier, and a barely noticeable spasm passed over his face again. He steadied himself for a moment, but then could hold out no longer and quickly lowered his eyes.

Stavrogin took his hat from the sofa.

'I'll come again sometime,' he said, with an air of extreme fatigue. 'You and I . . . I place a high value on the pleasure of conversation with you, and on the honour . . . and on your feelings. Believe me, I understand why some people love you so much. I ask that you pray for me to him whom you love so much . . .'

'You're going already?' Tikhon also stood up quickly, as if he hadn't at all been expecting such a quick departure. 'But I,' and he seemed to flounder, 'I was about to present a request to you, but . . . I don't know how . . . now I'm afraid to.'

'Oh, do me the favour,' Stavrogin promptly sat down, his

hat in his hand. Tikhon looked at this hat, at this pose, the pose of a man who had suddenly become a man of the world, both agitated and half-mad, who was giving him five minutes to finish his business, and he grew even more flustered.

'My request amounts just to this, that you . . . why, you are already aware, Nikolay Vsevolodovich (I think that's your given name and patronymic, isn't it?), that if you make your pages public, then you will ruin your future . . . in the terms of a career, for instance . . . and . . . in the terms of everything else.'

'Career?' Nikolay Vsevolodovich frowned unpleasantly.

'Why should you ruin it? What purpose does such inflexibility serve?' Tikhon concluded almost beseechingly, and with an obvious awareness of his own awkwardness. A pained expression appeared on Nikolay Vsevolodovich's face.

'I've already asked you, and I'm asking you again: all your words will be superfluous . . . and in general, our entire conversation is beginning to become unbearable.'

He turned significantly in the armchair.

'You don't understand me, now hear me out and don't get angry. You know my opinion: your heroic deed, if done out of humility, would be a very great Christian deed, if you could sustain it. Even if you couldn't sustain it, the Lord would reckon it as your initial sacrifice. Everything will be reckoned: not a single word, not a single spiritual impulse, not a single half-thought will be in vain. But instead of this heroic deed I propose to you another one, even greater than that, something that's unmistakably great . . .'

Nikolay Vsevolodovich said nothing.

'You are struggling with a desire for martyrdom and self-sacrifice. Subdue this desire of yours as well, lay aside these pages, and your intention – and then you will succeed in overcoming everything. You will put all your pride to shame, and your demon! You will end as a conqueror, you will attain freedom . . .'

His eyes began to burn. He folded his hands in front of him beseechingly.

'Purely and simply, you are very much averse to a scandal, and you're setting a trap for me, good Father Tikhon,' Stavrogin mumbled offhandedly and in annoyance, as he made to stand up. 'In short, you want me to settle down, perhaps get married, and finish out my life as a member of the local club, visiting your monastery on every holiday. Why, that's some penance! Although you, as a connoisseur of the human heart, perhaps can even foresee that this will undoubtedly come to pass and the only thing now is to beg me nicely for decency's sake, since that's precisely what I'm thirsting for, isn't that right?'

He gave an unhinged-sounding laugh.

'No, not that kind of penance; I'm preparing another kind for you,' Tikhon went on heatedly, not paying the slightest attention to Stavrogin's laughter or his remark. 'I know a certain elder, not here, but not far from here either, a hermit and anchorite, and of such Christian wisdom that neither you nor I could possibly grasp it. He will listen to my requests. I will tell him everything about you. Go to him in obedience, place yourself under his authority for five years, for seven, for as many as you should find necessary. Make a vow to yourself, and with this great sacrifice you will purchase everything you desire and do not even expect, for now you can't begin to understand what you will receive!'

Stavrogin listened to his last proposal very, even extremely, seriously.

'Purely and simply, you're proposing that I enter this monastery as a monk? However much I respect you, I should really have anticipated that. Well, I'll even admit to you that at moments of faint-heartedness the thought has flashed through my head: to hide from people, once these pages have been made public to all, in a monastery at least for a time. But I immediately blushed over something so base. But taking monastic vows – that didn't enter my mind even when I was feeling the most fearful and faint-hearted.'

'You don't have to be in the monastery; you don't have to take vows. You will only be a novice secretly, not overt, and you can do that while still living fully in the world . . .'

'Stop it, Father Tikhon,' Stavrogin interrupted disdainfully and got up out of his chair. Tikhon did the same.

'What's wrong with you?' he suddenly exclaimed, staring

at Tikhon almost in fright. Tikhon was standing before him his hands clasped in front of him, and for a moment his face went into a painful spasm, apparently the consequence of some great fear.

'What's wrong with you? What's wrong with you?' Stavrogin kept repeating, rushing to hold him up. It seemed to him as if the man were about to fall.

'I can see . . . I can see as if it were real,' Tikhon exclaimed in a voice that penetrated the soul and expressed enormous sadness, 'that you, you poor lost young man, have never stood so close to the most dreadful crime as at this moment!'

'Calm yourself!' Stavrogin kept repeating, positively alarmed for him, 'perhaps I'll still put it off . . . you're right, perhaps I can't hold out and in my rage I'll commit a new crime . . . that's all so . . . you're right, I'll put it off.'

'No, not after the pages have been made public, but before they have been made public; perhaps a day, an hour before the great step, you will throw yourself into a fresh crime as a way out, only to *avoid* making the pages public!'

Stavrogin even began to tremble with anger and almost with fear.

'Damned psychologist!' he suddenly snapped in a fury, and without looking back, he walked out of the cell.

List of Characters

All Russians have three names: the given name, the patronymic and the surname. Thus: Fyodor Mikhaylovich Dostoyevsky; Anna Grigoryevna Dostoevskaya (many female surnames end in *-a* (Stavrogina) or *-aya* (Virginskaya). The patronymic is the father's given name with the ending *-ovich* or *-evich* for males, *-ovna* or *-evna* for females. Patronymics can be abbreviated by omitting the *-ov/-ev*, as is often the case in this novel with Aleksey Yegorych, the Stavrogins' manservant, and this usually connotes a degree of familiarity.

Most given names have affectionate or diminutive forms, as in English. Thus, Pyotr: Petrusha; Darya: Dasha. In addition, in *Demons* the French equivalents of the Russian names are often used. Thus, Nikolay: Nicolas; Lizaveta: Lise.

One normally addresses a person one does not know by the surname, preceded by an honorific, for example, 'Professor' or 'Mr', and the formal form of the verb, second personal plural (*vy* – very much like the French *vous*). Some knowledge of the person, even with a great difference in age and rank, entitles one to use the first name and patronymic only, though the *vy* form of the verb is usually preserved.

CHARACTERS, IN ALPHABETICAL ORDER

(with accented syllable indicated)

By surname

Drozdóv, Mavríky Nikoláyevich (Maurice), a young officer, Lizaveta Nikolayevna's escort

Drozdóva, Práskovya Ivánovna, general's widow and Varvara Petrovna's childhood friend

Érkel (referred to by rank and surname: Ensign Erkel), a young officer, Pyotr Stepanovich's messenger

Gagánov, Artémy Pávlovich, Pavel Pavlovich's son, who wishes to defend the family honour

Gagánov, Pável Pávlovich, 'a man well along in years and even honoured for his service'

G—v, Antón Lavréntyevich, the chronicler

Karmázinov, Semyón Yegórovich, famous Russian writer who bids farewell to Russia and literature

Kiríllov, Alekséy Nílych, a civil engineer, just returned from abroad after an absence of four years

Lebyádkin, Ignát Timoféyevich, a retired staff captain, buffoon and composer of scandalous verse

Lebyádkina, Márya Timoféyevna, Lebyadkin's crippled sister

Lipútin, Sergéy Vasílyevich (also Vasílyich), a provincial clerk, member of the group of five

Lyámshin (surname only given), a minor clerk in the post office, member of the group of five

Shátov, Iván Pávlovich (Shátushka), Darya's brother, a former student

Shátova, Dárya Pávlovna (Dásha), Varvara Petrovna's ward

Shátova, Márya Ignátyevna (Marie), Ivan's estranged wife

Shigalyóv (surname only given), author of a utopian system, member of the group of five

Stavrógin, Nikoláy Vsévolodovich (Nicolas), Varvara Petrovna's only son

Stavrógina, Varvára Petróvna, widowed landowner and Stepan Trofimovich's patron

Tíkhon (surname only given), bishop living in retirement in the local monastery

Tolkachénko (surname only given), 'a strange individual . . . famous for his enormous knowledge of the common people, mainly crooks and thieves', member of the group of five

Túshina, Lizavéta Nikoláyevna (Líza, Lise), Praskovya Ivanovna's daughter from her first marriage

Ulítina, Sófya Matvéyevna, itinerant book-pedlar of Bibles

Verkhovénsky, Pyótr Stepánovich (Petrúsha, Pierre), Stepan Trofimovich's only son

Verkhovénsky, Stepán Trofímovich, a 'man of the 1840s', former tutor to Nikolay Stavrogin and others

Virgínskaya, Arína Prókhorovna, a professional midwife

Virgínsky (surname only given), a local civil servant, member of the group of five

von Blum, Andréy Antónovich, serves in Governor von Lembke's chancellery, also his distant relative

von Lembke, Andréy Antónovich, the newly arrived governor
von Lembke, Yúliya Mikháylovna (Julie), the governor's wife

Without surnames

Agáfya, Liputin's servant
Alekséy Yegórovich (also Yegórych), the Stavrogins' manservant
Fyódor Fyódorovich (known as Fédka the Convict), former house-serf
  of Stepan Trofimovich, now escaped convict
Iván Osípovich, the former governor
Nastásya (Stasie), Stepan Trofimovich's servant
Semyón Yákovlevich, a saintly fool, 'our blessed prophet'

Notes

I gratefully acknowledge my very large debt to the editors of the Academy of Sciences edition of Dostoyevsky's *Complete Collected Works in Thirty Volumes* (*Polnoe sobranie sochinenii v tridtsati tomakh*, 1972–90), and in particular the authors of the extensive Commentary on *Demons* to be found in volume 12 (Leningrad: Nauka, 1975). Quotations from Dostoyevsky's works and other contemporary source materials (journals, newspapers, letters, etc.), unless otherwise noted, are from this edition.

All translations of foreign-language text that appears in the novel are from French, unless otherwise specified. Quotations from the Bible are given in the Revised Standard Version, unless otherwise stated. Full bibliographical information is given in Further Reading. Material taken from Robert A. Maguire's translation of *Dead Souls* (Penguin, 2004) is identified as (*RAM*). Internal cross-references are in the form 'I, 2', i.e. Part I, chapter 2.

All dates, unless otherwise indicated, are given according to the Julian Calendar (old style), which remained in force in Russia until 1918. The Gregorian Calendar, adopted in the West in the eighteenth century, was generally twelve days ahead. Dostoyevsky's correspondence written abroad is supplied with both dates.

Ronald Meyer

[*Epigraph*]

1. *Strike me ... (1830)*: The first of the epigraphs, excerpts from 'Demons' by the master of Russian poetry and prose, Alexander Pushkin (1799–1837), gave Dostoyevsky the title for his novel. The folk imagery in Pushkin's lyric ballad provides a dramatic contrast to the demons of the biblical account in Luke. Pushkin, author of the novel in verse *Eugene Onegin*, was venerated by

Dostoyevsky: see his famous 'Pushkin Speech' (1881). See also I,
1, note 34.

PART I

CHAPTER I

Instead of an Introduction

1. *'exiled'*: 'Exile' within Russia's borders, that is, to Siberia or the
    provinces.
2. *Gulliver . . . small*: Eponymous hero of Jonathan Swift's (1667–
    1745) satire *Gulliver's Travels* (1726) is marooned on the island
    of Lilliput, whose diminutive populace measure half a foot in
    height.
3. *pleiad*: A group that traditionally numbers seven members, from
    the Pleiades, the seven daughters of Atlas of Greek mythology.
    The most famous in Russia of the 'generation just past' was the
    Pushkin Pleiad.
4. *Chaadayev, Belinsky, Granovsky and Herzen*: Seminal figures
    who helped to formulate the position of the 'Westernizers' in
    the debate in Russia with the Slavophiles (see note 8). Pyotr
    Chaadayev (1794–1856), author of the *Lettres philosophiques*
    (*Philosophical Letters*), the first of which was published in Rus-
    sian translation in 1836 in the journal *Telescope*, with the result
    that the journal was suspended, its editor was fined and Chaa-
    dayev himself was officially declared to be insane and put under
    house arrest; none of the other seven letters was published in
    his lifetime. The letters, which played a role in launching the
    Westernizer vs. Slavophile debate, were sharply critical of Russia,
    Russian history and Russian Orthodoxy, all of which Chaadayev
    unfavourably contrasted with Western Europe and Roman Cath-
    olicism. In his memoirs, Alexander Herzen recalls the astonish-
    ment occasioned by the publication: '[Chaadayev's] *Letter* was
    in a sense the last word, the limit. It was a shot that rang out in
    the dark night; . . . whether it was a signal, a cry for help, whether
    it was news of the dawn or news that there would not be one –
    it was all the same: one had to wake up' (*My Past and Thoughts:
    The Memoirs of Alexander Herzen*, tr. C. Garnett, ed. Humphrey
    Higgins, abridged by Dwight Macdonald (Berkeley and Los
    Angeles: University of California Press, 1982), pp. 292–30). Vis-
    sarion Belinsky (1811–48), the most influential critic in Russia

during his lifetime and early champion of Dostoyevsky, supported Westernizing views and socially engaged literature. The liberal historian and professor of history at Moscow University, Timofey Granovsky (1813–55), a prominent figure in the camp of the Westernizers, exercised considerable influence on his contemporaries, including Herzen and Ivan Turgenev (see I, 3, note 2). Herzen described Granovsky's lectures as a 'draught of freedom' in the Russia of Tsar Nicholas I (1796–1855). The character of Stepan Trofimovich Verkhovensky was first named 'Granovsky' in early drafts of *Demons* and is clearly modelled on him. The writer and editor Alexander Herzen (1812–70), a liberal Westernizer and socialist advocate, left Russia in 1847 and founded the Free Russian Press in London in 1853, which published revolutionary pamphlets, the journal *Polar Star* and the newspaper *Bell*. Herzen's memoirs, *My Past and Thoughts* (written 1852–68), his major undertaking in his later years and an enduring monument of Russian prose, bring together history, philosophy, politics and personal reminiscence in a narrative that is both personal and panoramic (see also II, 6, note 3).

5. *'whirlwind of concurrent circumstances'*: Perhaps an allusion to the phrase 'whirlwind of arisen circumstances' in *Selected Passages from Correspondence with Friends* (1847) by Nikolay Gogol (1809–52). See note 68.

6. *Rus*: Pronounced 'Roos'. The name, probably of Swedish or Finnish origin, given to the first Russian state, which arose in the ninth century and was centred in Kiev. It persisted until the fifteenth century, when *Rossiya* began to be used to designate the European part of the country, by then centred in Moscow. *Rus* has survived till the present day, but only as a poetic word or an appeal to patriotic sentiments. (*RAM*)

7. *Hanseatic significance ... Hanau*: The Hanseatic League was established in 1241 as an economic alliance of towns in northern Germany; Hanau is located on the Main River, east of Frankfurt. Stepan Trofimovich's dissertation ironically recalls Granovsky's on the history of medieval towns.

8. *Slavophiles*: In direct opposition to such figures as Belinsky, Granovsky and Herzen, the Slavophiles rejected the European orientation of the Westernizers in favour of national self-definition and believed in the unique destiny and mission of Russia and the Russian Orthodox Church. Slavophilism as an intellectual movement traces its origins to the 1830s, coming into

being, to some extent, as a rejoinder to Chaadayev's criticism of Russia's isolation from Europe, the Roman Church and European intellectual history.

9. *Dickens ... George Sand*: In the 1840s the liberal monthly *Fatherland Notes* published Russian translations of the novels *Oliver Twist, Barnaby Rudge, The Life and Adventures of Martin Chuzzlewit* and *Dombey and Son* by Charles Dickens (1812–70), as well as translations of half a dozen novels by the French writer George Sand (1804–76).

10. *certain knights ... age*: An ironic reference to Granovsky's essay on the French medieval knight, Bayard (1473–1524), known as the Knight without Fear and without Reproach.

11. *Fourier*: French social reformer Charles Fourier (1772–1837) advocated a utopian social framework that would reorganize society into 'phalansteries', that is, communities structured on cooperative principles to promote equality of wealth and resources, and collective harmony. The Petrashevsky Circle (see Introduction, Section I), of which Dostoyevsky was a member, avidly read and discussed Fourier's works.

12. *a long poem*: Dostoyevsky invokes the form and several motifs from the trilogy 'Pot-Pourri' by V. S. Pecherin (1807–85), which was published in Herzen's *Polar Star* in 1861. One part, entitled 'The Triumph of Death', includes choruses of winds, flames and stars, etc. Other works that influenced Dostoyevsky's ironic characterization include Granovsky's 'Scenes from the Life of Caliostro' (1834), a dialogue between Lorecini, an alchemist and astrologist, and the twenty-year-old Caliostro, which indeed is somewhat reminiscent of *Faust* (see following note), and 'Unborn Soul' (1835) by Evdokiya Rostopchina (1811–58), with its chorus of 'unborn souls'.

13. *Faust*: Allegorical figures abound in the second part of *Faust*, completed by Goethe just before his death. See note 66.

14. *Tower of Babel ... Olympus*: The tower is the explanation in the Bible for the phenomenon of multiple languages. The Babylonians decided to 'build ourselves a city, and a tower with its top in the heavens'. However, God confused 'their language, that they may not understand one another's speech' and they 'left off building the city' (Genesis 11:1–9). Mount Olympus, the highest point in Greece, home of Zeus and the mythical gods.

15. *people's poet ... and idealist*: Nikolay Nekrasov (1821–78), the foremost representative of the realist school in Russian poetry, was already being called the 'people's poet' during his lifetime.

The lines are from the 'civic' poem 'The Bear Hunt' (1866–7), which includes passages on Belinsky and Granovsky.

16. *'civic grief'*: The term enjoyed an enormous vogue in Petersburg in the 1860s. It referred to a social 'illness' brought about by intense anguish sustained in response to the deplorable conditions of society (e.g. prostitution, poverty, the plight of the peasantry) and was even given as the cause of death for some students and cadets.

17. *Maecenas*: Roman politician and patron of Horace and Virgil, Gaius Maecenas (70?–8 BC), whose generosity, by and large prompted by political aims, namely, the glorification of the reign of Augustus, has rendered his name the very personification of lavish patronage.

18. *cholerine*: Exact translation of the Russian *kholerina*, the diminutive of *kholera* (cholera), a word used as little today in Russian as in English. Cholerine signifies the condition of having mild symptoms associated with cholera, e.g. diarrhoea, but not the actual incidence of the disease – Stepan Trofimovich's illness is brought on by nerves, not disease.

19. *flesh of her flesh*: When Adam created woman, he said: 'This at last is bone of my bones and flesh of my flesh; she shall be called Woman' (Genesis 2:23).

20. *emancipation of the peasants ... circulate*: Rumours of the government's intention to emancipate the peasants had begun to circulate in Russia as early as the 1840s. The Statute on the Peasants was issued by Tsar Alexander II on 19 February 1861, a date that is mentioned more than once in the novel.

21. *Crimea*: The Crimean War (1853–6) pitted the Russians against combined British, French and Ottoman forces. In September 1854, Allied forces landed on the Crimean Peninsula, the north shore of the Black Sea, and commenced a year-long siege of Sevastopol.

22. *souls*: Before the emancipation in 1861, the value of an estate was calculated in terms of the number of adult male peasant serfs (souls).

23. *liquor franchisee*: In 1765, Catherine the Great made the franchise system of selling liquor binding on all of Russia, except Siberia. The liquor franchisee (*otkupshchik*), usually a member of the nobility, paid the state a certain sum of money in advance, and was granted exclusive rights to deal in alcoholic beverages and collect taxes on their sale. Many grew enormously rich. (*RAM*)

24. *Kukolnik*: An engraving of the portrait (1836) by the Russian artist Karl Bryullov (1799–1852) of the largely, and perhaps justly, forgotten poet and historical dramatist Nestor Kukolnik (1809–68).

25. *Tocqueville ... Paul de Kock*: The serious work of French historian and sociologist Alexis de Tocqueville (1805–59), author of *Democracy in America* (1835, 1840), is ironically contrasted to the racy, frothy and immensely popular novels of Parisian life by Charles-Paul de Kock (1793–1871).

26. *Moscow proved unsatisfactory*: In 1712, Peter the Great moved the capital from Moscow to St Petersburg, his 'window on the West', founded less than a decade earlier. Petersburg, designed from scratch on European models by European architects, thus became the political and administrative capital, as well as the cultural centre, while Moscow, with its traditional architecture (the Kremlin, the many churches, its winding streets) continued to be regarded as the traditional and spiritual centre – the tsars travelled to Moscow for their coronation even though the Court was in Petersburg. Russia thus had two capitals during much of the modern period. Dostoyevsky's *Crime and Punishment*, to name but one work, is set in Petersburg, but he portrays not the city of palaces, government buildings and magnificent parks, but the squalid rooming houses of the urban poor and stinking, dusty streets; see also the Appendix 'At Tikhon's'.

27. *Radishchev*: Alexander Radishchev (1749–1802) was sentenced to ten years of exile for publishing his *Journey from Petersburg to Moscow* (1790), a denunciation of the existing social order, the monarchy and serfdom, in particular. The book was officially banned until 1905.

28. *lyceum*: Also: lycée. In pre-Revolutionary Russia, an institution for men's secondary education, or post-secondary for law. Pushkin was a student at the lycée in Tsarskoe Selo.

29. *soirées*: A party, reception or other social gathering held in the evening.

30. *collective protests ... 'outrageous act'*: Writers' collective protests against 'outrageous' items in the press was a common phenomenon in the 1860s. In his memoirs the critic Nikolay Strakhov (1828–96) wrote: 'A protest meant to declare as a group in the name of *all literature* that such-and-such an act was considered base, ignoble, and had aroused indignation.' For example, a protest aimed at the journal *Spark* (see note 32) was signed by the entire editorial board and staff of *Russian Word*,

Fatherland Notes, Library for Reading and *Russian World*, as well as a number of writers.

31. *abolition of censorship . . . Krayevsky's house*: Censorship, spelling reform, women's rights, etc., were all burning issues discussed in the press of the day. The Arcade, known as the Passage, apart from shops, housed a theatre, restaurants, the Literary Fund and held exhibitions. Dostoyevsky's story 'The Crocodile' (1865) is set there. It remains a centre of public life in Petersburg today. Poland's boundaries have shifted greatly over the centuries. In the seventeenth century, the Polish-Lithuanian Commonwealth was one of the largest countries in Europe, incorporating substantial territory of present-day Ukraine and Russia. During the successive partitions of Poland in the eighteenth century, more and more Polish territory was ceded to Russian rule as Russia expanded westward. Dostoyevsky nurtured feelings of ill-will towards the publisher of *Fatherland Notes*, Andrey Krayevsky (1810–89), ostensibly as a result of believing that he had been exploited by Krayevsky early on in his career. Both *Fatherland Notes* and the newspaper *Voice* (see I, 2, note 7) had their editorial offices at Krayevsky's house at No. 36, Liteiny Prospect.

32. *illustrated magazine*: Nekrasov, 'the people's poet' (see note 15), was a contributor to *Spark*, an illustrated satirical journal published in Petersburg from 1859 to 1873.

33. *absurdity of the word 'fatherland' . . . religion was harmful*: Stepan Trofimovich's words here are in agreement with the programme of the followers of the Russian anarchist and political theorist Mikhail Bakunin (1814–76), one point of which read: 'Atheism – the abolition of all creeds, replacing religion with science, divine justice with human justice.' According to an article in *Voice* (2 June 1871), the International ratified this point and made it an obligatory part of its programme, as well as another article of faith, namely, that 'fatherland is an empty word . . . Nationality is an accidental result of birth.'

34. *boots . . . Pushkin*: Dostoyevsky takes issue with the utilitarian and materialist strain in Russian criticism as exemplified by the critic Dmitry Pisarev (1840–68). In his essay 'Mr Shchedrin, or a Schism among the Nihilists' (1864), Dostoyevsky wrote: 'From this it follows that boots in any case are better than Pushkin, because one can get by without Pushkin, but it's utterly impossible to get by without boots, and consequently, Pushkin – is a luxury and nonsense.' See also III, 1, note 17.

35. *On m'a . . . coton*: They treated me like an old cotton nightcap!

36. *laurel water*: Since ancient times, the laurel wreath has been conferred on poets, heroes and winners of athletic contests as a mark of honour (pp. 39, 533), but here laurel water is used for its medicinal purposes as a mild sedative.

37. *Vek and Vek . . . and Vek*: The opening lines of Dostoyevsky's satiric poem mocking popular journalism of the early 1860s. *Vek* (century, age; Russian) was a Petersburg weekly; Lev Kambek, a second-rate journalist, was the publisher of *Family Circle* (1859–60) and *St Petersburg Herald* (1861–2).

38. *Andrejeff (in the French spelling)*: The use of French was widespread in Russian society – Stepan Trofimovich peppers his speech with it. Characters are often called by the French equivalents of their names, for example, Nicolas for Nikolay.

39. *peut briser . . . en deux*: Can break my life in two.

40. *700 versts*: The equivalent of 746.9 kilometres or 464 miles. One verst equals 1.067 kilometres; 3,500 feet.

41. *Athenian evenings*: Allusion to *Athenian* [or *Attic*] *Nights* by Aulus Gellius (fl. 2nd century AD), a collection of materials in various disciplines structured in the form of dialogues. Stepan Trofimovich employs the original meaning of the expression; it later came to be a euphemism for 'orgy'.

42. *Sistine Madonna*: Painted (1513–14) during the Italian Renaissance by Raphael (1483–1520), it is housed in the Gemäldegalerie in Dresden, Germany. (It is referred to as the 'Dresden Madonna' in II, 4.) Dostoyevsky considered this painting to be one of the masterpieces of European art. The memoirs of his wife, Anna Grigoryevna Dostoyevskaya, record a visit to the Dresden gallery to see it: he insisted on standing on a chair to get a better look.

43. *en tout pays . . . ses veaux*: In every land . . . in the land of Makar and his calves. The Russian expression, which is translated two paragraphs later in the text, is roughly equivalent to 'back of the beyond', but also implies political repression, perhaps internal exile.

44. *je suis . . . de plus*: I am . . . and nothing more! Yes nothing more!

45. *'freethinking'*: Usually connotes scepticism in regard to religion, but might also encompass more general social issues, e.g. women's rights. As becomes clear later in the novel, Marya Shatova is one of the 'new people' (see I, 4, note 2).

46. *work-table*: A lady's table used to store the implements and materials for her sewing and needlework.

47. *chez les séminaristes*: Among the seminarians. Many of the

radicals of the 1860s, Nikolay Chernyshevsky (1828–89), for example, had been educated at seminaries, hence, the pejorative term 'seminarian'. (Education there did not necessarily mean the student intended to pursue a career in the church.) In one of his working notebooks from the 1860s, Dostoyevsky defines his understanding of 'seminarism': 'The seminarians are introducing into our literature a special sort of negation, one that is too complete and too hostile, too sharp and as a result too narrow-minded.' Negative references and attacks on seminarians can be found in his letters and his drafts for *Crime and Punishment*.

48. *the golden mean*: To take the middle path, to avoid extremes and embrace moderation.

49. *My dear friend . . . ancient Roman sentiment*: Dostoyevsky uses Virginsky's address to his wife to parody the artificial dialogue in Chernyshevsky's revolutionary novel *What Is to Be Done?* (1863). This plodding and mediocre work was literally the bible of the radical intelligentsia, but is the object of scorn in many of Dostoyevsky's works. The 'sentiment' is also taken from Chernyshevsky's novel.

50. *France, after Caesarism*: Military or imperial dictatorship; political absolutism. For Dostoyevsky's thoughts on the Third Republic, which was proclaimed in France in September 1870, see 'Musings about Europe' (March 1876), in *A Writer's Diary*.

51. *united Italy*: Victor Emmanuel II was proclaimed king of the newly united state of Italy in 1861; ten years later Rome was made the capital, and the Pope, formerly the sovereign of the papal states, which included Rome and surrounding territories, withdrew into the Vatican. For Dostoyevsky's anti-papal and anti-Catholic analysis of the state of Roman Catholicism, see 'An Expired Force and the Forces of the Future' (March 1876), in *A Writer's Diary*.

52. *Marseillaise*: Composed in 1792 by Claude-Joseph Rouget de Lisle (1760–1836) as the *Chant de guerre de l'Armée du Rhin* (*Marching Song of the Rhine Army*), it was adopted as the French national anthem on Bastille Day, 1795, though it was banned for much of the nineteenth century. See also II, 5, note 3.

53. *The muzhiks . . . will happen*: From 'Fantasy' (1861), an anonymous poem published in Herzen's *Polar Star*.

54. *Cher ami*: Dear friend.

55. *making a fuss over them . . . treasure*: In his survey of Russian literature for 1847, Belinsky appealed to writers to portray the Russian peasant, asking, 'Isn't the peasant a person as well?' The

1850s and 60s witnessed a number of such works, most famously Turgenev's *A Hunter's Sketches* (1847–50) and Nekrasov's narrative poem *Who Is Happy in Russia?* (1863–78).

56. *Komarinsky*: Designates a traditional Russian folk song in 2/4 time and the dance form *komarinskii*, but it is more usually referred to as *kamarinskaya*.

57. *Rachel for a muzhik*: Mlle Rachel (Élisa Félix, 1820/21?–58), French classical tragedienne who dominated the Comédie Française for seventeen years, included Russia on her European tours.

58. *bouquet de l'impératrice*: The 'Empress's Bouquet', an elegant French perfume, winner of a medal at the Paris World Exhibition in 1867, which in Russia was sold by the firm of L. Legran, 'perfumer to the Russian, French and Italian courts'. The empress in question is Eugénie, wife of Napoleon III.

59. *Anton Goremyka*: *Anton the Unfortunate* (1847), novel by Dmitry Grigorovich (1822–99), whose naturalistic depiction of the peasant Anton and the miseries of peasant life served as an indictment against serfdom, was greeted enthusiastically by Belinsky for ushering in a new age in Russian literature. Grigorovich, a friend of Dostoyevsky's since their days together at the Engineering Academy, is also mentioned in *The Idiot*.

60. *Anton Petrov affair*: The introduction of the Statute on the Peasants (see note 20) caused unrest in a number of provinces, which was harshly put down by imperial forces. In the village of Bezdna in Kazan Province, Anton Petrov, a peasant, took upon himself the responsibility of reading the statute to some 5,000 people from different villages who had gathered to hear him. He affirmed that all the land was being transferred to the peasants, and consequently they would no longer be required to pay taxes, etc. Forces were dispatched to Bezdna to restore order – many of the rebelling peasants were executed; Petrov was sentenced to death by firing squad. The events were reported in the journal *Time* (1861) and in Herzen's *Bell*.

61. *Peterschule*: St Peter's School, a German secondary school founded in the eighteenth century in Petersburg.

62. *pour notre sainte Russie*: For our holy Russia.

63. *pan-Slavisms*: Movement in the nineteenth century that embraced the political and cultural union of all Slavic peoples. In Russia, Pan-Slavism was appropriated by the Slavophiles, who advocated that all Slavic nations should band together to revitalize Western Europe, both politically and religiously.

64. *Prince Igor*: Two Igors come to mind. Igor Ryurikovich (d. 945),

Grand Prince of Kiev from 912, who united the Slavic tribes and made them subordinate to Kiev; and Prince Igor Svyatoslavich (1151–1202) of Novgorod-Seversk, the hero of the twelfth-century medieval Russian epic, 'The Song of Igor's Campaign', whom history, according to Vladimir Nabokov, 'remembers as an insignificant, shifty and pugnacious prince' (*The Song of Igor's Campaign*, tr. Vladimir Nabokov (Ann Arbor, Michigan: Ardis, 1988), p. 74). Here the allusion to Igor is used simply to signal a faraway time.

65. *mais distinguons*: But let's distinguish.

66. *I am an ancient pagan, like the great Goethe*: German poet Johann Wolfgang von Goethe (1749–1832), best known for his dramatic poem *Faust* (1808, 1832), held unorthodox views on religion and experienced a powerful attraction for the Greek classical world throughout his life, which is reflected in many of his works. The poet Heinrich Heine (1797–1856) called Goethe the 'great pagan'.

67. *George Sand . . . novels of genius*: Reference to the novel *Lélia* (1833) in which Sand addresses the problems of religion, marriage and woman's sexuality.

68. *Belinsky . . . 'some god'*: Nikolay Gogol, master of the short story and author of the novel *Dead Souls* (1842), severely disappointed Belinsky, his most important supporter, with his peculiar book *Selected Passages from Correspondence with Friends*. In his famous letter of 15 July 1847, Belinsky chastised Gogol for turning his back on his former liberal principles and adopting the reactionary world view evidenced in *Selected Passages*. Belinsky also took the opportunity to lash out at the Russian state and the Orthodox Church. The passage that Stepan Trofimovich alludes to reads: 'Superstition passes with the advances of civilization, but religiousness often keeps company with them too; we have a living example of this in France, where even today there are many sincere Catholics among enlightened and educated men, and where many people, who have rejected Christianity, still cling stubbornly to some sort of God' (*Readings in Russian Civilization*, ed. Thomas Riha, 2nd rev. edn (Chicago: University of Chicago Press, 1969), vol. 2). Dostoyevsky was arrested in 1849 for reading this prohibited letter at a meeting of the Petrashevsky Circle.

69. *Entre nous soit dit*: Just between us.

70. *Lenten oil*: During the Lenten fast, the longest in the Orthodox calendar, only vegetable oils may be used in cooking.

71. *Krylov's fable . . . than that*: Reference to 'The Inquisitive Man'

(1814) by the Russian La Fontaine, Ivan Krylov (1769–1844) (see also I, 5, note 11).

CHAPTER 2

Prince Harry. Matchmaking

1. *preceptor*: Teacher, instructor.
2. *horse guards*: Elite military unit in pre-Revolutionary Russia.
3. *Prince Harry . . . by Shakespeare*: Characters from Shakespeare's historical plays *Henry IV, Parts 1 and 2* (1597). They reappear, minus Prince Harry, in the comedy *The Merry Wives of Windsor* (1597). For Falstaff, see I, 5, note 15.
4. *reduction to the ranks . . . army's infantry regiments*: Stavrogin loses both his status as an officer and gentleman and has to leave his elite regiment for the regular army.
5. *In 1863*: The year would seem to indicate that Stavrogin took part in the suppression of the Polish Uprising.
6. *marshal of the nobility*: The elected representative of the gentry of a district or province who is charged with protecting the gentry's interests and who played a leading role in the organs of local self-government.
7. *Voice*: Krayevsky's daily political and literary newspaper, published in Petersburg from 1863 to 1883.
8. *attack of brain fever*: The phrase in Russian is *belaya goryachka*, which signifies *delirium tremens*, an episode of delirium usually brought on by a withdrawal from alcohol, although it may be induced as the result of heavy alcohol consumption.
9. *Considérant*: French socialist Victor-Prosper Considérant (1808–93) became the leader of Fourierism after the founder's death. His *Social Destiny* (1834–8), a systematic analysis of the master's views, immediately attracted the attention of Russian socialists upon its publication.
10. *grape cure . . . Vernex-Montreux*: An exclusive diet of grapes and grape juice was thought to cure cancer and other illnesses. Vernex-Montreux is a resort area, situated in the Swiss canton of Waadt, on the north-east shore of Lake Geneva.
11. *administrative ecstasy*: Dostoyevsky borrows the phrase from *The History of a Town* (1869–70), by satirical writer Mikhail Saltykov-Shchedrin (1826–89). In this parody of Russian history, the phrase is applied to the town governors, who are caricatures of Russian rulers and their ministers.

12. *excellente amie . . . son pouvoir*: *excellent amie*: excellent friend; *Ces interminables mots russes*: These interminable Russian words!; *Vous savez, chez nous . . . En un mot*: You know, among us . . . In a word; *pour vous montrer son pouvoir*: in order to show you his power; *mais c'est très curieux*: but this is very curious; *les dames charmantes*: the charming ladies; *vous savez ces chants et le livre de Job*: you know those songs and the Book of Job; *et il a montré son pouvoir*: and he showed his power. Passages from Job are read during Holy Week in the Russian Orthodox Church.

13. *quelle idée rouge*: What a wild idea!

14. *avec cette morgue*: With such arrogance.

15. *Vraiment*: Really?

16. *Bismarck*: Otto von Bismarck (1815–98), the 'Iron Chancellor', prime minister of Prussia, founder and first chancellor of the German Empire.

17. *ma bonne amie*: My good friend.

18. *Charmante enfant*: Charming child!

19. *the Last Judgement*: The day when the world comes to an end and God passes his final judgement on all individuals.

20. *Mais, ma chère*: But, my dear.

21. *Et puis . . . de raison*: And then, since one always finds more monks than reason. The phrase comes from the *Letters to a Provincial* (1656–7) by the French mathematician, physicist and philosopher Blaise Pascal (1623–62).

22. *Ma foi, chère*: Really, my dear.

23. *Irascible, mais bon*: Irascible, but good.

24. *c'est une . . . raconter*: It's a very silly story! I was waiting for you, my dear friend, in order to tell you.

25. *Tous les . . . soit dit*: *Tout les . . . en zapoi*: All men of genius and progress in Russia were, are and always will be gamblers and drunkards who go on drinking binges; *Mais, entre nous soit dit*: But, just between us.

26. *Mon cher, je suis un*: My dear, I am a.

27. *Lake Geneva makes the teeth ache*: According to his wife, when Dostoyevsky was suffering from toothache, he insisted that the pain was caused by the proximity to Lake Geneva and that he had read about this somewhere.

28. *Mais c'est une enfant*: But she's a child!

29. *'Tales from Spanish History'*: Granovsky authored a number of works on Spanish history.

30. *Oui, j'ai . . . c'est égal*: Yes, I chose the wrong word. But . . . it's all the same.
31. *Oui, oui, je suis incapable*: Yes, yes, I'm incapable.
32. *ce cher fils*: This dear son.
33. *c'est une si . . . de même*: *c'est une si pauvre tête*: he's not very bright; *c'est un pauvre sire tout de même*: he's such a poor creature all the same.
34. *Et enfin . . . Badinguet, un*: *Et enfin, le ridicule*: And finally, the ridicule; *Je suis un forçat, un Badinguet, un*: I am a convict, a Badinguet, a. Badinguet was the stonemason in whose clothes and under whose name Prince Napoleon Bonaparte (1808–73), the future Emperor Napoleon III, escaped from the fortress in Ham in 1846 to go to England.

CHAPTER 3

Another Man's Sins

1. *Molières and Voltaires*: Molière (1622–73), French comic play-wright, author of *Tartuffe* and more than two dozen other comic plays that exerted a profound influence on the world stage; Voltaire (1694–1778), French philosopher, novelist, dramatist, moralist, critic and leading figure in the Enlightenment, author of the philosophical tale *Candide* (1759) (see also II, 10, note 2).
2. *shipwreck somewhere . . . bodies pulled out*: The unflattering figure of Karmazinov is clearly meant to be a parody of the writer Ivan Turgenev (1818–83), author of the novel *Fathers and Sons* (1862), with whom Dostoyevsky maintained a difficult relation-ship. Many of Karmazinov's least attractive traits, ranging from his shrill, feminine voice to the way in which he offers his cheek in greeting are pure Turgenev. Karmazinov's article seems to beg comparison with Turgenev's sketch 'The Execution of Troppmann' (1870), in which the narrator is witness to an execution by guillotine, and with his late story 'A Fire at Sea' (1883), based on his own experience as a nineteen-year-old trav-elling to Germany aboard a steamship. Rumours reached Russia that Turgenev had acted the coward when the ship caught fire, and while the story was published after *Demons*, Dostoyevsky surely had heard them.
3. *stovepipe hat*: Man's top hat, made out of silk, where the cylinder was straight-sided, like a pipe, not wider at the top or bottom.

4.   *lorgnette*: Eyeglasses or opera glasses with a short handle.

5.   *prunella*: Strong worsted twill fabric used for the uppers of shoes and furniture upholstery.

6.   *reticule*: Small ladies handbag or purse.

7.   *Bukhara carpet*: Today the fifth largest city in Uzbekistan, Bukhara, renowned for its textiles and Persian carpets, was a major trading centre on the Silk Road, the ancient trade route that linked China with the West.

8.   *Teniers*: David Teniers the Younger (1610–90), Flemish painter, best known for his genre scenes of peasant life.

9.   *L'Homme qui rit*: *The Man Who Laughs* (1869), novel by the French Romantic author Victor Hugo (1802–85). The exotic cast of characters includes Gwynplaine, whose face was purposely disfigured when he was a boy so that it looks like a laughing mask, in order that he would have better success begging.

10. *Je m'en fiche . . . et témoin*: *Je m'en fiche*: I don't give a damn!; *Je m'en fiche et je proclame . . . la Lembke*: I don't give a damn and I proclaim my liberty. To the Devil with Karmazinoff! To the Devil with the Lembke woman!; *Vous me seconderez . . . et témoin*: You will support me, won't you, as a friend and witness.

11. *G—v (that's my surname)*: In Dostoyevsky's notebooks for the novel, the chronicler's surname is spelled out as 'Govorov' from the verb *govorit'* – to speak, say, tell, talk.

12. *c'est le mot*: That's the word.

13. *quelque chose . . . petit idiot*: *quelque chose dans ce genre*: something of that sort; *je m'en souviens. Enfin*: I remember that. Finally; *c'était comme un petit idiot*: he was like a little idiot.

14. *Comment . . . pauvre ami*: *Comment*: How's that!; *de ce pauvre ami*: of this poor friend.

15. *I, who have studied . . . does not know the Russian people*: Compare the following from Gogol's *Selected Passages from Correspondence with Friends*: 'You were counting on the fact that I know Russia, like the back of my hand; but I know absolutely nothing about it.'

16. *incidents of suicide in Russia*: The theme of suicide surfaces frequently in Dostoyevsky's notebooks and *A Writer's Diary*, where he explains the high incidence of suicide is due to the unsettled nature of Russian society in the transitional period following the reforms. See, for example, 'Two Suicides' and 'A Few Words about Young People' (October and December 1876, respectively), in *A Writer's Diary*.

17. *last peace congress*: The International League for Peace and Liberty was convened in Geneva in 1867.

18. *Mais cela passera*: But that will pass.

19. *Pechorins*: The protagonist of the novel, *A Hero of Our Time* (1840), by the Romantic poet and novelist Mikhail Lermontov (1814–41). Pechorin belongs to the class of Russian literary characters known as the 'superfluous man', individuals who seemingly possess all possible advantages, including position in society, talent, intellect, bravery, but who are nevertheless doomed to endless aimlessness, unable to find an outlet for their talents in Russia.

20. *de l'accident . . . n'est-ce pas*: To the accident. You will accompany me, won't you?

21. *O! Dieu qui est si grand et si bon*: O God, who is so great and so good!

22. *et je commence . . . je veux*: *et je commence à croire*: and I am beginning to believe; *En Dieu? En Dieu, qui est là-haut*: In God? In God above; *Il fait tout ce que je veux*: He does everything that I want.

23. *Enfin une minute de bonheur*: At last, a minute of happiness!

24. *Vous et le bonheur, vous arrivez en même temps*: You and happiness, you arrive at the same time!

25. *name-days*: In Russia, children were named after saints of the Eastern Orthodox Church, each of whom has a designated feast day in the church calendar. The celebration of the name-day in Russia was often more important than one's birthday.

26. *like a Kalmyk's*: The Kalmyk (also spelled Kalmuck) are a Mongol people who live in south-western Russia, west of the Volga River on the north-western shore of the Caspian Sea.

27. *Circassian*: From Circassia, a region between the Black Sea and the Caucasus Mountains. Its people go back to ancient times, were Christianized in the sixth century, but then converted to Islam when the region was taken into the Ottoman Empire in the seventeenth century. They came under Russian rule in 1829, and were hostile subjects, yet they have been widely celebrated in Russian literature for their bravery and physical beauty. (*RAM*)

28. *j'étais si nerveux et malade et puis*: I was so nervous and sick and then.

29. *C'est un pense-creux . . . homme du monde*: He is a local dreamer. He is the best and most irascible man in the world.

30. *et vous fairez un bienfait*: And you will be doing a good deed.

31. *icon*: In the Eastern Orthodox tradition, an image or representa-

tion of a sacred personage or event, usually painted on wood but also executed in murals and mosaics. The icon is placed in a corner of the room, and a lamp situated in front of it is lit.

32. *Emperor Nikolay Pavlovich*: Tsar Nicholas I, whose reign (1825–55) froze Russia with its thirty years of reactionary policies.

33. *I like tea . . . at night*: According to Dostoyevsky's wife, Kirillov is assigned his traits: Dostoyevsky 'liked strong tea, almost like beer . . . He particularly liked tea at night while he was working.'

34. *Sevastopol*: Allusion to the siege of Russia's main naval base on the Black Sea, during the Crimean War (See I, 1, note 21). On 11 September 1855 the Russians sank their ships, destroyed their fortress and evacuated the city.

35. *Enfin, c'est ridicule . . . tout de même*: *Enfin, c'est ridicule*: Anyhow, it's ridiculous; *Ce Maurice . . . brave homme tout de même*: That Mavriky . . . a good man all the same.

36. *Korobochka*: The acquisitive, narrow-minded provincial landowner in Gogol's *Dead Souls*. Her surname could be translated as 'little box', which helps to explain the chronicler's reply that in a magnified version she would be a 'trunk'.

37. *wet her head with vinegar*: Vinegar compresses have long been thought to possess medicinal properties, as in the English nursery rhyme, 'Jack and Jill': 'And [Jack] went to bed and covered his head / In vinegar and brown paper.'

38. *ce Lipoutine . . . un ingrat*: *ce Lipoutine, ce que je ne comprends pas*: this Liputin is something I don't understand; *Je suis un ingrat*: I am an ingrate!

39. *tout est dit . . . c'est terrible*: Everything has been said . . . it's terrible.

40. *pardon . . . un monstre*: *pardon*: forgive me; *C'est un ange*: She's an angel; *Ma foi*: Really; *Vingt ans*: Twenty years!; *C'est un monstre*: He is a monster.

41. *Ces gens-là . . . d'autre chose*: *Ces gens-là . . . ne sont réellement*: These people imagine that nature and human society are different from the way God made them and than they really are; *mais parlons d'autre chose*: but let's speak of something else.

42. *en Suisse*: In Switzerland.

43. *c'était bête . . . tout est dit*: It was stupid, but what can be done, everything has been said.

44. *Le bon Dieu*: God Almighty.

45. *si le miracle existe . . . soit dit*: *si le miracle existe*: if miracles exist?; *et que tout soit dit*: and let everything be said!

46. *ce qu'on appelle le*: What is called.
47. *laissez-moi ... voyez-vous*: *laissez-moi, mon ami*: leave me, my
    friend; *voyez-vous*: you see.

CHAPTER 4

The Crippled Woman

1. *Othello*: Shakespeare's tragedy (written 1602–4) ends with
   Othello strangling his wife Desdemona in a fit of jealous rage,
   whereupon he learns of her fidelity and kills himself.
2. *new people*: Chernyshevsky's *What Is to Be Done?* is subtitled
   From Stories about the New People, that is, people who espoused
   the new principles of materialism, socialism and utilitarianism
   and who regarded this novel as their manual (see I, 1, note 45).
3. *The literary undertaking*: In early 1869 Dostoyevsky wrote to
   his niece Sofya Ivanova about a similar idea for 'an enormous,
   useful, essential *annual* reference book for everyone' (*Complete
   Letters*, tr. D. Lowe, vol. 3, p. 126).
4. *infusorian*: Simple organism of microscopic proportions, often
   found in decomposing organic matter.
5. *lackeyism of thought*: The same phrase is found in Dostoyevsky's
   preparatory materials for *Crime and Punishment*: 'NB. Nihilism
   is lackeyism of thought. The nihilist is a lackey of thought.' While
   Turgenev did not coin the term 'nihilism', he certainly can be
   credited with creating its most famous representative in Bazarov
   in *Fathers and Sons*. As Arkady, Bazarov's young protégé,
   explains to his father, a 'nihilist is someone who doesn't bow
   down to any authority, who doesn't accept any principle on
   faith, no matter how revered that principle may be' (*Fathers
   and Sons*, in *The Essential Turgenev*, ed. Elizabeth Cheresh Allen
   (Evanston, Illinois: Northwestern University Press, 1994),
   p. 584). The term nihilist was loosely applied to radicals of all
   stripes in Russia during the 1860s, from those who questioned
   the existing state of affairs, rebelled against tradition and advocated reforms to those who sought the complete annihilation of
   the social order. Moreover, Dostoyevsky particularly loathed
   nihilism's materialist underpinnings, of which Bazarov's statement that 'a good chemist is twenty times as useful as any poet'
   (p. 587) is a good example. See also I, 1, note 34, and II, 1, note 5.
6. *There's also hatred here ... laughter that the world can see*:
   These words regarding hatred, it has been suggested, are most

likely directed at Saltykov-Shchedrin, whose writings Dostoyevsky admired, but with whom relations were frequently strained (see also I, 2, note 11). The narrator in Gogol's *Dead Souls* says that he is destined to survey life 'through laughter visible to the world and tears invisible and unknown to it' (*Dead Souls*, tr. Maguire, p. 150). In his 'Series of Articles about Russian Literature' (1861), Dostoyevsky writes that Gogol 'laughed all his life both at himself and at us, and we all laughed after him, we laughed so much that in the end we began to cry from our laughter'.

7.   *in order to try out for ourselves ... social conditions*: Taken almost verbatim from P. I. Ogorodnikov's travel essay 'From New York to San Francisco and Back to Russia' (1870).

8.   *spiritualism, lynch law ... took out my hairbrush*: Ogorodnikov devoted pages to spiritualists in Chicago, lynch law and the episode with the hairbrush.

9.   *lindenwood*: Also known as limewood, the preferred wood for icon painting; a soft wood that is also well suited for carving.

10. *Athos*: The Eastern Orthodox monastic community on Mt Athos, located in north-eastern Greece, dates back to the tenth century.

11. *I don't need ... for you*: These lines from Russian folklore are connected with Yevdokiya (Eudoxia) Lopukhina (1669–1731), first wife of Peter the Great, whom Peter forced into a convent in 1698; she took vows the following year.

12. *I have come ... I'll drink*: A grotesque parody of the frequently anthologized poem 'I have come to you with greeting' (1843) by Afanasy Fet (1820–92), who is best known for his lyrics on love and nature. The first four lines are Fet's (with only a minor variation), but then Lebyadkin hits his stride. Fet's poem ends with lines to the effect that he doesn't know 'what he shall sing, only that his song is ripening' – nothing about drink and drinking! The poem can be found in *The Heritage of Russian Verse*, ed. Dmitri Obolensky (Bloomington: Indiana University Press, 1976).

13. *recent year of famine*: Russia knew famine in 1867–8. In 1868 journals and newspapers printed articles and appeals for aid for our 'impoverished brothers'.

14. *Mais qu'avez-vous donc*: But what is the matter with you.

CHAPTER 5

The Wise Serpent

1. *Mais, chère ... quelle inquiétude*: But dear and excellent friend, in what anxiety.

2. *tic douloureux*: Painful tic.

3. *God's fool*: Also translated as 'fool-in-Christ' and 'holy fool', *yurodivyi* generally designates an eccentric individual who lives outside of society and its norms; does not have a fixed residence, but wanders, living on the charity of strangers; may be mad or may merely simulate madness; is able to divine truths or perhaps see the future; and delivers his message in parables or in symbolic language.

4. *enfin, c'est ... forçat évadé*: In short, he is a lost man and something in the way of an escaped convict.

5. *C'est un homme ... ce genre*: He is a dishonest man and I believe he is an escaped convict or something of the sort.

6. *one green banknote*: Denominations of banknotes were differentiated by colour; a green note was worth three roubles.

7. *Yermolov*: General A. P. Yermolov (1772–1861), hero of the war of 1812 against Napoleon, was commander-in-chief of Russian forces in the Caucasus from 1817 to 1827.

8. *Moscow Gazette*: The oldest Russian newspaper, published continuously from 1756 to 1917. Mikhail Katkov (1818–87) assumed the editorship in 1863 of this most influential newspaper of the period.

9. *Be still, my hopeless heart*: An inexact quotation from the poem 'Doubt' (1838) by Kukolnik (see I, 1, note 24). The original reads: 'Sleep, my hopeless heart'. The poem is better known through its musical setting by Mikhail Glinka.

10. *Montbars*: Montbars or Monbars (b. 1646), nicknamed the Exterminator, was a famous pirate in the West Indies, leader of the 'filibusters' (see also II, 10, note 3), and the protagonist of several dramas and novels, for example, *Monbars l'Exterminateur ou le Dernier chef des flibustiers, anecdotes du nouveau monde* (Paris, 1807).

11. *Krylov, to whom a monument has been erected*: The monument was officially unveiled in May 1855 and still stands today in front of the Tea House in St Petersburg's Summer Garden. The statue, designed by Pyotr Klodt, is decorated with bas-relief compositions of characters from Krylov's fables (see I, 1, note 71).

12. *'In this world a roach did dwell'*: Lebyadkin's grotesque fable is a parody of I. P. Myatlev's 'A Fantastic Pronouncement' (1834), which begins and ends with the words: 'As soon as the cockroach falls into the glass – he's done for. It's not easy to climb up glass.' Some scholars have seen a certain 'civic' strain (for example, the clamouring protests of the flies) in Lebyadkin's humorous verse, not unlike the numerous contemporary publications of satiric verse in which civic themes were vulgarized or trivialized.

13. *Denis Davydov*: Remembered today primarily as the 'Hussar Poet', Davydov (1784–1839) in his lyric verse celebrates wine, women and song, often on the eve of battle. Hussar regiments in Russia, as in other European countries, were named for the fifteenth-century Hungarian light-cavalry unit, the *huszár*. The hussar, in addition to his superior skill as a horseman, could be distinguished from men of other units by his elaborate and richly coloured uniform, which was matched by the wearer's fearless courage on the battlefield and reckless abandon in private life.

14. *Pierre, mon enfant*: Peter, my child. Here Stepan Trofimovich calls his son by the Russian diminutive form of Pyotr, Petrusha, and the French equivalent, Pierre.

15. *Falstaff*: The fat and witty Sir John Falstaff, the drinking companion of Prince Hal in Shakespeare's *King Henry IV, Parts 1 and 2*, expects to receive great favours when Hal becomes King – expectations that are not fulfilled.

16. *Gostiny Dvor*: The enormous shopping arcade in Petersburg, which dates from the eighteenth century, is on the city's main thoroughfare, Nevsky Prospect.

17. *Sodom*: The city of Sodom is destroyed for the sins of its inhabitants (Genesis 19:1–29). Here the word signifies 'disorder, excess'.

18. *Hamlet*: Eponymous hero of Shakespeare's great tragedy (1599–1601), famous for his indecision as given voice in the soliloquy that begins 'To be, or not to be'.

19. *Et vous avez raison*: And you are right.

20. *Horatio . . . Ophelia*: Hamlet confides to his friend Horatio what he has learned from his father's ghost, namely, that the king, Hamlet's father, was murdered by his brother Claudius. Spurned by Hamlet, Ophelia goes mad from grief and drowns herself.

21. *Decembrist L—n*: On 14 December 1825, some 3,000 military officers and nobles took advantage of the dynastic crisis following the death of Alexander I and gathered on Senate Square in St Petersburg to demand a constitution, peasant reforms and

other measures that would curb the abuses of the autocracy. The rebellion was quelled by forces loyal to the new tsar, Nicholas I; some sixty or seventy of the rebels were killed, five of the leaders were executed, while the remainder were exiled to Siberia or sent to the Caucasus. Mikhail Lunin (1787–1845), a Decembrist, had a reputation for engaging in reckless and senseless duelling, once initiating a duel to give his opponent an 'opportunity to experience the sensation of standing in front of a gun' (Irina Reyfman, *Ritualized Violence Russian Style: The Duel in Russian Culture and Literature* (Stanford, California: Stanford University Press, 1999), p. 78).

22. *rage . . . Lermontov*: Killed in a duel at the age of twenty-six, it was not Lermontov's first duel; in addition to his formidable talent as a writer, he had earned a reputation for his scornful and embittered view of people and society. See also I, 3, note 19.

PART II

CHAPTER I

Night

1. *Corsican vendetta*: A vendetta, or blood feud, between two groups, which are usually related in some way, initiated perhaps by murder and perpetuated through acts of revenge and retaliation. Groups often resort to vendetta when the rule of law is weak, as was the case on the island of Corsica for centuries.

2. *official capacity . . . confidentially*: In other words, an agent of the secret police.

3. *zemstvo*: The Great Reforms of 1864 continued Alexander II's modernization of Russia begun with the emancipation of the serfs. These reforms included a thorough overhaul of the judicial system and the reorganization of local government in the form of the zemtsvo, an elected district council in rural areas charged with the administration of such local concerns as education, medicine, hygiene, roads, food reserves.

4. *Il rit . . . Passons*: *Il rit*: He laughs; *Passons*: Let's move on.

5. *Bazarov*: The nihilist protagonist in Turgenev's *Fathers and Sons* scorns art, music and poetry; instead, he dissects frogs as he declares that nature is his 'workshop'. See also I, 4, note 5.

6. *Nozdryov and Byron*: Nozdryov, in Gogol's *Dead Souls*, is a

'windbag and chronic liar, whose name, derived from "nostril", suggests his lack of substance' (*RAM*). The Romantic poet George Gordon Byron (1788–1824) enjoyed immense popularity in Russia, as he did throughout Europe. Stepan Trofimovich makes an astute observation when he notes the affinity of Bazarov to the Byronic hero, a solitary character whose brooding, rebellious and contemptuous nature scorns society and its conventions.

7. *faire du bruit . . . rit toujours*: *faire du bruit autour de son nom*: to make an uproar around his name; *Il rit. Il rit beaucoup, il rit trop . . . Il rit toujours*: He laughs. He laughs a lot, he laughs too much . . . He is always laughing.

8. *Tant mieux. Passons*: So much the better. Let's move on.

9. *Je voulais . . . de louche*: *Je voulais convertir . . . Cette pauvre auntie, elle entendra de belles choses*: I wanted to convert him . . . This poor auntie, she will hear some pretty things!; *Il y a . . . de louche*: There's something blind and suspicious here.

10. *Ils sont . . . ce genre*: *Ils sont tout simplement des paresseux*: They are simply lazy; *Vous êtes . . . une impuissance*: You're lazy! Your banner is a rag, an impotence; *une bêtise dans ce genre*: stupidity of that sort.

11. *Vous ne comprenez pas*: You don't understand.

12. *keepsake . . . 'The Women of Balzac, with Illustrations'*: The English word 'keepsake' was adopted in Russian to signify a lavishly illustrated publication or album – here, presumably, portraits of heroines from Honoré de Balzac's series of novels, collectively known as *The Human Comedy* (written 1827–47).

13. *castrates*: The sect of the castrates (*skoptsy*) was created in the second half of the eighteenth century by Kondraty Selivanov, a peasant who was a member of the flagellant sect (*khlysty*) and who had posed both as Peter III and Christ. Self-castration (for both men and women) was introduced to root out the orgies that often accompanied the flagellants' ecstatic, orgiastic rituals. See also II, 8, note 8.

14. *If there is no God, then what kind of a captain am I after that*: Compare Voltaire's famous words: 'If God didn't exist, it would be necessary to invent him', in 'Letter to the Author of "The Three Impostors"' (1769). See also the *Meditations* of the Roman emperor Marcus Aurelius (AD 121–80), who questioned the sense of 'living in a world where there are no gods'.

15. *Internationale*: The International Workingmen's Association – the First International – was established in London in 1864. Karl

Marx was a founding father. In Russia the organization was often referred to as the Internationale (from the French). Soon after Bakunin (see I, 1, note 33) joined its ranks four years later, it split into two camps – headed by Marx and Bakunin.

16. *Charmeur's*: E. F. Charmeur, Petersburg tailor, is also referred to in *Crime and Punishment*, and according to his wife, was used by Dostoyevsky.

17. *my dear father shipped him off to the army*: The census of serfs, or souls, was used by the government to determine the number of conscripts each landowner must provide for the imperial army; this was, in effect, a tax on the landowner. Household serfs, like Fedka, were exempt from conscription, but Stepan Trofimovich voluntarily sent him, and received payment in return. Recruits served twenty-five years in the military at the beginning of the nineteenth century; reduced to twelve years mid-century.

18. *Pushkin wrote to Heeckeren*: On 26 January 1837, Pushkin wrote a letter to Baron von Heeckeren that was purposely offensive both to the addressee and his adopted son George d'Anthès. Pushkin was in a jealous rage over the supposedly unwanted attention his wife received from d'Anthès. The letter, which eventually led to Pushkin's fatal duel, was first published abroad in 1861 and appeared two years later in Russia, and thus was fairly new to the reading public.

19. *In the Apocalypse the angel swears that time will no longer exist*: Paraphrase of Revelation 10:6: 'And sware by him that liveth for ever and ever, who created heaven, and the things that therein are, and the earth, and the things that therein are, and the sea, and the things which are therein, that there should be *time* no longer' (King James Version; the Revised Standard Version has 'that there should be no more *delay*' – my italics).

20. *and his name will be Man-God . . . God-Man*: To some extent, Kirillov's concept of Man-God has its origins in the philosophical discussions of the 1840s, e.g. among the Petrashevsky Circle (see Introduction, Section I), many of whom were followers of German philosopher Ludwig Feuerbach (1804–72), who, in *Essence of Christianity* (1841), argued that God was the creation of man and that mankind should lay claim to those qualities he had invested in God. In other words, Kirillov's new theory is in fact what Stavrogin had earlier dismissed as 'Old philosophical commonplaces' (p. 262). For example, in the article 'On the Founding of Rome and the Reign of Romulus', read at a meeting of the Petrashevsky Circle, Nikolay Mombelli (1823–1902)

envisaged the future of mankind: 'Within man there is something ideal that brings him nearer to the divinity. I wish to believe in the good and believe that in the end good will triumph over evil, will destroy it, and then people will become moral divinities – absolute gods, only in a human body.' 'God-Man', the formula reversed, is the traditional characterization of Jesus Christ.

21. *vent window*: Windows in Russia have a *fórtochka*, that is, a single hinged pane that can be opened for ventilation without opening the whole window – a very practical arrangement given the cold temperatures. It has also been rendered in English as ventilating pane, ventilating window and casement.

22. *'God-bearing' people*: Shatov's philosophy has been traced, in part, to the neo-Slavophile views of the essayist and philosopher Nikolay Danilevsky (1822–85), author of *Russia and Europe* (1871). A former Fourierist and member of the Petrashevsky Circle, and later a 'repentant nihilist', Danilevsky wrote of the impending decline of Europe and the great future of Slavdom and Russia in particular.

23. *third temptation of the Devil . . . the fault of Catholicism*: For his third temptation of Christ in the wilderness, the Devil took Christ 'to a very high mountain, and showed him all the kingdoms of the world and the glory of them; and he said to him, "All these I will give you, if you will fall down and worship me"' (Matthew 4:8–9). For Christians, Antichrist is a false prophet who will oppose Christ, glorify himself, embody evil, seduce many believers away from their faith and will be accompanied by lawlessness and various disasters. His appearance signals the approach of the 'final hour' before the second coming of Christ, who will destroy him (e.g. 1 John 2:18–22; 4:1–3). In Revelation, the 'beast' is another name for the Antichrist (13:11–17; 20:10). Popularly but not accurately the Antichrist is often equated with Satan (*RAM*). Shatov's attitude towards Roman Catholicism owes a great deal to Dostoyevsky's own views. See, for example, his essay 'An Expired Force and the Forces of the Future' (March 1876): 'Roman Catholicism . . . sold Christ without hesitation in exchange for earthly power. Having proclaimed as dogma that "Christianity cannot survive on earth without the earthly power of the pope", it thereby proclaimed a new Christ, unlike the former one, one who has yielded to the third temptation of the Devil – the temptation of the kingdoms of the world' (*A Writer's Diary*, tr. K. Lantz, vol. 1, p. 405).

24. *you would rather remain with Christ than with the truth*: The

same sentiments are expressed in Dostoyevsky's letter of late January–February 1854 to Natalya Fonvizina (1805–69), wife of the Decembrist Ivan Fonvizin, who followed her husband into exile. She visited Dostoyevsky and other members of the Petrashevsky Circle in the transit prison in Tobolsk, an act of kindness he remembered ever afterwards. Dostoyevsky wrote: 'That credo is very simple, here it is: to believe that there is nothing more beautiful, more profound, more attractive, more wise, more courageous and more perfect than Christ, and what's more, I tell myself jealous with love, there cannot be. Moreover, if someone proved to me that Christ were outside the truth, and it *really* were that the truth lay outside Christ, I would prefer to remain with Christ rather than with the truth' (*Complete Letters*, tr. D. Lowe and R. Meyer, vol. 1, p. 195).

25. *'of living water'* ... *in the Apocalypse*: Shatov conflates two images of water from the New Testament, the 'living water' of John 7:38 ('He who believes in me, as the scripture has said, "Out of his heart shall flow rivers of living water"') and an episode taken from the Apocalypse: 'The sixth angel poured his bowl on the great river Euphrates, and its water was dried up' (Revelation 16:12).

26. *like Nozdryov, who wanted to catch a hare by its hind legs*: Nozdryov boasts that 'there's such an awful lot of grey hares that you can't see the ground. I myself caught one myself by the hind legs with my own hands' (*Dead Souls*, tr. Maguire, p. 81).

27. *Body of Christ ... Second Coming*: The body of Christ refers both to the community of believers in Christ as well as the mysteries of the Eucharist, where the bread and wine of the sacrament becomes the body and blood of Christ. Christ's Second Coming will mark his return to this world and the resurrection of the dead.

28. *Stenka Razin*: The Don Cossack Stenka Razin (1630–71) led a Cossack and peasant rebellion on Russia's southern borders. He was eventually captured by loyalist Cossack forces and turned over to tsarist authorities, brought to Moscow and executed by quartering on Red Square. Stenka Razin is a popular hero in Russian folklore, and the subject of numerous folksongs and tales.

29. *Marquis de Sade*: Comte Donatien Alphonse Sade, known as the Marquis de Sade (1740–1814), for whom 'sadism' is named, is the author of a number of erotic novels, including *Justine or the Misfortunes of Virtue* (1791).

30. *Tikhon . . . our Yefimyevsky Bogorodsky Monastery*: There were eleven monasteries in the vicinity of Tver, the prototype of the town in *Demons*, one of which was called Spaso-Yefimyevsky (Saviour-St Euphemius). Russia had three monasteries named for the Mother of God (*Bogorodsky*), one located in the town of Zadonsk on the Don River. In 1769 the former head of a Tver monastery took up residence there because of ill health, and became known as Tikhon of Zadonsk.

CHAPTER 2

Night (Continuation)

1. *like Martin gobblin' up the soap*: The source of this expression and a great deal of Fedka the Convict's language can be traced to Dostoyevsky's Siberian notebook, in which he recorded close to 500 sayings and expressions from prison folklore.

2. *bast shoe*: Traditional footwear woven from the bark of the linden or poplar tree, worn primarily by peasants and the poor.

3. *Zosima*: More than likely, not a reference to a real person; the name is used here as a synonym for a hermit.

4. *At night . . . as a poet of genius puts it*: From 'To the Memory of the Painter Orlovsky' (1838) by Prince Pyotr Vyazemsky (1792–1878), champion of Romanticism and intimate friend of Pushkin. Lebyadkin changes the verb in the first line to 'I blow', where the original has the second person singular (you).

5. *Akmolinsk*: Founded in 1824 as a Russian military outpost, today known as Astana, the capital of Kazakhstan.

6. *Gogol's 'Last Story' . . . from his bosom*: In *Selected Passages from Correspondence with Friends*, Gogol writes about 'A Farewell Story', a work that he was planning to write: 'I swear: I didn't compose it and didn't invent it, it came singing on its own out of my soul.' The story never materialized.

7. *Derzhavin*: Allusion to Gavriil Derzhavin (1743–1816), great Russian poet of the eighteenth century, and the well-known line from his ode 'God' (1784): 'I'm king, I'm slave, I'm worm, I'm God.'

8. *Grishka Otrepyev*: The first of the three pretenders to the throne during the Time of Troubles (1598–1613), Grigory ('Grishka') Otrepyev, a member of the gentry class, became a monk and then left his monastery. He claimed to be Prince Dmitry, Ivan

the Terrible's son who had died in 1591. In January 1605 Patriarch Job ordered that a decree be read in all churches, consigning this Pretender to eternal perdition.

9. *pot-house*: Drinking establishment or tavern, usually small and patronized by the lower classes. (*RAM*)

CHAPTER 3
The Duel

1. *char-à-banc*: Literally, a wagon with benches, a long, light carriage with multiple rows of forward-facing benches.

2. *corporal punishment from the Tsar*: Catherine the Great's Charter to the Nobility (1785) exempted the nobility, distinguished citizens, as well as merchants of the first and second guilds, from corporal punishment.

CHAPTER 4
All Wait Expectantly

1. *Neither duellist . . . had been bothered*: Duelling, of course, was illegal in Russia by this time. Peter the Great was the first to legislate against it, followed by Catherine the Great and her Manifesto on Duels (1787). See Reyfman's meticulous account in *Ritualized Violence Russian Style*, with a chapter on the duel in Dostoyevsky's works, including *Demons*.

2. *he couldn't very well challenge his own former serf to a duel*: The duel presupposes that the opponents are of equal social standing, and the distance between serf and master would seem to make a challenge impossible. And yet, as Reyfman writes: 'Shatov is Stavrogin's equal in other ways: having attended a university, he is Stavrogin's intellectual peer. Most important, they are both active in the radical movement, which does not differentiate between nobles and plebeians. Stavrogin thus has to decide whether to treat Shatov as his equal and challenge him to a duel or at least beat him up or kill him on the spot, as the novel's narrator half expects him to do . . .' (*Ritualized Violence Russian Style*, p. 240).

3. *new courts*: The Great Reforms of 1864 introduced a single court system for all classes of society and separated the judiciary from the administration. Trial by jury was established for serious

criminal offences; a system of justices of the peace dealt with minor civil and criminal offences.

4. *The lot of the Russian woman is dreadful*: The 'woman question' became a constant feature of debate in the periodical press in the 1860s and plays a major role in Chernyshevsky's *What Is to Be Done?* Dostoyevsky's sympathy can be seen in his letter of 1/ 13 January 1868 to his niece Sofya Ivanova: 'My dear, look after your education and don't neglect even a profession ... but you should know that the woman question, and especially that of the Russian woman, will definitely make several great and wonderful strides even within your lifetime. I'm not speaking of our precocious ladies – you know how I view them' (*Complete Letters*, ed. D. Lowe, vol. 3, pp. 18–19).

5. *tableaux vivants*: Literally, living pictures. A scene – from history or mythology, for example – is represented by actors in costume, who strike a pose on stage and remain silent as if in a painting. *Tableaux vivants* ranged from simple party games to elaborate royal presentations.

6. *quadrilles*: Fashionable dance of French origin, composed of four or five sections, and performed by four couples.

7. *that tribe*: For some reason, Russified Germans have often been objects of satire in Russian literature, for example, Hermann in Pushkin's short story, 'The Queen of Spades' (1834), and the landlady Amalia Ivanovna Lippewechsel in *Crime and Punishment*. All of the stereotypes about Germans are brought into play, for example, an overwhelming love of order and tidiness, a lack of imagination or perhaps intelligence altogether, and miserliness.

8. *calendar*: The 'General Calendar', which contained, among other things, information on population statistics with breakdowns according to nationality, religious affiliation, estate and age, was issued from 1867 to 1917. The 'Address-Calendar', an annual directory, listed civil servants and government officials and their rank.

9. *Fra Diavolo*: Literally, 'Brother Devil', a comic opera (1830) by the French composer Daniel François Esprit Auber (1782–1871). The title character is loosely based on a historical figure, an Italian brigand who figures in folk legends and is remembered for his resistance to the French occupation of Naples.

10. *church*: The Russian *kirka*, which comes from the German *Kirche*, indicates a Lutheran church.

11. *we are Tories, and you are Whigs*: The principal political parties

in eighteenth-century England. The Whigs later became the Liberal Party; the Tories the Conservative Party.

12. *activité dévorante*: Furious activity.

13. *bourru bienfaisant*: Benevolent boor.

CHAPTER 5

Before the Gala

1. *Stupidville*: Named after the town in Saltykov-Shchedrin's *The History of a Town*; Glupov in the Russian, from *glupyi*: stupid, foolish, silly. See also I, 2, note 11.

2. *reports about book-pedlars*: On 7 May 1870, *Voice* published a long article about book-pedlars, which reported an incident involving a 35-year-old book-pedlar, who had been 'offended to the point of tears in a certain tavern'.

3. *Qu'un ... nos sillons*: From the *Marseillaise*: 'Let their impure blood water our fields.'

4. *Mein lieber Augustin*: My dear Augustine (German), the title of a popular German waltz. Lyamshin's improvisation is a symbolic representation of the victory of the German petty bourgeoisie over the grand principles voiced by the French anthem.

5. *Pas un pouce ... nos forteresses*: Not one inch of our land, not one stone of our fortresses! Declaration by Jules Favre (1809–80), Minister of Foreign Affairs, made to Germany during the negotiations with Bismarck on the Treaty of Frankfurt (1871), ending the Franco-Prussian War.

6. '*A Liberal of the 1840s*': Describes Dostoyevsky himself. It became a commonplace in Russia to contrast the timid reforms discussed by the Westernizing liberals of the 1840s with the sweeping changes advocated by the utilitarian and materialist radicals of the 1860s.

7. *Château d'Yquem*: A highly prized and expensive Sauternes wine.

8. *Semyon Yakovlevich's*: According to Dostoyevsky's wife, based on a well-known holy fool who lived in Moscow, Ivan Yakovlevich Koreyshi (1781–1861), about whom a small brochure was published in the year of his death.

9. *Voltaire armchair*: Wide, deep, comfortable armchair with a tall back, named for the philosopher.

10. *some with sugar in the glass, others with a lump of sugar on the side*: Sugar in the glass for the more cultured tea-drinker, and

served on the side for the lower classes who would clamp the lump of sugar between their teeth and then drink their tea through it. In III, 7, Sofya Matveyevna drinks tea with the lump of sugar in her mouth, but Stepan Trofimovich decides to overlook this lapse in etiquette.

11. *Senate*: The highest court in the land, it also performed legislative and executive functions.

12. *What does this dream mean*: This question, a variation on Pushkin's 'What does your dream say?' from his poem 'The Bridegroom' (1825), enjoyed wide exposure in journalism during the 1860s. The use here is memorable, because Dostoyevsky returns to its original meaning. (The phrase reappears in *The Brothers Karamazov*.)

13. *kazachok*: Literally, little Cossack: a Ukrainian/Russian folk dance in which high kicks are executed from a squatting position, while the performer has his arms crossed on his chest.

14. *Oui, la comparaison . . . propre tombe*: Yes, such a comparison is permissible. It was like a little Don Cossack, who is dancing on his own grave.

15. *the mess of pottage you've sold your freedom to them for*: Esau sold his birthright to his brother Jacob for 'bread and pottage of lentils' (Genesis 25:33–4).

16. *Capefigue*: The work of the prolific and popular French biographer and historian Baptiste-Honoré-Raymond Capefigue (1802–72) more often represented hasty compilations rather than the products of original research and study.

17. *J'ai oublié*: I've forgotten.

18. *Alea jacta est*: The die is cast! (Latin). Words spoken by Julius Caesar as he and his legions crossed the Rubicon in 49 BC in defiance of the Senate, setting off the civil war that ended the Roman Republic and ushered in the Roman Empire.

19. *Filled with . . . delicious dream*: From Pushkin's lyric 'There once lived a poor knight' (1829). The poem receives extended treatment in Dostoyevsky's *Idiot* (II, 7).

CHAPTER 6

Pyotr Stepanovich All A-bustle

1. *'over whom this tongue of fire had blazed'*: From Pushkin's poem 'A Hero' (1830).

2. *Vogt, Moleschott and Büchner*: In the 1860s the works of

German natural scientist Karl Vogt (1817–95), Dutch physiologist Jacob Moleschott (1822–93) and German philosopher and physician Ludwig Büchner (1824–99) represented a bible of sorts for Russian radicals with a materialist world view.

3. *'cadet' ... Mr Herzen*: Refers to the episode in Herzen's *My Past and Thoughts* about Pavel Bakhmetev in the chapter 'The Younger Emigrants: The Common Fund'. In 1857, Bakhmetev, about to embark for the Marquesas Islands to found a socialist colony, gave Herzen a large sum of money, some 20,000 francs, to help finance Herzen's publishing concerns and other expenses connected with the Common Fund. In 1869, half of the money was given to revolutionary and conspirator Sergey Nechayev (1847–82); the remainder was sent to him after Herzen's death. Nechayev (see Introduction, Section II), the prototype of Pyotr Stepanovich, joined a radical student group in 1868 and took part in the orchestration of student unrest until March 1869, when he fled to Geneva. In Europe he made the acquaintance of Bakunin and Nikolay Ogaryov (1813–77), Herzen's long-time friend and co-editor, and firmly established his revolutionary credentials. Nechayev returned to Russia in September with a document signed by Bakunin, attesting to the fact that Nechayev was a member of the World Revolutionary Union; this was very useful for recruiting members for his revolutionary cells. See also III, 6, note 1.

4. *sans façon*: Without ceremony.

5. *sans que cela paraisse*: Without its being apparent.

6. *an axe was drawn on top*: Nechayev's Committee for People's Justice of 19 February 1870 had an oval-shaped brass seal, which featured the name of the organization and depicted an axe.

7. *A RADIANT PERSONALITY*: A parody of Ogaryov's 'The Student' (1868), which was published as a broadsheet in Geneva and dedicated to 'my young friend Nechayev'.

8. *from Smolensk to Tashkent*: In US geographic terms, 'from sea to shining sea'. The historic city of Smolensk is situated on the Dnieper River, 260 miles west of Moscow; Tashkent is the capital of Uzbekistan, the largest city in Central Asia.

9. *d.t.'s*: Delirium tremens.

10. *fougue*: Passion, heat, impetuosity.

11. *Avis au lecteur*: Preface or note to the reader. Here it contains a word of warning.

12. *Third Department*: The secret police in Imperial Russia. In the 1870s it was responsible for the arrests of many Populists

who had gone into the countryside to work and agitate among the peasantry. The department was abolished in 1880, two years after its head was assassinated by revolutionary terrorists.

13. *Ryleyev's Meditations*: The minor poet Kondraty Ryleyev (1795–1826) was hanged after the suppression of the Decembrist rebellion. In D. S. Mirsky's words, Ryleyev's 'patriotic and historical *Meditations* [1821–3], suggested by the similar poems of the Polish poet Niemcéwicz, proceed from a Plutarchian conception of Russian history as a collection of exemplars of civic virtue. With few exceptions the poems are stilted and conventional' (*History of Russian Literature* (Evanston, Illinois: Northwestern University Press, 1999), p. 103).

14. *only a lecturer . . . retired collegiate assessor*: In his memoirs, Herzen on more than one occasion refers to Granovsky as a docent, or lecturer, not a professor. Collegiate Assessor is Grade 8 in the Table of Ranks; the military equivalent is Major. Established in 1722 by Peter the Great, the table classified civil servants, military officers and court functionaries into fourteen ranks.

15. *sauntered up to exchange kisses, he merely offered his own cheek*: In his letter to A. N. Maikov, dated 16/28 August 1867, Dostoyevsky uses precisely these words to describe Turgenev.

16. *you always have several copies of your things made*: Again, an ironic poke at Turgenev, who was known for his lengthy and numerous revisions. In his letters Dostoyevsky complained more than once that he was forced to ruin his works by always having to rush to meet a deadline: '. . . but I won't start on it, because I want to work on it not for a deadline, but the way the Tolstoys, Turgenevs and Goncharovs write. Let at least one work of mine be written freely and not to meet a deadline' (Letter to Nikolay Strakhov, dated 2/14 December 1870, *Complete Letters*, ed. D. Lowe, vol. 3, p. 286).

17. *Wayfaring, or On the Way, or At the Crossways*: Parodies of titles of novels of the period, for example, *No Way Out* (1864) by Leskov. Dostoyevsky's notebook for 1864–5 has a short list of parodic titles: '*Whence?, Meanwhile, On the Eve, Tomorrow, What For?, Why?*'

18. *If Babylon really does collapse*: Reference to Babylon of the Apocalypse: 'Fallen, fallen is Babylon the great, she who made all nations drink the wine of her impure passion' (Revelation 14:8). See also Jeremiah 50–51.

19. *little huts on hens' legs*: In Russian folklore, Baba Yaga, the witch

with iron teeth, lives deep in the forest in a hut perched on chicken legs.

20. *'right to dishonour'*: A variation of the propaganda put out by Nechayev's Committee for People's Justice: 'We are guided by hatred for everything that is not of the people, we have no concept of moral obligations and honour in regard to that world which we hate and from which we expect nothing but evil.' The phrase 'right to dishonour' reappears in Dostoyevsky's discussion of the 'liberal fathers' of the current young generation ('Isolated Phenomena' (March 1876), in *A Writer's Diary*, tr. K. Lantz, vol. 1, pp. 422–3).

21. *Feast of the Protection*: The Feast of the Protection of the Mother of God is celebrated on 1 October.

22. *thalers*: Silver coin used as currency throughout Europe for 400 years.

23. *Gloomy dunderheads*: Dostoyevsky's notes for the novel *The Adolescent* (*A Raw Youth*) help to make sense of this formulation: 'The Nihilists – in essence that is what we were, eternal seekers of the higher idea. Now it's either indifferent dunderheads or monks. The first are "business-like", who nevertheless quite often shoot themselves, despite their business-like nature. While the monks are socialists who believe to the point of madness – these people never shoot themselves.'

24. *'sweetie-pie'*: In Chernyshevsky's *What Is to Be Done?*, the heroine Vera Pavlovna addresses her husband Lopukhov so often as 'sweetie-pie' that the endearment has ever after been associated with the novel.

25. *we'll seat ourselves in a barque, with little oars of maple . . . in the stern*: From a folksong of the Volga robbers, in which the 'beautiful maiden' has a prophetic dream that spells misfortune for the robbers.

26. *Se non è vero*: The first half of the Italian adage, 'If it's not true, it's well conceived' (*è ben trovato*).

CHAPTER 7

Among Our Own

1. *newly arrived Virginskaya . . . sheaf of papers*: Miss Virginskaya is modelled on the nineteen-year-old A. Dementyeva-Tkacheva, who provided the means for the Nechayev circle to set up an underground printing press. According to her testimony, she

printed a manifesto that was designed to arouse sympathy for the poor conditions faced by students.

2. *very young artillery man ... writing something down in his notebook*: According to a report published in the journal *Dawn* (1871), a 'half-literate young man' named Nikolayev, whom Nechayev represented as an 'inspector from a foreign revolutionary committee', attended the meetings, 'keeping his silence and writing something down all the time'.

3. *mazurka*: Lively Polish folk dance for a circle of couples, which is easily recognizable by the dancers' stamping feet and clicking heels.

4. *If you honour your father and your parents*: The girl student gives a very materialist twist to this commandment, which should read: 'Honour your father and your mother, that your days may be long in the land which the Lord your God gives you' (Exodus 20:12) – it says nothing about riches.

5. *Plato, Rousseau, Fourier, aluminium columns*: The three philosophers are named here ironically as creators of utopias. In his dialogue *The Republic*, Greek philosopher Plato (427?–347? BC), envisages a utopian society governed by philosophers; Swiss philosopher Jean-Jacques Rousseau (1712–78) emphasizes the importance of the individual in the utopian vision he sets forth in *The Social Contract* (1762); for Fourier, see I, 1, note 11. The aluminium columns are an allusion to the heroine's 'Fourth Dream' in Chernyshevsky's *What Is to Be Done?*, where the crystal palaces are decorated with them.

6. *One-tenth ... nine-tenths*: Dostoyevsky registered his impassioned protest on behalf of the nine-tenths in *A Writer's Diary*: 'I could never understand the notion that only one-tenth of people should get higher education while the other nine-tenths of people should serve only as their material and means while themselves remaining in darkness' ('The Russian Society for the Protection of Animals ... From the End or from the Beginning' (January 1876), tr. K. Lantz, vol. 1, p. 332). Variations of this division of society can be found in other works, for example, Raskolnikov's classification of 'ordinary' and 'extraordinary' people in *Crime and Punishment*.

7. *Cabet ... Proudhon*: In his novel *The Voyage to Icaria* (1840), French socialist Étienne Cabet (1788–1856) outlined his theories on establishing the ideal community. He, in fact, did found a settlement named Icaria in Illinois, but the reality never matched his theory. Pierre-Joseph Proudhon (1809–65), French

economist, socialist philosopher, anarchist and author of *What Is Property?* (1840), which contains the famous phrase 'Property is theft!'

8. *Dresden ... pocket Switzerland*: Dresden, known as 'Florence on the Elbe' on account of its art treasures, does indeed have a pocket Switzerland in its vicinity, namely, Saxon Switzerland, a mountainous climbing area and today a national park, which in the nineteenth century became popular with tourists and artists.

CHAPTER 8

Ivan the Tsarevich

1. *The first thing is to lower the level of education, science and accomplishment*: Here Dostoyevsky is parodying a number of the precepts found in Nechayev's 'Main Fundamentals of the Future Social Order' (1869).

2. *Cicero ... Shakespeare*: Cicero (106–43 BC), Roman statesman, philosopher and orator, did indeed endure exile and his tongue was cut out posthumously, a final act of revenge against his great gift of oratory. The Polish astronomer Nicolaus Copernicus (1473–1543), who put forth the theory that the planets revolved around the sun and not vice versa, was not blinded, nor was Shakespeare stoned.

3. *I'm your worm*: See II, 2, note 7.

4. *Littré's theory*: The French positivist philosopher Émile Littré (1801–81) is named here in error. The theory that 'crime is madness', popularized in Russia by the journalist and critic Varfolomey Zaitsev (1842–82), was developed by the Belgian mathematician and statistician Adolphe Quetelet (1796–1874).

5. *wilderness for forty years*: After the flight from Egypt, Moses led his people in the wilderness for forty years (Numbers 14 and Deuteronomy 29).

6. *Ivan the Tsarevich*: A popular hero in Russian folklore. The youngest of three sons, Ivan overcomes obstacles, completes the quest and generally succeeds where his brothers do not. For example, they fall asleep but Ivan captures the Firebird.

7. *The Pretender*: Russia has a rich tradition of Pretenders (see II, 2, note 8). As late as 1845 one made his appearance in the Orenburg region, claiming to be the son of Konstantin, the elder brother of Nicholas I; he promised to defend the peasants from the oppression of the gentry and government officials. Dostoyev-

sky may have become acquainted with this through an article in the *Herald of Europe* in 1868, 'Recent Unrest in the Orenburg Region', which includes the section 'The Pretender of 1845'.

8. *Ivan Filippovich, God of Sabaoth*: According to one legend of the castrates, their forefather would come from the East, mounted on a white horse, and would spread eunuchism in the West even among the French. Dostoyevsky seems to combine the names of two members of the castrate sect: Danilo Filippovich, who called himself God of Sabaoth, and Ivan Timofeyevich Suslov, who had declared that he was Christ. Sabaoth is the heavenly host, or army, which does battle with Evil and performs a number of duties, including guarding the gates of heaven, protecting the faithful and revealing the word of God.

9. *Solomonic judgements*: To exercise great wisdom, in the tradition of King Solomon, e.g. 1 Kings 3:16–28.

10. *Columbus without an America*: Dostoyevsky borrows this image from Herzen's characterization of Bakunin in *My Past and Thoughts*.

CHAPTER 9

A Search at Stepan Trofimovich's

1. *Enfin ... comprenez*: *Enfin un ami*: At last, a friend!; *Vous comprenez*: You understand?

2. *Pardon, j'ai oublié ... s'appelle Rosenthal*: Pardon, I've forgotten his name. He's not from here ... there was something stupid and German in his physiognomy. His name is Rosenthal.

3. *Vous le connaissez ... c'est cela*: *Vous le connaissez? Quelque ... roide et sérieux*: Do you know him? There was something dull and very self-satisfied in his appearance, and at the same time very severe, stiff and serious; *je m'y connais*: I know the type; *oui, je m'en souviens, il a employé ce mot*: Yes, I remember it, that was the word he used; *Il se tenait à distance*: He kept his distance; *enfin, il avait l'air ... comme ça*: in short, he seemed to believe that I was going to fall on him immediately and commence beating him to a pulp. All these people of the lower class are like that; *Voilà vingt ans que je m'y prépare*: It's twenty years that I've been preparing for this; *J'étais digne et calme*: I was dignified and calm; *et, enfin, tout ça*: and, in a word, all that; *et quelques-unes ... critiques et politiques*: and some of my historical, critical and political sketches; *Oui, c'est cela*: Yes, that's right.

4. *Il était seul . . . vous l'assure*: *Il était seul, bien seul*: He was alone,
    quite alone; *dans l'antichambre, oui, je m'en souviens, et puis*: in
    the entrance hall, yes, I remember, and then; *J'étais surexcité,
    voyez-vous. Il parlait, il parlait*: I was overexcited, you see. He
    talked, he talked; *un tas de choses*: a heap of things; *J'étais
    surexcité, mais digne, je vous l'assure*: I was overexcited, but
    dignified, I assure you.

5. *Savez-vous . . . tout-à-fait content*: *Savez-vous, il a prononcé le
    nom de Teliatnikoff*: You know, he mentioned the name Telyat-
    nikov; *qui me doit encore quinze roubles*: who still owes me
    fifteen roubles; *soi dit en passant. Enfin, je n'ai pas trop compris*:
    by the way. In a word, I didn't completely understand; *comment
    croyez-vous? Enfin, il a consenti*: what do you think? In a word,
    he consented; *et rien de plus*: and nothing more; *en amis, je suis
    tout-à-fait content*: as friends, I am completely satisfied.

6. *mes ennemis . . . et puis à quoi bon ce procureur . . . mon ami*:
    My enemies . . . and then what use is this prosecutor, our pig of
    a prosecutor, who twice has been impolite to me and got such a
    drubbing last year at the home of that charming and beautiful
    Natalya Pavlovna when he hid in her boudoir. And then, my
    friend.

7. *Quand on a . . . vous arrêter*: When one has such things in one's
    room and they come to arrest you.

8. *Éloignez-la . . . et puis ça m'embête*: Send her away . . . and
    besides it annoys me.

9. *Il faut être prêt, voyez-vous . . . chaque moment*: One must be
    prepared, you see . . . any moment.

10. *Cela date de Pêtersbourg*: This dates from Petersburg.

11. *Vous me mettez . . . de la lâcheté*: *Vous me mettez avec ces
    gens-là*: You put me on the same level as those people; *avec ces
    esprits-forts de la lâcheté*: with those freethinkers in cowardice.

12. *Savez-vous . . . je le sens*: *Savez-vous*: You know; *que je ferai
    là-bas quelque esclandre*: that I'll make some kind of scandal
    there; *Ma carrière est finie aujourd'hui, je le sens*: My career is
    finished today, I feel it.

13. *je vous jure*: I swear to you.

14. *Qu'en savez-vous*: What do you know about it.

15. *Siberia, Arkhangelsk*: Both destinations of exile – Siberia, to the
    east of European Russia, had been a place of exile for political
    prisoners since the seventeenth century; the city of Arkhangelsk
    (Archangel), is located on the Northern Dvina River, 30 miles
    from the White Sea.

16. *que dira-t-elle*: What will she say.

17. *Elle me soupçonnera toute sa vie*: She will suspect me all her life.

18. *c'est invraisemblable ... Et puis les femmes*: It is unlikely ... And then, women.

19. *Il faut être digne et calme avec von Lembke*: One must be dignified and calm with von Lembke.

20. *O croyez-moi ... de plus sacré*: O croyez-moi, je serai calme: Oh, believe me, I'll be calm!; *à la hauteur de tout ce qu'il y a de plus sacré*: at the height of everything that is most sacred.

21. *Allons*: Let's go!

CHAPTER 10

Filibusters. A Fateful Morning

1. *ordering artillery and Cossacks*: Allusion to incidents of putting down peasant unrest by force after the emancipation of 1861.

2. *Tout est ... mondes possibles. Voltaire. Candide*: 'All is for the best in this best of all possible worlds' – the words of Dr Pangloss in *Candide*.

3. *Filibusterov*: The character's name is actually *Flibusterov* (the Russian follows the French *flibustier*). However, it is Englished to emphasize the connection between Filibusterov and Andrey Antonovich's question: 'Filibusters?' The word, which derives from the Spanish for 'pirate' or 'freebooter', as it is used here signifies a military adventurer, originally applied in the 1850s in American English to those individuals who took part in Latin American insurrections.

4. *'Caps off!' ... 'On your knees!'*: Parody of the words spoken by Nicholas I to the people gathered on Haymarket Square during the cholera riots of June 1831, as recorded by an eyewitness: 'What are you doing, you fools? Where did you get the idea that you're being poisoned? It's God's punishment. On your knees, you blockheads! Pray to God!' Herzen's *Bell*, which printed Nikolay's speech in full, made the following observation, 'This captures Nicholas completely – genuinely, naively, naturally' (December 1865). Nicholas I shouted the command 'Caps off!' on 14 December 1825 to the rebelling troops gathered on Senate Square (the Decembrist Uprising).

5. *mon heure est sonné*: My hour has struck.

6. *Vous ne faites que des bêtises*: You're always doing stupid things.

7. *et comme on . . . de raison*: And since one finds everywhere more monks than reason. Cf. I, 2, note 21.

8. *C'est charmant, les moines*: That's charming, the monks.

9. *Karlsruhe*: Another oblique reference to Turgenev, who lived for a long period in this city, situated on the River Rhine in southwest Germany.

10. *all the shortcomings of the Westernizers*: A lampoon of Turgenev's essay, 'Apropos of *Fathers and Sons*' (1869), where he wrote: 'I derived particular satisfaction in depicting in Panshin (in a *Nest of Noblemen*) all the comical and vulgar aspects of Westernism; I made the Slavophile Lavretsky "destroy him at every point". Why did I do that – I, who consider Slavophile doctrine false and barren? Because *in this instance, as I saw it that was precisely* how life turned out and above all I wanted to be honest and truthful' (*Fathers and Sons*, tr. Ralph Matlaw, ed. M. R. Katz (New York: W. W. Norton, 1996), p. 163).

11. *one of our Shakespeares, in a private conversation . . . we great people*: Turgenev, after his break with Nekrasov's journal *Contemporary*, published a letter that he had received earlier from Nekrasov, who wrote that 'for the past several nights' he had 'seen [Turgenev] in his dreams'. Saltykov-Shchedrin cited this as an example, when 'a writer' had declared in print that 'he was so great that another writer saw him in his dreams'.

12. *et brisons-là, mon cher*: And let's say no more on the subject, my dear.

13. *others pointed their fingers to their foreheads . . . Lyamshin stuck two fingers above his forehead*: The traditional gesture of indicating that somebody is crazy; the cuckold's horns, which indicates an unfaithful spouse.

PART III

CHAPTER I

The Gala. First Part

1. *Tentetnikovs*: In Gogol's *Dead Souls* (Part II), Tentetnikov is an enlightened landowner, but 'belonged to that species of people who are in no danger of becoming extinct in Russia, and who formerly bore such names as sluggards, lieabouts and

couch-warmers, but who now should be called I really don't know what' (tr. Maguire, p. 292).

2. *Minervas*: Greek goddess of wisdom in Roman mythology, the counterpart of Athena in Greek mythology.

3. *Order of St Stanislav*: The Polish Order of St Stanislaus entered the Russian system of orders in 1831.

4. *literary matinée*: Literary readings became a frequent event in Petersburg after the Literary Fund was established in 1859. Dostoyevsky, Goncharov (see note 20), Turgenev and Nekrasov all took part in its benefits more than once.

5. *Belshazzar's feast*: Belshazzar, last king of Babylon, was renowned for his extraordinarily magnificent feasts. His guests drank wine from 'golden and silver vessels which had been taken out of the temple, the house of God in Jerusalem' (Daniel 5:3). At the last feast, Belshazzar sees a hand writing on the wall, which Daniel interprets as a sign that 'God has numbered the days of your kingdom.'

6. *orgeat*: Refreshing, cooling drink made from almond milk and sugar.

7. *A veritable oration got under way*: Karmazinov's farewell, which comprises the introduction and end of his 'Merci', parodies Turgenev's address to his readers in 'Apropos of *Fathers and Sons*'. The genre and composition of 'Merci' recall two short works by Turgenev: 'Phantoms' (1864), in the author's own words a 'series of scenes rather perfunctorily tied together', and 'Enough' (1865), a lengthy, pathetic, impassioned emotional monologue that is ripe for lampoon.

8. *Pompey or Cassius . . . Gluck*: Gnaeus Pompeius Magnus (106–48 BC), Roman consul, general and member of the First Triumvirate, known as Pompey the Great, suffered humiliating defeat at Pharsalus in battle against Julius Caesar; Gaius Cassius Longinus (d. 42 BC), a leader in the plot against Julius Caesar, suffered defeat in battle with Mark Antony at Philippi. Christoph Willibald Gluck (1714–87), German composer, best known for his operas *Orfeo ed Eurydice* (1762) and *Iphigénie en Tauride* (1779).

9. *en toutes lettres*: In full.

10. *Sukharev Tower*: Moscow landmark built in the Moscow Baroque style in 1692–5 (razed by the Soviets in 1934).

11. *Hoffmann . . . Ancus Marcius*: German Romantic writer E. T. A. Hoffmann (1776–1822), Polish composer Frédéric

Chopin (1810–49) and Ancus Marcius, legendary fourth king of Rome (642–617 BC).

12. *all these people who toil and are heavy laden*: 'Come to me, all who labour and are heavy laden, and I will give you rest' (Matthew 11:28).

13. *there is no crime . . . there are no righteous men*: Compare with Turgenev's 'Enough': 'Shakespeare again would have made his Lear repeat his cruel statement, "None doth offend", which in other words means: "None fails to offend"' (*Essential Turgenev*, ed. Allen, p. 761).

14. *grimace from Heine*: Verse from his *Book of Songs* (1827) has frequently been set to music.

15. *world rests on three fishes*: In Russian folklore the world rests on three fishes, much like Atlas in Greek mythology was commanded by Zeus to shoulder the weight of the heavens on his shoulders.

16. *c'est la bêtise . . . en parenthèse*: *c'est la bêtise . . . chimique*: it is stupidity in its purest essence, something like a chemical element; *en parenthèse*: by the way.

17. *Shakespeare or a pair of boots . . . socialism*: A variation on the debate on the utility of Pushkin (and art in general) or a pair of boots. According to Zaitsev in *Russian Word* (1864): 'There is no floor-polisher, no latrine-cleaner who is not many times more useful than Shakespeare.' Stepan Trofimovich takes up the position of an adherent of art for art's sake or pure art, thereby challenging the advocates of utilitarianism, whose position was articulated by Zaitsev: 'Contemporary admirers of art are turning both art and themselves into mummies, when they preach art for art's sake and make it not a means, but a goal. For two thousand years they have been in raptures over the Venus de Milo and three hundred years over Raphael's madonnas, without noticing that their ecstasies pronounce a sentence on art.'

18. *I shake the dust off my feet and curse you*: Stepan Trofimovich resorts to a biblical metaphor before uttering his curse: see Matthew 10:14 and Mark 6:11.

19. *the third reader, the maniac who had been waving his fist off-stage*: Platon Pavlov (1823–95), liberal professor of Russian history and the history of art at Petersburg University, served as the prototype. On 2 March 1862, Dostoyevsky heard his lecture on the thousand-year anniversary of Russia, which caused a sensation with the audience, but earned him the government's displeasure – he was exiled until 1869. According to contem-

poraries, Pavlov 'was not a completely normal man' and 'in conversation gave the impression of being mentally unstable'. The third reader's shrill loud voice that gradually turns into a shout and his gestures are drawn from Pavlov's manner of lecturing.

20. *Literature served at the pleasure of the censorship; close-order drill was taught in the universities*: A number of writers served as government censors, most famously Ivan Goncharov (1812–91), the author of *Oblomov*. In 1835 Tsar Nicholas I put Moscow University on a military footing: the students wore military uniforms, carried swords and military strategy was a required subject. Under Alexander II, the university statutes were relaxed in 1863.

21. *Cathedral of St Sophia ... thousand years*: A monument in the form of a bronze globe, the work of the sculptor M. O. Mikeshin (1836–96), was erected in 1862 near the ancient cathedral in Novgorod, to commemorate the thousand-year anniversary of Russia. It was frequently and vehemently attacked in the press, for example, by Saltykov-Shchedrin in his chronicle of contemporary life in Russia, 'Our Public Life' (1863).

CHAPTER 2

The End of the Gala

1. *Dieu vous ... de philosophie*: *Dieu vous pardonne ... vous garde*: May God forgive you, my friend, and may God protect you; *après le temps*: as time goes by; *quant à moi*: as for me; *ces pauvres gens ... de philosophie*: these poor people sometimes have charming expressions that are full of philosophy.

2. *O, ce sont ... voilà le mot*: Oh, they're pitiful little rogues and nothing more, little fools – that's the word!

3. *hier il avait tant d'esprit*: Yesterday he was so witty.

4. *quelle honte*: What shame!

5. *the Stock Exchange Gazette*: Popular Russian newspaper of the 1870s.

6. *A city ... cannot stand without seven righteous men*: In his attempt to save Sodom from destruction, Abraham in conversation with God first offered fifty righteous men, and then asked whether God would destroy the city if ten righteous men could be found there (Genesis 18:22–33).

7. *Vous me pardonnerez ... aux enfants*: *Vous me pardonnerez,*

charmante dame, n'est-ce pas: You will forgive me, charming
lady, won't you?; *aux enfants*: to children.

8.   *chasseur*: Soldier who served in a light infantry regiment.

9.   *pauvre mère*: Poor mother.

10. *'literary quadrille'*: Parody of a quadrille that took place in Moscow in February 1869, where the participants were dressed and
made up to suggest certain newspapers and journals in Moscow
and Petersburg. The three dancers have been identified: the
elderly gentleman with the hoarse voice is Andrey Krayevsky,
editor of *Voice*. 'Honest Russian thought' who carries an
'unsealed letter from abroad' is supposed to represent the Petersburg journal *Cause* (its title, *Delo*, could also be translated as
'case', 'affair' or 'matter', which explains the 'case' tucked under
his arm), published from 1866 to 1888, with ties to the Russian
revolutionary emigration. The 'formidable publication' is Katkov's reactionary *Moscow Gazette*, which regularly carried
attacks on the progressive press, including *Cause*.

11. *Zarechye*: Literally, on the other side of the river (Russian).

12. *Komarinsky unexpurgated*: One variant of the song (see I, 1,
note 56) opens: 'Oh, you son of a bitch, you *komarinsky* lout'.
In the 1860s satiric and revolutionary versions were published
in the free Russian press abroad and contained expressions that
could not be printed in Russia both because of the language and
the sentiment, e.g. 'Oh, you son of a bitch, you damned police
officer'.

13. *titular councillor*: Titular councillor is Grade 9 in the Table of
Ranks (see II, 6, note 14). The most famous titular councillor in
Russian literature is Gogol's Akaky Akakievich in the story 'The
Overcoat' (1842).

CHAPTER 3

A Romance Is Ended

1.   *Calendars always lie*: A quotation from the comedy *Woe from
Wit* (1823–5), Act III, Scene 21, by Alexander Griboyedov
(1795–1829). Many of its lines have become stock phrases in
the vocabulary of the Russian intelligentsia.

2.   *huge evil spider ... spend our entire lives looking at him and
being afraid of him*: Compare *Crime and Punishment* (IV, 1): 'We
always imagine eternity as something beyond our conception,
something vast, vast! But why must it be vast? Instead of all that,

what if it's one little room, like a bathhouse in the country, black and grimy and spiders in every corner, and that's all eternity is' (tr. Constance Garnett (New York: Macmillan Company, 1919), p. 263).

3. *Vox populi vox dei*: The maxim 'the voice of the people is the voice of God' (Latin) comes from *Works and Days* by Hesiod (*c.* 700 BC).

4. *Polinka Saks*: Belinsky championed the 'problem' novel *Polinka Saks* (1847) by Alexander Druzhinin (1824–64), which was greatly influenced by George Sand. The heroine is liberated by her husband to engage in an adulterous affair only to realize that she loves her husband.

5. *Vous êtes . . . et pardonner*: *Vous êtes malheureuse, n'est-ce pas*: You're unhappy, isn't that so?; *Nous sommes . . . tous. Pardonnons*: We're all unhappy, but one must forgive them all. Let us forgive; *il faut pardonner, pardonner et pardonner*: one must forgive, forgive and forgive!

6. *vingt-deux ans . . . qu'il est*: *vingt-deux ans*: twenty-two years; *chez ce marchand, s'il existe pourtant ce marchand*: at that merchant's house, assuming he exists, this merchant; *Mais savez-vous l'heure qu'il est*: But do you know what time it is!

7. *existe-t-elle la Russie? Bah, c'est vous, cher capitaine*: Does Russia exist? Bah, it's you, dear captain!

8. *the Voice writes about robberies*: Articles on murders and robberies began to appear in newspapers such as the *Voice* with the introduction in 1864 of public court proceedings.

9. *"poor" Liza*: Allusion to the story 'Poor Liza' (1792), a landmark of Russian sentimentalism, by Nikolay Karamzin (1766–1826). Liza, abandoned by her lover Erast, drowns herself in the pond that was once the witness of their love.

CHAPTER 4

A Final Decision

1. *struggle for existence*: From Charles Darwin's *On the Origin of Species by Means of Natural Selection* (1859).

2. *Tartar or a Mordvinian*: A Tartar is one of several Turkic-speaking peoples that for the most part are settled along the Volga River in central Russia and eastward to the Ural Mountains. Historically, the Mongol invaders of Russia in medieval times came to be known as Tartars. A Mordvinian is a member of a

people that speaks a Finno-Ugric language and which is largely
settled in the middle Volga River region of Russia.

3. *'from Smolensk . . . the student'*: See II, 6, note 8.

CHAPTER 5

A Woman Traveller

1. *Voznesenskaya . . . Bogoyavlenskaya*: The cabbie and Marie
   Shatova are having trouble keeping track of street names with
   religious derivations: Ascension and Epiphany, respectively. She,
   given her 'new people' credentials, would as a matter of principle
   scorn these religious landmarks.

2. *to open a bookbindery here, on rational cooperative principles*:
   Chernyshevsky's *What Is to Be Done?* launched a vogue for
   cooperative ventures of all kinds, following the example of his
   heroine.

3. *Frenchman in 1793*: The Reign of Terror began on 5 September
   1793; the Committee of Public Safety, whose most prominent
   member was Robespierre, exercised complete control over the
   government, initiating mass arrests, imprisonment and the
   execution of some 17,000 people.

4. *this is true, this is good*: In the account of the creation in Genesis
   1, in both the Russian Bible and the Revised Standard Version,
   God *sees* that 'it was good', but does not call it 'true'.

5. *there will be no childbirth, but all will be like God's angels*:
   Cf. 'For in the resurrection they neither marry nor are given in
   marriage, but are like angels in heaven' (Matthew 22:30).

6. *epilepsy*: According to Dostoyevsky's wife, Kirillov's account of
   the five or six seconds of eternal harmony is very similar to her
   husband's description of his own epileptic attacks.

7. *Mohammed's pitcher . . . on his horse*: According to the editors
   of the Academy edition, Shatov is referring to the traditional
   Muslim narrative from the life of Mohammed in which he is
   awakened in the night by the archangel Gabriel, who knocks
   over a pitcher of water with one of his wings. Mohammed travels
   from Mecca to Jerusalem and back, and then to heaven and back
   in an instant, returning in time to prevent the pitcher from falling
   over and spilling. A similar episode is briefly alluded to in the
   Koran (17, verse 1). Though dating back to ancient times, the
   charge that Mohammed was an epileptic is groundless.

CHAPTER 6

A Night of Many Difficulties

1. *It was a very gloomy place*: When a member of one of Nechayev's cells, I. I. Ivanov, a student at the Petrovsky Agricultural Academy in Moscow, declared his intention to leave the group, Nechayev ordered the other members to murder him. Ivanov was shot in the head after being beaten and strangled on 21 November 1869, in an isolated grotto on the grounds of the Academy, the model for this 'gloomy place'. Although his body was weighted with bricks and thrown into a pond, it was found four days later. By that time Nechayev had gone to Petersburg, from where he fled to Europe in December. The members of the cell were brought to trial in 1871. The following year Nechayev was extradited to Russia from Switzerland and imprisoned in the St Peter and Paul Fortress, where he died. See also II, 6, note 3.

2. *nothing secret that will not become manifest*: Kirillov paraphrases Christ's words to his disciples (Matthew 10:26; Luke 12:2).

3. *'Today you will be with me in paradise'*: Christ's words to the penitent thief who was crucified with him (Luke 23:43).

4. *Vive la république . . . la mort*: *Vive la république*: Long live the republic; *Vive la république démocratique, sociale et universelle ou la mort*: Long live the democratic, social and universal republic or death!; *Liberté, égalité, fraternité ou la mort*: Liberty, equality, fraternity or death!

5. *de Kiriloff . . . monde civilisé*: *de Kiriloff, gentilhomme russe et citoyen du monde*: de Kiriloff, Russian gentleman and citizen of the world; Kirillov assumes the French particle 'de', which often connotes noble origins; *Gentilhomme-séminariste russe et citoyen du monde civilisé*: Russian gentleman-seminarian and citizen of the civilized world!

CHAPTER 7

Stepan Trofimovich's Last Wandering

1. *ce marchand . . . grande route*: *ce marchand*: that merchant; *Vive la grande route*: Long live the high road.

2. *j'ai en tout . . . de même*: I have forty roubles in all; he'll take the roubles and kill me all the same.

3. *Grace à Dieu ... haut degré*: *Grace à Dieu*: Thank God; *et puis*: and then; *cela commence à être rassurant*: this begins to be reassuring; *c'est très rassurant*: this is very reassuring; *c'est rassurant au plus haut degré*: this is reassuring in the highest degree.

4. *moi c'est autre chose*: I am something else.

5. *Oui, c'est comme ça qu'on peut traduire*: Yes, it could be translated like that.

6. *C'est encore ... roubles, mais*: That's even better, I have forty roubles in all, but.

7. *C'est à dire*: That is to say.

8. *Elle l'a voulu*: She wanted it.

9. *un doigt d'eau de vie*: A finger of vodka.

10. *un tout petit rien*: Just a little bit.

11. *Je suis malade ... d'être malade*: I am quite ill, but it's not such a bad thing to be ill.

12. *une dame et elle en avait l'air*: A lady and she looked like one.

13. *mais je crois ... qu'on appelle*: *mais je crois que c'est l'Évangile*: but I believe that this is the Gospel; *Vous êtes ce qu'on appelle*: You are what they call.

14. *Je n'ai rien contre l'Évangile, et*: I have nothing against the Gospel, and.

15. *Renan's book, La Vie de Jésus*: The Life of Jesus (1863) by Ernest Renan (1823–92), who sought to employ a scientific historical method in his studies of Christianity and the life of Christ.

16. *Il me semble que tout le monde va à Spassof*: It seems that everybody is going to Spasov.

17. *Mais c'est ... tout pur*: *Mais c'est une dame, et très comme il faut*: But she is a lady, and very respectable; *Ce petit morceau de sucre ce n'est rien*: This little piece of sugar is nothing; *Le comme il faut tout pur*: Pure respectability.

18. *vous n'avez pas trente ans*: You can't be even thirty years old.

19. *Ces vauriens, ces malheureux*: Those scoundrels, those wretches.

20. *je deviens égoïste*: I'm becoming an egoist.

21. *Mais qu'est ce qu'il a cet homme*: But what's the matter with the man?

22. *Mais, ma chère et nouvelle amie*: But, my dear and new friend.

23. *Mais que faire, et je suis enchanté*: But what is to be done, and I'm enchanted!

24. *n'est ce pas ... le vrai peuple*: *n'est ce pas*: Won't you?; *J'aime le peuple ... vu de près*: I love the people, that's indispensable, but it seems to me that I never saw them up close; *cela va sans*

dire qu'elle est aussi du peuple: it goes without saying that also of the people; *mais le vrai peuple*: but the real people.

25. *Chère et incomparable amie*: Dear and incomparable friend.

26. *chère innocente ... chère ingrate*: *chère innocente. L'Évangile*: dear innocent lady. The Gospel; *Voyez-vous, désormais nous le prêcherons ensemble*: You see, from now on we will preach it together; *quelque chose de très nouveau dans ce genre*: something very new of this sort; *c'est admis*: this has been established; *à cette chère ingrate*: to that dear ungrateful (woman).

27. *Chère et incomparable ... cet argent*: *Chère et incomparable, pour moi une femme c'est tout*: Dear and incomparable lady, for me a woman is everything; *cela devient ... cet argent*: it's becoming too cold. By the way, I have forty roubles in all and here is that money.

28. *n'en parlons plus, parce que cela me fait mal*: Let's not speak any more about this, because it distresses me.

29. *parce que nous avons à parler ... Oui, j'ai beaucoup à vous dire, chère amie*: Because we need to talk ... Yes, I have a lot to say to you, my dear friend.

30. *Comment, vous savez déjà mon nom*: What, you already know my name?

31. *Assez, mon enfant ... me tourmentez*: *Assez, mon enfant*: Enough, my child; *nous avons notre argent, et après – et après le bon Dieu*: we have our money, and afterwards – and afterwards the good God will help; *Assez, assez, vous me tourmentez*: Enough, enough, you're tormenting me.

32. *Ce n'est rien, nous attendrons*: It's nothing, we'll wait.

33. *Vous êtes noble comme une marquise*: You are as noble as a marquise!

34. *I will turn my other cheek to her comme dans votre livre*: *comme dans votre livre*: As in your book. The 'book' is the Gospel; the reference to 'turning the other cheek' is from Christ's teaching in the Sermon on the Mount: 'Do not resist one who is evil. But if any one strikes you on the right cheek, turn to him the other also' (Matthew 5:39). Sofya Matveyevna later names this sermon; it is a summation of Christ's ethical teachings (Matthew 5–7).

35. *Est-ce que je suis si malade? Mais rien de sérieux*: Am I really that ill? But it's nothing serious.

36. *And to the angel of the church in Laodicea write*: Sofya Matveyevna reads from Revelation (The Apocalypse) 3:14–17.

iens, oui, l'Apocalypse. Lisez, lisez: Oh, I remember, alypse. Read, read.

s ensemble: We'll leave together.

These swine.

. comprendrons ensemble: *savez-vous*: you know; in this book; *une comparaison*: a comparison; *Oui, cette Russie, que j'aimais toujours*: Yes, this Russia which I have always loved; *et les autres avec lui*: and the others with him; *vous comprendrez après*: you will understand afterwards; *Vous comprendrez après . . . Nous comprendrons ensemble*: You will understand afterwards . . . We will understand together.

41. *Tiens, un lac*: Well now, a lake.
42. *Et je prêcherai l'Évangile*: And I'll preach the Gospel.
43. *C'est un ange . . . C'était plus qu'un ange pour moi*: She is an angel . . . She was more than an angel for me.
44. *Je vous aimais*: I loved you!
45. *Je vous aimais toute ma vie . . . vingt ans*: I loved you all my life . . . twenty years!
46. *une heure . . . un bouillon, un thé . . . enfin, il est si heureux*: An hour . . . some bouillon, tea . . . finally, he is so happy.
47. *Toute cette cérémonie*: This whole ceremony.
48. *Mon père, je vous remercie, et vous êtes bien bon, mais*: My Father, I thank you, and you're very kind, but.
49. *Voilà ma profession de foi*: There's my profession of faith!
50. *J'ai menti toute ma vie*: I've lied my entire life.

CHAPTER 8

Conclusion

1. *Shatov's cap . . . extraordinary carelessness*: A detail taken from the Ivanov murder: Nechayev grabbed the victim's cap instead of his own lambskin cap, which he left at the scene.
2. *Herzen . . . Canton of Uri*: Herzen took Swiss citizenship in the canton of Fribourg in 1851, when he was stripped of his rights and his return to Russia was no longer possible.

APPENDIX

At Tikhon's

1. *Spaso-Yefimyevsky Bogorodsky Monastery*: The name of the monastery is slightly different from when Shatov advises Stavrogin to see Tikhon, where it appears without 'Spaso' (Saviour). See II, 1, note 30.

2. *Archimandrite*: In the Russian Orthodox Church, a rank just below that of bishop; superior of a large monastery or group of monasteries (*RAM*).

3. *holy folly*: That is, an act of folly that comes about through one's saintly simplicity.

4. *étagères*: Sets of shelves.

5. *if you believe and you order a mountain to move*: Stavrogin refers to Christ's words to his disciples on the power of faith: 'Truly, I say to you, whoever says to this mountain, "Be taken up and cast into the sea", and does not doubt in his heart, but believes that what he says will come to pass, it will be done for him' (Mark 11:23).

6. *très peu*: Very little. See Dostoyevsky's 'Story about Father Nilus' (1873), in which a Paris archbishop during the French Revolution announces to the people that he has renounced his old ways, disowned the signs of his office (the crosses, vestments and chalices) and embraced Reason. A worker with his sword bared asks the archbishop whether he believes in God, to which the archbishop replies, 'Très peu'. To which the worker answers, 'That means that you're a scoundrel, and that you have been deceiving us until now.' And he splits the archbishop's head open with his sword.

7. *And to the angel . . . and naked*: Tikhon recites the passage from the Apocalypse in the Russian translation, the one that Sofya Matveyevna reads from in II, 9. However, since he is reciting by heart, there are minor inconsistencies – he incorporates a few words from the more archaic Church Slavonic translation that is still used today by the Russian Orthodox Church. For example, in two instances he substitutes archaic verbs, and these have been given here in the King James Version ('saith'; 'spue', the alternative spelling for spew).

8. *vice that Jean-Jacques Rousseau confessed to*: Soviet prudery prohibited the editors of the Academy edition of Dostoyevsky's

works from naming the vice Rousseau owns up to in his *Confessions* (1781–8), namely, masturbation.

9. *Petersburg Side*: Gorokhovaya Street, where Stavrogin has his room, is a major street in central Petersburg, running south from the Admiralty. The Petersburg Side is located on the opposite shore of the Neva, across from the Summer Garden and the Field of Mars and would be reached by Troitsky Bridge.

10. *Claude Lorrain . . . 'Acis and Galatea'*: *Landscape with Acis and Galatea* (1657) by Claude Lorrain (1600–1682), is indeed to be found in Dresden at the Gemäldegalerie. The subject, from Ovid's *Metamorphoses*, involves the shepherd Acis, who is loved by the nymph Galatea. The cyclops Polyphemus, in love with her, kills Acis by crushing him under a large rock.

11. *ten-year-old creature*: Note the discrepancy in Matryosha's age with p. 762, the difference making Stavrogin's crime all the more horrible.

12. *voluntary and involuntary sins*: These words appear in prayers asking forgiveness, for example, before and after Communion.

13. *'For whoso shall offend . . . little ones'*: 'But whoso shall offend one of these little ones which believe in me, it were better for him that a millstone were hanged about his neck, and that he were drowned in the depth of the sea' (Matthew 18:6, King James Version, which is closer to the Russian text).

14. *until his ways are made manifest*: The source of this quotation has not been established, but it is biblical in tone (e.g. 1 Corinthians 3:13, 'Every man's work shall be made manifest', King James Version).

Glossary

Some of the Russian words that have made their way into English are too familiar to require listing here, e.g. 'vodka', 'samovar'. Others, though now often listed in dictionaries, are still unfamiliar enough to require some explanation. Finally, a small number have been kept in the original because they have no English equivalents.

arshin (ar-shéen): 0.711 metres; 28 inches.

artel: A cooperative in Russia of workers or craftsmen.

boyar: Designation of members of the higher nobility from the tenth to the seventeenth centuries.

britska (britzka, britzska: bréets-kuh): An open carriage on springs, with a folding top, and room for the passenger to recline.

desyatina (dee-sya-tée-na): 1.092 hectares; 2.7 acres.

droshky (drozhki: drósh-kee): A low four-wheeled carriage, with no top, and with a narrow bench for passengers to sit astride or sideways with their feet on bars; often hired.

foont: Pound (weight), slightly less than the English equivalent.

kalach (kah-láhch): A bun shaped like a padlock or purse, with a (baked) dough handle.

kopeck: One hundred kopecks make a rouble.

muzhik (moo-zhéek): A male peasant; the general word, *krest'yanin*, includes males and females.

pood: 16.38 kilograms; 36 lbs.

rouble: The basic Russian monetary unit.

Rus See Notes for I, 1, note 6.

sazhen (sáh-zhen): 2.134 metres; 7 feet.

verst: 1.067 kilometres; 3,500 feet.

zakuski (zah-kóos-kee): Russian hors d'oeuvres.

THE STORY OF PENGUIN CLASSICS

Before 1946 ... 'Classics' are mainly the domain of academics and students; readable editions for everyone else are almost unheard of. This all changes when a little-known classicist, E. V. Rieu, presents Penguin founder Allen Lane with the translation of Homer's *Odyssey* that he has been working on in his spare time.

1946 Penguin Classics debuts with *The Odyssey*, which promptly sells three million copies. Suddenly, classics are no longer for the privileged few.

1950s Rieu, now series editor, turns to professional writers for the best modern, readable translations, including Dorothy L. Sayers's *Inferno* and Robert Graves's unexpurgated *Twelve Caesars*.

1960s The Classics are given the distinctive black covers that have remained a constant throughout the life of the series. Rieu retires in 1964, hailing the Penguin Classics list as 'the greatest educative force of the twentieth century.'

1970s A new generation of translators swells the Penguin Classics ranks, introducing readers of English to classics of world literature from more than twenty languages. The list grows to encompass more history, philosophy, science, religion and politics.

1980s The Penguin American Library launches with titles such as *Uncle Tom's Cabin*, and joins forces with Penguin Classics to provide the most comprehensive library of world literature available from any paperback publisher.

1990s The launch of Penguin Audiobooks brings the classics to a listening audience for the first time, and in 1999 the worldwide launch of the Penguin Classics website extends their reach to the global online community.

The 21st Century Penguin Classics are completely redesigned for the first time in nearly twenty years. This world-famous series now consists of more than 1300 titles, making the widest range of the best books ever written available to millions – and constantly redefining what makes a 'classic'.

The Odyssey continues ...

The best books ever written

PENGUIN CLASSICS

SINCE 1946

Find out more at www.penguinclassics.com